THE
QUEEN of SCORN

THE HELLBORN KING SAGA, BOOK THREE

A FANTASY NOVEL BY
CHRISTOPHER G. BRENNING

ACKNOWLEDGMENTS

What a long journey it has been. I first wrote the prologue for The Queen of Scorn shortly after finishing The Wrathbringer in 2022. In that time, three long years have passed. There are many reasons it has taken so long to finish this book: life, love, career, and even burnout.

Truth be told, the relentless grind of writing 200,000-word novels was getting to me. And worse, the pressure was on. After how well The Wrathbringer was received, I knew I had to raise the bar even higher. So, I doubled down, studied my craft intently, and took my time. The result is The Queen of Scorn, thus far, my crowning achievement.

My circle has grown smaller over the years, and not all of the friends who began this journey with me are continuing down the path. Even still, there are a few whose contributions made this book possible. I would like to thank Deb Gilbert for her honest feedback and for your support during this long process. I couldn't have done it without you. I would also like to thank my friend Dan for all of his suggestions and for helping me to become a better writer. You helped me sharpen my skills tenfold.

I would, as always, like to thank my mother, Karen, for her unyielding support and encouragement. Know this, Mom: I will never stop, no matter how difficult life becomes. My pace may slow, but I will never quit.

I hope you all enjoy The Queen of Scorn!

The Forlorn Sea
Rej Rhivoth
The Hinterwood
Teb River
Rit
Skaginlef
Siln River
Blackwolf Pass
Borjifa
Mot
The Bymist
Pelg
Khorrtal
Brimnora
Morden
Hok
Kepdon
The Plainhold
Dellhaven
The Great Sea
Mor Seveht
Greenwood Forest
Aret
Naxonnos
Bentmont
Cardale
Larssa
Vhos River
Willowsgrove
Glimmergulf
Corinope
Sothfort
Sommerwood River
The Everblue
CALDAKAS

CONTENTS

Acknowledgments iii
Prologue.............................1
Madelyn.............................10
Titan 17
Gareth.............................25
Udorn 38
Sylvia..............................45
Lucetta 54
Madelyn II 63
Sylvia II............................75
Titan II 85
Einarr.............................94
Udorn II...........................102
Gareth II 115
Sylvia III 127
Lucetta II 136
Udorn III 148
Madelyn III.......................164
Einarr II 176
Lucetta III 190

Aleksius............................202
Titan III 215
Sylvia IV 224
Udorn IV 235
Einarr III..........................248
Gareth III.........................255
Aleksius II 265
Lucetta IV 272
Madelyn IV.......................290
Udorn V...........................299
Titan IV 309
Sylvia V 318
Einarr IV..........................330
Lucetta V 337
Udorn VI 348
Sylvia VI...........................360
Aleksius III........................368
Madelyn V 380
Gareth IV.........................390
Sylvia VII 402

Lucetta VI 416
Udorn VII 426
Aleksius IV 434
Einarr V 443
Sylvia VIII 453
Gareth V 466
Lucetta VII 481
Sylvia IX 492
Madelyn VI 501
Udorn VIII 510
Einarr VI 519
Titan V 526
Lucetta VIII 535

Madelyn VII 542
Einarr VII 550
Udorn IX 558
Sylvia X...............................570
Aleksius V 587
Titan XI 598
Madelyn VIII 609
Einarr VIII 617
Lucetta IX 626
Gareth VI 642
Epilogue...............................653
A Word From The Author...661

PROLOGUE

"Where are they?" Svinn asked for the third time that morning. "They should have found us by now."

Voggar grunted, his teeth grinding. Nothanek were skittish creatures, he reckoned, too unnerved to ride with proper Rhivothi horsemasters. Still, after a crushing defeat on the Plainhold fields, their company would have to do.

"Enough with your mewling," Voggar commanded, his face turned sour. "These lands are crawling with Betanthians."

Despite his resolve, Voggar was every bit as worried as his brethren. He slept not a wink the night before, sleep proving as elusive as victory on the battlefield. Visions of the Blackthorn charge, an ungodly display of raw power, would be forever seared into his mind. And worse, their demise was heralded by the Eveldanyr, a woman many had given up for dead.

Indeed, such a calamity could only have been the work of the gods, their earthly emissary defiled in the most heinous ways. It was a violation Voggar and his kinsmen refrained from partaking in, but their punishment was the same regardless. Still, he was thankful to have his closest sword brothers riding beside him.

Hallvard Hearthammer was bruised and bloodied but otherwise

intact. Geir took an arrow to his left hand but seemed unbothered. Only Svinn and his Nothanek kinsman, Orjan, appeared unharmed, though they were the most distraught. Voggar winced as he secured his length of blonde hair with a leather band, the shaved skin on his right temple raked with a deep laceration.

As their patrol rode on, he thought of Rej Rhivoth and the beauty of its mighty forests. He pictured the foamy waters of the Forlorn Sea and longed to breathe its cool, salty aroma. With each thought of home, his resolve hardened further. Hostile lands were no place for a mind to wander, after all.

"Suppose they never find us," Svinn complained. "Do we return to camp?"

Voggar thought for a moment but decided otherwise. "No. Bethard scouts roam these lands. We must be Damien's eyes for as long as necessary."

It would have been a lie to say he was unconcerned. He spoke to Goran and his patrol not even a day prior. Now, their morning rendezvous was suspiciously delayed. But for a Rhivothi to lose heart was as likely as the sun never to rise, though it was certainly dark days for the warband.

"I may never sleep again after what I witnessed," said Orjan, a pimple-cheeked lad with tears of the Teb in his eyes. "The gods have forsaken us."

"Azldyr is loyal only to death, fisherman," Hallvard Hearthammer grumbled. His gnarled, hip-length hair appeared as brown snakes slithering in a southern breeze. "Blood is blood, no matter what vein it flows through. Ours or theirs, it makes no difference to the war god."

A fair statement, to be sure. Voggar had feasted on victory and defeat throughout his life, and their taste was often indistinguishable.

"Only the grave can defeat a Rhivothi," he said defiantly. "You would take heed of our warrior spirit, Nothanek. Trade your piety for sword work, and the gods will carry you to glory. Come, let us rest."

Together, the patrol found refuge in a grove of tall grass and twisted, dead trees. They ate salted meat and hard bread and drank modestly on warm ale. Conversation was fleeting, for they dared not betray their concealment. Thankfully, there was only the hissing of dry grass in a warm gust, a sign perhaps of coming rain.

After eating their fill, Voggar and his men returned to their patrol. While he longed to avenge his fallen sword brothers, there was comfort in knowing the Betanthians were slow to give chase. Perhaps it would allow Damien Dreadfire and the warband time enough to regroup and take up the fight once again.

Geir was beginning to sway in his saddle, his skin turning pale in the searing sun. He winced and gripped the wet, red wrappings around his hand. Loss of blood could best even the mightiest warrior, this much Voggar knew. He wheeled about, his horse jerking its head in protest.

"Has that little twig unmanned you, Geir?" he quipped.

Hallvard chuckled in kind. A proper challenge could ignite any Rhivothi's spirits, after all.

"Give me an axe over an arrow," Geir cursed. "The tools of cowards, I say!"

"Fear not, brother," Voggar said, lifting his chin. "Soon enough, you will deliver the axe blow yourself!"

Such encouragement seemed to do well enough, much to his satisfaction. Although, the sting of defeat loomed overhead like gray storm clouds. It was the unlikeliest outcome Voggar had expected, especially after hearing of victories throughout the past year.

The sacking of Castle Morden and the butchering of Betanthia's most infamous Commandant were reasons enough to join Damien Dreadfire's alliance. Tales of riches beyond imagination were as sweet as honey and enough to tempt even the craven to join the cause. The Nothanek he rode beside were undoubtedly proof in the flesh.

"If we even *have* the men to fight on. How many do you think survived?" Svinn asked, sounding like a petulant child. "Do you think any of the warchiefs made it out alive?"

"Only the gods know for certain," Voggar answered. "But I would wager my life that Dreadfire and Bonesplitter yet live. They must."

"Let us speak no more of this," Hallvard said abruptly. "We remain, as do many others. We must be their shield until our strength is recovered. Keep your mouth shut, fisherman, and your eyes open."

Silently, they rode, seeing neither friend nor foe on the horizon. The Nothanek continued whispering to each other, glancing over their shoulders like skittish cats. Geir was conspicuously silent, perhaps even asleep on his horse.

"How fares your wound, Geir?" Voggar asked with a grin. "A shame the womenfolk are not here to nurse you back to good health!"

When he heard no response, Voggar turned in the saddle and noticed Geir's horse was without its master. Perhaps his blood loss was more severe than it appeared. It was an unwelcome development, to say the least. Voggar wheeled about to retrieve his sword brother, but a sudden shriek pierced the air.

Orjan writhed in pain, eyes wide in horror, a quarrel shaft protruding from his collarbone. He shot Voggar a final, panicked glance before another bolt took him clean between the eyes. He slumped forward onto his horse's neck, then tumbled onto the parched earth.

"To arms!" Voggar roared, taking up both shield and axe. "To arms!"

Another quarrel whistled through the air, striking Hallvard's horse in the eye. The beast jerked about, screaming, throwing its rider before falling dead. Hallvard landed with a thud, cursing and spitting as he retrieved his maul.

It was impossible to see where the attack was coming from and how many were upon them. He searched desperately through the tall grass, hoping to spot their enemies closing in, but saw nothing. Svinn took off at speed, his horse racing north as fast as it would allow. It was disappointing to see a Nothanek flee, but not unexpected.

Coward! How quickly his bowels have turned to water!

Voggar spied a quarrel speeding through the air, its source nearby. Time seemed to slow as he watched the projectile arc gracefully through the air before planting itself firmly in Svinn's back. Another Nothanek had met their demise, leaving only two Rhivothi standing. Good enough odds on any day, Voggar supposed.

"Azldyr take you!" Hallvard Hearthammer roared in defiance, his battle rage building like a whirlwind. With maul in hand, he charged forward with reckless courage but found nothing lurking in the grass before him. By some miracle, Geir had regained his footing, a quarrel sunk deep into his chest. With sword and shield, he trudged into the fray but was cut down in a near instant.

All Voggar saw was a blur, a formless mass rushing past Geir like black lightning. A jet of blood erupted from his bicep, shooting high like a geyser. But the Rhivothi would not succumb. He loosed a mighty war cry, swinging shield then axe as the black haze returned. Voggar and Hallvard rushed forward to save their sword brother from the foeman, a furious melee of clattering steel and ripping flesh filling the air.

As they arrived, they spied Geir's neck open from ear to ear, a thick waterfall of blood gushing down his chest. A heroic death, one worthy of Sjenohor, no doubt. But there was no evidence of the assailant except for a trail of matted vegetation heading east. Voggar motioned with his shield, Hallvard nodding in kind. Together, the Rhivothi stalked forward, taking note of the tracks.

Show yourself, coward!

A gentle crunching of grass blades met his ear, the disturbance close behind. Voggar drew a slow, deep breath, gripping his axe handle so tightly the wood nearly splintered. Then, a sharp rustle followed by frantic footfalls. Voggar spun around, swinging his axe and bringing his shield forward.

The figure slid underneath his strike and made for Hallvard. With a beastly roar, Hearthammer swung his maul with frightening speed, but its head met only air. He roared again, but this time in agony; a long, deep gash opened wide across his thigh.

"Hallvard!" Voggar shouted, charging in with all haste.

In a flash, the figure re-emerged, eager to quench its battle thirst on Rhivothi blood. Hearthammer stumbled but managed to parry a downward slash with the handle of his maul. He answered with a rapid swing, but the black-clad foeman disengaged, diving and rolling back into the grass.

"Stand and fight; gods curse you!" Hearthammer spat.

"Come, Hallvard," he said softly, standing beside his sword brother. "Foul magic is at work here. We must get to open ground!"

Both men stood back to back, scanning the grass patiently, each hesitant to move. Voggar heard his kinsman grunting softly, the pain of his injury apparent. For a Rhivothi to show any weakness in battle was to dishonor himself and the gods, but Hearthammer kept his resolve intact. Minutes went by, each feeling like the passing of years, but the phantom had yet to reemerge. Sensing an opportunity, Voggar motioned to a small clearing with his axe, intent on escaping the ambuscade.

He managed no more than a step before a wet thump pierced the silence, followed by hissing and gurgling. Hallvard dropped his maul, fingers clawing at the hilt of a throwing knife protruding from his throat. Panic swept through Voggar's heart for the first time, his closest friend dying before his eyes.

"By the gods!" he cried out, stepping backward.

Suddenly, the grass shook as if taken by a swift gale. He spun around and saw the edge of shining steel bearing down with blinding speed.

Voggar's shield rose to meet the blade, its planks rattling and groaning from the impact. He answered with a wild, rapid swing, this time his axe tasting flesh. A sharp yelp rang out, not that of a man, but high in pitch and soft of tone.

A woman? Gods, could it be so?

Before he could make sense of the situation, another strike came raining in, followed by a sharp thrust. Each blow was met with thick Hinterwood spruce, his shield holding true. For the first time, he saw his attacker clearly. It was a woman's frame, no doubt, wide of hip and small of waist. Her face was masked with black linen, chin-length locks of black hair shrouding one eye. Despite having arms half his size, she was capable of blows mighty enough to stagger him.

Voggar saw she was tiring, his Rhivothi stamina winning out. Each strike felt a little less, until an opening presented itself. After parrying a slash, he landed a mighty front kick, sending the black-clad woman tumbling backward.

"Your trickery will gain you naught, devil!" he growled, stepping forward.

Despite staring down death, the woman appeared unfazed. Her eyes filled with black tar, a swirling, inky mess that halted Voggar in his steps. A dark mist began building around her, but whatever evil energies she harbored appeared to waver. He smiled, knowing his axe would soon drink its fill of blood.

As he stepped forward to deliver a final blow, the woman drew a knife and heaved it in the blink of an eye, the blade sinking deep into his hip. Voggar stumbled backward, growling like a beast, trying to wrench the knife free. Suddenly, his leg lost strength, sending him crashing to the ground. An unfortunate, cruel twist of fate if there ever was one.

With renewed vigor, the woman shot to her feet and charged in, both hands wrapped around the hilt of a short sword. A powerful downward slash followed, biting deep into Voggar's shield. The wood was faltering, a plume of splinters erupting like a nest of bees. He attempted to chop at the woman's legs, but she kicked his axe free, sending it fluttering into the weeds.

Just as she appeared ready to strike a final time, a thunderous charge drew their attention. Hallvard Hearthammer had not yet departed for Sjenohor despite a knife still protruding from his throat. With rivers of blood flowing down his chest, he swung his maul with legendary fury.

The woman made to parry out of instinct, but her sword was clubbed free, a shriek of pain following with it. She clasped at a battered wrist and dodged one swing after another in desperation. As Hearthammer pressed his attack, she drew another sword, the steel whistling as it cleaved through the air. With a diving roll, she drew its edge across Hallvard's abdomen, the soft flesh beneath his mail parting effortlessly.

Entrails spilled from Hallvard's gut, the light in his eyes flickering like a dying flame. Still, the mighty Rhivothi gripped his hammer in trembling hands. He looked at Voggar and sighed, knowing his soul was bound for the afterlife. Voggar struggled to rise, fumbling for his axe while agony burned deep in his leg.

Finding his weapon, he stumbled forward, axe raised, a fiery roar stinging his throat. The woman shot a scornful glare, a cold, blue eye staring back in hatred. She raised her blade and brought it down without hesitation, Hallvard's head tumbling off his shoulders moments after. She stepped back, pointed her sword at Voggar, and drew her left arm behind her back.

"Azldyr!" he screamed, axe and broken shield at the ready.

Despite the crippling pain, he surged forward, winding up a swing fierce enough to cleave a tree in half. The woman stood motionless, watching indifferently as his axe came down. Before it could greet her head, she stepped to the side and thrust with her left arm, a hidden knife finding its way between Voggar's ribs.

In an instant, his breath escaped and could not be recovered. In his mind, Voggar continued to fight, but his flesh was beginning to succumb. As he made to strike again, the black-clad woman slipped the knife free, then punctured his lungs several times with unholy speed.

It seemed that the gods were as absent now as they were on the Plainhold. Voggar crumpled to his knees, fighting to draw breath but finding none. A strange sensation began to embrace his body, not of pain but of serenity and acceptance. Perhaps the gods were preparing to carry him to the halls of Sjenohor, where every warrior was victorious in death.

"You'll… never… defeat… Dread…fire…" Voggar whispered, choking and drowning in blood.

He collapsed in a heap, shield and axe falling from his grasp. With a trembling hand, Voggar reached for his weapon, not to strike but to carry it to the world beyond. It was an act the woman seemed to understand well enough and made no move to oppose him.

Azldyr, forgive me for this defeat. Bring me home so I may fight eternally in your honor.

Pressing the axe to his chest, Voggar watched as light from the sunny sky began to dim. The mysterious woman stood over him, slowly removing her shroud. Chin-length locks of black hair fell across her cheek, stirred by a warm, gentle wind. The last thing mighty Voggar saw as his vision dimmed was a single steely-blue eye, gleaming in the darkness like cold starlight.

MADELYN

SHE KNELT IN THE TALL GRASS, VOMITING BLACK SLUDGE. FOUL LIQUID poured from Madelyn Everly's mouth in a bitter torrent, her stomach churning like a storm-tossed sea. Wracked with sickness, she barely registered the massacre sprawled around her. A northern patrol lay butchered—strong, brutish men, once capable of hammering iron with their bare fists.

Now they were nothing but corpses, husks of the proud warriors they had been. Gasping, spitting out another mouthful of stinking bile, she surveyed her handiwork with grim wonder.

What have I done? What am I becoming?

But there was no use dwelling on it. Every Northman dead was one less standing between her and Damien Dreadfire, the only man who truly mattered. Miles away though he was, each kill brought her one step closer to finding him.

Staggering upright, Madelyn turned to fetch her horse from the grove when a muffled groan broke through the silence. Short sword in hand, she pressed into the grass, every nerve taut.

A rustle made her heart lurch. She reached for the shadow realm but found no strength to cross the veil. No, this fight would have to be hers alone. Then a voice, faint and trembling, carried to her.

"P…please," a young Northman moaned. A quarrel jutted from his back like a banner planted in soft earth.

Madelyn sprang forth, sword poised, a burning hatred flickering behind her steely blue eyes. Yet as she prepared to strike, a pang of guilt caught her. Crawling across the parched earth was not a hulking Rhivothi nor a frothing Zylmacian. No—this was a youth, fair of complexion and slight of frame. A Nothanek, she supposed, perhaps the least vile of the Northern breeds.

To see a man beg for his life was pitiful, yet despite his tears and pleading, disgust surged through her, disgust bordering on hatred. Pious though they were, the Nothanek were no less guilty than Dreadfire himself. Yes, she decided. A madman's lackey deserved no pity.

"Kholdyr… please," he gasped. "Forgive me! I am not ready for Sjenohor!"

"Your gods cannot save you now," Madelyn answered coldly. "Every life your horde has destroyed, every bit of suffering you have sown… it has all come back on you."

"I fight only to protect my people! I—"

She cut him off with a furious step, the sword tip pressing his throat. "I will hear none of your lies! I am Madelyn Everly, the one you tried to break. I am a Commander of the Blackthorn Knights, a survivor of Morden, and the face of your ruin!"

"You…" the warrior stammered. "You are… the Eveldanyr? Why would you do this to your own people?"

"My people?" she spat. "I share no kinship with beasts. You are savages! Butchers! You inflicted horrors on me beyond imagination, and now you will answer for them. Tell me, where is Damien Dreadfire? Speak, or the last thing you feel will be my pain!"

She lowered the blade between his legs, inches from his manhood. His soft brown eyes locked with hers, a trembling arm lifted in a feeble ward. But no mercy lived in her gaze.

"I... I know nothing, I swear!" he pleaded. "Please, just let me live and I—"

"Silence!" Madelyn hissed, jabbing the sword just enough to draw a scream that split the dry plain.

"North! North!" The Nothanek writhed, clawing desperately at himself, his voice cracking in agony.

For half a heartbeat, she saw Corbyn Scott's sad, desperate eyes staring back at her, the eyes of her lost love. A rush of guilt stayed her hand, the memory of Castle Morden crashing over her like a tide. She blinked hard, trying to shake the haze, but sorrow coiled in her chest all the same.

"Please, spare me!" the warrior begged. "I had no part in what was done to you! My people believe in the sanctity of life. Please... show mercy!"

"Maybe your hands stayed clean," Madelyn said, voice low and bitter. "Maybe you took no part. But where were you while it happened? Why did you do nothing? Guilt clings to you all the same."

She raised her blade to strike—then faltered. His eyes caught her again. They were soft, caramel-colored, far too familiar. With every blink, the Nothanek's face shifted, morphing until it became Corbyn's, the same broken gaze she had seen on the day of his death.

No. This... can't be...

Her sword quivered, nearly slipping from her grip. The vision would not break. His lips curled into a mournful smile, and a faint whisper slid to her ears, so soft it seemed borne on the wind through the grass.

"Save... me..."

Gasping and choking, Madelyn stumbled backward, tears streaming like a gentle river. The same plea haunted her dreams for over a year. But no matter the scenario, the end was all the same. Corbyn was dead, his bones picked clean and bleached by a searing western sun, never to be recovered.

"I'm sorry," she sobbed, "I tried. I tried as hard as I could, my love. Please, forgive me!"

Madelyn rubbed the water from her eyes, and as she did, the vision dissolved. Light and shadow danced and flickered, spinning into a nauseating mess of color.

"W…what?" the Nothanek stammered, incredulous. He clawed backward, terrified by the madness spilling from her lips.

The familiar face was gone. In its place lay only a stranger—an enemy, a collaborator in the death of her beloved and of countless friends. Sorrow hardened to anger, and anger to hatred. Mourning would not raise the slain from their graves, nor would it end the war. Mercy had long since died—at Morden with her friends, and again on the night of her tribulation.

They will never stop until every last Betanthian is dead… until every city is razed, and every monument toppled. There will never be enough blood to quench their thirst. They will never stop… and nor shall I.

With all her strength, Madelyn drove her sword into the Nothanek's groin. His screams split the plain, sharp but mercifully brief. She stared down at the corpse, the vast emptiness in her heart unfilled by the bloodletting. This was not fair combat on a field of honor. It was murder, and her cold indifference was perhaps the most terrifying part.

The killing was necessary, even just—yet hollow. However, it would not change the war's course, nor bring Damien Dreadfire to justice. Only by pressing on could she hope to reach him. But being so close, yet still hopelessly far, was enough to fracture her stony facade.

A violent anxiety seized Madelyn's chest, choking off her breath. She staggered, legs turning to water, vision swimming. For a moment, she could not remember where she was or how she had come to this strange, blood-soaked place. Only the sight of slain barbarians anchored her, warding off a tide of panic.

Get a hold of yourself, Madelyn. Now is not the time for tears. Not when you've come this far… not when you're so close.

She wrenched her sword free from the corpse at her feet and began searching the bodies, desperate for anything that might point to Dreadfire's whereabouts. The presumed leader lay last among the dead, but his clothing yielded nothing—no maps, no orders, no clue worth the blood she had spilled. She cursed under her breath and turned to another when the ground itself rumbled.

The sound was unmistakable. Heart pounding, she sprinted to her mount, swinging into the saddle despite the agony in her joints. Rising above the tall grass, her eyes caught a banner through the sun's glare— difficult to make out at first, but then clear as fire: gold rippling against a black field. Shock prickled her skin.

The Order?! How could they have found me?

How had they discovered her here? Had they followed her? Or was this some wandering patrol, blind to her presence? Madelyn urged her horse east, spurring it hard into a gallop, unwilling to test the knights' intentions. The tall grass and brush soon swallowed her, granting cover enough to halt and watch.

From the shadows, she studied their column. Their numbers were staggering, a force that could mean only one thing: another battle loomed. Following them might reveal Dreadfire's position—but if she followed, she risked losing the one advantage that remained: the chance to strike him unaware.

"North," she said incredulously. "They're heading north. Do they know where Dreadfire is?"

It was an exhilarating thought that the Northmen might be so close. And who better than the Order to root them out amid the endless desolation of the Plainhold? As the riders came further into view, their heraldry became clear.

She recognized the banner, had seen it a dozen times in her youth at court—perhaps at a feast, or at the High Marshal's councils—but the name eluded her. Once, she could have recited every noble line from memory, their mottos and deeds like scripture. Now, she struggled even to recall faces, as though her old life had been scrubbed away by fire and ash. What did it mean for a woman of Betanthia to forget her own kin? To look upon the symbols of her country and see strangers?

Have I drifted so far from the woman I once was? Have I lost myself entirely?

Memories of her glory days on the battlefield drifted back, hazy as an autumn morning. Darker still were the shadows of her tribulation, ever-present, clawing at her mind. But amid the torment rose Gareth's face—his warmth, his love. Surely, his heart must have shattered into a thousand pieces when he discovered their wedding bed empty.

The thought nearly brought her to tears, but they dried as quickly as they came. She was something else now, something colder, unfamiliar. Better to have left, she told herself, than to remain a husk incapable of love.

He's a good man and will make a good king one day. He deserves more than what I can offer… he deserves better.

She remembered the day of their vows, when she still believed in warmth and in futures shaped by love. She had seen him then as not only a husband, but a partner, a shield against the storm. But that woman was gone. The one who rode northward now was carved hollow by grief and rage. Gareth would be king, and he would be loved by his people, and she would be remembered only as the shadow who abandoned him. Perhaps that was the kinder fate. Perhaps that was mercy.

Distraction threatened to unravel her. Indecision gnawed at her bones. She forced her gaze on the passing Blackthorn column, rigid as stone, until their banners faded from sight.

Only then did she press northward, visions of Damien Dreadfire burning in her mind. Perhaps claiming his head and returning victorious would banish the demons that haunted her waking hours. Or perhaps slitting the crone's throat and scattering her warband like ash on the wind would grant her peace at last.

The Plainhold stretched before her, endless and gray. She had crossed this wasteland before, shackled and broken, each mile a reminder of her helplessness. Now she crossed it of her own accord, yet the weight felt no lighter. Every step north carried her further from who she had been—Commander, daughter, wife—and closer to something else. Something born of shadow and vengeance.

Is this the woman I was meant to become? she wondered. *A revenant chasing ghosts across a dead land? Or is this the only truth left for me, that I cannot be Madelyn the wife or Madelyn the Commander, only Madelyn the avenger?*

She tightened her grip on the reins, the wind stinging her eyes. There was no turning back. There was only the path ahead, only the reckoning that awaited.

Perhaps, she thought, mustering the rage that was beginning to define her. *There's only one way to find out.*

TITAN

A DRY WIND KICKED UP A STORM OF POLLEN AND DUST, STINGING Tylar Bradshaw's eyes—an irritation on a stifling day, but not half as irritating as the company beside him. Conrak was babbling to a trio of Blackthorn Knights and a pair of Royal Guardsmen whose names Tylar couldn't be bothered to learn. Were it not for the sensitivity of their mission, he might very well have struck the lot of them.

"That is one thing you must never do," Conrak droned, "never underestimate them, even in defeat. A cornered dog is still dangerous despite his wounds."

"Eh, you're giving them too much credit," said Earlwick, a knight scarcely into his twenties. His smooth cheeks and round jaw made him look more like a boy than a soldier. "You saw how they broke and fled when we arrived. Cowards, the whole lot of them."

Tylar's teeth clenched. After everything he had witnessed, holding back his temper was nearly insurmountable. The nightmares of Castle Morden would never leave him. Worse still was the despair of losing Madelyn to the barbarians. Though she lived in the end, what returned was only a husk of the headstrong woman he had barely begun to know.

"Do you twats ever shut your mouths?" he growled. "This isn't some routine patrol. Show some respect for why we're here."

None dared to provoke his wrath. Many had seen what he had done on the battlefield, reckless heroics that spread through the camp like wildfire. Soldiers and knights alike came to understand why they called him Titan—and all were thankful to have such a man among them.

"Take heart, Bradshaw," Conrak said, stoic as ever. "She couldn't have gone far. Out here, there's nowhere to hide. We'll find her soon enough."

"I lost her once before," Tylar muttered, twisting the shaft of a lance in his grip, "and I swore I'd never lose her again. I'd tear the heads off each of your shoulders if it meant keeping her safe."

Masking the storm inside him was a monumental effort, though it was a wonder he could feel anything at all after years of loss. But there was still life in Tylar Bradshaw's cold heart—and wrath enough to outmatch even Damien Dreadfire.

"I can see how deeply you care about her. You two ever... uh..." Earlwick grinned.

Were it not for the importance of their mission, Tylar might have throttled him on the spot.

"The fuck are you implying?" he snarled, wheeling his horse about. "You think because I care for her, I'm fucking her? She's my comrade. Our bond was forged in battle. We bathed in the same blood—ours and theirs alike. Say that shit again, and I'll feed you your guts. Do you understand me?"

"Enough!" Conrak snapped, throwing up a hand. "Something's up ahead."

Tylar squinted into the distance. A figure loomed above the tall grass, still as stone. Weapons drawn, they spread into a loose line and advanced. An ambush could come at any moment, yet Tylar felt oddly calm.

As they closed the distance, his morbid suspicion was confirmed. A corpse stood impaled, a spear driven clean through and buried in the earth, its point jutting from the collarbone. The man wore a soiled blue tunic and black trousers—Blackthorn issue, straight from Castle

Thorn. Tylar had ruined plenty of the same linen with spilled liquor in years past.

"Fucking savages," he said softly.

Knives, birds, and insects had ravaged the corpse's face, twisting it into an unrecognizable ruin. Retribution for the Northmen's defeat, no doubt, and proof of their cowardice if ever there was.

The stench was worse than any battlefield Tylar had known: a sickly blend of spoiled meat and sun-baked rot. Flies crawled across the dead man's lips, wriggling into his slack mouth and buzzing furiously when disturbed. One of the Guardsmen muttered a prayer and turned his face away, while another spat into the grass, his jaw tight with unease.

"Let us not forget why we're here," Conrak said, bowing his head. "This is the fate that awaits us should we fail."

"You confuse the hell out of me," Tylar growled, drawing his horse alongside. He leaned in so the others could not hear. "Why aren't you with the Northmen? I'd think a Sacrithon, sworn to protect the Eveldanyr, would be better suited to their side. Wouldn't it be in your best interest to see Betanthia burn?"

"I'm on the side of peace, difficult as that may be for you to grasp," Conrak replied evenly. "I was once like you, Bradshaw. I saw the world in black and white. I hated the Northmen as much as you do. But I learned truths buried in time, knowledge nearly lost. That knowledge compels me to fight against a world gone mad."

Tylar jabbed a finger toward the mutilated corpse. "How's that working out for you? How'd it work out for him?"

Conrak's shoulders sagged. "In war, nothing is certain. Truth and lies blur together. I want peace, but I know it's a fool's hope. Too much blood has been spilled. One side must win." He paused, meeting Tylar's eyes. "That's why we must protect Madelyn. She may be the key to ending this war and bringing peace between all nations."

Hope was a cruel joke to Tylar. Every time he let it creep in, the world punished him tenfold. Still, he clenched his jaw. He'd be damned before he let fate dictate his end.

"You better be right," he mumbled. "You'd better truly believe in all that bullshit you spew."

Having seen enough, the men pressed on, leaving the body of their fallen brother to the crows. There was no time for rites or ceremony. It was a disgraceful end for a man who had given himself to the Order and its tenets—but such was the fate every fighting man accepted.

For hours, they saw nothing but rolling hills and seas of dry, brittle grass. Tylar began to wonder if they would ever find the Northmen, or if the bastards had been swallowed whole by the Plainhold's endless void. A skin of wine helped dull his boredom, if only slightly.

As the day waned, a haze of dust drifted on a stifling wind. Tylar thought little of it until the earth itself gave a faint, rumbling shiver. Conrak raised a hand, signaling the patrol to halt. One of the men immediately broke away, cresting a nearby hill. He froze, then came racing back, arms windmilling in warning.

"Riders approaching. Be on your guard!"

Swords hissed free as the patrol braced for contact. Tylar cared nothing for the odds. Whether ten or ten thousand Northmen, none would keep him from finding Madelyn.

Then, over the wavering plain, a banner rose black and gold: the sigil of the Order. Relief rippled through the men. Conrak smiled, sliding his sword back into its sheath, and spurred his horse to meet them. With a weary sigh, Tylar followed. Barbarian blood would have to wait.

As they drew closer, the sheer scale of the Blackthorn column became clear. Hundreds of knights rode two abreast, their banners snapping, their armor flashing dull in the Plainhold sun. At their head rode Gilliard Braand, a portly officer who looked as though he'd been pried from Castle Thorn's banquet table only yesterday. A gaggle of lackeys flanked him, their names unworthy of memory.

"Fancy running into you out here, Conrak," Gilliard snorted. His eyes slid to Tylar, narrowing at the strip of purple on his shoulders. "So, who'd you kill to wear such a fine color?"

"Does it sting," Tylar shot back, "knowing I sit at the right hand of royalty while you spent years fruitlessly licking the High Marshal's ass?" His gaze fell to the insignia on Gilliard's breastplate. "So you're the new First Lance. The last man to hold that title fought and died with more bravery than you could ever dream of."

Conrak's grin was immediate, though he masked it with a cough. He might have still worn the Order's sigil, but he clearly enjoyed Tylar's venom. "Gentlemen," he interjected, raising a hand. "Save the barbs for the alehouse. Have you located the Northmen?"

"We've a fair idea," Gilliard said with a shrug. "We've cut down some of their scouts. Others slipped away, and no doubt ran back to tell their masters we're coming."

"And Commander Everly?" Tylar's voice was flat, but the question burned hot in his chest.

"I've heard nothing," Gilliard said. "She's not our mission. My only concern is Damien Dreadfire and his horde."

Tylar was unsurprised. The Order had always treated its own as expendable the moment they stopped being useful. That the High Marshal's ward could be cast aside so easily was damning—but not shocking.

But Madelyn was *his* mission, whether the Order cared or not. Gareth had spared him from the noose, and that debt demanded loyalty. Yet even without it, Tylar would see her safe. And if his own countrymen stood in the way, then their blood would wet his sword as readily as any barbarian's.

"Then do what you must," Tylar growled. "But stay the fuck out of my way, or I'll—"

"Save it for the Northmen, Bradshaw," Conrak cut in, lifting his sword. "Because here they are!"

A detachment of barbarian cavalry crested the nearest rise, riding east in a loose column. Dozens at least, though they had yet to notice the Blackthorn line. Whether dulled by exhaustion or blinded by the Plainhold's glare, they rode straight into fate.

Gilliard took one look, barked a command, and spurred his horse into a gallop. The thunder of hooves gave them away, and the Northmen scattered like startled birds.

Tylar surged forward, his fury burning hotter than his mount could carry. A red haze crowded his vision, narrowing until he saw nothing but blood. He would have torn them apart with his bare hands—yet instinct cut through rage like cold steel. These were not harmless stragglers—lightly armored, yes, but dangerous.

The first arrows hissed past harmlessly, but soon volleys followed, black shafts peppering the ranks.

"Archers!" Gilliard cried out, his sword in the air.

"Spread out!" Conrak bellowed, veering east with Tylar at his flank. A half-score of knights surged after them, shields raised, lances couched.

The barbarians wheeled in panic, some fleeing, others fumbling to nock arrows. Tylar lowered his lance, his roar ripping across the field. The weapon found its mark with brutal precision, punching through a wildman's chest and lifting him from the saddle. Blood sprayed, the barbarian's scream cut short as he tumbled lifeless to the dirt.

Shards of bone and blood spattered across his arm as the skewered rider fell away, the lance splintering in Tylar's grip. He let it fall, steel already rasping free of its scabbard. The blade sang as he spurred through the ranks, hacking down anything in reach. Conrak and the others crashed in behind him, their charge scattering the savages like leaves in a gale.

The barbarian force was ill-equipped for a direct clash and broke as fast as their mounts would carry them. One rider's head leapt from his shoulders beneath Tylar's swing, a grisly trophy cartwheeling across the dirt, a fitting adornment for the battlefield if there ever was one. Yet for all his thirst, the fight bled out too soon, the Northmen vanishing in a whirlwind of dust and cowardice.

"Fucking cowards!" Tylar snarled, chest heaving. "Do I need to face their whole horde before they'll stand and fight?"

The last rider vanished over the ridge, leaving only silence and the smell of churned earth. Tylar sat high in his saddle, chest heaving, knuckles white on the hilt of his sword. Rage still roared through his veins, demanding more blood, but the field offered none. His fury had nowhere to go, and it curdled inside him until it became something heavier, something colder.

"Perhaps you should!" Conrak shouted back, his grin red with spatter. "Or maybe your reputation runs faster than they do?"

Tylar shot him a glare, the same mix of rage and weary tolerance he'd worn since their first meeting. "Eat shit. Madelyn's out there, and every wasted moment puts her further beyond our reach."

"Take it easy, Bradshaw," Conrak interrupted. "Finding levity at your expense helps to keep my mind sharp. I share just as much concern over her well-being as you."

The words rang hollow against the emptiness gnawing at Tylar's soul. Hours had passed since she slipped from camp, yet it felt like she'd vanished to the ends of the earth.

"Then quit flapping your gums," he muttered, eyes fixed northward. "Save your breath for splitting skulls. Come on, she won't wait for us."

"Slow it up, Bradshaw," Conrak warned, reining back. "The further north we push, the closer we come to the horde. Don't fool yourself, our little band wouldn't last a heartbeat alone. We need the Order, loath though you are to admit it."

The thought of riding under Blackthorn banners soured Tylar's gut worse than bad ale. Fighting alongside them felt like pissing molten iron. But if it meant finding Madelyn, then he would suffer it. The purple draped across his shoulders demanded obedience, whether men respected the brute wearing it or not.

"You'd better be right," he muttered darkly. "Because if anything happens to her, I'll leave your carcass out here for the crows."

Conrak exhaled, tired but steady. "The stakes aren't lost on me, Bradshaw. If we fail her, this wasteland becomes our grave as well—and the Plainhold will have two more ghosts before it's through."

GARETH

H E SAT ALONE AS DAWN BROKE, SORROW IN HIS HEART AND BOURBON in his belly. Pale light bled across the Plainhold, but it carried no promise of renewal. Gareth's gaze lingered northward, where the horizon seemed endless, a gray wall that mirrored the million fragmented thoughts poisoning his mind.

Marrying the woman of his dreams should have been the happiest moment of his life. But, as with every other good thing before, it had slipped away like smoke between his fingers.

Why would you do this? His thumb rubbed the edges of the folded letter, its creases worn soft from countless readings. *I don't understand. You came back after all those years, you gave me your vows... why, Madelyn? Why would you leave?*

He read the lines again, though he could recite them by heart. The sting of her words did not dull with time; it grew sharper, carving deeper into him with every pass. Even the bite of southern bourbon, the strongest he could find, dulled nothing. The bottle drained quickly, but his grief did not.

Gareth wandered through the waking camp, past rows of canvas tents sagging with dew, past men groaning in their sleep or whispering in pain as wounds were dressed by tired hands. Smoke from dying cookfires hung low, mingling with the sour stink of sweat and blood.

These men bore gashes, breaks, and scars—wounds of the flesh. Gareth would have traded places with any one of them. For all their pain, theirs could heal. Wounds of the heart always cut deeper, and his would never close.

At the edge of the camp, a group of soldiers clustered around an ale cart, their bodies swaying like stalks of grass in the Plainhold wind. Some lifted their mugs with shaky hands, others only stared, hollow-eyed, into the foam. Perhaps this was the only way left to steady themselves, Gareth thought bitterly. As he passed, they straightened and bowed, but the gesture rang hollow. Their eyes betrayed them, for they were still on the battlefield, fighting ghosts he could not banish.

Not that he cared for reverence. Victory meant little, even after leading men to triumph in his first true battle. Gareth had never felt more hollow, more defeated, the laurels of command rotting before they could be placed upon his brow. As he drifted aimlessly between rows of casks and stacked supply crates, a familiar voice broke through the haze.

"There you are!" Sir Edmund Thomas called, his silver hair plastered to his brow with sweat. He carried two wooden mugs of ale, foam spilling over the rims as he strode up. "I was on my way to share a drink, but I can see you've already beaten me to it."

"I don't feel like talking," Gareth muttered. He slouched against the casks and accepted the mug with reluctance, swirling the liquid though he had no taste for it.

Company, at a time like this, was as inviting as chewing nails. Even drinking felt like a chore. His thirst raged like a summer storm, but every swallow only seemed to settle heavier in his gut. Holding his composure before the men was becoming impossible, as if he were drowning in plate armor while the tide kept rising.

"Don't be so hard on yourself, lad," Edmund said, his voice softer than Gareth expected. He clapped a mailed hand against his shoulder, the gesture more paternal than martial. "You did nothing wrong."

"I hate her," Gareth said at last, the words leaking out on a sigh. His jaw tightened, the ale mug creaking in his grip.

The elder Guardsman tilted his head, studying him with calm, searching eyes. "Hate her, you say?" he asked. "Then tell me—why would you say such a thing?"

He wanted to cry; at least, his soul longed for it. But no tears came. Only emptiness remained, a hollow ache without escape.

"Because I was foolish enough to believe she truly cared," Gareth said at last, voice raw. "I gave in to my desires and let her into my heart, where she had always belonged. But I should have known better. I should have known she would never truly be mine."

"You mustn't blame yourself," Edmund said gently. "You had no way of knowing what she would do."

"I could have kept her safe! I could have given her the world and more!" Gareth's voice rose, sharp with desperation. "I would have burned the Hinterwood to ashes and brought her Dreadfire's head on a plate! What more could she possibly have wanted?"

Each frantic word seemed to drive a knife into Edmund's chest. Just as Gareth's heart was breaking, so too did the elder Guardsman's. For all his decades of battle, no consolation seemed great enough to mend such a wound.

"I wish I had the answers for you, lad," Edmund murmured. "Truly, I do. It's the not knowing that kills a man's soul. The mind fills the void with questions, with endless scenarios until madness takes root. Don't let it devour you. Madelyn is a tormented soul, and—"

"She's my wife!" Gareth snapped, eyes blazing. "And she swore to me!"

Despair and rage wrestled for dominion inside him, each clawing to be the first to break him. Assassins stalked his steps, the Northmen pressed from without, yet all Gareth's mind could seize upon was Madelyn. It was a hopelessness more dangerous than any sword.

"I need you to understand something, Gareth." Edmund laid a steady hand on his shoulder, guiding him toward a nearby bench. "You've stood on the battlefield only once. Tell me—how afraid were you?"

"It was the most terrifying experience of my life," Gareth admitted through clenched teeth.

"And rightly so. My first battle was no less harrowing. But you had the rare fortune of victory, and you lost no one close. Now imagine if we had failed, if Madelyn and I had been cut down before your eyes. How would you bear it?"

The question was so absurd he nearly scoffed. "Of course I would be distraught. I see what you're getting at."

"No," Edmund said flatly, his voice darkening. "You don't. You haven't the faintest idea what it means to watch those you love die in your arms. To know their last breath, their last plea, and carry it with you forever. And worse still, to suffer one of the most unspeakable violations any soul can endure. That is what Madelyn survived. That is why she is no longer the woman you remember."

It could not be true. Not to her. Not to Madelyn Everly, so strong, so unshakable. Gareth shook his head violently. "She's the love of my life, Edmund. I want to keep her safe, take her pain away. Doesn't she realize she doesn't need to fight anymore?"

Edmund straightened, weariness deepening the lines around his eyes. "Sometimes, Gareth, all a person has left is vengeance. Madelyn wants Damien Dreadfire to suffer as she has, and no one—neither you nor Bradshaw—will stand in her way. Accept that, and remember your duty. You lead this war, Lord Vakaro be damned. The men need a prince who is present, not drowning in grief." Think of the husbands who will never return to their wives if you lose yourself now."

It was one of many moments where, despite the ache in his chest,

Gareth knew Edmund was right. Truth rarely softened its edge, and tonight it bit deep.

"So… what do I do, then?" he asked, exhaling like a man already condemned.

"Bradshaw and Conrak are out there," Edmund said, steady as stone. "They're your best men, and you must believe in them. I know trust feels impossible—especially after an assassin's blade nearly claimed you in battle—but that is exactly why you must. Let them do what they do best. Let them hunt. Your place is here, keeping this army from shattering."

Gareth clenched his hands together, knuckles whitening. He had seen Bradshaw in the fray, a savage brute carved by war, and knew no foe could sleep easy with such a man in pursuit. And Conrak—slippery, unreadable Conrak—was clever enough to survive the gods themselves. Together, they were a terror worth loosing.

"You're right," Gareth admitted, his voice low. "I can't save Madelyn or win this war if Ridley's minions knife me in my sleep. You and I must keep our eyes on him, Edmund. He is the greater danger."

The elder Guardsman nodded grimly. "I know. But none of my men can get close. Lord Vakaro's circle is locked tighter than a miser's purse. His paranoia rivals his ambition."

Gareth's hand flexed, the bitterness in him searching for an outlet. "Then perhaps we turn one of his underlings. Fear, coin, honor—every man bends to something. We must find what that is."

The elder Guardsman paused, thumb brushing along his jaw. "It's possible. But with the zealotry of Ridley's men, it may do more harm than good. One wrong word, one misplaced coin, and we risk exposing that we know his designs."

The answer was no answer at all, and frustration swelled in Gareth's chest. He turned from Edmund and looked back over the sprawling camp. Cookfires smoked against the pale sky, soldiers shuffled in half-rest, half-unease, and the banners of Betanthia stirred listlessly in the morning wind. To him, it all felt distant, unreal, as if he were watching someone else's army.

"I suppose vigilance is all we have left," he said at last, starting down the row of tents, Edmund falling in step beside him. "If Ridley means to see me dead, it'll be on the battlefield. That's the only place he can strike with clean hands."

"Spoken like a commander," Edmund said with a faint smile. "Your mother's intuition runs strong. Keep yourself visible—not just for safety, but for the men. They need their prince to be more than rumor or shadow. They need to believe you stand where they stand." He adjusted the clasp of his cloak and gave a nod. "Now, I've a briefing to deliver. We'll speak again before nightfall."

The two embraced, brief but brotherly, before parting ways. Gareth drained the last of his ale and tossed the cup aside without care. For the next hour, he wandered aimlessly toward the northern perimeter. Hills rolled beneath a fortress of clouds, their slopes dark as iron, their crowns unbroken by even the faintest spear of sunlight. The day itself seemed to curdle, as though the heavens mirrored the shadow gnawing in his chest.

Gareth stared into the wilderness, praying Madelyn might emerge and end his torment. Each minute without her stripped another layer of hope, until despair hollowed him completely. Yet in that emptiness, a stubborn resolve began to stir.

The men could not see him broken. Nor could his enemies. Whatever storm tore at his heart, Gareth forced his face to remain stone.

Bury it. Bury everything. They'll never understand.

With a silent farewell, he turned back toward camp. The army was awake now, cookfires blazing, the smell of bread and broth drifting over rows of tents. Soldiers shook off their weariness, voices lifting in morning chatter, steel glinting as they readied for the march.

When they saw him, cheers rang out. Men stood straighter, pride warming their tired faces. Their strength lent him his own, stitching together the frayed pieces of his heart. For all his failings, Gareth was no longer only a prince. He was a banner in flesh, a living emblem of House Bethard—and perhaps, whether he wished it or not, the face of a kingdom.

Lord Anderton Kenfield approached, distinguished as ever. His armor gleamed in the sun, heavy with gold rings and chains, while Sir Edmund and a group of Guardsmen marched at his flank.

"My prince!" Lord Kenfield called, raising a jeweled hand.

"Good day, Anders," Gareth replied with a nod. "Tell me you bring good news."

"I've word that Lord Vakaro has dispatched a detachment north. Judging by their numbers, I suspect he may have found the barbarians."

On another day, Gareth might have bristled at the thought. But Ridley Vakaro's schemes had long since ceased to surprise him.

"Or he could simply be scouting," Edmund added. "I suspect the front has collapsed. We may no longer face one horde, but several."

The thought was tempting, though dangerous. Damien Dreadfire's strength lay not in his sword arm but in the way men followed him to damnation. Betanthia had already bled from underestimating him—Cedric Valens most of all.

"Wouldn't that be to our advantage?" Gareth asked.

"Yes and no," Edmund said. "Fragmented, they'd be weaker—but harder to pin down. We'd be forced to split ourselves in kind, risking our flanks and rear both."

Anders inclined his head. "A sound caution. Information is the true coin of war, my prince, and we cannot let Lord Vakaro hoard it for himself. If his patrol learns the truth, we must see it reaches you first."

It was a strange thing, Gareth thought, to watch palace intrigue play out on a battlefield. The common soldier would never know they were fighting two wars at once—one against the Northmen, the other for Betanthia's soul.

"Then it seems I'll be spending much of my time in his company," Gareth said darkly. "How ironic that I may be safer the closer I sit to the man who wants me dead. He wouldn't dare strike openly."

Or so he hoped. Nothing about Ridley Vakaro was ever certain. Like the weather, he shifted without warning. But even the strongest walls had cracks, and image and reputation were stones a clever hand could loosen.

"Perhaps not openly," Edmund said, "but a man like him would use poison. Or a knife in the dark. He's not above it."

"Then perhaps the answer is to stop skulking," Gareth muttered. "He expects shadows and whispers. But how ready would he be for a direct challenge?"

Anders paled. "No, my prince. Too bold. We cannot predict how he'll react if—"

"Which is why I'll do it." Gareth's voice was iron. He looked to both men in turn. "See to the soldiers. That is my command. I will handle Lord Vakaro myself."

Reluctantly, they obeyed. Edmund's glare lingered, sharp with disapproval, but he held his tongue. In another life, he might have defied Gareth outright in the name of duty. But those days were fading. More and more, it was Gareth, not his father, who bore the mantle of a patriarch.

As Gareth made his way through the camp, the stink of sweat and smoke carried him past a row of iron cages. Within them, barbarian prisoners huddled in silence, their eyes hollow, their bodies bruised and beaten. Most stared at the ground, resigned to whatever fate might come. But one cage held a shieldmaiden, her fair hair matted with dirt and blood, her glare unbroken despite the chains.

Two soldiers lingered too close, their laughter sour, their hands tugging at her ragged tunic. The shieldmaiden writhed, chains clattering, her eyes flashing with defiance even as fear trembled at the edges. Gareth's chest ignited with rage.

"Stand down," he barked, his voice cutting like steel on stone.

The soldiers froze, turning to see their prince striding toward them. He ripped one man away by the collar and slammed him into the cage, iron rattling. The other staggered back, face pale, muttering excuses that died under Gareth's glare.

"You shame the crown with this filth," he snarled. "These are prisoners of war, not spoils for cowards. If you'd dare force yourself on a helpless woman, then you have no place in my army. Do I make myself clear?"

The silence that followed was thick and merciless. Both men stammered their agreement, eyes downcast. Gareth let the one go with a shove, disgust heavy in his stomach.

When he turned back, the shieldmaiden's glare hadn't softened. But beneath it, he thought he caught a flicker—relief, perhaps, or the faintest recognition. It was gone in an instant, replaced by the cold defiance of a woman who had lost too much to show weakness. Gareth straightened, his anger cooling into shame. He bowed his head slightly toward the cage.

"My men's disgrace is mine as well. You have my word—no harm shall come to you while I draw breath."

The shieldmaiden's lips curled, her voice rough with scorn. "Words. Always words. Do Betanthians think vows mean anything to us?"

"What is your name?" Gareth asked, his tone steady, almost gentle.

For a long moment, she stared at him, silent, her brown hair hanging in a dirty curtain around her face. At last, with a reluctant rasp, she answered:

"Mikka. I am sworn to Sylvia Stormguard."

"Then hear me, Mikka," Gareth said, his hand resting on the cage's bars. "By my blood, by the crown of Betanthia, you will not be touched. Not by me, not by any man under my command."

She met his gaze, unblinking, then spat at his boots. "Keep your oaths. We will see how long they last."

Gareth did not flinch. "They will last as long as I do."

For a heartbeat, the camp seemed to hold its breath—the shield-maiden chained in defiance, the prince bound by his vow. Then Gareth stepped back, turning away with his resolve hardening like steel.

Ahead, Ridley's command tent loomed, its crimson banners snapping against the black of the Order. The colors bled together in the wind like a warning, yet Gareth felt an eerie stillness settle over him. Since uncovering the conspiracy, he had expected fury, dread, even panic. Instead, he felt a hollow calm. If Ridley drew steel and struck him down then and there, Gareth doubted he would feel anything at all.

All anger, grief, jealousy—every tangle of sorrow—had drained from him. Perhaps the misery would return, as it always did, but in that moment, only resolve remained. He would face Vakaro with nothing but strength and courage, because nothing else was left.

He tore back the tent flap and strode inside. "Lord Vakaro."

The Southern Commandant glanced up from a map strewn across the table. He gave a subtle nod, the bare minimum of courtesy. Around him lingered a gaggle of sycophants, men whose loyalties bent whichever way the wind blew. Their hesitation at Gareth's entrance was broken by a sharp throat clear—Sir Edmund's.

The elder Guardsman stood at Gareth's shoulder despite being ordered away, his very presence a quiet act of defiance. For a moment, Gareth almost smiled. Edmund had never been one to abandon a Bethard to face vipers alone.

To Lord Vakaro's left stood Commander Renald Fletch of the Blackthorn, slick as an oil stain—the man who had replaced Madelyn after her fall from the Order. To his right lingered Baron Richmal

Derricks of Sothfort, bald and beardless, his scalp leathery and scorched by the sun—an oddity for one bred in the shaded villas of the deep south.

"My prince," Ridley intoned. His gaze flicked toward Fletch, a silent signal. The Commander stepped smartly to a side table, filled a heavy chalice with wine, and presented it with both hands. Vakaro accepted but did not drink.

"Good morning, gentlemen," Gareth said, planting his boots squarely and lifting his chin. "I would have a full situation report—truthfully, if such a thing can be managed."

Lord Vakaro paused, chewing his tongue as though weighing every word. "Our scouts report the savages have broken north. Their ranks falter. We've already encountered stragglers to the east and west—likely deserters, or rabble lost after the rout."

Gareth said nothing at first. The battle had been chaos, a storm no man could weather. That any fragment of the horde still lingered was difficult to fathom; the Blackthorn's charge would be remembered as one of the most savage in Betanthian history.

"And the Order?" he asked at last, voice clipped. "Do they claim knowledge of where the Northmen march?"

Silence pressed on the tent as Vakaro's men shifted glances, each face a mask telling its own story. Whatever answer came would be varnished with lies—but even lies carried truth for those willing to sift it.

"My prince," Commander Fletch said at last, his tone oily yet steady. "The Order knows nothing more than you do. We sweep the Plainhold, scouring for the barbarians' main host. A force has been dispatched north, and Lord Vakaro's patrols guard our flanks. The moment their horde is found, you will be informed."

He sounded sincere enough, though Gareth knew sincerity came cheap among liars. The only certainty was that he could not let Vakaro and his jackals dictate the war's course.

"Sir Edmund," Gareth said, turning, his voice iron. "Begin preparations to move out by this afternoon. I won't allow the Northmen time to rally while we sit wasting ourselves on patrols."

"My prince!" Commander Fletch blurted. "What of our wounded? The field bled us dry as well. If we move them too soon, half will never survive the march!"

It should have been a cruel order, but Gareth felt no weight in giving it. "Better their kin receive bodies whole than bury them in this cursed soil. We cannot sit idle while the Northmen gather strength. Break camp by midday—we march."

Even Lord Vakaro flinched at the decree. It was the sort of cold command that belonged to a hardened general, not a young prince. Perhaps grief had calloused Gareth's heart, or perhaps desperation to reclaim Madelyn had driven him to harden where others broke.

Regardless of their true feelings, Gareth left the tent in silence, Sir Edmund falling into step beside him.

"I never thought I'd live to see it," Edmund said, eyes wide. "Cold words, lad. Cold—but kingly."

"I have to think bigger than myself," Gareth replied, almost fearful of the resolve in his own voice. "What would my father have done? My grandfather? They forged a peace that lasted years. If I falter now, Ridley's assassins will strike true next time. Better he wonders if I'm beyond his reach."

Edmund clapped his shoulder. "After that display, even his knives will hesitate. You may have bought us time. The closer we push to Dreadfire, the more desperate Lord Vakaro will become. Can't have you stealing his glory. We'll accomplish both objectives at once."

"You're wrong about one thing," Gareth sighed. "I have three goals: crush the barbarians, root out the traitors, and bring my wife home. I cannot fail at any of them."

Edmund's hand tightened on his shoulder. "Then we march by midday. I'll see the men ready."

Gareth returned to his tent, heavy with the knowledge that his order was a death sentence for many wounded. Yet this was war in its rawest form—glory and horror entwined. If conscience slowed him now, Betanthia would fall.

Perhaps I am more dangerous than I ever thought. Perhaps something in me has already died. And if so… may my enemies tremble.

UDORN

THE AIR OVER MOT WAS ALIVE, SO CHARGED IT SEEMED TO CRACKLE with thunder. Rarely had the Ubneri been so animated; their seasonal raids had grown into ritual, predictable as the tides. But now something greater called them—danger, adventure, and the promise of gold and glory enough to fill a thousand sagas.

Udorn stood grim at the docks while men heaved weapons and provisions into the bellies of longships. Their laughter carried like wedding songs, not war chants. Then again, the Ubneri seldom marked much difference between the two, for both had a way of ending in blood.

He had seen nearly fifty raids, more than he cared to count. Half the faces from those years were gone, claimed by axe or swallowed by the sea, their names preserved only in the smoke-thick mead halls of Mot. Glory lived forever in story, yes, but it did not ease the weight on Udorn's chest. He scratched the stubble of his shaved scalp and sighed.

"You look as though you've been sentenced, not set to sail," Dulkin One-Eye jeered, the leather patch biting tight across his brow.

Behind him lounged Thaul and Gaxas, inseparable as ever, sharing a laugh at their brother's quip. The two were so often at each other's side that men joked they were born from the same womb.

"Tell me again how you lost that eye," Udorn grunted. "Was it lack of skill in battle… or did your drunken tongue find the sharper blade?"

"You know the tale! It was in battle, but not for carelessness," Dulkin flared his nostrils. "Come, Udorn! This is a glorious day! We are about to embark on a raid the likes of which our people have never seen. Truly, history will be made by us!"

It was easy to boast of war. Gold and glory were the Ubneri's life-blood, and the only fate worse than death was to be forgotten. Udorn had seen and done terrible things, but pride in having his name carved into the stone of Mot's mead hall still stirred his heart.

"There's the slayer we remember," said Thaul, barrel-chested, arms like tree trunks. His brown hair hung loose to his hips, shifting as he laughed. "Your caution is well-founded, though. I've heard tales of Betanthia and their might. I saw their ships once—ten times the size of ours."

"It's true," Gaxas added, tall and lean beside his brother-in-arms. "We watched them on the horizon, hulking things they were. Must have lost their way. When they caught sight of us, they fled as fast as the winds could carry them. Imagine their terror when they see this fleet!"

Such tales always grew larger in the telling. At least this one was believable, Udorn thought, but not for the reasons his brothers believed. They mistook the Betanthians for cowards. The truth was far worse.

"The Betanthians are no cowards," Udorn said, turning away. "They will fight hard, and many good men will die. May the gods reward your optimism with good fortune."

Despite his reservations, Udorn knew he would sail south. To remain behind would brand him a coward, a shame that would cling to his bloodline for all eternity. Worse still, the gods themselves might scorn him, barring his place in Sjenohor when death at last came calling. No—he would sail, he would fight, and he would carve his name into glory. Before he could dwell further, a familiar voice called out.

"Udorn!" Rennek hailed, pushing through a knot of men hauling barrels.

Scars carved across his cheek and jaw caught the morning light, souvenirs from battles fought long ago. His eyes, sharp and weary, searched Udorn with the weight of a man who had buried too many brothers. Behind him strode Tharek, his firstborn, shoulders squared, his youth tempered but not yet broken. His dark hair was bound in a tight braid, and though his armor was battered, he carried it with pride.

"The whole of Mot is stirring," Tharek said. "It feels like every hand with a pulse means to sail. We would not miss it."

Udorn clasped Rennek's arm in greeting, then Tharek's. With Rennek, he had shared blood and battle more times than he could count, scars enough between them to fill a saga. Tharek, though, was untested—this would be his first true campaign. Yet his eager grip and wide-eyed fire steadied Udorn all the same, if only slightly.

Old, weathered planks groaned beneath Udorn's boots as he turned from the docks. Enough posturing, enough chatter—it was time to gather his own weapons and provisions. Though the day was young, the tide waited for no man, and by nightfall, half the fleet would be straining to push through the Plainhold surf. Better to be ready than caught lingering like a green boy.

But before he could step off the shaky dock, a stir ran through the crowd. Shouts rose, followed by a ripple of laughter and disbelief. Udorn paused, his brow furrowing as an unthinkable sight came heaving into view.

"By the gods," Udorn groaned. "What does he think he's doing?"

Lumbering onto the pier was Ragruk, chieftain of the Ubneri. Though years removed from his last raid, he was still a fearsome sight. Standing a head and a half taller than even Thaul, his sheer bulk commanded silence. A dozen slaves trailed after him, bent under the weight of chests, barrels, and, of course, his polished suit of thick armor.

"My lord?" Dulkin cocked his head. "Are you really—"

"Of course I am, you lout!" Ragruk thundered, a salty breeze rolling through his fiery red beard. "Did you lose your brains with your eye? Do you think I'd sit idle while my people set sail for the largest raid in history? Heh!"

An inconvenience if there ever was one, Udorn thought. The last thing he needed was to butt heads with a man such as Ragruk. After all, the chieftain had spent years feasting while others bled for his glory.

"Of course not, lord," Thaul said, arms crossed. "We would expect nothing less."

"Then be about your business!" Ragruk barked. "The waves beckon, and you sit here gossiping like women! Board and make ready, or I'll have you whipped!"

Udorn bit back a curse. It was a reminder of why he kept from Mot whenever he could — the man was as welcome as a boil on his ass. Still, at least they'd be sailing on separate ships. A small consolation, but enough to keep him from hurling himself into the sea.

He turned from the pier and made for his homestead, one of Mot's largest and properly suited for a man of his accomplishments. Guri stood in the doorway, anxiously awaiting his return. Smooth, green linen hugged her slender body, her thick, wavy blonde hair drawn into a single braid. It was a wonder how such a dainty woman was able to birth proper Ubneri children from a man such as him. Truly, the spirit of their people coursed through her blood.

As Udorn approached, she said nothing. Instead, Guri offered his shield, axe, and a leather satchel stocked with provisions. From her other hand dangled a small talisman of bone and twine, the edges carved with simple runes.

"I made this for you," she said, pressing it into his palm. "Carry it close, and may the gods remember my prayers when steel bites and waves crash."

They stared long into each other's eyes, neither daring to shame themselves with open grief. Still, it was proper for a man to love and honor his wife, and Udorn's chiseled arms drew Guri close with uncharacteristic gentleness.

"Go," she whispered, pulling back from their embrace.

A peal of laughter and screams echoed from behind their homestead. Their children were engrossed in some game, and though it would do him well to see all three before setting sail, it was better they not cry and plead for him to stay. There was no place for weakness in Mot, even from the tiniest babe. So instead, Udorn rubbed Guri's arm gently, tucked the talisman into his belt pouch, and turned back toward the docks.

Brave warriors greeted him as he came aboard a massive longship, some veterans of a hundred raids or more. Each carried the fury of the gods in his heart and the strength of the Ubneri in his sword arm. Their laughter and booming voices rose like storm winds, and Udorn felt his spirits lift at once. The bonds of brotherhood forged in battle were iron-strong, as binding as blood. In truth, he often felt closer to these men than to Guri or his children.

Perhaps in time, my boys will grow strong and earn their place by my side on the battlefield. Nothing would make me prouder than to have them carry my body home on my shield, to the sound of blowing trumpets and beating drums.

It was the highest honor an Ubneri could hope for—to be succeeded in life by his own blood. Legacy was the only treasure more precious than gold, and Udorn intended to set the bar as high as the gods would allow. Surely, his sons would face a great burden to surpass the tale he was about to carve into the histories.

A horn blast split the air, deep and commanding, rolling across Mot like thunder. The revelry died at once, every voice stilled. All turned as Ragruk, chieftain of the Ubneri, strode aboard Udorn's longship. His bulk seemed to darken the very bow, his arms raised high in a show of dominance.

"The time has come!" Ragruk bellowed, his beard flaming red in the salt wind. "All must bear witness and give thanks to the gods, for they have chosen us for this great task! Together we shall strike south, conquer new lands, and return with riches beyond counting!"

Mot erupted, cheers roaring so loud the gods themselves must have heard. Supplies were loaded with frantic speed, wives and sons offering their final farewells with stoic faces. Sons wondered if they would see their fathers again. Wives stared hard at their husbands, unwilling to let tears betray them. This was the Ubneri way.

For Udorn, the hardest burden was not leaving his home behind—it was enduring Ragruk's company. The chieftain ruled by right of blood, a chain unbroken for a thousand years, and that fact alone demanded silence. Yet Udorn's teeth ground in secret.

Insufferable oaf, he thought as he tightened the straps on his satchel. *I pray for swift winds and gentle waves, if only to be free of him sooner.*

Another horn bellowed. Longships cast off one by one, oars slapping the sea in thunderous unison. The great bay opened before them, and soon the Ubneri would be embraced by the endless blue waters of the Great Sea—a graveyard of countless souls, and the path to glory.

From the corner of his eye, Udorn caught sight of Guri and their three children at the water's edge. Though her cheeks were dry, he could feel the storm raging in her heart. Ubneri women were expected to be as stone when their men went to war, and Guri upheld that duty with unyielding resolve. Their eyes locked across the widening gulf, a silent pact passing between them.

Bring us gold and glory, or let the sea take you, her gaze seemed to say.

The fleet pulled away, sails snapping open as the wind pressed them seaward. Waves slapped the hull, and a cool spray kissed Udorn's face, carrying him back through a hundred memories of raids past. Each had begun like this—with horns, cheers, and high spirits—but none promised to be as great or as costly as the one now unfolding.

Still, he turned once more, feeling her eyes upon him. By his life or by his death, he would see his family cared for. Gold, slaves, and renown would be theirs in plenty—but only if he returned.

I will come back to you, my lady, he vowed silently, standing tall at the prow. *I will come back with gold and glory. Or else let the sea take me.*

SYLVIA

S HE SLEPT NOT A MINUTE THAT NIGHT. HER EYES STAYED FIXED ON the dark horizon, searching for a sign that never came. For days, Sylvia Stormguard had watched the wounded trickle into camp. Some limped. Some were carried. Some bore wounds that even the gods would not heal. Many had returned from the battlefield, but far more were feared dead. Among the missing were friends she loved too dearly to lose.

Zifnir, I beg for your mercy! Let them return unharmed. I would do anything to see them again.

But each warrior who passed by was a stranger. Kin, yes—but hollow, stripped of the jovial northern spirit that once defined them. Gone was the indomitable essence of their people. What returned now were broken men, ashamed of their defeat.

At least one companion had been spared. Ingryd Bjornsdottir stood with her at the edge of camp, her arm bound in a linen sling. Thick blonde hair, unbraided and unkempt, covered the cuts that lined her face. She looked older than her years, dark circles pooling beneath her eyes, as if even a month of sleep would not restore her.

"Do you think anyone else will return?" Ingryd asked. The question carried no hope.

Sylvia shook her head. "I have prayed more in these days than in all my years combined. Surely, one of the gods must hear."

Dawn bled across the eastern sky, crimson and orange spilling over the camp. In the growing light, more figures emerged—shadows turned to men. They had crept through the night to avoid Betanthian patrols, and now hundreds streamed into camp. Sylvia and Ingryd scanned each face, hearts pounding, clinging to scraps of hope.

But then, a face most familiar broke through the sea of strangers. Cropped black hair, eyes like frozen seas—Hilde. She had found her way back. Aside from a few gashes and bruises, she looked little worse for wear.

"Thank the gods!" Sylvia breathed, drawing her into a brief embrace. Yet even joy demanded restraint. As warchief, as Rhivothi shieldmaiden, she could not afford to weep.

"Thank them?" Hilde scoffed. "The gods delivered their faithful a crushing defeat. Why would they do such a thing?"

No answer could mend that wound. Sylvia herself had not yet come to terms with the rout, with the loss of so many kinsmen. Silence was all she could offer.

"But I am thankful they spared you both." Hilde's grip tightened on her shoulders. "Where is Mikka? Has she returned?"

Sylvia hesitated. To speak the truth was to risk shattering what little hope remained. Perhaps Mikka still lived, fighting to slip Betanthia's grasp. Perhaps.

"Not yet," she said at last. "But she will return. Of this, I have no doubt. Damien lives, so hope is not lost. But we must make ready. Our enemies give chase, and we are too stunned, too scattered to stand against them now."

Together, the three shieldmaidens pressed deeper into the camp. Everywhere Sylvia looked, sorrow lay heavy. The ground was thick with butchered bodies, strewn and heaped into wagons. Mournful groans rose from the wounded as surgeons cut and cauterized, filling the dawn air with the stench of charred flesh. Near the baggage train, movement caught her eye—Zander, striding with grim determination, as though already bound to some dreadful purpose.

"Make ready, and I will rejoin you soon." Sylvia touched Hilde's arm, gentle but brief, then hurried after the most despicable man in Caldakas.

Zander the Zylmacian. The very name stunk of treachery. Now he strode through camp with all the arrogance of a conqueror, intent on usurping Damien Dreadfire's command. Word of his challenge spread like wildfire, drawing eyes and whispers as he passed.

"You must not do this," Sylvia called, forcing her way through the crowd to keep pace.

Zander smirked, long strides unbroken. High noon would soon arrive, and with it, the hour of his challenge. A distasteful choice from a distasteful man—yet one she had suspected all along.

"Come now, love," he said, voice dripping with false charm. "Are you truly so blind? Damien led us into a slaughter. What would you have me do—stand idle while my people are massacred? You saw how those Blackthorn rode through us as though we were children. Even the gods cannot count our dead."

It would have been a lie to say Sylvia felt no sympathy. The wildmen had been cut down like dogs, their blood spilled in heaps before her eyes. For all their savagery, the Zylmacians had fought bravely. Even after watching their kinsmen executed, they had stood loyal beside Dreadfire. That loyalty, however, was now fading.

"Your people fought as bravely as any other," she conceded. "And we have suffered no less than you. But now is not the time for grievances. Betanthia is at our heels! We must remain united. If you—"

"United?" Zander barked a bitter laugh as he ducked into a refreshment tent. "Failure may unite the Rhivothi, but in Zylmacia, failure is married only to death."

He splashed a bowl of water over his face, streaks of mud and blood running down his jaw. The effort did little to cleanse him. Sylvia wrinkled her nose. She could not tell which reeked worse—the stench of the dying outside, or Zander himself.

"Zander, my people would never accept you as our warlord. The alliance would devour itself while King Bethard's hounds closed in. You cannot do this. Withdraw your challenge!"

He drained a mug of mead in one gulp, then turned on her. Daggers flashed in his eyes, a half-rotten smile curling his cracked lips. Something deeper lurked beneath that grin; an ambition long buried, now unmasked.

"The very fact you say such a thing tells me everything," he said, studying her like prey. "It tells me you fear I might actually beat him. Would that truly be so terrible, love? Would we not be better served under new leadership? Or would you have us all destroyed for the sake of loyalty to a failed man?"

Sylvia's jaw clenched. Damien's triumphs at Blackwolf Pass and Castle Morden felt like dust in the wind now. Even she could not deny the slaughter they had just endured. Yet her spirit hardened. If nothing else remained, she would fight for her oath.

"He is our warlord," she answered, voice steady, "and we have sworn ourselves to him. Would you break your word now, when it matters most? Is that the man you wish to be remembered as?"

Zander grinned wider, then shoved past her and strode back into the chaos of camp. All around, wounded still poured in, too many to count. Others began to pack and flee north without waiting for orders. The alliance shuddered like a dying beast.

"I am the man who will lead us from ruin to glory," he declared, pausing to rake his eyes over her from head to toe. "You are no fool. You know Damien does not stand a chance against me. So tell me, love—when I best the brute, will you take your rightful place at my side as chieftess?"

It was an offer as foul as swamp water. Sylvia turned away in disgust, curses flying. All she could do now was find Damien before it was too late. For all his wounds and weariness, he was a man who would diminish before no one, flee from no challenge. If the fates decreed it, Damien Dreadfire would march into Sjenohor with sword in hand.

And that is why I must stop this—for all our sakes!

"I would rather charge the battlefield alone than accept your offer," she spat over her shoulder. Then she ran, weaving through the camp at full haste. Word of the challenge spread like fire on dry grass, drawing men and women away from their duties despite the looming threat of Betanthian pursuit. Already, a crowd began to gather in grim anticipation of the duel.

Two Rhivothi guards stood at vigil outside the command tent. Their eyes were hollow, their shoulders heavy with defeat. These were men who once longed for Sjenohor, as all Rhivothi did—but after the calamity on the Plainhold, Sylvia wondered if they believed any glory could still be found in death.

She entered quietly. Damien stood shirtless, eyes closed, his breath coming in low, steady draws. Blood soaked through the bandage at his leg, seeping into torn trousers. His hands were raised, palms upward, lips murmuring a prayer. Before him on a table sat an effigy of Kholdyr, ringed with incense smoke and a linen-wrapped offering. The smell of ash and myrrh clung to the air. It was a sight all too familiar, and all too unwelcome.

"Damien," she pleaded, her voice breaking into the silence. "I beg of you. You must reconsider."

Slowly, the warlord turned. His face carried the weight of defeat, but in the depths of his eyes, the fire of purpose endured. Sylvia knew that look. She had seen it once before, years ago—when Damien first came to Rej Rhivoth, blood-soaked from the massacre at Borjifa.

"There is nothing to reconsider," Damien said, voice low but unshakable. "This path I walk is one I cannot stray from. I have come too far to turn back… even now, even after all I have suffered."

"Think of the greater good." Sylvia stepped closer, fighting to mask her desperation. "Our people need you now more than ever. If you were to fall, then—"

The supreme warlord's glare struck her like a lash, hot enough to scald the sun. "We have already fallen, Stormguard. There is no escaping the fate the gods have thrust upon us. But so long as I draw breath, no man shall ever challenge me. If it is my destiny to die by a Zylmacian axe, then I will enter Sjenohor with my head held high."

"Damien, you mustn't!" Sylvia cried. "You are too important. Should Zander strike you down, the Rhivothi will break from the alliance— likely the Nothanek with them. Our lands will be left defenseless. All will come to ruin!"

Damien limped toward the tent flap, every step heavy, bloodied. "By axe or sword, or the slow decay of time, I will meet my creator. My only desire is to die well and to have made him proud. The gods alone will decide the fate of the free tribes. If they demand my blood to keep our lands safe, then so be it."

In another moment, Sylvia might have found his resolve admirable. But not now. Not with so much hanging in the balance. Appealing to his reason was useless, though she had but one card left to play.

"And what of your family?" she pressed, forcing steel into her tone though her hands trembled. "Your wife and children… would they wish to see you slain? Would they want their legacy to end on a Zylmacian's blade?"

Dreadfire paused, eyes wide, his face drawn tight as a war drum. For the first time, Sylvia saw unbridled rage seize him. Not the measured fury of a warlord, but something raw, dangerous. It was a fear unlike any she had known in battle—one that made her very spirit tremble.

"Speak not of my family, Stormguard," Damien growled, sorrow trembling beneath the fury, "or I will tear your tongue from your mouth with my bare hands."

Before she could stammer an apology, a commotion rose outside. At first, Sylvia thought it was another Rhivothi brawl with the Zylmacians, but when she burst from the tent, she found no quarrel, only panic. A handful of men came sprinting from the south. Then more. Then a flood. A stampede of terror swept the camp.

"Knights!" a voice shrieked. "The knights are coming!"

Sylvia's breath caught. "Oh gods… Damien—they've found us!"

Dreadfire emerged, bastard sword in hand, gaze raking the chaos with cold bewilderment. Together they looked south, but the rolling hills showed only endless grass, bowing in the wind. Yet only days had passed since the slaughter, and Betanthian pursuit was certain. Damien's lips peeled back, teeth clenched like a sprung trap.

Without hesitation, he strode back into the tent. At once, he fell upon the heap of blackened steel that was his armor, strapping it on with ruthless efficiency. Though it might be his final battle, he moved with the unshaken certainty of a man unbroken. Sylvia lingered close, struck dumb by the sight. Even at the edge of ruin, he wavered not.

When Damien bent to bind his greaves, he faltered—just for an instant. His breath hissed through clenched teeth, the wound in his leg searing white-hot. In that sliver of hesitation, Sylvia saw past the legend. She saw the mortal man within, fragile and flesh, a shadow of fear flickering beneath the iron mask.

"Allow me," Sylvia said, moving to his side.

Damien bristled, turning away with a huff. He wrestled with the armor himself, jaw tight, refusing even this small mercy.

"There's no time!" she urged. "If this is our end, then we must steal every second we can to prepare."

At last, reason seemed to break through the iron wall of his pride. He gave a curt nod, lips drawn tight in anticipation of the pain to come.

Sylvia pressed a mug of mead into his hand, and he drained it greedily, amber spilling down his breastplate.

With a grunt, he allowed her to fasten the cuisse to his thigh. His eyes rolled back, breath sharp, as if caught between pain and some twisted ecstasy. To see a man of god-like strength so undone by wounds—it dimmed him in her eyes, however slightly. The thought struck her as absurd, and yet it clung to her still. Piece by piece, she encased him in steel, until at last he stood before her more statue than man.

"Ready?" she asked, though her own voice wavered.

Damien scowled but nodded, again seizing his bastard sword. When offered his helm, he waved it aside. He would meet his foes with his own face bared, that they might know the man who opposed them.

Together, they stepped out into chaos. Camp followers scrambled to heap what belongings they could into wagons. Wounded warriors staggered, some dragging others, while the helpless were left upon the ground. Terror rolled like a tide through the camp, yet still no enemy appeared from beyond.

Cresting the nearest hill came a band of riders, spurring their mounts as fast as the beasts could carry them. Dust trailed in their wake. A smaller group broke off, racing straight for the command tent, faces drawn and spirits frayed.

"My lord Damien!" one shouted, a nomad by his garb. "The Blackthorn give chase! We crossed them not two days past. We were no match! They cut us to pieces!"

Dreadfire said nothing. He only stared, incredulous. For a man so calculating, it must have been ruinous to watch every design unravel.

"How close?" Sylvia pressed, her voice taut. "How much time do we have?"

"A day, perhaps," the rider replied. "My lord, we must depart at once, before they discover us!"

Without waiting, the patrol tore off into camp, doubtless to gather kin and whatever meager belongings they could before fleeing north. Against the Blackthorn, with the alliance splintering and half the camp preparing to run, it would be folly to stand and fight.

"By the gods, I would give anything to slay our foes this day," Damien growled, his frown deepening. "But another path lies before us—for now. Come, Stormguard. We will see our people to safety. Then…" His black eyes burned. "Then I will show that Zylmacian dog that the might of old Borjifa has not yet diminished!"

LUCETTA

EACH HOUR DRAGGED LIKE A DAY, AND EACH DAY LIKE A CENTURY. Lucetta Eldon sat high upon the balcony of the Westwind Citadel's tallest tower, gazing out at the shattered landscape below. Cardale still smoldered. That surprised her. Its streets lay silent as a tomb — a far cry from the constant drone of the common folk.

A western wind stirred, pushing smoke out to sea. In its wake, the ruin revealed itself: buildings around the central square stood as husks, blackened skeletons of their former grandeur. The stench of burnt wood and charred flesh had sickened her at first. Now it rose to her like perfume, as fragrant as flowers in bloom.

There can be no creation without destruction, she told herself. *To heal, the rot must be burned away. If only I could leave this cursed palace, I would begin restoring this city to its glory.*

Few dared approach her except to deliver platters of food and jugs of water. She had refused Aldred's dinner table outright, in defiance of his decree to lock the wine cellar. Her thirst clawed at her unrelentingly; her hands shook as if plunged into ice.

And worse still, the woman in black had vanished. The shadow had not appeared in some time, leaving behind only a sea of unease. Every

stroke of Lucetta's grand design had been guided by that presence —
and now she was rudderless.

Please, do not abandon me. Not now. Not when I need you most.

When at last she dared to leave the tower, Lucetta descended the
stairwells like a storm. Servants scattered before her, trays clattering,
voices stammering, until she sent them fleeing at every turn. Never had
she despised the company of others more. In truth, her contempt had
grown so immense she could imagine Caldakas emptied of every soul
but her own—and she would welcome it. To endure the prattle of lesser
folk was nearly a fate worse than death.

That evening, she again refused Aldred's table, recoiling at the
thought of sharing space with anyone, and instead sought the highest
peaks of the Citadel. There she found her only solace: silence, lonesome
and absolute. For the first time in her life, she discovered a strange
comfort in isolation.

Hours passed as she gazed down at Cardale's corpse. Streets she
had walked, markets she had passed through, neighborhoods she had
known—all reduced to heaps of char and ruin. When despair pressed
down, memory rose sharper still: the ravenous mob, the priest's shrill
cries, their hands grasping for her mother's body.

*Who were they to make such demands of royalty? Who were they to
challenge the might of my House? Nobodies. Vermin. And now, heavens
willing, ash.*

The thought rekindled her fire, but only for a moment. It guttered
quickly. Escape was impossible; soldiers and purple cloaks prowled the
grounds like guard dogs. She was a prisoner, abandoned by her guardian spirit. And with Queen Charlotte gone, there was no one left to
confide in.

*I'm sorry, mother. I wish you were here. I wish none of this had ever
happened. If only the world still made sense instead of burning to cinders*

around me. You were the only one who ever loved me… and I destroyed the only good thing I had.

Later that night, Lucetta sat awake, rocking in her bed. The scabs of past wounds had long turned to scars, but still she clawed at them until her nails tore skin. Her tongue scraped across cracked lips. The thirst was unbearable. Days? Weeks? She could not remember the last time wine touched her mouth. The thought alone brought tears to her eyes.

I just want it to stop. All of it. Please… take this torment away from me!

Every minute alone was its own torture. The palace she had once called home now felt like her jailer, its walls closing in tighter with each passing hour.

If only I had wine, she thought, *then perhaps this suffering would ease. I do not care if Aldred forbade it. I must have wine. I'll get it myself if I have to!*

She slipped into the corridor outside her chamber, the stone floor cool and slick beneath her bare feet. Moonlight streamed through a high window, casting a pillar of white across the hall, orbs of dust drifting like fireflies. No sound stirred. The silence was tomb-like.

Lucetta crept toward the grand staircase, each step measured, each breath shallow, braced for a reprimand that never came. The palace was still—unnaturally still. Even at the latest hours, there was always movement, a guard patrolling, a servant bustling. Tonight, there was nothing.

Am I dreaming? she wondered. *No… this feels real enough.*

At the ground level, she slipped into the servants' wing, moving silently as a cat. Only the soft pitter-patter of her own steps betrayed her. A heavy oaken door stood ajar. Beyond it, rows of bunks stretched into the dark.

Servants lay upon them, each stiff as effigies, arms pressed neatly to their sides. Had their chests not risen faintly, Lucetta would have sworn she had stumbled into a mortician's house. It was one of the strangest sights she had ever beheld.

Nearly a dozen bunks in, a ring of keys glimmered on a worn wooden table beside a sleeping steward. Lucetta padded closer, heart hammering, careful to steady her breath. One hand lowered, hovering above the ring. Slowly, carefully, she slid her fingers over the cold iron. With her other hand, she lifted them free—no rattle, no sound.

She lowered her eyes to the ring, searching for the key she needed. Its crooked shape was unmistakable. Relief washed over her—the cellar would be hers, and at last, her thirst quenched.

Finally…

Lucetta lifted her head and froze. The servants were sitting upright. Dozens of men and women stared at her, unblinking, faces stiff as carved stone. A bolt of terror cut through her so sharply she nearly choked. Keys clutched to her breast, she began edging toward the door, each step measured, every muscle taut, as though any sudden motion would loose the pack upon her.

Their gazes never wavered. They crouched on the edge of pouncing, eyes darkening, whites turning red and raw. In the corner of her vision, one mouth stretched impossibly wide, curling into a grin that split from ear to ear. Lucetta's heart thrashed, fluttering so wildly she thought it might burst.

She dared a glance over her shoulder to measure the distance. Close enough. With a jolt, she broke into a run, lunging for the doorway— only to stop dead at its threshold.

What madness is this?!

The room was still. The servants lay flat once more, arms pressed to their sides, as if they had never stirred. She stood gaping, breath caught in her throat. Surely it was a dream. How else could such horror exist in waking life? Or had her thirst, her withdrawal, broken her mind at last? She wanted no answer.

Clutching the keys, Lucetta fled, hurrying through one corridor after the next. The sconces, usually ablaze day and night, were dead.

Only moonlight pooled across the stone to guide her steps. Yet in every corner of shadow, something seemed to move. Something watched.

At last, she reached the cellar door. The wood was ancient, swollen, and stained with time, the black iron hinges freckled with rust. Her hands shook as she fumbled with the keys, one after another, until—*click.* The tumblers gave way. With a faint squeal, the door opened, revealing an oil lantern hanging from a nail. Its flame was low but steady, enough to push back the dark.

Step by step, she descended, stone stairs slick with moisture beneath her bare feet. The air grew cool, her breath trailing in faint white wisps. Each sound—the scrape of her foot, the soft squeak of the lantern's chain—seemed deafening. She reminded herself again and again:

You can do this, Lucetta. It is only the wine cellar. Only that, and nothing more.

At the bottom, the gloom opened into rows upon rows of barrels, some so vast they could have been carriages, others small enough for a servant to roll with ease. The sight struck her like sunlight through storm clouds. For the first time in what felt like ages, she smiled. Against the far wall, a rack towered from floor to ceiling, bristling with bottles. Lucetta laughed—a sharp, broken sound—and nearly wept. At last. At last, her torment would end.

She snatched a bottle from the rack, its cork blackened with age, wedged deep in the glass. Her fingers clawed and twisted, grunting with effort, but her strength was pitiful, bled away by hunger and thirst. Minute after minute, she struggled until her hands trembled and the bottle slipped from her grip. Then it came.

A sound, faint and mournful, drifting from the back of the cellar. She ignored it at first, clutching the bottle to her chest. But as she turned toward the stairs, the sound returned—longer this time. A whimper. A sob. Her skin prickled. Every hair stood on end.

"Is… is that you?" she whispered, voice quavering, desperate for the woman in black. Strange that she longed for the entity's company, but in that moment, anything was better than the unseen.

She raised the lantern high, its glow trembling with her hand. Shadows stretched and shivered. The whimper came again, followed by a shuffle. Lucetta gasped, swallowing against the knot in her throat, her chest so tight it fought for air. From the far darkness, a shape lurched forward. Shambling, uneven, pale flesh catching the lantern's light. An arm extended out of the black, fingers cracking as they reached for her.

"Lucetta?" The voice was warped, groaning like old timbers, grinding like stone dragged across stone, yet she knew it. She knew it all too well.

"M…mother?!"

Impossible. Charlotte Bethard was dead. Lucetta had seen it with her own eyes—Pavlos' hands snuffing out her life, the funeral rites, the city tearing itself apart in mourning. There was no conceivable way the Queen could yet live.

But then the figure came into the lantern's light; her mother. And yet, not her mother. Charlotte's skin was pale as moonlight, stretched thin over jutting bone, cracked and flaking like old leather. The thick brown hair she once wore proudly had thinned to brittle gray strands that clung in stringy clumps. She lurched onward, tears spilling from sunken eyes, carving lines into a face hollow and raw.

"Lucetta… please!" the Queen groaned. As she spoke, teeth rattled loose from her gums, pattering to the floor like pebbles. "Don't leave me in the dark. Daughter… please…"

The sight was too terrible to comprehend. Lucetta screamed, dropped the bottle, and bolted. Glass shattered behind her, spilling its dark contents across the stones. Her heart battered her ribs as she sprinted, yet the cellar door stretched away, further with every step, retreating as if mocking her. She dared a glance back. Charlotte was coming fast, her broken body jerking, lumbering, closing the distance with unnatural speed.

"Come back! *Come back!*" she wailed, her voice rising shrill, cutting the air like a winter gale. "You left me! Why… why did you leave me in the dark?!"

Lucetta screamed, tears streaming in torrents as she bolted from the cellar. She slammed the door shut with desperate speed, fumbling the key into the lock. It turned with a sharp *click*. She pressed her back to the wood, chest heaving, sobs wracking her throat.

Please let it be madness, nothing more…

Then the thumping began. The door shuddered as though a dozen men had rammed it at once. Hinges shrieked. Wood groaned and split. A blow like thunder drove her forward, nearly spilling her onto the stone. Another followed, louder still, planks cracking under the strain. Surely the old wood could not hold.

"Daughter!" The groan rumbled through the door, mournful and hungry. "Come to me! Do not leave me in the dark! Join me—join me, and we will be together again!"

"I can't!" Lucetta wailed. "I'm sorry, Mother! Please… leave me be!"

"Come to me, daughter!" The voice sank into a rasp, deep and unearthly. "Come to me, and we will stay in the dark forever!"

Panic surged, carrying her limbs faster than thought. Lucetta fled, skirts tangling, her feet pounding up the grand staircase. Fear lent her strength she had never known, every heartbeat like a drum driving her onward. Three flights she climbed before daring to stop. From the balcony above, she looked down into the vast hall and froze.

Heavy footsteps echoed off the marble below. Wet, uneven slaps reverberated like meat against stone. Charlotte's decomposing body swayed and lurched, her head jerking as she sniffed the air like a beast on the hunt. Lucetta trembled, lungs burning. She had been holding her breath without knowing. Then it burst out of her in a sharp gasp— her hands snapping to her mouth a heartbeat too late.

The Queen halted mid-stride, her ruined head tilting toward the grand staircase. Then, step by dragging step, she began her ascent. One leg lurched stiffly, the flesh withered and pale, sloughing off in globs like melted wax.

Lucetta turned and fled again, climbing flight after flight until at last she reached the residential level. She darted into her chamber and shut the door with painstaking care, her sweat-slick hands fumbling with the skeleton key. The tumblers clicked, and relief bled through her in a shudder.

Two inches of oak now lay between her and the nightmare. But within moments came the sound—a slow pattering of footsteps, uneven and labored. Then the moan: low, guttural, groaning through the corridor like timbers bending at sea. Then silence.

Lucetta lowered to the floor, pressing her cheek against the cold stone. Through the narrow crack beneath the door, she strained to see, her breath shallow. Moonlight spilled across the corridor walls, empty and bare. For a fleeting instant, she believed it was over—that Charlotte was gone, returned to the crypt where she belonged, dust and bone and nothing more.

Then the shadow came. It slithered down the hall, long and thin at first, swelling with each step until it blotted out the light. Her pulse thundered in her ears. A rotting foot planted itself before the doorframe, pale and peeling. Lucetta's heart seized. The corpse bent low.

Terror-stricken, she tore herself back just as the Queen knelt, her ruined face angling for the gap, searching for her daughter's eyes in the dark.

Bony gray fingers scraped beneath the door, clawing and grasping. Long white nails ticked against the stone, their soft *tap-tap-tapping* pounding in Lucetta's ears like hammers. Shaking, she pressed her back to the wall, curling into a ball. She rocked, eyes squeezed shut like fortress gates.

This isn't real… this isn't real…

Then warmth touched her face. Sunlight. The first in days. Birds sang faintly beyond the window—or so she thought. Cautiously, Lucetta opened her eyes. The glare of morning seared them, forcing her to squint. Had she been asleep? How long? Was it all a dream?

The questions scarcely mattered. Relief washed over her in waves. She sighed and almost laughed, her lips trembling on the edge of joy. She stretched, joints aching from her cramped vigil. But then, something caught her eye.

She froze, dumbfounded, and leaned closer to the door. Beneath the gap, the stones were raked with long, fresh scratches. Thin and white, gouged deep. And there, among them, fragments of broken fingernails gleamed in the morning light. Lucetta's smile crumbled. Her breath seized.

The scream that tore from her throat shattered the silence. For she knew then, with a certainty beyond denial, what she had seen was no dream at all.

MADELYN II

S HE SAT BENEATH A DYING SUN, WEEPING. EACH TEAR STUNG LIKE A razor, stripping away another piece of who she once had been. Madelyn ran a hand through her hair — cropped short at the shoulders, nearly black from root to tip. The absence of her long braid reminded her of all she had lost, in flesh and in spirit.

It was only right for Gareth to have my braid. There was no other love left to give him…

But it was more than her adornment she mourned. Far more. Madelyn felt hollowed, displaced, as though her spirit had been wrenched from her body and thrust into a stranger's shell. Any sense of self, of the life she had lived before the war, was gone. Gone like her knights. Gone like her innocence.

For hours she rode, her body sagging in the saddle, until exhaustion dragged her to the edge of collapse. Even as the sun sank, the Plainhold burned hot as a furnace, nights offering little reprieve from day. And worst of all, water was scarce. To find it in this wasteland was like seeking warmth atop a mountain peak. Yet to the patient and the perceptive, the land spoke in its own tongue.

There were signs of life — even here, where death had claimed so much. A grove of withered oaks huddled together like mourners at a graveside, their trunks gray and rotten, their twisted branches thrust skyward in skeletal defiance.

She dismounted and sought shelter among them. There was no water, but their cover would suffice. She ached with fatigue—not just of flesh, but of spirit. She could have slept for a week and still woken weary.

"I am so tired," she murmured, voice breaking as she sank to the ground. "So… tired…"

Her muscles trembled with weakness, her eyes burned raw from sleeplessness. The more she thought on it, the more it dawned that days—perhaps even a week—had passed since true rest last touched her.

What if I never sleep again? What if my life is nothing but an endless waking nightmare?

The thought drove tears to her eyes, though it was a wonder she had any left to shed. As she wept, a glint of parchment caught her gaze— the edge of a scroll jutting from her horse's saddlebag. Hope, faint and fragile, flickered within her.

Madelyn hurried to retrieve it. The document was faded and brittle, its edges crumbling in her hands. Carefully, she unrolled it, though her heart sank. The ink bore none of the mystic luster she remembered from the Ivornorium's hidden cave. Its images did not shimmer or writhe with secret life; they lay dull and dead upon the page.

"Ancestors…" she whispered, closing her eyes tight. "Please… speak to me. I beg of you. I'm so lost. I need your guidance…"

She stroked the parchment with trembling thumbs, coaxing, pleading, desperate for some spark. Once it had felt alive beneath her touch; now it yielded nothing but the whisper of dry fibers and a ceaseless murmur of the Plainhold wind. Even with her eyes closed, her breath stilled, her mind reaching outward, the scroll remained lifeless.

Should I… Would it be wise? Is it the only way left?

The darkness inside her coiled, patient and eager. Its power was undeniable, swelling stronger with each summons. Yet every time she drank from its poison, some fragment of her former self withered. Still, desperation gnawed at her. Answers eluded her. And slowly, inexorably, shadow seeped into her eyes—black tears pooling at the corners, bleeding across the whites until they drowned in ink.

But before she could slip fully into that realm, the air shifted. Something stirred around her. Brilliant light bloomed around her, sparkling like a thousand lanterns cast into the barren grove. White orbs drifted through the night sky, glistening as if the stars themselves had fallen to earth. Madelyn exhaled, releasing the blackness from within her, and for the first time in what felt like an eternity, she smiled. A true smile.

The scroll in her hands shifted. The brittle parchment softened, rejuvenated, its surface smooth and supple. Ink brightened; its symbols seemed fresh-drawn, alive again. Daylight vanished, replaced in an instant by a sea of radiant stars. She gazed upward, lips parted, a strange warmth in her chest. She had not felt such peace since the march to Castle Morden.

Then the figure appeared. It came gliding through the grove, radiant with white fire, its form dissolving brush and bramble as though they were mist.

"You've come back!" Madelyn cried, tears of joy streaking her dirtied cheeks. She reached out, hand trembling, desperate for the touch of kin.

But something was wrong. The being did not rush to embrace her. It did not radiate the comfort she remembered in the cave. Instead, it stood still as a statue, its eyes unblinking pools of starlight. From it came not love, but disdain. Not warmth, but cold.

Madelyn faltered, arm falling back to her side. The spirit shook its head. Slowly it turned, as if to leave. Though its face was formless, she saw it clearly in her mind's eye: a straight beard thick as a curtain, hair pale and long, flowing past the elbows like a golden river. And the expression—it pierced her deeper than any sword. It was the same look the High Marshal had given her as a child, when her defiance had tested his patience.

"Why?" she pleaded, voice breaking. "Why do you shun me? What have I done wrong?"

The entity said nothing. Its gaze pierced her, searching the marrow of her soul, then turned away without word or gesture, as though disappointed. An avalanche of sorrow crushed her. It was as if all warmth, all light, all love had been stripped from her at once.

"Please!" Madelyn cried, collapsing to her knees. "Please, don't go! Don't leave me!"

But it was no use. The radiant figure receded. The orbs winked out, one by one, until only darkness remained. The ink upon the parchment stilled, brittle and lifeless once more. Though the air clung hot and heavy with humidity, a bitter chill swept the grove. Night pressed in again, and darker still were the shadows within her heart.

All her life, Madelyn had striven for righteousness—to achieve, to prove herself, to earn respect, to show she was more than she appeared. Yet for every effort, she had been scourged with suffering. Broken. Cast down. Alone. She curled beside her gear and wept until her body shook.

At last, exhaustion claimed her. Drowsiness thickened her limbs, and she drifted. First came darkness, an endless, absolute void without a hint of light. It was almost a relief to let herself sink into it, free of anguish, free of thought. But then, in the far distance, a faint glimmer appeared.

It grew. The light swelled brighter and sharper, until it consumed her. Blinding radiance enveloped her body, forcing her eyes open against its brilliance. She winced, raising a hand to her brow. Suddenly, daylight caressed her skin like a kiss.

Where... where am I?

She might have been drunk, so disoriented was she. Rising slowly from a bed of short, soft grass, she noticed something strange: thick leather bracers bound to her forearms, and across the backs of her hands, symbols of blue runic paint. The markings ran higher, curling over her biceps, intricate and unbroken. She rubbed at them in panic, but they did not smear. They were not paint, they were tattoos.

Dumbfounded, Madelyn tried to spring to her feet, but pain shot through her back and kept her pinned. She realized she had been lying on a blanket of long, golden hair—her own—miraculously restored. Panic surged. She seized great handfuls of tresses, rising to her knees as the weight of it slid down across her thighs, swaying like silken sunlight.

"What devilry is this?!" she whispered, her voice trembling.

Not only had her beloved hair returned, but her clothing had changed as well. She wore the garb of the Northmen: a simple linen tunic, brown trousers, and leather boots. Beside her lay a steel breastplate, an animal-skin cloak, a round shield, and a sheathed sword.

"This is a dream," she said, clutching her chest. "I know I must be dreaming…"

Terrified yet compelled, Madelyn bolted from the grassy cove to take in her surroundings. Before her stretched a sprawling city of tents, their banners snapping with runes painted in blood-red strokes. The air thrummed with deep drums, carrying on the wind like the beating of some ancient heart.

She was among the Northmen, that much was certain. But unlike her captivity, there was no dread here. The air felt… welcoming, almost reverent. She ventured past a patrol of spearmen, hulking men with sun-scorched skin and scarred flesh. Each lowered their heads as she passed, offering respect as though to a queen.

Beyond them stood a row of covered wagons laden with spoils. She drifted closer, curiosity tugging her on. Chests and sacks overflowed with wealth. Carved busts of marble peered out from the shadows, and wooden furniture gleamed with delicate artistry. The bounty of sacked villages lay piled high. She turned to leave, then froze.

A tall mirror leaned against the side of a wagon, and in its glass her reflection stared back. But it was not the woman she knew. The face was hers, yes—but sharpened, hardened. Her eyes glowed faintly with a steely fire, her hair flowing down her back like a golden river. Blue runes shimmered across her skin, pulsing faintly as though alive. She looked regal. Fearsome. Almost divine.

Madelyn's breath quickened. Her trembling hand rose toward the glass, but the reflection did not follow. It only stared, unblinking, as if to ask her a question she could not answer. She staggered back, the drums pounding louder, the banners snapping like whips.

"About time you woke," grumbled a familiar voice.

Madelyn turned sharply. Marvath Bonesplitter stood only paces away, arms crossed, expression soured as ever. His long beard and sandy hair whipped loose in the western wind, wild and untamed.

She did not know whether to embrace him or flee. In captivity, he had shown her an unexpected respect, a strange mercy. Though nothing like the bond she had shared with Tylar Bradshaw, there was something of the same iron in both men. Were it not for the war devouring Caldakas, they may have called each other friends.

"Well, don't just stand there," Marvath barked. "We take the field at any moment."

The hulking Rhivothi seized his great axe, hefting it easily in both hands, and strode southward. The earth already trembled. War cries rippled through the camp. Hooves beat the ground like drums, shaking it to its core. Madelyn's heart thundered. For an instant, she could not move, rooted between terror and awe.

Then instinct took hold. She scrambled for her breastplate, dragging it over her shoulders, then clasped the animal-skin cloak about her neck. With sword and shield gripped tight, she stumbled forward, breath ragged, as though she had run leagues. Past the tents she went, weaving through their dense ranks until the way opened, and before her stretched the northern host in all its dreadful breadth.

Before her stretched the might of the free lands. Nearly a hundred thousand strong, their host blanketed the horizon, a sea of shields and steel. Together they howled like beasts, axes and swords pounding against wood in a thunderous rhythm. Madelyn's breath caught. The sound, the energy—it rattled her bones, set fire to her chest. She could not help herself. A smile split her face wide, uncontrollable, and she joined the revelry.

She screamed until her throat burned raw. Her blade hammered against her shield, sending shocks into her arm, but she welcomed the pain. To be wild. To be unbroken. To stand among a people who would not bow. It was liberation, pure and savage.

Then, silence. The frenzy died all at once, swallowed by an ominous stillness. Madelyn blinked in confusion until she saw them. From beyond the rolling hills, another host descended. Tens of thousands. Perhaps hundreds of thousands. Their banners stretched like storm clouds across the plain: the eagle of House Bethard and, beside it, the black-and-gold of the Blackthorn Knights.

Her people, and yet not. A dread she had not expected crept through her. The sight of Betanthia's legions—disciplined, vast, merciless—filled her with no pride, no comfort—only fear. But the Northmen would not be cowed. Their warriors bellowed, horns bellowing, cries splitting the heavens. They howled for blood.

A mighty blast cut through the air, deep and long, and in an instant the host surged forward. Madelyn was swept up, legs churning, lungs searing. The field thundered beneath the stampede. Ahead, the Betanthians locked into formation, shields braced, spears bristling in a wall of death. The collision was inevitable.

What am I doing? Madelyn thought as she drew closer to the wall of shields. *These are my people... or at least... they used to be...*

But the thought slipped like sand through her fingers. Memories of Betanthia melted away like snow beneath a spring sun. Her days in the

Order felt like little more than daydreams now, pale beside the steel in her hand and the fire in her lungs. She could scarcely recall the High Marshal's name, nor even the face of Corbyn Scott, her fallen lover. His memory came like a flicker, then vanished, leaving nothing.

Arrows hissed overhead. The Betanthians braced. Madelyn saw it then—fear in their eyes. They had never faced such fury, such numbers, in all their long history. Then, impact. Flesh slammed against wood and steel, a deafening cacophony of shrieks and roars.

For the first time, Madelyn's sword drank Southern blood. Betanthian blood. It was thirsty, insatiable. She swung again and again, each blow cutting down another foe as effortlessly as scattering the seeds of a dandelion on the wind.

A barrel-chested spearman pushed into the line, a tower of polished steel that gleamed like a mirror. His southern shield braced, he lunged with lightning speed, the spear's tip snapping inches from her breast. Madelyn twisted, parried, the blade scraping sparks. He pressed her hard, strike after strike, until her arms screamed.

Then Marvath Bonesplitter came thundering in. His great axe cleaved the spear like kindling. Another swing, then another, shattered the shield into splinters. The soldier staggered back, howling as bone snapped in his arm. He turned to flee, but Madelyn was already upon him. Her blade slid across his lips, silencing him forever.

As brave as the Betanthians fought, they could not withstand northern ferocity. The barbarians seemed invincible, the strength of the Eveldanyr blazing through every warrior. They pressed forward with reckless abandon, undaunted by mounting casualties. Rhivothi axes carved into the wall of southern spears like bears shredding fallen timber.

The enemy line wavered, buckling first at its center, then crumbling at its wings. Madelyn watched as a mass of northern horsemen crashed headlong into the Blackthorn. For once, the Order found no advantage. A bannerman toppled from the saddle, a lance skewering his unguarded throat. The black-and-gold standard slipped from his grasp, tumbling to the dirt.

Madelyn felt nothing. No grief. No loyalty. Only a grim justice. The Order had earned this. Let every tear she had shed be repaid with a Blackthorn life. But then, she froze.

Titan Bradshaw loomed before her, broad as a fortress wall. His breastplate was streaked with gore, his shaggy salt-and-pepper hair matted in clots of blood. His eyes held no love, no kinship. Only a hatred fierce enough to burn through steel.

A knot cinched in her chest as the ground seemed to empty around them, warriors unconsciously giving space. The noise of battle dimmed beneath the weight of the moment. Titan moved first. His blade came down in a brutal arc, faster than his size should allow. She barely twisted aside, the strike carving air inches from her face. Another swing followed, crashing against her shield, rattling her bones.

"Tylar!" Madelyn screamed over the chaos, voice raw. "Enough of this! Tylar!"

Her pleas fell on deaf ears. Titan Bradshaw's hunger for vengeance was boundless. He had fought through hell itself to keep her safe, and the betrayal etched in his eyes could not be quenched. Every swing burned with rage, every blow bit deeper into her failing shield. Madelyn knew she could not endure him for long.

She searched desperately for an escape, but the horde pressed close on every side. All eyes were upon them—Northmen and Betanthians alike—the fighting in their quarter of the field grinding to a halt. There would be no flight, no reprieve. So, she embraced the darkness. Black mist bled across the whites of her eyes, and Titan faltered at the sight.

The earth rumbled as clouds thickened overhead, gray and churning. Madelyn clenched her teeth until her jaw ached, struggling to hold back the fury boiling within her. Titan lifted his blade, sensing an opening, but thunder cracked so violently it nearly sent him sprawling.

The air stank of lightning, and Madelyn let go. Her body dissolved into black fog, vanishing before the stunned host. Gasps rose from Northmen and Betanthians alike. At first, she hesitated. This was Titan, her protector, her brother-in-arms, their friendship forged together in the blood of Castle Morden. A bond such as theirs should never have been broken. But hesitation was death. She saw it in his eyes: if she faltered, he would not.

Grief hollowed her heart as she struck. One terrible swing, and Titan Bradshaw's head toppled from his shoulders. His massive body crumpled, crimson pouring into the thirsty earth. Warriors broke in panic at the sight, stumbling from the horror.

Goodbye, my friend. Perhaps we will meet again in the next life…

But no grief came—only rage, white-hot and searing. Teeth bared, eyes wild, Madelyn surged after the retreating southerners. This was Marcellus Bethard's doing, his endless hunger for conquest the true culprit. Because of him, Lord Cedric Valens and his son lay dead. Because of him, Corbyn and Hunter were gone. Because of him, she had slain her truest friend.

These aren't men. They're weapons of House Bethard. It's as simple as that. And no weapon that stands against me shall survive!

A strange voice cut through the chaos. At first, Madelyn thought it was just another dying soldier, or a foe begging for mercy before the killing stroke. But it came again, steady, familiar, and undeniable. Her breath caught, and she turned to find its source.

And there he was—Gareth Bethard, clad in the finest steel any smith could shape, his long brown hair knotted and matted with sweat, his face streaked with blood and anguish. He looked every inch the king he was meant to be.

"Madelyn?" Gareth uttered, his voice breaking. "What… what are you doing?"

Her throat tightened at the sight of him. Affection welled despite the carnage around them. Gareth had been the one constant in her fractured life; loyal, gentle, the man who held her through nights of torment. Innocent, in a world where innocence never lasted. And in his hand gleamed his sword.

The silver blade was radiant, gleaming as though forged from sunlight itself. Its long crossguard held twin sapphires, pale flames flickering in their depths. The grip was bound in dark leather worn smooth by use, and yet the weapon seemed untouched by time, ageless and eternal. The sight of it made her heart falter. A weapon fit not for a soldier, but for a legend.

With lips trembling, eyes blurring with tears, she stepped forward and laid her hand gently upon his cheek. Their gazes locked, and for a fleeting moment, the roar of battle melted away. Love had not yet died. She longed to fall into his arms, to shed every burden, to feel safe again.

Her breath quivered. She leaned closer, drawn by an aching need to press her lips to his, to let the world and all its cruelty fall away. But before she could bridge the distance, a Rhivothi axeman came roaring from the fray, his blade arcing straight for Gareth's neck.

Madelyn's scream caught in her throat—then she awoke, drenched in sweat and tears. The Plainhold's night lay cool around her, crickets singing under a blanket of stars. She was alone once more, lost in a world gone mad.

It had all been a dream, and not a pleasant one. Madelyn's spirit was torn in two, pulled hard in opposite directions, with no relief in sight. She was a woman of honor, a woman of loyalty, yet where should those loyalties lie? It was agony not to know where to call home.

Within moments, she was wailing again, her fists hammering against the rock-hard soil. But even as the sound tore from her throat, clarity dawned. She was in this forsaken land for one reason only. Short, black locks brushed her cheeks as she sat up, grim reminders of all that had come to pass.

Her mind raced through the litany of loss—her tribulation, the deaths of her friends, the High Marshal's treachery. Her tears dried, replaced by fire. Fingers curled into fists, trembling with a rage barely contained. She had done nothing wrong. It was the world that was wrong. And those who had taken part would answer for it.

They took everything from me, she thought, gathering her gear with steady hands. *Damien Dreadfire. The High Marshal. All of their ilk. If justice still lingers in this world, they will die screaming. And if there is no justice… then I will drag them to hell all the same!*

SYLVIA II

Only when the sun bled into the west did the warband dare to rest. Their march had been frantic and relentless, enough to sap the spirit of even the fiercest Rhivothi. Yet despite the dangers that lurked just beyond the horizon, Sylvia's thoughts lingered not on the pursuit but on what awaited them when camp was made.

The company of her shieldmaidens steadied her. Hilde and Ingryd rode close at her side through the day, and when night fell they helped raise her tent. Together they shared bread, salted meat, and a horn of mead beside a small fire. The flames were allowed only long enough to warm the food before being smothered, for even light had become a risk.

They sat together in the hush of the night. The heavens stretched vast above them, painted in rare hues of red, blue, purple, and green, a sky alive with wonder. Yet not even its splendor eased Sylvia's mind. She stared into the endless dark, as though searching for answers that would never come.

"You mustn't worry," Hilde said at last, sipping her mead. "Had Damien returned without an arm or leg, then you would have reason to fret."

"I do not know what has come over me," Sylvia admitted, her voice low, almost ashamed. "I was always so sure… so fierce in my convictions. But these past days, my confidence has faltered."

Her companions shifted uneasily. A Rhivothi, least of all a shield-maiden, was not expected to voice such weakness. Yet it was not wholly unexpected. For all their ferocity, the women of their people often fought with more than rage. They fought with love and hope, dangerous emotions to wield in a world that scorned them.

"We have all been shaken, no doubt," Hilde said at last, her cyan eyes catching the moonlight like shards of glass. "We mourn for Marvath, for Mikka, for all those we have lost. But their journey is done. They have gone to Sjenohor and are beyond the concerns of this world. Save your sentiment. The dead have no need of it."

It was a cold truth, but truth nonetheless. Sylvia bowed her head, recalling her station as warchief—how many eyes turned to her now for strength, for certainty, for a reason to keep fighting. With Marvath gone, who would stand as the Rhivothi's iron fist? Who would inspire both fear and wonder in their people?

"You are right," Sylvia whispered, nodding slowly. "It falls to me now to lead us from this darkness. I will pray and fast on the morrow, and seek strength from the gods. Not for myself, but for our people. I am only the conduit of their will."

"Conduit or no," Ingryd muttered, shifting forward, "you are flesh and blood as we are. And flesh grows weary." She gestured to the half-empty horn in Sylvia's hand. "Rest, sister. We will need your strength when the sun rises."

For a fleeting moment, warmth stirred between them; three women bound not by oaths alone, but by the weight of survival. Yet even that warmth could not keep the shadows at bay.

Sleep proved elusive. Every hoofbeat in the night set Sylvia's hand groping for her axe. Each creak of leather or whisper of canvas sent her heart pounding until she realized there was no danger. And then, with a weary sigh, she would drift once more into shallow dreams, only to wake again at the first tremor of movement.

At last, warmth touched her brow, the light of dawn prying her eyes open. There would be no more rest. Time was short, and the hour of Zander's challenge drew near. The Zylmacian would be denied no longer. She rose, muttered a prayer to the gods, and gathered her effects. Her shieldmaidens gave her solemn nods as she left the tent, the unspoken burden heavy in their eyes.

At the command tent, guards parted like temple doors, letting her pass without challenge. She cast back the canvas flap and stepped inside. Damien stood at the table, armored and grim, with Valerick the Red at his side. They spoke in low tones, words sharp but hushed, until they saw her. Silence fell, thick as fog. Both men stared, their eyes flashing unease.

"Let us speak no more of this," Dreadfire said, waving a hand dismissively, though the stiffness in his voice betrayed the weight of what had just passed.

Valerick bowed stiffly and departed, but not before fixing Sylvia with a grave stare. It was no look of hostility, no common enmity. His eyes carried something heavier—inevitability, as though he had already seen the end of all things. She refused to answer it with word or gesture, unwilling to give the omen power.

"Stormguard," Dreadfire said, lifting his chin. "Your interruption is most unexpected. Come, drink with me."

"Damien," she pressed, impatience straining her voice. "This is no time for mead. We must—"

"Enough," he cut her off, his tone sharp as steel. "Obey me now, as you once swore to do. Pour us a drink."

Her heart sank. Rarely, if ever, had Dreadfire spoken so to any of his warchiefs. It was a bleak sign, a shadow of finality cast upon his words. With a reluctant breath, she poured the mead into two tankards, placed one in his hand, and raised her own. Together, they drank in silence, a toast as somber as any funeral rite.

"You must not protest," Damien said at last, his black eyes glinting with suppressed fury. "Nor must you lose faith. All is as the gods decree. If my service has ended and I am summoned home to Sjenohor, I will go with joy and pride in my heart. Then it will fall to you, Stormguard, to fight for our people… to lead them if you must. Cleanse yourself of this despair. Root it out. It is poison, and it has no place in the spirit of a warrior."

It was a scathing rebuke, but a true one. Only when Sylvia paused to weigh his words did she see how far she had fallen. To be Rhivothi shieldmaiden was to rise above the common spirit; to be a warchief was to tower above even that. Doubt had no place in such a station. Her insecurities were hers alone to bury, no matter the cost.

Something stirred within her chest, faint but growing. Damien was right, to her annoyance. As warchief, she was not merely a warrior; she was a symbol, the standard to which their kin would rally. Marvath had gone to Sjenohor. Einarr's spirit had faltered. And soon, another would be claimed before midday. If she faltered too, all might be lost.

Their eyes met across the gloom of the tent, and this time no fear clouded hers. Only the unyielding northern fire. Together, they stepped out to face the morning. Several hundred had gathered in a great circle, the hush of expectation weighing heavy. Few spoke above whispers, and even those quickly fell silent.

Damien paused at the tent's edge, jaw clenched, his face rigid with discipline. Yet Sylvia could see the truth—each step sent fire racing through his battered body. The sheer force of will it took to hide such pain filled her with both dread and awe.

Then came the commotion. From the press of onlookers emerged a band of Zylmacians, more numerous than expected. At their head strode Zander, swaggering, eyes alight with cruel triumph. At his side marched Jollkud the Marauder and a clan of lesser kinsmen. They came like rabid hounds, snarling, howling, spittle flecking from their mouths. Their fury was plain, and Sylvia loathed to admit its root—they had cause enough for rage.

"Zander, you mustn't!" Arik Akselson cried, breaking from the crowd. "Betanthian scouts are everywhere! They could be upon us at any moment!"

"Enough of your sniveling, fisherman!" Zander spat. "This is no concern of yours. Go pray to your gods, or your trees, or whatever it is soft men like you do."

"We have all lost dearly," Arik pressed, arms spread wide. "But if we turn on one another now, all we've fought for will be ash. We can still win this war, but—"

Jollkud the Marauder shoved him hard, sending him sprawling into the dirt. A growl rose from the Nothanek nearby, uncharacteristic anger flashing in their eyes. Sylvia gasped, horror clenching her chest at the chaos breaking loose. She made to intervene, but a sudden silence fell.

Damien Dreadfire stepped forward into the circle, his bastard sword gripped in one hand. Pain twisted his face, and his limp betrayed him, yet he remained terrible and unbroken, the very force of nature his people feared and revered.

"Ah! He shows himself after all!" Zander jeered, twirling his axe. "But perhaps you've misunderstood, mate. Axes and shields, like the old ways."

Damien raised the sword to eye level, his gaze fixed on the worn leather of its hilt. "This blade was my chieftain's—Sanbaen, slain at Borjifa. It carries the weight of his story, of our people's struggle. Should I enter Sjenohor this day, it will be with this sword in my hand."

The wildman dragged his tongue across his half-rotten teeth. "Once again, the honorable Damien Dreadfire breaks his word! He bears no shred of honor. But no matter—I'll bury you with that sword, and with it the memory of your feeble tribe."

The two men advanced, each step heavy with purpose. There was no stopping them now. Sylvia could only watch, powerless, as their blood oaths collided. Zander lifted his shield with careless contempt, his scorn for Damien plain in every gesture. Dreadfire struck first, his bastard sword cleaving the air in a mighty arc, but finding nothing.

Zander slipped aside, nimble as a wolf, then trotted in a mocking circle. The gesture was infuriating, and Sylvia's hands itched for her axe. But to interfere would be to profane the gods themselves. So she clenched her teeth and prayed, silently, that some sudden misfortune might take him.

"Get him, Damien!" a Rhivothi nomad roared, breaking the deathly quiet.

The shout set the Zylmacians ablaze. They howled like pit-beasts, frothing and snarling, their voices rising in a savage chorus. Zander grinned at the frenzy, then feigned a rush. Damien stepped back—his bad leg faltering under him—and in that instant, Zander struck for real. His shield surged forward, his axe swinging with lethal force. Again and again, he chopped like a woodsman felling a tree. Each blow crashed against Damien's guard, steel shrieking, sparks flying.

The circle thickened as more warriors pressed close, eager for blood. Sylvia tried to keep her eyes fixed on the duel, but her gaze flicked again and again to the crowd. Every new face was another threat, another risk. A Betanthian patrol could appear at any moment, thundering down upon them. Were that to happen, their warband would be cut apart as easily as wheat beneath the scythe.

A thunderous clash yanked her focus back. Damien had turned the tide, launching his own barrage. His blade fell swift and merciless, but Zander's shield absorbed every strike. He danced, he deflected, never overreaching, content to wear Damien down. It was plain to Sylvia what would happen: he would circle, parry, and wait until exhaustion dragged Damien's guard low… and then the killing stroke would come.

Her chest tightened. Her prayers felt useless. And in desperation, Sylvia did the only thing left to her.

"Borjifa!" Sylvia roared, the cry tearing from her lungs like fire. "Borjifa! Borjifa!"

Her voice broke the air, and others joined at once. Axes hammered against shields, feet stamped the earth, the chant swelling into thunder.

"Borjifa! Borjifa!"

A spark lit in Damien's black eyes, then a blaze, stoked by the cry of his kin. A sheen of water welled there, born of rage and grief and the terror of failing both tribe and family. He drew every pain, every wound, every betrayal into his heart, and fed the fire. Zander sneered, contempt curling his lips, and lunged again. He slithered side to side, axe whirling in savage arcs.

But Damien moved like water—sudden, unstoppable. He flowed around each strike, turning aside every blow, then crashed back with terrible force. A front kick slammed into Zander's shield, staggering him. The wildman raised his axe to meet the overhead swing, but Damien's sword fell quicker than lightning.

With a roar that shook the circle, the bastard sword split through wood and iron. Zander's axe snapped in two. For a heartbeat, time held still. Both men froze, the crowd silent, every eye fixed upon them. Then blood appeared, a red smear along the sword's edge.

Zander staggered. His knees buckled. And with one final twitch, his head toppled from his shoulders. His body crumpled to the dirt, blood gushing like mead from a shattered cask. A pitiful end to a pitiful man.

The circle was deathly quiet. The Zylmacians stood, stunned and motionless as stone. Zander, the most infamous wildman the Bymist had ever birthed, was gone. Sylvia scanned their faces. She expected fury, vengeance. Instead, she saw only despair. The Westerners' spirit, it seemed, was breaking.

Gods, I pray this was the right decision. I pray we have not damned our cause by way of petty pride.

"It is finished," Jollkud said at last, his face tight with displeasure. "The will of the gods has been made known. For our part, we will abide by their decision."

Sylvia found the words curious. Incivility was the Western way of life, yet even the lowliest of creatures clung to honor. And so it seemed with the Zylmacians. Still, many stared at Zander's headless corpse as though his passing had marked the end of an age for their people.

Damien staggered back, dragging breath into his chest. His eyes lifted toward the heavens, scanning the dreary veil of clouds overhead. Was he searching for the gods' approval, or their forgiveness? It was impossible to know. And Sylvia, truth be told, did not wish to. The alliance he had bled to build, year by year, had splintered in mere moments.

She stepped into the clearing, but few spared her a glance.

"Let this duel bury our quarrels," she said, her voice steady. "Let them be ended, so we may turn again to the true war. Betanthia gathers against us. The Zylmacians must choose a new warchief, one who will speak at Damien's table."

No answer. Not a voice among them. Some began to drift away, their shoulders bent, their faces hollow. They turned their backs on the cause for which so many had fought and died. To see such men lose heart when resolve was most needed cut deeper than defeat on the Plainhold.

"Jollkud," Sylvia pressed, her gaze fixed upon the Marauder. "Your people respect you. If the choice falls to you, know that I will give my endorsement without hesitation."

"Every man here stands by his own will," Jollkud said grimly. "And I cannot compel them to stay—not by whip, nor gold, nor oath—should their hearts turn elsewhere. For our part, Zylmacia has given its last."

For a people she once thought treasure-hungry and brutish, they seemed now every bit as human as any other. Perhaps their famed ferocity had always been nothing more than a mask, a shield against a gnawing sense of inferiority. It was hard to know.

"We must convene a council," Damien rasped, breath ragged like a wounded beast. "Summon the others… at once."

Step by step, he forced himself toward the command tent, every movement wrenched by pain. He tried to mask it, but the limp betrayed him. Sylvia hurried close, desperate to shield him from so many prying eyes. At least Zander's corpse still held the warband's attention.

"Summon the other warchiefs!" she barked to a nearby guard before slipping inside. She turned on Damien, alarm sharp in her voice. "Your leg! Let me—"

But he stilled her with a raised hand. Seizing a pitcher of mead, he drank deep, gulping as though it were water in a desert. The wound burned, his body screamed, yet he gave nothing more than a grunt. He would not allow weakness to be seen. Not here. Not even by Sylvia.

Moments later, Arik Akselson and Valerick the Red arrived, their silence carrying more weight than words. Both took up grim positions at the table, eyes shadowed with doubt. Then came Dhuuld, storming in with fury written across his face.

"Damien!" the Khorrtalli chief roared. "What have you done?! The alliance is in tatters—the Zylmacians desert by the score!"

The news was no surprise, though no less distressing for it. If the Betanthians struck now, their battered warband would not withstand the blow. Sylvia steeled herself, knowing one careless word could splinter what little remained.

"We cannot trouble ourselves with the wildmen," she said firmly. "We must turn to our own and regroup before the enemy finds us scattered."

But Arik pressed on, ignoring her. "My lord… what is to be our fate, now that the Zylmacians have abandoned the campaign?"

Silence answered first, broken by a dry hiss of wind tugging at the canvas. Damien wiped sweat from his brow, his eyes fixed on a map spread before him. Then the flap stirred, and Jollkud strode inside. Every gaze followed as the marauder filled a mug, drank deep, and claimed a place at the table.

"Do not think my people so easily undone," he growled. "Many have swallowed their last humiliation and returned to the Bymist, aye. But those who march beneath my banner have come too far to turn back. Not even this defeat will sate our golden hunger."

It was encouragement, faint though it was, the first in many days. Yet the air remained thick with unease.

"What of Lazilyth?" Arik asked at last, his voice low. "Where is the crone? Why does she not show her face?"

Sylvia's lips parted. Her own encounter with the woman had left her wary, the mystique frayed, her faith shaken. Perhaps Lazilyth was no soothsayer, only a manipulator cloaked in shadows. Yet... she had seen things. Terrible, inexplicable things, beyond any parlor trick. Before she could answer, Damien's voice cut through the tent.

"The power of the Eveldanyr has shown itself," he said, dark and solemn. "Lazilyth's sight was blinded by a force not of this world. Of this I am certain: powers move against us, powers beyond mortal reckoning. But we must not bend. Betanthia closes in for the kill. We cannot be caught unawares."

He slammed his palm upon the map, black eyes blazing. "Come. We must shield our people while time yet remains!"

TITAN II

OUGHT TO KILL EACH AND EVERY ONE OF THEM...

The thought gnawed at Tylar as he endured hour after hour of witless chatter. Each empty word was another nail hammered into his skull, and Conrak seemed to have an endless supply of them. This was torture, every bit as cruel as the cell beneath Castle Thorn.

Tales spilled from Conrak's mouth like cheap ale in a barracks, each one more bloated than the last. Brave deeds, impossible feats, wild encounters—whether truth or fancy no longer mattered. Tylar had ceased caring. His patience was bled dry. The night did little to help. It was a starless black, so thick he could scarcely see the outline of his horse's head. The air was heavy, oppressive, and his mood soured with every mile.

"And that was when we found them," Conrak said, his voice dripping with smug nostalgia. "Nearly thirty Zylmacians gathered round a fire in the central square. Seems wildmen don't care for walls or roofs when they eat. We waited until nightfall, and they were drunk as lords."

"Thirty?" Earlwick scoffed. "And how many were you?"

"A dozen, perhaps," Conrak mused, scratching his chin. "We slipped into their camp quiet as foxes, slit their throats one by one. They noticed only when we reached the last ten. After that, well… it was butcher's work."

Tylar had heard the tale before. Once, twice, perhaps more. Each telling with new flourishes, new boasts. Conrak's lies were like flies: swatting them away only brought more. Better, then, to stay silent. And so he rode, eyes fixed on the dark horizon, watching for the faintest sign of movement. The night pressed in on all sides, and with each league behind them, Madelyn's trail grew colder. Doubt crept in—perhaps the path had gone too cold already. Perhaps they would never find her again.

Just when hope seemed ready to desert him, the sky broke open. Clouds peeled back to reveal a swollen moon, its pale light spilling across the parched earth. The world sharpened into view, every ridge and shadow laid bare. Tylar almost scoffed aloud. Were he the sort to heed omens, he might have taken it as a sign, perhaps even proof that the strange power within Madelyn bent the land to her will. The thought curdled in his gut.

They pressed on, the Plainhold's tall grass parting around them in whispering waves. Conrak and his fools prattled still, blind to the way the growth thinned into a sudden clearing. Tylar's gaze caught something—a detail out of place, wrong enough to set his teeth on edge.

"Would you shut the fuck up?" he snapped, his voice raw and vicious. "We've got company."

The laughter died at once. Horses stamped nervously, and the patrol froze, each man's breath locked tight in his chest. Earlwick's face drained of blood; his bulging eyes looked fit to pop from his skull.

"He's right," Conrak muttered, all humor gone. "Something's there."

Tylar's eyes narrowed. A faint wisp of smoke curled upward through the grass, the blackened stalks charred as if kissed by flame. The smell hit him next—acrid, bitter, unmistakable. Burnt flesh. He slid from the saddle in a heartbeat, drawing his blade before his boots struck dirt.

Better to have steel in his hand than a broken leg beneath a horse when the trap sprang.

Conrak followed, shield already up, eyes scanning the shadows. Northmen were as treacherous as they were fierce; it would be no surprise if they lay hidden, waiting for the chance to bleed them dry. Step by careful step, Tylar advanced. The silence held, heavy and unnatural. No sudden rush. No battle cry. Only a faint stink of death on the wind.

As they broke into the clearing, a flock of carrion crows burst skyward in a black wave of wings. Tylar flinched, his body tensing before he forced it still. The farther they pressed on, the clearer the horror became. Bodies lay strewn across the dirt, some hacked apart by steel, others half-eaten by the birds. No Betanthian patrol had reached this deep into the Plainhold. Curious… troubling.

"Who could have done this?" Tylar muttered, his voice low, wary of the silence around them.

Conrak crouched, studying the lay of corpses, tracing shapes in the dust as though his mind could rewind the carnage. His gaze fell to a hulking brute, a mountain of a man still clutching a giant maul.

"Must have taken a fair number to bring that one down," Conrak said, almost admiring. His mouth curled into a grin. "Might have proven too much even for you, Bradshaw."

Any other time, Tylar might have answered steel for jest. Instead, his thoughts went elsewhere. Not to patrols or warbands—to Madelyn. She had half a day's lead, perhaps more. Enough rage to split stone, enough fury to cut down any who stood before her.

"You don't suppose the girl was here, do you?" Tylar asked, though it was little more than a thought spoken aloud.

"I wouldn't rule it out," Conrak admitted, sliding his sword back into its sheath. "If so, then we're close. I spy tracks to the northeast."

Hope lit Tylar's chest like fire. Without hesitation, he turned, striding hard toward his horse. Perhaps he was only hours behind her now. The battle here would have cost her time—time he could close. As he crossed the hard-packed earth, his eyes caught another body, and he slowed. A Northman lay apart from the rest, his corpse strangely undisturbed.

The warrior was flat on his back, a one-handed axe clasped against his chest. This was no twisted, broken husk but a death of honor, a courtesy the battlefield seldom granted. Tylar frowned. Hard to believe Madelyn, with her wrath unbridled, would have spared such mercy. Yet perhaps… perhaps a woman's kindness had not yet burned away.

"There's a village not far from here, if memory serves," Conrak mused, stroking his chin as though divining secrets from the air. "I suspect we might find more evidence of Madelyn there."

"How can you be so sure?" Earlwick scoffed. "Is there anywhere you haven't been?"

Tylar exhaled through his nose, rolling his eyes. The mystique Conrak spun around himself was insufferable—a web of half-truths and swagger. It might awe green boys fresh to the sword, but not him. Not a man who had spent decades knee-deep in war.

"No, I don't believe I have," Conrak replied with a grin, unbothered. "But I've wandered the Plainhold more than once. Ask Bradshaw about it sometime!"

Tylar's leg throbbed, a dull ache flaring and vanishing just as quickly. A cruel reminder of chains, of humiliation, of how narrowly he had escaped the noose. Healed though the flesh was, the scar still burned like an old insult.

"Eat shit, Conrak," Tylar growled. "How many men did it take to bring me down, starving and half-dead? You should've faced me on a good day."

"Easy now, Bradshaw," Conrak chuckled, shaking his head. "I'm only getting a rise out of you. And gods, you make it far too easy. Perhaps you ought not to take life so seriously."

Humor was as foreign to Tylar as the Bymist. He had no patience for banter and found it more distasteful than wildmen. There was little left in the world worth laughing about, and even less so of late. Pride was the only currency that mattered; a man's reputation was dearer than gold.

"Enough of this," Arhan muttered at last, breaking the squabble. The older Blackthorn rode with a weariness honed by years. His graying hair hung to his shoulders, half tied back, the strands falling across a ragged scar that split his throat.

Some claimed bandits had nearly severed his head. Others whispered his own mother had tried to murder him. Still more said he had dangled from a noose, breathing through broken flesh for minutes before the rope gave way. None knew the truth, and Arhan never spoke of it. Silent, scarred, steady—he was the sort of company Tylar could abide.

Another hour passed, mercifully in quiet. Conrak strained to follow the trail, but the darkness was near absolute. Torchlight faltered, swallowed by the Plainhold's void. Yet Tylar's eyes caught something ahead; not trees, nor grass, but shapes. Still, human shapes. Flesh and bone.

"Get ready," he said, raising a gauntleted hand toward the horizon. "I see something."

The patrol drew to a halt. The figures were faint, half-swallowed in the dark. Tylar slid from his saddle, shield and sword in hand. The others followed, for no man with sense would stay mounted at night, not in a place such as this.

"Drop your weapons!" Conrak barked, steel flashing free.

Earlwick and Arhan raised their bows, strings drawn taut, waiting for the first twitch of movement. But the figures ahead did not stir. They stood motionless, eerie as scarecrows in the moonlight.

"Drop them!" Conrak bellowed again. Silence answered.

Tylar's gut clenched. He narrowed his eyes, the truth settling cold in his chest. With deliberate calm, he slid his blade back into its scabbard.

"They're dead," Tylar muttered, shoving past the others.

He knelt by the remains of a northern patrol, the truth plain in the moonlight. Three men lay in disarray about a dead fire pit, its embers long since smothered. Two corpses sprawled mere feet away, throwing knives jutting from their flesh like cruel ornaments. A third sat slumped before the ashes, a quarrel lodged clean between his eyes.

"Indeed, you're right!" Conrak said, sliding his blade back into its sheath. "The trail's not cold at all. If anything, it's heating up."

"Hell of a way to die," Tylar grunted. "A warm meal, a pint of ale— the only joys left in a shit heap like this. Only worse way to go would be with your breeches down, pissing in the dirt."

The Blackthorn shared a short, uneasy laugh as they moved among the corpses, checking for survivors and supplies. It was clear Madelyn had been here. The bodies were stripped of anything worth taking. Maps, dispatches, provisions— all gone. At least she had the sense to know food and drink were coin in this wasteland.

Darkness fell hard. The sky was choked of stars and moon, a lid of black clouds sealing them in. No wind, no rain. Just the suffocating stillness of the Plainhold. Even the bugs seemed to have abandoned the earth.

Tylar's eyes caught a neat pile of split logs by the fire pit — not enough to last the night, but enough for flame. He knelt, stacking wood over dry grass, then struck his flint. Sparks leapt, and within moments, a hungry fire clawed upward. Orange light spilled across the clearing, chasing shadows back to the grass. Conrak set down his weapons and crouched close, smiling into the blaze as though it were an old friend.

"What are you so happy about?" Tylar scoffed.

"We're alive despite the odds," Conrak replied, tearing open a ration of salted meat. "Take care not to overlook the little things, Bradshaw. How many of our fallen brothers would trade places with you in an instant?"

The words struck not with comfort but with venom. Tylar's frustration boiled over. He glanced at the corpse of a barbarian sprawled mere feet away, body stiff, eyes glassy.

"If you asked him, what do you think he'd say? You think he'd want one more day of this shit existence? No… he's the lucky one. No more hunger, no more fear. No more anything."

Conrak leaned toward the fire, the flames painting his face in restless orange. "Tell me, Bradshaw, do you believe in a world beyond this one?"

"No," Tylar snapped. "And when the day comes, I'll welcome it. I'm tired, and death will be a relief. But not yet. Not until the girl is safe. She's the only thing left that matters."

Saving Madelyn had become his obsession. Not because she was helpless—she had proved the opposite. But because Tylar could not lose another friend. Not the last true one he had. Conrak had earned a measure of brotherhood through fire and steel, but it paled beside his bond with her. They were the same—two idealists who had stomached horrors for causes never truly their own. And for her, he would see this cursed land burn before he allowed it to claim her.

"Is that why you throw yourself so carelessly into battle?" Conrak asked, cocking his head. "Are you seeking death?"

"Death is the only thing worth seeking," Tylar answered without pause. "What do I care for kings and their empty crowns? I wipe my ass with their nobility. I've failed everyone I ever cared about, but I won't fail her. Once Madelyn is safe, then I can rest."

Conrak looked away, lips tight. After a long silence, he took a swig of ale. "I get it, Bradshaw. Your intentions are pure. You've made them plain enough. You may think me a trickster, and aye, I have my ends. But there's honor in what you do. The men see it.

"Don't put my name and honor in the same breath," Tylar muttered darkly. "I know what I am. A brute. A killer. Hated by my own. Forsaken by the Order. And that suits me just fine."

Wearied of talk, he rose and left the firepit, wandering the edge of the clearing. Darkness pressed like a weight, thick and impenetrable. Beyond the bonfire's glow lurked only the Plainhold's silence, and with it the promise of danger in every shifting shadow.

He passed corpses where they had fallen, Northmen sprawled in death, hacked and broken. Madelyn's handiwork, no doubt. She had become a storm, cutting down warriors with a precision and fury that rivaled his own. Tylar slowed, uneasy. Even he, butcher that he was, felt a pause at the sheer swiftness of her wrath.

What horrible thing has taken hold of you, I wonder?

Then—a shimmer. Mist swirled in a small clearing ahead, pale as breath on a winter night. At first, he thought it was heat rising from the parched soil, or a trick of tired eyes. But the haze twisted, coiling into form, until a shape stood before him. Familiar. Too familiar.

Tylar's chest seized, his breath catching in his throat. "Madelyn?!" he gasped, wide-eyed, staring into the ghostly image.

But the specter did not see him. Its gaze swept the clearing, movements sharp and cautious. It slinked from shadow to shadow, advancing like a lion on the hunt. Tylar followed, breath held, watching every ghostly motion.

The apparition drew a crossbow, string already taut. A quarrel slid into place, loosed in a blur. It vanished into the dark with a hiss. Then knives—two, hurled quick as thought. Then steel—a sword flashing, each strike falling with inhuman speed. Madelyn moved like lightning, savage and unrelenting, though no foe stood before her.

Tylar's instincts flared. His own sword sang free as he spun in circles, panting, searching the shadows. But there was nothing. No enemy. Only the phantom of his friend, reenacting carnage that had already been written into the dirt.

"Damn it, girl," Tylar rasped, shaken. "Why the fuck would you leave after all we bled through? Why didn't you ask me to come with you?"

The apparition halted. Slowly, its head turned, and its eyes locked with his. The glare was venom, cold enough to freeze his marrow. Then, with impossible swiftness, it lunged. A hand like ice clamped around his throat. Tylar's breath caught; terror rooted him where he stood.

"Leave… me…" the figure hissed, voice thin as winter wind. Its gaze snapped northeast, then back to him—a silent command, or a warning.

And then it was gone. No mist. No tracks. Nothing. Tylar stood trembling, his heart a hammer against his ribs. But fear gave way to something fiercer: certainty. Madelyn lived. She was out there, and with every moment wasted, she slipped further from his reach. He all but ran back to camp, haunted by a thousand desperate thoughts.

"What's the matter, Bradshaw?" Conrak chuckled from the fire, grin sharp in the glow. "Something got your hackles raised?"

Tylar ignored him. He stormed to his bedroll, snatched up his gear, and strapped it tight. Earlwick and Arhan stared as he threw himself into the saddle, eyes wild, body taut as a drawn bow.

"Shut the fuck up and stay out of my way," he roared, spurring his horse into motion. "I know where Madelyn is."

EINARR

H E RACED ACROSS THE DESOLATE EXPANSE, LOW ON SUPPLIES AND with no companion, save the gods. Einarr Rollfson knew not where to find the warband beyond the vague direction of south, yet some unseen hand seemed to guide his steps. Anticipation gnawed at him in every waking moment, as though a great tragedy waited at journey's end.

Something had gone wrong — horribly wrong. Why else would the gods draw him out from peace and prayer into this endless waste? There had to be a reason. So he pressed on, following faith across the merciless Plainhold. At times, he spied disturbances in the earth that suggested an army had passed. At others, he rode with nothing but trust to steer him.

His horse fared worse than he, ribs showing through its hide, each stride weaker than the last. If it fell, so too would he. Einarr's own skin was red and cracked, lips parched, face stinging as if a smith's bellows blasted hot air against it.

Zifnir... I beg of you. Spare my life, that I may spare others in this war.

That night, Einarr consumed the last of his rations. He gave the final mouthful of water to his horse — without it, survival was hopeless. Dread hovered close, yet beneath the fear came an odd calm. The sky stretched wide and cloudless, strewn with stars that burned like watch-ful eyes.

Green and blue lights flickered faintly, a shimmering tide across the heavens, as he had once seen above Skaginlef. He gazed upward, and for a fleeting moment felt comfort. Perhaps the gods had not turned away from him after all.

His dreams were little more than fragments—Alina's face flickering like candlelight against a backdrop of shattered stone, the butchered dead, the atrocities he could never outrun. A great raven circled a cathe-dral of pines, its caw echoing over a floor of sun-bleached bones. And always, just before waking, came the glowing eyes and gaping maw of the great cat, that feral spirit still on his heels.

Yet his dreams no longer crushed him as they once had. The horrors lingered, but they left behind a strange resolve, as though each night-mare was fuel, each terror a torch in the dark. In truth, the visions were the only thing keeping him alive.

Starving, lips cracked, his body shaking, Einarr mounted again at dawn and pushed forward into the unknown. From morning until noon, he wandered, every horizon the same barren sweep of earth and stone. Delirium clawed at his mind. He thought he saw Alina ahead of him, arms outstretched, beckoning. At first, she seemed to call him home. But when his vision steadied, she was pointing—not behind, not above, but to the southeast.

"I'm sorry, my love," he gasped, voice ragged. "I tried… I tried…"

With the last of his strength, Einarr nudged his horse toward the direction of her phantom hand. Hill after hill, each crest only revealed more desolation. He was ready to surrender to despair, until the smell came. Smoke. Horses. Men. The warband.

At first, he thought it was a mirage, a cruel trick of hunger and thirst. But the stench on the wind was too heavy, too real. Alina had led him true again, even from the grave. He pushed closer, but before he could reach the outer ring of camp, a dozen riders thundered forth like hornets loosed from their nest. Spears leveled, bows strung, voices sharp.

"Halt!" cried a Northman. "Come no further!"

Einarr pulled his horse short, but thirst had made him fearless. He saw the tremor in their grips, the unease in their eyes. Strange, that a dozen hardened men should fear one lone rider.

"It is I... Einarr Rolffson," he croaked, voice ragged. "Where... where is Damien?"

At first, the riders did not recognize him. How could they? He looked more corpse than man—skin scorched and cracked by the Plainhold, body shriveled to bone. His horse staggered beneath him, ribs jutting, every breath a shudder.

"Einarr?" one of them gasped, disbelief heavy in his tone. The man looked to be Nothanek, though in the dim light it was hard to tell. "By the gods... what are you doing here?!"

They rushed forward, and the Nothanek flung him a water skin. Einarr's hands trembled so badly that he nearly dropped it, but at last his fingers found purchase. He tore it open and drank greedily, the warm, stale water spilling down his chin, soaking his beard. Never had he tasted anything so divine.

"You must... take me to Damien," he managed between gulps.

The men exchanged looks, but they offered no protest. A moment later, they were escorting him into camp. Unease seized Einarr almost immediately. This was no longer the warband that had shattered Lord Cedric Valens at Blackwolf Pass or sacked Castle Morden in fire and fury. No, this was something else, something broken.

"What... happened here?" he whispered, though part of him dreaded the answer.

The riders said nothing. They guided him silently, and one by one peeled away until only the camp stretched before him. What he saw stopped him cold.

Tents sagged under the weight of death. Everywhere he looked lay the wounded, groaning and bleeding, their bodies stitched and seared in crude attempts at survival. Wagons overflowed with severed limbs and blood-soaked bandages, black flies clouding so thick they seemed like a second plague. The stench was unbearable—iron, rot, and smoke mingled into one suffocating haze. Einarr's heart pounded. He had prayed for reunion, but not like this.

"You there!" he called to a camp follower staggering past with a bundle of rags. "Where is Damien? I must speak with him at once!"

It was as though his words were carried off by the wind, heard by none. Warriors who once stood tall in defiance of an empire shuffled like shades, their shoulders bent, their faces gray. The fire that once burned in them had guttered, leaving only ash.

Einarr pressed deeper into the camp, each step heavier than the last. The stench of sickness clung to the air. He passed heaps of broken shields, rows of wounded groaning on filthy bedrolls, and pyres stacked high with corpses waiting for flame. At the heart of the camp rose a sprawling pavilion draped in tattered banners—Dreadfire's tent.

Two burly guards flanked the entrance, silent and unmoving as carved stone. For the first time, Einarr faltered. His hand trembled against the reins. What if Damien lay within, lifeless? What if the gods had claimed him and the alliance as well? He forced himself forward. But before he could reach the guards, a voice cut through the camp.

"You!?"

He turned. Sylvia Stormguard stood there, her face hollowed by sleepless nights, her eyes ringed dark as bruises. The years seemed to have weighed on her in mere days. Their reunion carried no joy, only exhaustion and anger sharpened to a blade's edge.

"What happened here?" Einarr asked, disbelieving. His voice cracked, broken by thirst and dread. "Where is Damien?"

Sylvia chewed the inside of her cheek, choosing her words with care.

"We met the Betanthians south of here. At first, the day was ours. Victory was within reach. But then the Blackthorn came… cutting through us like a storm. At their head…" Her lip curled, hatred burning where weariness had dulled all else. "The Eveldanyr bitch."

Einarr's stomach sank. His worst fears coiled into life. His mind leapt to Skaginlef, to his people, and the doom now looming over them all.

"By the gods…" he whispered.

"You abandoned us," Sylvia hissed, her voice ragged with grief. "You left us to our fate when we needed you most."

Einarr flinched but only for an instant. He had not come this far to wallow in shame. The path he walked—strange, merciless, and guided by unseen hands—had not been chance. Every step, every trial, had purpose.

His eyes met hers, steady and burning with resolve. "My absence was not without meaning. The gods have spoken to me, Stormguard. They have shown me wonders… and horrors. Damien must hear what I have seen."

He took a step toward her, but his legs gave way beneath him. Darkness crept in at the corners of his sight, and for a heartbeat, it seemed he might crumble to the ground entirely. Sylvia caught him before he fell, her grip tight but straining against his dead weight.

A trio of Nothanek rushed to help. One pressed a skin of water into his hand. Einarr drank until his chest ached, heedless of how pitiful he must have looked. Yet even in that weakness, he knew any man who crossed the Plainhold alone earned respect, no matter the state in which he returned.

A crust of bread followed, devoured in seconds. Slowly, strength returned to his limbs, enough to straighten his back. Sylvia pointed toward the great pavilion at the heart of camp, her gesture sharper than words. Einarr pushed inside.

The tent was thick with incense, smoke curling in ghostly ribbons that stung his eyes. The air smelled of iron and ash. At the center, Damien Dreadfire sat slumped upon a wooden chair, his massive bastard sword upright before him, both hands draped across its hilt. His gaze was fixed on the effigy of Azldyr set upon the table, the god's image flickering in firelight.

But it was not anger that clung to the warlord. Einarr felt it instantly: despair, shame, the weight of defeat pressing down like an avalanche. For a man carved from stone, to see such sorrow was almost unbearable.

"Damien," Einarr said, his voice tinged with apprehension. "Thank the gods you yet live."

Dreadfire turned, eyes burning with the hostility of a cornered beast. The glare was not born of hatred, but of pride wounded deeper than flesh. With a grunt, he rose, a red-stained bandage binding his leg, the dark blotches betraying a grievous wound beneath.

"Son of Rolff," the warlord rumbled. "So you have returned… gods be praised."

They embraced briefly, though the gesture carried no warmth. It was the duty of comrades, not the relief of brothers. A heartbeat later, Sylvia swept in behind Einarr, her stare hard enough to cut stone. The air grew taut with her silent reproach. Einarr did not flinch from it. He had known the welcome would be cold. His hand, as much as Damien's, had forged this alliance—and with it, the calamity that followed.

"I regret I was not here to fight beside you," he said at last, eyes dropping to the floor. "The shame of cowardice weighs heavily on me for walking away."

"As it should," Sylvia snapped, arms crossed like a judge pronouncing sentence. "We lost more than you can count… Bonesplitter among them."

Einarr's breath caught, his stomach plunging like a stone. For a moment, the words refused to take root. Marvath—who had stood like a mountain in every storm, whose silence carried more weight than another man's roar—gone? The thought alone felt impossible. Surely only the gods themselves could have struck him down.

"Gods be good…" Einarr muttered. "May his soul find its way to Sjenohor."

"Zander is dead as well," Stormguard added, her tone as cold as iron. "He dared challenge Damien for the right to lead once the battle was lost."

Einarr stiffened. Another shock, though not entirely unexpected. Zander had always reeked of treachery, no more trustworthy than a serpent in tall grass. Bonesplitter had warned of such treason, and the man's end only proved him right.

"And for his boldness, I took his head," Damien said flatly, his scowl carved deep. "His kin broke with us soon after. Only Jollkud remains… what few he still commands. You will come to know him soon enough."

One Zylmacian was as good as another in Einarr's eyes. He had warned Damien against the gamble from the start. Wildmen were fierce, indeed, but ferocity without loyalty was a blade with no hilt—sooner or later, it cut the hand that wielded it.

"I know there are no words to mend what you've endured," Einarr said, stepping nearer. "But the gods have spoken to me. They led me down a path no man should walk, and in it I was shown many things. I return now to tell you the truth of what I have seen."

"There is no time," Sylvia cut in sharply. "We linger too long, and Betanthian scouts close the gap with every hour. We must move, or they will fall upon us again!"

Damien gave a weary nod, silencing her with a flick of his wrist. She swept from the tent at once, barking orders as she went, the crack of her voice carrying through the camp. The Supreme Warlord lingered only a moment longer, then strode out after her without so much as a glance.

Left standing alone, Einarr felt the words he had carried across the Plainhold wither in his throat. He would not let them die unspoken.

"Damien," he called, forcing strength into his voice. "I must share something with you—something for your ears alone."

He motioned back toward the tent. After a pause, the Dreadfire turned. His face was carved from stone, unreadable save for the weariness behind his eyes. For a moment, Einarr thought he might refuse him outright. Yet, perhaps out of respect for the blood they had once shed together, Damien relented and stepped back inside.

"Speak, my friend," Dreadfire said, lowering himself stiffly into his chair. "What troubles you so that it could not wait?"

"After I left Skaginlef, I journeyed to Khorrtal in search of your trail," Einarr began. "There, I crossed paths with a man named Niddeg—one of Dhuuld Lurrson's retainers. I told him I sought you… and he tried to kill me."

Damien's black eyes widened, the flicker of fear breaking through his stony mask. He shook his head slowly, as though some suspicion long buried had just been confirmed.

"You must believe me, Damien," Einarr pleaded, his voice raw. "We are betrayed!"

The air thickened, hot and oppressive, as though the sun itself had descended into the tent. Fury overtook the despair in Dreadfire's face. His fists clenched, the tendons standing out like ropes, trembling with the strain of barely contained violence.

"Then let us put this to the test beneath the sight of the gods," Damien growled, his voice low and thunderous. "If your words prove true, Einarr… then blood shall rain from the heavens, enough to wash this treason from the earth!"

UDORN II

A briny mist kissed Udorn's face as he stood at the ship's bow, tall sails fat with an afternoon breeze. Behind him, a hundred shield brothers waited—lean, hungry men who longed for blood and plunder. The sea heaved and snarled, but Udorn's stomach was an iron cauldron; no wave could unseat him.

He might have even savored the voyage, had Ragruk not been aboard. The enormous chieftain's voice carried across the deck without rest, a constant barrage of curses, boasts, and barked orders. His presence was like a stone in the boot: tolerable for a time, but unbearable for long. Udorn consoled himself with the thought that land would soon rise on the horizon. It had been many years since he last sailed south, yet he knew these waters well enough—their prows cut toward Betanthia.

"Gods, does he ever stop?" Dulkin One-Eye muttered, scratching at the patch strapped across his face. "He'll rouse the whole coast before we even see it."

"Careful," Udorn said quietly. "If he hears, you'll be fish-bait before sunset."

The truth was, he shared the sentiment. A Betanthian spear almost seemed a kinder fate than another hour under Ragruk's tongue.

"Udorn!" Ragruk bellowed, the deck groaning as he lumbered forward. "How long until we make landfall? My coffers will not tolerate such emptiness for long!"

"There is a city to the south along the coast," Udorn replied evenly. "It sits beside a deep harbor and is ringed by high walls."

"And?" the chieftain grunted. "You speak as though fear has seized your heart!"

Udorn's mind drifted back to the one time he had seen Dellhaven, captured aboard a southern freighter. Its fortifications were no idle boast. A reckless strike would bring their undoing.

"It is no fishing village," Udorn warned. "It is a city of stone, defended by an army. To charge its harbor headlong would be folly."

Ragruk spat over the rail and crossed his massive arms. "And is that not why we came south? What would you have me do, plunder farmers and fishermen? Bah!"

The urge to clobber him rose like a tide, but even the mightiest blow would do nothing but further incense the brute. For now, his taunts would have to be endured.

"I suggest we land half our force and keep the rest at sea," Udorn said, eyes fixed on the fading west. "Once a foothold is secured, we march on the city. We strike their walls when the moment is right, drawing their garrison to the landward fight. Then our ships slip into port and take them from behind."

"A clever scheme," Ragruk mocked, throwing his arms wide, "but it squanders our greatest weapon—surprise! No. We raid the port, seize the city, and claim our plunder before they even know the gods have forsaken them. You have grown soft, Udorn... soft and afraid!"

The chieftain stomped to the stern, satisfied in his madness. Around them, few dared to voice doubts. Victories past had bred arrogance, so much so that most could not remember the last time Ubneri blood had spilled without a banquet after.

Arrogant fool. Has it been so long since he sailed the high seas? So long since he bloodied his hands in honest combat?

As day surrendered to night, the sea grew restless. A harsh wind swept in from the west, whipping the waters into jagged chop. Udorn's longship bucked and groaned, its sail snapping like a beast's hide beneath the lash. He glanced back at the men, each standing firm and unshaken. It was said the Ubneri could sail before they could walk, and even the sea's fiercest tantrum could not bend their iron stomachs.

If anything, the storm fed their spirits. Udorn braced himself at the prow, a grin cutting across his face as the ship carved its way through foaming waves. The oarsmen pulled in flawless rhythm, their twenty-foot blades biting deep, while the sail ballooned and strained near to tearing. To a southerner, it would have been torment, but for raiders, such turmoil was a homecoming.

"Glorious, is it not?" Dulkin One-Eye bellowed, stumbling across the slick deck, his good eye alight. "Azldyr gives us his blessing!"

The heavens split with fire. Lightning clawed across the black canopy, and thunder rolled so violently it seemed to rattle the marrow of every man aboard. For a fleeting moment, the night was banished, sea and sky revealed in blinding brilliance. Udorn's heart soared. The storm was a hymn, a reminder that he was alive, and that the war god still watched. He cupped his hands to his mouth and loosed a wolf's howl, drunk on the raw ecstasy of the moment.

But storms are fleeting things. As suddenly as it had come, the tempest broke and passed. Swells lingered, crashing against the hull through the night and into the following day, but their fury waned with each hour. For three more days, the fleet pressed south until the winds betrayed them and died. Then came the groan of timber and the sweat of labor, hundreds of oars chewing the sea in place of the vanished gale.

When darkness fell again, a coastline emerged—too familiar for comfort. Dellhaven. The great harbor city loomed in the distance, its silhouette bristling with towers and walls. Udorn's gut soured at the sight. Were it not for the shroud of night, horns would already be sounding and the fleet's intrusion challenged. Instead, they advanced in eerie quiet, broken only by the dull cawing of gulls drifting over black water.

Silence ruled the fleet. The Ubneri crouched at their benches, hands resting on hilts and hafts, eyes glinting like predators waiting for the order to spring. Even the restless sea seemed to hush in anticipation. At the prow of the lead ship, Ragruk loomed, his bulk framed against the moonlit horizon. He squinted toward Dellhaven's harbor, lips curling in greedy calculation.

"It appears empty," the chieftain muttered at last, his tone thick with satisfaction. "We strike while the night cloaks us. By dawn, this city will belong to us!"

"If it is your will," Udorn replied evenly, his contempt buried behind a mask of obedience. "I will lead the first strike from Thaul's ship. I claim this burden as mine."

Ragruk lifted his chin, studying him with narrowed eyes as though weighing his ambition. After a long pause, he rumbled, "So be it. Bring us gold. Bring us glory. Bring us victory!"

Udorn lifted a hand, and Thaul's oarsmen pulled carefully, bringing their ship alongside. The longships kissed silently, boards creaking as they pressed together. With practiced ease, Udorn mounted the gunwale and vaulted across, landing with surprising grace for a man of his size.

A second thud shook the deck behind him. He turned, teeth bared, and found Dulkin One-Eye rising to his feet, a wolfish grin plastered across his scarred face.

"You fool," Udorn hissed. "What use is a half-blind man in a night raid?"

"Come now," Dulkin said, brushing the salt spray from his tunic.

"You'll need me, and you know it. We've painted the seas red half a hundred times together — or has your memory gone soft as Ragruk's belly?"

Udorn clenched his jaw but said nothing. He could not deny the truth. Dulkin's ferocity was legendary, his one good eye sharp enough to see where other men went blind. How many battles had they survived together? How many foes had felt their blades? Yet, each fight carved its own path, and Dellhaven promised dangers unlike any that had come before.

"Are you prepared for this?" Udorn asked, his voice low and grave. "We will lose many tonight, and the fight will be hard indeed. Put aside your zealotry and answer me true."

"Yes, Udorn," Dulkin said with a single nod. "I have bled enough at your side to know when your words carry weight. I am ready to meet the gods if this is to be my last raid. But until that moment comes, you have my axe and my loyalty."

Despite every misgiving gnawing at his gut, Udorn drew his axe and raised it skyward. The dim moonlight licked along its edge as he cast his gaze over the longships and the silent warriors awaiting their signal. At his command, oars slipped into the water, dipping smooth and deliberate so as not to betray their advance. The fleet crept forward like wolves on the hunt, gliding toward the northern edge of the harbor.

Gods, protect us. Grant us your favor, and we shall carve your glory upon this city of stone.

For a brief, tantalizing moment, Udorn believed they might land unchallenged. Half the distance to shore closed beneath their prow without alarm, the harbor as still as a graveyard. But such hopes were folly. One by one, pinpricks of light appeared along the battlements, swelling into a chain of glowing orbs. Then, with a sudden blaze, massive braziers flared to life, bathing the docks in golden fire.

A horn split the night air—shrill, piercing, unrelenting. Another answered it, then another, echoing in dreadful chorus. Dellhaven was awake.

Udorn roared, his axe high, every sinew in his neck straining. "Row, you swine! Row! ROW!"

Twenty longships burst forward like horses loosed from the gate, their oars biting deep into the black water. The Ubneri roared their approval, voices raw with hunger for plunder, baying like wolves in the night. It was not the cleverest of ambushes, but subtlety was a weapon long forgotten by their kind. If the gods were merciful and their backs held firm, they would be ashore before the Betanthians could muster a proper defense.

The rush was intoxicating. Udorn's heart hammered, his pulse quickening until his whole body felt light as smoke on the wind. He gripped the prow with both hands, his nails digging splinters from the wood. Fury and glory both filled his chest until the night split apart.

A shrieking *whoosh* tore the air, forcing him to stumble backward. For a blink, he caught the outline of iron streaking high above, vanishing into the dark. Then came the crash.

The bolt smashed through the mast of a neighboring ship, splintering the thick pine as though it were no sturdier than glass. Men screamed as the heavy spar toppled, snapping rigging and canvas in its fall. Some hurled themselves into the waves, others were caught beneath the wreckage, their bodies broken like twigs under an avalanche.

Another shriek cut the sky. A second bolt rammed clean through a ship's hull, splitting the keel with a sound like thunder. The vessel lurched, its oarsmen spilling into the sea as water rushed in to claim them. Udorn's stomach clenched. He longed to look, to fix the sight of his kinsmen's fate in his mind, but there was no time. More bolts streaked overhead, each one a death sentence if his gaze lingered too long. He barked orders instead, forcing his ship to hold steady.

"Udorn!" Thaul roared from midship, his voice nearly lost beneath the chaos. "We must turn about! This is folly!"

"Hold fast, men!" Udorn bellowed, his voice like iron over the chaos. "The gods are with us! Hard to starboard! Put your backs into it!"

Oars dug deep, straining as the longship surged through a storm of iron. Bolts hissed overhead, smashing the water in violent plumes, others clattering against the hull with bone-jarring force. Every heartbeat felt drawn out, every stroke of the oars an eternity. Time itself seemed to twist, stretching each second until Udorn swore he could count the droplets leaping from the bolts as they struck the sea.

Then he saw it—a shadow rising where the harbor mouth yawned open. At first, he thought it was smoke or drifting wreckage, but the moon betrayed the truth: a chain, thick as a wagon, studded with cruel spikes long enough to gut a horse. It crawled upward out of the black water, barring their path.

Udorn's stomach plummeted. They cleared it by the breadth of a hair, their keel scraping just above the iron teeth. "Turn about! Turn about, you fools!" he roared, throat raw with desperation.

Too late. Two ships behind him struck the snare broadside. The crash was deafening, wood shrieking and splintering as if the sea itself had swallowed them whole. Raiders were hurled screaming into the waves, others crushed beneath collapsing timbers. The water boiled with limbs, shields, and shattered oars, and over it all came the relentless shriek of more ballistae.

Udorn forced his eyes forward, heart clenched like a fist. There would be no saving those left thrashing in the water, not with death raining from the ramparts. His ship alone had made it clear, fifty men against the wrath of Dellhaven. Arrows whistled down, peppering the sea and hammering into the hull. Oarsmen crouched low, faces pale in the firelit rain. Even the bravest among them shrank against the benches, making themselves small as frightened children.

"To the north!" Udorn bellowed, lifting his axe high, the blade catching the lantern-glow like a shard of lightning. "Row, damn you! Row!"

A ballista bolt screamed past, so close it nearly sheared four oarsmen in half. The men flinched, ducking low—all but one. Dulkin One-Eye had slipped into the place of a fallen kinsman, and instead of fear, he threw his head back and laughed. His lone eye gleamed in the firelight, wide with madness.

"Azldyr!" he bellowed, voice hoarse with joy. "I'm coming home!"

The raiders roared with him, their spirits feeding off his frenzy. Death and glory were rewards every Ubneri yearned for, but Udorn clenched his jaw. Let others lust for a warrior's grave—he would rather see his sons grow into men, his lands remain free of Betanthian chains. Still, if the gods called him tonight, he would not meet them cowering.

A shadow loomed at his flank. Another longship had slipped past the harbor chain, keeping pace with his own. For a moment, Udorn felt a rush of relief. Fifty men against a garrison was madness, but two ships, two warbands together, might yet carve a foothold.

The strangers rowed with savage precision, their prow cutting the waves like a spear. Soon, they surged ahead, hungry to claim first blood. Udorn squinted, straining to see the face of their captain in the chaos, but the night kept its secrets. No matter. They were shield-brothers, and their courage lit a fire in his chest.

But the gods are cruel. The Betanthians fixed upon the boldest target. Ballistae shrieked, quarrels hissing down in a deadly swarm. Iron rained into the longship's hull and flesh alike. Men toppled like wheat before a scythe, their cries drowned in a crash of wood and water.

"Faster, men!" Udorn snarled, taking up his shield. "Faster! And ready yourselves! When we strike land, every man off this ship at once!"

The sea answered with a groan as jagged rocks tore into their hull. The ship lurched, timbers splitting like bones under an axe. Raiders pitched forward as the deck heaved, waves rushing up over the bow.

Udorn didn't wait for the wreck to claim them. He slung his shield across his back, roared to his brothers, and hurled himself into the surf. The water was shockingly shallow. His boots sank into sand and stone, the shore only steps away.

He spied a storm of movement atop the walls, shadows moving swiftly in torchlight as archers and men-at-arms scrambled into position. Dellhaven's defenders poured across the parapets like ants to a carcass, desperate to repel the raiders who had slipped their chain. For a heartbeat, Udorn almost mistook it for Sjenohor itself, the torchlight gleaming gold as though the gods had opened their halls to him.

Then the arrows fell. Shafts hissed into the sea, black fletching biting through foam and flesh. Udorn thrashed against the salty tide, every stroke of his arms a fight against the weight of his sodden mail. Raiders splashed alongside him, their war cries drowned beneath the shrieks of the wounded.

A thunderous crack split the night as two ballista bolts struck home, tearing through the wreck of their ship. The timbers burst apart as though struck by lightning, the deck exploding in shards of oak and iron. Men were not men in that moment, but meat—shredded, pulped, hurled screaming into the froth.

Udorn drove himself onward, teeth clenched, every stroke dragging him closer to the stone line of the harbor. His limbs felt as heavy as anchors, his cloak like a net pulling him down. Yet the thrill of battle, the nearness of blood and glory, kept him afloat.

At last, his boots struck stone beneath the shallows. He staggered upright, half-crawling through the surf until he pressed his back against an inlet in the harbor wall. The shadow of its arch gave him cover from the falling shafts. All around him, survivors dragged themselves ashore, coughing brine, clutching axes, spitting blood.

Less than forty. By all the gods, may the fallen watch us now from Sjenohor's tables!

"Udorn!" Dulkin wheezed, hauling himself from the water with all the grace of a drowning ox. His patch glistened, seawater rushing down his face as he staggered to stand. "We made it! But where are the others?"

Ragruk and the fleet lingered far out in the black water, their sails ghostly in the torchlight. For all his roaring bluster, the chieftain seemed content to watch from safety while Udorn and his men bled beneath Dellhaven's walls. It was unbecoming of an Ubneri—cowardice dressed as command. But Udorn had expected no better. Selflessness was never the way of the privileged, and Ragruk's pomp was worth less than the salt in the sea.

"We're here, Udorn," Thaul panted, dragging himself onto the stone lip of the inlet. Gaxas slumped beside him, still gripping his axe, though blood trickled down his brow. "But I have seen no others."

Udorn scanned the wreckage of the bay. Less than forty souls remained, and every one of them was already half-dead from the crossing. Yet in the shifting shadows, he found two more familiar faces—Rennek, limping, and his son Tharek, teeth bared in a grimace as he hauled another wounded man clear of the surf. Against all odds, they too had survived.

"We need to move," Udorn declared, his voice low and firm. "There's little cover here, and the Betanthians will be upon us soon."

The truth rang in the distant clamor. Horns wailed across the harbor, and shouts echoed from the walls as soldiers scrambled to finish the slaughter. Time had shrunk to embers, and every ember risked snuffing out.

Then Udorn saw it—a rusted grate set into the seawall, half-hidden in shadow—a drain, corroded with salt, bars clinging on by little more than memory. With a sharp wave of his arm, he motioned the men forward.

Gaxas and two more burly raiders seized the rust-bitten metal and heaved. Iron shrieked in protest, then gave way, falling with a splash into the black water below. One by one, they slipped into the narrow channel, bodies pressing close in the wet dark. Udorn led from the front, shoulders scraping against damp stone, his hand steady on the haft of his axe.

Ahead, through the suffocating black, a pale shaft of moonlight pierced the grate above—a promise of direction, faint but enough. He gritted his teeth and pressed on, praying that light would not betray them to the enemy above.

Disorienting as it was, Udorn pressed his men toward the faint glow ahead, though each step brought them deeper into a suffocating dark. He halted suddenly as footsteps rattled from above. Betanthian soldiers scurried along the harbor road, their armor clinking, their voices sharp and hurried as they dragged engines of war into place. An assault was coming, and Ragruk had left them to rot beneath the city's skin.

A rank stench rolled through the cramped passage, fouler than a battlefield left to fester in the sun. The air reeked of filth and excrement, coating the back of the throat until even hardened raiders gagged like green boys. Udorn shoved the man behind him hard in the chest. A warning, silent but stern. Noise here would mean their deaths.

Overhead, boots ground gravel into stone. Dozens, perhaps more. The weight of an entire garrison seemed to thunder just above their heads. Udorn clenched his jaw until his teeth ached, praying that Ragruk had the sense to slip the fleet beyond sight before Dellhaven's garrison swept the shore clean.

"Be still," he rasped, the whisper clawing against his throat. "Breathe quiet."

The command was easier spoken than followed. Men who would grin at the prospect of steel in their bellies fought like children against their own bodies—choking, coughing, shoulders heaving with the effort of restraint. Each muffled gag echoed like a warhorn in Udorn's ears.

He shut his eyes, forcing his mind northward, toward home. The forests thick with pine. The crash of waves against black stone. His children's eager eyes scanning the eastern shore, waiting for sails that might never return.

I will not die tonight. Not here. Not in this sewer. Not like this. Not even the gods will keep me from home… or glory.

Time bled away. The clash of steel above ebbed, leaving only a mutter of voices and the thump of boots growing distant. Victory or slaughter, Udorn could not tell, but the silence that followed was no reprieve. Silence meant the Betanthians would now be hunting.

He pressed forward. The pipe stretched on and on, broken only by faint pillars of moonlight that leaked through grates above. A mile, perhaps more, until at last he spied an opening. Rust had eaten deep into the iron rungs of a ladder fixed to the stonework. He placed his hand upon it, the metal slick beneath his palm, and began to climb.

Never one to send another where he himself would not go, Udorn ascended first. Every movement was deliberate, every breath held as he reached the cover above. Muscles strained as he pressed his shoulder into the heavy disc of corroded iron. It groaned softly, a sound that made his blood freeze. But the lid shifted, and with a grunt, he cracked it open just enough to peer into the world above.

The street was quiet, too quiet for a city under siege. Dellhaven should have been a hive of panic, its avenues choked with screams and chaos. Yet here, there was only stillness, the silence heavy as a shroud. All the better. Udorn pushed himself from the sewer's mouth and drew his axe, the steel catching a sliver of moonlight. Fresh air filled his lungs at last, clean compared to the filth below, though it stank of ash and fear.

From the sewers, his men emerged one by one, slick with grime, coughing and gagging as they climbed into the open. Udorn motioned for silence, his eyes burning as he scanned the avenues around them.

"Thank the gods," Dulkin wheezed, doubled over with exhaustion.

"Any longer down there, and I'd have begged for a Betanthian spear to end it."

No one laughed. The air was too thick with danger, too heavy with the weight of unseen eyes. Shadows moved across the distant walls where soldiers hurried to their posts, voices echoing off stone. Time, Udorn knew, was as thin as a frayed rope. He tightened his grip on the axe and gathered his men with a sweep of his arm.

"We move, and we move swiftly," he said, his voice iron. "If the Betanthians don't take our heads tonight, Ragruk surely will, come the dawn. So steel yourselves, brothers—pray Azldyr's hunger for southern blood is far from sated. For by the morrow, we will feed it well."

GARETH II

"**I** LOVE YOU," SHE WHISPERED, HER VOICE SOFT AS SILK.

Madelyn's eyes were an endless ocean, blue and fathomless, so deep Gareth thought he might gladly drown in them. He brushed a stray lock of golden hair from her face, his fingers lingering against her cheek. In that moment, nothing else in the world mattered—not Damien Dreadfire's horde, not the throne, not even the gods themselves, if they existed. There was only her.

"I love you too," he said, smiling. "Let me take you home, Madelyn, back to Cardale. You're safe now. I'll see to it that nothing can touch you again."

For a heartbeat, she seemed to soften. Her lips parted, as if she might lean forward and melt into his arms. Gareth felt his chest lighten, daring to believe love might win out over fury. But then, just as swiftly, the warmth in her gaze curdled. Her eyes hardened like storm clouds overtaking a clear sky.

The muscles in her jaw tensed, and her hand lashed out, slapping his away with startling force. Madelyn rose from the bed in a sudden flare of motion, the shift so violent it made Gareth flinch. The softness he thought he saw was gone—burned away in an instant, replaced by a tempest barely contained beneath her scarred, beautiful skin.

"I will not rest until Damien's head is in my hands," she said, her voice hard as steel. "Neither you, nor the King, nor death itself will keep me from my revenge."

Her words struck Gareth like a blade. Love, it seemed, could not quench the fire in her heart; if anything, his affection only fanned the flames.

"You don't need to fight anymore!" he pleaded, voice breaking. "You're my wife now. Let me restore your honor. Let our generals do what they were born to do. Please, Madelyn… just come home."

But she would not hear him. With a sudden motion, she strode across the chamber to where her armor lay scattered on the floor. Even scarred, her form was breathtaking, her every curve a cruel reminder of the woman he yearned to protect. Gareth's eyes followed the sway of her hair against her thighs, and for a moment, he was lost in a trance of desire, even as dread twisted in his chest.

He only understood the change when Madelyn stood fully armored, straps cinched, weapons locked to a thick leather belt with the precision of a practiced soldier. Gareth shot to his feet, panic hot in his throat, desperate to stop the woman he loved from vanishing again into the thing she had become.

"Madelyn, please. Stop this!"

She turned. The woman who had been all softness and light a moment ago was gone. Her hair was cropped close now, the color of midnight. The blue wells of her eyes had gone black and hard, glinting with something colder than sorrow.

"Get away from me!" she snarled, voice razor-edged and layered with strange undertones, as if several emotions spoke at once. "Who are you to deny me my vengeance? Who are you to deny me what is mine?"

"I'm your husband," Gareth said, his voice breaking. "I know what was done to you was monstrous. I can never take that back. But please—let go of this hate before it consumes you. Let me do it. Let me kill Damien. Let me take that burden from you."

Madelyn regarded him with a look that bordered on contempt, a hatred so cold and absolute it stunned him. No plea, no promise, no wealth he could offer would sway her. How could anything he had done or could do ever be enough?

He reached for her arm only to be hurled backwards as if struck by a storm. Her shove sent him sprawling across the tent floor, breath knocked from his lungs. She turned without a backward glance and strode from the canvas with the grim purpose of a blade leaving its sheath. Gareth landed hard, coughed, and fought to rise, but his legs betrayed him; strength had emptied from his limbs.

Madelyn!" he cried, panic ripping through his voice. "Come back! Please — don't leave!"

He was still on his knees when the dream snapped shut. Gareth exhaled with a hollow sound, eyes wet with tears he did not bother to hide. He glanced to the empty side of the bed where she should have slept; the space yawned like a wound. The void there felt larger than any chasm he'd seen, deeper than any loss.

But grief curdled fast into something harder. Anger like a living thing rose in him — hotter, sharper than sorrow. He found himself hating everything: the Northmen and their butcher-warrior Damien Dreadfire; Aldred for his timidity and the ruin it invited; and, with a shock that made his stomach drop, Madelyn herself.

Why do I feel this way? he wondered, dismayed by the unfamiliar ferocity within him. *What is happening to me? These thoughts are not mine... and yet... they are...*

Half an hour passed before he could haul himself from the bed. Each minute he lay there he weighed the world and its betrayals: how he had come to this point, and what cost he might yet pay. The burden pressed down like iron, but something in him refused to yield. He rose at last, the resolve in his chest heavy and cold as a drawn sword.

Knowing Sir Edmund or a Guardsman messenger would barge in

at any moment, Gareth rose and dressed in a black silk tunic, blue trousers, and supple leather boots. On the table beside his bed lay the remnants of last night's supper—wine, bread, and a plate of fruit. He forced himself to eat, though each bite felt tasteless, swallowed more from habit than hunger.

As expected, Edmund arrived, punctual as ever. The old knight's presence filled the tent with quiet authority, his sharp eyes narrowing at once. He could read Gareth like a book; no veil of stoicism could hide what weighed on him.

"Good morning, lad," Edmund said. "Is everything well?"

Gareth lowered his gaze, hands stilling over his half-eaten bread. "I had a dream," he said softly. "And I don't know why my thoughts torment me so. I find no peace... not even in sleep."

Edmund's expression gentled, though his tone stayed firm. "Aye. We like to think ourselves masters of our fate, but the mind often strays where it will. Be careful, Gareth; do not become your own abuser."

The words struck him harder than expected. Gareth sighed, running a hand through his hair.

"It isn't that. I've never been an angry man—you know this. But lately..." His voice caught. "Lately, I feel hatred. A darkness creeping into me. It frightens me, Edmund. I'm not sure I recognize myself anymore."

The Guardsman's weathered hand came down upon his shoulder, heavy but steadying. "You're walking a path every man must walk. Your father should have guided you through it, but he was too broken to do so. Now you bear it alone. This is you becoming the man you were always meant to be. But be warned, boy—you may not like all that you become. Life will twist your ideals and crush your hopes. The trick is to guard the good within you, lest the darkness take it all."

Gareth sat motionless, Edmund's hand a weight of truth across his shoulder. The words should have comforted him. Instead, they left him staring into the cup of wine at his table, unsettled by the thought that perhaps the man he was becoming had already stepped too far into the shadows.

"I have neither the time nor the energy to dwell on this further," Gareth said, his voice flat with exhaustion. "Come. We must get moving."

He had endured enough lectures for one morning. With grim resolve, he stepped out of the tent and prepared to ride. Days bled into a week, perhaps longer. In the Plainhold, time ceased to have meaning. One barren horizon looked much the same as the next, broken only by the occasional parade of dark clouds. Yet even those passed in silence, stingy of rain, leaving the earth below cracked and hard as baked clay.

The men looked at him differently now. Gareth still drew admiration, the kind reserved for a prince who bled beside his soldiers. Yet in the quiet, whispers followed. His decision to abandon the wounded gnawed at camp morale. Many understood the necessity, but understanding brought little comfort.

Several physicians had chosen to remain behind with the injured while a small caravan set off toward Mor Seveht in search of water and clean bandages. Whether they would return in time—or at all—was a question no one dared to ask aloud.

When Gareth climbed onto his horse, pain seared through his thighs. Fresh sores rubbed raw against leather, burning like live coals. It amazed him how the Blackthorn Knights could endure weeks mounted without breaking stride, their bodies forged into iron by years in the saddle. Gareth was not so hardened, though pride forbade him from showing weakness.

That afternoon proved merciless. The sun blazed white and cruel, shimmering against the endless waste. His vision blurred, the world fading at the edges. At last, he raised his hand and ordered the column to halt. Tents went up quickly, weary soldiers moving with the efficiency of habit.

A foraging party was dispatched, more to soothe the men than in expectation of success. They would comb the rocky ground for roots, scrub plants, and perhaps the faintest trace of a spring. In the Plainhold, hope itself was a kind of sustenance.

A mug of warm red ale beneath a canopy's shade felt like heaven. Gareth sat propped against a grain cart, unburdened at last by the weight of steel. His boots lay discarded nearby, toes splayed against the dust. Even the insects, relentless as they were in this cursed land, had retreated from the heat, granting him a rare peace.

He drank in silence for nearly an hour, one mug after another draining into him. The ale dulled his throat but did nothing to quiet his thoughts. They came ceaselessly, like waves against stone—memories of Madelyn, visions of battles yet unfought, doubts whispered in his own voice. Every dark possibility pressed upon him with the weight of a blacksmith's anvil, and the harder he tried to banish them, the more they returned.

Only Sir Edmund dared to approach. The elder Guardsman cut his usual imposing figure, clad in gleaming plate with a purple cape flowing from his shoulders. Yet the sheen of sweat across his brow betrayed the toll of the Plainhold's relentless heat. When he spied Gareth nursing a mug, a grin creased his weathered face—relief, plain and human.

"As happy as I am to see you, lad, I'm even happier to see that!" Edmund chuckled, though it ended in a dry cough. He wasted no time filling a mug to the brim and easing himself down beside Gareth with a groan. "You're not stuck inside that head of yours again, are you?"

"It's difficult to come to terms with the fact that the world isn't what you thought it was," Gareth said, swallowing a mouthful of ale. His eyes drifted across the plain, unfocused. "I never imagined life would lead me here. I thought by now I'd be married, raising children, dreading palace debates and court intrigue. I never cared for the throne, yet I always knew it would come to me one day. But not like this. The world has turned upside down, and I hardly recognize it anymore."

"And it's fallen to you to set it right," Edmund replied, his tone steady. "No simple task, I admit. But if you study history as I have, you'll see that greatness is most often thrust upon reluctant men. Destiny doesn't wait for readiness. It comes when you're least prepared. What gives me hope is that, despite it all, you've embraced it as best you could."

A score of soldiers passed by, smiling, nodding, some calling Gareth's name with the affection reserved for brothers-in-arms. Their loyalty was almost unsettling. He was still their crown prince, but the admiration he felt in their eyes wasn't for the crown, it was for him. Yet the weight of that loyalty clashed with the darkness gnawing at his heart.

Behind every smile was a man with a family, a life, a story. Fathers who would never see their sons grown. Husbands who had already sacrificed more than Gareth ever had. Palace life, for all its constraints and cruelties, had been nothing compared to theirs. It was humbling… and shameful.

"I would see this war ended," Gareth said firmly, voice sharpening. "I would see Damien Dreadfire broken, his horde ground into dust, and Lord Vakaro strung from a rope. I want my wife to return to me whole. I want peace, Edmund. But I see now there is no peace without blood. And if the gods demand it, then I will stain my hands red until peace is bought."

"You're hardly the first Bethard to feel this, lad." Edmund refilled their mugs, the old man's hands steady as a smith's. "Your grandfather fretted over legacy and whether his peace was worth the cost. It lasted only so long, but it was peace nonetheless. Your father chased a different dream—vanquish the wicked, purge the land. We all know how that ended."

The name sent a coldness through Gareth, a blush of shame that lingered at his throat. Marcellus Bethard had once been a figure of honor; by the end, his rule had bent toward madness and cruelty. The shadow of that ruin was a fate Gareth swore he would not inherit.

"I refuse to be another link in that chain," Gareth said, voice low and resolute. "I never asked for this war. I never asked for my people to be butchered or for Madelyn to be broken. But I will not step back now. I will see this through, to whatever end it demands."

"Now there's the spirit!" Edmund laughed, clapping him hard on the bicep. "Keep that fire. Every leader stumbles; it's how you rise that matters."

The fire in Gareth's veins felt real enough to scorch. Where once depression had been his constant companion, anger now sat beside him like a wolf poised to spring. It frightened him and steadied him all at once.

"Indeed, which is why I will no longer remain passive, not while my enemies close in. I will make my own fate from this moment forward. Summon Lord Vakaro at once. I wish to have a word with him."

Sir Edmund's face went ashen; his mouth fell open, the protest already forming. "Gareth, that is most unwise, lad. We must be cautious, we must—"

"Summon Lord Vakaro," Gareth said again, sharper this time. "I will not say it again."

Reluctantly, the elder Guardsman obeyed. Gareth felt the weight of what he'd set in motion yet, oddly, a calm settled over him. He retired to the royal tent and went about adorning himself—metal first, habit next. The breastplate on the wooden bust gleamed like a mirror, its surface scored with chips and deep scrapes.

Those blemishes had names. Each nick was bought on the battlefield, each gouge told where a man had been spared by luck or steel. The scars in the metal would say more to Ridley than any speech or purple cloak ever could. He did not intend to frighten the southern lord; he intended to make him doubt.

When Ridley crossed the threshold, the tent felt smaller. The Commandant wore his finery as armor: a burgundy tunic, black hose, and an ornate silver breastplate that threw light back like accusation. A black cape was draped over one shoulder; his hair lay slick and dark. He lifted his chin as if the world owed him an explanation.

"What is the meaning of this?" Lord Vakaro demanded, chin high. "I have important matters to attend to."

"Silence." Gareth's answer was curt. "We'll spare the courtesies. I know your heart, Lord Vakaro. I know you would gladly be rid of me. There is no use hiding that."

Ridley said nothing; he only shook his head, lips pressed thin as if clearing a nuisance. "My prince, I am here to finish this war. My commission comes from the king. With his blessing, I will do whatever it takes to crush this barbarian menace and restore order. Your meddling will only endanger that work."

Gareth met the words without flinch. He let the armor speak, let the scars do the insulting. The contest was now a matter of wills; Ridley had chosen to meet it publicly. Gareth answered with something colder than anger—a promise.

"And there we have it," Gareth said, spreading his arms. "I applaud your honesty, Lord Vakaro. I would expect nothing less from a man of your temperament. Now listen."

He crossed the tent with the gait of a man who meant what he said and stopped within inches of Ridley's face. Though half a head shorter, he did not look small; whatever fear had lived in him once had been burned away.

"I know what you've done and what you intend to do," he said, the scowl tightening his mouth.

Ridley's eyes narrowed. "Tell me, my prince, what is it you think I have done?"

If Ridley had a weakness, it was not in courage. He answered evenly, as if the ground itself could not surprise him.

"You sent a man to kill me on the field," Gareth said. "A blade disguised as one of ours. For that, you deserve—" He let the rest hang, the sentence shaped by the metal at his hip and the men who listened. "Whether you like it or not, Betanthia will pass through my line. I will not watch a usurper wipe out the legacy my House has kept."

"That is a grave charge," Ridley replied, disturbingly composed. "I would have thought House Bethard would show more gratitude. If not for my efforts, Damien Dreadfire would already be at Bentmont's gates."

Trading barbs with him proved as useful as smashing one's head against a wall. Gareth exhaled through his nose. He would not relent. If Ridley would not break now, perhaps he could be found out later—caught in the act rather than scoffing in the tent.

"Let us come to an understanding, then," Gareth said. "You serve at the pleasure of House Bethard. Remain faithful and you may keep your command to the end of your days. Like my father before me, those who guard the interests of my line and the Kingdom will be rewarded. You will uphold your oaths and your duty, will you not?"

"Indeed… my prince."

Lord Vakaro turned on his heel and left without another word. Gareth watched him go, the tent feeling suddenly too small and too hot. He could not tell if the confrontation had secured anything but trouble; a sour suspicion lodged in his gut that he had made things worse. Rather than despair, a raw, hungry anger rose through him like wildfire.

His sword lay on a nearby table, its silver hilt catching the light. The fantasy was simple and bright — loosen the blade, run after Ridley, and press steel to the back of that arrogant skull. It pleased him in the imagining, as satisfying as a wound well struck. But the notion was poison in action; such indulgence would cost lives and invite a chaos he could not afford.

So he buckled the scabbard at his hip instead and stepped from the tent into the white hot oppression of the Plainhold. The heat hit him like a hand; the day offered no forgiveness. Edmund stood a few paces off, arms crossed, regarding him with a look a man wears when he measures another's folly.

"Dare I ask what passed in there?" the old guard said.

"An arrogant fool," Gareth muttered, moving toward the stables. "I called him out for the ambush on the field. He neither owned it nor had the courage to deny it cleanly."

Edmund slapped his palm to his forehead. "Unwise, lad. You've thrown away the element of surprise. If Lord Vakaro is as treacherous as you reckon, he'll change his habits—move where you won't expect him. You must harden the watches, vary your routines—"

"What difference does it make?" Gareth snapped, stopping so suddenly that Edmund nearly bumped into him. "If the man wants me dead, he'll strike when he can. Better he know I'm on him than that he catches me unawares. At least now—at least now—he may hesitate. He may think twice before he pulls the next cord."

Together, the two men walked toward the stables. Gareth's horse stood in a patch of shade, nose buried in a heap of hay. A stablemaster looked up at their approach, bowed quickly, and set about saddling the mount without a word.

"I understand your reasoning," Edmund said quietly, "but I've dealt with men like him longer than you've been alive. You would not be the first Bethard to be assassinated. Your twice-great-grandfather, King Hugo, took a knife in the back from his most trusted Guardsman. He'd grown drunk on power and crossed the wrong men. The throne stayed in Bethard hands—but only barely."

Gareth knew the story well. Hugo's son, Corrin Bethard, had rallied a loyal handful of Royal Guardsmen and cut down the usurpers before dawn. In a single night, the dynasty had come within an inch of ruin. Perhaps history was circling back.

"I have trusted you without reservation since this war began—and for years before it," Gareth said as he swung into the saddle. "But now

I need you to trust me. I need you to stand by my decisions. For better or worse, I'm writing my own story now—my own legacy. And I'll be damned if anyone else pens even a single word of it. Let them write their own eulogy instead."

SYLVIA III

BY MIDDAY, THE WARBAND WAS READY TO MARCH. THE SHADOW OF Marcellus Bethard's host loomed ever closer, a creeping blight across the inhospitable land. Many of the Zylmacian wildmen had already taken their leave, acolytes of Zander who had stomached their final humiliation. Their absence brought relief to some, but others worried they would descend on unprotected villages during their retreat to the Bymist.

Not even Einarr's return was enough to restore confidence. A handful of the Nothanek welcomed him, but most greeted him with wary silence. Sylvia, at least, found comfort in his presence; he had been her friend once. Yet something gnawed at her—he had not spoken of the knowledge he had carried to Damien, and his uncharacteristic silence was troubling.

Before the column could move, business remained unfinished. Damien summoned the surviving warchiefs and the heirs of those who had fallen. Sylvia came early, but found she was not the first.

Einarr stood at Damien's side, bent in quiet conversation. When she entered, both men glanced at her, but neither stopped speaking. She knew better than to intrude and instead poured herself a mug of mead from the table along the wall.

The others filed in one by one. Jollkud entered next, his bald head bronzed and peeling beneath the Plainhold sun. The sight of any Zylmacian still among them after Zander's death was remarkable—a faint credit to what scraps of honor a wildman might yet cling to, she thought.

Then came Valerick the Red, trailing his stench of carrion. It had been some time since the hulking Rhivothi had bathed in the blood of beasts, but the odor clung to him still. He strode to the mead without hesitation and upended an entire vessel, swallowing until the froth ran down his beard.

Dhuuld Lurrson and Arik Akselson followed soon after, taking their places around the table. Arik looked as restless as ever, though the Nothanek had proven their valor time and again. The Khorrtalli chieftain wore only a plain gray tunic and black trousers—his usual wealth of gold ornaments conspicuously absent.

"Welcome, honored friends," Damien said, placing a hand to his chest with a shallow bow. "We must be brief. The wolves of King Bethard are upon us, and our people cannot face them again in the open field. We must choose our course together... for the sake of all."

A hush fell across the tent, heavy but fleeting. Einarr gave a solemn nod, then turned to the map spread before them.

"I am grateful to stand among you once more," he said. "I regret my absence these past months. I know many of you resent me for it, and I will accept whatever judgment you give. But my time away was not wasted—the gods themselves spoke to me."

The warchiefs barely stirred. Even for men steeped in piety, faith had lost its edge against grief. Belief could not bring back the dead, nor could it mend the ruin of their clans. Yet Sylvia held to it still. Perhaps she was a fanatic, as her detractors claimed. But if so, she would bear it gladly. Few could question her devotion.

"The gods are mysterious," she said, letting her voice rise above the silence. "They lead us down dark and winding paths, often without revealing their purpose. But my faith has not faltered. Despite all that we have suffered, I do not believe we have been forsaken."

"Spare us your righteous babble," Dhuuld snapped. "I have seen enough of my kin cut down. I will not stand here and listen to sermons while our enemies close in. Speak plainly, or I will take my leave."

Damien and Einarr exchanged a quick, guarded look—an economy of motion that meant more than words—and only Sylvia caught the slight tightening at Damien's jaw. She had learned to read the small betrayals of body language; tonight, they spoke of plans not yet voiced.

"Very well," Dreadfire said, leaning forward on the table. The wood flexed and grunted under the weight of his palms. "We must head north and put as much distance between ourselves and King Bethard's minions as possible."

"You would send us closer to our own lands?" Arik blurted. "If we turn north, we give the Betanthians an easier road to our villages should we fail. We bring the danger to our doorsteps."

Sylvia and several of the chiefs inclined their heads; the logic was plain and whoever proposed it would be branded a fool. Damien and Einarr did not flinch. Their faces held an unreadable calm that only made Sylvia more certain something else lay beneath the words.

"True," Damien admitted after a breath. "We must make space between King Bethard and the north. If we can lure his force into the Bymist's embrace, we may buy our people time... even if it costs us dearly."

Dhuuld barked a laugh that was more fury than humor. "You would damn my people for your stratagems! Khorrtal sits square in their path—no walls, no respite! I will not be the one who leads my clan to slaughter!"

Heat and tension thickened the air until it felt like a thing in itself.

Sylvia could feel her pulse drum in her throat. She watched Damien and Einarr closely, searching their faces for a tremor of truth. When Einarr's hand eased toward the haft of an axe at his hip—slow, casual, careful—her stomach tightened. The motion was deliberate enough for her to catch it; her heart told her the quiet gesture was a signal.

"Your concerns have been noted. But before this meeting is concluded, there is another matter we must discuss." Damien's mouth tightened into a hard line. "There is something you must know, something that touches every life that marches beside us. Our defeat on the Plainhold was not born of misfortune or cunning alone. It was made possible by treachery."

Hostile looks snapped around the table. Men's hands drifted to hilts; faces went hard. Sylvia felt the room tilt for a breath—fear and a terrible, expectant hope tangled in her chest.

"Treachery?" Valerick barked. "Who would damn us so? Who among us would hand the enemy our throats?"

"Yet it was done," Einarr said, the axe haft a slow, deliberate anchor in his fingers. "When I rode from Skaginlef, I went where I might learn your whereabouts. In Khorrtal, a petty chieftain—Niddeg—set upon me. He aimed a blade at my throat. Kholdyr answered with fire, and he burned their hall for the attempt."

Dhuuld's mouth tightened into a sneer. "Niddeg? Bah. You always did attract trouble, son of Rolff. What provocation did you offer an honorable man to act thus?"

"Provocation?" Einarr's voice sharpened, and the axe moved an inch in his hand. "There was none from me. The attack was deliberate. Niddeg did not act on a whim—his men were organized, his scouts had guides. Such an order does not happen without an instruction. Your retainers would not strike me except by command. Someone in Khorrtal signaled them."

A bitter laugh escaped Dhuuld. "You point fingers at my household?

I have bled for Khorrtal—my clan dies to keep the Bymist safe. You would insult me with such an accusation?!"

Tensions in the tent had grown solid, like stone walls pressing in. The heat swelled with it. Valerick's fist opened and closed on the table, the knuckles whitening as if he weighed whether to bury his axe in the Khorrtalli's skull. Only Damien's unyielding presence seemed to restrain him.

Sweat poured down Jollkud's face, his heavy chest rising and falling like a war drum. The wildman looked ready to leap over the table and claw out Dhuuld's eyes. Sylvia knew well—if he moved, stopping him would be suicide.

"Your fondness for Betanthian gold was my first misgiving," Einarr said evenly. "Easy to excuse it as plunder, or tribute from Lord Valens to keep Khorrtal docile. But perhaps there is more to it…"

A sudden chill slithered through the air. The canvas rippled as if brushed by winter's breath, and outside, the sky dimmed beneath bleeding clouds. Sunlight faded to shadow, and fear crept into the tent with the cold. Damien alone was unchanged. A grin spread across his stone-hewn face as his eyes drifted toward the flap.

"There will be no more talk of accusation," the warlord said. "Instead, we will have truth."

The Rhivothi guards drew back, and Lazilyth entered. She moved like a nightmare given flesh, sunken eyes gleaming out of a face waxen and corpse-like. A dusty gray shawl hung from her head, veiling the brittle strands of white hair that dangled like cobwebs down her bent spine.

It was the first glimpse of her since their shattering defeat, and her absence had stoked countless whispers. Had the crone misled them? Had her black arts failed, or betrayed them? No one knew, though theories had spilled freely over mugs of mead.

Her presence alone stilled the tent. Even Dreadfire fell silent beneath her weight. Lazilyth sniffed at the air like a beast, her clouded eyes sliding from face to face, hunting, measuring. When her mouth split into a grin of broken teeth and rotting gums, bile rose sharp in Sylvia's throat.

"Darkness I see…" the crone hissed. "Darkness I taste… like salt on a storm-tossed sea."

She tottered forward, and the warchiefs recoiled as if from fire. An unseen force pressed against them, heavy and choking. Only Damien did not stir, though the glint in his black eyes promised horror yet to come. Nothing good ever followed the old woman's steps.

"Tell me, Lazilyth," Damien commanded. His voice was a growl, a demand given to the abyss. "Tell me what truth the fates hide. Speak the treacheries they whisper."

With a creaking groan, she lifted her arms. Her fingers unfurled, nails long and yellowed, jagged as rusted blades. A bitter wind howled through the canvas, toppling a stack of parchments and sliding the map across the table.

Sylvia caught movement at the edges of her sight—shadows swirling like carrion birds, gathering just beyond the light. When she turned her head, they vanished, only to reappear the moment her gaze slipped away. The other warchiefs twitched and craned their necks, muttering under their breath as they too glimpsed the phantoms.

"Silver… and gold…" Lazilyth moaned, her neck twisting in grotesque arcs. "I see them gathered… circling like vultures… appetites sharpened by gold…"

Dhuuld's righteous mask began to melt, his face sagging like wax before a flame. His eyes betrayed truths that only Sylvia seemed to notice; the rest were spellbound by Lazilyth's convulsions, her jerking movements growing more violent with every breath.

"Tell me what they speak of, crone!" Damien thundered, his voice shaking the canvas. "Tell me!"

"Blood… and betrayal…" Lazilyth hissed. "Promises broken… our people scattered like chaff… a traitor enthroned upon the ashes…"

"Show me!" Dreadfire roared, his hand thrust toward her. "Show me the one!"

Lazilyth's fluttering hand stilled, curling into a fist before one crooked finger extended like the branch of a dead tree. Slowly, it drifted across the circle of warchiefs, lingering on each face, before stopping—unyielding, damning—upon one.

Her eyes cleared in that instant, pale clouds lifting to reveal a terrible lucidity. Silence fell like a blade. Fear rooted the tent in place. Then, one by one, the warchiefs turned their heads to see who had been named. Dhuuld.

His mouth fell open, aghast. Babble spilled from him in a frothy rush, words crashing over themselves, desperate and incoherent.

"I... I..."

Fear burned away into fury. Steel hissed free from scabbards as the warchiefs drew their weapons, circling like wolves. Vengeance flared in their eyes. But before blood could be spilled, Damien lifted his hand.

"Not yet," the warlord said, his voice like frost. "He will not escape so easily. Death is a mercy, and mercy is denied until the debt of treachery is paid in full."

"It is the muttering of an old fool!" Dhuuld spat, panic twisting into defiance. "If her visions were true, then why did she not see our ruin? Why did she not save us from defeat? Why did she lead us blind into the Plainhold slaughter?"

It was a fair question. Many had already mocked Lazilyth's theatrics in private; some had never stopped. For a breath, Sylvia felt the same doubt curl in her chest. Had they all been following superstition while the true threats wore faces and boots?

"Dark forces work here," the crone rasped, voice thin with strain. "The Eveldanyr's wrath grows. This war is not only of steel and blood. We fight on fields the eye cannot see."

"So you deny it?" Einarr asked, though no one expected a different answer.

"Of course I deny it!" Dhuuld cried, voice cracking with indignation. "I am no traitor. I have bled for Khorrtal! I have always bled for it!"

Damien's fingers met his lips in a sharp whistle. The sound snapped through the tent like a blade. In an instant, a cluster of Rhivothi guards shoved aside the flap and flooded the space, spears level, shields braced.

"Then we will learn the truth beneath the weight of pain," Damien said, voice flat as a grave.

"Allow me," Jollkud said before anyone could stop him. His tone carried no plea, only the promise of vengeance. "The Zylmacians have lost more than most. Though Zander was a bastard, he was kin. Thousands of my people lie unburied across the Plainhold. Let me take the Thal'akur."

Sylvia had never heard the word spoken in counsel; it landed like a stone. The Zylmacians were not a people known for their mercy. The name meant rites older than their language, an honor and a sentence both.

"Very well," Damien conceded. "Bind him. If any of Khorrtal rise to protest, bind them too. Let none interfere."

Chains were produced with the same efficiency as swords. Men moved to obey, faces cruel with the taste of judgment. Sylvia watched, stomach turned cold. The tent smelled of leather and iron and a sharp tang of fear. Outside, the plain waited, indifferent. Inside, men were about to do what men do best: punish the one who has been pointed at.

Without hesitation, the Rhivothi surged forward and overpowered Dhuuld; he writhed and screamed like a worm on a hook. Men seized him, bound him, and dragged him from the tent with Jollkud shadowing every step—no haste, no mercy.

"What does he intend to do?" Sylvia asked, though the question might have been born of naivete. "What is the Thal'akur?"

"A ritual of pain," Damien said, voice flat as a grave. "A practice so savage even the gods would turn away. I know it by reputation only, for its rites are not given lightly. But this betrayal that has cost too many lives, Dhuuld deserves no gentler fate."

The thought of it made Sylvia's anger harden until it was iron. Memories of the Plainhold flared: friends hacked down, kin left unburied… things that would not be forgiven.

"I, for one, am eager to see it done," she said, breath tight, fighting the urge to smile at the thought of retribution.

"Be careful," Damien warned. "What you will witness will stain you. Give thanks, ask forgiveness, pray to whatever gods you trust—and pray they will wash these images from your memory. There is no glory in what comes next, only judgment."

LUCETTA II

SHE STOOD ON THE CITADEL'S HIGHEST BALCONY, TOES DANGLING over the edge. The courtyard below was a pinprick in the haze, so far away it seemed unreal. Lucetta's chest fluttered as she stared down. Death was a final answer—permanent, irreversible—but at times it felt like the only escape from the palace and its haunted halls.

Have I gone completely mad? How did my life twist into ruin? Where are you when I need you most?

The woman in black had not appeared in days. The entity's absence grew more disturbing with each dawn. Perhaps Lucetta was truly losing her mind. The thought alone brought tears to her cheeks. She had risen so far, accomplished so much in the blink of an eye, only to find her so-called divine mission ending in shadows and silence.

She walked the halls only when the sun was bright, when the Citadel seemed a living place instead of a tomb. Even then, terrors pooled behind curtains and gathered in every darkened corner. Visions of the Queen stalked her waking hours, and at night, when the palace held its breath, Lucetta sometimes thought she heard a mournful wail threading through the corridors.

There was only one solution left. It frightened her more than dying, but the alternatives were annihilation or eternal confinement.

I have to do this. There is no other way out. If you're watching… give me courage.

She whispered the prayer to the absent woman in black, drew a shuddering breath, and stepped back from the balcony. Then, gathering the ragged pieces of her composure, she left her chamber and set her feet toward the King's chamber. Speaking to Marcellus was a prospect as ghastly as the visions themselves, but Aldred had left her no choice.

Two Guardsmen flanked the royal chamber doors, standing rigid in spotless armor. Their purple cloaks were as bright as the day they had been woven, ornate short swords at their hips, each man gripping both shield and spear. Why they had pledged their lives to guarding an old fool was anyone's guess. To Lucetta, it seemed more noble to fall on one's sword than waste breath protecting a drunken womanizer.

They stepped aside without a word. Despite her confinement, Lucetta still carried the Bethard name, and that courtesy alone spared her humiliation. A poor consolation, given what the family name had rotted into. She cast the guards a wary glance, then slipped past them, mindful that every step might be reported to Aldred.

She entered the chamber and stopped cold against a wall of stench. Coughing, hand clamped to her nose, she fought the bile rising in her throat. For a heartbeat, she thought Marcellus was already dead, slumped over his desk like a corpse forgotten.

"Father?" she managed, voice pinched. "I… I hope you are faring well."

The King did not stir. His gaze was fixed on an empty wine chalice, its ghostly contents already running through his veins. Far too early in the day to be so drunk, even by her lenient measure.

"I need to speak with you, father." Lucetta edged closer, stepping carefully through the clutter that choked the floor. "It is urgent… the fate of the kingdom—"

"My daughter…" Marcellus mumbled, his words thick with spite.

"Ungrateful bitch. You come to me only when there is something to take. Such dutiful children I've sired."

The exchange was nothing new. Every attempt to speak with him dissolved into venom. Still, he was her father—the King—and if she hoped to survive the palace, she would need to navigate the wreckage of his mind with care.

"I am only safeguarding your legacy, Father. Cardale is in ruins! When the city burned, I rode at the head of your army to crush the rebellion in your name... our name. Yet Aldred fears Bethard initiative. He's locked me in this palace like a criminal! Please, Father, tell him I cannot be kept here like this!"

"Bah!" The King spat the word like phlegm. "You've done nothing for my name but drag it through the filth. You are a selfish whore of a daughter, as corrupt as the rest! When have you ever come to me out of concern? When have you asked how you might serve me? You use me for your own ends, just like the whole pack of ingrates that fills my court. Get out! You will get nothing from me. Nothing!"

Tears burned down Lucetta's cheeks. Even after years of venom, the sting of his words never dulled. But her sorrow hardened under a rising heat; anger curled in her like a serpent as Marcellus hawked his throat and spat.

"Spare me your insincerity, girl. You only ever cry when you want your way, just like that bitch of a mother of yours."

A dark current rippled through the chamber. The candelabra flames guttered, flickering as though wind had found them, though the windows were shut tight. From the far corner of the room, shadows deepened, then moved.

The woman in black stepped forth, eyes glinting orange-red like coals. Dark hair spilled around her waist, swaying in unseen currents, her gown a haze of black linen rimmed by drifting mist. Lucetta's breath caught. A wicked smile began to edge her lips.

Finally! Oh, how I have missed you!

The woman in black grinned—a terrible grin, cruel enough to unman the bravest knight. Yet for Lucetta, it was an anchor, a comfort hidden inside menace.

She leaned on the desk, palms flat against the grimy wood. The surface complained under her weight as if it bore the press of a dozen men. The woman in black hovered close and laid a cool hand on Lucetta's shoulder; the touch was soft, but it felt like frozen leather.

"Now you listen," Lucetta said, the words coming out low and unfamiliar, as if another voice rode them. "Do as I command, you wretched old man, or I will unleash cruelties upon you so foul that even the Northmen would turn and flee."

Marcellus's face went slack with sudden comprehension and raw fear. The dementia that usually blurred his features thinned like mist; something clear and terrible had cut through. He recoiled, groping for the chalice as if it might be armor.

"You will order the Guardsmen to return me to Cardale at once," she continued, each sentence a blade. "You will see me free of Aldred's custody. If you deny me, if you call for men to seize me..." Her voice hardened to stone. "I will tear the eyes from your skull and drag that tongue from your mouth."

The woman in black drew closer and, with a movement like a veil settling, slipped into Lucetta's skin. Heat and flame roared behind her lids; her teeth felt as if they were sharpening into knives. Laughter—low, new, and seismic—built in her chest until the floor seemed to tremble beneath it.

Marcellus scrambled back from the desk and toppled from his seat with a sickening thud. He clawed at the air, incoherent pleas spilling free, but his voice could not bind what now moved through his daughter. Lucetta rose as if buoyed, drifting a hand toward him; she hovered a half-step above the floor, an accusation made visible.

"Now," she said, pointing with a finger as precise and merciless as a spear. "Do as I say, father. Obey me, or I will tear your soul to shreds!"

The experience felt more like a nightmare than waking life. Lucetta watched herself from somewhere outside her body, powerless, horrified at the spectacle she had become. To move without will, to act without control—it was a terror greater than any vision. Slowly, as if surfacing from a dream, her limbs grew her own again, and she drifted gently back to the floor.

Dear heavens! What has come over me?!

How the entity had seized her body was a mystery too dreadful to contemplate. Yet there was no mistaking it; the woman in black was growing stronger with each passing day. The thought of what she might do next sent a cold ripple down Lucetta's spine.

"Guards!" the King bellowed, sweat coursing down his wrinkled brow.

The chamber doors burst open, and the two purple-cloaked sentries stepped inside. Their faces betrayed unease, as though they too sensed the lingering malice that clung to the room.

"Y… yes, my king?" one stammered, eyes darting over the chamber.

The woman in black appeared beside Marcellus, studying him with eerie fascination. Behind her burning eyes, some devious intent was taking shape. She raised a single finger and pressed it to the King's brow. At once, his features shifted. Clarity flooded back into his gaze, the fog of years scattering. For the first time in memory, light returned to his eyes.

"You are to return my daughter to her estate without delay," Marcellus declared, his voice startlingly firm. "She is to go unmolested in her affairs henceforth. Her comings and goings will be questioned by no one."

Lucetta turned toward him and sneered, clearing her throat with deliberate sharpness. The King flinched at the sound and cast her an uneasy glance, as if reminded that his sudden clarity had been borrowed, not earned.

"And furthermore," Marcellus rasped, "she is not to be disturbed by Aldred under any circumstance. He is to remain within the palace until Cardale's safety is no longer in doubt. This is my command."

"Thank you, Father," Lucetta said with a smile that only deepened the King's dread. "You have been most generous."

She swept from the royal chamber with an oppressive air trailing in her wake. The Guardsmen recoiled as she passed, gooseflesh prickling their skin as if winter itself had brushed them. Lucetta walked with a confidence she had never known before. Her guardian spirit had returned in triumph. She was safe again, free to resume her divine mandate.

Descending the grand staircase, she entered the great hall, where guards and messengers moved in hurried streams. Tension coiled in the cavernous chamber, the security doubled and redoubled since the devastation beyond the palace walls.

Lucetta did not falter. She strode toward the towering front doors, their weighty panels cracked just enough for two men to slip through abreast. A Guardsman stepped forward to block her path, his hand raised in stiff formality.

"I'm sorry, princess, but I cannot allow you to—"

"Silence!" Lucetta cut him off, her wrist flicking with regal disdain. "The King has commanded my return to my estate. I am free to conduct my business as I see fit."

It was not the first time she had made such a claim, and the man's expression showed it. He smirked, tongue pressing at his front teeth as if chewing on insolence.

"Princess," he said, annoyance edging his tone, "you must understand... I am under strict orders not to—"

"She's right," one of the trailing purple cloaks said at last, his voice reluctant but firm. "I heard it from the King himself. We are to return her to her estate at once. By royal decree, she is free to go about her affairs."

The guard blocking her path stiffened, then stepped aside with a resigned shrug. Duty bound him more than preference, and honor left him no choice. Another barrier had fallen before her, but Lucetta's heart only pounded harder. With every step forward came the weight of certainty: a reckoning loomed, and it would be uglier than any manifestation of the woman in black.

Crossing into the courtyard, her knees turned to water. Dozens of Guardsmen patrolled the walls, bows and crossbows drawn taut. The palace grounds thrummed with the same frantic energy as the day of the rebellion. Even the air carried that same acrid blend of charred wood, burnt flesh, and pulverized stone. Memories came unbidden, flashing sharp behind her eyes.

She drew stares as she moved across the yard, purple cloaks frowning at the sight of her beyond the Citadel's doors. From a tower's shadowed entrance, she caught a glimpse of two burning orbs and the curl of a devilish smile.

All the reassurance I could ask for, she thought.

"Lucetta!" The voice cracked like a whip. Aldred stood, hands planted on his hips, his face caught between disbelief and outrage. "What in the hells are you doing? Have I not told you, again and again?"

She did not answer. She kept walking until his hand clamped around her arm. Before she could react, another Guardsman stepped in and tore Aldred's grip away.

"What is the meaning of this?" he roared, eyes wide with disbelief.

"I'm sorry, my lord," the Guardsman said, voice stiff with unease. "But these are the King's orders. The princess is to return home, free in her comings and goings."

Husband and wife locked eyes. There was no passion in it, only a grim clash of wills. Aldred's jaw clenched so tight his teeth squealed against each other like grinding stone. At length, he stepped back, relenting. But Lucetta knew this was no surrender. This was only the beginning.

Heavens... I have never seen him so angry in my life.

There was truth in the old saying: weak men were the most dangerous of all. And Aldred was weakness incarnate. For all his bluster, the past year had stripped him bare—powerless before Gareth. A drunkard without discipline. Helpless against the barbarian tide. Unable to keep Betanthia's crown jewel from fire and ruin. And now, humiliated by his own wife.

"We will discuss this in private," Aldred growled, his rage burning through her like heat from a forge. "When we return home, we—"

The Guardsman cleared his throat. "I'm afraid you are to remain at the palace, my lord. The King has commanded it."

The light in Aldred's eyes dimmed to something cold and flat. Stone replaced fury. Lucetta felt triumph in her chest, but unease crawled in its shadow. A man could only be stripped so many times before he broke. Pride and dignity gone, he was a husband in name only, a stranger wearing Aldred's face.

Still, she knew better than to let anger fester unchallenged. Enemies too close were the most dangerous of all. She would need to soothe him, even if only with token gestures. A bone tossed to a beaten dog.

"I know you will take good care of the city," Lucetta said, forcing a smile that never touched her eyes. "Don't worry about me. I'll be fine. A little time at home will do me good. The last thing you need is me underfoot while you're trying to restore order."

She leaned in for a kiss, but Aldred turned away. The rejection struck her harder than she expected. There was no affection left between them, but the slight still stung, only because so many Guardsmen stood watching. Perhaps it was wounded pride, not love. No matter.

With two dozen guards in her train, she left the walls of Westwind Citadel. A carriage would have been wiser, but the streets were too choked with rubble to allow for it. Archers tracked her from the battlements, bows nocked, until she passed from their range.

Auburn Row still stirred with life despite its ruin. Merchants rebuilt stalls with one hand and peddled scraps with the other, unwilling or unable to surrender a day's trade. Even in peace, they lived hand to mouth; now, necessity had turned them iron-hard.

For the first time, Lucetta felt at ease walking Cardale's streets. The sight of a purple cloak scattered commoners like vermin, heads bowed, shoulders hunched, desperate to avoid notice. The Royal Guardsmen had left their mark well enough—their swords practically still wet with Cardalean blood.

And yet, amid the torched shells of homes and shops, Lucetta saw opportunity. Every blackened wall and broken beam was a chance to reshape the city in her own image. No doubt her greedy brother Trace saw the same golden promise. He would need to be managed in time, but that was a problem for another day.

I must gather myself and those loyal to me. I have already let precious time slip away.

Lucetta cursed herself for surrendering to despair. Yet perhaps her suffering had been the very summons the woman in black required. The entity had proven again what terrors it could unleash—but even that power was nothing beside the man she needed most.

Pavlos. I must find him…

At last, her estate rose into view. Lucetta exhaled, relief loosening her chest. Here she would resume her divine mandate in peace, free of Aldred's incessant prattle. Trace was no doubt barricaded inside his bank, clutching at his coin like a drowning man to driftwood. The thought that no one would meddle in her affairs brought a rare calm.

But then, eyes. She felt them. Turning south, she scanned the ruined lanes and rubble-strewn alleys. For a moment, nothing stirred, until sunlight caught on a familiar flash of gold. Pavlos.

He leaned against a charred wall, hood drawn, his Guardsman armor gone. A plain brown cloak hung from his shoulders, but the glint of that golden smile betrayed him. As her entourage marched on, Pavlos slipped from the wall and followed at a distance, careful to mask his pursuit. Lucetta fought the urge to squeal aloud, her heart hammering in secret delight.

I knew he wouldn't abandon me! This is the most glorious day!

The sight of the Droethien thrilled her more than the gates of her own estate. A crude checkpoint bristled before her, spearmen at the ready and archers perched above the wall. The Guardsmen stationed there looked bewildered at the sudden arrival of their mistress.

"Open the gate!" one of her escorts barked. "By order of King Marcellus, Princess Lucetta is to maintain residency here. She is to come and go as she pleases, without question or hindrance."

Lucetta was greeted with puzzled glances and stiff bows, each servant careful to mask their thoughts. To displease their lady could mean a lashing from her sharp tongue, or a quiet death, their body left to float in the Camsby. Few dared to tempt either fate.

Once she dismissed them, Lucetta hurried into the gardens, her steps quick and unsteady. She hardly knew why she'd come here, save that her intuition burned hotter than the woman in black's eyes. A soft rustling by the arborvitae along the outer wall caught her ear. From the shadows stepped Pavlos.

The Droethien smiled, his golden teeth flashing in the light. The sight struck her like cool rain after drought.

"Pavlos!" she gasped. "How ever did you make it inside?"

He chuckled, low and confident. "Such tiny walls cannot keep Pavlos out for long. I scaled them with ease. Princess, perhaps you should build them higher, yes?"

Alarm never touched her, only comfort. Not only had the woman in black returned, but now so had her champion. With Aldred stripped of his power, little remained to bar the destiny promised to her.

"I am so happy to see you again," she said, breath quick with relief. "I was imprisoned in the palace, forbidden to leave until I bent my father's will. I feared you had abandoned me… forsaken your loyalty and gone elsewhere."

"Oh, Princess…" Pavlos shook his head, his golden smile glinting. "What sort of man runs when he is needed most? A Betanthian soldier, perhaps, but never a Droethien. And never a man of the White Spear. Pavlos has sworn himself to you always, yes?"

Faint chatter spilled from the banquet hall, startling her for a heartbeat. But the momentary panic passed. She moved now beneath a new mandate. None could contest her. Not Aldred. Not the King. Not after the terror she had placed in his heart.

"We must speak in private," Lucetta said carefully. "There are too many unfriendly ears here."

"Then perhaps we must change that, yes?" Pavlos answered with a sly grin.

Together they entered the estate and climbed to the second floor, heading for her study. The thought lingered with her—how could she ever replace every guard and servant without drawing eyes? Absurd, perhaps. Yet as she considered it, she realized nothing truly barred her from doing so.

Her study stood untouched. Every book and scroll, every trinket and painting, rested exactly as she had left them. A full flagon of wine waited by the window, likely placed there the moment word of her return spread. Whether it had been done out of duty or fear, she neither knew nor cared.

She strode to the table and poured a chalice, drinking it down with the thirst of a desert wanderer. Pavlos chuckled softly, plucked the flagon from her hand, and refilled her cup to the brim before pouring one for himself.

"To good fortune," the Droethien said, raising his chalice high.

"I prefer to make my own fortune," Lucetta replied with a sly grin. "Still… I have a feeling all will bend toward my favor. Cardale lies in ruin, the people still restless, but our divine mission cannot fail. Tell me, Pavlos, have you any word from the north?"

"When last I heard," Pavlos said, "the work continues. Your slaves clear the earth; your people raise the palisade. More come each day—from miles around—seeking a new life beneath your banner."

Relief warmed Lucetta like a flash of sun. Time was everything; a single wasted day could let Betanthia fill with barbarians and cost her the breathing room she needed to strike.

"Most pleasing," she said, lifting her chin. "I always knew I could rely on you. Once Aldred's suspicion eases, I will ride north to inspect the works myself. Even with him confined, eyes will watch my every step."

"Then we will break those eyes," Pavlos replied with a dry chuckle. "If your husband proves too troublesome, perhaps his neck will break as he sleeps, yes?"

The thought should have disgusted her; instead, Lucetta found herself oddly indifferent. Murder was unpleasant, but necessity wore no conscience. If Aldred threatened her safety or her designs, he would be dealt with when the moment demanded it.

"We will deal with him in time," she said, settling at her desk and tapping a map. "For now, gather every man you can. Send riders north and south; rally the Droethiens and any who swear to the White Spear. The hour grows late, and labor waits for no one. My queendom will be born—by will or by blade."

UDORN III

THEY MOVED THROUGH THE DYING DARK LIKE WOLVES ON THE HUNT, swift and silent. Dellhaven lay deathly quiet, but Udorn knew they were not alone. At every corner lurked a Betanthian patrol, restless and ready to spill Northern blood.

Though unfamiliar with the city, Udorn kept the sea to his right. Northward was the only direction that mattered. Dellhaven looked younger than he had expected; scaffolds and half-finished works stood at every turn, timber stacked in neat piles, mortar still wet in places.

Riches gleamed here in abundance. The scale of the buildings, the ornament of their facades—Dellhaven was a city swollen with wealth. Were their lives not balanced on a knife's edge, one raid could have fed Mot's clans for generations.

But gold meant nothing if they were left as butchered corpses in these foreign streets. No treasure could be carried to Sjenohor; only blood and glory counted as coin in the afterlife. With that truth steady in his chest, Udorn pressed on, eyes searching for a way clear of the city's maze.

A rumble carried down the avenues—a sound any man of war knew well. Hooves. Steel. An armed host was closing. Against such numbers, even Ubneri ferocity would be ground to dust.

But Dellhaven had places to vanish. Pride might balk, yet survival demanded it. Unfinished structures loomed on either side, too weak to hold an assault but strong enough to hide shadows. Udorn signaled his men onward, axe drawn, ready to carve down any who barred their way. The streets were still drowned in night, dawn's light not yet risen over the rooftops. In that blackness, Udorn spotted what he sought—a sanctuary ahead, a chance to live and fight another day.

"There," Udorn whispered, raising his axe toward a nearby estate.

It was no castle by Dellhaven's standard, but the three-story brick chateau sprawled wide enough to hide a band of raiders. They closed in quickly. The front gate loomed tall, its iron doors shut fast. Even the strongest among them would break before such a barrier.

But not every obstacle was solved with steel. Udorn remembered years past, when survival meant creeping, stealing, and outwitting. Every Ubneri boy learned that lesson: failure was death, success was manhood.

The walls were stout, but Betanthian pride had left its flaw. At the top, wrought-iron ornamentation was more show than shield, a weakness born of decadence. Dellhaven had known luxury, not siege.

"Hefnir," Udorn murmured, pointing. "Go over. Open the gate."

The raider stepped forward—compact, muscle knotted thick as timber. He studied the wall, then took three quick strides and bounded upward. Hands seized the ledge. With a grunt, he hauled himself onto the balusters and slipped over. A heartbeat later came the muffled thump of his landing.

Udorn's gaze swept the street, every nerve taut. Time thinned around them; any moment, the sound of hooves could break through the dark. Then, metal groaned. The latch clanged. One of the iron doors shuddered and swung wide enough to admit them. Hefnir stood within, grinning through the gloom.

"Move!" Udorn hissed, waving his men forward while he kept watch on the empty street.

Moments before he slipped inside, Udorn caught the tramp of boots—a Betanthian patrol closing fast. He ducked through the gates, and his men heaved the iron doors shut behind them. Silence fell. They crouched in the courtyard, chests still, breath shallow. The footsteps passed, fading into the distance. Only then did Udorn loose a long breath.

They had entered a palace in all but name. The chateau's brick and stone gleamed even in shadow, its facade dressed in marble pillars and archways—Southern wealth carved into permanence. A smile flickered across Udorn's lips. Riches lay within, though gold was no concern tonight. Survival came first. Shelter had to be secured.

He crossed to a set of double doors at the heart of the house. Carved from stained wood, embossed with birds and wild horses, they looked as though they had been meant to awe, not defend. One heave of his axe shattered the latch. The doors groaned open beneath his shove.

A rush of scented air washed over him—bergamot and oud, heavy and cloying. The fragrance turned heads among his men, for such luxuries rarely drifted north to Mot. Candles glowed inside, their light trembling across the walls. For a moment, the place seemed deserted.

Then, metal scraped. Armor clattered faintly in the hall. Udorn signaled his raiders back and pressed himself against the shadow of a tall sculpture. A lantern's glow spilled across the foyer as a guard descended the corridor, stepping out from behind the grand staircase. His eyes caught the open door.

"Is someone there?" he called, hand sliding to the sword at his hip. "Hello?"

He managed only a handful of steps before Udorn lunged, swift as a hawk stooping from the sky. His axe bit deep. The lantern flew, shattering, the steel of the man's armor ringing against the floor. The sound echoed shrill and sharp through the halls, loud enough to wake the dead.

Udorn motioned, and his men poured inside without a thought for subtlety. In an instant, the house became a storm: raiders fanned through rooms, shouts and steel clashed, then, as quickly as it began, the noise curdled into a grim silence.

"On your knees, swine!" Dulkin's bark rolled down from the upper floor.

Udorn sprinted up the grand stair and found another guard dead, a servant girl collapsed nearby with her throat cut ear to ear, blood spread like ink across the floor. Men rifled chests through and overturned drawers, tossing silks and plates aside, but Udorn kept his eyes on the living. Hostages mattered more than silver.

"Who are you?!" an elder lord stammered, hands trembling. "What is the meaning of this? I—"

"Silence your tongue," Udorn snapped. "Cooperate, and your family walks. Refuse, and I will make sure you speak no more."

"Father?" a girl wept, her voice thin and raw.

"Beatrice, hush. Everything will be alright," the lord croaked, flinging himself into useless comfort. "Name your price. Gold, jewels, spices—take it all!"

The raiders laughed darkly at the supplications. Such pleading never failed to amuse them; it was a low, human sound that broke no bones and bought no honor, only coin and cowardice.

"I would have your name," Udorn said, stepping toward the cowering family. "And I would have it the first time. I never ask a second."

"L–Lord Edwin Drakeford," the man stammered. "Please, I beg you—spare my family, I—"

"Enough." Udorn knelt, drawing a knife that caught the candlelight. "I care nothing for your riches. A fleet of my kinsmen lies offshore, ready to turn this city into ashes. I am among the more merciful of my people. Do not test my patience. Be still now; this will be over soon."

Day bled into night, and the city lay silent in the wake of slaughter.

Patrols had not returned, nor had any reinforcements arrived. A handful of Ubneri kept watch from the estate's windows, scanning the streets for danger. None came.

That evening, they feasted like kings. The Drakeford pantry yielded delicacies beyond imagination: spiced meats, honeyed fruits, rich cheeses, bread baked golden. Udorn gorged until his belly ached, still cramming food as though it might vanish. For a fleeting moment, he felt he had crossed into Sjenohor itself, Kholdyr's Hall laden with an eternal banquet.

"Udorn!" Dulkin One-Eye bellowed, arms spread wide and grin split across his scarred face. "I would almost sail home without spoils. The food, the drink—they are feast enough to raise a horde!"

"Indeed," Udorn said, smirking. "I can only imagine Ragruk gnawing his stale bread and raw fish while we glut ourselves."

They both laughed and lifted tankards of Betanthian ale. Mead was the gift of the gods, but even Udorn admitted there was weight and craft in southern brews. Thick, hearty, layered with taste; it filled his mouth and belly like no drink of Mot ever had.

"To the brave go the spoils," Dulkin declared, draining his tankard. "You were right to lead us here, Udorn. Whatever doubts you had, cast them aside. This raid will be sung for generations—short though it has been."

Rennek lifted his own mug in answer, his grizzled face lit with rare cheer. "Aye, Dulkin speaks true. I never thought I'd live to taste such delicacies. And to think my son fights here beside me... by Kholdyr, that is worth more than any jewel in this cursed city."

Tharek, still young but blooded, flushed at the words. He raised his cup high, voice steady though his hand trembled with excitement. "I only did as you taught me, Father. Today I stood shoulder to shoulder with our kin. Today I felt the gods watching."

Rennek clapped a heavy hand to his son's shoulder, pride gleaming brighter than the candlelight. "And they will watch you still, boy. You brought no shame to our name. One day, it will be you leading men through fire and steel. I could not ask for a finer heir."

The raiders roared in approval, tankards slamming against the table. Udorn allowed himself a small smile at the sight. Blood and ruin surrounded them, but here—among kin, with bellies full and pride alight—the Ubneri felt untouchable.

"I pray I can see our people out of this place alive," Udorn murmured, staring into the dregs of his tankard. "A feast is little consolation if none of us live to see home again."

Dulkin moved beside him, heavy hand pressing against his shoulder. "You must not be so hard on yourself. Think of the men who drowned in the bay hours ago. You led us from that slaughter. And here we sit, with food in our bellies and hope in our hearts. The men believe in you, Udorn. It's time you believe in yourself."

Strange words from Dulkin, a man who mocked weakness as easily as he drew breath. Yet the more Udorn turned them over, the truer they felt. He had always been his own harshest critic, never satisfied, even when victory lay in his hands. Perhaps it was that restlessness—those gnawing defects—that kept his men alive where others would have perished.

Across the hall, Rennek raised his cup, grinning as Tharek matched his gesture beside him. "Hear that, boy? Even the mighty Udorn doubts himself! Yet you and I, we stood with him, and the gods will remember it."

Tharek flushed, pride bright in his eyes. "I will not forget it either, Father. To fight beside you, and beside Udorn—it feels as though Kholdyr himself watched us today."

Rennek's laugh rumbled like thunder, and he pulled his son close. "Aye, and may he watch you tomorrow too. Whatever comes, Tharek, you have made me proud."

Udorn felt the warmth of the moment settle in his chest. Doubt would never leave him, that much he knew. But seeing Rennek and Tharek together, he understood why he bore the weight so heavily. It was for them, and for all their sons, that he would carry it.

Gradually, the sun crept over the horizon; a small victory, but a victory all the same. The raiders had supped and slept with full bellies, and now they stirred with renewed vigor. Laughter and jeers echoed through the chambers, as though they had forgotten they lay in the heart of an enemy city.

Udorn rose groggily, rubbing grit from his eyes, incredulous at the noise. He opened his mouth to rein them in, only to be beaten to it.

"Silence!" Thaul hissed, his hand cutting the air. He rushed to the window, easing the curtain back with care. "Betanthian patrol," he muttered. "Headed this way!"

Udorn raised a finger to his lips, his glare sharp enough to cut. At once, the chamber fell still. Even the noble family seemed carved in ice, Lord Drakeford's forehead slick with sweat as his gaze darted between his wife and daughter.

The sound came first: a steady crunch of armored boots, the rattle of mail, the creak of leather straps. Each step rang louder, swelling until it seemed to fill the very walls of the estate. Then, mercifully, it began to fade. Thaul exhaled hard, letting the curtain fall back into place. He gave a curt nod. A ripple of relief moved through the raiders, an unspoken prayer to the gods that the moment had passed.

Beatrice's face went pale, her thin frame shaking like a beaten dog. She looked to her parents with wide, frantic eyes, sensing an opportunity slipping away.

"Help us!" she shrieked, voice cracking as she screamed toward the street. "In here! Help us!"

Udorn moved in a flash. His knife carved across her throat, spraying a red arc onto the chamber wall. The girl crumpled, thrashing weakly, her hands clawing at the wound as blood poured through her fingers. Lord Edwin and his wife wailed, rushing forward, only to be seized and held fast by raiders.

"That was *her* choice," Udorn growled, pointing his bloodied blade at the grieving pair. "And if you dare make another sound, you will join her. Do you understand?"

Neither answered. They could only stare, frozen in horror as Beatrice spasmed once, twice, then fell still in a spreading pool of scarlet. Lady Ann Drakeford pressed both hands to her mouth, her muffled sobs shuddering through the silence.

"Here they come!" Thaul hissed from the window.

"Positions, men!" Udorn snapped, his voice low but commanding. "Do exactly as I say. We will not see Sjenohor without a fight!"

From the street below, a chorus of shouts rang out, then silence. It was the kind of silence that meant strategy. Udorn slid to another window, peeling the curtain back with a finger. Betanthians swarmed outside, steel glinting in the morning light. They were spreading, encircling, their eyes fixed on the house, patient as wolves scenting blood.

They were trapped and surrounded, with nowhere to run. Decent odds on any day, Udorn supposed, but here they held a strange advantage. The garrison would not dare to smoke them out with fire, not with Lord Drakeford and his family inside. Truly, it was a blessing from the gods to have chosen such a refuge.

Before long, dozens of soldiers, perhaps a hundred, poured into the surrounding avenues, shields locked and spears bristling. A company of archers followed in their wake, longbows and crossbows nocked and ready. Formidable though their numbers seemed, they were not enough to break Ubneri spirits.

"Whoever shelters inside this estate," came a booming voice, "I demand you show yourselves at once!"

A man in worn but well-kept armor stepped boldly from the ranks.

His beard was streaked with iron and black, his frame broad as a wall, his pale gray eyes cold with resolve. The purple cloak of Betanthia's royal house, faded with years of service, clung to him still.

Dulkin exchanged a glance with the raiders nearest him, fighting back a bark of laughter. The sheer arrogance of such a demand, with hostages so near, was almost comical. Still, Udorn knew this was no time for amusement. If they were to survive, this moment must be seized.

"And who would issue such a demand?" he called, stepping onto the balcony with fearless poise.

At once, bowstrings creaked as archers drew taut. Arrows hovered, ready to fly, but the sight of the Ubneri chieftain standing proud seemed to give them pause. Even the spearmen shrank behind their kite shields, as if expecting him to hurl thunder from the sky.

"I am Commander Albin Marrick of the Dellhaven Garrison," the veteran bellowed, voice hard as quarried stone. "This city belongs to House Bethard; your presence here is an abomination. Throw down your weapons and surrender, or be destroyed!"

Though the raiders suspected the threats were hollow, they looked to Udorn all the same. Honor demanded an answer; even faced with near-certain death, he could not let the challenge go unanswered.

No…I cannot. How will I be remembered should this campaign end with our demise?

"Stay your arrows," Udorn ordered, jabbing a stern finger down. "If you fell me, my men will cut the heads off your precious lord and his family."

Gaxas stepped out onto the balcony with Lord Drakeford in his grip, a blade pressed cold and bright against the old man's throat. A dozen archers twitched toward their strings, then froze; despite their numbers, they had no clean shot that would not cost the hostage his life.

"No—please!" Edwin pleaded, voice breaking. "They… they killed my daughter! Do not provoke them!"

"Stand down!" the commander snapped to his men, then fixed Udorn with hard eyes. "State your demands, savage. But be warned: shed one more drop of blood and it will be your undoing."

Udorn watched the soldiers below—saw the tremor in their hands, the white of fear in their faces—and felt, oddly, a calm settle over him. The advantage was slim and the danger real, but for all that, there was a clarity to the moment.

"I demand safe passage to the north," he said at last, leaning against the balustrade as if the world were his to steady. "We keep Lord Drakeford and his family as hostages until we have cleared the city. Only once we are free will we return them to you."

Commander Marrik's mouth tightened as he weighed the demand. "Your terms are unacceptable," he said at last, the anger in his voice thin as paper. "How can we trust you won't break your word once you're free? We'd be fools to simply let you march out of Dellhaven."

"They're bluffing," Dulkin growled from just behind Udorn, eyes fixed on the patrol below. "Do not relent. Keep your foot on their throat, or they'll test you."

There was truth in the warning. Udorn moved with a calm that hid the racing math in his head. He slipped into the master bedchamber where his men stood breathless, and with one cold, decisive motion, he seized his axe. Without ceremony, he brought it down across Beatrice's neck.

Lady Ann's gasp turned to a cry as the girl's head rolled free. Udorn grabbed the hair in one blood-slick fist and strode back onto the balcony, holding the severed head high for all to see before tossing it. A wet thud punctuated the street as it struck stone and spun to a stop; a ripple of gasps and curses ran through the ranks below and then, like a struck chord, hushed into frightened silence.

"If you would measure wills," Udorn said, voice flat as iron, "know that I outmatch you. Meet my demands, and your lord walks. Test me once, and they all die—then you will join them. Do we have terms?"

The sight was enough. Albin's posture sagged; the commander sheathed his sword with a reluctant hand and signaled his men to stand down. "We have terms," he conceded, voice tight. "But mark my words—"

A few of the raiders laughed, the sound ugly and bright in the cold morning. The threat and the show of brutality had stripped the garrison's bravado thin as parchment. Udorn gave a small nod, then turned back toward the bedchamber.

Inside, Thaul's grin was broad and proud; Gaxas moved to bind the hostages. Lady Ann lay unconscious, slack and pale—securing her hands with a length of rope was a grim, simple affair. The raiders worked with the efficient, hungry focus of men who understood that terror, once sown, must be tended until the harvest.

"Please..." Lord Drakeford whimpered, voice thin. "Be true to your word. Let my wife and I live. I beg you!"

"You will live to see the new dawn," Udorn said, his hand heavy on the old man's shoulder. "So long as no effort is made to oppose us."

"N... no! Never!" Edwin stammered. "They would never risk my safety! I am too important!"

With an outstretched arm, Udorn motioned toward the door. "Then you have nothing to fear."

The raiders moved down the staircase with their prisoners in tow. Udorn counted men with a quick, practiced glance, making sure none were left behind. When he was satisfied, he seized Lord Drakeford by the shoulder and steered him toward the front door.

"Relax," Udorn told him, giving a firm shove. "This will be over soon."

He cast one last look across the foyer, etching each face into his memory. They might very well be marching into death; he would not forget them. Dulkin fell in at his side and nodded.

"We're ready, Udorn."

A mischievous light danced in Dulkin's eyes despite the grimness of the hour, as if the thought of Sjenohor's halls—of feasting, drinking, and slaughtering in the company of the gods—made his blood sing. It was the proudest hope for many men. Udorn felt it too, but his hunger was different: not for eternal revelry, but to live long enough to see his children rise and take the spear in his stead. That, he thought, would be a far truer victory.

"I have seen that look before, old friend," Udorn said quietly. "But you will not be dying today... not if I have any say in the matter."

"You know me too well!" Dulkin chuckled, the sound rough but oddly warm. "Yet how could I long for Sjenohor after feasting on the delights of this world? A man could grow old and fat here, aye—if he weren't chased by spears every hour."

Some would call their retreat a defeat, for no flames blackened the sky above Dellhaven and no treasure wagons groaned behind them. Yet Udorn had lost not a single man, and to him that was triumph enough.

"Fear not," he grinned, voice pitched for all his kin to hear. "We will return! Tell me, have you filled your pockets?"

The response was a thunderous cheer, shameless laughter rolling through the chamber like a storm breaking. To raid and return emp-ty-handed was disgraceful; to escape with spoils, however small, was the Ubneri way.

Lord Drakeford flinched at their joy, distraught at the ransacking of his home. Yet, protest was useless. His life was still his own, so long as the Betanthians kept to their bargain. Udorn clapped him on the shoulder, then hauled the door wide.

Blinding sunlight spilled into the foyer, forcing them to squint as they stepped out. The courtyard gates loomed ahead, still barred and heavy, but for now they shielded the raiders from the hungry eyes beyond.

"On your guard, men," Udorn commanded, leading them toward the gate.

The latch groaned, the doors heaved open—and beyond, a sea of spears greeted them. Rows of anxious faces peered over kite shields, waiting, quivering for the slightest excuse to strike. Then, with deliberate slowness, the ranks parted, opening a narrow lane that pointed north.

It was almost comical to behold the terror etched across the soldiers' faces. For many, it was their first time standing so near to a Northman. Others masked fear with poorly contained rage, but none dared act, not with Lord Drakeford's life hanging in the balance.

Thaul found the spectacle even more amusing than Udorn. He prowled along the line, jeering at the Southerners with open contempt.

"Such obedient dogs you are!" he bellowed.

He seized the rim of a soldier's shield and rattled it hard, laughter booming as the man flinched. The taunt rippled through the formation, shaking the nerve of those with weaker wills; a few looked on the verge of breaking entirely. Udorn would have preferred discipline over mockery, but the provocation served its purpose. These men had no stomach for fair combat. If a fight did erupt, only the most fanatical few would stand their ground.

The streets of Dellhaven stretched before them, eerily deserted. Only the clatter of armored boots and the whisper of arrows being shifted in quivers broke the silence. Cityfolk peered through shuttered windows, wide-eyed, before vanishing as quickly as they had appeared. To them, this grim procession must have looked like a parade of ghosts.

Since when did Betanthia become a kingdom of cowards? Why do they not offer battle?

Regardless, the thought emboldened him. Perhaps they would march from Dellhaven without losing a single man. Perhaps Ragruk had already mourned him as dead—and perhaps that mistake would raise him higher still. A hero's name could be a dangerous crown, but for now, it was his to seize.

Gradually, the streets thinned into the countryside, vast tracts of open land unfolding before them. Sprawling estates dotted the horizon, each mansion more brazen than the last—some taller than the grandest temple in Mot, others broader than its legendary mead hall.

"How can men build such things?" Dulkin muttered in awe.

Udorn's grin was fleeting. He had seen wonders greater than Dellhaven, yet even so, every detail was worth noting. The city was not only stone and mortar—it was armor, ranks, supply, and will. He burned each sight into memory, down to the cut of the soldiers' shields and the forge-markings on their mail.

"One day, my brother," he said, voice low, "I will show you sights to shame even Sjenohor."

At last, the outer walls loomed, a great spine of stone girding Dellhaven. Dozens of archers scrambled along the parapet, bows nocked, strings ready to be drawn taut. Udorn tightened his grip on Lord Drakeford's neck, pulling the old man close until the edge of his knife rested just shy of flesh. None would dare release an arrow with their prize so near death.

Cavalry thundered past, sabers flashing, lances held ready as riders streamed toward the gate. Every step forward felt like a heartbeat too long, peril wound so tight that the faintest mistake could end them all. The gates creaked wide under the strain of chains and gears, and Betanthian faces glared with naked fury as they allowed the Ubneri their passage. The raiders pressed through, flanked by a tide of soldiers.

Commander Marrik appeared at the vanguard, his brow shadowed, his voice sharp as flint. "We have met your terms, savage. Now unhand our lord!"

"Indeed, you have," Udorn said with a nod. "But who is to say you will not ride us down the moment the exchange is made? I think not. We Ubneri are not beasts—we are men of logic and lethal cunning. Your lord stays with me until we are given enough horses to make good our escape. Deny me, and I will water this earth with his blood. Or perhaps hers."

In a blur, Dulkin seized Lady Ann by the hair, yanking her head back and pressing a blade to her throat. The sight of cold steel at soft flesh was all the persuasion the commander needed.

"Don't argue with them, you fools!" Lord Drakeford cried. "Give them the damn horses and be done with it!"

Albin Marrik's jaw worked furiously, but he knew he had been bested. With a sharp motion, he signaled a subordinate, who galloped back toward the city. A few raiders laughed openly, marveling at how easily the Betanthians yielded. If Ragruk had witnessed so much as a moment of this exchange, he might have sworn to raze the kingdom to its roots.

Perhaps, Udorn thought, his kinsmen were right all along. Perhaps the Southerners truly had become the cowards they claimed. These were not the same men who had once chained him. Betanthia was a shadow of itself.

After a tense wait, Dellhaven's gates groaned open once more. This time, a herd of saddled horses emerged, wrangled by over two dozen riders. Udorn's eyes narrowed with satisfaction as he watched them driven forward. The hostages were shoved into view, Lord Edwin and Lady Ann pale and trembling with their hands bound high.

Both sides moved with painstaking care, every man poised to strike at the faintest sign of treachery. But no such spark came. The Betanthians yielded the horses, and the Drakefords stumbled into the arms of their soldiers, alive.

Tension rippled across the ranks. Each side held its prize, and for a heartbeat violence threatened to erupt as men eyed what they had just surrendered. Then, as quickly as it came, the panic ebbed—every man on the field knew he would see another sunrise, and that alone was the greatest prize.

"Enough of this," Commander Marrik snarled. "Leave our lands at once. Begone!"

"You kept your word, Betanthian," Udorn said, smiling. "And we have kept ours. Know this—should any of you give chase, we will not only slay you, but I will order our fleet to return and burn Dellhaven to ash. Test me, and let Lord Drakeford's daughter be your reminder of my resolve."

Albin wanted vengeance, his face a knotted thing of fury, but reason held his hand. He watched, seething, as the Ubneri mounted and surged away in a thundering line. Cheers and howls rose behind them—lessons of terror and triumph braided into a hard-won victory.

"Udorn!" Gaxas bellowed, voice booming with approval. "May the gods remember this day—the day you conquered our enemies not by steel, but by words!"

It was no small thing for men who measured worth by blade and blood. Udorn ought to have reveled; instead, his thoughts slid like a shadow to Ragruk. Glory invited envy, and a hungry chieftain could be as deadly as any sword. The crown of a champion sat light and warm—and dangerously visible. Being the man of the hour was a precarious perch. Ragruk might see this as a threat and move to snuff him out before his fame grew too bright.

All I crave is hearth and kin. Yet if that fool dares to block my path, I will turn his pride to ash, and I will wear his skin as a cloak!

MADELYN III

SMOKE AND REVELRY DRIFTED FROM THE MEAD HALL'S CHIMNEY, rising like a beacon in the dusk. It was a strange sight—these barbarians celebrating after their ruin on the Plainhold. But nothing, not even defeat, seemed to dull Northern spirits. Madelyn watched from afar, lips curling at their foolishness. Perhaps it was not courage but stupidity that kept them so merry.

She had wandered the wastes for days, driven by instinct more than reason. Every wrong turn brought with it a dreadful anxiety, a cold hand gripping her gut until she veered back to the unseen path. Only when she was true again did the pressure ease. And now, by those strange tugs of fate, she had found a garrison of Damien Dreadfire's marauders.

She tied her horse to the dead limb of a gnarled oak, then scanned the settlement. A few dozen warriors lounged in the dirt streets as if war were leagues away. But her sharpened eyes, no longer bound to mortal limits, caught the truth—hidden sentries peppered the perimeter, shadows within shadows. To an untrained eye, the village might seem lax. To her, it was a clever trap.

Still, not clever enough. An open assault would scatter the survivors and alert Damien too soon. Better to be patient. Better to strike with precision, unseen and unheralded. Had her appearance not changed so completely, she might never have dared attempt such infiltration. But clad in black leathers, her hair as dark as a raven's wing, she looked more Rhivothi than Betanthian now. Disguise alone would not save her, but it gave her a chance, and a chance was all she needed.

You cannot be timid, Madelyn, she told herself. *There are men down there who did what was done to you. Keep that thought foremost.*

She checked her gear once more, then stepped from a tangle of weeds and dead trees. Chin up, steps measured, she walked toward two spearmen on patrol. They halted as she neared, brows knitting as they weighed whether to challenge her.

"And where did you come from, eh?" one grunted. Despite his weathered face, he was Nothanek through and through, as was the man beside him.

She could have cut them down and moved on, but murder now would light the whole village. Better to test their gullibility. Madelyn spat, a hard, hateful sound, the taunt stripped of any pretense. The Nothanek flinched and took a step back.

"Easy there!" the other muttered.

"She must be one of those Rhivothi shieldmaidens," the first said, curiosity edging his tone. "I've only seen one once. She lives up to the talk, by the gods."

They stepped aside without further fuss. Heart pounding, vision thinning at the edges, Madelyn pressed on toward the mead hall. A few heads turned, then dropped—suspicion slackened at the outer patrol, but danger still lurked within.

Inside the hall, smoke and the smell of stale ale struck her like a wall. The air stung with tobacco and crushed herbs; under that lay a sour reek of spilled drink and old piss. She tightened her face into a mask and forced herself forward. The room teemed with Rhivothi and Nothanek, a scattering of Zylmacians too; the closeness of wildmen made something cold twist in her gut.

At the hall's far end, a row of tapped kegs leaned on a shelf. The tavernkeep moved from tankard to tankard with a nervous efficiency, his eyes flicking over the crowd. Madelyn pushed between two grizzled Rhivothi at the bar—boldness that in less fortunate times would have cost a man his head—and planted herself where she could watch everything.

The ruse seemed to hold. A few warriors glanced her way, but their interest quickly bled back into drink and dice. Only a Rhivothi woman could be that brazen and still walk away intact.

Don't get comfortable, she reminded herself. *Any one of these beasts could know your face.*

Her cropped black hair and dark garb masked her well enough, but she moved carefully, letting her eyes wander while her body carried the guise of indifference. Slowly, she circled the hall, measuring each man by his weapons, his stance, his swagger. None of the faces stirred memory, which stung, but it was too early to despair.

Near the center, a gang of warriors played at dice, golden Betanthian coins stacked like bait in front of them. Madelyn snatched a mug of mead from a nearby table and leaned against a post, watching the game. The rules were half-familiar, half-foreign, but the rhythm was easy to follow. She sipped and studied, her pulse calm as she slipped deeper into the masquerade.

Nearly thirty of them crowded the hall—too many to cut down at once, even if she loosed the darkness in her veins. No, brute force would be suicide. She would need precision.

"You there." A heavily tattooed Zylmacian sneered at her, his voice carrying over the dice clatter. "Rhivothi bitch. You mean to stare all day, or will you sit and wager like the rest?"

Madelyn snorted, masking a sudden jolt of fear. She roughened her words in the northern tongue. "Games are for children."

"I can think of a few games I'd play with you." The man grinned wide, golden teeth flashing in the firelight. He grabbed his crotch with one hand and raised his tankard with the other. "But I'm no child. I am Drakka, and you'd do well to remember that name."

Dozens of eyes tracked her, weighing every twitch of her face. Only one path could keep the ruse alive: bury her dagger in Drakka's skull. But no, the time was not right. She forced the urge down, snarled instead, and claimed a chair at the table, slamming her mug hard enough to slosh its contents.

"Got any gold?" the Zylmacian asked, his grin filthy. "Or would you rather wager something more… appetizing?"

Without breaking his gaze, she slipped a hand to her belt pouch and spilled a small pile of coins onto the table—mostly silver, a few bright gold pieces glinting among them. Laughter rippled through the men, each already savoring the chance to strip her purse and perhaps more. Satisfied, Drakka rattled dice into a leather cup and gave it a shake.

"You must be one of Stormguard's," said a blond Rhivothi brute across from her. "I am Skarik, kinsman to Marvath."

Madelyn offered no words at first, only a thin smile and a raised chin. At the name, her stomach clenched. Sylvia. Chains biting her wrists, nights freezing alone like an animal, the weight of a child never meant for love. The memories pressed like iron.

"Aye," she forced out, "I was separated in the rout. I do not even know who lived."

Skarik's voice softened, his eyes dropping. "It should pain you to hear that Bonesplitter fell. His body still rots on the Plainhold. He deserves a pyre, not the pecking of crows."

Despite every reason to hate these men, the words struck her. Marvath—cruel as the rest, yet he alone had shown her moments of pity, even risked defiance to shield her from Zylmacian filth. Grief cracked her mask, dragging her gaze to the table.

"You have my condolences," Skarik said. "His death wounds us all."

"Are we playing," Drakka spat, breaking the moment, "or do you mean to sit here weeping like children?"

It was curious to see how the Rhivothi kept a watchful eye on her, as though she were truly one of their own. They were perhaps the fiercest warriors in all of Caldakas, yet there lingered in them a strange streak of honor. Still, their regard would not be enough to spare them when the time came.

I must learn where Dreadfire is hiding, she thought. *One of these beasts has to know.*

After another round of mead, the warriors' tongues loosened. Some slurred their boasts, others shouted so loudly the rafters shook. Their drunkenness made them no less dangerous—perhaps more so—but it offered her a chance. Careful words could pry secrets from them where steel could not.

"How long do we plan to rot in this sty?" she asked, rolling dice into the shaker with practiced ease. "We should not stray too far from the others."

"As long as Damien requires," Skarik replied. "He needs our eyes and ears."

Cryptic and unsatisfying, but a thread nonetheless. Madelyn forced a nod, though bile rose in her throat at even uttering the name. "Stormguard will be wondering if I still draw breath," she added, letting Sylvia's name fall like bait. "I must get back to her with all haste."

It was a gamble, and a sharp one. None of these men had ever seen her among their ranks, and one slip would burn her disguise to ash. For now, though, the haze of drink dulled suspicion.

"Fuck Stormguard," Drakka spat, ale dribbling from his chin. "None of you northern whores belong in a proper army anyway. If I were warchief, my first order would be to—"

"Mind your tongue, Westerner," a hulking Rhivothi cut in, his scowl dark as storm clouds. "I would take any one of our women over your best men, and twice as quick."

Boisterous laughter rumbled through the mead hall. The Zylmacians seemed as amused as they were insulted, but the barkeep's endless stream of mead kept their tempers dulled.

The dice game dragged on, and Madelyn was bleeding coin. She had played its Southern cousin before, but these rules twisted in ways she struggled to follow. Still, she had hoped victory might loosen tongues. Now, with her last coins on the table, that chance was slipping away.

Drakka slammed the shaker down, his smirk as vile as the stench of him. The roar that followed told her all she needed to know.

"You lose," he sneered. "Unless you've got something else to wager, get the fuck away from my table."

Retreat would have been sound—but the eyes of the Rhivothi said otherwise. Her ruse would wither if she cowered now. Better to fight one wolf at a time than the whole pack at once.

"I do have something more for you," she said, half-grinning. "Hold out your hand."

Chuckling, Drakka slapped his palm flat on the table, eager to mock her. Madelyn slipped a dagger from her belt and drove it clean through his hand. His eyes bulged wide as saucers, though not a scream escaped his throat.

"You Bymist rat," she spat, savoring the old insult Marvath once used.

Before the hall could erupt, she rose, drew her second dagger, and buried it in the crown of Drakka's skull. His body stiffened, eyes rolling back as she twisted the hilt slowly side to side. The Zylmacians froze, staring first at their fallen kin, then at her—dogs on the edge of frenzy.

"You filthy bitch!" someone roared.

In an instant, a dozen wildmen shot to their feet, steel flashing in the torchlight as they clamored for vengeance. Madelyn's eyes flooded with black liquid, though she refused the safety of the shadows. Instead, she tore her dagger free and hurled it into the chest of the first Zylmacian who charged. As he collapsed forward, she ripped his axe from his grip and buried its edge across another man's face, splitting bone and teeth in a spray of blood.

But they were too many, too fast. If she meant to live, she would need the darkness. A mist bled from her skin, curling like smoke across the floorboards. The tavern roared with fury.

Then came the Rhivothi. With knives, axes, clubs—and bare fists—they hurled themselves upon the Zylmacians. Rage long stifled erupted all at once, their battle cries thunderous, their blows merciless. A few Nothanek shrank back, unwilling to stand between wolves and prey.

The leaner wildmen were no match for northern muscle. Flesh split, bones broke, and blood sprayed in sheets. Madelyn seized a jagged shard of plate from the wreckage and drove it into the throat of another, feeling his body convulse and seize before he crumpled at her feet.

And then—silence. The frenzy burned out as quickly as it had begun. The tavern floor glistened with gore, the air heavy with death. Nearly a dozen Zylmacians lay in ruin, their last breaths rattling. A few Rhivothi nursed shallow wounds, their eyes blazing with triumph.

"Begone, you filthy rats," Skarik spat, skewering a dying foe through the belly. He turned to her, blood dripping from his blade. "How fare you, kinsman?"

Madelyn's eyes still swirled black, though the mist coiling around her dissipated. She bent, reclaimed her blades, and wiped them clean with deliberate care.

"I'm still standing," she said, breath ragged but steady. A faint grin curled across her lips. "Killing these dogs is thirsty work. What say we drink to our victory?"

Smiles and victorious cheers were all the approval she needed. If there was one truth about Northmen, it was that their thirst never waned—especially after slaughter. Madelyn slapped her palm against the oak bar, demanding another round. The barkeep nearly tripped over himself, sweat streaming as he rushed to comply.

Mugs were filled and raised. The Rhivothi drank deep, some sloshing mead over hands still slick with blood. Madelyn lifted her own mug, feigning a swallow. Her other hand moved faster than the eye—steel flashing, throat parting. The warrior beside her dropped his cup with a clatter, clutching at the torrent spilling from his neck.

By the time the others turned, she was already in motion. A knife drove into another man's eye, her free hand ripping the axe from his slackening grip.

"Treacherous bitch!" someone roared.

She spun, the axe heaving into the skull of the first man to charge. The blade buried deep with a wet *clunk*, splitting bone and brain. He toppled, twitching, leaving only three. Two swayed drunkenly, dumbstruck by what they saw. The last, steadier than the rest, drew his sword and came on with a howl.

Madelyn's black eyes burned, the mist coiling tighter around her like smoke from a pyre. In the space of a breath, she vanished. The swordsman faltered mid-step, confusion breaking into fear.

"What devilry is this—?" His words choked off as his throat opened ear to ear. His corpse collapsed like a felled tree.

From the shadows, two knives whistled. Both struck true, one in the ribs, the other the neck. The last pair of Rhivothi clawed weakly at the serrated blades, gurgling, before sagging lifeless to the blood-soaked floor. Madelyn faded back into view, her blackened eyes dimming, the mist receding like smoke after fire.

One of the warriors bled out quickly, the torrent from his throat painting the floor in frothing red. Madelyn strode to the other, planting her boot on the knife's pommel and pressing down. The blade slid deeper with slow, grinding resistance. The man gurgled, eyes bulging, hands clawing desperately until they stilled and dropped limp.

Silence settled over the mead hall, broken only by the ragged, panicked breaths of one still living. Madelyn wrenched her blade free, the sound of tearing flesh echoing obscenely.

"Come out," she commanded, her voice rumbling like an earthquake.

The barkeep rose from behind the counter, trembling, his hands high. "Please… don't kill me."

Leaving no witnesses would have been sound, but a spark of humanity pricked at her rage. Even the few Nothanek left seemed beneath her attention—pitiful cowards who would never dare raise steel.

"Go now," she said. "Gather those you love and flee. There is nothing here but death."

He needed no further urging. Bowing low, he bolted for the door, vanishing into the night. Madelyn's gaze fell on the half-dozen Nothanek who lingered, their faces pale and stricken. They stared at her as if she were something not of this world.

"Who are you?" one of the fisherfolk whispered.

Another swallowed hard, dread in his voice. "I know who she is… She's the Eveldanyr. I'd stake my life on it."

A chill fluttered through Madelyn's chest, tightening her breath. Her tribulation was no secret. Her humiliation was remembered. And though she had bested every man in the room, the weight of being *known* made her feel small again—small and afraid.

"I am," she whispered, shame burning in her throat. "And I am what you have made me."

The Nothanek recoiled, hands raised as if to ward off the specter of her vengeance. They were not monsters—she had learned that in her captivity. Yet none had stepped forward on that cursed night. None had lifted a hand to stop the atrocity. None had the courage to defend a woman's honor.

"Please," one of them stammered. "It was the Zylmacians who did it, not our people. The gods punished them at the Plainhold—punished them until the earth ran red with their blood!"

"The gods shed not a drop," Madelyn hissed. "That blood was mine to spill. And, gods willing, I will spill plenty more. Live with your shame—the shame of watching and doing nothing. If you wish to absolve yourselves, then tell me where Damien has gone."

But their eyes fell away, cowardly and blank. Whether it was ignorance or blind faith, none dared utter his name.

"Very well," she signed.

She strode toward the door. None barred her path. None even breathed too loudly. Madelyn stepped into the night, the eastern sky painted with a wash of clouds. The first pale thread of moonlight shimmered above, heralding the long dark to come. A cool wind whispered from the west, carrying the dry scent of rain yet to fall.

Closing the door behind her, she lingered in silence, the weight of the massacre pressing down on her shoulders. Dozens lay dead, yet she was no closer to finding Damien Dreadfire or what remained of his horde. Still, the swelling numbers of northern patrols meant she was close, perhaps closer than she dared hope.

Beside the doorway, two torches leaned idle against the wall. Madelyn stared at them, thoughts colliding in her skull. Those men inside might have been guilty of nothing more than standing on the wrong side of war. But her rage burned hotter than reason, urging her hand toward the flame.

Was mercy shown to me when I posed no threat? Was any hand raised in my defense?

The answer throbbed like a wound inside her chest. No mercy. No aid. Only silence and shame. The black void within her coiled and hissed, demanding retribution. Every Northman, every Zylmacian carried a share of guilt for that night—whether by deed, by word, or by cowardly inaction. And guilt, she decided, was enough to warrant death.

Her eyes fell upon an abandoned cart, its axles bowed with age, its horse long gone. Madelyn dug her fingers into the frame and heaved. Muscles burned, joints popped, but rage lent her a strength that felt more than mortal. The massive wheels shrieked against the earth as the cart groaned backward, inch by inch, until it crashed against the mead hall's doors, locking the survivors inside their tomb.

With a few strikes of flint, she conjured life back into the waiting torches. Fire leapt eagerly to her call, tongues of orange and gold dancing and twisting with ravenous hunger. She lingered in their glow, staring into the heart of the flame. There was no fear, no hesitation, not even triumph—only a strange hollowness, as though her soul had already been consumed.

From within the hall came the muffled shouts of the Nothanek, banging futilely against the barred door. Each cry was a reminder of her own screams, unanswered in the darkness of that night. Her grip tightened on the torch until her knuckles ached.

The tramp of boots drew her head sharply—an approaching patrol. The time for reflection had ended. Without another thought, Madelyn cast the torch onto the thatched roof. Flames surged with a deafening roar, spreading greedily across the timbers. The hall became a blazing inferno, a beacon of her vengeance. The air filled with a crack of timber, the shriek of the dying, and the chaos of men rushing to intervene.

Madelyn turned from it all. She drew her blades with ritual calm, the steel whispering as it left the scabbards. Darkness welled up around her, clouds of black haze curling like smoke from a funeral pyre, swallowing her shape until she was little more than a shadow with burning eyes.

Against the backdrop of fire and screams, she strode into the night. Not as the broken woman she had been, but as something else—something the gods themselves had loosed upon the earth. Cthenir's hunger was her own now, and the world would bleed until it was sated.

EINARR II

Coldly, Einarr observed as the Zylmacians dragged timber and iron into place. With a frenzy bordering on madness, they raised a tall post, crowned at its peak with a crude crosspiece. Burlap sacks were lashed together in the shape of a man, stuffed with horse dung until it bulged grotesquely. Einarr wondered what fresh horror the wildmen meant to conjure with such an effigy as they hauled Dhuuld forward, the chieftain thrashing and shrieking like a cornered boar.

"Unhand me, you beasts!" Dhuuld bellowed. "Do you know who I am? Unhand me at once!"

But his kinsmen were nowhere to be seen. Einarr suspected many of the Khorrtalli were already fleeing for their lives, fearing chains or the noose as conspirators to their lord's treachery. Their absence mattered little. After all the warband had suffered, the loss of a few hundred spearmen was hardly worth a passing thought.

The Zylmacians had come by the hundreds, wild-eyed and braying like jackals. At every step they struck the captive with fists, whips, and cudgels, each eager for a taste of vengeance. By Jollkud's command, Dhuuld was flung onto a crude wooden table and bound fast with thick bands of leather, his limbs stretched taut until he could scarcely twitch a finger.

"If you think the Rhivothi savage," Jollkud spat, leaning close to smear contempt across the chieftain's face, "wait until you see how the Bymist punishes betrayal. Your screams will echo for a thousand years."

A shudder pricked down Einarr's spine, though he betrayed no emotion. Beside him, Damien Dreadfire stood unmoved, black-eyed and silent, as if he had already foreseen what was to come. A leather satchel was brought forth and unfastened on the table. Within gleamed cruel instruments of torment—so sharp, so wickedly devised, they looked fit to carve the soul itself into pieces.

Jollkud produced a small axe, its edge honed not for battle but for butcher's work. He lifted it high, displaying it to the horde. The Zylmacians erupted with ravenous cheers, their eyes glittering with bloodlust. Dhuuld thrashed against his bindings, but the thick leather straps bit deep into his wrists and ankles, holding him fast.

"Will we truly learn the truth from him?" Einarr asked, his gaze steady on the table. "Or will he only scream what we wish to hear?"

"In truth, it matters not," Damien replied coldly, his arms folded across his chest. "Your word already carries the weight of a thousand warriors. And Lazilyth's vision is proof enough for any man with eyes. If there was folly, it was mine—for trusting those who still bent the knee to House Bethard."

Einarr exhaled slowly, his fingers clenching. "There was no way to know. We thought all Northern blood yearned for freedom. But it seems the shine of Southern coin can blind even the proud."

A vast crowd had swelled around the spectacle—Rhivothi and Zylmacians shoulder to shoulder, Nothanek too, though their numbers were thin. Morbid curiosity had overcome hesitation, drawing every eye to the condemned chieftain. The air was feverish, thick with anticipation, as though the whole warband hungered to watch treachery carved apart before them.

"Now then…" Jollkud twirled the axe lazily in his hand, his lips curling into a grin. "Will you speak the truth, Dhuuld Lurrson of Khorrtal? Or will your silence damn you further?"

"I have no other truth to speak!" the chieftain cried, desperation sharpening his voice. "I have only ever served this alliance in good faith!"

The words barely left his lips before the axe flashed downward, too swift for the eye to follow. A spray of blood erupted across the table as four fingers of Dhuuld's right hand clattered away like discarded meat. For a heartbeat there was no pain, the edge biting so cleanly that his body lagged behind the horror. Then the shock seized him, a strangled gasp breaking from his throat as he stared wide-eyed at the mutilated stump where his fingers had once been.

But then, he screamed. It was a shrill, piercing cry—haunting, unnatural—most unfitting for a man who once carried such a heavy, booming voice. The sound drew jeers and howls from the crowd, their appetite whetted by the breaking of a chieftain.

A Zylmacian flesh-stitcher hurried forward, his scarred hands working with practiced precision. He looped a leather band tight around Dhuuld's wrist, twisting until the blood ceased its flow and the stump turned the color of deep night. Moments later, a glowing iron was pressed hard against the ruin of his hand.

Flesh hissed and popped as smoke curled upward, filling the air with the foul stench of charred skin. Dhuuld's body thrashed in agony, but the straps held firm. The stitcher withdrew, leaving the wound sealed but raw. The wildmen had no intention of letting their victim slip mercifully into death.

The severed digits were carried solemnly to the grotesque effigy—the burlap figure stuffed with manure. With almost ceremonial reverence, they were affixed to the mock hand, turning the thing into a vile parody of its owner. In that moment, Einarr understood fully. The Thal'akur was not merely torment, it was mockery. A punishment meant to strip a man not only of his flesh, but of his dignity, piece by piece.

"He'll never talk," Einarr muttered under his breath. "He knows death will find him, whether by our hand or King Bethard's, should he confess. He will carry the lie until his final breath."

"He will talk," Damien said, his tone low and certain. His dark eyes glittered like obsidian. "All men speak in the end. Pain has a tongue sharper than steel. And the Zylmacians…" he allowed himself a small, cruel smile, "they are its masters. Do not mistake savagery for simplicity. There is skill in their cruelty—an artistry that can stretch suffering for days."

Digit by digit, the butchery continued. Dhuuld's remaining fingers were hewn away, each one nailed to the dung-stuffed effigy. Then the toes, hacked free and mounted in turn, until his extremities were gone. Sweat ran in streams down his wrinkled brow, and though his chest heaved like a bellows, he clung to life with surprising tenacity. Age had not made him fragile; it had made him stubborn, and the gods had cursed him with endurance enough to taste every horror.

But when the axe began to bite deeper—first at the wrist, then the ankles, then inching up toward the elbow—his strength began to wane. Dhuuld's cries were raw now, hoarse from endless screaming, the sound rattling across the plain like the wail of a dying beast.

"Give him the tea!" Jollkud thundered.

A witch doctor slithered forward from the crowd, his painted face ghastly beneath the searing sun. In his gnarled hands he carried a frothing mug, its contents a foul stew of herbs and unholy tinctures. The stench alone was enough to make Einarr's stomach turn—bitter roots, sour fungus, and something acrid that burned the nostrils. He had heard whispers of such a drink during his years among the warband. The Rhivothi had their mushrooms, taken before battle to dull fear and sharpen rage. The Zylmacians, not to be outdone, had their own concoction.

"Tengaar," Damien muttered darkly, folding his arms. "A brew that twists the mind and keeps a man hovering between life and death. His torment is far from over."

Metal instruments forced Dhuuld's jaw open. The witch doctor tilted the vessel and poured. The steaming slurry choked its way down his throat as he gagged and sputtered. He coughed violently, nearly drowning in the mixture, yet no mercy awaited him in suffocation. Soon the brew did its work. His eyes rolled back, fluttering as if chasing some vision only he could see, then snapped forward with unnatural clarity. His head swayed side to side like a reed in the wind, but his voice—broken and halting—was suddenly lucid.

"I want a name!" Jollkud demanded, pointing a bloodied knife. "Give me the name!"

"I… I will speak…" he croaked, blood and spittle flecking his lips. "Lord… Valens paid me… handsomely… for my… cooperation. With his passing…" he wheezed, "Lord… Vakaro became… my benefactor…"

A ripple of outrage coursed through the onlookers. Some hissed, others spat, and still others bared their teeth in feral snarls. The name of Ridley Vakaro was poison in their ears, and yet it was no surprise. Betanthian gold was a venom that seeped into every crevice it touched.

"And what were you promised?" Jollkud pressed, his voice low and venomous. He set aside his broad knife and took up a smaller instrument, a slender blade honed to a needle's edge. He twirled it slowly, letting the crowd drink in the malice. "What prize was so great that you would barter away the blood of your people?"

The circle tightened, the sea of faces looming in hungry silence. Dhuuld's chest rose and fell in ragged heaves, each word rasping like the bellows of a dying man.

"He… promised me… the north…" he gasped. "All of it… after the war…"

Murmurs exploded into curses, the mob surging forward until Damien raised a hand and steadied them with a single, chilling glare.

"After we are slain," Jollkud spat, "and our homes left to vultures and carrion. Treachery to the marrow." His lip curled in contempt. "Give him more tea. We will send this dog to the underworld—the Zylmacian way."

Einarr's face tightened. For a flicker of a moment, pity stirred in his chest. Among the Nothanek, even the most wretched of souls were afforded reverence in death. All life, righteous or wicked, bore the breath of the gods. But that mercy evaporated as quickly as it came. He remembered the night of his near death, when assassins came for him with steel. He remembered the beastly cat, eyes glowing like twin stars, that had saved him from the shadows.

No, this was not cruelty. This was the will of the gods, made manifest. *Just as that night was meant to be, so must this. Steel your sympathy, Einarr. You are not the naive man you once were.*

Jollkud drove the razor into Dhuuld's crown and pulled it down toward the neck. Einarr flinched but kept his gaze. To look away now would be to give his doubts breath, and he had already collected too many questions since Skaginlef.

Skin came away in slow, slippery strips, revealing slick, pale muscle that glistened in the sun. Einarr watched Damien without flinching; there was a look in the warlord's eyes that belonged to men who had watched too much ruin. The memory of Borjifa passed like a shadow across Dreadfire's face—a grief that hardened into defiance. For all the warband's mockery of Nothanek piety, Dreadfire's faith was fierce in its own brutal way.

It was a testament to the indomitable Borjifan spirit, which could never be conquered. Even in the face of defeat and treachery, Dreadfire remained defiant. While many in the warband derided the Nothanek for their piety, the Supreme Warlord held the most faith of all.

When the last scrap of flesh was peeled back, Dhuuld lay open-mouthed, ragged breaths rasping through fluids and frayed words. The

Zylmacians roared their victory and paraded the flayed hide like some vile trophy. Einarr felt bile at the sight; the skin, dark and reeking, was draped over the dung-stuffed effigy and lashed into place until the scarecrow looked grotesquely human.

Severed limbs were mounted where hands and feet should have been; the mock-man faced its maker, a hideous monument to the gods. Dhuuld, clinging to a thread of life, turned his head and saw his mutilation arrayed before him. He tried to speak, but only a rasp came.

Jollkud spat in contempt. "When your soul reaches the underworld, tell them Jollkud sent you," he sneered. "May you wander the pits forever."

Damien stepped forward and silence fell like a cloth over the crowd. He signaled for a massive two-handed axe—a blade with the hunger to fell horses—and took it up with slow, deliberate motion. The warlord's voice cut through the hush: low, final, a verdict delivered from a throne of pain.

"Before you leave this world, son of Lurr," Damien said, each word a struck blow, "know this: you have paid for your treason with your life. But treachery breeds beyond one throat. Your kinsmen tried to murder my friend. For that, I will see Khorrtal burn to the ground—and your people wiped from the face of this earth."

The threat hung in the air, a promise of fire and ruin. Around Einarr, the warband murmured and tightened; somewhere between justice and vengeance the line had been crossed, and the gods—if they watched at all—would have to bear witness.

"Let that be your final thought," Dreadfire concluded, lifting the axe high. "Your people will be joining you soon enough."

With a single, brutal heave, the blade fell. Dhuuld's head rolled free and thudded onto the earth, a dark fountain of blood pouring from the severed stump. A riot of cries rose from the crowd as the head was held aloft, then impaled atop the dung-stuffed scarecrow as a blasphemous crown.

Damien gave a satisfied sneer and stepped back from the gore. Wildmen surged forward, surrounding the remains and spitting upon them; some urinated at the base of the stake in a final, obscene blessing. Einarr moved through the crowd, glad the spectacle was done though the taste of it lingered in his mouth like rust.

"Thank the gods that menace was purged from our ranks before more damage could be done," Einarr said, his voice steady though his jaw tightened. "There is another matter I must speak to you about—one that affects all of us."

Dreadfire nodded, recognizing the unusual edge in Einarr's tone, and motioned him toward the command tent. Inside, he poured each a cup of strong, dark mead. It warmed the hands but not the mind; nothing could wash the image from Einarr's eyes.

"Now tell me, my friend—what troubles you?" Damien asked, settling into a battered chair that groaned beneath him.

"I care not for what happened to Dhuuld." Einarr shook his head firmly. "Even the gods know it was just. What I must say is something different—and it must be said before every warchief. With your leave, I will summon them here."

Dreadfire's brows lifted, his lips pressed thin. It was no small thing for Einarr to demand such an audience, least of all from him. Yet after a moment's study, Damien gave a single nod. A runner slipped away to carry the summons. Silence filled the tent in his absence, broken only by the dull creak of chairs and the steady slosh of mead being sipped. Both men sat as if measuring the other, steel in their eyes.

For the first time since they'd forged their brotherhood, Damien seemed unsettled by Einarr. Perhaps he had always thought the Nothanek too pious, too simple, incapable of the ruthless cunning demanded by this age. But now, something had shifted—a fire in Einarr's voice that gave even the Supreme Warlord pause.

One by one, the warchiefs filed in, their faces lined with suspicion.

The stink of death outside and the howls of revelry carried with them an air of chaos, and more than one man wondered if the alliance itself was about to break. Only Jollkud was absent, still presiding over the spectacle of pain he had authored.

"I thank you all for coming," Einarr began, his gaze lingering on each man in turn. "Many of you believe our cause to be lost—and I would not fault any of you for it. We have bled dearly, and hope grows thinner by the day. But I bring a message… one I alone was charged to deliver."

"You speak of hope?" Sylvia said, arms crossed and voice sharp. "Yet you were the first to lose it. You abandoned us and returned home."

"Indeed, I did." Einarr inclined his head, unashamed. "But in Skaginlef, the gods revealed themselves to me in ways I could never have foreseen. And what I witnessed there may yet be our salvation."

Despite the fervor in his tone, the other warchiefs remained unmoved. Their faces were stone, carved by hardship and disbelief. Only Damien studied him closely, and for Einarr, that single gaze was all the assurance he required.

"Tell me, fisherman," Valerick the Red rumbled, his arms folded like iron bands. "How can the gods speak of victory when they hand us a defeat beyond repair? Are the gods so fickle?"

"I am no priest, Rhivothi," Einarr snapped back. "Not even the wisest can untangle the gods' designs. They see what was, what is, and what will be. We see only the moment before us. Our defeat was a trial, nothing more. Their favor has not left us. If we endure—if we hold to one another—then the mandate of the divine will yet be fulfilled."

The tent flap burst open, and in stormed Jollkud, chest heaving as though he had sprinted from the edge of the world. Blood streaked his arms to the elbows, and a smile split his brutal face. He snatched a linen cloth, smearing it red as he wiped, then reached for the cask. A mug brimmed, and half of it vanished down his gullet in one pull.

"My apologies," he growled, wiping froth from his beard. "Thirsty work, peeling a man's skin."

He claimed a place at the table, and for the first time no sneer or whispered insult followed him. His cruelty had done what no speeches ever could—mending, however briefly, the Northmen's contempt for Western stock.

"We were discussing the path ahead," Einarr said, steadying his voice. He leaned forward, eyes burning as memory seized him. "One of the visions granted me was of a mountain—taller than the sky itself, its peak white with snow. Not a range, no. A single spire, rising from the land like the finger of a god."

Sylvia paled, her breath catching as if her very soul recoiled. "Morvhalgr…" she whispered. "The Mountain of Souls."

Valerick the Red shifted in place, his features betraying unease more than anger. Even for a Rhivothi, the name carried the weight of dread and reverence.

"Tell me," Sylvia urged, her tone sharp as steel. "Tell me exactly what you saw. What claim do you make of the gods?"

Einarr met her gaze without faltering. "I saw two figures trudging through snow so deep it swallowed them to the waist, guided only by torchlight and the stars. I called out, but my voice was carried away on a wind that howled like the dead. I know not what it meant… only that the figures were you and Damien."

Stormguard and Dreadfire locked eyes across the table, their silence more damning than any word. A thousand unspoken truths hung in that brief exchange, and Einarr could feel their weight even if he did not understand them.

"It would have been wiser to hold your tongue until the proper time," Damien said, his voice colder than usual. "Such visions are not for every ear to hear."

"But it has been spoken now," Valerick pressed, stepping closer, his voice rising. "And you know as well as I that the Mountain of Souls is no place for jest. The legends say that when the gods claimed victory in the first great war, they demanded tribute. Kuggvord the Grim gave it freely—he climbed Morvhalgr and never returned. That was the price of divine favor, and none since have dared follow him. Every man who has tried has been swallowed by the mountain. No one has returned to tell the tale."

The tent grew quiet as his words settled like falling snow, each warchief uneasy beneath the weight of the legend. Einarr felt the chill of his vision anew, colder now than the Plainhold wind.

He drew in a breath, steadying himself. "Still, the gods have set a path before us. I do not claim to understand all of it, nor will I pretend to. But what I have seen is more than fever dreams. I saw visions of a great beast… a giant and fearsome cat who appeared to me in moments of danger."

Jollkud stroked his beard, eyes burning like hot coals. "Visions, omens, beasts of old Droethien lore… aye, these are things best not dismissed. You speak of Azu'raah as if it were more than flesh and fang, as if the gods themselves wear its skin. That is a tale my people know well."

A cold chill crept down Einarr's spine. He thought such visions would be met with ridicule, but, much to his surprise, they were embraced with fear and wonderment.

"And I have seen it more than once," Einarr said hesitantly. "There are other visions as well, though I fear to speak of them just yet. I feel the gods have not intended me to reveal all of their wisdom. But, Damien, you must take heed of what I have said."

Dreadfire and Stormguard locked eyes once more, their silence speaking louder than any words. A heaviness filled the tent, as though even the torches strained to burn against the weight of unseen forces.

Sylvia's mouth tightened, her expression torn between suspicion and belief. "But Morvhalgr is not just a tale. The mountain is real, and what sleeps upon its heights has always been beyond our reach. You must know the weight of what you've spoken, Einarr. If the gods have set their eyes upon you, then this burden belongs to you as much as it does to Damien."

"I have known Einarr longer than anyone aside from his kinsmen," Damien interjected. "There is no one I trust more. Despite my reservations, I do not believe he speaks falsehood. Son of Rolff, I believe what you have seen. To turn from what the gods have shown you would be to invite our ruin."

Not all faces softened. Arik's brow beaded with sweat; Jollkud drank deeper and harder, agitation showing in his grip on the mug. The tent hummed with nervous energy.

"So what then?" Jollkud cut in, breaking the fragile quiet. "Who leads us while you are gone, Damien? Will it be you, Rolffson?"

Einarr felt the weight of hostile eyes for the first time since his return. The alliance needed a steady hand, not fractures. He swallowed and spoke plainly.

"No, Jollkud. It is not my fate to lead our host. If the great cat is what the gods showed me, my path lies elsewhere. The beast is what saved me from the assassins. I must ride south into Droethien lands… to follow where the visions point."

Sylvia's posture stiffened. Fear prickled the edge of her voice. "Then who will lead us in your absence? If Damien and I march north and you ride south, who keeps our people whole?"

Damien cut through the question before it could fester. "We will not fracture. Jollkud—take your hosts west. Lay waste to Khorrtal. Leave no refuge for traitors or for Betanthian influence to hide behind our lines. Do this, and keep whatever spoils you find."

Jollkud's grin widened until it split his face. "A fitting retribution for betrayal," he snarled. "Khorrtal will be scrubbed from the map. I will return when the work is done, and I shall bring trophies to prove it."

Einarr's stomach tightened at the image of smoke and children among the ash, but the warband could not be left with a festering wound at its flank. How many more would die if a nest of traitors remained to whisper in the dark? The choice, terrible as it was, felt inevitable.

"Let it be so," Damien said, the word falling like a gavel. "Stormguard and I will lead the host north at first light. Jollkud rides west. Einarr, you will go south and into Droethien lands to follow your vision. Who will rise and steady our alliance in our absence?"

Einarr watched the warlords closely. He had rehearsed the answer in a hundred sleepless nights. "Arik," he said at last. "Let Arik hold the line. He is patient and steady. He thinks like a man who weighs risks rather than leaps at blood for sport. I trust him to keep our people intact while the rest of us seek what must be found."

A ripple of incredulous murmurs passed through the tent. Arik himself sat straighter, sweat pearling along his temple. The man's eyes darted from face to face, as if measuring whether he'd been set-up for mockery. Still, Einarr's tone left little room for argument.

I know they think me mad. But I pray, dear gods, I pray you let them see reason!

"And what would your visions have me do, Rolffson?" Valerick said, lifting his chin.

"You must come with me to the lands of Droethia," Einarr answered, meeting the Rhivothi's gaze. "I know not what we will discover there, but I have no doubt the gods will see us through to whatever end."

There was doubt aplenty throughout the tent—so abundant that if it were food, it might have sustained the warband for a month. Yet even in the midst of suspicion, there remained faith, not only in the gods but in Damien Dreadfire himself. Despite their defeat, the warchiefs turned their eyes to him, waiting for an answer that might be their salvation… or their final undoing.

"We must hold fast to our faith," Damien declared, leaning forward against the table. "Not when it is easy, but when it is hard. I have believed in this cause from the beginning, and I will not turn away now. Do not be afraid, my brothers and sisters. Do not let despair take you. The gods walk with us wherever we march. As for me—" he struck a fist to his chest, "—I will go to the ends of the earth with courage in my heart. Who among you has the faith to follow?"

The response was thunderous. Pride swelled in every chest as fists rose high and battle cries shook the canvas walls of the tent. Einarr pressed his lips into a thin line, burying the storm of feeling that welled up inside him. He knew he might be leading his dearest friends to their doom. Yet as quickly as those doubts surfaced, he crushed them down.

"Then let us part in faith and friendship," he said, resting a hand on Sylvia's shoulder. "And let us return whole—our sword arms filled with the gods' strength, and our souls burning with their fury."

LUCETTA III

S HE DRESSED IN HER FAVORITE GOWN OF CRIMSON LINEN, THE NECKLINE low and the waistline tight. As she smoothed the skirts, Lucetta studied her reflection in the mirror. Gone were the scars and scabs that streaked her arms and neck; her skin shone pure and radiant as sunlight. The heavy circles beneath her eyes had lifted, clearing like storm clouds at dusk.

Am I dreaming, or is this some trick of my mind?

Even the years had fallen away. Time's slow, merciless creep seemed to have reversed. Her auburn hair had thickened like a forest canopy and spilled nearly to her tailbone. Youth and beauty had returned in abundance; the woman in the mirror was almost unrecognizable.

Tears welled as a smile tugged at lips that had known only frowns. Strange energy coursed through her body, alive and uncontainable. Perhaps the woman in black had imparted its otherworldly power when it entered her. Whatever the truth, she had become the best version of herself.

I knew you would uplift me and never steer me wrong. Now the world will know the real Lucetta Bethard!

But when she turned from the mirror, her breath stopped. At the end of the hall stood a figure, blacker than the deepest chasm. Though sunlight streamed through the estate, the being stood like a blight—an infection against the sun's warmth.

A stench of rotten meat rolled down the corridor, gagging her. Lucetta choked, fighting the urge to vomit. From the balcony drifted a fly, then another, buzzing past her face toward the source. Soon, a swarm gathered, dark wings swirling around their decaying host.

"Daughter…" wheezed a mournful voice.

The figure stepped forward as a frigid wind screamed down the hall, revealing Charlotte Bethard's withered face. Sunken eyes glazed with death, greasy skin tinged green-gray, hair a tangle of stringy white knots. Her yellow nails curved long and sharp as daggers. She was exactly as Lucetta had seen in her nightmare.

Suddenly, Charlotte thrust out an arm, a shriek ripping from her gaping maw. She glided forward without a step, feet squealing across the polished floor. Blood and insects spewed from her mouth in a torrent, the sickly-sweet stench of rot blasting like a hurricane.

Lucetta staggered back and clawed at the latch. With trembling hands, she slammed the door shut a heartbeat before Charlotte struck. The wood boomed and flexed, hinges nearly snapping loose. Again, the Queen hurled herself against it, driving Lucetta to her knees.

She screamed, tears streaming like spring rain. Even daylight could not ward off her mother's vile essence. Gasping, Lucetta panted like a beast dying of thirst. Then—a crawling tickle against her ankles.

A pale tide of maggots spilled from beneath the door, writhing at her feet. She recoiled with a strangled cry, nearly forgetting the terror pounding on the other side. Yet there was nowhere to run. If she fled, the Queen would break through and unleash unspeakable horrors.

"Go away!" she cried. "Leave me be!"

But then, the noise ceased, and the gut-churning stench thinned into nothing. No insects writhed at her feet, and no trace of Charlotte lingered. Another cruelty of the mind. Despite her calloused heart and hardened resolve, Lucetta whimpered and nearly broke.

Just as despair began to claim her, the far corner of the bedchamber grew dim. Yet instead of terror, the bleeding darkness carried a strange comfort, almost familial, even nurturing. From it emerged the woman in black, her orange-red eyes unblinking, burning straight through Lucetta's soul.

Relief loosened Lucetta's chest. Her guardian spirit had come. The entity drifted forward, its elegant gown billowing as though moved by an unseen current, long black hair flowing around her like a living shadow.

"Why does my mother torment me so?" Lucetta asked, fighting back tears. "Is she real, or do these visions exist solely in my mind?

The woman in black was silent at first, her eyes smoldering with a malicious fire. "What is real and what is not? This is a question not even I can answer. You have become something else, Lucetta Bethard. An instrument of the gods. The visions you see and the horrors you endure are part of their divine mandate."

"Can you make them stop?" Lucetta pleaded, clasping her hands together. "Please—make them go away!"

"Alas, I cannot," the woman said, gliding closer. She placed a cold hand against Lucetta's cheek. "What you witness serves a greater good. It is for you to endure, to search for meaning even in the darkest of trials. No torment is wasted if you dare to learn from it."

Hardly a consolation, Lucetta thought, but perhaps enough to still her trembling mind. She sighed and reached for her wine glass. Yet before she could drink, a new sound rose beyond the door—heavy, deliberate footfalls, too deep to belong to any woman. When she turned, Pavlos stood there, golden grin gleaming as he bowed his head.

"Good morning to you, princess," the Droethien said. His gaze lingered over her with intrigue, head cocked. "You look radiant this day, yes?"

Pavlos reached forward and took Lucetta's hand, pressing a delicate kiss upon it. It was the first time he had ever acknowledged her so intimately, and it unsettled her. Perhaps the reflection in the mirror had been real after all, and not merely a figment of wishful imagination.

"Everything is alright, yes?"

"I'm fine, thank you," she answered quickly, pulling her hand away. "Now, we have much to discuss and little time. My father has decreed that my movements are to be unrestricted, but I fear Aldred will not take this lying down. I saw it in his eyes. He will do everything in his power to keep me under his thumb and avenge his humiliation."

"You trouble yourself needlessly, princess. Pavlos should cut his throat and be done with it."

As liberating as the thought might be, the notion of killing Aldred still made Lucetta tremble. "No. As wretched as he may be, he is still my husband. At least… I would prefer not to go down that road unless it became necessary."

"As you wish," Pavlos said with a shrug. "We must leave Cardale at once. The fewer eyes upon you, the better. Yes?"

It was a sensible decision—and one she intended to make anyway. Too many eyes lingered on her, even here, even in her own home. Surely, Aldred was already scheming his next move, feeding on humiliation. Refusing to waste another moment, Lucetta swept toward the courtyard. Pavlos followed close behind, himself eager to be free of Cardale. As they crossed the estate, a servant approached, his posture bent, eyes cast low—like a whipped dog bracing for the next blow.

"You there," Lucetta snapped, flicking her fingers. "Summon a carriage and driver, and ready my bodyguard. I depart for Dellhaven at once."

"I would, my princess… but—" the servant stammered, bowing and fidgeting with an unsealed scroll. There was something about him that set Lucetta on edge: the same sad, glassy eyes she'd seen in Gareth, the look of a man worn hollow by drink.

She motioned for the dispatch, annoyed by the interruption. Before she could break the seal, the servant's voice pitched up with an odd, urgent tremor.

"Dellhaven is under attack from the sea," he blurted, chewing his lip. "Dozens—perhaps hundreds—of ships from the north have laid siege to the port. Their Commander has sent word to Brimnora requesting immediate reinforcements."

The words hit like a blow. For a moment, Lucetta stood rooted, the world narrowing until only the sentence existed. Dellhaven—the kingdom's most fortified harbor, funded and manned by Cardale's finest—could not simply fall. It was inconceivable.

"What treachery is this?" she snarled, jabbing a finger. "Speak true, or I will have him rip your tongue from your mouth!"

Pavlos cracked a smile and flexed his knuckles. The servant, eyes wide, gestured to the scroll.

"Please, Your Highness, don't believe me! Read for yourself!"

Lucetta tore the parchment open, praying it was some cruel jest. If it were, she'd cut the jester's head clean off and set it on a pike. But line by line, the dispatch confirmed the worst: burning, ships at anchor, men flooding the docks. Her chest tightened until breath was difficult. She dismissed the servant with a hiss and lashed out, her nails flashing near his face.

"How… how could this be?" she whispered to Pavlos, voice cracking. "Dellhaven… under attack?"

"This is a most disturbing development, princess," Pavlos said, stroking his forehead. "If Dellhaven falls, our efforts may falter. But perhaps we should take matters into our own hands, yes? With time and preparation, your vision will still come to fruition!"

His calm tone grated against her ears. How could anyone meet such news with composure?

"This is an utter disaster, Pavlos!" Lucetta shrieked, stamping her feet like a child denied her toy. "Do you not see? Even if Dellhaven is saved, it will be crawling with my father's soldiers! Every inch guarded, every eye searching. It is only a matter of time before I am discovered! Leave me—I must think."

Pavlos only shrugged, though the shadow of a smirk tugged at his lips. The sight alone nearly drove her into a frenzy. Lucetta stormed off and slammed her husband's parlor door with all her strength. No one would dare intrude now—not even the boldest.

Aldred's study, at least, offered one salvation: shelves lined with the kingdom's finest bourbon. Though she preferred wine, it would have to suffice. She seized a crystal glass, filled it nearly to the brim, and drank deep.

The burn hit instantly. It took every ounce of will not to spit it back across the floor. The bourbon was fine—delicious even—but it was meant to be sipped, savored among dignitaries, not swallowed in desperation. Still, the warmth slid down into her chest, dulling the panic that had threatened to consume her.

"Do not let yourself be troubled, my child," the woman in black said, emerging from a far corner like smoke. "Even now, when all hope seems to have faded, you remain on the path destined for you."

Lucetta laughed—a cruel, barking sound that nearly turned to bile. "I don't believe you, demon," she snapped. "Whenever you promise sunshine, only storm clouds follow. Betanthia falls to ruin all the same, and you would have me believe my efforts do anything but hasten its demise!"

The woman's orange-red eyes flared. Long black hair whipped around her like a cape, and the light itself seemed to recoil. The walls melted into a lake of fire and molten rock; she stood as if in the mouth of hell. Still, Lucetta planted her feet, though her spirit quivered beneath it.

"Did I not speak this prophecy once already?" the entity asked, drifting forward on a cloud of flies and ash. "Did I not tell you that for your queendom to rise, the kingdom of your forefathers must be destroyed? Why doubt me as my words come to pass? You are the same weak, foolish child you have always been!"

Once, such words might have sliced her through. Now something fiercer burned in Lucetta—rage, or resolve; either would do. The entity's threats hardened her, made her sharper.

"You deal only in lies and delusions!" she spat. "Everything I have done at your behest has brought me misery. I prostituted myself to win favor. I murdered my mother to hide the truth. And now my country burns because of what I have done. I have gone too far. I will end this myself!"

The woman in black watched in silence; her eyes smoldered like embers. After a long moment, her anger cooled to a measured stillness. Lucetta turned and strode from the room. Pavlos fell in step, barking for a carriage and an escort as they swept toward the courtyard.

"Princess, do you think it wise to travel to Dellhaven? Pavlos cannot guarantee your safety in the midst of battle!"

"I don't intend to go there. Not yet," Lucetta said, folding her arms. "We must recruit more soldiers, and quickly. Tell me, Pavlos—where might we find them? Surely you must know."

The Droethien paused, brow furrowed. "The White Spear keeps a camp outside the city where we rally, but I have received no word for some time. Yet Pavlos knows of another place where men may be found. We will travel there now, yes?"

Lucetta nodded just as an armored carriage rolled into the outer courtyard. A handful of Guardsmen stood nearby, their faces tight with unease. They had grown accustomed to her sudden whims, and duty compelled them to serve regardless of doubt.

Within minutes, the royal caravan was prepared. Though she knew the entity was watching, Lucetta's heart leapt. To step again into a city that had tried to kill her brought a flood of memories—terror, suffocation, the taste of death—but also a strange exhilaration. As the carriage lumbered past the gates, she giggled under her breath like a girl unshackled.

The city that once seethed with danger now bristled with soldiers. Armed patrols lined even Cardale's darkest quarters. Peasants shrank from the sight of purple cloaks, scattering into hovels like mice before a torch.

Most of the ruin was contained to the city center and the eastern district near Westwind Citadel. Southward, there were signs of a skirmish, perhaps against the watch, but nothing like the inferno that had nearly swallowed the jewel of Betanthia whole.

At the southern gate, Lucetta and Pavlos were met by a contingent of troops behind spiked barricades. Scores of archers lined the parapet overhead, bows nocked and ready to loose at a heartbeat's notice. Only the eagle sigil of House Bethard was enough to soothe their taut nerves.

"Open the gate at once," Lucetta commanded, her tone leaving no room for challenge. "I will return before evening. I expect obedience upon my arrival."

The watchmen, dumbfounded, hurried to lift the massive wooden beam that barred the reinforced doors. Hinges shrieked as the gate groaned open—its first movement since chaos had overtaken the city. Beyond Cardale's walls lay an astonishing sight: another city altogether, though not of stone or timber. A sprawling sea of tents, shanties, and stalls stretched to the horizon, shifting and alive like a restless tide.

"What is this?" she demanded. "Why are so many camped outside the walls?"

"Ah, princess," Pavlos replied, "this is where travelers trade without paying the city tax. Here the White Spear gathers, and many others, serving many masters."

Fury burned in her chest. Another blight upon Aldred's already tarnished rule. That such disorder thrived within sight of Cardale's gates was unthinkable for so calculating a man. But railing against it now would only waste time. She had a mission to see through.

Pavlos led the royal column westward, down crude tracks choked with tents and rickety stalls. Smoke and spice filled the air, mingling with roasted meat and the reek of animal dung—an unholy stench that made Lucetta gag. She pressed a handkerchief to her nose, though it did little good.

"Most curious, princess," Pavlos said, scratching at his chin. "It seems the great companies have taken their leave, yes?"

"What nonsense is this?" Lucetta scoffed. "You promised me men-at-arms, and yet there are none? What is the meaning of it?"

Indeed, the ground bore signs of a once-bustling camp: fire pits cold, trampled earth littered with scraps of canvas, and tents mostly dismantled. Only a handful remained, and not a single mercenary stood in sight.

Pavlos, however, spotted an olive-skinned man seated at a weathered desk inside one of the last tents. His face was as dark and lined as old leather, a deep scar splitting from brow to chin. One eye was milk-white and blind. He wore a cloak of exotic, night-dark fabric, and across his chest ran a black leather bandolier studded with throwing knives and pouches.

With a broad smile, Pavlos dismounted and spread his arms wide. "Ah, Draxios—it is good to see you, yes?"

The mercenary barely lifted his gaze. His nostrils flared as he glanced at the royal caravan, then dismissed them, turning back to the loose parchments on his table. His indifference set Lucetta's skin crawling. Pavlos looked over his shoulder at her and shrugged.

"How fares your company, my friend?" Pavlos pressed, stepping closer.

"Friend?" Draxios grumbled, his voice rough as splintered wood. "Speak not of such things. Your friendship is as trustworthy as a nest of scorpions."

Lucetta blinked, astonished. It was the first time she had seen Pavlos rebuked so sharply. For a moment, she thought the Droethien might answer insult with steel. Instead, he only chuckled, golden grin masking the glint of anger in his eyes.

"Come, come," Pavlos said, flicking his wrist. "Let us get down to business, yes?"

"There is no business," Draxios spat. "The city garrison has driven me out—driven *everyone* out! Can you not see? None remain!"

Lucetta's heart sank at the exchange. It was only natural that the watch would forbid mercenaries so near the walls after the chaos that had nearly consumed Cardale. And yet she knew whose hand had written the order. Another affront from Aldred—always Aldred.

"Come now," Pavlos said, still hoping to salvage the moment. "There are many cities in Betanthia, yes? Perhaps you will find better fortune in Bentmont?"

"I would find better fortune in Larssa, for all Betanthia has cost me," the outlander growled, shoving a stack of parchment into a thick ledger and slamming it shut. " I shall remain here no longer. Lord Eldon has banned all hired swords from the city. Only men who wear the King's colors may bear arms."

A hot dizziness swept through Lucetta, followed by a storm of rage. Of course, Aldred would be behind it. His life's mission seemed nothing but obstruction.

She pictured her hands around his wrinkled throat, fingers digging deep, muscles tightening as his breath rattled and failed. The fantasy came often, each version bloodier than the last. Perhaps killing him was the only way to be free. Yet to strike such a man down would be all but impossible.

Her lips peeled back into a scowl, a low growl rising in her throat. Neither Pavlos nor Draxios mattered in that moment; their stares were gnats buzzing in her periphery. Only vengeance mattered—first upon her meddling husband, then upon the invaders threatening to strangle her queendom in its crib.

"There are dark signs about her," Draxios muttered, waving a hand as if to cast away the shadow she carried. "Go now. I will speak no more of this."

Reality snapped Lucetta from her murderous visions. The moment was slipping away, and if this stranger could not aid her directly, perhaps he knew someone who might.

Bentmont was out of the question, for the Order kept a chokehold on the flow of mercenaries. Betanthia's other cities lay too far, and what few prospects remained had long since traded freedom for a soldier's wage.

With a reckless burst, Lucetta threw open the carriage door and leapt out, nearly tangling herself in her skirts.

"Wait!" she cried. "You mustn't leave!"

Draxios barely spared her a glance, swatting at the air as though brushing away a fly. He continued stuffing his belongings into wooden chests, preparing them for the road west.

"I am told you are a man of great means," Lucetta pressed, her fingers twitching. "I require what you have to offer."

"Have you heard nothing I've said?" Draxios thundered. "There are no fighters to be found here! I must go elsewhere to ply my trade. I have not the means to remain."

Something in his words rang false. In a kingdom of millions, poverty was endless. Desperate men could always be found, willing to bleed for coin. Surely, amassing a company should have been simple. Lucetta's gaze cut to Pavlos, pleading for one of his vaunted solutions. But the Droethien only shrugged, uncharacteristically at a loss. That left her with but one path to turn this man's will.

"Rest assured," she said at last, her voice steadying, "I have means of my own.

With a deep sigh, Lucetta slipped the gem-studded ring from her finger and held it up. Once it had promised Aldred's fealty and the protection of House Eldon; now it was little more than a bauble to be traded. She extended it, breath held.

Draxios's blind eye widened at the sight of the treasure. He rose, moving slowly toward the ring while casting a suspicious glance at Pavlos. After a measured hesitation, he snatched the band and turned it in his hands, inspecting each facet.

"You have my attention," he said in a sudden change of tone.

"I am Princess Lucetta Eldon, daughter of King Marcellus Bethard," she announced, straightening. "Those who serve me well will be richly rewarded."

Pavlos's grin flashed, his golden teeth catching the light and holding Draxios's gaze. The outlander stood uncertain—bow or sneer—before greed decided for him.

"If it is my husband's meddling you fear," Lucetta continued, "then be assured: serve under my banner and you will rise beyond your station. Your trade will not be punished. Now, there is more to your tale. You must know where men-at-arms can be found."

Draxios glanced once more at the ring, then eased it into his pouch. "If you insist, my princess. Many may be called. After your husband's decree, most left for other cities or other work, but they can be summoned back to Cardale and set to your defense."

A mischievous curl tugged at Lucetta's mouth, quashed almost as quickly as it came. It felt too easy—manipulating men with trinkets and titles—but the result was what mattered.

"Cardale does not concern me," she said, turning toward her carriage. "My interest is to the north. Be swift, Draxios, for I require an army."

ALEKSIUS

D AWN CAME THIN AND GRAY, THE KIND OF MORNING THE BORDERLANDS had worn for thirty years. Aleksius of Naxonnos rose and squinted through the east-facing window of his provincial house. The silk curtains hung half-drawn; beyond the Vhos, the Blackthorn paced the riverbank like a slow, black tide.

Blackthorn Knights. Curse them, each and every one. To a thousand fiery deaths, I curse them.

The sight put bile in his mouth. Foreign swords had become as common as bread, more visible than the levies that once answered the king. Their morning patrols stood as proof: the life had been stripped from Naxonnos and trampled beneath outsiders' boots.

He yawned and rose. Kyra still slept; the bed beside him was a calm island. He pulled on a plain blue tunic trimmed with gold, laced his worn sandals, then ran his fingers over the rings on the silver dish before dividing them between his hands—a private, grounding ritual. His black hair lay in stubborn curls; combing it would do no good.

A slave boy set a modest breakfast before him: a heel of hard bread, some dried figs, and a goblet of wine. Aleksius waved him off with one flat motion and ate alone. Lately, solitude was a better company than talk.

There was little to be found in Naxonnos. Once a bustling city of a hundred thousand, it had withered to barely ten thousand souls—soldiers counted among them. From the balcony outside his bedchamber, Aleksius watched the ruin that had been his forefathers' pride.

A small tributary of the Vhos cut through what had been the governor's central plaza; now it served as a last line of defense. Across that strip of water, he could see the palace's other half—walls toppled like broken teeth, marble columns scattered into heaps by Betanthian siege engines. The sight felt like sacrilege: the shining jewel of the Republic reduced to rubble and ash.

As a child, he'd feasted in the plaza beneath olive and fig trees, the air thick with birdsong and the steady drone of cicadas. Now, the grounds were dangerous to cross unless one wore full armor and brought soldiers. The Bethards had visited ruin on Naxonnos, and each shattered archway and collapsed portico stuck in his gut like an accusation he could not shake.

Kyra stirred beside him as he chewed his wine-soaked bread. She had always been steady, loyal, soft with reassurances.

"You blame yourself too much, Aleksius," she had told him long ago. "Were it not for you, Betanthia might have overrun us. You kept our people safe, whether they know it or not."

Words that might once have comforted now felt thin. Under his watch, the eastern Droethien armies had been beaten again and again by Marcellus Bethard; the losses were so many that the Senate had to step in or risk the Republic's collapse. Naxonnos had stood once at the province's center; now it lay hollowed, a shell pressed to the front lines of a weary war.

Aleksius drained his goblet and finished the last of his breakfast. He left the bedchamber slow and careful so Kyra could keep sleeping. Often, he paused to watch the soft curve of her shoulder or the way sleep smoothed her face. In those moments, there was no fear or blame, only a quiet purpose that steadied him.

Descending the grand stair, he peered at a freshly repaired breach in the wall. The hole was nearly large enough for a carriage—a signature wound from a Bethard trebuchet. The patched stone shone cleaner and brighter than the older blocks around it, a pale scar against the ruined masonry.

A scrawny, middle-aged slave hurried after him with a hardened leather breastplate and dressed him with practiced hands. The man's fingers moved sure and quick; straps were tightened and buckles clicked into place. Aleksius avoided donning his ornate steel cuirass or helmet when walking the outer lines—too bold an invitation to a Blackthorn archer hunting heads.

Dozens of servants swept and tended the morning chores. At his passing, each stopped, bowed low, and kept their heads down. Their obeisance was automatic; he barely noted it except as a fact of rank.

Outside, the courtyard crunched underfoot like a bed of dead leaves. The plaza had not borne green since the sieges—no grass, no life; the soil itself seemed poisoned and thin. He remembered lazy afternoons beneath olive trees, cicadas droning, the earth soft under his back. Those memories felt like relics from another life.

The orchards were gone. Only charred stumps remained, the trunks blackened and snapped where flaming pitch had taken them. A fat black crow watched from a broken limb, croaking its contempt at the soldiers below. Aleksius could not conjure the old peace; the place he had once loved now kept only echoes and ash.

The Bethards took more than my city and my home when they came with steel and fire. They took my soul as well.

A thin line of sentries paced a crude wall of timber and cobble—Tiberion's men, posted under the Senate's authority. Most of Aleksius's soldiers had bled out in the great battles for Naxonnos or in the slow grind of skirmishes that followed. Each time the blue-and-bronze banners of the Senate snapped in the wind, shame rose in his chest. How could he govern properly without an army to hold his province?

The morning calm fractured as Tasos Calellis barked orders. The senior officer thundered at a cluster of men supposed to guard the riverbanks; they were chatting when they should have been watching the Blackthorn across the Vhos. The short, burly Loxarchon—Aleksius's fiercest enforcer—lashed at them with a leather scourge, spitting curses. Sunlight winked off his half-bald head as he worked the men into line.

"On your feet, you fools! Now, before I flay you and feed your carcasses to the wildmen!" he roared.

A Droethien's dread of Zylmacians ran deeper than fear of Betanthians; at the mention of "wildmen," the soldiers snapped to attention and scrambled back to their posts. Once, the spectacle might have drawn a grim smile from Aleksius. Now it only underscored how hollow their cause had grown; even his men had little faith left. More than once, he'd thought of stepping down and letting a stronger hand take the reins for the good of the people.

"Sire," Tasos said then, thumping his chest with a balled fist, "a thousand apologies. I have been too soft on these men. They've grown lazy. I will peel the flesh from their backs if I must, yes?"

"I cannot blame them," Aleksius muttered. "Many have lost their homes. Naxonnos is a shadow of what it was. No wonder they ask themselves what, exactly, they are defending."

Tasos's brow tightened. "Pardon me, Sire?"

"Pay me no mind. My mood is sour today."

No rain could wash the smell of ash from the air. Each step outside dragged his mind back to the day Naxonnos nearly fell to Betanthia. The men's faces carried that same hollow look, a mirror of his own doubt.

"With your leave, Sire—the briefing is ready. I was on my way to deliver it before those lazy fools distracted me." Tasos unrolled a piece of parchment dense with notes.

Briefings. Reports. The same litany every morning—another accounting of loss, another reminder of how thin the Droethien hold on the city had grown. The Blackthorn guarded their half of the Vhos, and their barricade on the far bank now stood more as a statement than a serious defense. Aleksius had no stomach for sorting them out; everyone knew it.

"Unless you have some new development, I wish for you to spare me. I have no stomach for it today."

"Forgive me, Sire." Tasos rolled the parchment and tucked it into his cloak.

"Every day these foreigners defile our lands is another insult," Aleksius said, scowling. "Why the gods have visited such despair on our people, I do not know."

"Worry not," Tasos replied with fierce certainty, "Atysus will see justice done."

Atysus, the sun-god, was the Droethien's anchor—patron of Naxonnos and the name mothers whispered when children fevered at night. In a temple atop a nearby hill, priests beat bronze bowls and set great coils of incense to smoke until the air tasted faintly of citrus and ash; votive shields of beaten brass caught the morning light and threw it back like promises.

How such a god could allow ruin to come down on his faithful was a mystery that hollowed Aleksius out. Nights filled with prayers had given him no reprieve; no thunder from the sky, no spear of light to cleave their enemies. The more he prayed, the more the silence felt like abandonment. He had begun to suspect that either the gods had turned away, or else they never listened at all.

"Do you believe such things, Tasos?" Aleksius asked, jaw tight. "When you look around, do you see the Shield of Fire? Do you see the Spear of Light set upon our foes?"

The old ritual images—fiery shields and lances of dawn—seemed now like childish comforts.

"Such hope is the hope of a fool. We have been forsaken, my brother. By the gods and by the Senate. Naxonnos is a lost cause."

Tasos spat into the dry dust, the sound ugly and final. "Such talk is unbecoming of you, Sire. When the time is right, we shall have our revenge." He tried to wrap conviction around the words, but his fingers twitched as if he, too, felt the chill of doubt.

"If the gods are just, then perhaps," Aleksius replied, but his voice carried none of the certainty he once owned. "I have seen little evidence to believe they are as such."

The memory came back as if it had only just happened—the report that read like a sentence. A Betanthian host under King Marcellus Bethard had crossed the Plainhold, not with some light raiding band, but with an army like a rolling ocean: one hundred thousand men, and at their flanks several thousand Blackthorn auxiliaries. For weeks, their tide had crashed and burned through the countryside, leaving smoke and screaming behind.

At first, the numbers had been impossible to accept. No eastern king had ever mustered such force against Droethia, at least not in living memory. Their banners had been a forest of colors on the horizon, the beat of a hundred thousand boots like a coming storm. The Blackthorn, with their foreign discipline and steel, rode where the plain allowed and fed men to the siege engines that tore stone from stone. Siege engines—trebuchets the size of houses—cast boulders into their lines; the air had been full of splintering timber and the sick, metallic tang of blood.

Aleksius had been slow to act. He raised thirty thousand men and scraped together another fifteen thousand levies, but it was scarcely a match for the mass that came to meet them. The first clash ended in ruin: two-thirds of his host ground down in the carnage, and of the remainder nearly half broke and fled to save wives and children left choking in the smoke.

The retreat to the Vhos had been chaos: men stumbling through mud, wagons overturned, cries for the fallen mixed with a hiss of arrows.

Boats groaned as they took on bodies; bridges were choked with men who could not, or would not, return.

I was a fool, a reckless fool who sent many good men to their deaths that day. Perhaps this is why Atysus has forsaken me.

It was a far cry from his father's day when he had fought Betanthia to a standstill and borne the weight of the Republic on his shoulders. King Torben Bethard's campaigns west had ended in death and defeat more than once; Aleksius felt the sting of that wasted struggle as a private shame. If only his father were alive now—how disappointed he would be.

Those thoughts were like poisoned water. The more Aleksius drank, the deeper he sank into a slow, sinking despair.

You must not do this to yourself again, he told himself. *Your people need you. You are all they have left. And Kyra… she needs you. You are all she has.*

The palace's dreariness offered no cure. He decided he needed to be out among the people for a while, if only to remind them that someone still stood between ruin and order. Even a broken palace could not be an excuse to cower within it.

"Come, Tasos. Walk with me."

Tasos snapped his fingers and four spearmen answered, armor gilded a dull gold, shields broad and oval like portable bulwarks, spears long and counterweighted. These were the backbone of a Droethien formation—steady, disciplined—and their presence before the small party did more for morale than any speech. Two men marched ahead; two closed ranks behind. The display was theater, perhaps, but better a reassuring theater than no reassurance at all.

The people should see strength in their leader and draw hope from it, Aleksius thought, though he found it hard to borrow the feeling for himself.

Outside, the outer palace had been remade into trenchworks and stakes, a hardened camp where once there had been orchards and fountains. They filed through rings of defenses and out into streets that still smelled faintly of smoke. The city had been reshaped by siege and by time; what remained was all edges and ash.

Street names meant little now—blocks had been renamed by ruin. Here, a market had been; there a bathhouse; the trebuchet's scars ran across what had been avenues. People lived where they could: in the gaps between collapsed arches, under canvas tarps slung from ruined columns, in tents braced against stone. The scene was a ragged, stubborn life trying to root itself in rubble.

It was impossible to see such ruin and not feel anger. Naxonnos would not recover in his lifetime—perhaps never. Buildings could be rebuilt, roads relaid, but people changed. Year after year, the population thinned: some fled to strange lands to scratch out a living, others stayed and learned to live on scraps of hope.

Aleksius had heard what Betanthians said of them, and none of it was kind. The Droethiens were spoken of as vermin, an infestation many would gladly purge. Thousands of his people had scattered across Betanthia, hawking trinkets and thin stews to survive. The irony bit: the very realm that had burned their fields had become the only place offering work to those who escaped the ash.

From the Betanthian view, Droethiens were backward and savage, a people akin to the Zylmacian wildmen. In some brutal way, the image fit: refugees drifting into towns with nothing but the rags on their backs, looking like beggars more than citizens. Naxonnos had once been different—temples of marble, streets lined with shade trees.

Those Khorrish dogs were building driftwood hovels on the beaches where they landed, while we were building temples of marble into the heavens. Who are they to think themselves superior?

It stung him that the other governors had stood idle while the Bethards marched through. Only when Naxonnos nearly burned did the Senate stir, and by then the damage was done. The people had seen, in ash and smoke, how little the western governors cared—how easily they'd trade a quarter of the Droethien folk to spare their own provinces. That realization, cold and blunt, hardened something in Aleksius. It was not only grief he felt, but also betrayal.

Cowards. Every last one of them. I see why the Bethards continue to set themselves upon our lands.

"Tell me, Tasos… do you ever wonder why we bother? Why we cling to a hope that feels so damned futile?"

Aleksius's face had closed like a drawn blade. Walking the shattered streets cost him; still, he did it because the people needed to see a leader who would not hide.

"I'm not sure I follow, Sire." Tasos rubbed at the month's stubble that had taken the place of his usual clean jaw. The man had started growing a beard, perhaps to answer for the hair he'd lost on top. Small comforts, Aleksius thought.

"Look at this," Aleksius said, voice low. "So much despair, so little I can do. Sometimes I think—maybe I should give Marcellus Bethard what he wants and be done. If selling out spares my people another winter of hunger and body-count, would that not be mercy? This place—this graveyard—maybe it's kinder to let it go."

Tasos spat, the sound flat and angry. "Nonsense. You know as well as I that if we give them a morsel, they will swallow the whole feast. King Bethard's appetite is never satisfied."

He was right. Even now, the Blackthorn and their hirelings prowled the opposite bank, waiting like wolves. Treaties would mean nothing; walls and spears were the only language those men seemed to understand.

"I cannot watch my people suffer more, Tasos. I cannot let them starve for pride or for the bones of a city," Aleksius said, the words tasting like iron.

"Many fled. Many died," Tasos said, softer now. "But they remember this: you did not run. Not when the walls burned. Not when your home broke around you. That stubbornness—call it folly if you will—keeps them going. It gives them a shape to hold onto." He nodded toward a cluster of women hauling a worn cart. "They see you, and they go on."

Aleksius watched the women, their shoulders bent but moving, and felt the old, familiar pull of responsibility.

They look none too inspired to me, he thought, but he kept the judgment out of his mind. It was easier to lead with a steady hand than with despair.

A newborn's wail cut through the ruin like a bright blade. In a place full of endings, the sound of new life felt like a small mercy. Aleksius gave a sad, gentle smile and knelt beside the woman holding the child.

"Sire." She dipped her head with the weary respect of someone who had learned not to demand.

"What a beautiful child. His father must be proud."

Her face broke. Tears ran hot and steady down cheeks already hollowed by hunger.

"His father is dead… killed by a Blackthorn arrow." She fought for composure and lost. "I am broken without him. Please, Sire, avenge him. Make the Bethards pay with blood!"

It was the same plea he had heard a hundred times, each one raw and terrible in its own way. Aleksius wanted nothing more than to drive the foreigners from the Vhos and sink spears into every man who had taken a life he loved.

"I promise you, the gods will see justice," he began, but the woman cut him off.

"I do not want to wait for the gods. I want vengeance now!"

Her cry shook the child; both mother and baby sobbed together, a tiny, terrible duet. There was little he could offer that would staunch such grief.

As do I, my poor woman. As do I.

Two guards approached with hempen sacks slung over their shoulders.

Aleksius rose and drew a round loaf from one, offering it with steady hands. The woman accepted it, still trembling. Food was a small, blunt cure, and it was all he could give freely, often at the cost of going hungry himself so Kyra might eat. He had learned that charity kept more than bellies filled; it kept the fragile thread of hope from snapping entirely.

Nearly all the fertile fields that once rolled east to the Plainhold had been seized by Betanthia; much of the land lay salted and fallow. A thin ribbon remained—patches kept to feed the garrisons—but it was a pittance. If Aleksius had fifty thousand spears, he might hope to retake the farms and bring real relief to his people. But he could not. He had barely five thousand.

With the Senate's backing and their troops at hand, an assault might be possible, but the costs would be terrible. Betanthia was the continent's hammer for a reason; their veterans had crushed Aleksius's best time and again. The thought of dragging more suffering into Naxonnos curdled him. He could not stomach ordering a campaign that might clear fields for one spring and leave a thousand grieving widows in its wake.

Further along the rubble-choked road, he saw the ruins of the Temple of Etros, one of the city's oldest places of worship. While marble had shaped much of Naxonnos for two thousand years, this temple predated that glory—gray stone hewn by hands long dead. Its shattered portico and sunken roof were a wound that bled hope and, paradoxically, sometimes healed it; for some, the mere fact that the house of the gods still stood at all was proof the world had not entirely ended.

A man in a dirtied white chitin led a small prayer at the temple steps, his voice low and rough as rope. A handful of the faithful clustered around him; women with threadbare shawls, a child clutching a piece of bread, an old soldier whose one good eye watched everything with the slow patience of habit. The smell of smoldering incense tangled with smoke and the acrid tang of siege; a few candles guttered in browned holders, throwing a weak light over cracked stone.

Tasos Calellis closed his eyes and mouthed the final verse of a prayer, then drew the old sign: middle and ring fingers touching between brow and sliding down to the chin, finishing where they began.

"May Atysus shine his mercy down upon us," the priest intoned. He saw Aleksius and bowed low. "And may he grant our Governor the strength to drive back the evil that has poisoned these sacred lands."

The words should have warmed him. Instead, they felt like knives—praise that cut because he feared he did not deserve it. Still, there was solace in the sound: the congregation's thin chorus, a child's uncertain voice, the rustle of shawls. For a few heartbeats, the city was not only ash and hunger; it was people holding a stubborn, fragile hope.

After the last of the bread was handed out, Aleksius and Tasos returned to the Governor's house for a quiet midday meal. Kyra waited at the table. They ate simply: a few lamb chops lacquered in wine, potatoes browned and coarse. Where other nobles would have feasted, Aleksius let such luxuries pass; every scrap spared from his own table could be sent to a family that needed it more.

When the plates were cleared, he climbed the narrow stairs to the palace's upper rooms. From there, he could see the Vhos and the Blackthorn on the far bank, their banners like a dark smear against the day. He hated them with a steady, cold hatred—every man in that foreign steel. He hated what they had done: the burned orchards, the broken temples, the children who would never know a spring without fear.

He imagined, as he often did, a line of spears thrust across the river and the Blackthorn falling back—images of swift, brutal justice that comforted and terrified him in equal measure. For now, those were only imaginations. Duty called first: reports to read, men to muster, a city to keep breathing another week.

He lingered a moment at the window, letting the small ritual of watching the river settle his mind. Then he turned, squared his shoulders, and moved to the work that might yet matter more than prayers or promises: the day's hard, provincial labor of keeping what little remained alive.

I see no army, or reinforcements, or siege engines. No, if there were to be an attack, we would be aware of it.

The standards, however, continue to change. The Blackthorn's black-and-gold banners are a constant blight across the far bank; the king's colors, by contrast, have grown rarer. That shift may not have meant much on its own, as Betanthian commanders often rearranged forces to meet Zylmacian raids. Tiberion had sent Senate troops north to blunt the wildmen more than once—but patterns are a governor's map. Read them right, and they tell you where the danger lies.

Sometimes Aleksius used the enemy's movement as a crude bell-weather: if the wildmen failed to break Betanthian lines, they often turned south to pillage what remained of Naxonnos' lands. Perhaps another strike was coming. Perhaps it was only the itch of an overly cautious mind. He felt the same old stirring in his bones—the small, stubborn warning an old man learns to trust before a storm arrives.

Whatever the threat, whatever its shape or source, Aleksius of Naxonnos would not be caught unready. He would watch. He would count banners and listen for the roll of wheels beyond the trees. He would stand, vigilant, until either hope returned or the last light went out.

TITAN III

A HAZE OF DARK SMOKE HUNG OVER THE LOWLAND, THE AIR THICK with the scent of blackened wood and rotting men. Tylar's heart jumped; the smell told him they were close. His hand went to his sword by reflex, then dropped. If Madelyn had struck again, nothing living would be left to find.

They picked their way down the rolling hill, each step cautious and careful. Shapes resolved out of the veil of smoke—faint outlines of houses, a sagging roof, a crooked wall. A standing settlement this far into the Plainhold was odd, though its presence might be a clue.

Arhan rode a little apart, cloak pulled tight, his face a map of old campaigns. Tylar knew him by reputation—steady, watchful, a man who kept to the work and did not squander words. He watched the ruined plain with a slow, careful eye.

"Where the fuck are we?" Tylar muttered. "We've gone too far east."

"Not so fast, Bradshaw." Conrak slid from his saddle, fingers already on the hilt of his arming sword. "East we are, but not off course. We must have just missed her. Let's secure the area—there'll be signs. Tracks, patterns, something."

"If she even came this way," he protested. "How do we know the girl was here? Maybe the Northmen sacked the place."

Conrak shook his head. "No, she was here. I'd stake my life on it. I feel her, like she's standing beside us." He sounded certain in a way Tylar found unnerving.

Tylar kept his hope small. Experience had taught him that hope and disappointment traveled the same road. Better to expect the worst than be undone by the best.

Just another waste of time. The girl is likely miles from here and heading to who the fuck knows where.

"And what makes you so certain?" Tylar shot back.

"I'd have thought you learned a thing or two by now." Conrak's mouth was a crooked line. "I don't carry Madelyn's power in my blood, but years as a Sacrithon taught me to read the Eveldanyr's essence. She was here. Maybe we'll find where she went."

They moved into the ruined settlement with measured steps. Earlwick looked pale and skittish, as if the sight might topple him; the Guardsmen kept stony faces, weapon-ready and taut as bows. Smoke clawed at their throats, and the ash underfoot made each step sound loud.

Arhan dismounted quietly and began scanning the ground, his heels dragging through the ash. His gaze passed over crushed beams and broken wheel-ruts as if reading a book of sorrow.

The destruction was worse than anything Madelyn had done before. Where a meeting hall or tavern had stood, there was only a shell: thatch collapsed into cinders, timber reduced to gray heaps. Flames had leapt from house to house, the center of the village a black wound. A wrecked cart lay upended before the entrance, iron twisted, spokes charred—an ugly testament to sudden violence.

Tylar felt the chill settle into his spine. This was no petty raid. If Madelyn had passed through, whatever possessed her had hardened into something far darker than mere vengeance. He dismounted, hand on his sword, every sense tightening. A patrol of barbarians might still be near; smoke could carry for miles across the Plainhold.

"There's nothing here," Earlwick said, voice thin as he crouched and picked at a scorched beam, searching for survivors.

"No—no, there isn't," Conrak replied, running a hand through the ash at the hall's threshold. "But you'll want to see this, Bradshaw." His tone was flat, the kind that made Tylar's teeth ache.

Conrak's seriousness was unsettling—he wore chaos like a second skin, but this gravity was different, measured and certain. Tylar frowned; reading the man was never easy, yet something in his stance told Tylar this ruin hid more than burned wood. With steel in hand, he stepped closer to the hall, the smoke parting like a curtain, bracing for whatever waited inside.

"Fuck…" he grunted.

Dozens of charred bodies lay twisted across the stone floor, limbs contorted into grotesque angles. Fire did terrible things to flesh; whether these men had been alive when the blaze took them mattered little now, for the result was ash, bone, and silence.

He had seen carnage before, but never as the work of one hand, and never at the scale of this. Tylar stood rooted, feeling a conflict split him open: horror at the sight and a terrible, private responsibility.

Arhan crouched beside a collapsed beam and pressed a careful finger to the floor where embers still smoldered. "Fast fire," he said quietly. "Not the usual torch-and-run. Whoever did this knew how to use flame—close, choking, no chance to run." He looked up at Tylar with a single hard nod: "This was done with intent."

"This is beyond the pale for someone like her," he said, voice raw. "It's my fault. I should never have left her at the Mord. I should have climbed those walls with my bare fucking hands and carried her away. Now look—what has she become? A butcher."

"All is as the gods will it," Conrak said, sheathing his sword with a slow, practiced motion. "You cannot punish yourself for what came before, during, or after the siege, Bradshaw. There are forces at play you do not understand. We are pawns in something larger than our grief."

Tylar's grip tightened on the hilt until his knuckles turned white. He wanted to throw the sword, to drive it through the smoke itself. "This is no game, you zealous cunt! This is Madelyn. She never asked for any of this. I would have taken ten thousand deaths to save her. The more I give, the farther she falls."

Around them, each corpse carried its own ruin: a face frozen in a scream, hands curled as if still gripping some vanished tool, a man's limb small among the ash. Even reduced to charcoal, some forms hinted at monstrous size—men who must once have been hulking, boulder-chewing fiends. How a woman could have cut them down so utterly was a question that burned in Tylar as fiercely as the embers beneath their boots.

Conrak said nothing. His jaw worked. For once, the man's usual chaos-tinged grin had nowhere to hide; seriousness sat on him like armor.

Tylar stepped closer to a collapsed beam and found, half-buried in cinder, a scrap of a man's tunic—threadbare, singed at the edges. The sight opened something raw in him: not just anger, but grief that had no neat target. He turned away and swallowed the taste of ash, knowing that whatever Madelyn had become, it could not be undone by curses or vows. Only action might answer what had been done.

Tylar sighed, sheathed his sword, and moved through the village, scanning for any trace of her. The streets were a litter of blackened bodies and singed debris; many lay as if felled mid-task, faces slack with surprise. Each corpse deepened the hollow in his gut—this was not swift justice, it was a slaughter that left questions smoking in its wake.

One figure appeared fresher than the rest. A hand clutched at a ragged slash from collarbone to belly; dark soil stained the ground beneath him, as if his blood had only just begun to soak into the earth. Tylar rifled through the man's few belongings, seeking maps, dispatches, anything that might point to where the attackers had come from or where they were going.

As he rolled the body, it made a low, ragged groan that jerked him back. The barbarian was alive, but barely. Instinct and habit pushed Tylar's hand to his sword; the steel whispered from its scabbard, and its point hovered a breath from the wounded man's throat.

"P…please…" the barbarian rasped, voice a dry scrape.

Tylar's frown set. He was not a man given to mercy in the field, but neither was he blind to suffering. Still, this place demanded answers more than pity. He leaned close so the man could smell the smoke on his skin and hear the hard edge in his voice.

"Tell me what I need to know, and I'll end your pain," Tylar said, each word a cold promise. "Refuse, and you'll suffer like never before. Where is she?"

"S…she?" the barbarian spluttered, face twisted. "I… I never—didn't see it come. We were—attacked—and—"

His hands, slick with blood, trembled as he tried to form the sentence. The Northman's voice broke into a wailing that curdled in Tylar's gut. Men unraveled here; he'd watched it a thousand times. It was always the same: fear stripped a man down to bone and sound.

"Shut the fuck up and listen," Tylar barked, pacing the ragged breath between them. Time thinned like paper. "Which way did she go? Tell me. Now."

"N—north!" the barbarian gasped, finger wavering before falling limp.

The answer was vague and useless—true in the way a fever dream is true—and Tylar felt the heat of frustration climb his neck. Survivors and solid leads were dwindling with every second. He scanned the ruined lane and spotted a hovel whose door hung broken but, strangely, unburned. The little house had escaped the flames; something in its untouched interior felt like an accusation.

He pushed inside. Chairs lay toppled, a crude table stained with ash. An iron cauldron sagged over a dead hearth, its congealed contents a gray slick. The place smelled of smoke and old sweat; it held the small, stubborn life of a morning interrupted. Tylar rifled through cracked chests and overturned bundles—not out of hope for treasure, but because the hovel might hold a scrap of direction, a bootprint, a hastily-scribbled note. Against the plainness, every overlooked detail could be the thing that saved them.

He searched for another ten minutes and found nothing. His men had regrouped at the village center, voices low as they argued next steps. Though morning still clung to the hour, a dark bank of clouds rolled in and stripped the day of light, dragging noon toward dusk.

Bad weather was part of the Plainhold's insult. The land seemed to resent them here—wind and sky conspiring to shove them off it. Tylar felt the same appetite for ruin: he would have been glad to see every last acre turned to ash. He watched the cloud mass thicken into a black wall, its edges grinding together like some great, slow mill.

A heavy mist slid up the lane, a ribbon of gray that pooled and swirled with a will of its own. Tylar's chest tightened; the movement was too deliberate to be mere weather. Shapes twisted inside the fog—pale, blurring outlines that rose and fell with the breath of the air. For a heartbeat, he thought himself mad, until a scent crawled up his nose and made his skin pimple: the faint, impossible tang of singed linen and smoke—and something else, an iron-sweet note he had learned all too well.

"Is that—" he whispered, and could not finish.

What stepped from the mist was not quite flesh and not quite memory. Madelyn's shade moved down the street with a catlike grace, all hollowed cheekbones and wind-tossed hair. It paused beside a stack of barrels, head cocked as if stalking prey. Tylar crept forward on the balls of his feet, every nerve strung taut, even as his mind tried to argue the sight away.

A spectral hand slid to a hip as if to draw a blade. In a single fluid motion, the figure sprang from cover and crashed onto an unseen foe, the phantom arm falling with terrible, practiced force. The motion replayed the massacre he had just witnessed, only now it moved like a memory replaying itself, inevitable and obscene.

Tylar could hear, in the mist, the echo of bodies collapsing—an impossible, hollow clatter that belonged to a dream. He steadied himself against a ruined post and forced his breath small, waiting for what would come next.

"Damn foolish girl," Tylar muttered. "You and your bloody vendetta. You couldn't wait and let us do the killing with you. No… you thought only of yourself."

The words landed hard, and hypocrisy stung even as they left his mouth. Tylar lived by revenge; he had fed men to causes that bore little honor. In fits of fury, he'd sent good men to die, and the truth of that cut him sharper than any blade.

Madelyn heard him. She stopped, turned, and fixed him with those obsidian eyes—aware, patient, and somehow vast. For a heartbeat, she cocked her head, then sprang. One arm slammed into his chest with a shove that knocked the breath from him. He stumbled back, the blow rattling through his ribs like a bell.

He should have called it a trick—smoke, fever, the afterimages that follow war. He'd known ghosts of memory before: the faces of the dead, the taste of blood on a winter night. This felt different, though. Too close, too present.

"What the fuck are you?" he breathed.

Madelyn's face rippled. Skin shifted like wet paint caught by wind, features smearing into something not-quite-human. Her eyes hollowed into pits that drank the light. The air around her curdled; a foul, wet rot bled out, a stink that made his mouth water and his stomach lurch.

This was not the girl Tylar had known. Something unnatural had eaten at not just her flesh—as the Plainhold had shown—but at whatever lay beneath it. The creature's mouth curled into a grin of crooked, dagger-like teeth, blackened and lost to rot.

"I don't know what you are, or what you've done to Madelyn," Tylar said, his voice tight with a fear he could barely hide. "But unhand her now, or there's no hole deep enough, no realm far enough, where I won't come to cut your fucking head from your shoulders."

The dark thing said nothing. It continued north, moving with an almost lazy certainty. After a few paces, its shape collapsed, unraveling into a buzzing cloud of flies that scattered like kicked ash. The stink left with them, and the oppressive dread that had knotted his chest loosened. He hadn't realized he'd been holding his breath until he gasped for air.

Then a hot, sharp pain cracked across his right pectoral. He stared down and saw a dirty smear, the outline of a hand pressed into his steel cuirass, exactly where the ache flared. An unfamiliar chill threaded through him. Whoever, or whatever, had touched him had been real.

Conrak and the others hurried up at the sound of his curse. "What's the matter, Bradshaw?" Conrak asked, brow creased. "You look like you've seen a ghost."

"Because I have, you fucking dolt," Tylar snapped, though his face felt hollow and far away.

Earlwick laughed at first, thinking it a jape. The sound died on his lips when he caught the look in Tylar's eyes and the smear on the armor. Mockery was a dead man's sport here; no one touched it.

"What are you saying, Bradshaw?" Conrak cocked his head. "You mean to tell me you saw—"

"I saw her!" Tylar snarled. "I fucking *saw* her as if she stood beside us. But something was wrong inside her. It was… corrupt. Evil. And it left its mark on me."

He jabbed a finger at the black smear on his cuirass. A few knights bristled with skepticism—this land was full of soot and blood; marks happened. Conrak, however, stepped forward and studied the stain. He licked a thumb and tested the edge, then scowled as if tasting soot.

"It looks like you may be right," Conrak said slowly. "The mark's stained into the steel. I can't wipe it off. Gods… could it be so?"

"What the fuck else are you holding back?" Tylar roared, fists tightening. "Why am I seeing visions of her if she's alive? How can she touch me like she's flesh and bone?"

"As much as I'd like to have answers, Bradshaw, I don't," Conrak admitted, scratching at his stubbled chin. "We live in strange times… strange as any in the old tales. Maybe centuries. Maybe longer. Who can say? We're pawns in a game played by powers beyond our comprehension."

The answer nearly split Tylar open with rage. He had grown tired of riddles and platitudes. He stalked to his horse, the sack of questions turning to iron in his gut. Madelyn needed him more than ever—no sermon, no theory would keep her from whatever fury held her now.

"Where are you going?" Conrak called after him, hands thrown wide.

"Games are meant to be won," Tylar snarled without looking back. "I'll play by my own rules. I'll find her—by god or by blade—even if I have to kill every god in the heavens to do it."

SYLVIA IV

S HE WOKE TO A BLOODY SUNRISE, THE SKY A SMEAR OF BRUISED RED that felt like an omen. Dawn carried with it a cold dread, for today they would do the unthinkable: break their force and scatter into the unknown. Sylvia thought it madness to divide when unity was the only bulwark left.

Her faith was fierce, but even zeal could not make sense of Einarr's visions. Every instinct in her body screamed against leaving. Yet Damien had already bent to the vision. Defeat had shaken him, yes, but not his conviction. That steadiness unnerved her more than any enemy.

She packed slowly after a frugal breakfast of dried meat, stale bread, and a cup of ale. She placed her long, brown hair into a pair of loose, twin braids, then prepared to ride. But then, Hilde burst inside like a thrown spear.

"You're leaving?!" Hilde's arms folded, cyan eyes flashing, anger and fear twisting through her voice. "After everything… after all we've lost… you and Damien just pack up and go where? Where?"

"Be still, Hilde." Sylvia's patience had been thinned to a razor. "This is something I must do. I can scarcely explain it… but I must have faith."

"Faith in what?" Hilde shot back. "Faith in visions? What about faith in kin? You'd leave us with a Nothanek at the helm? Arik? He's not a leader. He'll be picked apart by the wildmen the moment they smell weakness."

Indeed, leaving a Nothanek in charge of the warband felt reckless. Arik was skittish as any of his kin, but he had a rough intelligence and a stubborn streak that might keep the fighters from falling apart—the least terrible choice, if there were no better.

"We have no surplus of options," Sylvia said, hefting a strap of her pack. "We must trust Einarr and the visions the gods have given him."

Hilde ran a hand through a chin-length lock of black hair, jaw tight. "How can you trust a man who so easily deserted us?"

Sylvia's patience snapped like a frayed cord. "Have you heard nothing I've said? We cannot face Betanthia in the open. We must take this leap. I will petition Taug for reinforcements once we reach Rej Rhivoth, and perhaps Einarr will find what he seeks in the south."

She slung a leather sack over her shoulder, tested the weight of her weapons, and searched for parting words that would steady them all. Hilde's fear was plain; she would not voice it, but the tremor in her hands said enough. Still, beneath the fear, something like hope burned, small and stubborn.

Sylvia stepped toward the tent flap and found Einarr waiting outside, reins looped across his arm. Her horse stood saddled, packs bulging with carefully tied satchels and extras—water skins, salted meat, a roll of spare cord. He wore a different sort of quiet; the same callused frame, but with a look in his eyes that bespoke a man who had been touched by something larger than himself.

"Time is short," he said, handing her the reins. "I gathered everything you'll need. May the road keep you in better company."

Sylvia took the leather and let her fingers rest on Einarr's arm. "Thank you," she said softly. "You are a good man. I am ashamed I ever doubted you."

Apologies were hard for the Rhivothi; pride bled like an open wound and was easier to parade than to heal. Still, she meant the words. Einarr's calling was not born of vanity but of something he believed to be a higher law. Now it was her turn to walk the next stretch of that road—unseen, dangerous, but necessary.

"All is forgiven," Einarr said, meeting her eyes. "Visions only point a way; they do not hold every step. I know not who will stand at the end or how many will fall, but we have given too much to turn back now."

A procession drifted toward them. Damien led it, wrapped in linen and leather, his blackened steel set aside in a wagon, so the heat would no longer consume him. The wound across his side had been cauterized, but it took from him hour by hour; he walked like a man learning to breathe through fresh pain.

"Do you think he will make it?" Sylvia asked, voice low.

"He must," Einarr said, though his answer lacked ease. He drew a long breath and then, as if unable to hold it inside, spoke what he had seen.

"It came to me when I passed the ruins of Castle Morden," Einarr said slowly. "Not a dream, but a thing pressed into my sight. I saw a colossus born of bone, tearing up from the lowest pits of the earth—taller than any tree, its limbs dripping with melted flesh. It was the most gruesome sight I have ever borne. I know not what it means, but it cannot mean anything but ill. I cannot shake the sense that this vision was not meant for me, but for you."

The image of the colossus lodged in Sylvia like a cold stone. The image of the bone giant—ribs like arches, limbs dripping with melted flesh—left no comfort. She pressed a small, fierce hand to Einarr's forearm; the gesture said more than words.

"I will take comfort in your faith, Einarr, and keep it with me. I will need something to hold onto."

Warriors spilled from camp by the hundreds to watch Dreadfire ride;

some saw surrender, others saw purpose. No fanfare met them, only the hush of men who understood the weight of what was being done. Sylvia mounted, snapped her reins, and rode out into the great unknown.

You cannot look back. You must remain focused on the road ahead. Gods know you will need every ounce of strength and wit to survive what is to come...

The first days on the Plainhold gave them little—long, sun-flat miles between them and the Betanthian host, whose columns so far showed no hurry to pursue. The ground bore the imprint of war: wheel ruts, flattened grass, soil churned and disturbed. They traveled steady, leaning into the wind, each day a small test of exhaustion and will.

By the fourth day, Damien had begun to fail. Lack of decent food, sleeplessness, and the Plainhold's hard miles had taken their toll on his injured leg; the linen wrap no longer hid the creeping rot. Color leeched from his face until his skin looked like old parchment, and he rode with a slow, hollow sway.

"Damien," Sylvia pleaded as they rode, voice tight with fear, "this is madness. You must rest. You cannot go on like this."

"There is no time," he answered, voice as thin as parchment. "We must continue."

"For all the years I have trusted and followed you without question... I need you to trust me now," she said, firmer. "If we do nothing, that wound will kill you."

Shame flared in him for a breath—pride and pain braided together. Even a man of his legend was flesh and blood, vulnerable to steel like any other. He nodded at last, reluctant and small, and Sylvia let herself believe it was enough.

They found a hollow ringed by dead trees and great boulders and made a cautious camp. Sylvia wasted no time. A small fire took from flint and dry kindling, smoke curling thin into an empty sky. Fire in the Plainhold was a risk—the tinder-dry grass and wind could turn a

cookfire into an inferno in minutes, and any light might draw beasts…
or the keen eyes of Betanthian cavalry scouting the wastes.

Hours passed with little trouble. Then a dry gust from the west
snatched at the flames and died; she coaxed the embers with flint and
twig until a larger blaze caught and crackled. Night here was a thief—
cold enough to bite and quick to creep into bones—so they banked
their shelter close and huddled near the warmth.

Once Damien settled enough to breathe freely, Sylvia unrolled an
animal-skin map. The leather smelled faintly of smoke and salt; inked
routes and merchant markings glimmered in the firelight. Finding
their place in a landscape stripped by war was hard, but merchants had
recorded trails and notched landmarks that could be read by one who
knew how.

"Here," she said, tracing a route with one finger. "If we keep this
heading, we could make it to Skaginlef. It would add no more than two,
maybe three days to our journey. We can resupply and rest properly. It's
a detour, but it buys you time."

"No," Damien muttered. "Time is what we do not have. Every hour
we stall risks our people. We must make for Rej Rhivoth."

She looked at him, at the thin set of his mouth, the stubborn line
of his jaw, and felt the old argument crease between them: prudence
or urgency. Silently, she weighed the days against the wound and the
vision that rode them like a shadow.

"I do not think it wise," Sylvia sighed. "The Hinterwood is still wild.
There are wolves and bears in abundance. If we're set upon, I fear we'll
have neither strength nor time to fight."

"I will not deviate," Damien growled, low and flat. "And I will not
speak of this again.

He lay back on a wool blanket, head on a saddlebag, each breath
a small battle. The argument closed as quickly as it had flared. She
wanted to insist, to force food into him, but his spirit had hardened;

pressing him now would only widen the wound between them. So she kept quiet and watched him sleep, the worry knotted under her ribs.

By the seventh day, the heat at last began to break. Sylvia's skin had burned and begun to peel, a raw pink that stung when she moved. The Plainhold's outer reaches were near, their charts promised; with every mile her hope thinned, then hiccupped back into life.

Gods, hear me. I will not die in this forsaken place. I will die on the field with axe in hand. I will be greeted in Sjenohor as a hero. Mark these words, o gods.

At midday, a dark shape circled above. For a long, hollow second, she feared a vulture had come for the scent of Damien's rot. But the bird rode the wind with a different grace—an Embercrest eagle, native to the Hinterwood, brown wings broad and patient. She watched it with a hollow ache of homesickness that made her chest tighten.

When she finally looked away from the bird, the forest revealed itself: the tops of mighty pines slicing the horizon. There was no sight sweeter to a Rhivothi. The Hinterwood meant shelter, shade, and the clean smell of sap instead of smoke. For the first time in days, a real smile crossed her face.

"By the gods, we've made it!" she breathed.

Even Damien's spirit seemed to lift. The sharp scent of pine strengthened any Northman's heart—more than a reminder of home, it was an argument for everything they had fought to keep.

An opening in the dense forest yawned ahead like a gate. They passed beneath an arch of white-barked aspens, trunks polished pale as bone, the path beneath them packed hard from centuries of feet and hooves. Someone, long ago, had worn this track into the land, and now it welcomed them back.

"This is our road home," Dreadfire rasped. "We ride until sunset."

His stubbornness could have been madness, but Sylvia had neither the will nor the words to argue. For a breath, she let herself feel safe. The war was still out there, and their kinsmen bled on other fields, but the sight of trees and solid ground steadied her like a hand on the small of her back.

They pushed deeper. A narrower trail, carpeted with soft sedge and the fall of last year's needles, took them into quieter woods. Deer and horse tracks scored the damp earth; sometimes the forest looked new from one season to the next, as if the land itself kept changing faces to test those who walked it.

Humidity closed around them, heavy and slow, but the pine canopy offered a merciful shade. There were no swarms of biting flies—dry months had thinned the usual pests—and the quiet was almost luxurious. Best of all, water still ran here: a thin stream, dark and cold, would be enough to wash bandages and ease thirst. For the first time since the Plainhold, the road felt less like punishment and more like purpose.

Praise be to you, Kholdyr, for keeping us safe on this perilous journey. I only pray that you remain with us when we reach the mountain...

As the sun slid west, Sylvia steadied herself in the saddle. They rode north, she knew that, but the track ahead felt strange, a path she had never walked. These pines stood differently here; tall as towers and planted in unnerving, precise rows, trunks marching like sentinels into the sky. The sight pricked at some half-remembered thing inside her.

It was enough to conjure memories of tales she had heard around bonfires as a child, when the Wisemen of Rej Rhivoth would recite the history of their people. Stories rose up from the corner of her mind, those old bonfire nights when the Wisemen of Rej Rhivoth spun histories and warnings into the smoke.

"I have never seen this place," she said softly, "and yet it feels like something I have dreamed."

Damien's face creased with pain and impatience. He glanced about, seeing only trees. "Surely you've ridden these ways before, Stormguard?"

"No," she answered, shaking her head. "Not in waking hours. I only know the tales of how the Hinterwood came to be. The words sit in me as though I had heard them yesterday."

A cool gust slid past, full of pine-sap and shadow, an honest blessing after the Plainhold's dust. It kissed her cheek and left her steadier.

"The elders said the Hinterwood was once nothing but open plain," she began, the story tasting like old bread. "A man named Dolvargan wandered here seeking shelter. He carried seeds of every kind, but only pine and spruce would take root. The rest withered. He planted, and the trees rose like a watch over the land."

The memory warmed her. She let the story carry her back: the smell of smoke, the comfort of meat on a skewer, the tilt of a father's laugh. At ten, she had stolen sips from his mug until she was caught; instead of anger, he poured a little into a wooden cup and they drank together, his hand large and sure around hers. It was a simple thing, but the taste of that night—honeyed ale and a father's quiet pride—remained hers like a charm.

For a moment, she let herself live there, in that small, bright memory, before the present closed again like a door. Her memory of first drunkenness rose like a warm, embarrassed fever. The mead had tasted sweet then, burning only a little on the tongue, but the sweetness had turned her stomach and sent her retching in the straw. She did not sip again until adolescence, when the same drink felt like honeyed nectar and a small sacrament.

"An interesting tale," Dreadfire said, flat and unamused. "The creation story of your people differs greatly from that of mine."

A flicker at the edge of her vision stole her words. Sylvia pulled the reins, and together, they halted. She shaded her eyes against the slanting sun and scanned the trees. The disturbance was not animal at all but human-made.

"Do you see that?" she asked, hand near her axe, unsure whether to draw it.

Damien peered through the branches, black eyes narrowing. "A dwelling of some sort, if my sight has not failed. We should take a look."

They rode closer with caution. The structure had long been abandoned. Only a low stone foundation remained true, while the timber walls had rotted and fallen in, a tangled heap of mossed beams and collapsed rafters. It looked, from a distance, like the ribs of some great beast buried by time.

Sylvia's neck prickled. She eased from her saddle and strapped her axe to the belt, the metal cool against her palm. Inside the hollowed shell, there was only leaf and dust—no smoke, no sign of a living hearth.

"We should make camp here," Damien said, surprising her with the softness in his voice. "I must rest and find my strength."

It was a small, human admission, a statement of frailty she had not heard from him before. For a moment, she forgot the war and the visions and simply felt the odd comfort of shelter: a hollow made safe by the mere act of taking it. The ruined cabin, for all its decay, offered a pocket of quiet in a landscape still raw from march and battle.

Old, dilapidated places often carried a sour, watchful air, but not this ruin. Sylvia felt instead the same easy peace she had known as a child among old relatives: a warmth that invited rather than warned. The hollowed shell smelled of spruce and dry aspen, and a chorus of crickets and distant owls sang the woods to sleep.

She made a crude bed on the packed earth, a roll of cloak for a blanket, and her saddlebag for a pillow. Though it was high summer, the evening was crisp enough to wake the blood but not to make her shiver. A thin veil of cloud thinned to silver and then to turquoise; moonlight poured down not pale but ocean-hued, strange and beautiful. Sylvia sat up and smiled despite exhaustion. Even after years among these trees, the Hinterwood could still surprise her.

Gods! she thought, stepping carefully past Dreadfire as he slept. *What beauty... the wonder of your creation never ceases to amaze me...*

Tiny blue mushrooms decorated the moss in the eerie light, each cap pulsing faintly like buried stars. Fireflies stitched themselves through the trunks—slow, lazy constellations drifting above the forest floor. For a whisper of a moment, she thought of waking Dreadfire, of drawing him to this small miracle, but she let him lie. He needed sleep more than wonder tonight.

She padded between the standing pines, laughing very softly, a child again for an instant. The night was cool, and the humidity that had clung to them all day lifted. Somewhere, smoke of incense hung in the air, a dry, resinous note mingling with cedar and pine. It felt like a benediction left by hands that had passed this way not long before them. Sylvia breathed it in and let the small, private joy settle into her chest.

Whatever could that be? she thought, curiously pulling her forward.

A soft blue orb hovered in the gloom, unlike moonlight or the phosphorescent mushrooms, one steady point of light that seemed to breathe. Cautiously, she followed it between trunks, pausing with every step. The Hinterwood wore strangers; it sheltered beasts and old things better left undisturbed.

Through a stand of jackpine, she peered and froze. An old man, bent and white-haired, moved among the saplings. Two baskets hung from his hips on a worn leather belt; a small iron trowel flashed in one hand. He scooped gentle holes, set saplings in the earth, and brushed loose soil around each fragile stem with a tenderness that made Sylvia's throat tighten. After a moment, he stepped on, planting again and again in a patient rhythm.

Could this be Dolvargan himself—one of those firelight tales made flesh—wandering the Hinterwood and raising its trees for all time? The sight fit the stories too well to be a mere coincidence. She opened her mouth to call out, then thought better of it, for even the kindest spirits, she'd been taught, could sour when startled.

As each sapling settled, its stem flushed a living green in the blue light; thin golden threads crawled up from the dark soil and wove through needles like a blessing. The air smelled of sap and something older—incense and loam—and Sylvia stifled a laugh at the impossibility of the scene. It was a sight not even a dream could have arranged better.

The old man paused, trowel halted mid-stroke, and turned. His gaze found hers. For an instant, nothing moved but the breath in her chest. Then a slow, pressing drowsiness slid over her like a tide. Her legs failed first; her vision blurred and rolled inward. She could not say when she fell, only that the world narrowed to a bright blue point, then closed.

"I have only seen the dead sleep so well," Damien said, arms crossed as he loomed over her. "Come, Stormguard, we must delay no longer. With every minute, Betanthia draws nearer to our people."

Neither Rhivothi mushrooms nor any ale could have produced such a debilitating hangover. Sylvia clutched her aching temples and pushed herself up, knees buckling as she crawled to her feet. The fog in her head peeled away as quickly as it had come, and when it cleared, she felt unnervingly alert—brighter than she had in days. The touch of whatever had reached for her in the grove lingered at the edges of her skin like a faint warmth, proof that something not wholly of this world had laid a hand on her.

She shook herself as if to dislodge the last of sleep and busied about gathering her things. Nothing appeared disturbed until she lifted the flap of a saddlebag to check for maps and the small comforts they carried. She stopped short and took an involuntary step back. Nestled in the leather, its root ball wrapped in coarse burlap and bound with twine, was a small pine sapling—fresh green, the needles still soft, soil clinging to the roots.

UDORN IV

"**G**ODS, BE GOOD!" DULKIN ONE-EYE CACKLED, VOICE RAW WITH disbelief. "Can you believe it, Udorn? Can you believe we made it?"

Few among them could. Udorn still tasted the iron of close death on his tongue and felt the aftershock of adrenaline under his skin. Maybe the gods had smiled upon them; maybe it was only the sloppiness of Southern decadence. Either way, they had slipped from a perilous fate without losing a man.

"Give thanks and drink while you can," Udorn said, level and blunt. "We will not be so lucky twice. Fortune runs as deep as a mead mug."

The raiders heard him. Each man knew how near they had come to the headsman's axe; gratitude and relief moved through the band like heat. Udorn glared at the thought of Ragruk in command—no subtlety there. If the lumbering chieftain had led, Udorn thought, they would have already knelt before the axe.

"I would suggest we drink to our victory," Thaul said with a crooked grin, "but alas, we have no mead!"

Provisions had been an afterthought when they fled Dellhaven. They carried what they had grabbed from Lord Drakeford's pantry: a few salted hams, loaves of bread, jars of things that smelled of sweetness and rot in equal measure. It would see them a day or two at most. Still, Betanthia was broad, and the land was full of villages; a place to steal a proper meal would appear soon enough.

They rested but briefly, then rode hard north. As the hours uncoiled, the green of cultivated fields thinned and the signs of human life grew sparse. Udorn's map-sense, usually sharp as a hawk's eye, fuzzed at the edges; the borders of kingdom and county blurred into scrub and track. A dangerous thought snaked up his spine: they might have left civilization behind altogether. If so, the next misstep would not be down an alley but into a trap the like of which no feast or mead could fix.

We must find food and water soon, Udorn thought, though he kept his worry like a folded blade at his side. He would not survive swords and spears only to perish by inches from thirst.

They rode for hours without complaint. No man questioned the heading, but Udorn felt the worry in the set of their shoulders and the way eyes flicked to the horizon. These were strange lands—thin, uncultivated, full of their own small dangers—but a cloudless sky and the sinking western sun gave him a compass he could trust. That was enough to keep morale from snapping; lesser men might have mutinied after what they'd endured.

"Worry not, Udorn!" Dulkin crowed, grin wide and shameless. "The gods would not have carried us through certain death only for us to die of hunger! Our axes will sing soon enough!"

Udorn nearly groaned at the fools' cheer, but if Dulkin's bluster kept men from slipping into despair, it was a tolerable sound. Pride was a stubborn thing to swallow; Udorn had rarely drunk from that cup. Even in Betanthian chains years ago, he had kept his temper and his teeth.

As dusk bleached the sky, faint columns of smoke rose on the far horizon. Dulkin spotted them and waved, abrupt and eager. The band pulled to a halt, breath held. Udorn reached for his weapon before common sense overruled, then relaxed when he saw nothing hostile in the smoke's gray curl. It was the welcome sign of people, not enemies, and for the first time since Dellhaven, the thought of a proper meal felt not just possible but near.

"You must have been praying under your breath," Udorn said, more light than he felt. "The gods have answered. Your eye did the work of two tonight."

A ripple of grunts and low cheers answered him, but the men's composure stayed taut. Relief eased them, not boisterous amusement.

"And not a moment too soon," Gaxas muttered, his face turned sour. "Another hour and I would have made this beast my supper." He slapped his mount's neck and barked a laugh that tried to sound brave.

Udorn felt hunger like a living thing gnawing at his gut. His Ubneri resolve was being tested; long marches and thin rations had turned his stomach into a hollow place that only food could fill. Still, he forced a measured tone.

"We must be cautious. Thaul, ride out and scout ahead. The rest of you, make ready and take cover. We will need every ounce of strength we can muster."

They parceled the last of the rations and settled in the pined shade. Conversation thinned to silence—men conserving energy and appetite alike. Some closed their eyes and drifted off to sleep, others lay back and watched the slow roll of clouds across a clean blue sky.

For a few soft minutes, Udorn let himself drift, thinking of Mot and the family waiting for him. He pictured Guri's face when she heard of Dellhaven, the children wide-eyed at their father's tales. Rennek and his boy Tharek sat nearby, talking in low voices; seeing them whole and breathing felt like salt in a wound—bitter but welcome.

Thaul's sudden return cut the quiet clean. The men were up in an instant, weapons in hand, formations snapping into place.

"What news do you bring?" Udorn asked, eyes sweeping the gloom for any sign of pursuit.

"It is a small settlement," Thaul said, a grin cutting across his face. "Entirely undefended."

Relief moved through the raiders like warm blood. They wasted no breath; men threw their packs together and mounted on instinct. Each knew the rhythm—wait, strike, vanish.

"Are you certain?" Udorn asked, sliding his axe into its loop. "No guards? No patrols?"

"None," Thaul replied. "Simple farmers and hunters. Maybe a spearman or two at most. They will not see us until it is too late."

Udorn raised a finger and circled it once, signaling them to prepare. The anticipation left a dry, bitter tang at the back of his throat; his pulse quickened, and sweat beaded along his palm.

They spread out into a wide crescent, axe-hafts and spearpoints glinting in the waning light. The camp rolled toward the clearing like a living shadow. Through the pines, the thatched roofs and wooden sheds of the settlement showed themselves: low huts, a yard scattered with tools, herds of sheep and goats grazing with the careless calm of the unprepared. Gold might be scarce, but food would be plentiful.

Time thinned as the sun dropped, the world narrowing to breath and step and the soft rustle of underbrush. Only the low, impatient rumble of his stomach broke the quiet. The horse shifted beneath him, eager.

"The beast thinks you're going to devour it instead!" Dulkin smirked.

Hunger could make men savage, but these were Ubneri, bred for discipline as much as rage. Even weary and worn, Udorn and his raiders kept their oath: never break, never yield, never betray the blade. Tonight, they would test that vow on luck and the sweat of farmers' brows.

Udorn hefted his axe, pointed once, and the line surged. Dry pine needles burst up like a cloud as hooves hammered the forest floor—the raiders came through the trees like an avalanche of flesh and iron.

Screams split the air when the line fell on the hamlet. The Ubneri moved with brutal speed; only when they hit the clearing did the silence shatter into a madness of shrieks and battle-calls. A snake-thin grin slid across Udorn's face—combat had him once more.

They butchered with a merciless rhythm. A half-dozen villagers tried to stand, but their tools were no more than ragged promises of defense. They were cut down or thrown aside like stalks in a scythe's path.

Udorn dropped from his mount and took a shield, preferring the steadiness of the ground. An older peasant, nearing fifty, pitchfork in hand, rushed him with a courage that might have been noble in another life. Udorn met the first wild thrust and let the man swing, deflecting and dodging with a practiced economy of motion.

He could have ended the fight in an instant, but there was a strange courtesy in letting the man strike one last time. The old farmer's breath heaved, and when his strength failed, Udorn brought his axe down onto the man's forehead.

Another villager lunged, young, wiry, scythe raised. He sidestepped a flailing overhand strike and answered with a quick, clean blow to the ribs that folded the youth into the dust. The sweep of battle moved on, knives glinting and axes finding their mark, the small settlement breaking like thin ice under the raiders' weight.

The raiders spared neither woman nor child in the frenzy. Dulkin and a handful of men swept through the hovels like wolves, prying open doors, snatching what could be carried, and breaking resistance with a practiced cruelty. Occasional screams flared and died; soon the hamlet settled into the hard silence that follows a storm.

When it was over, bodies lay scattered in the yards and between broken carts, some missing heads or arms, others simply still. The huts stood, their thatch intact in many places. Plunder had been taken, but the settlement itself had not been razed—enough remained to feed a band on the move.

Udorn ignored petty trinkets. He moved instead toward the barn, where the real prize waited: grain sacks, salted hams, and, most importantly, casks of brew. He cracked the lid on a barrel of mead, and the sweet, honeyed scent hit him.

Thank the gods, and not a moment too soon.

Without ceremony, he dipped his lips to the cask and drank. Mead ran down his chin; warmth spread through him like fire under a skin. He scooped a smaller, sealed cask and slung it over his shoulder, a private trophy for the road.

The raiders made no great fanfare that night, but they ate and drank and kept a wary smoke on their fires. Celebration was tempered by sense: Dellhaven's garrison might be searching, or a hunting patrol could have picked up their trail. Udorn's triumph tasted fine on his tongue, but the shadow of retribution lay close. Tonight, they rested; tomorrow, the road would decide which of them lived to boast of the night.

"Tell us true, Udorn," Dulkin said around a mouthful of bread. "Do you know where we are headed, or are we just wandering?"

"And what of Ragruk?" asked Gaxas. "Surely, he celebrates our demise prematurely. Yours especially, Udorn."

Doubt circled them despite the miracle of their escape. Faces that should have been thinking of home were lit instead by the old hunger for glory. What was survival without a story to burn in other men's ears?

"Come now, brothers," he replied. "We have the ocean to our east. That is all the guidance we need. Should we find nothing until we reach Mot, we will get another ship and show that fat pig we have not yet departed for Sjenohor!"

It drew a roar, true enough. Better a boast that steadied a man than silence that ate him from the inside. If a man must die, better that he die in memory than fade to nothing.

"Then we must move at first light," Thaul said. "Ragruk might be wasting good men trying to batter that harbor."

"We know who should have led," Gaxas growled. "That bloated fool nearly sent us to our deaths. Too much drink has rotted his mind."

Some had considered banning the practice of mead-making a generation ago, given the destruction it could wreak on a man's body and soul. It was only through the heroic discipline of Varnak the Ironfather that Mot was saved from itself.

Varnak did not outlaw mead outright, but he hammered Mot with reforms so hard the village still felt the echo. With fanatical priests at his shoulder, he turned drink into ritual: measured rations, fasting before rites, public casks counted and sealed, penalties for those who slipped. Mead became something sacred and watched, not an excuse to drown a man's wits.

Still, the rules were for the common man. The ruling class thumbed their noses, their private cellars and velvet cups forever hidden beyond the reach of the Ironfather's patrols. Ragruk wore decadence like a banner—lavish feasts, braggart shows, a man convinced his weight and wine made him clever.

Udorn had seen men undone by less. Perhaps that was why the chieftain's head had rolled so easily in Udorn's mind: swagger bought with mead was no substitute for sense and skill.

"Drink can make a man fierce or foolish," he observed. "It is wise never to allow such a thing to conquer you."

There was a stretch in Udorn's life when the slow death of mead almost took him. But what soothes the flesh dulls the mind; what is denied strengthens both. It was a lesson hard-learned, for the truth is no gift—it is a burden the weak drop and the strong carry.

"Speaking of drunken fools, who remembers Brannok?" said Herwight, grinning. He was perhaps the shortest raider among them, though no less fierce because of it. Both sides of his head were shaved, and the length of his curly, blonde hair was drawn back with leather bands. A runic tattoo on his left cheek was marred by a deep scar from a decade ago or more.

The name drew a ripple of chuckles. The tale of Brannok was an old favorite; the band never tired of it.

"Allow me!" Dulkin hiccupped, draining another mouthful of Lord Drakeford's wine. He lurched to his feet and cleared his throat, fighting to hold back laughter. "One evening, Farnhald and his men were camped not far from Ravenmarsh."

"Why do you always get to tell the story?" Thaul protested. "You weren't even there!"

"Because I tell it best!" Dulkin shot back. "So, there they were: forty strong, fresh off a raid of some backwater shit heap of a village. Farnhald thinks they're safe and sets up camp in Greyfen Wood. Little does he know, this village was a trade depot under the authority of some local warlord."

Udorn felt the familiar curl of a grin. He watched his sword-brothers light up as they remembered. Brannok—big, brutish, given to sudden, clumsy violence—lived in all their stories as both comic and caution. Some joked the man was dropped on his skull as a babe; others swore he'd been born with a war-ax in hand. Whatever the truth, Brannok's appetite for trouble was legendary.

"So, as evening approaches, the men settle in for the night," Dulkin said, hands carving the air. "Meat and ale are flowing like water, and Brannok does what he always does: damn near drinks himself to death. So, he stumbles to the edge of camp to relieve himself, not knowing the warlord was tipped off to their location and was closing in with a full war party."

Gaxas jabbed Thaul in the ribs; everyone knew the part that was coming.

"Farnhald starts screaming for everyone to gather their arms," Dulkin went on, grin widening. "Brannok picks up his axe and charges straight at the riders with his cock still hanging out, screaming like a madman. He's swinging that axe with everything he has, but he still hasn't emptied himself of all that ale."

Laughter erupted around the fire. Udorn took a swallow of mead and let the sound roll through him.

"Blood and piss are flying everywhere," Dulkin choked out, wiping his eyes. "And as he goes to charge at the warlord, his britches drop to his ankles, and he falls right on his face. By the gods, he landed with all the grace of a fallen tree… his arms splayed out as… he… fell…"

One-Eye folded over, roaring with laughter as if hearing the tale for the first time. Udorn's belly shook with it, but their joy died as quickly as it came. Brannok's story always ended the same, funny, then sharp.

Sadly, as Brannok struggled to rise, the enemy warlord raked a saber down the length of his back. It was a wound not even the fiercest could survive. He died brave and ridiculous both, and now rode in Sjenohor, where every warrior is king.

Silence fell, but it was not sorrow that held them. If anything, the band felt a sour envy. Brannok had won what every Ubneri coveted most: a quick, certain place at the god's table. Better to die with a name than to survive nameless.

"Fear not, kinsmen," Udorn said, voice even. "Each of you will earn your place in Kholdyr's hall. But not before we carve our names into history, and leave our families richer for it!"

"Aye!" came the cry, mugs and horns lifted high.

"To Brannok!" Dulkin bellowed again. "May he look down upon us with the same merriment as when we tell his story."

With somber pride, the Ubneri lifted their horns and drank to their kinsman's memory. The silence that followed was not wholly sorrow; there was a hard edge of envy in their eyes. In their world, to die on the field with a name carved into men's mouths was the only true immortality. If a blundering fool like Brannok could win the gods' favor and find a place in Sjenohor, what then of those who lived on—quiet, old, and forgotten? That thought sat sourly in their stomachs.

It was the old conundrum of Ubneri life and death, and it twisted at Udorn more nights than he would admit. Part of him wanted to see Guri's face again, to watch his children grow stubborn and strong in Mot; to take the small, stubborn comforts of a life lived well. The other part burned with a hunger for a glorious end—the sort of death that carves a man's name into song and stone. He wanted both and knew the gods offered only one without bargaining.

When the revelry thinned, Udorn let himself drink enough to steady the men but not so much that he would be wasted. He slept with one eye half open and woke with a swim in his head and the bite of overindulgence in his gut. Stale bread and a scrap of salted meat made a poor but honest breakfast, and by first light they had packed the barns' grain and the petty silver into their packs.

With Udorn riding point, the raiders threaded through wide stretches of farmland, hedgerows thick as walls and treelines like black teeth. Rows of crops stood months from harvest—a cruel sight for men who'd expected to fill bellies, not wait. Betanthia showed its wealth in the open plains; Mot had never been so generous.

At midday, a scouting party slipped out under a cool fog drifting in from the east. The mist helped hide them, but it also risked sending men wandering blind. With enemies likely on their trail, a stray hour could be the difference between life and a burial ground.

By midafternoon, the sun burned off the murk, slow and sure, and the fields resolved into the familiar shapes of farmsteads and flooded furrows. The land felt known and foreign at once, like a country stripped of its name, and Udorn let himself hope the horizon held good news.

To his surprise, the patrol returned a gallop, horse flanks steaming as they thundered up. Their pace was frantic but not panicked; hope rode with them, though caution still clung to their faces.

"Udorn!" Thaul shouted as he rode up, breath ragged. "There is a river to our west, not far!"

"We made it!" Herwight whooped, grin wide. "Gods be praised. They have use for us yet!"

It could mean only one thing: the Siln River lay close, and with it the chance of boats, trade, and the way east. No more wandering aimlessly—salvation, or as close to it as a band of raiders could hope. The men tightened their grips on reins and weapons alike. Tonight, they would sleep with the river at their backs and a plan on their tongues.

"Take heed of these lands, my brothers," Udorn called, chest puffed with sudden swagger. "We will know these fields well in the years ahead. Now, let us find a ship and reunite with our kin!"

Laughter rolled through the band. It was not the quip that pleased them so much as the thought of rubbing Ragruk's nose in their survival. The fat chieftain had nearly bled them dry with his folly, and their return would be a loud, bloody rebuke.

There was no time for scheming, though. Udorn turned east, and they followed the Siln's snaking bank, the low sun sliding toward the horizon. Dusk would come soon, but the river promised food and boats, everything a hungry raider could want.

Then a smear of gray rose in the eastern sky—thin trails at first, then more, a ribbon of smoke that multiplied. Udorn pulled his mount up short, and the men slid to a halt behind him. The land ahead looked chewed and scarred, as if some calamity had passed through. A treeline crouched not far off, enough to hide the whole company if need be.

"What is it, Udorn?" Udorn answered, nodding toward the trees. "Are there enemies ahead?"

"I am uncertain," he replied, motioning toward the treeline, "but we must find cover and fast. We are not home yet. This place smells of trouble."

They galloped for the ruined woods without question. Stumps

pimpled the clearing—trees cut hard and recent, pale sapwood glaring where trunks had been stripped. Someone had been at work here: shipwrights, perhaps, or men hewing timber for rafts and barges. That meant hope and danger both—if the work was fresh and the crews were nearby.

"You see," Udorn observed, "this could be the means of our salvation. There is activity here. Let us continue on foot, but be ready for battle."

As if any Ubneri needed convincing. Speak of blood and blades and their feet would follow. They secured the horses and slunk north, every eye and ear angled toward the smoke and the ruined timberline ahead.

The palisade rose like a jagged tooth-row from the grass. Udorn dropped to a crouch and crept through tall stalks, straining for a better look. Beyond the fence, men moved: tall, olive-skinned fighters cloaked in rich purple, longbows resting in ready hands. The place looked half-built—an ornate stone structure pushing above the palisade and, beside it, an older mead hall with weathered shingles. Nothing about the compound made sense, but that did not slow the Ubneri bloodlust.

"What schemes are you weaving now?" Thaul whispered as he slid beside Udorn.

"I have seen those cloaks before, during my time in captivity," Udorn said, voice low, the memory sour. "We must take care and strike only when the time is right, or else we risk the ruin of all we have accomplished."

The warning landed like a hand on a shoulder—meant to steady, not to scare. It was a fine thing to remind the men of prudence, but prudence was a thin shield against hunger and pride. Already, the raiders' breaths came sharp with appetite for the kill.

"Then let us strike at nightfall," Thaul suggested. "These soft Southerners will have no idea of what awaits them."

Udorn watched the compound one long breath more and let the plan settle. Night would bring their cover; cunning would do the rest.

"Agreed." Udorn nodded. "Tonight they will sleep soundly in their beds, only to awaken in the afterworld! Come, brothers. Let us eat and make ourselves prepared. We would hate to keep the war god waiting much longer!"

EINARR III

FOR THE FIRST TIME SINCE THE WARBAND'S FORGING, THEY RODE without a chosen leader. Damien had ridden north with Sylvia Stormguard and left a hollow where certainty once stood; here and there, men drifted for home. Desertions came in trickles, not a flood—a handful of men gone, the rest clinging to whatever ember of purpose remained. A scant few true hearts were enough to keep the flame alive, however faint.

Einarr rose before dawn and stood while the light came. He had not taken a quiet moment like this since Skaginlef, not since the world tightened to the single, hard business of marching and fighting. Watching the eastern sky thaw from gray to coal to burnished gold felt almost obscene in its beauty, and holy: a small mercy he accepted with a bowed head.

I hear your voice, oh gods, even in this forsaken land. I know you walk beside me at all times, and in all places.

After a plain breakfast of hard bread and salted pork, he wandered back through the camp. Rumors tracked like flies: whispers of missing scouts, of Blackthorn closing in, and murmurs of men questioning the road. Anxiety passed from tent to tent; he could not blame them. Each man carried defeat's map on his face and the old hurts under his armor.

A border guard stood watch as he passed, where the ground opened to plain. Lances glinted, arrows stacked like waiting teeth. From the small rise, he could see for miles, and the guard's eyes missed nothing. A Nothanek rider gave a stiff nod, that of a man who had kept too many watches; his courtesy was polite, but the warmth had been stripped out by the same cold wind that moved through every tent.

"Take heart, my brothers," Einarr called, voice steady. "Like a snake shedding its skin, we will grow harder and more fierce than before. The gods are not finished with us yet."

A wall of indifference met him—stoic faces and folded arms—but here and there a man's jaw tightened, as if the words had landed where they were needed. Great causes often begin as a single stubborn spark, and Einarr meant to tend it.

The command tent was half undone by the time he reached it. Warchiefs lounged in a protective ring of Rhivothi, axes and spears leaned like a palisade. They spoke in low tones, the murmur of their counsel no louder than the hum of bees. A small table stood at the center, wooden mugs of mead sweating in the morning air, each cup filled for a toast that might be final.

"Good morning to you all," Einarr said, inclining his head. "The gods have granted fair weather today. A small mercy in this land."

"We have larger matters to settle, Rollfson," Valerick the Red replied, folding his arms. "This plan of yours looks ill for us all."

Doubt shadowed every face. Arik Akselson, set to assume command, was not a man of speeches; he brought steadiness where others offered fire. Einarr relied on that steadiness—Arik's cool judgment would hold the remnants of the warband together when courage alone would not suffice.

"Are you sure this is right, Einarr?" Arik asked, brow lifted. "If the Betanthians strike again, what hope do we have? Dreadfire and Stormguard have ridden north, and now you and Valerick leave us to hold the line."

Einarr slapped Arik's shoulder with a friendly, grounding force. "I would not ask it if I did not believe you could do it. You will have Jollkud to keep the men in line. He will return shortly and keep order until I come back." His tone left no room for argument; it was permission and command folded together.

The warchiefs exchanged looks, the weight of choice settling on them like a cloak. Beyond the circle, the camp moved with a weary efficiency—bundles gathered, mounts readied, a people preparing to test whether faith or fate would see them through.

The mention of the Zylmacian warchief did little to boost Arik's confidence. He twisted his face in protest. "You mean, the man who fled when the fighting was fiercest?"

Einarr felt it then; a small, sharp otherness despite all he had done to bind the warband together. He had helped forge these men, yet now, with the costly battle fought without him, a distance had opened. Dreadfire still named him first among equals, but the title felt thin this morning.

Arik's fear was understandable. He was a good fighter—steady, sensible—but command was another weight entirely. To hold other men's lives in one's hands was to wear a burden many could not bear.

"I know why you are afraid," Einarr said, turning on his heel so his cloak fanned the air. His voice was blunt, without flourish. "And you are right to be. Any fool who took this without doubt would be a worse fool for it. That is precisely why it must be you. When Dreadfire returns, you will have kept our people whole. The gods have set this hour before us, and none are exempt."

Arik stared, then scratched the back of his neck as if to reassure himself. "You are right, Einarr," he said at last. "I am not the sort to sing of valor. Still, I will do all I can to steer our folk through this storm. Perhaps the gods pick the least likely to carry their charge."

Truer words had never been spoken, and Einarr felt the reminder settle into him like a good, steadfast stone. He was a humble servant of the gods, one who despised power yet found it laid into his hands again and again. Duty did not flatter; it merely asked for work, and he would answer.

"Indeed, old friend. Indeed." Einarr's voice fell soft. "Time and opportunity grow short. I must be gone. Trust your instincts, Arik. Keep Jollkud close when he returns, and you will have little to fear from the wildmen. Pray to the gods that we are reunited when this is done."

"Have you two finished chattering like women?" Loth grunted, cutting through the calm. He was another monstrous Rhivothi—skin pale as drifted snow, waist-length hair streaming like a white banner. Indigo eyes stared from a face mapped in old scars; his bulk was a living cliff of muscle and battle-hewn stone.

Loth rode under the knotted-circle sigil of Ulfroth, god of the hunt: green and tan cloth trimmed with leather, hemp braids, and carved charms swinging at the staff. A nomad of the deep Hinterwood, he was of a lesser tribe, but a sort so fierce they kept wolves at bay. Einarr had seen few banners so plain and yet so dangerous.

"Patience, brother," Valerick said, voice low. "I pray you know what you are doing, fisherman. This plan of yours could be the ruin of us all."

The doubt gnawed at Einarr, as it had since the first hard morning after returning. What if the North had been meant to fall? What if Betanthia's iron reach would not be stayed, and Caldakas would bend and break beneath its tread? Such thoughts were the dark ones that lived between breaths—unwelcome visitors that tempted a man to despair.

"Perhaps," Einarr admitted, and the word was not hasty. "But I have traveled far and seen more than I dared hope. I have watched gods move in strange ways and men stand when they should not. We are here for a reason. By the grace of the gods, we will see the next day and the day after. I once came near to losing my faith; I will not let that happen again. I must not."

"You Nothanek truly are as pious as they say," Dolsigg of Rej Rhivoth rumbled, voice like a stone rolling. The man was as brutish as any of his kin—bald, scarred, and wearing a heavy black beard that fell in a tangled curtain over his chest.

"Perhaps not enough for our own good," Einarr shot back. "Come, the road before us is long and perilous. We march west to Mor Seveht… the last place to take on supplies before we cross into old Droethia."

Only Valerick had known of their destination beforehand; for most, it would be the farthest from home they had ever gone. The Rhivothi guards around them tightened like a living wall: shields locked, spears lifted, eyes sweeping the tree-line. The camp's laughter and low talk drew to a hush as readiness replaced mirth.

"What treachery is this?" Loth snorted, nostrils flaring. "Does this dog bring a message from his master?"

A lone Zylmacian rider broke from the long grass and cantered into the clearing, shoulders squared beneath a crude, well-worn saddle. Einarr studied him for a long breath, unsure what the wind had carried in. The horse was heavily laden—too much for a simple courier.

"I am here at the behest of my chieftain," the wildman said, bringing his mount to a sudden halt. "I am Hyleth of Vrakult. I have been ordered to serve as your guide."

"Guide?" Dolsigg grunted. "We need no guide, savage. The stars will steer us true enough."

Hyleth said nothing; his face set like carved rock. He was large even for a Zylmacian—broad-shouldered and a head above most—an odd testament to a life spent abroad and a diet not wholly of grass and dung. The horse huffed and stamped, hooves sinking into the baked earth.

"You will, at least, where we are going," Hyleth replied, voice low, nudging his mount with a bootheel. "To reach Mor Seveht, we ride west and cut through the Bymist at the mountains of Shar'halak. There is no easy road."

The line of men stiffened. The map of their plans folded inward as the name of the mountains fell between them. Einarr watched disgust and weary calculation pass over the faces of his men. They had signed up for hardship, but this pushed farther than any had imagined. They would be the first Northmen to press so deep into those ranges.

"You will lead us to our graves, Rollfson," Valerick muttered, shaking his head. "I would sooner die beneath a northern sky, my ashes in the pines, than march into some foreign maw."

"All is as the gods will it," Einarr answered, blunt and steady. "I have seen horrors clearer than your waking fears. Give the gods their praise and hold your spears. Though this road is harsh—though it will test us—Stormguard and Dreadfire have already taken the harder path. Which would you prefer? Fade into memory here, or take the chance to shape what comes after?"

His question hung in the air unanswered, and for a long beat, no man spoke. Doubt nibbled at resolve, but defeat had taught them the price of timidity. If they did nothing, Betanthia's shadow would creep until the Hinterwood itself fell silent.

"You Nothanek are better orators than fighters," Loth finally said, crossing his arms. "I pray your sword arm is as righteous as your mouth."

"Be at peace," Valerick said sharply. "I have fought beside Einarr from the first. Let no man here doubt his skill in battle. He has sent more Betanthians to the underworld than I can count. Bonesplitter trusted him to the end, and so shall I."

Loth gave no reply, only a slow flare of indigo eyes. He drew the hood of a tattered brown cloak up over his head, a pale sentinel shading himself from the sun. It was a cruel thing for such a fair man to travel so far south—the heat did not favor snow—but he sat unmoved.

"And I as well." Dolsigg nodded. "We have traded enough words. Time grows short, and our people are in need. Let us drink to good fortune and the gods' favor."

They raised their cups in turn, each man meeting the other's gaze before drinking. Einarr let the warm, bitter northwoods ale settle in his chest—the taste of home and of what might be lost. Even as the clink of wood cups faded, the vision that had shadowed him across Caldakas tugged at the edge of his mind: the great cat, ever waiting... ever watching...

GARETH III

By midday, the ground trembled under the march, a dull rumble like some great beast awakening beneath the Plainhold. The army had been mustered despite the toll; wounded men were being sent back to Bentmont, the hopeless left to whatever mercy the world would grant. It was a hard, cold calculus, and one that still gnawed at Gareth.

Perhaps it would slow Lord Vakaro long enough to turn the tide against the Northmen. Ridley's schemes had already chewed through more than one plan; to count the Commandant out would be reckless. Gareth knew every slight would demand an answer ten times harsher—ruthless, precise, unavoidable.

From his mount, he watched tens of thousands of Betanthians fan out across the parched plain. Dust rose in wavering sheets, banners snapped in the dry wind, and the eagle of House Bethard flew bright and proud above it all. The sight of his kingdom's standard brought a homesickness that tightened his chest—an ache for a simpler order of days.

Sir Edmund rode up beside him, reading the shadow on Gareth's face like a line of scripture. "What troubles you, lad? Is it Madelyn again?"

Madelyn hovered at the edge of his thoughts as she always did, but she was not the root of this ache. Gareth's worry had a different shape today—less a single name than a weight of consequence, of decisions taken and men counted as necessary losses. He tightened his jaw and watched the plain swallow men and banners alike, feeling insignificant beneath the vast, indifferent sky.

"No." He shook his head, voice low. "She is always on my mind, yes. But it is my mother I miss most. It pains me to know she is gone. Even out here—in this blasted waste—I would be steadier if I knew she was waiting for me at home. I would give anything to ride back through the Citadel's gates and find her smiling at the steps."

"Aye," Edmund said. "Losing a parent is a terrible thing. Natural or not, it feels cruel. I lost mine so long ago, I barely remember their faces. My father was no help in that; bastard that he was."

Gareth could only half-smile. It was one of the small things that bound them: both men too familiar with loss, both too fond of strong drink as a remedy. Edmund's taste for bourbon had corrupted many nights, but there was something in trading poison for truth that felt like unburdening, even if it hurt the liver.

"The fates are cruel," Gareth sighed. "They claim a woman who deserved a long life and allow a man who deserves death to continue. My father squanders his days and shames his family and his people. If I had the power, I would have them trade places in a heartbeat."

The words sounded stranger now that they left his mouth. War had begun to reshape him—some changes welcome, others he did not like. He caught himself and turned his gaze back to the camp. Tents clustered like wounds in the plain; inside many lay the wounded he had ordered left behind. Good men. Loyal men. By his decision, they would be left to the carrion and the elements. The thought sat in his gut like cold iron.

"Instead," Gareth said, voice tight, "I hold power over men whose names I will never learn. I have damned good soldiers to death… men with wives and children and whole lives built on small, stubborn things."

A few caretakers had stayed by choice, binding wounds and whispering prayers as if their hands could barter time. It was a selfish kind of bravery, Gareth thought, selfish because he could not ask every man to do it, yet noble all the same—small lights in a dark work.

"I don't envy you for one second, lad," Sir Edmund said. "That is not a choice to be made lightly. Every man here knows that."

"Truth be told, there's only one man I worry about," Gareth grumbled. "Every time I try to snuff him out, he wriggles free and finds another knife."

"Indeed." Edmund's mouth thinned. "Such is the burden when dealing with men of means. Still, your calling him out bought us breathing room. You confronted Lord Vakaro directly despite my counsel—and we are all the better for it. That will cost him, and it will give us the time we need to find the Northmen and end this."

Edmund's reassurance landed, but did not settle the stones in Gareth's gut. He knew how cunning the Commandant was; the quiet war of influence was as deadly as any pitched battle. No hour would be easy; no night would be wholly safe.

"Still," Gareth admitted, "I have a feeling he will try again, and soon. Do you still have men planted within the army?"

"Aye," Edmund said, pride flickering in his tone. "Quiet blades in quiet places. Their secrecy holds."

"Good," Gareth breathed out. "Keep them near. If another assassin comes, I want it stopped before it reaches me. My place is with the men on the field. That is where I must lead, but that is also where I am most exposed."

"Perhaps not exposed as you fear," Edmund offered. "Lord Vakaro has played the assassin once; he will know we are watchful. If he strikes, it will be in the dead of night or during some ordinary hour when men lower their guard. Expect cunning, lad, never the obvious."

Perhaps it was for the better that Charlotte was dead, Gareth thought, for the Queen surely would have died of worry if she knew half of the danger surrounding him. More likely, she would have taken up the sword herself to spare her eldest son.

A rider barreled into the camp like a wind-lashed messenger, cloak snapping behind him. Dispatches came and went at all hours, but the young man's face carried a thin, frantic edge that raised Garet's hackles. He wheeled his mount over the churned earth, dust trailing in the hot air.

"Your Highness!" the rider gasped, sliding from the saddle. "We took a group of men coming from the west. I was sent to report their capture."

West? Gareth blinked. The Plainhold lay open to the north and east, where the Northmen prowled—who would be moving in from the west?

"Take me to them," he ordered before Sir Edmund could speak. The elder guard gave a quick, tight glance—concern framed in a soldier's discipline—but did not object. Gareth trusted his gut more than the safe counsel of caution.

They rode to a staging ground off the army's main column where a hundred riders idled, mounts stamping and nostrils flaring in the heat. Men clustered in the shade of canvas and wagons, voices low, blades glinting like a waiting tide.

"Spare me your lies!" a lieutenant snarled at the group on the ground, a short, angry man with rage in his voice. He leaned close to a row of seated prisoners, his hand on the hilt of a longsword. "Tell the truth, or I will take your eyes!"

"Enough!" Gareth cut through the noise. Men bowed their heads at his voice like reeds in a gust. "Who are these men?"

Six sat propped on their haunches, wrists bound with rough cord. Their horses and a small cart stood nearby, its contents dusted with the same pale powder that covered the camp. Their skin was olive, their robes bright with hues of indigo and rust and gold—silks out of place among the battered tents. Droethiens, by the look of them: traders or perhaps refugees. Gareth's eyes narrowed. Curiosity and suspicion warred in his chest.

"Could be spies, Your Highness," the lieutenant replied. "We caught them riding straight toward us. Can you imagine it? Why else would they be so bold?"

One of the captives sat unfazed. He met Gareth's stare with a cool, almost easy familiarity—as if two old acquaintances had happened on each other in the dust. The look put the stirred crowd on edge. Gareth swung down from his horse and stepped forward, cloak brushing the churned earth.

"Do you speak our tongue?" he asked, not without a measure of suspicion.

"Yes, nearly as well as my own," the man replied clearly, the words falling with a polished ease that hinted at travel and long acquaintance with many lands.

The lieutenant, hot with anger, kicked the prisoner as if to remind him of his place. "You will call him Your Highness or Prince Gareth, you filth!" he barked.

"That is quite enough," Gareth snapped, his command cutting through the jeers. The man flinched back, and quiet returned for a breath. "Now—who are you, and what are you doing this far from home?"

The captive bowed, hand to his breast in a practiced gesture. "Nikkos, Your Highness." His silks were threadbare at the seams but still spoke of distant markets—faint saffron on the cuff, a spice-smell clinging to the fabric. "We are simple travelers, nothing more. Fate placed our cart in your path this day, yes?"

It was a claim Gareth heard a thousand ways in a battlefield's life— truth, lie, bargaining—but the man's face told little of deceit. There was a steady, ordinary dignity to him that made the veteran lieutenant scowl and the younger soldiers lean in a little closer. Gareth kept his courtesy, if only because a ruler must be one in deed as well as name—Sir Edmund's lesson, worn into him like armor after long years of drills.

"Not all fate ends well," Gareth said, voice flat. "You are lucky you crossed my path and not that of a less merciful lord. We will search you for weapons or contraband. If we find nothing, you may go on your way."

The order drew curious looks, Edmund's most of all. Letting men from a neighbouring realm move freely when talk of spies and assassins hung in the air was a risky grace. Still, Gareth's command was followed. Soldiers emptied saddlebags onto the sun-cracked ground and ran careful fingers along seams and straps; boots were overturned, cloaks upended, belts checked for hidden blades.

Nikkos watched with the same calm confidence. When the last pouch was opened and nothing more than food, wine, and a handful of trinkets clinked out, the lieutenant grunted and shrugged. The captives had no weapons, no suspicious documents—only the small inventory of traveling men.

Nikkos bowed slightly, then smoothed his silks and let his gold and gems chime faintly as he moved. "You have my gratitude, Your Highness," he offered. "Many call your house butchers, yet you have shown us mercy. Proof, perhaps, that rumor is a poor judge."

The words pricked at something Gareth could not name. He had heard a thousand flattering accounts of Marcellus, each polished for court and council. He had also seen the other face of power—decisions made in shadow, favors granted for costlier returns. The truth sat between those versions like a stone: clear, heavy, and cold. He returned Nikkos a guarded nod and turned away, the weight of command settling back onto his shoulders.

To punish a man for speaking a truth he did not know seemed petty, and Gareth let the remark slide. There may be a grain of truth in the foreigner's words, or merely the reflection of a man who had seen too many roads. Either way, the insult demanded no further attention.

"I cannot answer for my father or the men that came before him," Gareth said, even-voiced. "I am not them. I am my own man, and I will answer only for what I choose to answer for. Those who earn my wrath will find no mercy. Now go, and be at peace."

The Droethien cocked his head and smiled in a way that was neither cruel nor courtly, something quieter and sharper.

"You have good vethrath, my friend," Nikkos said, fingers making a little circle in the air. "But your mind, it is always turning. The wheel does not stop."

Gareth's brow arched. "Vethrath? What is this you speak of?"

It seemed like another silly Western superstition, judging by its name. Still, for accosting the man, he was owed a bit of conversation.

"It is the sum of your deeds and your thoughts," the man explained, patient as if teaching a child a new weave. "Your vethrath is strong and good. Yet you have not reached what you might be. You will not find peace while that wheel spins. You must learn to let it rest."

Gareth said nothing immediately; the foreign word hung between them like a small, bright coin. It was easy enough to dismiss—another stranger's superstition—but the idea burrowed at the edge of his thoughts. He watched Nikkos for a long moment, then inclined his head once as if accepting a challenge rather than a prophecy.

"You will never find peace until you can break out of this cycle," the Droethien continued. "Always your mind, going, going, going. You must cease this."

"Easier said than done," Gareth sighed. "You do not bear the weight of a kingdom, nor a family splintering beneath you. You are not fighting a war for your survival."

Nikkos waved his hand dismissively. "These are matters of flesh, not of the spirit. Let those who are ruled by impulse quarrel over slights.

You were made for stillness, not the storms of ego. You must not carry the weight of the dead, for it will slowly suffocate you. And you must empty your heart of those who do not seek to make a home in it."

The words landed with the awkward clarity of a thrown stone. They echoed in Gareth longer than any trumpet-call. He had never hungered for crown or scepter. There had always been a stubborn part of him that longed for smallness: an evening in the Hollow Stone, beer on the breath of companions, a walk under the stars. The throne felt less like a prize and more like a cell with gilded bars. He had already watched power rot men's faces—Lord Vakaro foremost among them—followed by a crawling court of flatterers.

Yet those were easy judgments. The stranger's insight had cut deeper, into places where logic had no path. How could a man plucked from the road know the architecture of Gareth's nights, the precise angles of his anxieties? Something else—something that did not care for councils or lineage—seemed to be at work.

"Release these men," Gareth said suddenly, the command sharper than he intended. The words startled even him; they tasted of mercy and of a ruler trying on a different shape.

"I would advise against it, lad," Sir Edmund snapped, breaking his usual reserve. He stepped forward, eyes narrow with professional worry. "These are men from a foreign realm. They may be our enemies in disguise, or spies who will sell our positions to the highest bidder!"

Although caution would have justified harsher measures, something in Gareth balked at the thought. These men did not feel like a plot; rather, their arrival had lit a curious ember in him. How could a stranger from a distant land know the shape of his nights so precisely? If Nikkos truly carried such insight, Gareth found himself wishing for more of it.

"They might," he said, voice even. "But I do not believe they will. I think this man knew we would cross paths."

Nikkos only gave a faint, almost private smile. The lieutenant grumbled, but under Gareth's order, the soldiers untied the captives, repacked their saddles, and even slipped loaves of bread and skins of wine into their hands before sending them on their way. The kindness sat poorly with many—an unpopular mercy in a hard camp—but Gareth felt the weight of it as a different sort of command.

"This is how a man proves himself, Your Highness," Nikkos said as he mounted, gold and jewels chiming softly. "Not by the banners you fly, but by the dignity you keep when your temper is tested, and the mercy you show when wrath sits close at hand. Remember what we have spoken."

Gareth watched the Droethiens ride east under the rising dust, and the camp's mutters rose like a dry wind. By every metric, these were enemies; history's pages were written in blood on both sides. Still, they were not the Northmen—these riders carried manners and a civility that unsettled him almost as much as it intrigued him.

When the outlanders had passed from sight, the army folded back into its ponderous march. Curious glances followed Gareth, some admiring, some suspicious, but leadership often carried that lonely exposure. Mercy, he had learned, was the heavier thing to shoulder. It marked a ruler more than a soldier.

"This may come back to haunt us," Sir Edmund warned, settling his reins beside Gareth. "They could betray us. The campaign's security is at risk."

"Indeed, it may," Gareth admitted. "But my integrity will not allow it. I am not my father. I cannot sentence men to death for merely crossing my path. If you are to stand with me when the crown comes, you must accept what kind of king I intend to be."

Edmund brushed a sweaty gray lock from his brow. "You have a good heart, lad. No man can deny that. But I have lived long enough to see many hearts bent by power or turned to stone. I admire your idealism, but beware of being so rigid. A king must sometimes bend for the good of his people, not for the comfort of his conscience."

Gareth felt the words, both necessary and unwelcome. Perhaps it was the heat, or perhaps the grinding grief that had hollowed him these past months, but patience was a scarce thing. Rule was a lonely mountain that few could climb.

"I am tired, Edmund," he said finally. "Tired of defending every choice. For once, I need you to stand by me. Counsel me, yes, but I will not be at odds with you every time a difficult decision is made. I cannot be."

The elder Guardsman pursed his lips, then nodded. "Very well then, lad. I merely try to caution you, because these eyes have seen many things. I know you have a good heart and a strong mind. You will have nothing but my unwavering support… until whatever end."

The promise settled between them. It stung that Gareth must harden in ways he had not wished, but silence was no longer an option. For all the darkness he felt pressing in, he would not let it swallow what little light still remained.

"To whatever end," Gareth echoed, staring toward the distant horizon. "And there is no other man I would rather be beside."

ALEKSIUS II

"**B**ACK TO YOUR POSTS, YOU DOGS! OR I WILL HAVE YOU WHIPPED!"
Tasos Calellis cursed as his scourging whip cracked the morning air, the leather singing a harsh, familiar note. It had long been part of the dawn: Tasos' screams and threats, the ritual of chastising men who'd grown lax in a ruined city. Aleksius took a small, private pleasure in that sound. It proved, however faintly, that Droethien spirit still pulsed in the bones of Naxonnos. The men expected the spectacle now and feared Tasos a little less each day—his promises to flay and skewer rarely leaving the realm of noise.

In the end, they obeyed, not only for fear of the lash but out of loyalty to Aleksius. Why any of them kept faith with him after the loss of province and pride was a question he rarely answered aloud. Still, every morning when he stood at the window and watched them move—the sweep of armor, the clank of boots—it stirred something in their leader and in them that compelled duty onward.

They have lost heart, this I can see.

Aleksius and Kyra broke their fast on eggs, leftover bread, and wine; far from sumptuous, but enough. Each morsel on Kyra's plate reminded him of what he'd failed to preserve. Once he had lavished her with gold and finery, but now she ate like any peasant in the rubble. Yet her gaze was steady.

She loved him still. That constancy—her devotion, the children's laughter in the corridors—was one of the few true things left to fight for. Seeing his sons and daughters grow up in a palace of soot and shattered marble felt like penance and purpose at once.

I do not deserve such rich blessings, but I am thankful to have them.

The day sagged under an overcast sky, gray and horribly stifling. A low, hot ceiling of cloud offered no mercy from the summer heat; if anything, it made the air feel heavier. Aleksius had lived his whole life in Naxonnos, yet the climate still wore on him. He longed for a time when his family might flee to kinder lands and spend their last years in peace, an honest dream that, tragically, felt destined to remain only a dream.

Two slaves fanned him with slow, rhythmic strokes while he read the morning dispatches. The reports were a parade of the same failures: troop dispositions along the Vhos, ration shortages despite tight management, a creeping plague in the western quarter, and another supplication to the Senate that would likely return with little more than polite words. If only there were more wine, he thought, then perhaps the day would taste less bitter. But no cask could stitch the city back together.

Sakis and Magia burst into the room, laughter and shouts tearing through the heavy air and breaking Aleksius's brooding. He paused and let himself watch them. Sakis, at eight, had his mother's fair skin and soft brown hair; his eyes were dark and quick. Magia, at six, was Aleksius's twin in miniature—long, tight black curls and a temper to match. Her eyes were an impossible blue, a small mystery in a household of familiar faces. They tumbled about the den, and for a moment, the ruined palace felt less like a tomb and more like a home.

"Give it back! I won!" Magia squealed as she darted around the desk, curls whipping with each turn.

266

"No, I won! You cheated!" Sakis shot back, sticking out a defiant tongue.

"Did not!"

They tussled over a small painted-ivory bird, its wings chipped but still bright with flaked pigment. For a few minutes, the den filled with the honest noise of children—the sort of sound that could make a man forget ash and siege engines.

Aleksius watched them with a smile that softened the hard lines around his mouth. He let them bicker and scuffle, letting the small magic of their play push aside the palace's gloom. When the scuffle tipped toward the earnest sort of wrestling that risked real tears, he rose.

"All right, enough," he said, voice gentle but firm. "Take it to your mother."

"But father—" Sakis protested, before Magia shoved him and both launched for the door.

"Be still, now. Go on and find your mother. I have important work to finish."

They were out in a blink, laughter trailing them like a bright banner. The sound left an ache in Aleksius that was part gratitude, part sorrow. These were the only proofs he had that anything good remained here: their small, stubborn joy. He forced himself back to his desk. Duty waited. Always duty.

Hours slipped by in a blur of parchment and signatures. He read petitions and troop reports until the ink seemed to swim; each reply felt like a bandage on a wound that would not close. When the last dispatch was finally set aside, he poured himself a cup of wine and let the liquid warm his belly. The thin comfort of it steadied his nerves a little, but did not erase the sight beyond the window. Across the Vhos, the enemy stood like a black sea—ranks and banners rippling in the hot air.

Damned Blackthorn. Gods damn them all. Every time I look outside, all I see are their accursed banners.

He stared until the wine had gone stale in his mouth. Then the thought that had been forming at the edge of his mind came cleanly into focus. There were only the Blackthorn standards—no king's sigils, no bright banners of Betanthia flapping in the wind. Not a single royal color to be seen. The absence felt like a new kind of threat: not merely occupation, but a settling, a permanence.

Aleksius felt his chest tighten, a fist of cold worry settling beneath his ribs. The decline in Betanthian numbers along the Vhos had been gradual, but this—this emptying—felt deliberate. He stepped onto the stone balcony and squinted across the river. The field of Blackthorn standards wavered in the heat like a dark tide, and yet the eagle of House Bethard was nowhere to be seen.

A complete absence of royal colors was not the idle happenstance of summer. It smelled of stratagem, the sort he'd learned to dread. Deception had taken Naxonnos once before, and he would not be so blind again.

He clapped his hands, the sound sharp as a whip. A slave hurried in from the corridor, a middle-aged man whose skin hung like old leather and whose shoulders stooped under the discipline of years. He bowed so low that his forehead nearly met the stone floor.

"Summon Tasos—at once," Aleksius ordered, voice tight. He waved the man away, then turned back to the river.

His eyes tracked the sparse patrols, the gaps between them like yawning mouths. A wind lifted his hair and carried with it the tang of smoke and dust; for the first time since the siege, he realized how exposed the palace perch truly was. One arrow, well-placed, and all the fragile order he had left might unravel.

He slipped behind a heavy silk curtain and let the fabric cloak him. From that shaded vantage, he watched as if stalking prey, counting standards, measuring distances, searching for the twitch that would betray intent. The stillness beyond the Vhos felt wrong—too quiet, a pause before the strike.

A knock came at the door, and Tasos stepped in, brows raised as if he'd expected trouble.

"Sire?" the Loxarchon said, scratching at his stubble. "What ails you? You look as if you have seen a ghost."

Aleksius only motioned with two fingers, too unsettled to voice the thought that had taken root. He had stared at House Bethard's eagle for years and could read its absence like a missing line in Kyra's face.

"No eagle," he muttered, mostly to himself. "No blue. No silver. Nothing but the black and gold of the Order."

Tasos leaned forward and squinted toward the river. "Perhaps they have been moved—rotated to another front. They do that, yes? Swap banners to suit a maneuver?"

Aleksius shook his head slowly. "Lesser lords, perhaps, but not like this. Not all of them. And not without leaving something in their place. House Bethard survives on spectacle and fear as much as it survives on the strength of arms."

A long silence passed between the two men. They watched a Blackthorn officer trot by, cool and carefree as a pigeon. To an untrained eye, such confidence would seem like just that. However, Aleksius knew his enemy well enough. The Order was always bellicose, always strutting and taunting. But not today.

"So what does it mean?" Tasos asked.

Aleksius chewed on his lip. He turned from the window and began pacing. "It means... something has changed. But whether it is to our fortune or our doom, I do not yet know. Send word to our scouts and have them ride to Mor Seveht. I want eyes on the northern trade roads. If Betanthia has pulled out of Naxonnos, then they have gone *somewhere*. Surely, someone will have seen the movement of so many soldiers."

Tasos bowed and turned on his heel. "Yes, Sire. I will double the watches tonight and make certain every man is prepared to fight."

Was war only a sunset away? Only the gods knew for certain, and their guidance was spoken in omens and other riddles of nature. For all of his failures, Aleksius knew he could not fail this time. Not if Naxonnos truly stood on the eve of battle. This evening would either be his finest hour or the final nail in the city's coffin.

Hours dragged like wounded beasts. Reports came and went, but none from the scouts. Their findings would be days away at best. Aleksius could not eat, nor could he rest. He lingered in the tower chambers, staring across the Vhos as the afternoon sun faded behind clouds like bruises.

He studied every movement, every detail, analyzing what others might consider mundane: fewer torch patrols. No fresh campfire smoke. No banners rotated. No sign of Betanthian supply caravans. Only the Order. A strange stillness clung to the eastern bank, like the stillness before a scream.

By the time the first stars began to pierce the murk overhead, Aleksius donned his cloak and left his chambers. Flickering gold danced on the stone walls as torchbearers lit the passageways ahead. His footsteps echoed in cold silence. When he reached the outer yard, Tasos was already there, overseeing watch rotations.

"Any word from the scouts along the river?" Aleksius asked, leaning in close.

"Yes, Sire. Their findings are… unremarkable. It is as we saw earlier, Blackthorn, and nothing more."

Aleksius gave a silent nod and gestured for his helmet. One of the guards produced it from a nearby stand; bronze, crested, plain but polished. Aleksius did not wear it often. Tonight, he would.

"Sound no alarm," he said quietly. "But light every brazier along the wall. I want the city to burn bright tonight. If the enemy means to come in shadow, let them see we are watching. I want the signal horns to sound at the slightest provocation."

The two men walked the barricade together, crickets and snapping torchlight their only company. Behind them, the streets were quiet. Most of the people had gone to sleep hungry and unaware that it might be their last night in the city. Aleksius placed a hand on the scorched rampart, its stones and crude planks stained by flame and siege.

"Do you feel it?" he asked. "Something is coming."

Tasos said nothing for a long while. "I feel… absence. Like the moment a hawk flies overhead and all the songbirds forget how to sing."

Aleksius breathed deeply, his tongue recalling the taste of ash and ruin in the air. "Then ready the wall. Whatever comes, Naxonnos will not go quietly. Tonight, our spears will sing."

LUCETTA IV

A NEW DAY CAME AFTER ANOTHER SLEEPLESS NIGHT. LUCETTA SAT AT her desk long before dawn, ruling a queendom that existed only in her head. Building a nation from nothing was tireless work—farms, granaries, trade routes, defenses—each need spun off a dozen questions. She forced herself through them, one stubborn list at a time.

Parchment piled up around her like a small, paper city: maps, ledgers, hastily scrawled orders. Servants left bread and wine on a side table and only knocked once, as if afraid to breathe while she schemed. The silence suited her; it let the plans cohere, if only for a moment.

Draxios's absence gnawed at her. The outlander had taken her ring like a down payment on an army and then vanished as if theft were a clerical error. The jewel on her finger had once meant comfort; now it felt like a ledger entry gone wrong.

I live in a land of imbeciles! How difficult could it be to find an honest man of means in this forsaken hellhole?

Even Pavlos irritated her. The Droethien had once been useful, but now he lingered over wine and women as if ambition were optional. If men like him could grow soft in an age that demanded steel, what hope did she have?

The answer hardened inside her: no one was coming. So she would build what was needed herself. She uncapped her pen and began to write orders that would turn coin into spears and rumor into a muster. Let the world call it sordid — she would call it necessary.

There truly is no one coming to save me. I will have to do the difficult work myself… the dirty, unsavory work meant for dirty and unsavory men.

Despite a fierce will to do what was necessary, the means remained maddeningly elusive. Had Lucetta possessed enough coin, every problem would be solved at a pen stroke. Instead, more money had been spent than earned, and Draxios—fiend that he was—had taken her greatest asset.

House Bethard's treasure sat behind steel and guards at Westwind Citadel; House Eldon's holdings barely paid for the estate's upkeep, wine bills included. There had to be a way to make new wealth, she told herself.

She spent the morning and most of the afternoon rifling through Aldred's things in the master suite. The old miser must have kept trinkets and tucked-away coin somewhere, she thought. Drawers were emptied and cabinets upended; nothing was left unturned. Noon softened into late afternoon, and casually, she drifted down to Aldred's study. The door clicked shut behind her as she turned a skeleton key on the post, closing the world out with a soft, decisive sound.

She worked with the graceless efficiency of a woman who had nothing to lose. Papers flew like startled birds; ledgers were upended, envelopes torn. Beneath a clutter of invoices and brittle receipts, she found a handful of coins and a few small gold things—enough to be worth keeping, if not enough to bankroll a campaign. Each glittering scrap seemed to expand in importance.

In the corner, a tall mirror sat shrouded beneath a white sheet, the fabric oddly reverent. Lucetta tugged the cover free and, for a moment, felt a tiny spike of disappointment: it was an ordinary mirror, plain glass in a plain frame. Strange, she thought, that Aldred—no believer in omens—would bother to hide it. She frowned, set the sheet aside, and returned to her search, the room smelling faintly of ink and old tobacco.

Lucetta breathed through clenched teeth, fighting the hot sting behind her eyes. She had searched every drawer, every seam, every false bottom she could imagine—and found nothing. It felt like another shaft of failure, another proof of her own smallness. In a flash of rage and humiliation, she seized a heavy inkwell and hurled it at the mirror. The glass answered with a sharp, satisfying crack as the inkwell smashed the upper corner to glittering shards.

The crash echoed, but beneath it came a second sound—a cold, metallic clank that stopped her breath. For a moment, she simply stood, pulse hammering in her throat, then crept toward it. Behind the fractured pane, where only plaster and frame should be, was a door of thick gray steel, set into the wall like a secret kept too long.

Heavens! she thought, holding a hand to her gaping mouth.

Fear and excitement warred in her chest. Every nerve screamed to bolt; every plan in her head insisted she stay. Instinct won. She tossed the sheet back over the mirror, scooped up the larger shards, and shoved them into a cupboard as if hiding contraband. She scraped the smaller bits away with the heels of her hands and flicked them into the wastebasket, pacing the floor until the sound of clinking glass was only a memory.

I have to get out of here! I must!

After a moment to steady her face, she turned the skeleton key in the lock, the metal clicking softly. She moved with purpose down the corridor, shoulders squared, footsteps measured—servants glanced up from arranging plates and silver, eyes quick as mice but hands steady. They dared not interfere, for a lady's ire had a way of making the household hold its breath.

Before she reached the courtyard, Pavlos stepped out to meet her.

His usual golden grin was gone; concern had set in the lines of his face like ink staining fine paper.

"Princess," the Droethien said, bowing with an anxious quickness, "your brother is coming. He wishes to speak with you, yes?"

"Trace?" Lucetta frowned, mouth pulled tight. "What on earth does he want with me?"

It struck her as odd that her brother would leave the relative safety of his bank after the riots. Trace and Esma had shoved themselves behind thick walls and steel doors long ago—prudent people, those two—so his sudden appearance at the estate smelled of something other than mere family concern.

"Pavlos overheard the guards speaking, yes? Your brother will be arriving at any moment!"

Before she could weave a plan, Trace entered like a blue-and-gold storm, puffed and pompous in silks that strained politely against his rotund frame. Half a dozen Guardsmen flanked him; his sausage fingers flashed with ring after gaudy ring. A cloud of heavy perfume trailed in his wake—wood and musk—and Lucetta suppressed a sour curl. He was, in every seam and manner, a Bethard through and through: prosperous, cautious, and stubbornly allied to coin before kin.

"Sister," he thundered, clapping until the room seemed to shiver, "we must speak privately." The command sent servants and bodyguards scattering like frightened mice. "Tell your manservant to wait outside."

There was an audacity to him she had rarely seen. Lucetta's suspicion prickled. Whatever had dragged Trace from the stone safety of his vault must be worth more than a family parley.

"Very well," she said, the words clipped and cool. With a deliberate flick of her wrist, she dismissed Pavlos, who gave her one last worried look before retreating.

They climbed the grand stairs in silence. Rather than head to Lucetta's study, Trace veered left toward his private chambers, doors she had rarely crossed since childhood. He fumbled at his silks, produced a key from a leather pouch, and worked the old lock until it sighed open.

The room smelled of neglect and old perfume. Trace set the curtains just so, fetched an ivory stick of incense from an alabaster jar, and lit it with a small iron tinderbox. A thin blue haze curled through the air, bringing musk and bergamot and a note Lucetta couldn't place. For a moment, she allowed herself the small mercy of thinking: at least his taste is not entirely tasteless.

Trace produced a dust-furred bottle from a shelf and poured himself a single cup of wine. He settled into a chair that complained under his weight and sipped without offering her so much as a sniff. In a Bethard house, such an omission was an insult.

"I hear you are quite busy these days," Trace said, his eyes locked on hers. "Your comings and goings are quite numerous, or so I'm told."

"And what makes you think that?" she snorted, arms crossed. "I have never known you for one to delight in rumor, brother."

Something about the conversation felt off—Trace was not his usual placid self. The man who normally wore indifference like armor now radiated an edge, a careful hostility coiled under polite words. He sipped his wine slowly, watching her as if measuring risk.

"It is the curse of being a Bethard," he said finally, voice smooth as silk. "Our lives are never private; every action draws a thousand eyes. But do not mistake me... I do not come to lecture you on ambition, sister. That is yours to bear. I have come about a different matter altogether."

A sudden tightness squeezed her throat.

"As you wish, brother," she said, forcing her voice small.

Trace did not bother with pleasantries. He rose and leaned on the desk, palms flat against the polished, dust-dulled wood. "My time is short, so I will be blunt. After your visit to my bank, a sizable amount of gold and jewels vanished. Of course, you would know nothing of it, would you, dear sister?"

A parade of childhood shame marched through her — the old ache to earn her parents' approval, the memory of her brothers' loftier looks, the small humiliations that had made her desperate to prove herself. Tears welled before she could stop them.

Something else moved in the room. The warm stale air of incense shifted as if a slow hand had swept across it. From beneath Trace's desk came the soft, impossible light she had come to dread and crave: the woman in black, eyes glowing like coals and that thin, uncanny smile. Today, the smile was a blade. It fed the heat rising in Lucetta and fanned it into fury.

"You accuse me of theft?" Lucetta's voice snapped, wolfish and stunned all at once. "How dare you. Do you imagine me so base that I would steal from my own blood? Where would I hide such things? Do you not see me — have you not seen how I have wasted away with worry? After all I have lost, you ask this of me?"

The tears ran hot and shameful down her cheeks, but she kept her shoulders squared. Her fury was a mask over something finer—humiliation, outrage, a brittle pride refusing to be broken. In the tense hush that followed, Trace's eyes flicked to the shadowed corner beneath the desk where the woman in black lingered, and for a heartbeat, Lucetta thought she saw those ember-eyes brighten as if pleased.

"Sister…" Trace said, pinching the bridge of his nose. "I was only asking. You know I keep meticulous records of my clients' investments. You were the only visitor logged that day, and I would be remiss if I did not—"

"Damn you, Trace!" she shrieked. "All I have ever wanted is the approval of my brothers, since Father would never give it. And you question me like I am some common thief? After everything I've done to protect our family and this city—this is the gratitude I get?"

As she spun to go, Trace rose and hobbled after her with a grunt; his knees popping in protest of each step. "Lucetta, wait!"

She paused a beat, then let a faint, hard smile play at her lips, the performance working as she'd hoped. Turning slowly, she folded her arms and met him with cool indifference.

"I know what you did for our family and for Cardale," Trace said, smoothing his silks. "Everyone knows. I do not mean to belittle your service; I am only exercising due diligence. Let us speak no more of it. I have an important meeting I must attend to."

With that, he waddled toward the door, locking it behind him with an exaggerated clack. Bethard men had once again proven how soft their spines were when pressed. Lucetta stamped down the hall to her chamber, slamming the door hard enough to rattle the upper rooms. She stood with her back to it a moment, chest heaving. Guilty as sin though she might be, the sting of being accused was no less maddening.

The encounter left her hollowed out, the blood seeming to drain from her limbs. There was, of course, a remedy for such weakness: wine. She crossed the room with deliberate, slow steps, fingers finding the bottles and glasses as if by muscle memory. One generous measure later, the comforting burn chased the paleness from her cheeks and pushed the edge from her breath.

Anger curdled into something hotter, something close to hate. It was one thing to endure men's incompetence; it was another to be judged by it.

"I hate him," she whispered, hands balling tightly into fists. "He's no better than Gareth, just more of a simpering worm."

"Do not let yourself be troubled, child," the woman in black said, gliding up through the tablecloth's shadow. Her gown hung like a tide of night; long, ink-dark hair spilled over her shoulders and down her back, moving as if caught in its own wind. It hovered on a haze of smoke, eyes aglow like embers. "One brother is as insignificant as the other. But you must be vigilant. They are not your true concern."

The entity's words were the same shape as always—cryptic, clipped, never generous with instruction. Lucetta wanted something plain, a map drawn in charcoal on a tavern table; instead, she received riddles wrapped in silk. Frustration tightened her jaw.

"Speak plainly, I beg you," she said, voice fraying. Tears pricked at the corners of her eyes. "My mind and body are tired. I could sleep a thousand years and still wake hungry. Please… just tell me what to do!"

For a beat, nothing came but the scent of bergamot and ash. Then, contrary to Lucetta's expectation of rebuke, the woman in black drifted toward the door and extended a single hand. Its skin was cool and coarse, like weathered leather, and the nails were neat as if manicured by moonlight itself.

Apprehension and a sense of need warred in her chest. Lucetta hesitated only a moment before taking that chill hand. The touch sent a shiver through her, and for an instant the room narrowed to the point where their palms met and the rest of the world fell away.

"There are many paths that lead in many directions," the entity said, "And along those paths stand many people. Some will steer you true; others will lead you astray. One such person is downstairs as we speak. He is with your brother at this very moment."

A flutter of anxiety stirred in Lucetta's stomach. Perhaps this meeting would mark a turning point, a long-awaited step toward the prosperous future she craved. She followed with wary steps, yet the entity's path veered not toward the stairs.

"W…where are you taking me?" she whispered, tugging faintly at the cold hand.

The woman in black's grip did not yield. Lucetta flinched as the figure glided through a solid wall, dragging her along as if through a sheet of water. Fear paralyzed her as brick and timber swam into view, then melted away, leaving a forgotten crawlspace beyond. Dust thickened the narrow air, cobwebs trailing like torn banners.

Onward they sank, slipping through the ceiling until they stood in the parlor. Servants moved about their chores, oblivious to the terror in their midst. Lucetta shuddered at the thought of being seen—then stared in horror as her own flesh grew pale and translucent, her body nothing but mist and outline.

Dear heavens... what is happening to me?!

"The more you witness, Lucetta Bethard, the more you doubt," hissed the woman in black. "Put aside your childish fears. See the world as it truly is. Come. Your brother is with his guest."

Together they drifted down the hall, sliding through a servant girl's frame. The girl shivered violently, head snapping about to find no one there. Lucetta nearly gasped, only to realize she had not drawn breath at all. Before she could reckon with that horror, the pair slipped through the heavy door of Aldred's study.

It was curious that Trace had chosen this room, though it was indeed the most secure in the estate. To Lucetta's surprise, Sir Tristan Conway of the King's council sat opposite her brother, looking far too at ease in Aldred's chair.

What in the world is he doing here? What business could he possibly have with my brother?

Her fingers clutched tighter around the woman in black's cold, lifeless hand as both men raised chalices in toast.

"I do apologize for the delay," Trace said, dabbing his mouth with the back of his finger. "My sister has grown quite the burden of late."

"So I have heard," Sir Tristan murmured, sympathy tinged with scorn. "Grumblings reach the palace often enough. It seems her marriage is as unstable as our fine city."

Trace dragged a weary hand down his face. "Whatever you've heard is but a fraction. Even before our mother passed, her mind had begun to fray. Afterward... well, it has thoroughly collapsed."

Their words stung, yet Lucetta felt nothing. No anger, no sorrow, not even shame. The hollow weight of flesh had slipped away, leaving her spirit strangely detached.

"Indeed." Sir Tristan swirled his wine with lazy disdain. "And her theatrics during the riots—unfathomable. Do not mistake me, Trace, I admire her courage. But a Bethard princess in the thick of such carnage? Unthinkable. A scandal that refuses to quiet!"

"And still, the madness goes on," Trace sighed. "But enough of my sister. Let us go to the heart of it—what is the Citadel's plan for Cardale's reconstruction?"

The woman in black turned with a sneer, as if she had known of this meeting long before. For all the wonders and horrors the entity had shown, Lucetta still found belief hard to muster.

"To be frank, the crown cares little for rebuilding." Sir Tristan gave a dismissive shrug. "Aldred is far more concerned with security, with keeping tensions from rising again. With the war draining our coffers, the Kingdom cannot risk another such upheaval. Peace must be held at any cost."

"I see." Trace tried to hide a devilish smile behind the rim of his chalice. "You require resources, and I have them in plenty. If the Council granted me its blessing... and a free hand... I could aid the city's reconstruction. Of course, there would be... changes to the districts in question. We would not want them overrun with the destitute once more, would we?"

They shared a chuckle and poured themselves fresh wine. To Lucetta, it was difficult to fathom—gentle, pliant Trace cloaked in such corruption beneath his soft, doughy frame. Perhaps he had been misjudged after all. Accustomed as she was to men of brute savagery, it struck her strange that her brother wielded cruelty of a quieter, shrewder kind.

"There is another matter to resolve before you depart," Trace said at last, the merriment fading from his voice. "I must decide what to do with my meddlesome sister. I cannot be burdened by her if I am to serve as Cardale's benefactor."

"Indeed." Sir Tristan nodded gravely. "I have heard Aldred lament often of his wife's instability. And that reckless display during the riots… none of us can make sense of it."

Trace groaned and wiped his brow. "Do not remind me. Her foolish antics endangered our entire House. Can you imagine it? A Bethard princess charging into battle like some… some low-born armsman?"

Lucetta squeezed the woman in black's hand, fire coiling in her chest. For the briefest heartbeat, even the entity seemed troubled, wary of the fury kindling in her half-formed shape. The urge to let go and confront them burned hot—but another voice within urged caution. This was only the surface of a deeper plot, one that might involve more than these two men behind closed doors.

"Her emasculation of Aldred seems only to worsen," Tristan said with a sly grin. "Perhaps it will open the way for change within the Council."

"Far be it from me to sabotage family," Trace muttered, heaving himself toward the door. "But I suspect change is coming regardless. In the meantime, keep your ear low and remain in the shadows. In time, the Council may yet find itself under… firmer hands."

The young councilman lifted his glass in salute and drained the last of his wine. As he turned to depart, Trace cleared his throat and lifted a ring-studded finger.

"Sir Tristan! One final thing. My sister—have her followed. I want to know what mischief she pursues."

"Easier done than said," Tristan replied, smiling. "One might even say… such a thing is already in motion. But now I must bid you good day. Other matters await." He bowed and left.

Trace smiled after him, toasting the empty air before draining his cup. Were she in flesh, Lucetta would have seized his flabby throat and squeezed until her palms met. But before rage could claim her, he waddled into the hall and locked the door behind him.

Never would anyone have suspected gentle, aloof Trace of such schemes. Yet in that moment, he had shown himself the most ruthless Bethard of them all. The revelation left Lucetta reeling, bafflement a rare affliction for her. She drifted about the room, pacing, though her feet no longer touched the ground.

Just as House Bethard had underestimated her, she too had underestimated Trace. If such a harmless man could weave deceit, who was to say Gareth might not do the same? Panic surged, each thought feeding the next until her mind swarmed with terrors. Her gaze snapped back to the fractured mirror—and to the hidden door beyond it.

"Come now, child," the woman in black hissed. "Return to your study. You have seen all that is necessary."

"Wait." Lucetta's voice was thin as paper. "I must know what lies beyond that door. Please… show me."

The entity studied her, ember eyes flaring in silent judgment. "Very well. But you will never be the same after what you will witness. Do you find this an acceptable trade—knowledge for misery?"

The cryptic warning gave her pause, but desire outweighed caution. With a single, fearful nod, she agreed. The woman in black seemed almost sorrowful, as though already mourning the wound about to be dealt. Yet it gripped her hand once more and pulled her through the mirror and the iron door.

Darkness pressed close, thick with a stench of mildew. With her free hand extended, the entity conjured a spark—first a fragile ember, then a swelling flame that blossomed into a bright, golden orb. Its glow struck Lucetta's eyes like daggers. She gasped, for before her rose a hidden vault: shelves stacked high from floor to ceiling with gems, coins, and ingots of precious metal.

It was wealth enough to buy an army—perhaps even a kingdom.

Aldred had been hoarding treasure for years, all while crying poverty and tightening household coffers. Likely, he had used this fortune to purchase influence and favors, the coin that had bought him a seat at the King's side. His rise among Betanthia's elite, it seemed, had been paid for in gold, not earned in merit.

Such betrayal cut deeper than a Zylmacian axe. Years wasted in penny-pinching austerity, when all the while she might have lived as a princess should. Surely this was only the surface of a rot that ran deeper. And now, with Trace's schemes laid bare, it was clearer than ever how diseased House Bethard had become.

They are all liars… they are all deceivers… each with their own agenda. How could I have been so naive? How could I ever have been so trusting of their intentions?

"Enough of this," the woman in black said. "You must focus your attention elsewhere."

With a blink, Lucetta was back in her study, as though she had never moved. Yet the musty scent clinging to her silks proved it was no dream. As her mind reeled to catch hold of what had just transpired, she remembered: Sir Tristan was still in Cardale, walking its streets, plotting the next step of his conspiracy.

Urgency surged through her. She threw open the door and swept down the stairs, skirts threatening to tangle her stride. At the bottom, she gathered her dress with quick hands, smoothed her expression, and strode calmly past the dining room into the grand hall. Pavlos lingered in a side parlor with a tankard of ale, which he emptied in two great gulps when he saw her.

"Ah, princess!" the Droethien said, smiling. "I have been meaning to—"

"Shut up," Lucetta snapped, keeping her voice low. "It's Sir Tristan. He was meeting with my brother just moments ago. I have to know where that cretin is heading and who he is conspiring with."

Pavlos blinked at her sharpness, his grin fading to a frown. "Princess, this is most irregular. Pavlos has heard nothing of any… conspiracy. Perhaps instead we should focus on Draxios. Surely he must be returning any—"

"Gods damn you!" she hissed, teeth locked like castle gates. "Remind me again why I pay you. Was it for your counsel, or to obey my command? No wonder your people scrape their lives from the sand."

Like a winter sunset, Pavlos' golden grin faded. Violence flickered in his eyes, enough to chill her heart. She knew too well what this man was capable of. He had cut down Sir Bryce Whitewood and even the Queen without a whisper of suspicion. What would stop him from ending yet another noble life?

"Perhaps the princess is tired, yes?" Pavlos grunted, his expression soured.

"Do forgive me," Lucetta said quickly, masking her fear. "My nerves are frayed by worry. I fear my brother and his accomplices have discovered us. If we do not act quickly, we will likely be clapped in irons and headed to the gallows!"

The grim warning cooled his anger but did not sway his caution. "The city is still dangerous, princess. We must bring your bodyguard. Pavlos can only fight so many men at once, yes?"

"Very well," she relented. "But we must hurry before he gets away!"

They crossed the foyer and stepped into the courtyard. Lanterns flared along the avenues, evening settling fast over Cardale. Doors shut, voices dwindled; the city withdrew into itself. Time was thinning before Sir Tristan reached his destination.

"I am sorry, my princess," said a middle-aged officer, voice firm. "I cannot in good conscience allow you to roam without a proper escort. The city remains on edge, and the guilty still haunt the streets."

"Ever diligent in your duties, Captain," Lucetta replied with scorn.

"Gather your men, but keep your distance. I have sensitive matters I wish to discuss with my… associate."

A troop of eight purple cloaks gathered and trailed Lucetta into the dusky streets. They were few, but their ferocity was worth ten times their number. Polished breastplates and razor-tipped spears kept onlookers at bay.

Yet even these hardened men seemed uneasy in her presence. When Lucetta glanced back, she caught their whispers and sidelong stares. Let them fear her—fear was a leash strong enough to bind even the most violent beasts.

With Pavlos at the fore, they wound through empty avenues and narrow alleys. Rubble and refuse littered the cobbles, some charred black, others still stained red from those grim days of riot. A pair of vagrants scattered like rats at the sight of Pavlos, his golden grin and clenched hand on his arming sword enough to send them running.

Time dragged on with no sign of Sir Tristan. Surely he would avoid the main avenues, for conspirators scurried like cockroaches, preferring shadows to the open street. So far, his tactics had worked.

"Perhaps he has gone this way, princess," Pavlos said, pointing to the west. "He would not have turned that way; the neighborhoods are too dangerous, yes?"

Deflated, Lucetta nodded, pressing on down a dim-lit lane. They quickened their pace, but Tristan remained unseen. Somehow the councilman had slipped them—or perhaps her champion had blundered.

"Curses!" she spat, throwing her arms wide. "Now we might never discover who that cretin consorts with!"

"Worry not, princess," the Droethien said with a grin. "Pavlos will find him and reveal his deepest secrets, yes?"

But Lucetta felt no comfort. Not even the woman in black could persuade her of fortune's favor now. Luck seemed as fleeting as a stray cat, and aging as poorly as raw meat. She turned away in disgust, her gaze falling on the Guardsmen shadowing her steps.

They were watching, taking note of all. Their loyalty was coin, not kin. If not for her ties in the north, she would have preferred the White Spear at her side—those men would have walled her in so tightly that not even Northmen could break through.

Her thought was cut short when one Guardsman crumpled onto the cobbles. The dim light masked the cause, and she sighed, ready to lash out at such clumsiness, when two more toppled like sacks of stone, armor clattering across the street.

Shadows erupted with life. A swarm of men poured forth, robed in filth, armed with bows, crossbows, and truncheons. Lucetta gasped, breath stolen from her lungs. Pavlos's sword sang free in a single motion, steel flashing as he shoved her behind him. The surviving Guardsmen scrambled to form ranks, but their resolve faltered beneath the audacity of the ambush.

"Stand down!" a thunderous voice bellowed down the empty street. "Drop your weapons, I say!"

Pavlos only grinned, twirling his blade with one hand while shielding Lucetta with the other. Warrior composure clung to him even in the face of certain death. His Betanthian counterparts wavered, but though their spirits shook, still they refused to cast aside their arms.

"You *will* die here like dogs," the voice rasped as the speaker stepped from the dark. "Drop your arms, and your lives may be spared. Do not, and—"

"Do you fools not realize who you challenge?" Lucetta shrieked, much to Pavlos' horror. "I am your princess! I am…"

The words ripped from her before she could contain them. In that instant, she knew she had made a terrible mistake. Those robes—she had seen them at the Temple of the Dawn, on the day fanatics had nearly seized her mother's body. The Harbingers had not been cleansed after all.

"We know who you are, Princess Lucetta."

The man drew nearer and dropped his hood. His face was a rough map of burns and scars, raw and pink at the edges. A linen bandage wrapped his forearm from elbow to wrist, dark with old blood.

"Then you must know what I have done to those who opposed me," she snapped. "If you will not let me pass, the same fate awaits you."

She prayed, privately and desperately, for the woman in black to manifest as she had before—to rend the fanatics by spirit or by miracle. Whether such wrath belonged to the living world or only to her fractured sight mattered little; Lucetta had come to rely on that impossible defense.

"Princess," Pavlos whispered, "you must be silent now, yes? There are too many."

A sour chuckle cut the night. Unmoved by her threats, the leader strolled closer, his men pressing behind him like a living hedge.

"You are not in a position to make demands," he said flatly, urging his followers forward. "Either your guards stand down, or we will water these streets with their blood."

As more ragged men revealed themselves, Lucetta's bravado bled away. Even Pavlos—formidable as he was—could not hold a path against dozens. The solution was bitter and immediate.

"Lower your weapons," she said at last, her voice thin as fog.

The strange man smiled, his teeth the color of rotten meat. "You have made a wise decision, princess. Now, if you will, come with me. Hesgrin would like a word."

Lucetta nearly fainted as fear surged through her. That vile fanatic had survived not only the burning of Cardale but the purge that followed. As his followers closed in, she could not stop her mind from conjuring the horrors that awaited her in the grip of such a deranged man.

"I will not let them take us alive," Pavlos growled, twirling his sword with a predator's ease, ready to strike.

"Be still," she said sharply, catching his arm. "If we resist, they will cut us down where we stand. We cannot die in the streets like dogs. There are greater works yet to complete."

Reluctantly, Pavlos let the steel fall from his hand and lifted both arms in surrender. The fanatics pounced, binding him in irons alongside the Guardsmen with brutal efficiency. Lucetta swallowed hard as her captor loomed closer, a black hood clenched in his scarred fist. When the coarse cloth descended, she felt hot tears streak her cheeks. Darkness swallowed her whole—her most dreaded prison, a place where even her voice could not follow.

MADELYN IV

S HE RODE FOR DAYS BENEATH A SEARING SUN, THE HORIZON shimmering like molten glass. The trail had long since gone cold. More than once, Madelyn tried to double back, to recover her bearings, but each attempt only deepened her frustration. The Plainhold offered no guidance, only a vast sameness that swallowed all direction. Hour by hour, the desert drank away her water, until her mouth felt as dry and brittle as the earth beneath her horse's hooves.

"Where am I?!" she cried, the sound cracking against the endless sky. No tears came, for her body had none left to spare.

Her mount fared little better. The beast's flanks heaved with labored breath, its once-proud stride now a weary shuffle. Every step felt like it might be the last. The sight carved into her heart, for she had leaned on the animal as her one companion in this forsaken land. With dusk descending, it seemed both rider and steed might soon share a final sunset.

Death lurked in every fold of the land—behind each rolling hill, in every dry blade of grass, beneath the shadow of every twisted tree. It coiled around her like a serpent waiting to strike. Yet as exhaustion weighed down her limbs, her fear of death dulled. Numbness crept in where terror once lived.

290

At last, delirious and near collapse, she sought shelter among a cluster of towering rocks. They rose like the tombstones of forgotten giants, offering her a place to crouch against the wind. She cobbled together a pitiful camp from what little she carried, no fire, no comfort, just a semblance of safety in a world that had none to give.

From her saddlebag, she drew the pilfered scrolls. They had been her one prize from the Ivornorium's secret cave, but here in the open waste their power had guttered out. Whatever strange force had clung to them, it withered the farther she traveled from that hidden place.

Perhaps removing them had been folly, she thought grimly. The Plainhold devoured all things in time, and these fragile relics would be no exception. Already the parchment showed signs of decay—cracks spreading like spiderwebs across the face of a scroll that peeked from the bag's mouth. She ran her fingers gently over the brittle surface, mourning its fragility. It was another cruel reminder that her good intentions seemed to end only in ruin.

"Is this what my life has become?" Madelyn whispered, her fingers tracing the fractured lines of the scroll. "Is everything I touch doomed to die?"

No—it could not be so. How could it? She had lived her life with a clean conscience, always putting others before herself. She had chosen the harder path, again and again, when compromise would have been easier. If the gods truly watched, there must be a purpose in such suffering, a noble thread woven through her pain. Men like Damien Dreadfire were the very opposite of good—corrupt, cruel, and merciless.

"I am nothing like him," she said, lifting her eyes toward the barren heavens. "And yet that villain still poisons the earth, still murders Betanthians without consequence, while I… I wander this wasteland aimlessly. As though this place was meant to be my grave."

The thought curdled in her stomach, sickening as stagnant water. She forced herself to push it aside. There had to be an answer—she would accept nothing less. If light and prayer had failed, then she would seek truth in the darkness, fool's errand though it seemed. It was the only path left to glimpse what the fates had in store.

She gathered the scroll in both hands as though it were a fragile child, then settled cross-legged on the hard stone. Closing her eyes, she drew her breath long and deliberate, each one rocking through her chest like a ship at port.

The sensation came swiftly, a sickly current coursing through her veins. It soured her tongue, knotted her gut, and crawled across her skin until every nerve recoiled. Even a Zylmacian might gag on such bitterness. Yet she endured it, even welcomed it. Strange as it was, the corruption no longer felt wholly foreign.

Though her eyes remained shut, she sensed a darkness building behind them—a tar-like film spreading across her pupils, seeping outward until her entire skull throbbed with alien force. The Plainhold, the horse, the world itself seemed to slip away. Whether it was sleep or something deeper, she fell into a state that was neither dream nor waking—a trance that bound her spirit to what lay beyond.

When she awoke, there was only nothingness. A vast, endless void stretched from horizon to horizon, blacker than midnight seas. For a breathless instant, she thought her eyes were still closed—that she remained adrift in a dream. But then the weight came. A crushing pressure bore down from every side, squeezing her chest, her limbs, even the marrow in her bones.

She fought against it, straining as though the air itself were iron. At last, she forced herself upright, though her legs felt shackled with siege stones, every step an act of rebellion against the void.

Then came a flicker—white smoke curling thin as a thread, followed by a dull pulse of orange light. Shapes stirred on the empty skyline, shadowy manifestations twisting the blank canvas into something both real and unreal. The distance to them yawned wide, infinite, as if the horizon itself mocked her.

Madelyn pressed forward. Each step tore at her muscles, but strangely, with each movement, the heaviness began to ease. The void seemed less intent on crushing her, as though it yielded bit by bit to her will. Perhaps she had grown stronger since her last encounter with the Fate Realm... or perhaps it was not strength at all, but surrender. The abyss itself might have been drawing her deeper, guiding her step by step into its heart.

As she pressed onward, the mist thickened and churned, swirling into a veil so dense it swallowed even her breath. Memory stirred at the edges of her mind—hazy, fragile recollections of her first time in this cursed place. Only when faint outlines of stone tables took shape in the fog did she anchor herself, regaining the smallest sliver of perspective.

Yes... This is it. The pieces on the table... I remember now...

No mortal had ever walked such ground, and perhaps none ever would again. Even the gods seemed far removed from this realm; no starlight pierced the void, no divine warmth reached its cold expanse. Motionless effigies sat upon the slabs, carved of dark stone into poses deliberate and solemn. Each one told a story, a memory of things long passed, etched into the silence like scars.

Madelyn drew on her will and surged forward, determined to reach the impressions of what was yet to come. But before she could, the path itself betrayed her. The road split open. A single narrow way fractured into six, branching like the limbs of a blackened tree. Each path was swallowed in mist, darker than a moonless night. She froze at the threshold, her spirit arrested by uncertainty.

Beside her stood another table, this one etched with effigies of Blackthorn knights—stone soldiers locked in a frozen charge against the barbarian horde.

The gods are giving me a choice, she realized, the thought reverberating like thunder inside her. *But which path do I take?*

As she edged closer, her eyes caught a new detail. Along each shadowed avenue hovered dim orange orbs, soft lights that flickered and strained against the suffocating dark. They were fragile, forever assailed by the surrounding gloom, yet none extinguished. For all their weakness, they endured.

A subtle motion stirred at the edge of her vision. Madelyn froze, then slid into cover behind a stone table, her body as rigid as the carved effigies beside her. Out of the mist drifted a figure. It emerged from one path, then slipped into another, moving with a strange, deliberate rhythm. The frame was frail and hunched—an elderly woman draped in a flowing gown of tattered gray linen. A long train dragged behind her, churning up swirls of mist with every step.

Madelyn's chest tightened. The figure was not bound by the Fate Realm's forward pull. It wandered freely, at will. Such command of the abyss could only belong to something powerful, perhaps something terrible. Like a stalking cat, Madelyn crept on, careful to keep her distance. Each step felt like blasphemy in this silent place, but her hunger for answers pressed her forward.

The crone moved with eerie calm, unbothered by the suffocating weight of the void. Where Madelyn strained under its pressure, the old woman seemed to wear it like a familiar cloak. Pain flared in Madelyn's skull, a pulsing ache that made her grit her teeth, yet she dared not falter.

At another table, the old woman came to a halt. With one gnarled hand, she extended a crooked finger, gliding it across the stone effigies as though choosing between them. Her glassy eyes darted, twitching from one to the next with unsettling speed.

Then, without warning, she stopped. Her head lifted. Blind-seeming eyes rolled and narrowed, searching for something unseen. Instead of finding, she inhaled sharply, sniffing at the air like a beast on a trail. A smile cracked across her ruined face, exposing teeth blackened and broken with rot.

"I smell you…" The raspy hiss echoed from everywhere at once, filling the void. "The powers you meddle with are far beyond your comprehension, girl."

Panic seized Madelyn. She tried to sever her tether to the Fate Realm, to wrench herself free, but found herself bound fast, as though an unseen hand clenched her in its fist. The old woman turned, toddling forward with dreadful slowness. Mist scattered at her approach, rolling away from her broken frame. In the glow of the hovering orbs, Madelyn saw her clearly—and her heart froze. Lazilyth.

"So… it is you," the crone snarled, her decrepit features twisting into fury. "You, who dare intrude upon this sacred place. You, who tore the fabric of fate itself! Tell me, child… tell me how you bent the course of the future!"

Madelyn's body screamed with heaviness, but desperation lent her wings. She broke into a frantic sprint, legs dragging as if weighed with iron. Stone tables flashed past her—effigies of long-past wars and triumphs ignored in her terror. She dared not look; to linger even a moment might mean her undoing.

Behind her, the crone followed. Though slowed by the same oppressive weight, Lazilyth's presence clung like smoke, choking and relentless. Madelyn glanced over her shoulder, daring hope that she had slipped free, only to see the hag still advancing, faster now, gliding upon a swelling cloud of ash and gray vapor.

Lazilyth's ruined face stretched into a terrible smile, both arms extended in a parody of welcome, as though to draw Madelyn into an embrace that would never end. The path ahead stretched dim and narrow, the only route left to her. No escape but forward.

"Come to me, child!" the crone shrieked, her voice cutting through the mist like a winter gale. "You cannot resist… you cannot flee! The knowledge you hoard will be mine. I will rend the fabric of time and stitch it anew, by my hand alone!"

Madelyn's chest heaved. With no other choice, she turned from the narrow path and cast herself into the black. It yawned on either side, an eternal void where no light flickered and no sound was born, a crushing darkness heavy as the sea's deepest trench. She knew her spirit would be seized if she hesitated, so she plunged into the unknown.

Agony struck her instantly. Her skull felt crushed beneath the weight of a falling castle. Her eardrums popped and bled. Her eyes throbbed as if ready to burst. Each bone within her body crunched and splintered like autumn leaves trampled underfoot, her blood thickening until it crawled through her veins like tar. Every step became torment, each movement heavier, slower—until she could bear no more.

Ancestors… please… forgive me. Save… me…

She collapsed, chest striking hard against unseen ground. Her lungs flattened, refusing breath. Each gasp came up empty, each attempt at life smothered by the void. Death's shadow loomed closer with every heartbeat. Her eyes drifted shut—perhaps for the last time—when the blackness stirred. A ripple ran through the void, widening, approaching. Its outline suggested a mortal form, but the haze made certainty impossible.

Just as her strength gave way, arms strong and sure gathered her up. They wrapped around her with fierce resolve, holding her as though she were weightless. Fear clawed at her, yet something within the embrace felt achingly familiar. Faint rays of golden light broke through the void, spilling like dawn across the abyss. They shone as beautiful as a Cardale sunrise—then faded, leaving only memory behind.

Then suddenly, warmth brushed her face—a kiss of summer sunlight. Madelyn winced, recoiling, raising her hands to shield against the unseen blaze. When she dared open her eyes, the vision had vanished.

Only the still, barren Plainhold stretched before her. The scattered rocks of her camp surrounded her as though she had never moved at all. Perhaps it had been nothing but a nightmare, a fever-dream spun from exhaustion.

A faint crunch of dry grass broke the silence. Madelyn stiffened, her hand twitching toward her weapons, but her body refused to move. Just a few paces away, the air itself rippled. A human-shaped outline shimmered with pulsing energy, its edges wavering like heat rising from stone. She could see through it, yet the world beyond bent and warped, distorted by its presence.

Her breath caught. Could this be the presence that had torn her from Lazilyth's clutches? The one who had lifted her when all else failed?

"Who… who are you?" she stammered, dragging herself backward across the dust.

The spirit gave no answer. It only regarded her with an eyeless gaze, its silence heavier than words. Then it came—a sudden wash of emotion, sadness so deep it pressed on her chest, disappointment as sharp as a lash. Madelyn trembled. She knew. Or at least she understood what it must be. An ancestor. One she had already met.

"Oh gods…" she gasped, realization shaking her voice. "It's you… from the Ivornorium… my blood… my family. You saved me. But why?"

The figure quivered, as if agitation rippled through its form. It stepped forward, and though half-translucent, its energy weighed enough to flatten the brittle grass beneath its feet. Madelyn recoiled like a scolded child, hands raised, wincing in fear of judgment. But the spirit did not strike. It stood still as stone, its silence more condemning than any blow.

Tears welled and spilled down Madelyn's face. The ache in her chest was not the sting of wounds but the deeper wound of disgrace—the same judgment the High Marshal would hand out: never a broken bone, but a disappointment that cleaved cleaner than any axe.

"I'm sorry!" she cried. "I did what I thought was right. You saw what those monsters did to me—how they butchered the innocent—and yet they walk free. Why must I be the one punished? Am I not owed my honor?"

The ancestor said nothing; its answer came in a single, devastating motion as it turned away. In that motion, Madelyn felt the verdict settle in her bones: retribution belonged to powers higher than her. It was not for her to wield the gods' justice. She had been placed here, the spirit implied, to serve some colder design. The wicked would suffer in time, but not by her hand.

As the apparition thinned and drifted into the heat-haze, a hard, bleak sorrow gripped her. This was not the path she had hoped for. No ancestor had stepped forward to champion her cause. They watched, aloof and patient, allowing evil to fester while goodness sat sidelined. The discovery cut deep, and then snapped something inside her into iron.

"Is there no justice in this world?!" she roared, voice jagged as flint. "If you will not avenge me... if you will not right these wrongs... then damn you all! Gods and ancestors be damned!"

UDORN V

HE SPENT NEARLY AN HOUR STALKING THROUGH THE TALL GRASS, studying the endless stretch of the wooden palisade. The wall seemed without end, winding and snaking as far as the eye could follow. Udorn reckoned he could wander for a week and still not reach its end. Whatever treasures it guarded must have been of great worth.

Patrols of archers and spearmen paced the parapet, their silhouettes shifting against the night sky. Perhaps their numbers were few. Perhaps they felt so secure behind timber and iron that no more were needed. Either way, the place demanded caution, or avoidance altogether.

Knowing his band was too small for a true assault, Udorn resolved to bypass the stronghold and press on toward the sea. From there, they might return home with tales of their kinsmen's demise, or else seize new ships and rejoin the war. He favored the latter. Only those who found Sjenohor earned remembrance.

No greater shame existed than to crawl back to Mot and live soft and long. The notion of dying in a warm bed, wrinkled and forgotten, chilled Udorn more than the thought of losing all he loved. For an Ubneri, the path to immortality ran slick with blood.

"What are we waiting for?" Thaul smirked, his voice eager. "This is our chance! We must strike while the night still permits it."

Though his men hungered for plunder, Udorn held to caution. They had skirted death once already. Surely, the gods would not grant them the same mercy twice.

"I do not disagree," Udorn said, tone threaded with reluctance. "But we must tread carefully. I did not fight my way out of certain death only to perish for want of patience. If we strike, it must be in silence."

Such methods were familiar to the Ubneri; from childhood, they learned to use any edge the world offered. Whether by crashing tide of steel or a quiet blade at a throat, their swords would taste Southern blood. The night smelled faintly of salt and damp earth, and that thought steadied him.

"Imagine the glory that awaits us!" Dulkin One-Eye cackled. "We, the forgotten few, cast into the fire and left for dead, sack this settlement and return with a mighty prize! Stories of this will be carved in stone and told for generations. Think of it, Udorn!"

Udorn could not deny the lure. The idea sat warmer in his belly than a boar over a spit. Done right, the raid would not only fix their names in history but also cut at Ragruk's insufferable sway over Mot. Many wished for such a day and kept their mouths shut.

"Your tongue is perhaps your sharpest blade, One-Eye," Udorn conceded. "If we do this, we use our wits. These Southerners guard their walls against wild raids. We will become shadows. We will take them unawares and send them to Azldyr as proper tribute."

Smiles rippled through the men; Udorn had been called too cautious before, and now his decision pleased them.

"We must pick our kills and silence as many guards as we can," he continued. "This settlement could house hundreds, and our numbers are few. Only if we are found do we unleash hell. If that happens, we move fast—set flame to everything and spread terror quicker than the blaze."

Muffled chuckles and low grunts of approval answered him. The plan had teeth.

"Imagine if we are successful in taking such a place," Thaul said, lips wet as he licked them in hunger for battle. "The glory that awaits us will be legendary!"

But Udorn knew not every man would share in the glory. They had no baggage train and no camp followers to tend to the spoils or keep watch. Alone in a hostile land, they were at the mercy of its vast, merciless power.

"Someone must stay and guard the horses," he said, voice reluctant. "We cannot lose our provisions or the little plunder we have earned."

As expected, silence followed. None wished to volunteer. To remain behind was an insult. To be first over the wall and into harm's way was a far greater honor than to sit idle and watch from the rear. Still, a choice had to be made, and swiftly, for the good of all.

"Dulkin," Udorn said with a sigh. "I must ask this of you."

"I cannot!" One-Eye screeched, near enough to betray their hiding place. "I will not! After all I have suffered at your side, you would cast me away and deny me my rightful glory?!"

"Be still, my friend," Udorn said, raising his hand to calm him. "We strike under deep darkness. Every man must be aware of his place. With one eye, you are a danger not only to yourself, but to each of us."

Few sights struck harder than denying an Ubneri his place on the battlefield. Dulkin's pride guttered like a candle in a draft. An insult such as this was one no man should endure.

"You dishonor me," One-Eye said as he turned and stormed away.

The choice cut Udorn more deeply than any blade, but it was necessary. To bar a shield-brother from battle was a wound no sword could inflict, yet to risk the company on stubborn pride would be folly. Dulkin's bitter retreat was proof enough that Udorn had chosen rightly.

"Look on the bright side!" Gaxas sneered. "If we are slain, you will be the richest man in Mot!"

Riches were no comfort against the weight of eternal glory. Dulkin said nothing, trudging toward the horses. Udorn felt his friend's rage, but duty bound him to the many. Their survival in this strange land outweighed the pride of one man.

Hours bled away until the sun sank to its death. A crescent moon rose, only to be veiled by a wall of clouds. Darkness ruled the field, broken only by torchlight flickering along the parapet. Perhaps Azldyr had granted them a gift of shadows.

Udorn and his raiders smeared their skin with wet soil, the loam still damp from recent rain. They looked less like men and more like phantoms. Any foe unlucky enough to glimpse them might die of terror before steel even found flesh.

Though their supplies were scarce, Thaul knotted lengths of rope into crude ladders. The air carried a faint tang, the river whispering close and masking their movements. Silent as a tide, the Ubneri gathered beneath an unmanned watchtower.

Udorn raised his hand, signaling Thaul to cast the rope. The palisade would not remain unguarded forever. Their window was narrow, and hesitation could doom them. He chose to climb first, dagger clenched between his teeth, bare feet gripping the wood. He moved upward with the grace of a spider.

At the summit, he peered over the sharpened stakes, eyes sweeping the shadows. A distant orb of torchlight glowed faintly down the wall, far enough to mask them for now. With a gesture, he beckoned the others. One by one, they rose after him—then in greater numbers, spilling over the palisade like a black wave.

With his kinsmen safely over the top, Udorn signaled toward a set of switchback stairs. They slipped down single-file, noses to the wind, ears tuned for patrols.

"Where now, Udorn?" Thaul whispered, thin as a buzzing fly.

A quick sweep showed a city taking form. Shaped stone and neat piles of timber sat on budding street corners. Scaffolds hugged frames of brick and masonry like a forest of ribs. The place was larger than any frontier hamlet—more a staging ground than a village. Udorn's gaze found a supply depot and did not like what he saw.

"I fear we may have underestimated this place," he said, quickly motioning to a supply depot.

Stone roads ran between buildings like veins through a corpse—too straight, too planned for a mere fishing outpost. Every stacked plank, every cart of bricks spoke of Southern designs. That truth chilled him deeper than a hundred guards ever could: this was not a prize to be plundered. It was a foothold of an empire.

"We must do something," Gaxas said, voice tight. "The night will not hide us forever. We need to be gone before dawn."

Udorn inhaled slowly, measuring the hour. Time had turned traitor. One watchman, one raised cry, and the sleeping beast of the settlement would wake. They had to bleed it before it stirred.

"Listen to me carefully," he ordered. "We must split into pairs and destroy their guards quietly and with all haste. If we are discovered, this entire city will be upon us before morning."

In a choice between gold and the glory of Sjenohor, Udorn was uncertain which weighed heavier. Either way, his men smiled as they broke into smaller units, slinking into the dark with scarcely a whisper. Beside him knelt Tharek, perhaps the youngest among them. His father, Rennek, had already vanished into the murk.

Udorn would have preferred a seasoned warrior like Thaul at his side, yet he bore the weight of every life under his command. Tharek was no helpless boy; he had already proven his steel in the raid-turned-survival. His dark hair was bound in a tight braid, streaked with mud, while his battered armor clung stubbornly to his frame. The only thing Udorn could see unmistakably were his blue eyes, bright and piercing as fallen stars, shining all the more against his youth.

With axe in hand and knife ready, Udorn motioned toward a blossoming boulevard, its stonework finer than anything Mot could raise. Some of the emerging structures would tower stories high once finished. How such grandeur had sprouted near the Teb was a mystery he did not care for.

A glow of fire wavered against a wall up ahead—a sign of a patrol. By fortune, the garrison seemed complacent, content with their walls and their distance from any true threat. Only lone men wandered the night. Udorn pressed back into the yawning mouth of a half-built structure, Tharek ghosting at his side. Together, they blended with the dark.

Azldyr, let my steel be swift and silent...

The guard shuffled into view, cloaked in rich purple and armored in a polished breastplate that shimmered like sunlit glass. A jeweled longsword swung at his hip. His olive skin and sleek black hair looked strange for a Betanthian, though to Udorn, one Southerner was much the same as the next.

He slipped from the shadows like a wolf from the brush. His axe struck with brutal speed, splitting the man's face. Tharek caught the corpse before it fell, driving his knife behind the Southerner's ear to finish the task.

They dragged the body into a building and tucked it against a corner. One foe down, though how many more prowled the night, Udorn could not guess. In the distance, torches winked out one by one—his kinsmen's silent work. Yet the city was not wholly asleep. From somewhere far off came music, laughter, and the clink of mugs, revelry spilling from a tavern even at this late hour.

While the thought of a crisp ale tugged at him, there was butcher's work to be done. Udorn and Tharek moved like ghosts, slipping from cover to cover beneath the weak glow of street lamps. The drunken locals noticed nothing until Udorn stood nearly among them.

"Remain here," he instructed, voice low and sure. "You will know when."

Tharek obeyed, melting into shadow, braid catching a smear of moonless light. He watched Udorn stride down the avenue's center as if daring the world to stop him. Lantern-glow painted the veteran in wavering gold, but the revelers were too wrapped in drink and anger to see.

"I ought to kick your teeth in!" a portly man slurred, fists clumsy. "You cheated me, you fuck!"

"The hell I did!" another snapped, knuckles white. "You lose every time, Yorick. You drink and gamble away a week's pay and then cry theft. I will not stand for it!"

Likely a dice row, Udorn thought — a perfect mask for what he intended. He closed to within twenty paces of the cluster, the crowd a half-dozen strong and thick with sweat and song.

"You are like every other Southern cheat," the first man spat, jabbing a finger in accusation. "You take a man's honest coin with lies!"

"Perhaps I can settle this," Udorn said, stepping forward, calm as a blade before it falls.

With axe and knife in hand, Udorn struck. Two men fell in silence, their throats opened, warm blood spraying in arcs. Before the others could grasp what was happening, he brought his weapons down again, splitting skulls with swift precision. The crowd collapsed in a heap of crimson, leaving only the belligerent drunk to stare, dumbstruck, at the carnage.

"Fucking hell!" the man belched, then let out a laugh. "Serves you right, you cretins!"

Udorn wrenched the mug of ale from his hands and drank deep. The edge of his knife raked across the fool's throat as he swallowed, the man choking out his life in wet gurgles. The ale was warm, spiced, bold—far finer than he expected from Southern swill.

"Thank you for the drink," he said, dropping the empty vessel on the corpse's chest.

It seemed a shame to waste such spirits by torching the tavern, yet time was their enemy. Had fortune allowed, he might have butchered each patron as they staggered into the street. Instead, he would see them all slaughtered before a single alarm could rise.

He signaled for Tharek to emerge from hiding—yet the night flared bright with sudden fire. A column of flame roared in the south, ripping their stealth to shreds. Udorn cursed through his teeth and rushed to his kinsman.

"What in the name of the gods is this?" he hissed. "What have you seen?"

"I… I know nothing," Tharek stammered, his resolve wavering.

Together they slipped back toward the palisade, hunting the source of the blaze or a path to escape. As the inferno spread, cheers carried on the wind, not cries of alarm. Victory's roar, Udorn realized, though the battle had scarcely begun.

Down the street strode Gaxas, grinning, dripping gore, the severed head of a woman clutched in his fist. His axe ran red as if dipped entirely in blood. A single look told Udorn what he already feared: their covert raid was lost, betrayed by savagery.

"What have you done?!" Udorn roared, stepping from the shadows. "You have betrayed our position! You endanger us all!"

Gaxas threw back his head and bellowed with manic laughter. "Soft, Udorn? We have slain their garrison! The city is ours for the taking!"

Udorn faltered. The truth struck hard: the garrison had been wiped away, the settlement caught unawares. There would be little treasure in such a half-formed place, yet supplies enough might be seized to see them home, if the flames did not devour every inch first.

Tharek grinned, eyes alight. He was too young to crave anything but the rush of slaughter. Udorn longed for Sjenohor as any man did, but he would have kept the gods waiting. A return to Mot, to his hall and to Guri's arms, felt richer than any hoard. Yet fame and fortune wore different faces to different men.

From the square rose a tide of chaos—screams, the clash of steel, the roar of fire. Udorn and his companions rushed toward it, finding the avenues lined with corpses, the stones running red.

"Gods, be good!" Tharek cried, near delirious with bloodlust.

The raiders had cut through the town like an army ten times their size. No true warriors had lived here, only the thin garrison now slain. The feat was as staggering as their survival at Dellhaven. Perhaps the War God himself smiled upon them.

Flames leapt higher, racing along scaffolds and half-built beams, feeding on stacked timber and cartloads of supply. From afar, it must have seemed as though hundreds had poured into the settlement, not a few ragged survivors.

"Come, Udorn!" Thaul roared, driving a sword into the gut of a peasant man. "Azldyr's thirst has been quenched this night! Let us drink! Drink to the war god's victory!"

Despite the danger that still prowled the night, pride and savagery welled within Udorn's chest. He would not be counted a bystander on this fateful eve. No—he hurled himself into the chaos, axe high, heart thundering with the promise of glory.

A frantic mob of townsfolk scrambled to escape, trapped between a wall of flame and the thirst of Ubneri steel. One by one, they fell, their blood spilling across the freshly laid cobbles, screams drowned beneath the clash of iron. The air stank of charred wood and opened bowels. Men, women, and even children were trampled as scores more stampeded toward the gates, desperate to live another hour.

Hunting them down would have appeased his kinsmen's lust, yet

Udorn knew better. Let the survivors flee, for their terror was a sharper weapon than any axe. To reveal how few the Ubneri truly were would invite ruin. Better that the Southerners scatter like rats from a sinking ship, leaving their infant city strangled in its crib.

When the last cries had faded, Udorn stood amidst the wreckage. Torchlight licked his axe blade, hot and hungry. Around him, his brothers exulted, their voices raised to the gods. Yet his eyes fixed on the open gates, black against the fire, where the final villagers had vanished into the wild.

"Let them run," he muttered, voice steady as stone. "Let them scream to kings and lords. Let them carry word of what we have wrought." He turned to Thaul, fire dancing in his gaze. "We will not waste breath in chase. Our mark has been made."

Thaul nodded, though unease dulled his grin. "They will come for us—the Betanthians, perhaps even Ragruk, when he learns of this night."

"They always do," Udorn said darkly.

Already, the survivors would be carrying word of the massacre across the countryside. There would be retaliation, vengeance, even. But that suited him well enough. The more enemies he drew to his blade, the more plunder and glory he and his raiders would acquire.

And when the reckoning came—when blood debts were settled and the South lay scarred and trembling—it would not be Ragruk's name the bards set to song. It would be his.

TITAN IV

IN THE QUIET HOURS, HIS MIND DRIFTED, DRAGGED BACK TO battlefields that had long gone silent. Steel on steel. Screams swallowed by winter wind. Blood that soaked the ground and turned it to rust. Yet even here, in the wasteland's stillness, true quiet proved elusive. Conrak filled every moment with his chatter, a relentless rasp of words. The man loved the sound of his voice more than his own heartbeat; not even a headsman's axe, Tylar thought, would the Sacrithon, it seemed.

Memories of Castle Morden dogged him as faithfully as death trailing an old man. Rumination had become a habit—what was, what might have been, what should never have been—all gnawed at him as the Plainhold gnawed at his body. Picking at those thoughts was like tearing at a wound that would never heal.

Why do I bother? Why does it matter to me so fucking much? Will finding her change anything? It seems like she doesn't even want to be found...

It was a bitter truth to imagine Madelyn willingly walking toward the grave. Yet Tylar knew the feeling; many times he had prayed for death's embrace himself. Even now, riding through this forsaken expanse, it seemed a mercy. Something stronger than despair drove him onward—perhaps redemption, perhaps simple refusal to give up—but it was a tether he could not cut.

I know you want to die, he thought, examining the barren terrain as he rode. *I get it. You think it will take the pain away. And it will... at least, for you. But what about the rest of us? Having known what I have experienced trying to save good men from death, you would still do this to me? You and your damn stubborn pride. You selfish bitch...*

Weeks of fruitless wandering had begun to crack his iron resolve. The thought crept in like rot: Madelyn might already be dead, bones picked clean and hidden from all but the gods, if such loathsome beings existed.

Arhan rode a few paces ahead, a black silhouette against the dim sky. Unlike Conrak, he spoke little, a scar of a man whose silence had weight. Tylar could not decide if Arhan was a blessing or a curse—an omen of survival or a herald of the grave—but the man had been at his side through every inch of this barren crawl north.

"I thought you said you knew where she was?" Earlwick complained. "At this rate, we'll be dead before the week is out!"

Tylar grunted. The man was not wrong. Their rations had dwindled to scraps, and what water they had left carried the taste of rot. Duty and loyalty might drive a man into the storm, but neither filled his gut nor quenched his thirst.

"If you don't shut your fucking mouth, we might be feasting on Earlwick fillets this evening," he rasped. "I know we're not going to find her. But I had to try, for the girl's sake. Fuck what the rest of you think."

"It's alright, Bradshaw," Conrak said, trying to wet his cracking lips. "Nobody can say we did not exhaust ourselves trying. If we find nothing by midday, I would suggest we head south. If we intend to live, we should resupply and take up the search once more."

Failure rode heavier than hunger. It gnawed at him, more bitter than Earlwick's whining or Conrak's endless babble. For it was easy, too easy, to forget the Plainhold's cruelty until it bared its fangs. This wasteland was no mere stretch of earth—it was a beast, and none could tame it. Not even Titan Bradshaw, not even the strength that had shattered armies and stormed castles. Nature itself mocked his might.

They rode on until the sun had climbed high and hammered the world with light. Midday crept close, and Tylar kept glancing over his shoulder, hungry for the relief of camp and a proper ale. He could have strangled the King himself for a jug and a bench to sit upon. Heat baked the air, dust clinging to skin and cloth, every breath tasting of grit.

Damn you and your foolish pride, girl. Did you learn nothing from my stories? Did you listen to my regret and become hellbent on making the same mistakes I made? Are you really so stupid?

Just as the last scrap of hope frayed, a distant haze rose to the northeast. At first, he blamed the wind lifting the Plainhold's dust, but the cloud held a shape and purpose that did not belong to mere weather. It resolved into form: movement, mass.

"Are you thinking what I'm thinking?" Conrak said rhetorically. "Come, but be careful."

Tylar dug his heels in until his mount nearly bucked, then drove it forward. A hard jerk of the reins, and he galloped for the hillcrest, Conrak close behind. Arhan rode a little apart, quiet as ever, hood pulled low; he watched but did not speak. Any mistake here could be their last.

They crested the rise and peered down through a tangle of scrub and thorn. Below, the barbarian horde spilled across the plain like a living river. Thousands moved in ragged columns—men, beasts, carts—slow but inexorable. At its center, a near-endless train of wagons and packs crawled along, heavy with the spoils of conquest.

"Fuck me…" Tylar breathed, the whisper barely a rasp. "We found the fuckers. After all this searching, and here they are…"

"It's only a matter of time before they find us," Conrak cautioned. "We must have exploited the only gap in their outer perimeter. If we don't leave now, and fast, their scouts will give chase. And believe me,

Bradshaw, they will send everything they have our way. Can't have us reporting their location, eh?"

Hope was a terrible thing, especially in hopeless circumstances. A hot shame rose in Tylar's chest, a blow to pride that gnawed at him worse than hunger. He would not—could not—abandon the search for Madelyn, not now, not when the thought of her stepping into that sea of barbarians chilled him to the bone.

"I'm not leaving without the girl," he said defiantly. "If we discovered them, then surely she has. I know she's near, and I won't let her face these animals alone."

The fantasy of riding headlong into a barbarian host and cleaving a path to her side flickered bright and terrible in his mind. He imagined steel taking men by the score, shields splintering, the ground slick with blood—heroic, and awful. He knew the dead had paid such prices before; honor and loyalty had been carved into flesh and bone in countless fields. Death was an obstruction, nothing more, to the duty he had sworn.

"Damn it, Bradshaw!" Conrak snapped, voice ragged with fear and reason both. "I know what Madelyn is to you beyond the war. You would move the heavens for her. But we cannot if we are corpses! We cannot stand against that horde alone, even if she were to appear beside us in all her fury!"

Tylar felt the force of the logic like a palm against his sternum. Rage and love did not change the arithmetic; ten thousand steelheads still bested a handful of tired men. Earlwick and the other knights pushed their mounts into a retreat, the animals stumbling over scrub and stone as if eager to flee the coming teeth of war. Tylar held, stubborn, to pull one last scrap of meaning from the field, one more glance to mark their enemy's disposition before they melted into shadow.

Where are you, you fucker…

The horde filtered into the distance under a veil of dust; at times, the line blurred into a single living wall. He hunted for the one figure who had tormented his nights—Damien Dreadfire—seeking the hulking silhouette and black armor that would give him purpose. The chieftain, however, did not show.

Seconds piled into a small, dangerous heap. Every heartbeat was a bell, every breath a risk. Knowledge, accurate and carried back to safety, was worth more than a freighter of gold. With a last, reluctant pull on the reins, Tylar turned. The pull to live, to report, to plan, carried the same weight as his vow. They would live, and then they would return. The warband's location would be worth more than any ill-fought charge.

Make no mistake, you lumbering piece of shit... I will find you. And I will beat you to within an inch of your life so you can watch me lay waste to everything you hold dear. And after my work is finished, I'll pry that bald head off your shoulders with my bare hands. Mark my words...

"Come on, Bradshaw!" Conrak hissed, voice strained but urgent. "We must warn Prince Gareth!"

Duty snapped through Tylar like a whip. Madelyn was his heart's true aim, but to leave Gareth blind to the Northmen's position would be a betrayal of a different sort. Gareth had spared him from the rope; that mercy demanded repayment in truth. If their sighting could turn the tide of a greater battle, then it was no small thing—but no less necessary than finding a single woman in a wasteland.

Everything is so fucked. How can it be that we're winning on the battlefield, yet it seems like we're on the losing end? And why am I wandering through this fucking shithole searching for the girl when she doesn't want to be found? Is there even anything left in her worth saving?

Tylar flinched at the memory of darkness in Madelyn's steely-blue eyes—an uncanny void that had nothing human in it. The vision haunted him: a light gone wrong, a thing that had reached in and planted itself where a soul ought to be. The more he turned the image over, the less certain he felt it had been real and not some cruelty of his own mind.

The sad truth, he admitted to himself, was that despite blood-bond and shared battle, he knew little of her life beyond what she chose to show. Maybe she had been born cracked—cursed in the cradle, a brittle thing from the start. Perhaps the world simply ground the good down and let the wicked bloom. He had watched both truths play out too many times to pretend otherwise.

I've seen more than my share of good men die, and wicked men flourish.

Reluctantly, he eased his mount into retreat. Miles fell away like ash—weightless, present, inevitable. Every hoofbeat struck the hard earth like a drum marking some private failure. He had not spoken since they left the ridge; words would have been cheap measures here. The sun slid toward evening, and a thin, gritty wind bit at exposed skin like broken glass.

When night came, they made camp beneath a cluster of jagged boulders, teeth of stone hunched against the sky. No fire. No clamor. Only a low gnaw of hunger and the soft scraping of cloth as men shifted to sleep. Tylar stared into the black until the world thinned and sleep took him, though not before a single thought stalled in his mind.

She's out there. And she's still fighting. I have to believe that. For her sake, but for mine as well. What's a man to do when he has nothing left to fight for?

Dawn found him raw and stung, nipped awake by insects that had settled like a living rash. His lips peeled like old leather; his mouth felt like driftwood. The Plainhold wanted him dead in small, petty ways as much as in great ones. Before he could entertain the thought of surrender, a sharp rustle at his shoulder snapped him upright. Steel came free from its sheath in one practiced motion.

"Easy with the blade. Not to spoil your brooding, Bradshaw," Conrak muttered while picking through a tangle of thornbrush, "but unless you've started pissing fresh water and shitting dried beef, we'd best find something before we all start eating boot leather."

Insufferable as the Sacrithon was, there was no denying the gravity of their situation. Their rations were stretched thinner than an old man's skin, their water supplies nearly exhausted. Soon, they might be forced to butcher a horse for meat and blood to drink, though such actions would mark the beginning of the end.

"Why don't you just fuck off and let me die?" Tylar grumbled. "Being eaten to the bones would be far more enjoyable than remaining in your company."

Conrak smirked. "At least your charming personality hasn't suffered much. Come on, we need to get moving while we still have the energy. I think if we head that way, we might have some luck. There's a cluster of green vegetation in that depression over there. It's probably our best bet at finding water."

For all of his mockery, the man knew how to survive. And survival, in a place like this, was no small feat. Together, their patrol broke camp and took to the starving, parched fields once again. Tylar was too exhausted and hungry to protest, for following another man's command was as foreign to him as the Droethien language.

They crossed the dust-caked flatlands, the sun glaring like an open furnace overhead. Every hoof beat sent up little clouds of powder-fine dirt that clung to their boots and stung their eyes. Flies gathered in thick clouds, sensing weakness, yet finding men whose resolve had not yet broken.

A thin patch of green slowly came into view, just a smear of color against the dreary world. Tylar squinted, thinking it might have been a trick of the light, or perhaps hope playing games with a dying man. They reached the edge of the depression, more a shallow basin than a true valley, and found a source of life hidden among a tangle of weeds and tall, reed-like grass: a spring, bubbling gently beneath the surface.

The water was shielded by a thicket of stone and bramble. It was not much, but it was enough.

One of the younger scouts, barely more than a boy, dropped to his knees and began scooping muddy water into his hands. Conrak cuffed him hard across the back of the head.

"Let it settle, idiot," he snapped. "Or you'll be shitting yourself to death by nightfall."

The scout muttered an apology and crawled back. Tylar, watching the exchange, said nothing. He knelt beside the spring and ran a hand over the damp ground. Cool to the touch. Real.

"Fuck me…" he whispered.

It was no miracle, but in that moment, it felt like one. They took turns drinking in silence, Conrak overseeing the process with gruff efficiency. Tylar drank last, partly out of discipline, partly out of shame. The water was gritty, metallic, but he could have wept for the taste.

Conrak, to his credit, had proven far more resourceful than he could ever have imagined. It was perhaps his one saving grace, for the man's mouth never seemed to shut for more than a few moments. The Sacrithon was able to scavenge food and water in the unlikeliest places, meager as his findings were. Still, it was enough to sustain them.

I would stab any number of them for a plate of potatoes and seared meat. And an ale… a proper red ale. And perhaps a pipe packed with herb…

Tylar was beginning to wonder if there was indeed truth to the fanciful tales Conrak often told. He was never one to believe in fate or a power higher than man. But to survive for as long as they had in such a forsaken place was nothing short of a miracle.

He would have twisted the man's head off his shoulders before ever admitting it, but the past years certainly felt as if they were authored by an invisible hand. From life in the Order to being a deserter on the run, to capture and near death, Tylar now found himself serving the highest cause. For better or worse, every action and event seemed to have a purpose.

Knowing his life was not an utter waste was a reassuring thought. But despite this, nothing would stop him from sacrificing his life if it meant keeping Madelyn safe, nor sacrificing the lives of his so-called brothers in the Order.

They can die and rot for all I care. But in the end, I'll show them what Tylar Bradshaw is truly made of. I'll make them wish they never fucked me over.

Truly, his fallen brethren were looking down on him with pride in their hearts, if a world beyond even existed. But for the sake of their memory and in honor of their sacrifices, Tylar began forcing himself to believe not only in himself, but in the possibility of brighter days beyond the storm clouds.

If nothing else, surviving this hellish landscape might bring him one step closer to avenging the past and serving punishment to those who deserved it most. He ran a hand across his stubbled jaw and surveyed the great distance while the others gathered every drop of water they could carry.

"Madelyn's still out there," he muttered, just loud enough for Conrak to hear. The Sacrithon glanced his way, but said nothing. "And I'll find her, because we all know where she's going. But she'd better be quick, because I'll tear Damien Dreadfire's head off before she can even draw a blade. Come on, let's ride."

SYLVIA V

THEY TRAVELED BENEATH SUN AND STARS, THE DAYS BLEEDING INTO one another without distinction. The journey was long and grueling, yet the Plainhold's wrath had at last subsided. Now and then, a cool breath from the north revived Sylvia's weary spirit. It was a promise of home— the Hinterwood's trees whispering their welcome like long-lost kin.

Water and forageable food grew more abundant, easing their march. Death's shadow had lifted from the Plainhold fields, life returning in fragile but undeniable force. To Sylvia, the contrast was staggering— how one corner of the gods' creation could be so merciless, and another so nurturing. Comfort tempered her heart, though she knew the Plainhold would demand their return one day.

As the miles wore on, she began to see the cost borne by Damien. He hid his pain masterfully, his mask convincing to all but the most watchful. After a meal of berries and roasted meat, they pressed forward once more.

"I thought I would never see the forest again," Sylvia sighed. "Thank the gods we made it this far, against every odd."

Damien gave no answer. His stride only quickened. The trails leading north came back to them with ease. To the east lay Skaginlef, perhaps two days' ride. To the west waited Blackwolf Pass, cradle of their most decisive victory. The thought of thousands of Betanthian bones still rotting in its depths gave Sylvia reassurance. It reminded her that Betanthia was not invincible.

Cedric Valens had been broken, and his castle reduced to rubble. Hok had been sacked in a single night, its treasures scattered among the warband. Through toil, blood, and the gods' favor, they had achieved what once seemed impossible.

I feel you speaking to me, she thought blissfully. *Thank you for reminding me of your presence, for I know I never walk alone. You are here, and you have always been... even in our darkest hours. Something within me suspects our defeat was merely part of a grander plan...*

They pressed north after a brief respite beneath towering pines, following cart trails and deer paths well-worn with memory. The scent of needles filled the air, a fragrance that drew a rare smile to Sylvia's tired lips. Birds trilled from high branches, and squirrels darted through the underbrush. To be surrounded by life again—true, familiar life—was a blessing after the desolation of the Plainhold.

But as the hours slipped by, it became clear the Warlord was faltering. His posture sagged, his frame bent beneath invisible weight, his face contorted with suppressed pain.

"Are you alright, Damien?" Sylvia guided her horse closer, ready to catch him should he fall.

Dreadfire gave no reply, only a low grunt. To see such a man show weakness was like watching a wound seared shut—ugly, but necessary. Still, his endurance shone like iron in a forge. It seemed nothing short of the gods themselves driving a spear through his chest could bring him down.

By midday, the trees began to thin, surrendering to a veil of mist. Smoke curled upward from chimneys and pit fires, drifting into the cool sky. Out of the haze emerged Rej Rhivoth, its stone hovels and thatched roofs spreading across the land like a specter made solid.

Though they crept with caution, their presence did not go unnoticed. A half dozen riders came upon them swift as falcons, cloaks of heavy furs streaming behind them like banners. Each bore a lance of sharpened steel, eight inches of lethal point mounted on shafts long enough to skewer a line of men.

Sylvia could not help but admire the patrol's vigilance. Even in the depths of the Hinterwood, danger always lingered, and intruders were never far. At first, the riders failed to recognize her, their eyes hard with violence, hungry for a clash of steel rather than words.

"Good of you to keep the place intact while I was away," she called out, her tone steady and sharp. "I feared we had taken our best south and left only the riffraff."

"Stormguard?" The lead rider lowered his lance by a fraction. "You have returned?"

It was nothing like the triumph Sylvia once imagined. In her mind's eye, the warriors of Rej Rhivoth would have marched home under banners heavy with spoils, greeted with feasts and songs lasting for weeks. Instead, her welcome was confusion—lukewarm at best.

"We must speak with Taug at once," she said. "There is no time to waste."

"Where are the others?" another rider pressed, agitation rising in his voice. "Why have you returned alone?"

Sylvia exhaled sharply, her patience thinning. "Take me to Taug, and you will have your answer. I have neither the time nor the will to explain myself twice."

The riders traded uneasy looks before turning toward the heart of the village. Sylvia and Damien followed, their progress watched by wary eyes. Rej Rhivoth was a place of rugged men, as harsh and unyielding as the land itself.

An icy gust swept in from the Forlorn Sea, its gray waters only a short march away. A thin crust of snow frosted the rooftops, heralding autumn's approach. To Sylvia, it was a blessing—a reprieve from the Plainhold's blistering heat, which had felt fierce enough to melt stone. She had always favored the cold, and here in her homeland, the chill was constant, a companion year-round.

They trotted down a well-worn avenue, the dirt beaten flat and frozen hard as stone beneath the hooves of their mounts. The air hung thick with the scent of fish and silt, drifting from merchants who bellowed their wares at crooked market stalls. Others displayed trinkets of silver and gold, their craftsmanship rivaling even the Betanthians. Bolts of dyed cloth fluttered in the chill, and racks of blades and steelwork gleamed in the weak light—signs of a thriving economy, as rugged as the people who had built it.

Ahead stood Sylvia's favorite tavern, one of many scattered through Rej Rhivoth but unmatched in character. Oldheart Hollow was no ordinary hall; it had been hewn into the trunk of a titanic, long-dead tree. Its vast canopy had fallen centuries ago, branches buried beneath layers of soil and undergrowth. Time itself seemed to cling to the place.

The tavern's name, carved in worn runes above the entrance, was almost lost to the years. Inside, the Hollow offered the finest ale in the north, brewed with fresh juniper berries. Mead, as in any Rhivothi hall, flowed freely, joined by fruit wines that warmed the bones on bitter nights. Yet what set the Hollow apart was not its drink, but its form

Glass-paned windows glowed from high along the trunk's height, each one a lantern against the dusk. Where once a gaping wound had marred the tree, a balcony now jutted outward, fitted with tables and chairs. The balustrade crawled with flowering vines, stubborn even in the cold. Leaning against it, two hulking Rhivothi passed a pipe of herb between them, their eyes tracking Sylvia's every step.

Few places in Caldakas matched the Hollow for wonder. Legend claimed the tree was once the greatest in the world, felled in a godly contest for dominion over Rej Rhivoth. Azldyr, the god of war, and

Nymvarrik, the god of the sea, clashed with such fury that the earth split and the waves boiled. Azldyr struck the final blow, winning the people's devotion—but the land bore the scar of that struggle forever.

A smile touched Sylvia's lips for the first time in what felt like ages. She remembered long nights spent within Oldheart Hollow—drinking and laughing with shieldmaidens and sword-brothers until dawn's light spilled across the horizon. She could almost feel the hearth's heat on her cheeks, hear the thrum of drums and the cry of strings echoing through its trunk. But that reunion would have to wait.

They pressed on until Bryndraskar came into view. The sight never failed to steal Sylvia's breath. Unlike any hall of the north, it rose not from timber or thatch but from the bones of the earth itself.

Hewn from a mountain's stone, its cavernous heart had once been stripped for ore and rock, feeding countless smaller structures over the centuries. When the void grew too vast to ignore, Brok the Vengeful, the great Chieftain of his age, decreed it be transformed into a hall worthy of gods and men alike.

Sylvia often wondered if the Rhivothi were descended from miners, for their skill in shaping the land to their will was unmatched. They were no sailors nor farmers of renown; their passions—apart from the glory of battle—were bound to craft and creation, producing wonders their kin could scarce imitate.

"Magnificent, is it not?" she said, her voice alight with pride. "It feels like only yesterday when you arrived here."

A shroud of moss draped the stony roof, its thick green blanket softening the harsh lines of rock. Smoke curled from a broad, stunted chimney, carrying with it a rich scent of roasting meat. Sylvia's stomach roared in protest, snarling like a starved wolf at the promise of a feast.

"Its beauty will never be wasted on me," Damien replied, his words heavy with fatigue. He straightened in the saddle, straining to hold fast to his image of iron strength. "I pray its master greets us in good spirits."

A fool's hope, Sylvia thought. Taug was as jagged as the land itself, and no friend would he be to their return. He had pledged Rej Rhivoth's finest to Dreadfire's campaign, only to see his warlord stagger home with nothing to show but wounds. Betanthian cavalry were fierce foes, but Taug's temper—quick to ignite and slow to cool—was fiercer still.

Eight spearmen stood watch before Bryndraskar, ringmail polished bright beneath cloaks of heavy blue linen that rippled like banners in the sea wind. Their helmets of steel were reinforced across brow and nose, though the jaws lay bare—for no Rhivothi beard would ever be caged, lest it snag and tear.

Among them loomed Kaldor Wolfbane, his arms thick as tree trunks, a single blond braid hanging down the breadth of his back and resting upon his honorary cloak. With him were Aldrik, Sigvald, and Odhran—veterans all, chosen for the chieftain's honor guard.

They saw Sylvia and Damien's approach yet gave no word of greeting, no nod of respect. The silence was an omen. For a named warrior such as Stormguard to be ignored was no small slight—it was an insult that stung as sharp as hornets.

Ahead, Bryndraskar's great doors yawned half-open, smoke drifting outward in lazy plumes. Whether Taug's welcome came cold or cruel, the customs of the north still bound him: they would be offered meat, drink, and fire, the courtesies owed to any Rhivothi who bore arms.

Sylvia slid from her saddle and hissed at the sting in her thighs, rubbed raw from long days astride. Damien fared little better, though the grim set of his jaw betrayed only a faint limp. The wound he carried from the Plainhold was ghastly, yet his iron will burned hot enough to sear the pain away. From her saddlebag, Sylvia withdrew a tiny sapling wrapped in cloth—the gift of Dolvargan. She cradled it carefully in her hands. Whatever came, this would be her offering.

Bryndraskar's cavernous hall lay mostly barren, its emptiness echoing louder than any feast. Only a cluster of councilmen lingered at the far side, gathered near a long oaken bar stacked to the rafters with casks fit for gods and kings. From a shadowed corner, a trio of musicians plucked strings and beat their drums in somber rhythm, their chants rising as hymns to the honored dead.

At the hall's heart, the pit fire smoldered weakly. Only a meager handful of logs fed its flame—a pale shadow of the roaring inferno it could become, bright enough to melt the frozen earth. The emptiness seemed deliberate, a cold reflection of its master's mood.

Upon a throne of polished oak sat Taug, chieftain of Rej Rhivoth. His chestnut hair and beard were streaked with gray, the marks of age failing to soften his presence. Though years pressed upon him, he remained every bit the beast his people feared and revered, his very stillness radiating menace.

The music faltered, then died as Sylvia and Damien entered. Merriment turned to silence, eyes narrowing in disbelief. No one had expected their return—at least not so soon, and certainly not so diminished. Yet custom demanded respect. Stormguard was named, and by law and blood she could not be met as less.

"What is the meaning of this visit, Stormguard?" Taug's voice cut through the hush, sharp as an axe-blade. His gaze shifted to Damien, cool and merciless. "And you. When last we spoke, you bore two thousand warriors at your back—nomads and Nothanek alike. Now you crawl home with none. Explain."

"Chieftain," Sylvia dropped to one knee, then rose again, her hand pressed to her breast. "We—"

"Silence!" Taug thundered, rising from his oak throne. His voice rattled through the cavernous hall like stone grinding on stone. "I was not speaking to you. I can only assume the purpose of this intrusion. Tell me—has some great calamity befallen you on the field? Hm?"

Though the chieftain's fury radiated across the chamber, Damien did not flinch. Ally or not, defiance here would mean blood. With a measured bow of his head, he stepped forward.

"The gods have quenched our thirst for victory many times," he said evenly. "But the gods are fickle, and their generosity finite. I will not veil the truth—our alliance bleeds. The war teeters on ruin, and destruction breathes at our necks."

Taug sank back into his throne, his face darkening. "And so you come begging for more flesh to throw onto the pyre? I once welcomed you, Dreadfire. I gave you the spears of all who would follow. But no more. Rej Rhivoth will not send its last sons to die for a hopeless cause. I will not see my people fade from this world! It would take generations to recover—if we ever did."

Yet Damien's gaze never wavered. He had not come for swords. His purpose lay deeper.

"I have not come seeking warriors," he said, his voice low but unyielding. Confusion rippled through the gathered elders. "Those who remain in this fight do so by choice. We ask no more. What I seek is rest and replenishment. For when I depart, it will be for Morvhalgr—" his words hung in the smoky air "—to scale the forbidden mountain."

The hall erupted in gasps. Shock and dread rippled like a wave through council and warrior alike. Men who had faced cavalry charges without a tremor now glanced sidelong, unsettled, their hands tightening on the hafts of their spears. Rej Rhivoth had lived in the mountain's shadow for millennia. Its terror ran in their blood, as old as their name.

"And what do you hope to find in such a place?" Taug asked at last, hesitation softening the edge of his voice. "What does Morvhalgr hold that you would seek so recklessly?"

The answer was etched into every Rhivothi's blood. From cradle to grave, their people spoke of the mountain's secret.

"I have come seeking Ruin," Damien said boldly. "It is the only means of our salvation, for it has once saved our people from Betanthia's hunger."

Taug's fingers curled through his beard, stroking in thought. "And who is to say the blade endures? Perhaps the gods reclaimed their weapon after it was laid to rest. Perhaps it is nothing but legend."

A fair doubt, one Sylvia had wrestled with herself. Would this quest prove folly? Would it bleed them of strength when Damien's hand was needed most at the warband's helm? Such questions haunted her in the long hours of night.

"We cannot know," she blurted, drawing the ire of both men. "Faith is all we have. Faith may seem a frail thing when the world unravels, but it is then we need it most. Einarr Rollfson has been touched by the gods. He has seen the path laid before us, and that path leads to Morvhalgr."

Taug's gaze hardened, unimpressed. "You have always spoken with fire, Stormguard. And I will not deny a free Rhivothi their right to walk where their will drives them. But I cannot permit you to carry whatever dwells within that mountain back to Rej Rhivoth. Go, if you must. But do not return here."

For a moment, it seemed he yielded. Yet assumption was a treacherous trap. Beneath every word, Taug's impulse was plain: to shield his people at any cost. Who could fault him? A Rhivothi chieftain ruled only by the consent of those he swore to protect.

"I am no savior," Damien said. His voice carried no boast, only the weight of truth. "No prophecy marks my coming. No ancestor foretold it. I am only a man—a man who gives his life freely for his people. Borjifa may live now only in memory, but those who bled beside me are my kin. For them, I would make the ultimate sacrifice."

It was as convincing an argument as any she had heard, yet Taug's face remained carved from stone. He beckoned his council close, and low whispers rippled between them like the murmur of a cold tide.

Sylvia held her tongue and folded her hands, offering a silent prayer to the gods for her kinsmen's mercy. Faith had been a distant stranger to her of late. Once she had been Rej Rhivoth's fiercest zealot, ready to skewer a man for the faintest blasphemy. But years of war and the taste of bitter defeat had dulled that edge. Only now, standing in the hall of her ancestors beneath the shadow of Morvhalgr, did her faith stir again, warming her like a buried ember.

"The quest you are about to undertake will be your last," Taug said at length, his voice low but implacable. "There is no return from the mountain. Every soul who has climbed it has vanished. You risk certain death for hope—but hope, my friend, is no strategy."

Dreadfire lowered his eyes briefly, then met Taug's gaze once more. "No, it is no strategy. But it is necessary. So much has been lost, and faith is all I have left. I cannot falter despite all we have suffered. I *must* not."

Taug's hand drifted through his chestnut beard, his eyes heavy with reluctant respect. "Very well. Rej Rhivoth's hospitality is yours. Take what you need, rest as long as you require. I suspect this may be our last meeting, Damien Dreadfire. But know this—before you go to certain doom, I gave as much as I could."

"You have our thanks," Sylvia said. "May the gods bless you and your House in all the coming days. I bring you a gift from the forest. May it grow and flourish in our memory."

She set the sapling gently upon the table, her eyes lingering on it with quiet reverence. The councilmen exchanged uneasy glances but spoke no word as she turned away. Together, she and Damien departed Bryndraskar's hall. On any other night, they might have drunk the casks dry, but the road ahead promised no such indulgence.

Outside, Damien managed only a handful of steps before a guttural growl escaped him, low and raw as a wounded beast. His hand clamped over his leg, the wound throbbing even after the sear of cauterization. Sylvia slipped an arm around his broad back as his stride faltered, sparing him the shame of collapse. To stumble here—in sight of Rej Rhivoth—was to court ruin.

"Take your hand off of me," Dreadfire whispered in an unsteady voice. "I will walk these streets unaided… or may the gods strike me dead where I stand."

It was fair, and she nearly flushed with shame for presuming to steady him. Damien's name was worth as much as a thousand ravenous warriors, and even the hint of weakness could sow doubt.

Yet his endurance left her in awe. To watch him summon fire from a body so broken was to witness something nearly divine. Truly, Kholdyr's hand was upon him. Together they pressed on toward her hovel, though the distance seemed an endless gauntlet. Damien's black eyes glazed, rolling back as though consumed by unseen flame. His spirit guttered and flared in turn, like a torch in a blizzard, unyielding even as the storm pressed to snuff it out.

When they reached the hovel, Damien nearly pitched forward through the door but caught himself on the frame at the last instant. Sylvia ushered him inside quickly, shielding him from any prying eyes, and guided him to a bed of straw stuffed with goose feathers. He collapsed onto it with a heavy sigh, the tension in his leg easing at last, and for a heartbeat he almost smiled.

"Bring me drink," he muttered. "And make it plentiful."

By fortune, several unopened casks of mead still lay in the corner, their contents preserved by the perpetual cold. Sylvia tapped one, filled two oversized wooden mugs to the brim, and handed one to Damien. The mead's scent was sharp and clean—aged, but unspoiled.

"Let us drink to our people and to the gods," she said, raising her mug. "For we may never see home again. You and I are about to walk the most dangerous road of our lives. If we are to meet our end on Morvhalgr, then I will die without regret. Surely the gods will be pleased with what we have done in their service."

Damien drank slowly at first, then upended the mug, swallowing the rest in one long pull. "This will not be our end, Stormguard. The gods still have use for us. We are imperfect servants—angering and disappointing them more times than there are stars in the heavens—but that imperfection binds us to them. It makes us strive to rise above ourselves. Not every man can give himself to a cause greater than his own life."

They ate and drank in near silence after that, each alone with their thoughts. The mead warmed them, but it could not ease the knowledge that come dawn, their lives would belong not to themselves, but to something vast and unseen.

Forgive me for my shortcomings, Sylvia prayed before turning in for sleep. *I have only sought to serve you, oh gods, and live my life in your service. I ask only for your protection from what is to come so that I may serve you further. But if my time has come, then so be it. Let me be welcomed into the halls of Sjenohor to the sound of blowing trumpets!*

EINARR IV

Of all the accursed places he had experienced, Einarr thought the Plainhold was the worst. It was a dry, desolate, unforgiving landscape, inhospitable to life itself. The gods themselves seemed to despise such a place, perhaps even creating it as a means to torment both enemies and nonbelievers.

That was, until he encountered Zylmacian hill country. Hyleth led them westward for weeks, carefully skirting the land between Mor Seveht and Castle Morden. It had become a no-man's land since the stronghold was reduced to ruin. Undoubtedly, Jollkud and his marauders had exacted their vengeance on Khorrtal by now, removing yet another civilization from existence.

Despite the ever-present danger, Einarr remained in faithful company. Hyleth appeared to recognize every hill, dead tree, and stone along their path. Given how indistinguishable the terrain was, it was difficult to imagine how anyone could know such a place so well, but their Zylmacian guide remained true.

Conversation was fleeting, for every man knew to keep their guard up at all times. Only when the land flattened and appeared less imposing did they dare to break the mundane silence. But as the gods would have it, their first conversation would not be about strategy or even home and its comforts.

"Fucking heat," Dolsigg complained. "Fucking flies. Fucking worthless land."

Even among the Rhivothi, such vulgarity was frowned upon. Valerick the Red shot his kinsman a look of disgust—a telling thing, given it came from a man known to bathe himself in animal blood.

"Is this your first time outside your forest hut, Northman?" Hyleth asked, his voice carrying more boldness than courtesy. "You look as though the sun itself offends you."

"Give me a winter gale any day," Dolsigg grumbled, scratching at the flaky skin on his bald crown. "I wager you Westerners would freeze stiff in minutes."

If anything was as sure as an eastern sunrise, it was a conflict between a Zylmacian and a Rhivothi. Perhaps the gods created them to be mortal enemies, to fight and die in perpetual struggle until the end of time. Like fire and ice, night and day, they were as opposite as one could imagine, down to their very core.

"Tell us again," said Loth, his tone edged with impatience, "why we must wander through this forsaken nightmare?"

Unlike Dolsigg, whose complaints were as constant as flies, Loth's words carried weight. A grim-faced warrior, broad of shoulder and slow to jest, he rarely spoke without reason. He had survived more campaigns than most men could dream of, and when he gave his thoughts voice, even Einarr listened.

"I do not trust the safety of Mor Seveht," Hyleth said dryly. "Long has it been a sanctuary for the weary traveler, free of Betanthia's tyranny or that of some petty lord. These days, it is far too dangerous for us to be seen there. We would be killed on sight, surely. But if we must venture there, then we must."

Einarr suspected as such and offered no protest. Indeed, their presence in the south would draw unwanted attention, betraying the very nature of their mission. Dolsigg grumbled something under his breath and fell quiet. Even he knew better than to question Hyleth's judgment when it came to this land. His instincts had kept them alive thus far. Still, the Rhivothi had a way of taking silence as an invitation to brood.

As the afternoon sun unleashed its vengeance, weariness and agitation began to boil inside them. Even Einarr's calm demeanor was challenged under such conditions. They rode in a single file now, a serpent of sweat-drenched men on worn horses. The wind had died entirely. Even the insects seemed reluctant to stir. Dust clung to every fold of cloth and every crease of skin. No one spoke.

Einarr stole a glance at Hyleth. His eyes were narrowed, mouth pressed into a hard line. If he feared what lay ahead, he did not show it. Fear was a foreign concept to the Zylmacians, a credit to their culture, but one Einar would dare not speak aloud. Their gallant charge against the walls of Castle Morden and the vastness of their corpses left behind would be forever seared in his mind.

He remembered the way they charged—shields raised, voices howling, not one of them hesitating even as arrows blackened the sky. It was not courage. It was something colder. Something deeper. The kind of resolve that came only from lifetimes of being born beneath a blade. Yet even Hyleth was not fully immune to the wear of the land.

As the sun dipped lower, the hills changed again. The soft curves of soil gave way to stone and spine. Jagged outcroppings rose like broken teeth from the earth, casting long shadows across the trail. Some rocks leaned unnaturally, as though shoved there by a colossal hand. No trees grew here, only dry grass, browned and brittle, rasping underfoot with every step.

Dolsigg's horse began to fidget; first a snort, then a jolt. The beast tossed its head and stomped at the ground, muscles twitching beneath its sweat-slick hide. He gave the beast a kick in a bid to silence it, but some unforeseen disturbance continued to agitate it.

Einarr turned in his saddle. "Hold your reins," he said.

"Damned flies," Dolsigg muttered. "They're biting worse now."

But the flies were gone—all of them. Not a single buzz remained.

"It seems even your horse has grown tired of your company!" Valerick quipped. The remark was quite amusing for a man not known for his humor.

"I'll run the damn thing through if it doesn't settle down," Dolisgg grunted.

Having witnessed enough slaughter, Einarr knew to trust a horse's instinct. They could often sense trouble long before it was visible to the human eye. Hyleth seemed keen on the disturbance as well, turning in his saddle and eyeing their surroundings.

"Make yourselves ready, Northmen," the Zylmacian said, drawing his saber. "These hills are fraught with danger."

Einarr scanned the terrain frantically, searching for any sign of predators or foes. Instinctively, he drew his arming sword and held it aloft. Dry grass crunched and shook as if taken by a sudden wind, yet there was no sign of any adversary.

From the rear of their column came shouts and shrieking of horses. Chaos broke out among the ranks as horse and rider scattered in every direction. Small, dark blurs shot across the rocky hills, making it difficult to focus. Only when shrill screams pierced the air did Einarr see the source of the assault.

"Close ranks!" Hyleth shouted over the chaos, charging toward his embattled brethren. "Close ranks, I say!"

A pack of beasts descended upon them like a swarm of locusts. Einarr supposed they were wild dogs, given their large ears and small snouts. But something about them seemed unnatural, as if the land's hostility had imparted unnatural size and strength as a means of survival. Only when he charged in to aid his kin did he notice they were anything but dogs.

They moved like mountain lions but bore little else in common.

Their limbs were longer, their gait more unnatural, like they had too many joints bending in the wrong directions. Coarse, patchy fur clung to muscular frames, grey-brown and matted with old blood.

Their eyes glowed faintly amber in the sunlight—too intelligent, too fixed in their hunger. Long tails whipped behind them like lashing cords, and when they snarled, their mouths split wider than any natural beast, revealing double rows of black, needle-like teeth. They were not born of nature, it seemed.

Valerick let loose a fiery war cry, ready to fight on foot. A few mangy animals seemed hardly a fitting challenge for all the men he had slain, and fighting while mounted seemed a coward's tactic.

"AZLDYR!" he roared like a lion.

He dismounted in one fluid motion, landing with a thud that sent dust flying around his boots. Axe in hand, he charged headlong into the fray, laughing like a man possessed. One of the beasts lunged at him— he sidestepped and brought his weapon down in a wide, brutal arc. Bone cracked. The thing's body crumpled into the dirt like a torn sack.

Another came at him from the left. Valerick twisted and caught it mid-leap with the haft of his axe, then buried the blade in its back before it could recover. His blood-soaked tunic clung to his chest, face streaked with dirt and gore, red hair whipping wildly as he turned to find his next kill.

To Einarr, it was as if some ancient spirit of war had taken form in flesh—unstoppable, untamed, and utterly merciless. In that moment, he was reminded of Marvath Bonesplitter. He could nearly see the Rhivothi nomad now, his sandy-colored hair flowing like a banner. But it was just an illusion brought by fear and dehydration, for the Warchief lived only in memory.

One of the monsters charged in with lightning speed and leaped upon a Rhivothi rider, toppling both man and steed. Its dagger-like claws and menacing teeth sank deep into the warrior's flesh, ripping and tearing and sending jets of blood into the air. Despite such grievous wounds, the Rhivothi fought on, slashing and stabbing until his sword was knocked away.

Out of sheer instinct to protect his brethren, Einarr jabbed his horse with a bootheel and charged into the fray. Before he could reach the embattled Rhivothi, a ferocious beast came speeding in, nearly taking him unawares. Only a swift downward slash was able to repel the vicious animal, which thrashed about and pawed at its savaged face.

Before Einarr could regain his senses, a heavy mass slammed into his back. The force nearly knocked him from the saddle, his horse screaming and thrashing about violently. A deep snarl sounded so close it was practically inside his head, a searing sting erupting across his upper back.

The pain was white-hot—blinding. Einarr roared through gritted teeth, nearly dropping his sword as blood soaked through his cloak. His horse reared in terror, hooves flailing at the air. Somehow, he clung to the saddle. The beast behind him was heavier than he expected. Its claws dug in deeper, searching for purchase, its snarling breath wet against his neck.

In desperation, Einarr twisted his torso and slammed the hilt of his sword backward. Once. Twice. The third strike landed with a crunch and a pitiful yelp. The creature fell away. He turned, gasping, barely able to lift his blade. Another was already bounding toward him.

Then came Valerick, howling, red-eyed, cleaving the two-handed axe through sinew and skull. The beast collapsed mid-leap, twitching at his horse's hooves.

"You live, fisherman?" Valerick shouted.

"Not for long if we stay!" Einarr growled back, the pain immeasurable.

Around them, the skirmish was turning desperate. Several horses lay shredded, their riders dead or disarmed. Dolsigg had taken up a spear and was driving it repeatedly into the chest of one beast while another clawed at his back. Hyleth fought on foot, surrounded but unyielding, his saber flashing like a serpent's fang. Einarr wiped blood from his brow. Holding the hill would prove fatal.

"Hyleth!" he bellowed, voice cracking. "Fall back! Rally north of the ridge!"

The Zylmacian offered no response, but heard well enough. He slashed through one more attacker, then signaled with his blade—a retreat. The Northmen broke free in ragged clusters, bloodied and breathless, dragging the wounded behind them. The beasts did not pursue far. They seemed to vanish as swiftly as they had appeared, melting into the rocks as if they had never existed.

Einarr rode last, clutching his sword with a trembling hand, vision darkening at the edges. His breath came ragged. Each heartbeat thudded in his ears like war drums, slower and heavier than the last. Blood poured from his shoulder, soaking his belt and dripping onto the soil below. Then he saw it. Not a beast. Not a man.

Atop the ridge stood a shape, tall and motionless, cloaked in shadows that the sun should have burned away. It had no features he could name, only the vague suggestion of limbs and a head. But it watched. He knew it was watching. The great cat, the spectral guardian, it seemed, had returned.

And then, in the blink of an eye, it was gone. Einarr's grip slackened. The world tilted sideways, and everything went dark.

LUCETTA V

A FOUL STENCH WRENCHED HER FROM SLEEP, GAGGING HER AWAKE AS though filthy fingers clutched at her throat. Warm light flickered beyond a blackened hood, but a gnawing chill crawled over her skin. Drops of fetid water pattered into a nearby puddle; rats scratched and skittered in the dark, their noise defiling the silence like blasphemy in a chapel.

Lucetta rose on trembling legs. A sharp, stabbing ache pained her neck, nearly drawing tears. Stagnant water clung to her skirts, reeking of rot, a slimy crust caking her legs. She gagged, swallowing back bile, forcing her mind to clear.

"Pavlos?!" she called, her voice hoarse but measured, wary of the zealots who had taken her.

No answer. Only her ragged breath and pounding pulse. A pitiful whimper trembled at the back of her throat. She lunged forward in panic, only to feel iron bite into her wrists—the cold weight of shackles. Chains rattled softly, echoing through the cavernous dark.

"Please… save me," she whispered to the woman in black, praying the entity still heard her.

But the sewer answered only with its stench and its vermin. A wet shuffle echoed from a nearby passage, joined by a faint voice. Lucetta's heart thundered. The disturbance grew louder—more footsteps, more bodies. And then came the laughter, high and mocking, a prelude to torment. It was the same laughter she had heard before, a reminder of her violation at the hands of Sir Bryce Whitewood.

"Princess Lucetta," a man's voice rang out at last, smooth and familiar. The villain who had taken her stepped into the glow. "I am Sorrith. I trust you have not been too greatly discomforted?"

She said nothing, only wincing as his boots struck closer. Fear gnawed through her defenses despite all her efforts to remain unshaken. A bright jingle of keys broke the silence, followed by a sudden tug of iron biting her wrists. The tumblers clacked, and the shackles fell away with a heavy thud.

Relief surged through her veins, but it was laced with no safety. With shaking hands, she tore away the hood. Tangled strands of auburn hair fell across her face, sticky with damp filth. She blinked against the light and found herself surrounded. Roughly a dozen men ringed the chamber—clubs gripped in their fists, one brandishing a whip. Their eyes burned with resentment, their gazes hungry and hateful.

"Where am I?" Lucetta barked, her voice breaking between defiance and tremor. "I demand you release me at once, or else—"

"You are in no position to demand anything, princess." Sorrith laughed, the sound slick and mocking. "No one will find you here. No one even knows these halls exist, save for us. We are the forgotten."

Intimidation, Lucetta told herself. The age-old tactic of weak men desperate for power. None of them would dare lay a hand on a royal daughter, not when the King's wrath would fall not only on them, but on every loved one they had.

Besides, the woman in black was never far. Surely, this was no more than another trial of spirit, a crucible through which she must prove herself. The entity would not permit real harm. Even the King had witnessed her strength and lived to fear it. That thought steadied her trembling hands and lent her a boldness she would not have other-wise dared.

"State your terms, vermin," she hissed. "I have greater concerns than this dung-heap, and I will not be penned in your sty another moment!"

"She truly is the bitch they say," one of the men sneered.

A flick of Sorrith's hand silenced him at once. "Hostility will earn you nothing, princess. Yet your eagerness to bargain is most encourag-ing. Come, walk with me."

At another time in her life, Lucetta might have collapsed into hys-teria. But not here. Not now. Even in the shadow of such peril, she gathered herself, lifted her chin, and followed her captor. She brushed past the zealots with a look of disdain, as if they were no more than beggars in her way.

They moved through winding corridors where sconces wept pale light against damp stone. Slime clung thick to the walls; cobwebs sagged from the ceiling in long, silken veils. A rat's carcass lay bloated in black water, beside bones of a man long picked clean.

At last, the passage widened into a cavernous hall. Great braziers roared with heaps of coal, casting the walls in restless shadows. Long tables stretched bare, untouched by feast or council in years. Shelves towered from floor to vault, their books little more than dust pressed between rotting covers.

But the racks made her breath hitch. Rows of cruel instruments gleamed beneath the firelight—iron pincers, saws, spikes of wood and steel. Freshly whetted, freshly oiled. Their purpose was unmistakable. Yet Lucetta felt no fear. The woman in black was with her still. No tor-mentor's hand could touch her—not truly.

Then her gaze found them. Her Guardsmen stood shackled to the wall like dogs. Their armor and cloaks were stripped away, leaving bodies welted with lashes, mottled blue and purple with bruises where truncheons struck them. Each pair of eyes met hers, torn between duty and dread. Even so, beneath the broken flesh, the spark of warriors still burned.

As her eyes swept the chamber, Lucetta froze. Pavlos knelt at the far end, his head caught in the grip of a wooden stockade. Bruises marred his face, one eye swollen shut, his chin stained with the dried smear of blood. The sight of him—usually so composed, so indomitable—struck her like a whip.

Heavens… what have they done to you?!

Fear clawed at her veins, but Lucetta stood unyielding. Her hands balled into fists, her scowl fierce enough to cut stone. Were the woman in black beside her, she would have torn through this rabble like a wolf loosed among hens.

"Release these men at once!" she commanded, her voice cracking against the vaulted chamber. "You will have nothing from me until their freedom is secured. Your quarrel is with me, not them!"

Of course, Pavlos was the one who mattered most—the Droethien was the linchpin of her designs. The rest, though loyal, were expendable in comparison. Yet her captors did not know that, nor would she ever let it show.

Sorrith merely crossed his arms, a smirk tugging at his lips. "The rumors prove true," he said with venomous amusement. "You are every bit the insufferable bitch they claim. That no one has wrung your neck like a rope is a wonder. But enough of your empty threats."

Before Lucetta could spit her reply, a shuffle echoed from the darkened edge of the hall. From the corner of her eye, she caught movement—three figures stepping forward. One limped, his arm bound in a linen sling, while another was little more than skin stretched over bone.

Then the torchlight revealed the third. Lucetta gasped, her breath catching in awe. The face that emerged from the shadows was one she knew well. Hesgrin.

"My, my…" the old priest groaned, his voice a rasping croak. "Princess Lucetta. I feared my ears deceived me."

He was more monstrous now than when last she saw him. His beard, once long and wiry, had been burned to uneven stubble. The skin of his left cheek was raw and cracked, weeping from a flame's kiss. A rank stench of charred hair and melted flesh clung to him, so pungent it could turn even vultures away.

"You!" Lucetta gasped, her mask of stoicism slipping. "How dare you abduct me into this pit! I ought to—"

"You will do nothing," Hesgrin spat, then winced as pain lanced through his jaw. "Neither wealth, nor status, nor that insufferable tongue will save you. Your House holds no sway here. Not in these halls. Not in the domain of the forgotten."

He gestured to the Guardsmen chained like animals, their bruised bodies a testament to his cruelty. But there was no honor in it. The Harbingers struck from shadows, striking like jackals, never meeting their prey in a fair contest.

"Hurting these men moves me not," she said coldly, folding her arms across her chest. "Release them, and perhaps you might earn my good graces."

"Your good graces?" Hesgrin gave a wheezing chuckle, only for the burned flesh of his cheek to flare with agony. His grin twisted into a grimace. "My child, if your heart were pure, you would have yielded. You would have delivered the Divine Mother into the hands of her faithful! Instead, she lies in darkness—alone, with only rats and insects for company!"

Rage welled inside Lucetta like rising fire. She prayed for the woman in black, begged for that otherworldly strength to manifest—to strike down these wretches and scatter them like chaff. But the shadows yielded nothing. She was alone, bound not by chains but by her own helplessness. Her tongue, sharp as any blade, faltered into silence.

"For centuries our faithful have endured beneath the heel of your godless dynasty," Hesgrin snarled, his voice growing stronger with each word. "The House of Bethard spurned the old ways, casting us into an age of corruption and ruin. We prayed for deliverance—for faith, for reason—to return and set the world right."

Zeal blazed in his eyes, dulling the sting of his burns. He shuffled toward a table bristling with iron instruments and leather restraints, each made for one grim purpose.

"When word came of the Mother's death," he rasped, his fingers trailing across blades and hooks, "we listened closely. They said her body lay unspoiled for days in the summer heat, yet no decay touched her flesh. That was when we knew our prayers had been answered. She was immaculate."

"Give them nothing, my princess!" a Guardsman cried out, his voice ragged but unyielding. His face was split and swollen, his hair clotted with blood.

Two zealots descended upon him with fists and truncheons, their strikes landing wet and heavy. The blows cracked through the chamber, each one hard enough to make Lucetta wince. At last, his defiance was beaten silent. They dragged him across the stone floor, unshackled him, only to bind him anew upon the waiting table—his wrists and ankles strapped fast in the cruel loops of leather.

Lucetta knew well the horrors about to unfold. She fixed her gaze on Hesgrin, her eyes daggers, while the purple cloak strained futilely against his bonds. The priest's face twisted in a sneer, every movement tugging at his burned flesh, filling the air with the sour stench of charred skin. With deliberate care, he lifted a cat-o'-nine-tails, its strands tipped with jagged shards of steel.

"Now then, princess," he croaked, shaking the whip so the shards clinked against one another. "If you are truly the people's champion—as your false posturing would have them believe—you will yield to my demands. Do so, and I will spare this man. Refuse…"

With a sudden, violent snap, Hesgrin lashed downward. The steel barbs sank deep into the table's wood, splintering it inches from the Guardsman's leg. Broken chips scattered like autumn leaves as Hesgrin wrenched the weapon free. The purple cloak's eyes found Lucetta's, desperate for strength—clinging to her as the last reminder of his purpose.

"House Bethard does not bow to the whims of any man," she declared, her voice ringing sharp despite the tremor beneath. "Not lord, not priest, nor peasant. Strike them if you must—the more harm you bring upon my servants, the more—"

The second crack came swiftly, tearing across the Guardsman's shin. His scream ripped through the chamber, yet Lucetta's eyes did not waver. Her jaw clenched, her defiance unbroken.

"This ends with a word," Hesgrin hissed, tearing the whip free in a spray of blood.

Still, she stood resolute. Undeterred, the old zealot struck again and again, scourging flesh from ankle to knee until bone gleamed wet in the torchlight. The Guardsman's body thrashed and twisted, his cries breaking into guttural groans, each breath a war between life and surrender.

Lucetta's mind drifted—an instinctive shield against the spectacle. She envisioned Pavlos in the city square, blade in hand, dragging Hesgrin to the block. She saw the priest's lips quiver in pleas, his robes fouled as his first layer of skin split and bled. The image comforted her. In it, justice was assured.

Satisfying as those fantasies were, they changed nothing. Lucetta watched helplessly as the scourging continued—each strike so cruel it seemed intent on tearing limb from bone. The purple cloak finally went limp, pain dragging him under into unconsciousness. Whether the grave would claim him was a question the room would not answer.

"This is what we signed up for, lads," one of the Guardsmen croaked, staring at his fallen comrade. "To die for House Bethard is an honor!"

For such devotion, a truncheon kissed his cheek with brutal force. Blood and shattered teeth spat across the flagstones; the brave man slumped, suddenly still. Their heroism earned little more than fresh lashes—most of the others had already made their peace with a grisly end. Lucetta felt guilt like a hot stone in her chest for men who knew her only through oaths and duty.

Through the torture, she stole a glance at Pavlos. He knelt in the stockade, helpless against its iron locks and stubborn planks. His stillness might spare him now, but not forever; sooner or later, the Harbingers' attentions would turn to him.

You must deliver me before any harm can befall him, she thought, channeling her energy toward the woman in black. *Should he die, then this path you have led me down will have been for naught. Tell me, spirit… tell me this cannot be so!*

Perhaps this was another test. Lucetta, to her shame, had sometimes missed the larger visions the woman in black revealed. After all that had been taken and all that had been demanded of her, to break faith now would be madness. This was her crucible: the hour to prove her devotion was not mere vanity but a thing to be sacrificed for.

After what felt like an hour, the chamber went still. The Guardsman on the table scarcely resembled a man—his flesh torn to ribbons, reduced to bloody pulp. At least the scourging had granted him a grim mercy; if there was a world beyond, his spirit had surely fled to it.

Lucetta's eyes drifted to the other soldier who had dared to speak. He still drew breath, but it was thin and ragged, a wager no dice-thrower would take. The Harbingers unshackled him from the wall and laid him upon the blood-slick table, a lamb awaiting the same slaughter.

"I say again," Hesgrin rasped, his breath uneven, "this can end by your hand. But it will continue as long as necessary."

Every demand only stoked the furnace inside her. Defiance was instinctual—born of youth, of rebellion, of years learning never to bow. Even when compliance might serve her better, submission felt like degradation, like being ordered to scrub a latrine.

Why have you not appeared? she pleaded inwardly. Why must you remain hidden now, in my darkest hour?

The pattern was undeniable now. The woman in black did not vanish; she concealed herself. She had done so before, and each time it had been to test Lucetta's mettle. Perhaps she was still watching, ensuring no true harm befell her—but the absence cut deep all the same.

Fear and insecurity had blinded her to the truth. The entity would continue to place her in peril until she embraced faith—not as a shield, but as surrender. Only in that surrender could she seize destiny. Only then would the door to something brighter stand open.

Yes, she thought, a strange calm washing over her. I see now what I must do. And I know you will keep me safe.

With sudden boldness, Lucetta lunged forward and snatched a wooden mallet from the table. Its weight nearly buckled her arms, but she lifted it all the same. Hesgrin froze, his burned face slack with surprise, while the Harbingers around him snarled and reached for their weapons. Lucetta retreated to the table, standing over the ravaged Guardsman who still clung to a thread of life. Her voice cracked like a whip.

"You seek to intimidate me?" she barked. "You think the lives of these men mean anything to me? They are nothing but sworn swords. Nameless, faceless defenders of my father's House. If you think you can threaten me with their deaths, then you have sorely underestimated me!"

With a scream of fury, she raised the mallet high and brought it down. The hammer's head crashed into the Guardsman's face with a sickening crunch. Blood sprayed. Bone split. His limbs jerked wildly before falling still. She struck again, and again, until his features were nothing but a red slurry beneath her blows. The chamber stood stunned. Hesgrin's mouth twitched in disbelief. At his signal, the Harbingers lowered their weapons, their faces ashen with shock.

Lucetta drew in a sharp breath, the taste of copper heavy on her tongue. She licked her lips, smeared crimson across her fingers, and grinned. The exhilaration pulsed through her, dark and heady, nearly sweet in its ecstasy. With renewed strength, she lifted the mallet once more, laughing as she struck the corpse again and again.

"I think that will suffice," Hesgrin said tightly, trying to mask the unease in his voice. "Whatever point you wish to prove—"

"*Another!*" Lucetta shrieked, her eyes wild. "Bring me another! If you think me false, lay the next man down. Go on! Cowards!"

Then she saw them. Two glowing orbs of orange-red, watching from the shadows. Subtle, fleeting, but unmistakable. The woman in black was here.

Lucetta's grin widened. *Yes... I am learning.* The Harbingers, once menacing, now looked pathetic to her—pitiful shadows playing at strength before true power.

Cautiously, Lucetta glanced at Pavlos. Through the blur of pain on his face, he managed a small, crooked grin. Heeding him now would be dangerous—his true worth must remain hidden—so she turned her stare back to the stunned captors.

"Enough for one day," Hesgrin sighed at last, pushing himself upright. "Let her rot in a cell for a few weeks. Perhaps then she'll be more compliant."

Suddenly, the wind in her sails died. Weeks? The notion was stupefying—utterly beyond what she had expected after such a violent declaration.

Two Harbingers seized her arms and hauled her along the slick corridor, their grip a pair of iron jaws that would not relent. Shock ebbed and left raw panic in its wake; Lucetta's legs lashed out, boots pounding the flagstones as she screamed until her voice shredded. It did nothing.

"Unhand me, you beasts!" she screamed, the words torn from throat and pride. "I am Princess Lucetta of Betanthia! You will die for this if you do not release me!"

The gate screeched open, revealing a pit fit for carrion. Rusted bars gaped like jagged teeth, framing a floor strewn with mold-choked hay. A black puddle festered in the corner, its reek thick with mildew and rot. The stench struck her like a blow—old, damp decay, the sour tang of things long broken. Whatever fury had braced her spine faltered into a thin, frightened sound. They hurled her inside like refuse, and the iron slammed shut with a brutal, final snap.

"Welcome to your new palace, Your Highness," Sorrith said, lantern swinging. Its oil flame threw a small, muttering circle of gold that made the shadows look deeper by contrast. "Do make yourself comfortable; I'm afraid you will be with us for some time."

Alone, Lucetta watched as the lantern's flame guttered and fled, as the last smear of light was swallowed by the black. Darkness pooled around her, thick as wool, pressing at her ears until each breath sounded loud and obscene. Her chest pounded; her vision blurred with tears and sweat; the room's stink rose to fill her mouth. For the first time since she could remember, the rage that had been her armor failed to shield the small, animal part of her that wanted only to be safe.

"Let me out!" she shrieked between panicked sobs. "I'll kill you! I'll kill you all! LET... ME... OUT!"

UDORN VI

BY DAWN, THE INFANT CITY LAY BLACKENED AND BROKEN, ITS PROMISE smothered beneath a shroud of smoke. Ash drifted like snow across the scorched earth, coating every beam and body in shades of gray. What had stood hours ago—walls, homes, lives—was now a graveyard of glowing coals and skeletal remains. The scent of charred flesh clung to the air, cloying and heavy, crawling into every breath like a curse.

Udorn strode through the wreckage with deliberate steps, the heel of his boot crunching embers beneath him. All around, smoke coiled like spirits mourning the dead. He made no sign of sorrow. Only awe. Not at the ruin itself, but at the scale of it. For all its youth, the place had been vast; too vast, perhaps.

How many Southerners had called this place home? Only the gods could know. Many had fled the Ubneri onslaught, but many more remained here forever. Riches were scarce, though food and water were plentiful. Yet greater than plunder was the prize all men sought: glory.

In the town's center—no more than a half-made square—Udorn found his warriors gathered. They greeted him with shouts, mugs of frothy ale thrust high, their just reward for a night well-fought.

"By the gods!" Gaxas cried, his face still caked in dried mud. "Can you believe it? Another battle, and we still draw breath!"

It seemed true at first glance. Raiders trickled back from the perimeter, swelling the crowd with weary triumph. Yet not all were at ease. Some scanned the smoke-stained horizon with unease, and Tharek paced like a caged beast, his emotions surging toward a breaking point.

"Perhaps not," Udorn sighed, suspecting the unthinkable. "I pray the reality is anything but."

With all but a few men accounted for, the raiders bowed their heads in reverence. They knew all too well what Rennek's absence meant. He was diminished by the relentless march of time and age, yet still blessed with a warrior's fury. Should the unthinkable be true, then his spirit was already in Sjenohor, drinking and feasting alongside the gods and revered ancestors of old.

Initially, Udorn held out hope that Rennek had simply become distracted with pillaging. It was every Ubneri's right to keep what he fought to attain, after all. But when he saw a pair of raiders carrying a body, reality quickly set in. Despite their crushing victory that night, they had suffered a heavy loss.

Tharek held his composure, excruciating though it was. Such stoicism as was expected of any man of Mot. Even though he had been dealt the most terrible loss a son could endure, his Ubneri spirit maintained its dignity. He watched as Rennek's body was placed in the city square, eyes still open and staring lifelessly at the heavens.

Tharek knelt beside the corpse, resting a hand on his father's chest. For a long moment, he said nothing, only bowed his head and closed Rennek's eyes with trembling fingers. No tears came. They were not the way of their people. Instead, he leaned close and whispered something only the dead would hear. A final rite, perhaps. Or a promise.

One by one, the other Ubneri circled the body, offering silent nods, solemn grips of the shoulder, or brief, whispered prayers to Kholdyr. Gaxas muttered a battle hymn beneath his breath, barely audible, his voice low and raw with reverence.

Udorn stood apart, arms crossed, staring down at Rennek's still form. So many years of war, so many enemies slain—and still, loss found him here, in a forgotten corner of the world. Not in vain, Udorn thought. Never in vain.

At last, Tharek rose, face like carved stone. "He died as he lived," he said. "On his feet. With steel in hand."

The raiders let out a low, unified hum, neither cheer nor chant, but something ancestral, deep and grounding—a farewell from warriors to one of their own.

After a brief, solemn ceremony for their fallen brother-in-arms, the Ubneri turned their focus back to survival. Grief would have to wait. They were deep in enemy lands, surrounded by unfamiliar terrain and unknown threats. Every man knew that to linger in mourning too long was to invite death upon them all.

Though they had taken the settlement without destroying its outer defenses, their hold was tenuous. The palisade still stood, but its sheer size stretched far beyond what their small company could effectively guard. As Udorn surveyed the battlements, weighing strategy against their meager numbers, a figure emerged from the smoke. Rorn approached with a troubled gait, the look in his eyes like a man who had glimpsed something best left unseen.

He was built like a seasoned raider—broad of shoulder and hard of jaw, but there was something quieter beneath his brawn. Rorn seldom spoke unless necessary, his presence usually marked by silence and a kind of brooding watchfulness. He bore no ornament, no trophies, only the steel at his side and scars that told his story. As he came to stand beside Udorn, it was clear something had rattled him... a rare thing, and never to be taken lightly.

"Come," he said grimly. "There is something I must show you."

Sensing unease in Rorn's voice, Udorn gave a curt nod and fell into step beside him. A handful of raiders followed at a distance, doing little to hide their curiosity. They moved through the skeletal remains of several wooden shanties—hastily built shelters for the settlement's laborers, now collapsed into smoldering wreckage. Beyond the last of the charred timbers, the devastation gave way to a wide clearing, strangely untouched, as if the flames had chosen to spare it.

"Look," Rorn said, pointing. "Something important was happening here, no doubt."

A few meters back from the outer palisade sat a stone wall, or at least, the foundations for one. This was to be the city's true fortification, though its completion was years away. It was no coincidence that such a structure was situated north, facing the Teb.

"Perhaps we will never know what these Southerners had planned for this place," Udorn said, running a hand across his facial hair. "But they were most certainly not expecting an attack from the south. They were preparing themselves to defend against what lay beyond the river."

Rorn approached a massive wooden watchtower, tall enough to command the area for miles. Without a word, he began the ascent, and Udorn followed. The structure creaked beneath their weight, its timbers scorched but still holding firm. From the top, the world unfurled around them: ashen ruins to the south, dense forest to the west, and to the east, a faint shimmer on the horizon. Although the ocean was miles beyond their sight, its unmistakable aroma meant they were one step closer to home. From there, they might rest and rearm, then return to the sea.

At first, the people of Mot might think them cowards for returning from the campaign so soon. But once tales of their grand adventure were told, it would forever secure their place in history. The mead hall would bear new inscriptions and depictions of their glorious escape and the sacking of not one but two settlements.

Before daydreams could consume his mind, movements along the Siln's surface drew his attention. Udorn squinted and strained to see through a cloud of smoke. As it passed, he saw tall masts and furled sails of many dozens of longships, their oarsmen rowing in near-perfect harmony.

"It cannot be!" he muttered, doubting his own eyes.

Rorn looked on incredulously, then darted down the tower stairs to alert the others. Thaul and the small band of onlookers raced in every direction to spread the news of the fleet's unexpected arrival. Before long, raiders were emerging from every corner of the settlement, eager to see the arrival of their kinsmen.

It was a shame they carried no banner, as its presence would inspire utter disbelief. The Ubneri surely had given up Udorn and his men for dead. Perhaps it would have been for the better, he supposed, as their survival might come with unintended consequences.

Ships began disembarking their raiders one after another, the Siln's width allowing them to reach the shore in quick order. Were these men not kin, their arrival would have been the stuff of nightmares. It was a rare opportunity to witness such a thing from the perspective of a hapless villager or soldier, watching as death quickly closed in from the waters.

A mighty horn blast cut through the silence, so shrill it nearly made him wince. As the formation advanced toward the settlement, Ragruk's distinctive red hair appeared. The lumbering chieftain was in the lead, though his display of bravery was most definitely a farce. Were the young city not belching smoke into the heavens, he might have reserved such courage for another time.

Gods… why must you curse me with the presence of this man? Was his ignorant attempt on my life not punishment enough?

There was something oddly satisfying about watching Ragruk huff and pant as he crossed the wet terrain. All the while, Udorn stood on the tower's peak, comfortable and savoring the moment the chieftain laid eyes on him. He would not have to wait for long.

"Is that..." Ragruk grumbled, his bellowing voice loud enough for the dead to hear. "Do my eyes deceive me, or am I seeing a ghost?"

A few chuckles were heard from the raiding party, but nearly all were silent in awe. Their disbelief hung in the air like smoke, thick with the weight of uncertainty. Whispers passed between the men, some in reverence, others in dread, for they had all heard tales of Udorn's fall. Yet here he stood—unbowed, unbroken—a ghost returned not to haunt, but to judge.

"I suppose I could say the same," Udorn said, arms folded and leaning against the tower's edge. "How did you manage to find this place?"

"After the siege ended, we sailed north to resupply," Ragruk said, though his voice had no joy. "We raided a few measly villages until we saw smoke drifting from the west. So, we sailed up the river, and here we are."

Judging from the sour expressions of the others, their raids appeared to have been unfruitful. Udorn knew there to be only fishing villages along the Siln's mouth.

"Now," Ragruk continued. "Show us inside. We must rest before setting out again."

"How did the siege end?" he asked, though suspecting what the answer might be.

"There will be time for discussion later," the warchief grunted, his brow lowering. "Open the gates at once!"

Udorn said nothing at first. He let the silence fester, let the weight of command shift back onto the shoulders of the man who had cast him aside. His eyes narrowed, the flicker of a smirk barely suppressed, as if savoring the moment before a blade's plunge.

"There are no gates in this direction," he said smugly, trying to mask a grin. "I am afraid you must march around the southern side to find one... unless you care to batter down the wall here instead?"

Udorn's men chuckled, but Ragruk and the army did not share in their amusement. Their faces were long with exhaustion, and likely, the taste of defeat was still fresh in their mouths. Only by the grace of the gods did he not find himself in a similar position. No, despite every unfavorable odd, they had survived.

Perhaps there was a greater purpose behind their survival. It was a romantic thought, for every man would like to believe there was a reason for their existence. Udorn watched Ragruk and the army make the long slog around the palisade, studying their movements carefully. Even though their spirits were low, they were far from true defeat.

Open gates awaited the Uberni to the south. They entered the once-blossoming settlement, unimpressed by the ruin. To them, it appeared hardly different than the farming communities and fishing villages they were used to despoiling. Had the city been given a decade to flourish, their attitudes might be drastically different, he thought.

As the horde settled for the night, Udorn collected the city's remaining provisions. Thankfully, Southern folk held the same affinity for strong drink as their superior Northern counterparts. Casks of ale were rolled out by the dozen, though the Ubneri would have preferred the sweet taste of mead. It was the god's favored drink, after all.

Legend told that the goddess Zifnir once wearied of wine and sought a new delight to sate her thirst. For a time, she found nothing until a queen bee landed upon her arm and promised a gift unlike any other. Zifnir gave her blessing, and from the hive's labor flowed honey—sweet nectar the goddess deemed worthy. From it, the Ubneri fashioned mead, and so the tradition endured through the ages.

Udorn often wondered if such tales were no more than bedtime fancy for children. Yet after all he had seen and endured, he had learned to grant truth its shadows—every story bore some fragment of it.

Ragruk, true to form, wasted no time burying his face in ale. As night draped itself over the settlement, he ordered fires lit and music raised, as though the raid were but a prelude to revelry. He seemed eager to drown himself in song and feast, forgetting the rigors of war with the indulgence of a sailor long at sea.

Udorn kept to the periphery, content with a single mug in the company of his chosen few. Dulkin One-Eye was conspicuously absent, no doubt seething at his exclusion from the battle. It had been a hard decision to keep him back, but in truth, one that spared them all needless risk.

"Why do you look so miserable, Udorn?" Thaul asked, holding mugs in each hand. "The gods have brought us this far. We have been blessed with survival and good fortune when most men would certainly have perished."

"Because we are with insufferable company," he replied, then drank a mouthful of ale. "Were it not for our kin along with him, I would like to have seen that fool swallowed by the sea. We would be all the better for it."

Such words, if spoken openly, could earn a man the headsman's block. But after betrayal, abandonment, and survival against all odds, Udorn found he cared little for Ragruk's wrath. The gods had spared him for more than silence.

"You would not be the first to think it," Thaul said with a shrug. "But I want answers. Why were we sent forth while the rest stayed behind? The only men bold enough to follow in that second ship now rot on the beaches."

The questions gnawed, but brooding on them now was folly. They still marched on hostile ground, surrounded by enemies whose numbers dwarfed their own. Division among the Ubneri would mean death, yet many clung fiercely to Ragruk, fattened by the coin and tribute his raids delivered.

Still, treachery could not be buried beneath feasts and ale. Cowardice was not the Ubneri way—it never had been, no matter the odds. To ignore such a slight would mark Udorn as less than a man. What tale would his sons inherit if he bowed his head in silence?

Legacy was worth more than gold. Trinkets passed through countless hands, loyal to none. But the stories of men—of courage and principle, of standing firm in the face of betrayal—outlived their owners. Steel and stone eroded; words endured.

I will not tuck tail and keep my silence. How can these men continue to fight by my side if I allow Ragruk's hubris to remain unchallenged? Will my sons be proud to carry on my name if I do nothing?

The ale warmed him, but his mind cut clear through the haze. He had guided them out of Dellhaven's jaws when any lesser captain would have perished. By all rights, he should have been hailed a hero, not discarded like refuse. The thought was an anchor—and a spur.

He drained the last of his cup, set it down with a final thud. "Worry not," he said, his voice low and steady. "I will not see our struggle diminished, nor our glory forgotten. When the time comes, I will need you and the others at my side."

With grim resolve, they marched toward the city's heart, where a massive bonfire roared against the night. Its glow washed over the ruins, banishing shadow and painting the dead settlement in flickering gold. Only the revelry of Ubneri raiders gave the place breath—shouts, drunken laughter, the crash of mugs raised in triumph. A mountain of casks lined the square, tapped one after another as though they meant to drain the city dry before dawn.

Thaul lengthened his stride, beckoning their shipmates to follow. Though some still drank, the scorn on their faces was plain. None seemed surprised at what was about to unfold.

At the square's center, Ragruk sprawled atop a wooden platform, a dozen retainers forming a wall at his back. His words slurred and swayed like a longship in heavy seas, his body lurching as though he might spill from his seat at any moment. Yet his temper burned hotter with every gulp of ale, fire feeding fire.

Udorn advanced, teeth grinding, every step striking the packed earth with purpose. His tread drew eyes from every corner, voices dying into silence as he passed. The revelry soured, tension thickening into a hush that felt like the pause before a storm breaks.

"Ragruk," he bellowed. "We have a conversation that is yet to be concluded."

Merriment in the chieftain's face died like unfavorable winds. He squinted and snorted, then gulped down nearly an entire mug of ale. Scores of nearby Ubneri hushed themselves, curious and half expecting violence at any moment.

"Conversation, you say?" Ragruk belched. "I recall no conversation."

He let the words hang, as if daring Udorn to shrink beneath them. But Udorn did not flinch. He climbed one step closer, his voice steady, cold.

"Of course, you have forgotten," Udorn said, his voice cutting through the square. "For it is a topic you would rather bury. You never told us how the battle ended… what truly transpired… nothing."

The words struck like sparks in dry brush. Several of Ragruk's retainers stirred, hands sliding to the hilts of their weapons. The sight drew more Ubneri toward the bonfire, curiosity thickening the crowd until the square pressed close with bodies.

Ragruk shifted in his seat, fighting to regain some measure of sobriety. "Of course I did! Have you turned simple, Udorn? I said we sailed north to resupply and—"

"You explained nothing," he boldly interrupted. "After we sailed ashore, did you give chase? Did you attempt to join us in battle, or did you sit comfortably on your perch while we nearly drowned in blood?"

The chieftain gaped, too flabbergasted—and too deep in his cups—to muster an answer. He stammered, lurched upright, then fell back into his chair. The timbers groaned beneath his bulk, threatening to splinter.

Udorn pressed on, his words striking like hammer blows. "After our ship landed, we took refuge in sewers choked with filth. From there, we stormed the estate of a nobleman and took him hostage. We escaped only by the gods' grace… while our kin chose safety… chose absence!"

The square erupted with sound, a guttural rumble coursing through the gathered mass. Many frowned, some muttered in disbelief, and others bristled at Udorn's fury. The air thickened with heat and sweat, no room to move, no room to breathe. Yet still, most held their ground—waiting, watching, hungry to see which way fate would turn.

"Do you call me a coward?" Ragruk bellowed, his eyes wide and wild in the firelight. "Do you dare? I should have you skinned for such an insult! It is not your place to accuse your chief!"

One of his retainers stepped forward. Tall, lean, and soft-armed, he had the look of a man long spoiled by privilege. Udorn knew him at once—Skomm, a parasite who never walked Mot's streets without escorts. He descended the platform as if from a throne, chin high, voice dripping with disdain. Rings glittered on every finger, jewels flashing in the firelight—a mockery of calloused hands that had truly earned their place here.

"By what right do you speak to your chieftain in such a manner?" Skomm demanded, voice ringing with false authority. "Mind that tongue of yours, lest you—"

"Lest I what?" Udorn roared, his voice shaking the night. He stepped closer, eyes black with fury. "You posture, you threaten—but you would have others bloody their hands for you. If it is my tongue you seek, then take it yourself. If not, then hold your peace!"

His shipmates grunted and chuckled, for flickers of past savagery began to emerge from places where it had long been buried. The Udorn of old was returning, a man who could channel fury so destructive it could scorch the heavens.

"You feast tonight in the wake of *our* victory!" Thaul said, emboldened. His massive hands were clenched so tightly they could batter down fortress gates. "By old rite, it is we who should be celebrated,

Skomm! Take you and your pretty silks and fine jewelry to the brothel, where all the whores belong!"

The square erupted. Roars and jeers thundered through the crowd, steel rings of mugs clashing as laughter tore from men unaccustomed to such levity. Even hard Ubneri—stone-born, storm-forged—doubled over with wheezing guffaws.

It was never the blade that struck head-on that was the most deadly. A dagger was perhaps the most treacherous weapon, for it could strike quickly, quietly, and at any moment. Though it was not their people's way to kill from the shadows, it was nevertheless the method of choice for inferior men.

Before Ragruk could muster a reply, Udorn's shipmates swept him up from behind, hoisting him high and parading him through the firelit square. The scene echoed the triumph due a conquering hero, though the campaign had yet to taste true victory. Farming villages and shanty towns could never sate the thirst of the War God. Only the blood of Dellhaven would suffice.

Faces flickered past in the glow of the bonfire—some laughing, some scowling, others unreadable. As Udorn met their eyes, unease stirred beneath his pride. Was it wisdom to provoke so boldly? What of his kin, should some treacherous hand seek vengeance in the night? Assassins, poison, the quiet end of a legacy—such thoughts pressed upon him. And yet… perhaps there was safety in standing at the edge of danger, daring fate to act.

Who would dare to strike at me now, after all we have achieved? Let them come, be they assassins, kings, or the gods themselves.

SYLVIA VI

THEY TRUDGED THROUGH SLEET AND SNOW, AN ARCTIC GALE BITING to the bone. Damien and Sylvia rode as far as their horses would allow before continuing on foot. The terrain had transformed into a craggy, inhospitable nightmare, treacherous for even the most able-bodied. The mighty Hinterwood itself began to wane in the shadow of Morvhalgr, its trees becoming sparse.

Damien's leg appeared to be faring better, but their pace remained painfully slow. Proper rest at Rej Rhivoth seemed to have done him well, though his strength was many days from returning. But the further they drove west, the more his lingering injury made itself apparent.

During the previous night, Sylvia thought she spied a trio of shamans silently entering Dreadfire's room. At first, the encounter felt like nothing more than a lucid dream, for the healers moved gracefully and without sound throughout her hovel. Perhaps an excess of mead had dampened her senses, but Damien was all the better for it, regardless of the reality.

Snowdrifts thick as walls swallowed the trail, each gust of wind blotting their progress anew. The Hinterwood vanished behind them, leaving only a bleak plain of permafrost stretching beneath a star-pricked sky.

Clouds rolled in to smother even that faint guidance, forcing them into halts and detours that clawed at their patience.

Sylvia drew her cloak tighter, fur stiff with ice, sleet biting into her cheeks until her skin burned raw. She glanced at Damien. He leaned hard on a walking stick, shoulders squared against the storm, his jaw clenched like iron. Stoic, unyielding, even here at the edge of the world, with only her eyes to witness his pain.

"We should make camp and rest," she said, tightening the hood of her fur cloak. Sleet stung her cheeks and eyes, turning them red with irritation.

"No," Damien grunted. "We must continue, or we will find ourselves buried come the morning."

After another hour, the storm relented. Snow tapered off, clouds drew back, and a full moon spilled silver across the wastes. Yet the light vanished ahead, devoured by a looming shadow. Sylvia's heart froze, then pounded in her chest. Morvhalgr had revealed itself.

The mountain was every bit the terror of legend. A single colossal peak, its base miles across, thrust skyward as if to pierce the heavens. No ridges, no neighboring formations—only a lone titan rising from a sea of snow. Clouds circled its summit in endless swirls, hiding the crown from mortal sight.

Even Damien faltered at the sight, his black eyes narrowing. No warrior, no matter how feared, could stand before that mass of stone and not feel small. Yet he pressed forward, torchlight flickering against the night, a fragile flame defying a mountain.

The trail widened into walls of carved stone, weathered but unmistakable. No hand of nature shaped them. Ancient masons had once labored here, and Sylvia gazed in awe, humbled at walking ground untrodden for centuries. But the awe curdled quickly into unease. Whatever power had built this place, it lingered still.

The path led to a towering archway, half-buried in drifts. Snow piled high against its flanks, but the road itself remained strangely clear. As they stepped through, a deep groan rolled across the land, as though Morvhalgr itself exhaled in warning.

A blizzard erupted without warning, spilling down the mountainside with lightning swiftness. Winds shrieked, carrying sleet as sharp as razors. Damien and Sylvia hunched against the gale, forcing their legs onward through drifts that swallowed the trail. Sylvia was no stranger to winter—she had been born into its cruelty, raised in Rej Rhivoth— but even she felt the terror of Morvhalgr's fury.

Every step became torment. The wind bit like the teeth of a starving bear, tearing through cloak and flesh, gnawing deep into bone. Sylvia shivered uncontrollably, her mouth chattering like stones in a sack. Heat bled from her skin until she felt hollow, emptied, devoured by the mountain's hunger.

"We must seek shelter!" she cried, pulling her hood tight. "If we continue, you will surely—"

"I will not!" Damien barked, defiant even as he staggered. "Neither man nor storm will conquer me. Not even the icy grip of death itself will stand in my way!"

Snow spun in clouds that stung like hornets, blinding her eyes, searing her cheeks raw. Fear clamped down on her heart. Even the Plainhold, with all its chaos, had seemed to obey some law of the living. But here the land cared nothing for blood or loyalty. Morvhalgr's only law was death, and only the gods could rule it.

"You must believe me!" she shouted, fighting for breath against the gale. "If we do not find shelter, we will die here! None who enter such a storm ever return! Please, Damien!"

Damien pressed on, spirit burning, though his body faltered. Through the white haze, he searched, step after step, refusing to yield. At the moment hope seemed lost, the storm split open as if by divine hand.

Sylvia gasped. For an instant, looming through the snow, stood ruined walls and broken towers, ancient stone dark against the blizzard. Then the curtain of white swept back in, hiding it once more. The stories she had heard as a child were true. A stronghold *did* exist within the mountain.

"There!" she hollered, pointing to the northwest. "Just a little further!"

They plunged into the drifts together, each step heavier than the last. Damien's stride faltered, his breath harsh and ragged. The walking stick bore nearly his whole weight, and when it slipped, he nearly toppled. Sylvia slid beneath his arm, heaving his bulk across her shoulders. Her knees buckled, but she forced herself upright.

Just... a bit... further...

The fortress loomed out of the storm, black stone rising like the bones of a dead giant. Time had chewed its walls and snow had buried half its height, yet the place endured, defiant. As they neared a broken tower, a void appeared at its base—a hole in the blizzard's white curtain. In that void, a shape resolved: a door of ancient wood, banded in black iron.

Sylvia's heart surged with desperate hope. She clawed toward it, half-dragging Damien through the gale. The iron knob froze her skin at a touch, but the mechanism held firm, untouched by centuries. Their only hope was force. She set her shoulder against it and rammed. Once. Twice. Again.

The impacts rattled her bones, each weaker than the last, fatigue dragging at her arms and legs. Still, the planks groaned under her assault, cracking, splintering—until at last they yielded with a shriek. She stumbled through, collapsing to her knees on stone damp with age.

The air inside reeked of must, old hay, and long-forgotten rot, but it was air free of knives of sleet. Damien followed, dragging himself in and pressing the door shut. It hung crooked, broken from its frame, but he wedged a rotted barrel across it until the howling storm was reduced to a muffled roar. For the first time that night, they could breathe.

Damien sagged against the wall, clutching his leg. Sylvia forced herself to move, scouring the chamber for anything burnable. Though abandoned for centuries, the place was not empty: splintered furniture, withered shelves, the tattered corpses of books. She gathered it all into a pile, struck flint to steel, and coaxed a spark to life. Flame caught, smoke curled upward, and warmth—faint but real—spread through the ruined hall.

They huddled close, palms spread toward the fire. Heat stung their raw fingers as thawing nerves screamed in protest. Buckets of snow melted into drink, salted meat hissed as it warmed above the flames. Survival here was meager, harsh, and fragile—but survival all the same.

"We should stay as long as we can," Sylvia urged, tugging her cloak tighter. "You'll need every scrap of strength, and the road ahead is long."

Damien's lip curled. "My anger is all the strength I need, Stormguard. Trust in that."

That fury—impossible, inexhaustible—was a thing of legend, carrying him beyond mortal limits. Every Northman knew the tales of Borjifa, the night the Dread Fires burned. Yet the truth of it remained veiled. What had he seen? What had forged Damien into the man whose soul-name came drenched in blood? Curiosity gnawed at Sylvia, dangerous though the question was.

"Damien..." she said at last, her voice trembling despite herself. "I know your past compels you. Tell me what happened that day. Tell me what you saw at Borjifa."

The pain in his leg seemed to vanish, as though consumed by a darker memory. His black eyes fixed on hers, heavy with grief, rage, and a storm unbroken by years.

"I have spoken of it to no one," he said softly, the words like stone dragged across stone. "I would have been content never to speak of it again. But here—at the edge of the world, with death itself at our heels—I will tell you what I saw."

Mead would have suited such a tale, but all they had was melted snow. Damien stared into the fire, its glow dancing in the depths of his black eyes.

"Marcellus Bethard brought his horde to Borjifa, eager to drive us into the sea. They came by the thousands, demanding we abandon our homes without struggle. Sanbaen, our chieftain, wavered between appeasement and resistance. In the end, he knew—even an ocean of blood would not sate Betanthia's thirst."

The flames leapt suddenly higher, as if the story itself had stoked them. Sylvia's heart raced, her breath catching, as though she were standing on that field herself, about to face the doom of Borjifa.

"Our council chose to strike first. In the dead of night, we nearly ended King Bethard's life. Had the blade struck true, perhaps fate itself would have bent. But dawn came, and with it came battle. My riders and I waited in the western woods, descending on their horsemen with no mercy. Yet it was a ruse. Their true cavalry swept in from the east…"

Sylvia felt her chest tighten, a sudden rush of dread. She knew what was coming—every Northman knew—but hearing it from his lips was like watching a wound open before her eyes. She still clung to a futile hope, as though the tale might edge toward mercy.

"We saw Borjifa burning," Damien continued, voice low, heavy. "We could do nothing. Thousands of Betanthian blades fell on our army, our kin, our children—until nothing remained but the riders at my back. Only when they departed did we return. I found the ruins still warm, and knew for certain my family had perished. It was as if the gods sought to harden me for horrors yet to come."

Sylvia clenched her hands in her lap, fighting to master the tide rising in her chest. Her sorrow was nothing compared to his. So she held her tongue and listened.

"My home was ashes, but I searched still, clinging to hope," Damien said, his voice low and jagged. "I found nothing… until I came upon a grove. There, against a boulder, lay the woman I loved most. King Bethard's men had defiled her, then cut her down with sword and axe, hacking until she was scarcely flesh at all."

A tear welled in Sylvia's eye, but she forced herself to hold it. All of Rej Rhivoth knew the tale of Borjifa, yet none could fathom the torment borne by Damien Dreadfire.

"And then I saw them." His eyes grew distant, black pools void of light. "My children. Their bodies lay broken nearby, their heads dashed against the stones until nothing remained. My son, my daughter—murdered like dogs. My legacy extinguished in a single morning. I gathered them in my arms and howled to the gods, begging them for vengeance."

"The gods were cruel to allow such suffering," Sylvia said softly, averting her gaze. "I will pray to Zifnir that your family feasts in Sjenohor. And I will pray to Azldyr that he grants us the strength to end this war."

Damien rose with a grunt, his face carved into a scowl. He paced the chamber, searching for something—release, remedy, an answer—but finding none.

"The gods do not serve men," he said at last. "Their designs are their own. We are tools, Stormguard, not masters. They may guide us, but the path must be walked by our own strength. This fight is ours alone. Come—we must continue."

Though exhaustion clawed at her, Sylvia nodded. She stamped out the fire, gathered their scant provisions, and followed Damien into the night. The storm had broken, leaving the mountain awash in moonlight. Morvhalgr's face towered above them, immense and cold. High on its flank yawned the dark mouth of a cave, their only road forward. It would be a climb few had dared in generations.

Damien pressed on, each step a struggle, yet unbowed. The Dread Fires of Borjifa blazed within him still, hot enough to melt the frost clinging to his soul. That fire would be their only shield against whatever waited in the black abyss of the cave.

Gods preserve us, Sylvia thought, as the shadow swallowed them.

Within lay a gate of stone, colossal and cruel. Intricate carvings coiled across its surface, flanked by towering columns and statues of forgotten warriors. The wooden doors rose twenty feet high, iron spikes jutting from them like the teeth of some great beast. The keep itself seemed alive, aware, its silence thick with despair. Sylvia felt it in her bones—the place *knew* them, and it hated them.

Damien stood before the ancient doors, measuring himself against their grim enormity. For a moment, he was still, then the corners of his mouth twitched into a grin.

"Fear not, Stormguard," he said, his voice carrying like a war-horn. "Neither beast nor demon shall prevail against us. Not while our arms hold strength, and the fire of Borjifa burns in our hearts. Now, let us cross this accursed veil, and show the gods what Northern courage can achieve!"

ALEKSIUS III

H E SAT AWAKE WATCHING THE VHOS, WINE IN HIS HAND AND WORRY in his heart. Aleksius had barely slept in days, nervously anticipating an attack that never came. With each passing sunrise, Naxonnos remained as it always was: a burnt-out husk, yet still clinging perilously to life. Soldiers along the barricade appeared far less uncertain, their movements relaxed and their state of readiness dwindling.

Even Tasos began to lose faith in his command. The Loxarchon began to strike less and less until his whip fell silent as well. Under the faint light of a waning crescent moon, Aleksius spied him dozing off against a watchtower. Even the most dutiful among them, it seemed, were unconcerned.

I do not have such a luxury. Let them resent my command if they must. But if it keeps Naxonnos alive for another day, then I will do whatever it takes. Damn my pride.

Despite his hardened resolve, sleep was an adversary no man could conquer. Exhaustion lay its hand upon his brow, turning his eyelids as heavy as lead. Short bursts of darkness overtook his vision, despite both eyes remaining open. It was the most drained he had ever felt, even more so than when Sakis was born.

Kyra was in labor for nearly an entire day, he recalled. Even the most skilled Droethien physicians thought his son would arrive still-born. Aleksius had never felt such profound fear in his life. But, by the gods' grace, Sakis drew breath moments after coming into the world, and Kyra survived the ordeal as well. Such memories were reminders that courage and faith should never be forsaken.

As his weary mind began to wander into the realm of dreams, a sudden commotion arose from the north. Aleksius thought little of it at first, supposing it was the coming of another, all-too-frequent nightmare. But the shouting did not fade. It grew louder. Closer. Sharp voices rang across the upper terrace—guard voices. Real ones.

Aleksius jerked upright in his chair, sloshing wine down the front of his robe. He blinked twice, mind sluggish, heart pounding. The goblet clattered to the floor.

This is no dream…

He rose, slow and stiff, joints aching from the night's vigil. By the time he reached the outer hall, a pair of sentries were already hurrying up the stairwell, torches blazing in the dark. In that terrible moment, every one of his worst fears appeared to be manifesting. Such haste could only mean one thing.

"Sire!" one of them called. "A rider has returned. From Mor Seveht."

Aleksius said nothing. He nodded once and swept past them like a shadow. Down in the torchlit yard, the scout was dismounting, his horse trembling and foam-laced. The rider was little more than a boy, barely into his second decade—his cloak torn and face caked in dust. He dropped to a knee the moment he saw Aleksius approach, averting his eyes to the parched ground.

Tasos stood nearby, his face painted with disappointment, but not for the news the scout had provided. Aleksius had seen such a look before. It was the face of shame for falling asleep at such a critical time. But there the Loxarchon stood like a looming monolith, stony and grim.

"My lord… forgive the hour," the rider said.

"Speak," Aleksius said. "Quickly."

The scout's eyes remained low. "Mor Seveht was overrun with panic, Sire. Traders from the west say Castle Morden has been in ruins for a year now. The Northmen have crossed through the heart of the Plainhold. Betanthia is at war!"

A long silence followed, perforated only by the restless snorting of the scout's horse and a distant hiss of torches in a humid breeze. Aleksius could barely believe what he was hearing. In his exhausted and near-delirious state, he thought of flogging the scout for such trickery. But the sullen faces of the men around him gave validity to the words that were spoken.

"Are you certain? Morden fell one year ago?!"

The boy nodded. "I heard it from three tongues. A man from Moltvar claimed to have seen it himself. The fires, the bodies. He spoke of a mighty host, nearly a hundred thousand strong, coming down from the Hinterwood. Zylmacians are among them, forming the backbone of their horde. They say the Betanthians rallied their full strength northward to meet them."

Aleksius glanced at the barricade, a small, pathetic obstacle compared to the great Bethard fortress. "Castle Morden… gone…"

The loss of such a formidable structure could not have been possible, he thought. Throughout the years, travelers brought tales of the stronghold's size and presence, some even presenting intricate paintings that left little to the imagination. Only the gods could have been capable of toppling Morden's walls, or so he had heard from those who laid eyes upon it.

But now, Betanthia's greatest fortress lay in ruins. Truly, the Northmen must have found some clever deception or method to exploit an unforeseen weakness, for such massive, thick walls could never be destroyed by brute force alone. Or so he thought.

Aleksius turned slowly, his gaze drifting from the flickering torches to the scorched stones beneath his feet. For a moment, he said nothing, too dumbfounded to speak. "Do you understand what this means, Tasos?"

The Loxarchon approached with caution, his jaw tight. "It means Betanthia bleeds. For the first time in many years, yes?"

Aleksius gave a bitter laugh, low and joyless. "It means their back is turned."

Tasos grunted. "You sound almost pleased."

"No, only wary. A wounded lion is not a lion to pity. It bites harder when you press too close. It will fight beyond its strength to the death of itself and its prey."

He walked a few paces toward the open yard, as if the night air could offer clarity. Tasos followed after dismissing the scout and soldiers with a flick of his wrist. Although the night was particularly oppressive, it seemed as if a bitter chill had arrived on the wind.

"A hundred thousand men," Aleksius reflected. "Zylmacians among them. Gods preserve us. If they truly march together, then Betanthia's eyes will be locked to the north for seasons to come."

"Which means they have little left for us," Tasos added.

Aleksius turned to him sharply. "Or it means nothing at all. You think they will simply let us be? That the Blackthorn will up and vanish? No, Tasos. We are still a thorn in their side… still the humbling scar they have not yet erased. And should they best the northern tribes and their Zylmacian allies, then what? They will turn their attention westward and snuff our people out. Caldakas will be their domain, uncontested from sea to sea."

Tasos was silent for a time, then nodded. "So what would you have us do?"

Aleksius looked beyond the walls, beyond the Vhos, into the dark horizon where the first slivers of dawn were cutting through the humid mist. "Nothing yet, not until we know more. But if Betanthia is truly besieged… then the world is changing. And not in our favor. This is not over, Tasos. It just became more complicated."

Both men stood in silence for a while, watching as the ghostly mist clung stubbornly to the Vhos like a shroud. The first pale hues of morning began to stretch their fingers across the sky, casting the ruined city in soft, indifferent light. Soldiers along the barricade had resumed their patrols, though their movements remained slow and listless. Aleksius doubted any of them understood the gravity of the news delivered only moments ago.

"If I may, Sire," the Loxarchon said, the wheels inside his head turning.

"We should not speak of this here," he murmured, eyes scanning the nearby archways. "Too many ears. Come."

Tasos followed without question, boots echoing faintly against the worn marble as Aleksius led him through a colonnade, past sleeping sentries and prayer alcoves long unused. The silence inside the palace was thicker than the air outside, laden not with fog, but with memory. Ghosts of better days lingered in every corridor.

They entered a narrow chamber near the old war room, its stone walls cloaked in faded banners of gold and blue. Once the most powerful and secretive room in the palace, it was now little more than a storage space for forgotten maps and cracked amphorae. Aleksius lit a small oil lamp in the corner, then lowered himself onto a bench by a window. The sun was rising, slow and merciless.

"Speak freely," he said, not bothering to meet Tasos' eye. "I would know what thoughts churn inside your mind."

Tasos crossed his arms. "I believe this is the gods handing us a blade."

Aleksius tilted his head slightly, curious but guarded.

"Their army is gone," Tasos continued. "Drawn north to meet an enemy they did not expect. The Blackthorn are few, spread thin across this front. If we were ever to strike… *ever*… this would be the hour."

Aleksius exhaled through his nose. "Strike with what? Starved men and broken spears? Our garrisons are undermanned. Our stores are depleted. The Senate sends us crumbs. How are we to face the might of Betanthia with so little?"

"The people are weary," Tasos agreed. "But they still believe in you. Let them fight. If we take back the fields across the Vhos, even for a season, we can feed them. We can give them hope."

"And if you are wrong?" Aleksius stood, his voice remaining calm but cold. "If this is a trick? If the Northmen falter and the Bethard's wolves come roaring back and baying for blood? What then? We will have spent the last of our strength for a handful of farms. And my wife and children will die screaming behind these broken walls."

Tasos said nothing for a moment, his face growing long with disappointment. For all of his will to fight, it must have been soul-crushing to hear Aleksius speak in such ways. Droethiens were warriors from birth and were the first to tame the wild lands of Caldakas with their spears. To appear so defeated must have felt like a greater loss than if their people were to be wiped out in glorious battle.

Aleksius knew he would face criticism no matter what he decided. Hardliners and soldiers like Tasos Calellis would prefer the sword and spear, no matter what the cost, a simple solution for simple men. But governing was another matter entirely. For every warrior yearning for battle, there were dozens of civilians desperately clinging to whatever existence they could scrape out. How could any man of reason risk the lives of so many innocents to appease the bloodthirst of so few?

Having said his piece, Aleksius stood and made to retire. He felt a strong hand on his arm, stopping him abruptly. He froze, not from fear, but from the sheer audacity of the gesture. In all their years together, Tasos had never laid hands on him without invitation. The tension between them thickened like smoke in a sealed room.

"Sire," Tasos said, quieter now, though the fire in his eyes remained. "You are not wrong to fear. But you *are* wrong to let that fear become a chain."

Aleksius turned, jaw clenched. "Do you presume to lecture me on fear, Tasos?"

"I presume nothing," the Loxarchon replied, his voice steady. "I have seen you bleed for this city. I have followed you into defeat, and I have followed you into ruin. But this… *this*… would be the greatest defeat of all: to do nothing while the world shifts beneath our feet."

Aleksius regarded him for a long moment. The words were not those of insubordination, but of a man too loyal to remain silent. He stepped back, straightening the folds of his robe, regaining his calm with the measured breath of a practiced statesman.

"For your many years of faithful service, I will forgive this… indiscretion," he said, barely masking his nervousness. "I fear if we attack, we may be lulled into a false sense of security. If Morden indeed fell a year ago, how likely is this war to still be raging? Would Marcellus Bethard stand idle while his mightiest fortress was reduced to ruin? No, Tasos. The Bethard's response was likely swift and decisive. Perhaps they have already defeated the Northmen and driven the Zylmacians back to the Bymist…"

"It is possible," Tasos acknowledged, his gaze falling to the ground. "But I believe we have been too passive, Sire. If you do not wish to sally out with all of our might, then we must broaden our gaze. Let us send out many eyes beyond our borders and learn the truth of what we may face."

A sound precaution, he supposed. Better to know the whole truth of what mysteries the Plainhold fields held. Under less trying times, Aleksius might not have batted an eye at sending dozens of riders forth, but now, every soul mattered.

"We take a significant risk with our horsemen, few as they are," he said, sighing. "But we take a greater risk in inaction. Yes, Tasos, I am in agreement. Send them out far and wide. If our enemies take notice and see provocation, at least we will be prepared. And prepare a carriage and detachment, and send my wife and children to Larssa. They must be kept safe."

Tasos raised his brows but said nothing. The decision needed no explanation. The Loxarchon stepped back and vanished into the shadows, leaving Aleksius alone with the dimming lamp and the gnawing weight of his choice. As a new day began, he left the broken palace grounds and retired to what remained of his home.

Aleksius walked the long corridors in silence, the walls lined with faded banners and ash-choked sconces. His boots tapped gently on the stone, and for once, he did not mind the sound. It grounded him, reminded him that he was still alive, still a man, not merely a relic of a dying cause.

A reinforced door to the family quarters was slightly ajar. Warm lamplight spilled out onto the floor, though its glow was quickly overtaken by the rising sun. He stopped just outside and listened. Inside, Kyra's voice carried with a calm, practiced cadence.

"And what's the duty of a Loxarchon, Sakis?" Her voice was as sweet as honey.

"The Master of Soldiers!" the boy answered a little too loudly.

"Correct!" Kyra said proudly. "And below him?"

"The Dekarchon. He commands ten decades."

Aleksius could not help but smile. Her voice was so steady, so composed, as if the world beyond these walls was not collapsing inward. How he would ever be able to survive without her warm presence within the palace was a thought too torturous to imagine. But yet, keeping her near was too great a risk.

"Good," Kyra said. "And a Triarchon?"

"Three hundred," Sakis recited. "Usually the forward guard, or the flanks if the field is wide."

"And who commands all of them?" she asked softly.

"The Stratarchon," Sakis replied, nearly in awe of speaking such a title.

"And who commands him?" came Magia's tiny voice.

Kyra laughed gently. "The gods, I suppose."

Such moments nearly brought tears to Alekisus' eyes. He opened the door slowly, beaming with pride. They turned at the sound of the old hinges whining, Magia running to him with arms outstretched. Aleksius knelt to catch her, lifting her off the ground and holding her close, breathing in the scent of her unwashed hair and warm skin. She laughed and squealed as he spun her once before setting her down gently.

Sakis stood straighter, beaming as if he'd just won a great battle. "I remembered all the ranks this time, Father!"

Aleksius smiled. "You'll be a fine commander one day, my boy."

Kyra remained seated by the window, sunlight streaking across her robe and casting soft gold into her hair. She looked up at him, eyes searching his face, sharp as ever. "You have been up all night, again."

"I have had worse nights," he said quietly.

She stood, crossed the room, and placed a hand gently on his arm. "But few more uncertain."

He looked around the room, silently taking in every inch of it. The threadbare rug beneath his boots. The weathered trunk they brought from their first home in the city. The wooden horse Magia had chewed on as a baby. Every piece was a memory. He had to say it now before he lost his nerve. Kyra sat on a red linen sofa and beckoned him to join.

Aleksius sat down beside her, careful not to disturb the children's excitement. Magia curled into his side, humming a little song to herself, while Sakis began recounting, unprompted, the duties of a Triarchon again, proud as a rooster in spring. He let them speak. He let the warmth of their voices wash over him like a dying fire, knowing it might be the last time for a long while.

"How about you two go find Leona," Kyra said gently, brushing

Magia's hair with her fingers. "See if she has found that fox carving you lost."

Sakis opened his mouth to protest, but a glance from Aleksius softened his resolve.

"Yes, mother," he muttered, and took his sister's hand. They scampered out of the chamber with the slap of bare feet on stone and the echo of laughter that always lingered too briefly. When the door clicked shut behind them, the warmth left with it.

Kyra watched him for a long moment after the children had gone. She did not speak, not yet. Only studied his face the way a physician might examine an open wound. After what felt like an eternity, she rose and drew the drapes on a far window halfway. Using the light of the quickly diminishing lantern, she lit a pair of incense sticks, placing them into clay holders near the sofa.

Aleksius studied the curves of her body through a blue silk gown, nearly entranced. Despite decades spent together, he craved her with the hunger of a lion. Her intoxicating femininity was nearly enough to make him forget the somber nature of his visit.

"You used to smile more when you came in here," she said softly, fanning the glowing embers on the incense.

Aleksius gave a small, humorless chuckle. "I used to have more to smile about."

"Your morning reports must bring ill news." Kyra's eyes masked a barely contained desperation. She knew something was amiss, although she did not know what.

He ran a hand along the sofa, fingers tracing the worn fabric like a trail through memory. He did not meet her eyes when he spoke. "I will spare you the details, for they will only worry you more. What you need to know is that a rider has returned from Mor Seveht... bringing news from beyond our borders. Castle Morden fell one year ago, and Betanthia is at war with the Northmen."

Kyra's lips pursed and valiantly tried to mask her erupting worry. She was a good and kind woman, strong and fierce, yet fearful for her family.

"War?" she uttered, her voice thin as morning dew. "Aleksius…"

Before her mind could run away like stampeding cattle, he raised a hand. "They say the Northmen and their Zylmacian allies descended like fire. Traders spoke of smoldering stone and fields littered with corpses. Betanthia has turned its gaze north and away from our borders. At least, for now."

She sank down beside him, hands folded tightly in her lap. Trails of incense coiled lazily into the air, sweet and sharp. "What does this all mean?"

"Only the gods know for certain," he replied reluctantly. "Our best hope is for Betanthia to be defeated and driven back across the Plainhold, diminished for generations. But hope is a fickle mistress. My greater fear is that Betanthia is continuing their expansion through the heart of Caldakas and—"

Kyra clutched his arm. "And if they defeat the Northmen, then… we…"

Neither spoke, but both understood perfectly. Judging from the water filling in her eyes, it would have been better to say nothing. But now was not the time to spare feelings, not when sparing lives was far more pressing.

"Until I know the truth of what dangers we face, you must take the children and leave for Larssa," he said, each word a torment all of its own.

Kyra chewed on her lip for a moment, weighing the gravity of Aleksius' decree. "I know why you ask this of me. But… I fear I am not strong enough to be without you."

He placed both hands on her cheeks without a second's thought. "Never speak such things."

She leaned into his touch, closing her eyes, fearing the moment might vanish. "And if I never see you again?"

"You will," he said. "Because I will not allow the world to end without you in it."

Kyra's lip quivered, but no tears fell. She was Droethien—grief was a private thing. Instead, she nodded once and kissed the inside of his palm. Not out of duty or respect to his title, but out of love. True, undying love.

"Then you must promise me," she whispered, "that you will not die behind these walls. If the end comes, you will ride out to meet it."

Aleksius nodded, though the words caught like thorns in his throat. "I swear it."

They held one another for a long time, letting silence speak where words could not. The incense burned low, its fragrance beginning to fade, and the morning sun finally broke through the eastern window.

When Kyra rose, she did so with quiet dignity. "I will pack what is needed," she said. "And I will explain it to the children."

Aleksius remained seated as she moved through the chamber. He watched her with a strange detachment, as though this were a dream already slipping from his grasp. And when she disappeared into the hall to prepare the children, he sat alone in the half-lit room, listening to the fading sound of their laughter echoing faintly down the hall.

He would remember it for the rest of his life.

MADELYN V

FOR THE FIRST TIME SINCE LEAVING HER WEDDING BED, MADELYN felt she had strayed from the true path. Her trail was littered with bodies and blood, yet Damien Dreadfire's head remained beyond her grasp. With every barbarian cut down, vengeance seemed to drift further from reach.

Nearly two weeks had passed since her blades tasted Northern flesh, though in the Plainhold's grip, time had no meaning. Here, distance stretched and hours dissolved. The land itself was a punishment—a barren crucible where food and water vanished as quickly as her prey. Even Northern patrols, once her constant shadow, had melted into nothing.

Her instincts were failing. Or so it seemed. Perhaps she had been a fool all along, chasing phantoms into a wilderness that bore only hunger, heat, and death. After mile upon mile of torment, she yielded to exhaustion and stopped in a grove of withered trees. Their skeletal canopy partially broke the afternoon sun's punishing glare.

She considered building a fire, even reached for the last of her rations, but withheld. Strength still clung to her frame; better to save what remained for the moment she truly needed it. Instead, she tied her horse and tried to rest, though sleep had become a rare luxury.

Am I cursed? she thought, barely clinging to fragile hope. *Am I doomed to wander for all of eternity? And for what? What has all of this suffering brought me, except for more suffering?*

The air itself stung like a hive of bees, heavy with heat and humidity. Madelyn shifted restlessly, sighing at her own futility. Yet slowly, mercifully, the dream realm crept upon her. Darkness claimed her senses, easing her weary body for the first time in weeks.

But her slumber did not last. Madelyn winced as blistering sunlight seared her steely-blue eyes. She raised a hand to shield herself, groaning as the radiance pressed harder, until she thought she might cry out. Then, suddenly, the light relented. A rush of lavender and sea salt swept over her, fresh and sharp, soothing the pain.

When she opened her eyes, the Plainhold was gone. She stood upon a carpet of blue and silver thread, its weave so soft it seemed to breathe beneath her feet. Alabaster vases brimmed with flowers at either side, their fragrance mingling with the salt air. Silk curtains swayed in a dry, sweltering breeze, the fabric so fine it was nearly transparent.

Where am I?! What is this place?

A lavish bed loomed nearby, dark wood polished until it gleamed like black glass. Fresh linens lay draped across it, immaculate and inviting. Beside it, a half-open wardrobe revealed gowns of silk in vibrant colors, garments worthy of queens or goddesses. Someone lived here— someone powerful. But who?

Cautiously, she crossed to the window. Beyond lay a shoreline of pale sand, waves foaming as they met the beach, the air rich with seaweed and fish. Paradise, perhaps. A refuge conjured by the dream-world to spare her from endless horror.

"Good morning," a soft voice said.

Madelyn's heart leapt. She spun around and nearly stumbled. A young woman stood before her, no older than twenty, with thick hair like molten gold falling to her elbows. She wore a simple white linen dress, its long sleeves clinging gracefully to her frame. Too plain for such beauty—yet in its simplicity, almost divine.

"Who are you?" Madelyn demanded. "What is this place?"

The young woman smiled faintly. "I would have hoped you'd recognize your own. It is good to see you, Mother."

It was an impossible revelation—yet undeniable. Madelyn had not seen her child since the moment of birth, yet the young woman's features mirrored her own so perfectly that it was like looking at a memory made flesh.

"I'm dreaming," Madelyn muttered, almost pleading with herself. "Nothing more. Another cruel trick of the mind… or perhaps the gods punishing me for my misdeeds."

"Are you certain this is a dream, Mother?" the young woman asked, voice as calm as the tide. "You have walked in places beyond time, into realms where even the dead cannot tread. You have seen what no mortal should. Do you feel any less alive now than you did in those forbidden places?"

A fair question—and a terrifying one. Had she crossed into the future? Was this only a glimpse of what might be? The thought sent a tremor through her chest, a quickening of breath she could not control. Yet her senses spoke no lies; she felt more awake, more *present* than she had in years.

"What is your name?" Madelyn asked at last, her voice catching.

The young woman drifted to a vanity with a round, polished mirror. She took up a boar-bristle brush and ran it down her golden hair, each stroke deliberate, echoing like a ritual. "My name will remain hidden," she said evenly. "You never honored me with one. For now, Daughter will suffice. Though the word is not without irony."

Madelyn's shoulders sagged. "It is true. I never wanted to be a mother. I was raised by the High Marshal, among knights. All I ever wanted was to lead, to command. Those I cared for most were slain because of my ambitions."

"Go on," her daughter said, folding her arms.

"I was never born to be a mother or a wife," Madelyn whispered, her voice breaking. "It was never my destiny. And I… I…"

Fighting back tears proved as hard as holding off the Northmen. One by one, drops of remorse slipped from Madelyn's eyes. Yet no comfort met them: no embrace, no sympathy, only her daughter's cold indifference.

"Say it," Daughter pressed, her voice sharp as steel. "Admit the truth you've locked away."

"You were not born of love!" Madelyn burst out, teeth clenched, eyes burning red. "I was broken—violated day and night until I could no longer tell one face from the next. They defiled me, stripped me of everything. Death would have been a mercy, and I begged for it as many times as there are stars… but the gods left me there to rot!"

"I understand your pain," Daughter replied, stepping behind a changing screen. Her voice did not soften. "And I know I am the reminder of it. But I live. I am my own. I did not choose the manner of my birth. It was *you* who abandoned me, and for that, I carry my own burden. Thoughts, doubts, resentments—I wrestle with them every day."

Her pale gown fluttered over the top of the screen, cast aside. Madelyn heard the faint rustle of fabric as her daughter dressed anew, though her words cut far deeper than the act.

She turned back to the window, watching waves break and foam against a flawless shore. For the first time, the thought whispered to her—perhaps a simple life here was worth more than all the hollow glory she'd pursued. History seldom remembered the true hands that shaped it; her deeds, however grand, would fade into dust or be ascribed to another. After all she had endured, a quiet shore and a life unremarkable seemed a trade she might accept.

"The path I walk now is my own," Daughter said, stepping from behind the screen. She was no longer robed in linen but clad in leather and steel, a knight born of Madelyn's blood. An arming sword hung loose at her hip; pouches and knife-holsters lined a weathered belt.

Madelyn's chest seized. She could not name the feeling at first—fear, grief, pride all at once—but seeing her daughter armed for battle made the thought of losing yet another piece of herself unbearable. Fate, it seemed, had an endless appetite for cruelty.

"No, please," she whispered, voice cracking. "Do not make the same mistakes I made. Every oath I swore led only to ruin. I've become something I scarcely recognize. Down this road, there is nothing but darkness and death!"

"It is not your choice to make, Mother," Daughter answered. Her eyes blazed like tempered steel. "I will avenge what was done to you. I will make them pay for the misery they've wrought on my life. This has been my desire from the beginning. Who are you to tell me otherwise—a woman who swore oaths to everyone but her own blood?"

Madelyn could not answer. Every objection tasted of hypocrisy. Her thoughts flicked to her own mother—how aghast she would be to see what Madelyn had become. Every parent wanted a child to succeed where they had failed; Madelyn had only passed her wounds forward.

"I'm sorry," she breathed, fighting for air. "The greatest mistake of my life was discarding you, though you should never have come into this world in such horror. You should have been born of love. Even still, I wish I had stayed with Gareth and raised you beside him. He is a good man. He would have cared for you. You would have wanted for nothing. I'm sorry I stole that future from you…"

"Apologies will not change what has been done—or delay what will come," Daughter growled, her voice like tempered iron. She seized a painted round shield, its surface scarred by forgotten wars, and gripped it tight. "Stand aside, Mother. I will carve my destiny in the blood of those who wronged us."

She stormed to the door and flung it open. The dream shifted violently. Beyond lay a grassy plain already ruined, smoke and fire clawing at the horizon. A city smoldered in the distance, its bones collapsing in flame. Above, black clouds strangled the light, choking day into a false dusk.

Before them, battle raged beyond counting. Millions clashed like a sea of iron, so vast they blurred into an unending swarm of ants. The ground was a carpet of bodies, crimson earth churned with limbs and heads. The stench of blood and rot rolled thick as fog, so strong Madelyn gagged on it.

Tattered banners drooped in the lifeless wind, each propped up by the corpses of its bearers. Spears jutted from the soil like a forest of dead trees, each root sunk in flesh. Northman and Betanthian alike lay broken together, nameless in the vastness of slaughter. It was carnage that dwarfed even Castle Morden's fall—chaos unbound, multiplied a hundredfold.

"No!" Madelyn shrieked, lunging forward, arm outstretched. "Come back! Please—don't go!"

Daughter turned, and for one terrible instant, love and hatred mingled in her smile. "For you, Mother. For us."

She drew her arming sword, its blade shining with uncanny recognition. A simple weapon, its crossguard adorned with twin sapphires that glowed faintly in the dream-haze. Madelyn's heart faltered—she *knew* that sword. It was not her daughter's at all, but Gareth's. Then Daughter hurled herself into the tide of steel.

Madelyn rushed after her, panic tearing through her chest. But before she reached the threshold, an eruption of ash and ember burst from the battlefield, striking her like a siege engine. She was flung against the wall, lungs emptied, gasping like a fish in sand. The door slammed shut with a thunderous crack, its iron latch clamping fast.

"What… what have I done?" she sobbed, clawing helplessly at her face as the echo of battle rolled on without her.

Through the haze of grief, a realization surfaced. She had committed the same sin once done to her. Madelyn had been unloved, abandoned, left to drift without anchor or belonging. Life at Castle Thorn was marked by sadness and the hollow ache for a parent's embrace. The High Marshal had raised her dutifully, yes, but never let her forget she was not of his blood. And now, she had condemned another Everly child to the same fate.

Must it be so? she wondered. *Must this cycle of misery never break?*

The vision dissolved like mist at dawn, leaving her once more in the Plainhold's endless desolation. Bleak hills, dead grass, and the foul taste of betrayal—nothing had changed. The Northmen still roamed. The High Marshal's treachery still festered. The world remained the same malignant thing it had always been.

But her daughter—her child—was still a babe. Still untouched by the madness. Still free of the scars that had hardened her mother. There was time yet to turn from the abyss, time to choose a different path. Madelyn rose, her body heavy but her spirit drawn taut with resolve. A new purpose, fragile but fierce, called her forward.

"I know what I must do," she whispered. "I have to return home."

The thought was almost laughably simple. Retiring from war was no riddle of gods, no trial by steel. It was as easy as loosening her grip on a sword. No oath compelled her to remain—words sworn in noble company had never weighed more than dust in the mouth of a starving man. Leaving it behind seemed, suddenly, as natural as drawing breath.

She turned with newfound determination, reaching for her horse's reins—when a sudden gale lashed across the Plainhold. Cold as the grave, it tore through the tall grass, whipping it into a frenzy. Her skin pebbled to ice at once, as though the very breath of life had been sucked from her veins.

Slowly, stiffly, she turned back. There, beneath a dead tree, stood a shape darker than shadow itself. Blacker than black, it seemed to drink the light around it. One spindly arm clutched the withered trunk; the other rose slowly, curling long fingers to beckon her forth.

Madelyn's body shook in terror, her lips quivering against words that refused to form. She shook her head, a fragile gesture of defiance. The figure spoke no word, yet its will slid coldly into her mind. She knew it. She had seen its terrible likeness before, sketched in ink across forbidden parchment. Cthenir. The Accursed. God of Death, whose name was scarcely dared even in whispers.

"No," she whimpered. "No… I will go no further. I have spilled blood in your name. I have done everything you demanded of me—everything! But no longer!"

The abyss of his eyes yawned wider. White, writhing maggots pooled and churned in each socket, their foul sweetness wafting on the gale. His mouth split into a grin, jagged and cruel, teeth like blackened spikes pressed tight in mockery of joy.

Then his arm began to stretch. The spindly limb slithered outward like a serpent, joints bending wrong, skin like tar peeling from bone. Fingers splintered into hooked talons, jagged and lengthening, reaching… reaching. Madelyn gasped, panic ripping through her chest. She tried to run, but her feet clung to the earth, held fast as if the very soil had betrayed her.

She looked down—and nearly screamed. Slithering entrails writhed up from the soil like rotten seedlings, coiling tight around her legs. They dripped black bile, reeking of melted flesh and death long past.

"Let me go!" she cried, thrashing against their grip. "I have fulfilled my pledge! I will serve no longer!"

But the words meant nothing. She reached deep inside herself, desperate to summon the darkness she had wielded before—but there was nothing. No current, no spark. Her power had never been her own. Cthenir gave, and now Cthenir took away, leaving her as helpless as a deer in a snare.

The god's spindly arm drifted closer. A single finger touched her brow, pressing, forcing its way through flesh and bone. White agony exploded in her skull. She shrieked, grinding her teeth until they squealed. Her eyes rolled back, ink spilling into them until they were two black pools.

Light fractured. Colors whirled. Then, all dissolved into a blank, terrible nothingness. Out of that void came a vision, thundering toward her like a stampede of wild horses. She saw Gareth. She saw Titan. Both stood tall upon the battlefield, steel in hand, cutting a path through a sea of Northmen. They moved like gods of war, shields and blades painting death across the horde. Victory was within reach; the enemy wavered, seconds from collapse.

From a lake of steaming gore, a figure rose—Cthenir, slender and towering, levitating above the heap of corpses. His arm stretched skyward before descending, hand swelling until each finger was long as a pike, palm wide as a canopy of war.

With lightning speed, his fingers drove through Gareth and Titan. Their bodies convulsed, pinned like insects, screams ripped from their throats. Flesh blistered as though set ablaze. Titan's great frame withered in moments, collapsing into a skeletal husk. His iron spirit fled, leaving only a twisted face frozen in terror—an end so cruel it mocked all he had been.

Gareth's torment did not end quickly. Madelyn tried to shut her eyes, but they were forced open as if by iron hands. She watched his limbs wrench backward, bones shattering with sick, terrible cracks. His spine twisted in grotesque, impossible angles; his screams shredded the air—soundless howls lodged in her chest long after the vision faded.

Cthenir would not permit death as release. The cruelty escalated, a slow, meticulous undoing: joints pulled from sockets, flesh torn until it hung in hot, ragged strips. Each break sounded like a twig underfoot. Madelyn could not stomach it; bile rose, and with it a plea.

"Stop!" she whimpered when their eyes met. "Leave him be! He is innocent—take me instead. I will fulfill my pledge. Just make it stop…"

The nightmare tore away as suddenly as it had come. She was back in the Plainhold, the vast, gray nothing pressing in on every side. Only her horse and the wind bore witness. The black stain of Cthenir receded into the sky like a storm bank, but its weight lingered in the air.

Madelyn swung into the saddle and felt a hot sting along her forearm. She drew back her sleeve. A row of long, dark marks ran diagonally across her skin—bruised, weeping drops of dark blood. The edges of each wound were rimmed in black, as if rot had already begun to claim her flesh.

Cthenir's hold had left its mark. It felt absolute—an iron bargain until the debt was paid. Perhaps only an ocean of barbarian blood could sate a god like him. The thought hardened something in her chest. She did not flinch from what must be done.

If it brings me home, I will strike every last Northman where he stands. she vowed inwardly, voice like flint. *If it keeps Gareth safe, I will suffer as I must.*

And a final promise, darker than the rest: *But when my oath is fulfilled, you will release me. If not, Cthenir—you will be the one I hunt next.*

GARETH IV

THE MORNING SUN ROSE LIKE A VULTURE'S EYE OVER THE HORIZON, piercing, hot, and watching. Gareth rode in exhausted silence, his armor dusted with the grit of days unwashed and nights unrested. All around him, the Plainhold stretched on like a dried-out wound, cracked and groaning beneath the weight of thousands of boots.

The stagnant, dry wind was still. Deathly still. There were no birds, nor breeze, just the heavy breath of marching men and a chiming clink of steel. He had not slept in what felt like ages. Not really. The ache in his ribs from battle had long outlasted the bruises, and the ache in his heart longer still.

Then came the horn. A sudden, shrill blast rippled across the desolate plain. Gareth's head jerked toward the northeast, his eyes quickly scanning the distant hilltops. Immediately, the Royal Guardsmen formed a perimeter around him, shields and lances at the ready.

"Come now, lad," Sir Edmund said, wheeling his horse about. "Time to get to work."

The lead column shifted in unison, defensive ranks snapping into place like a flock of birds veering mid-flight. Behind the shields, scores of archers raised their bows, the strings nocked and barbed arrowheads poised to loose.

Gareth's heart stilled, then slammed inside his chest as if trying to break free. He drew his silver sword and lifted it aloft. The blade flared in the sun, sharp as ice and blinding as fire. For a moment, a thought flickered—death might be a kind of freedom. Freedom from the weight of command, from the torturous thoughts that cut deeper than any spear. Perhaps there was peace to be found there, Gareth supposed.

"I will not diminish, now or ever!" Gareth cried, spurring his horse to ride just behind the shield wall. "Let them come!"

The army lurched toward battle order, though sluggishly. Officers barked like dogs in a frenzy, wheeling about on horseback, trying to wrench order from the chaos. Light cavalry broke away in a spray of dust, their bows raised, eager to delay whatever advance threatened them.

Gareth's eyes narrowed. The skirmishers slowed. Their formation wavered, yet there was no panic—only hesitation. It was too familiar a rhythm, and too calm. Then came a horn, faint but clear, its pitch a sound he knew as well as his own heartbeat.

Sir Edmund exhaled like a man freed from the gallows. "It seems your hunger will not be sated this day."

From the far hill, the eagle standard of Betanthia rose, carried by a gang of riders. They swept down in practiced unison, dust trailing their hooves. At their head loomed Titan Bradshaw, his broad frame unmistakable even at a distance. Gareth's stomach plunged.

Oh heavens… Tell me he found her… Tell me she's alive…

But no. Madelyn was not among them. The hope that leapt in his chest curdled at once into despair. It was foolish to think she might return to him from this barren hell. Foolish—and cruel. Better, perhaps, had it been the Northmen cresting the rise, for at least then the pain in his chest would be sharpened by battle, not poisoned by longing.

Ranks loosened as swiftly as they had formed. Shields lowered. Spears dipped. The host sagged back into its endless march. Men muttered their discontent, restless for a clash to end this purgatory of trudging heat and insects. Victory or death—either was preferable to the gnawing emptiness of the Plainhold.

Titan and Conrak rode hard to him, their faces flushed red, cracked with wind and heat. Men seldom returned from such a mission, yet these two had—proof again of the iron that made their names feared.

"My prince," Conrak said, pressing fist to breast with a shallow bow. His voice carried urgency, not ceremony. "Time is short. We crossed paths with the Northmen only days ago and slipped away unseen. They are not far now."

The report should have quickened Gareth's blood. Instead, his gaze fell to Titan Bradshaw. The giant's face, usually carved from stone, was dark with something closer to sorrow.

"Tylar," Gareth said, dread tightening his throat. "You didn't find her… did you?"

Titan met his eyes square, chin lifted, his pride unbroken. "No. But she lives. Of that, I am certain. She has carved her way through the Plainhold like a storm. What I've seen… no man could mistake it. She is no longer the girl you remember. She's a beast now."

The words struck harder than any spear. Gareth clung to the vision of Madelyn as she had been—bright, idealistic, gentle beneath the steel. To think of her as savage, as lost, was worse than defeat. Worse than death itself.

"That is my wife," he said, his voice defiant, near breaking. "And I will see her brought home. Your courage is noted, and your service honored. Now, come. We will speak further in private."

He turned his horse with a sharp tug, forcing himself forward. Rage and grief threatened to break through his ribs, but he would not spill them here before the men. Titan, though, was not finished.

"The fuck I will," Tylar snapped. "She's gone, you hear me? We scoured half the fucking Plainhold! And if by some curse we did find her, she wouldn't be the woman you remember. She's become something else… something you don't want. Talk about all you like. Me? I'm off for a brew."

With a snarl, he tore his reins and thundered off toward the camp followers, already hunting ale to drown his fury. Gareth sat frozen, his mouth half-open. If anyone had a right to rage over Madelyn, it was he alone—not Tylar, not anyone.

For a prince raised in courts and halls, tavern insults were still alien. His blood boiled at the audacity of a common man spitting truth in so crude a tongue. Yet grace had to be given: men of steel spoke with steel, and their words cut like blades.

"I'm sorry, lad," said Sir Edmund, his voice low with sympathy. "But you've kept steady. You've kept your eyes on the greater good."

Gareth's gaze chilled. "Tylar's right. Enough of her. I must focus on what matters: ending this war and bringing our men home. I will not walk my father's path. I will not be selfish, blinded, or reckless. I will not. I cannot put my desires above the greater good."

Edmund gave a slow nod. "Then you're becoming the man you were meant to be. History does not speak kindly of selfless kings. They burn themselves away chasing legacy, trying to outshine the dead. But if you hold to this path… perhaps you will outshine them all."

A noble praise, but hollow to Gareth's ears. He did not crave his legend carved in stone. He wanted love. He wanted Madelyn. Yet fate stripped her from him, petal by petal, until nothing remained but the thorns. How cruel, he thought, that a man who sought only good was dealt such ruin.

There was one solution, Gareth thought: end the war decisively, and purge traitors from within his own ranks. Hunting the Northmen through sea-high grass would be slow and costly, and executing the Southern Commandant prematurely could doom the army. The answer lay in control and speed—root out treachery before it could strangle them all.

"Summon Lord Vakaro and his officers at once," Gareth ordered. "If we meet the Northmen in battle, there must be no misunderstandings. They ride under my banner. Any treachery will be answered with terrible retribution. I will not tolerate disunity… or let that snake try to claim my life again."

Something inside him was beginning to harden, a necessary closing-off against the constant battering of disappointment. Violence had become the logic his grief would accept: strike the monsters before they could remold him into one of their own.

"I would argue otherwise, lad," Sir Edmund said slowly, "but perhaps you are right. If this is your will—so be it."

Edmund left with an uncharacteristic haste, a curt motion that felt more like a rebuke than counsel. Gareth felt the sharp sting of doubt. Even his closest men now seemed ready to question him when he showed resolve, too pleased at his earlier uncertainty.

Such leniency was dangerous. Sir Edmund bore blame for the blade that had come so near Gareth's throat; his purple cloaks had failed to root out Lord Vakaro's circle or to guard the prince from plots. That negligence could cost them all.

Lord Kenfield proved no wiser, lost in his usual aloof stupor. Gareth wondered why he even tolerated such a fool at his side. The thought churned, sharp and bitter, until a grim realization surfaced.

These are incompetent, incapable men. Years of peace and opulence have dimmed their wits and softened their resolve. Even the mighty Titan is little more than a simple brute. Perhaps I should be looking for others —others who are driven not by greed or a lust for power, but by sheer loyalty.

It was a dangerous notion. Trustworthy men were rarer than water in the Plainhold, and to place faith in the wrong hand could be fatal. Yet the seed was planted, and it would take root in time. For now, Gareth wheeled his horse about and retired, the day's march heavy on his shoulders.

He passed wagons of wounded, bodies swaddled in bloody bandages. Some lay shaded beneath sagging canvas, others blistered under the pitiless sun. Once, he might have grieved for them; now, they blurred into one faceless mass. Each had a name, a story, but all were spent as coin for Betanthia's safety. He told himself they marched not only for House Bethard but for their own hearths and families—an easier lie to live with.

When the host at last halted and a perimeter was set, Gareth sought the camp's heart, where his tent rose from the dust. Safest in theory, most exposed in truth. Northern blades were one threat, but shadows and whispers were worse. Assassins wore no banners.

He sat beneath a canopy, nursing a mug of warm beer that tasted no better than horse piss. Hours dragged on with no sign of Vakaro. At last, Lord Kenfield stumbled into view, armor cast off, his tunic soaked and clinging, sweat running in rivers down his pale face.

"Anders," Gareth said, motioning for him to sit. "What news do you bring?"

The portly lord pursed his lips, unusually subdued, his jowls slick with sweat. He glanced about as though the shadows themselves might be listening before waddling closer.

"News, my prince? I... I have very little. None, in fact. Our efforts to infiltrate Lord Vakaro's inner circle remain frustrated. I am here on related business, but—unfortunately—"

Gareth leaned back in his chair, studying him. Watching a grown man squirm might have delighted others, but Gareth found it distasteful, pathetic. His patience, already frayed, thinned further.

"Just say it, Anders," Gareth sighed, pinching the bridge of his nose.

Lord Kenfield wrung his soft hands together, voice dropping. "Well... Sir Edmund sent me to inform you that... Lord Vakaro has refused your summons. And he is nowhere to be found. We suspect he is either with a patrol, or—"

Gareth's jaw tightened. Evading a royal summons was insult enough, but Anders' shifty eyes betrayed something worse. His gaze fell to the dirt, words clogging in his throat.

"You would do well not to lie, Lord Kenfield," Gareth snapped. "You aren't any good at it. Out with the truth—quickly."

Anders swallowed hard. "My prince… he received your summons. To your face, he would not refuse, but to Sir Edmund's? He laughed. Said your demands were a waste of time with the Northmen so near. He claimed there were 'more pressing matters' than answering you."

The words struck like a slap. Gareth sat still, lips pressed white, teeth grinding so fiercely his mouth ached. Yet he gave nothing more than a flick of the wrist, dismissing the bumbling lord.

He could have roared. Could have throttled Anders across the face for daring to carry such venom to him. But anger was exactly what Ridley wanted—a prince ruled by temper, easily mocked, easily undone. Gareth forced it down, though it curdled within him like poison.

Instead, he did the only thing that made sense. He sought an ale cart. The camp was settling into dusk, a sea of tents and weary men stretching across the Plainhold's cracked earth. Fires hissed to life, shadows thickening at the edges of the world. Gareth sat beneath a canopy with a mug of southern red ale, bitter and warm, but still drinkable. One mug turned into another, each mouthful loosening the knots inside him, each drop stirring ghosts.

He thought of Queen Charlotte—always Charlotte, her memory dogging him like a funeral dirge that would not end. Every smile recalled was a knife. Every laugh was a wound. The woman he had loved most haunted his hours like music in a key of regret.

If only he had been more attentive and not so drunk on grief, not so mired in the swamp of self-pity. How many days had he squandered? How many moments of love left unspoken, laughter never shared? The thoughts came not as sharp edges, but as blunt stones—dull, heavy, endless echoes that returned again and again, never fading.

Charlotte's death left a hole in him so wide that joy itself fell into it, swallowed before it could ever take root. Even victories, fleeting moments of triumph, even the loyalty of good men—none of it filled the void. It was the ache of a love forever unfinished, and it haunted him more than all the corpses the war had laid at his feet.

I hope you're proud of me, mother, he thought bitterly. *I am sorry I could not be there when you needed me most. Sorry that all I have ever done is fail you. Whatever crown I wear, whatever lands I claim, none of it will change that. I will always be your failure, no matter how many banners I raise or enemies I cast down.*

The same tortured voices sat beside him as daylight died, giving way to a moonless night. The ale churned inside him like a storm-tide, bitter and hot, rising into his throat. Yet no measure of drink was enough to wash away the memories—or the *what ifs.* Each swallow only brought more of them.

Above all, his mind circled back to the living—to those who had not yet left him. Edmund, most of all. A truer friend had never walked at his side, and still Gareth had snapped at him like a spoiled child. Their bond was rarer than gold, stronger than the finest steel, yet Gareth had treated him like any other court lackey. If misfortune should take Edmund from him, Gareth thought, then he would be truly alone in this world.

I owe him an apology. The admission gnawed at him, sour and unrelenting. *My tone was unworthy of the trust he has given me. My people deserve better. The few who still care for me deserve better.*

For an evening on the Plainhold, the air was surprisingly crisp. Not cold enough for a cloak, but cool enough to wash away the sting of the day's furnace heat. Gareth walked freely among the rows of tents, his thoughts heavy as the earth beneath his boots. Torchlight was scarce, their captains unwilling to betray their presence to any Northern eye. The waxing moon did what it could, slipping through shreds of cloud to silver the ground and sketch the outlines of men and canvas.

Edmund has been faithful all my life, Gareth thought. More faithful than blood, more patient than any man has right to be. How can I lash out at him? He deserves my apology, not my wrath. If our roles were reversed, he would be the better man—he would have already spoken of peace. Why should I do less?

The more he turned it over, the worse the taste grew. Judging the elder Guardsman sat in him like spoiled meat. It was not Edmund who had allowed Lord Vakaro to humiliate him again. Nor was it truly Edmund's fault that an assassin's blade had come within a breath of his throat. The threats they faced were unlike any Betanthian host had endured: Northmen prowling the edges of the dark, and worse still— treachery festering in their own ranks.

Ahead lay Edmund's tent, pitched close to his own for convenience and vigilance both. Since the attempt on his life, Gareth had doubled the guard without making it obvious. His purple cloaks remained visible, stalwart in their patrols. The rest were disguised as camp followers, mule-drivers, and men-at-arms dressed down to seem beneath notice. It was a veil of normalcy—but one born of necessity, for in a world where blades hid in every shadow, even the semblance of safety had to be crafted.

Despite the precautions, there was no such thing as safety on the Plainhold. The land itself seemed to conspire against them—heat and drought by day, gnats and sickness by night. But worse than nature, worse even than the Northmen, were the men who marched under his own banner. Gareth found his shoulders stiffening whenever he neared those whose loyalties were uncertain, his hand unconsciously drifting toward the hilt at his side.

Yet, not every face stirred suspicion. Passing a trio of Guardsmen, he felt a flicker of comfort. These were men who had stood watch at the palace for years, who had seen him stumble through boyhood into manhood, and now into the bitter mold of command. They bowed their heads briefly as he passed.

"My prince," one murmured, before his eyes flicked back to the dark horizon, vigilant as ever.

The sight steadied him until he reached Edmund's tent. A low lantern glow pulsed against the canvas walls. Curious. The elder Guardsman prized his rest almost as much as his whiskey, and both were usually taken together. For him to be awake at such an hour meant some fresh trouble had landed in his lap.

But what Gareth saw unsettled him more than any imagined crisis. Two silhouettes shifted within, their shapes warped and stretched by the lantern's angle. The gestures were too sharp, too sudden—more struggle than conversation. A grunt carried through the canvas, followed by the smash of glass and the clang of metal. One shadow lurched, then vanished altogether. Gareth froze outside the flap, heart quickening. Whatever was happening inside was no ordinary council.

A shout rang out from within—Edmund's voice, though garbled, broken into sounds too muddied to decipher. Before Gareth could move, a surge of Guardsmen thundered past him, swords and spears flashing in the torchlight. He froze, heart hammering, every instinct screaming to rush in, yet his legs felt nailed to the earth.

The camp erupted. Shouts rolled like surf across the Plainhold night, colliding, overlapping, multiplying into chaos. Purple cloaks burst from Edmund's tent in all directions, some brandishing steel, others shouting orders. The sight jolted Gareth free. He lunged forward, desperate, only to be met with the gleam of a spear tip inches from his eye.

"Halt!" a Guardsman barked, voice raw with panic. "Stop right there—hands up!"

For a heartbeat, Gareth's mind went blank. His hands shot skyward on instinct, the soldier before him too keyed for hesitation.

"Wait!" Gareth cried. "It's me—your prince!"

Recognition stuttered across the man's face, torn between reflex and reason. The spear wavered, dipped, then dropped as shame and fear fought for dominance in his eyes. He caught Gareth by the shoulder with a grip like iron, yanking him half off his feet before shoving him behind.

"Inside, my prince! Now! It's not safe!"

All around them, the camp boiled alive. Torchlight streaked across canvas and steel as men scrambled into armor, shouting of Northmen and treachery, each rumor birthing two more. Gareth ignored them all. His world narrowed to a single thought: Edmund. Was he alive? Was he dying? With a single breath to steel himself, he seized the tent flap and threw it wide.

"Prince Gareth!" a purple cloak barked as he shoved through the flap, announcing him as though ceremony still mattered.

The sight inside struck Gareth like a hammer. Sir Edmund sat hunched on the edge of a bed soaked through with blood, both arms braced on his knees to keep himself from toppling over. A savage cut split his brow, blood running freely into the white of his beard and staining his torn tunic a deep, spreading red. His hands were shredded, the flesh raw and ragged from grappling bare steel.

Two Guardsmen bent over him in frantic work, bandaging leaks as fast as they opened. Another shouted hoarsely for a surgeon, his voice cutting sharply through the tent.

"What..." Gareth stammered, eyes wide, his throat dry. "Why? Edmund—what's happened?!"

"I was a heartbeat away from the grave," Edmund rasped, his words thick with blood and whiskey. "Might still be, yet. But I gave as good as I got—worth a pint or two in the telling."

"Why would anyone come for you?!" Gareth's voice broke, torn between rage and disbelief. "What sense is there in this?"

Edmund's gaze lifted, weary but unwavering. "The sense is simple, lad. That knife wasn't meant for me." He coughed, spat red, and steadied his breath. "No, I was only the wall in the way. Whoever sent that bastard wanted you. But the coward knew he'd have to carve through me first. I reckon he thought he'd find me asleep. Instead, I was up for a piss. Imagine that—saved by the very vice that'll kill me one day."

Gareth's heart thundered. Ridley Vakaro. The name clawed at his thoughts, impossible yet inescapable. Could the snake truly be so brazen? To send assassins into the royal tent, under his very nose?

A roar of commotion split the night outside. Steel scraped, men shouted like hounds loosed on a fox. Amid the tumult came a voice Gareth knew at once—Lord Kenfield. Anders protested in shrill panic, his words tumbling over one another, but the purple cloaks showed him no courtesy. Every man was a suspect now, and no rank or title would buy his safety.

"We'll find the fiend responsible for this, mark my words, Edmund," he said, hands tightening into fists. "We'll find him and make the bastard talk. And when he spills his guts, I'll spill his blood... and that of his master."

SYLVIA VII

A HOWLING GALE CHASED THEM INTO THE CAVE'S GAPING MAW, THE wind shrieking like a beast denied its prey. Inside was no warmth, but it spared them the knives of frost that had gnawed their flesh and souls alike. Sylvia bent double, lungs clawing for air, while Damien leaned against the wall, rubbing his ruined leg with slow, steady fingers. Their eyes met—exhausted, disbelieving.

"We made it," Sylvia gasped, her teeth clattering like woodpeckers against bark. "By the gods, Damien…"

Dreadfire nodded, though his expression carried no triumph. "We are not at journey's end, Stormguard. Not yet. These halls have not known footsteps in centuries. I know not what lies ahead."

This was no simple cavern, she realized. Legend told of endless tunnels and cunning traps, snares designed not only to take a man's life but to bind his soul. Her eyes strained against the dark until she dug into her satchel. By fortune, the thick seals had spared her flint and torch from the storm's bite.

Sparks leapt at the stone's strike, and the torch flared to life. Firelight licked the walls, driving shadows back just enough to reveal what waited: another entrance, vast and deliberate. Its facade was no work of nature. Hewn from the mountain's own bones, the doorway rose on pillars the size of oaks, crowned with an arch etched in ancient glyphs and watchful statues.

Though the craft bore her ancestors' mark, the air soured as if in warning. Rage, grief, and despair clung to the stones like mildew, seeping into her chest until her throat tightened with tears. Whatever dwelt beyond was no ghost, but something far worse—something alive.

"I do not feel good about this, Damien," Sylvia muttered, trying to mask the tremor in her voice.

Dreadfire gave no reply. His black eyes bored into the abyss, unblinking, as if he might pierce its veil by sheer will. If doubt lingered in him, he did not show it. His face was carved from stone.

"Steel yourself, Stormguard," he said at last. "We have come too far to turn back. After all we have endured, here we still stand. The gods are with us, even in a place as cursed as this."

With sudden resolve, Damien wrenched the torch from her hand and strode into the dark. Sylvia froze, breath caught, then forced herself onward. To falter now would shame not only her but her ancestors. Better death than dishonor beneath their watching eyes.

She hurried after him, the torch's glow painting trembling halos across the walls. The passage yawned ahead, every surface carved in runes from floor to ceiling. Sylvia's breath quickened as she traced them with her eyes. They were not Khorrish—not anything she knew—but stranger, older, a tongue whispered before the first stone halls of the North were ever raised.

She caught up to Damien, who stood studying a relief carved into the wall. Even through layers of grime and cobweb, the story was clear: two armies clashing, one beneath the blazing sigil of Azldyr. Thousands pressed against thousands, the fray carved with such precision she could see the links of mail, the edges of swords.

Another panel unfurled beside it, the battle raging in brutal detail—axes hewing, spears splintering, swords dripping with death. And at the far end, the tale's climax: a single towering figure, triumphant over the fallen, raising a colossal greatsword high above his host. The stonework itself seemed to revere him.

"Is that..." Sylvia breathed. "Kuggvord?"

"No, Stormguard," Damien grunted. "This sanctuary is far older than any of us could have imagined. It has stood for perhaps a thousand years or more before the time of Kuggvord."

The thought staggered her. Could Caldakas be older, far older, than any tale had dared suggest? Doubt gnawed at her, yet wonder stirred all the same.

"How can you be certain?" she pressed, brow furrowed. "No tradition of Rej Rhivoth speaks of this. We have no scrolls, no totems, no carvings of such days. We are raised on the sagas of Kuggvord, of the tribes who came before him. But nothing of this..."

Her words trailed off as understanding crashed over her like surf on stone. She stared into Damien's black eyes, their depths reflecting the torch's restless flame.

"That is because our true history has been taken from us," he said, voice heavy as iron. "The Bethards burned our parchments, shattered our monuments, ground our stories into dust. They have erased centuries— millennia, perhaps—of our birthright. What remains is only what they allowed to survive."

A sickness of sorrow welled in Sylvia's chest. She could feel her ancestors here—pride mingled with grief—etched into every rune, every figure locked in frozen battle. Their struggles had been titanic, their victories monumental... yet time and tyrants had buried them beneath silence.

And still, the walls spoke. Their story endured in this palace of ice and stone. Part of her longed to stop, to trace each rune and commit it to memory, to carry this revelation back to Rej Rhivoth. But the fire of purpose reminded her: they had come for something greater, and time slipped away with every beat of her heart.

"Then we must honor them by ensuring their struggles were not in vain," Sylvia said, her voice hard as steel. "We must press on."

Dreadfire nodded, the firelight deepening the hollows of his face. "We must, yes. Perhaps one day these lands will be safe again, and our people may return to uncover the secrets buried here. But for now, Stormguard, more than the living count on us."

Another weary hour passed before the cavern widened into a chamber of staggering scale. It was no common hall, but a feasting place fit for a mountain king long turned to dust. Damien's torch swung slowly, casting restless shadows across the walls until it caught the iron mouths of sconces and the great braziers clustered near a massive stone slab that had once been a table. He lit them one by one, and the room came alive in waves of flame.

The chamber stretched vast enough to house half a thousand souls. Against one wall stood a towering rack of weapons, entombed in cobwebs so thick they looked spun of wool. The cleared stone at their base suggested contests of arms had once echoed here. Sylvia's breath caught in her throat.

I can only imagine the events these walls have witnessed...

Damien brushed aside webs and dust, revealing the head of a brutal axe, its edge still keen despite the centuries. Relics, yet deadly all the same. Sylvia joined him, eyes wide with reverence as she traced the haft of a war spear carved with faded runes.

"Marvelous, is it not?" she murmured. "These look as though they were forged in Rej Rhivoth but a year past."

"A testament to our Khorrish history—and the pride of our ancestors," Damien said with quiet reverence.

He pressed deeper into the hall, torch flaring as he lit every sconce and brazier along the way. One by one, fire bloomed across the chamber until the vast room shone in a golden blaze. Yet the warmth did not comfort; it only made the silence more terrible. Sylvia's skin prickled. Something in that cavernous dark felt watchful.

At the hall's far end rose a dais of cracked stone. Upon it sat a throne, grim and gray, catching firelight across its filth-cloaked surface. A shape slumped within it—motionless, regal, and wrong. Sylvia's hand slipped to the haft of her axe without thought, her breath catching in her throat. Centuries might have passed since this place last drew breath, but she swore she was not standing in an empty hall.

Damien slowed, his torch angling forward. "Stay close." His voice echoed like iron on stone as he climbed the short steps. Sylvia followed, each heartbeat crashing in her ears like a war drum.

The light peeled back the veil of shadow, revealing the withered husk of a man. His skin was parchment pulled tight across yellow bone, his frame locked in a crooked slouch. Dust clung to every joint, yet his empty sockets seemed to stare, presiding over the ruin of his hall.

"Gods…" she gasped. "It cannot be!"

Carved into the throne's crown blazed the rune of Kuggvord the Grim. The warlord of legend. The Ruin of Betanthia. His name had been whispered in fireside tales for centuries, dismissed by many as myth. And yet here he was—dead, but not forgotten.

"And so the stories are true," Damien said, voice low, reverent. "Here lies the scourge himself."

Propped against the stone seat lay his weapon, the greatsword Ruin. Even from the steps, its majesty struck her dumb. Torchlight played across its edge, keen as if it had been honed that very morning. Dust lay thick on the hilt, but the fuller glowed faintly—an ember-red gleam, unnatural, pulsing like the memory of blood.

Sylvia's mouth fell open. "Gods, Damien… there it is. We've found it."

It was the greatest discovery of her life—greater than any hunt, any raid, any rite of passage. Ruin was not just steel; it was proof. Proof that the gods walked among men once, that the tales of elders were not fanciful stories told to warm firesides but fragments of truth, carried down through centuries like sacred embers.

"Then it is true," Damien murmured, voice hushed as if afraid to break the spell. "Our faith is not some empty ritual passed blindly through the ages. This blade was touched by the gods themselves... perhaps by Azldyr's own hand. Forged for one purpose. A purpose reborn this very hour."

He clenched his jaw, eyes dark and troubled. "And yet—for all that I am, for all the terrible things I have wrought—I am unworthy to carry it."

He turned from the sword, his shoulders heavy with the weight of his confession. Sylvia's heart tightened at the sight. She understood well enough: this weapon was more than iron and fire; it was legacy. It was burden. To wield it meant shouldering the fate of thousands. And who among mortals could be worthy of that?

"You must gather yourself," she said, gentler than a command yet edged with urgency. "Our people bleed with each passing moment. Whatever the gods have decreed, we cannot linger."

Damien stood rooted, but Sylvia's eyes wandered. The hall whispered to her as though it still remembered its revels. Two vast tables stretched nearly the full length of the chamber, flanked by ranks of chairs—enough to seat two hundred or more. She almost heard the clatter of platters, smelled mead and roasted meat, and caught the echo of laughter rolling from men long dead.

But the illusion faltered with every heartbeat. Shadows reclaimed the corners. Dust weighed heavily. There was no time for reverie. Whatever secrets the mountain held, they would have to remain secrets, for delay was death.

A thick ledger sat on a smaller table, its leather cover cracked and stiff as old bone. The spine bulged with nearly six inches of parchment, each page yellowed and brittle as frost-burnt leaves. Perhaps it once held the names of kings, of guests long dead, or decrees of a forgotten age. Sylvia reached for it—then froze. The parchment seemed so frail that a breath might scatter it into dust.

"There are many mysteries here," Damien said, his voice low, startling her. "One day, we will return and reclaim them. Our people deserve to know the truths buried in this mountain."

For a moment, they lingered in reverence, staring at the book as though it were the heart of their stolen history. To carry it now would mean almost certain ruin, yet leaving it behind felt like betrayal.

Then came the sound. A scrape. A shuffle. The faint drag of something brittle across stone. They froze. Neither dared turn at first. The air thickened until Damien shifted, pushing Sylvia firmly behind his broad frame. Torchlight flared across the throne—and the impossible revealed itself.

The corpse stirred. Kuggvord sat upright, parchment skin stretching over bone, empty sockets glistening faintly as though wet with decay. A groan leaked from his throat, brittle and thin, as his desiccated frame struggled to rise. Dust cascaded from his limbs, yet still he stood. Sylvia's lips parted, but no sound came. The tales of Kuggvord had been nightmare enough. To see his corpse lurch into motion was beyond nightmare—beyond reason.

Kuggvord's teeth scraped against one another with a hideous creak, the sound like wet bone grinding on stone. Empty eyes fixed on them, or perhaps beyond them, weighing not flesh but soul. Slowly, the corpse's withered hands closed around Ruin's hilt.

The sword flared to life. A deep, bloody glow pulsed along its fuller, casting the chamber in a hellish light. As Kuggvord heaved it overhead, the air itself seemed to rip apart—Sylvia swore she heard screams, faint and dying, carried on the swing.

"Stand aside, Stormguard," Damien growled, black eyes narrowing. His bastard sword hissed free of its scabbard.

The warlord bellowed his defiance and charged. His roar shook the rusted chandeliers, scattering webs and dust like storm-spray. His blade came down in a savage arc—only to meet Ruin in midair.

Steel screamed against steel. Sparks burst like stars as the shock shuddered up Damien's arms. He staggered, gritting his teeth against the impossible force driving him back. Kuggvord pressed with inhuman strength, snarling through split lips, before shoving him aside as though he were nothing more than a child.

Damien reeled, bracing himself against a cobweb-draped Khorrish idol, gasping through clenched teeth. He would not hold long, not wounded, not weakened. Sylvia's fear sharpened into fury. She ripped her axe from its loop and darted toward the wall, seizing a dust-caked shield from its iron hook. The weight nearly toppled her, but she hefted it with both arms and set her stance.

Azldyr, give me courage! Give me the strength to vanquish this nightmare!

With fear thundering in her chest, Sylvia let out a raw, defiant cry and hurled herself forward. Her axe carved through the air and buried itself in Kuggvord's shoulder with a crunch of brittle bone. For a heartbeat, she thought the strike was true—until the corpse simply turned its hollow gaze upon her.

Gods! she thought, panicked. *What have I done?!*

The backhand came like a storm. Kuggvord's withered arm lashed out with monstrous strength, and Sylvia flew across the chamber like a rag doll. She hit the stone floor with a bone-jarring thud, her breath torn from her lungs in a single brutal gasp. Gagging, clawing for air, she struggled to rise, but her body betrayed her.

Damien's roar split the hall. He surged back into the fray, his bastard sword screaming through the air. Ruin rose to meet it, and this time the clash shattered his steel. The blade snapped in a spray of sparks, fragments skittering across the flagstones. Damien froze, wide-eyed—the first flicker of fear Sylvia had ever seen in him.

Ruin came screaming down again. Damien dove aside, the cursed edge cleaving empty air by inches. He raced to the rack and snatched a spear, bracing it with both hands, trying to gain the reach he desperately needed. But the dead mocked the living. Kuggvord spun Ruin in a blur, and the sword bled into a spear of its own, its shaft seething with black smoke and a hateful crimson glow.

"Damien!" Sylvia cried, clutching her ribs. "We have to go!"

But she could only watch, helpless, as the two warriors circled—two predators in a pit of stone. Spears darted and clashed like striking serpents, their fury echoing through the vast hall. Then, with a savage thrust, Damien drove his point clean through Kuggvord's chest, iron bursting from the corpse's back in a spray of dust and decay.

But the spear through its chest did nothing. The corpse neither faltered nor fell. With a groan that rattled the rafters, Kuggvord lifted Ruin high. The weapon writhed in his grip, lengthening, unraveling into a whip of iron tails. A dozen barbed ends glowed like coals pulled straight from a forge. The lash cracked through the air, close enough that Damien felt the sting of heat across his cheek.

Snarling, the corpse wrenched the spear out of its ribs and cast it aside. Damien seized a great axe from the rack, his face slick with sweat, his breath ragged but unyielding. Desperation burned in him now—yet desperation had always been the fuel of his victories. He charged, reckless and unbowed.

The whip came again, a storm of shrieking tails. Damien braced, catching the coiling strikes against the axe's haft. Wood groaned, but the snare gave him his chance. With a roar, he surged in close and smashed a fist into Kuggvord's skeletal jaw. The blow staggered the ancient one, brittle teeth clattering against stone. In the same motion, Damien twisted hard on the axe haft, tearing the cursed weapon free of its master's grip.

Dear gods! Sylvia thought, too anxious to breathe.

Ruin coiled and shifted in Damien's hands, shedding its whip form and swelling back into the greatsword of legend. Its crimson light flared brighter than before, spilling across the throne room in a molten haze. Kuggvord reeled, groaning deep in his withered chest, his maw splitting into a scream that was half-wail, half-windstorm. And still Damien did not strike. He raised the blade high, the weight of history burning in his eyes.

"My quarrel is not with you," he growled, voice low but ringing with command. "We are kin. Ancient Khorria flows in my veins as it did in yours. You kept these lands safe through conquest. Now the same foe has risen again. I ask not for your death… but for your strength. For your wisdom."

Kuggvord's head cocked to one side, like a hound puzzling over its master. The light in his sockets dimmed, flickering. Sylvia, clutching her ribs, staggered to her feet. Her first thought was to circle behind and bury her axe in the creature's spine, end it before it could strike again. But something in the air stayed her hand. The hall had grown hushed, heavy, as though the gods themselves leaned close to witness what might unfold.

"Betanthia has risen again to break the free North," Damien thundered, his voice echoing against the vaulted stone. "The sacrifice you made to shield our people now lies in peril. King Bethard stands on the edge of victory, his armies grinding us into dust. Our kin fight with courage, but their strength is waning. I came here to find what you once found. To shoulder what you once bore. To make the same sacrifice."

The hall fell still, silence pressing like a shroud. Torchlight guttered, shadows stretching long across the runes. Kuggvord's rotten face fixed on him, unblinking, the ember glow within his sockets faltering as though stirred by memory.

Slowly, almost painfully, the corpse's jaw worked, the remnant of a voice rattling deep inside his throat—but only a dry rasp came forth. No words. No language left. Realization weighed on the ancient one like chainmail. Kuggvord's head sagged, a warrior shamed by the truth of his own decay.

Damien lowered Ruin slightly, not in surrender but in reverence. His voice softened, steady, carrying the weight of oaths. "I ask not that you rise again to wage this war. You have done your part. Now it falls to your blood, to your heirs, to me. Grant me your blessing, Kuggvord the Grim, so I—Damien Dreadfire—may finish what you began."

Sylvia's chest seized, breath caught sharp in her lungs. *Blessing?* The word struck her like a hammer. Their mission had been simple: find Ruin, seize it, and return. Yet here was Damien, baring his soul to a corpse, begging not just for a weapon, but for its master's mantle. Horror and awe collided within her, leaving her trembling. Had he planned this all along? Or was the mountain itself reshaping his fate before her eyes?

Slowly, impossibly, a smile crept across Kuggvord's withered face. It was not the leer of a revenant but the weary smile of a man finally released from chains unseen. Centuries of exile, of unending vigilance, had come to an end. Relief shone through rotted flesh.

He lurched forward, eyes fixed on Ruin. Damien dropped to one knee and held the greatsword upright in both hands, offering the hilt like a son returning his father's heirloom. The corpse's brittle fingers traced the fuller, bones rasping against steel in a sound both tender and terrible—an ancient warrior saying farewell to the weapon that had defined him. Were it not for the river of dread coursing in her veins, Sylvia might have wept at the sight.

Then Kuggvord raised one trembling hand and extended a single, skeletal finger. With infinite slowness, he pressed its tip between Damien's eyes. The cavern roared. Stone shuddered and cracked as if the mountain itself recoiled. A stink of rot and old blood flooded the air. Sylvia's stomach turned. Then came the light—piercing, blinding, a bolt of raw blue fire that burned from Kuggvord's fingertip straight into Damien's skull.

"ARRGGHHH!" Damien roared, jaw locked so hard she swore his teeth would shatter. Ruin slipped from his hands and crashed against the stone, its ring reverberating like a funeral bell.

A wind swept through the chamber, wild and unnatural, tearing at banners long rotted to threads, scattering centuries of dust. At its heart stood Kuggvord, smiling faintly even as his bones cracked apart. One by one they splintered, collapsing into a pile of brittle fragments. The Ruin of Betanthia was gone, his spirit freed at last to drink and feast in Sjenohor's eternal hall.

Sylvia let out a shaky breath, relief flooding her chest until it ached. Limping forward, she fell to Damien's side, her eyes locked on the mound of dust. She could not decide what terrified her more—the collapse of the greatest warlord who ever lived, or what his final gift had just done to Damien.

"Are you alright?" she wheezed.

Dreadfire did not answer. He stood like a statue, black eyes unfocused, staring into some abyss only he could see. It was as though his mind had been thrust beyond the veil, shown things no mortal ought to behold. A faint film clouded his eyes, like water glazing glass, before vanishing just as quickly. The storm had passed—or so it seemed—but Sylvia felt a chill coil in her gut.

"Come," she pressed, forcing her voice steady. "We must leave this cursed place."

He did not move. Not at first. He only stared, hollow and silent, while the braziers crackled faintly around them. Minutes passed like hours before Damien stirred. Slowly, deliberately, he knelt and lifted Ruin from the floor. The blade throbbed in his grip, its red glow pulsing like a heartbeat. Sylvia froze as a whisper coiled through the chamber—faint, tortured cries, the wailing of hundreds, perhaps thousands, bound to the weapon's soul.

Dreadfire gazed deep into that glow as though transfixed. His lips parted in something between awe and hunger. "Yes," he said at last, his voice quiet but firm. "The hour grows late, and our people remain in danger. But before we depart, there is something I must do."

He turned from the throne and strode deeper into the hall, Ruin's glow painting his shadow long across the stone. Sylvia followed hesitantly, her breath quickening with unease.

At another table sat offerings untouched by time: chests of coin, small barrels, tarnished platters heaped with treasures. He swept aside gold and jewels without so much as a glance, the wealth of kingdoms clattering to the floor like gravel. What mattered was not the treasure, but the vessel. From the pile, he pulled forth a heavy chest, empty now, its cracked binding still sturdy.

He knelt beside Kuggvord's remains and set the empty chest at the corpse's side. With hands both reverent and shaking, he swept ash and brittle bone into the box — a crude, fitting burial for the greatest Khorrish warrior to ever walk Caldakas — then tucked the chest beneath his arm like a solemn prize.

Temptation, however, is a patient thing. Sylvia drifted from his shadow toward the offering table and, with practiced fingers, filled her belt-pouches with gems and coins. The soft clink of metal was almost lost beneath the hall's echo, but not to Dreadfire's ears.

"Do not burden yourself with riches, Stormguard," he warned, voice low. "The mountain is treacherous enough without their added weight."

"This is not for me," she answered, tightening the pouches. "These could help pay for the entire war. They'll keep our people alive."

He said nothing more. Together they turned for the cave mouth and began the long, lonely trudge back through corridors that seemed to drink the torchlight. Though Sylvia bore a living flame, Ruin's glow threw a deeper, colder light through the stone; its radiance seemed to pull the dark apart and set it moving.

Shadows writhed on the walls—not cast by her torch, but conjured by the sword itself. Figures rose and fell in a ghostly reenactment of fights long ended: armor clashed, blades rang, men fell and were pulled up again to fight as though the stone remembered blood better than time. The images came only from Ruin, and they carried a stench of iron and old fury.

What malevolence had been hammered into that steel? Had the gods poured spite into the blade when it was forged? Questions like spear-thrusts lodged in Sylvia's mind.

What have we done? she pondered as they approached the grand foyer. *And what are we about to do? Are we merely pieces on some divine board?*

Whatever the gods' designs, they were now walking back into the world carrying a force unseen for centuries. As they stepped into the frigid air, Ruin's heat steamed the night, hissing off the snow. The sword did not simply reflect light; it seemed to think, to hunger—its red heart burning with the fury of a thousand suns.

May our enemies be scorched… and may our people be spared from this terrible fate…

LUCETTA VI

WEEKS OF STINK AND SOLITUDE GNAWED AT HER FRAGILE MIND. Time itself had slipped from her grasp—day and night blurred until she wondered if years had passed. The air was thick with mildew and rot; her only measure of change was the crawling of vermin through cracks in the stone. Meals came rarely, tossed like scraps to a dog: a lump of stale bread, a strip of meat already turning sour. Even starving beasts would have recoiled.

Hunger had become less an affliction than a companion. She barely noticed the twisting ache in her gut anymore; the greater torment was her own mind, wandering endlessly through a labyrinth of schemes and punishments. Every daydream ended the same: her enemies broken, her betrayers writhing beneath her heel.

After three days without another living voice, a spear of lantern light lanced through the black. Lucetta squinted, her eyes raw from disuse, as a Harbinger slouched toward her cell with a tin platter of filth. His water skin swung at his hip, green with stagnation. He lifted the lantern deliberately, letting its glare sting her eyes.

Lucetta met it with a feral glare, her lips peeling back from her teeth. She hissed, then lunged at the bars with a rabid fury that rattled the iron.

"Easy now, princess," the Harbinger mocked, smirking. "Maybe a little longer in the dark will sweeten your manners."

He slid the plate through the bars and sauntered off, his laughter echoing as the lantern's glow dwindled into nothing. Alone again, Lucetta stared at the meager offerings. Bread crumbled to powder in her fingers; the strip of meat reeked of rot. Tears stung her eyes as she forced the bile down.

Was this the cost of good intentions? Would she have fared better had she simply stood aside, watching the world burn without interference? Such questions gnawed at her unraveling psyche until even sleep offered no mercy. Her dreams were not of joy or memory, but only mirror images of her prison—endless dark, endless cold.

Then came the sound. A pitiful groan, low and ragged, drifting from the far corner of her cell. Lucetta froze, breath caught in her throat, telling herself it was her fractured mind at play. But then it came—a faint ripple of pinkish-purple light seeping from the stone, cold fog curling across the floor and prickling her skin like nettles.

She crawled backward on hands and knees, panic clawing through her chest, until her back struck the wall. From the glow rose a figure, long-limbed and spindly, dragging itself upward as if climbing from the underworld. Strands of knotted hair swayed like rotted vines, stirring in an icy gale that had no source.

"No, please!" Lucetta shrieked, tearing at the bars with bloodied fingers. "Whoever you are… whatever you are… leave me be!"

The light flared suddenly, flooding the cell from floor to ceiling. It should have blinded her, but her eyes drank it in, soothed even as terror strangled her. The radiance was almost holy… but at its center loomed the specter that ruined it.

"Daughter…" A frail voice sobbed from the light. "Why?"

Lucetta's mouth went dry, her heart hammering against her ribs.

In her nightmares, the Queen haunted her, whispering venom, tearing at her sanity. But this was no dream. She was awake. She was certain of it.

"Why…" moaned Charlotte Bethard, face pale as grave wax, eyes like wet glass. "Why did you leave me in the dark, daughter?"

The Queen's flesh was olive green, stretched taut across jutting bones. Black pits and sores pocked her face where worms and flies had long since feasted. Her once-lustrous hair, now brittle and white, clung to her scalp in ragged tufts. But worst of all were her hands.

Charlotte's fingers had grown twice their length, warped and gnarled, nails jutting out like rusted daggers. Her mouth sagged into a drooping frown as flesh sloughed away from her jaw, strips of skin peeling like wet parchment. The sight was more revolting than the corpse Lucetta once saw rotting on the Camsby bridge.

"Mother… please!" she whimpered, voice cracking. "I'm sorry for what I did to you. It was… it was necessary. I only did what I had to, to save our family, to save our people!"

But the eyes that stared back were not her mother's. Cold, glassy, and unblinking, they carried no love, no familiarity—only malice. Perhaps this was not Charlotte at all, but some darker spirit that wore her face. Or perhaps the woman in black had conjured this vision as yet another torment.

For what purpose? Lucetta could not guess. Charlotte's death had already been her doing. Why twist the knife further? Hunger and solitude gnawed her sanity thin, leaving her thoughts muddled and frantic.

"You were my first and only daughter," Charlotte said, tears of blood spilling down her sunken cheeks. "The best of me made flesh… yet my greatest disappointment. My undoing."

Lucetta's tears spilled freely despite her thirst. Since childhood, she had only ever yearned for her mother's pride. Marcellus had been kind once, attentive, even loving. But it was Charlotte—ever graceful, ever radiant—whose approval she coveted most. And here she was, damned by it, denied it even in death.

From her earliest memory, Lucetta had carried the weight of failure. Even after she bloomed into womanhood, beauty glimmering like her own cruel weapon, she still withered in Charlotte's shadow. How could any daughter rival the most celebrated woman in Betanthia? Bards sang her praises in taverns, poets scrawled her charity on parchment, and courtiers whispered of her grace as if she were a goddess in mortal flesh.

The thought lit a fire through Lucetta's despair. Pavlos had been right to end her. It was not Lucetta's crime that her mother lay rotting, but Charlotte's own ceaseless meddling—always prying, always judging, always prodding deeper than need be. None of the others had endured it. Only she.

"None of this had to happen," Lucetta spat, nostrils flaring, hatred drowning her fear. "If you had only kept to yourself. If you hadn't tried to chain my every choice! I didn't kill you—you killed yourself with your meddling. Why couldn't you just leave me be?"

The Queen only stared, her eyes black wells without a ripple. Then her slack lips curled, first into a smirk, then into something twisted, gleeful, hungry. She lurched forward on all fours, bones cracking, joints snapping like kindling.

"You little cunt," Charlotte hissed, her voice no longer her own but some guttural thing from the grave. "All I ever did was love you—watch after you—and this is my reward? You cast me into the dark! You left me... in... the... DARK!"

Her skeletal fingers snaked forward, clawing for Lucetta's face. There was nowhere to flee; the cell swallowed her whole. She flailed, batting away the bony talons, but they kept coming. Charlotte's jaw sagged wide, spilling a gush of black bile, dripping with squirming white worms.

"Go away!" Lucetta shrieked, curling tight against the stone. "Spirit, protect me! Please—I beg of you!"

Suddenly, Charlotte's claws faltered. Her ruined face slackened, and for the briefest moment, the horror bled away, replaced by something heartbreakingly human. Life flickered back into her hollow eyes—memories, love, and a thousand lost years shimmering in the sickly violet glow. The rage and malice drained from her features until only grief remained. She looked like a mother again.

"No… Mother… please, don't leave me," Lucetta choked, reaching out though her shackled arms would not carry her far enough. "I pushed you away because I thought I was unworthy of your love—because I was afraid of you—and now I've done it again. Please forgive me! Don't leave me alone!"

But the Queen only lowered her gaze. She crept back across the stone floor, each movement slower, dimmer, as though some invisible cord of anguish were drawing her into the corner. The light around her dimmed with every step. Her outline broke apart, wisp by wisp, until nothing remained but a scent—wildflowers, faint and forlorn, a fragrance Lucetta remembered from her childhood. It lingered like an unanswered prayer.

A raw sound tore from Lucetta's throat, half scream, half sob. She convulsed as she cried, shaking like a child lost in the dark. She had driven her mother away again—driven everything good away. Perhaps she was cursed. Perhaps she destroyed all she touched. The cell closed around her like a coffin, and the thought came unbidden: death would be easier than this.

Her gaze fell to her own wrist. The quickest way would be to gnaw through it. Painful, yes—but it would be over in moments. No more hunger. No more shame. No more ghosts. She pressed her teeth to the tender flesh and braced herself for the bite.

"There, there, child," a voice cooed from the shadows, low and familiar, smooth as silk. "You must not despair."

A pair of orange-red eyes flared to life at her side, bathing the cell in a hellish glow. Out of the blackness stepped the woman in black at last, her face pale and inhuman, her presence heavier than chains. She laid one leathery hand on Lucetta's shoulder and, with the other, brushed a matted lock of hair from her cheek.

"I am a horrible daughter… a horrible person," Lucetta sobbed, body quaking. "I betrayed those who loved me most—and for what? To rot in this pit until they decide to end me? I've failed. I always fail…"

The woman in black's sigh rattled like dry leaves. "So fragile still. I have given you every gift, yet you let sentiment foul your heart and blind your eyes. Perhaps you will never assume your true potential."

Rage, sudden and wild, flooded Lucetta's veins. She lunged, fingers locking around the entity's throat. Nails dug deep into cold flesh, but the woman did not flinch.

"I hate you!" Lucetta shrieked, shaking with fury. "I'll kill you! I'll kill you!"

Laughter spilled from the creature, a chorus of voices layered in discord, shrill and deep all at once. With effortless strength, it tore Lucetta's hands away.

"Good," the woman said, rising. Her shadow spread like oil into the corners. "Now you are ready. Ready to hate. Ready to kill."

Lucetta collapsed, heaving, her sobs echoing off the damp stone. One by one, torches along the hall blazed to life, flooding the dungeon with firelight. Iron squealed as her cell door groaned open, its lock undone by unseen hands.

The entity had vanished, but its absence weighed no lighter. The air pressed in around her, thick and suffocating, as oppressive as a Cardale summer. For a heartbeat, Lucetta longed to abandon her campaign, to crawl away from the madness that had swallowed her whole. But deep down, she knew the truth: there was no retreat. Every soul who had interfered in her grand design would have to pay.

Murderous intent steeled her trembling frame. She rose on unsteady legs, swaying like a drunkard, and stumbled from her cell. Hunger clawed at her insides, dizziness buckled her knees, and bile threatened to rise. The torchlight blazing along the walls burned her eyes raw, white-hot as if she stared into an afternoon sun.

Then came the voice. Soft, melodic, eerily familiar—drifting down the corridor like perfume.

"Come…" it whispered, thin as mist. "Come here…"

Lucetta froze, ears straining. The voice was female, but it was not her mother. Nor the woman in black. For an instant, she thought it might be her own voice, echoing back from some fractured corner of her mind—or from a future self calling through the veil. A haze coalesced in the dark, a misty outline with an arm stretched forth, beckoning.

Fear should have rooted her where she stood. Instead, fire churned in her chest. She followed. Step by hesitant step, she shadowed the blur as it glided down the hall. Its voice grew clearer, higher in pitch, lighter, younger.

"Who are you?" she whispered hoarsely. "Where are you leading me?"

The figure brightened, solidifying. Not a phantom, not some faceless shade—no, it was a child. Small, dainty, clad in a purple gown trimmed in white. Lucetta's breath hitched as recognition struck her like a spear. It was *her.*

"I've been waiting for you," the little girl said, smiling.

"W… waiting for me?" Lucetta stammered, retreating a pace. "Why? For what?"

A small, warm hand slipped into hers. The touch was impossibly gentle, soothing as a draught of red wine. For a fleeting instant, her mind was flooded with memories she had long buried—childhood laughter, the warmth of hearthfires, the sweet simplicity of being wanted. The young Lucetta only giggled, then pointed with her free hand to the left.

"For you to come home!"

Home. The word struck her like a switch. Foreign, alien—something she had always feared would bind her, cage her. Yet in this moment, it was the thing she yearned for most. A home. A place not built of iron bars and hunger.

The little girl tugged gently, leading her deeper into the dark, as if her small eyes could pierce shadows grown impenetrable. Lucetta stumbled along, each step heavier than the last, but her guide never faltered. Soon, they came to a stop before what felt like a warped frame of wood. Her fingers traced its damp, uneven surface, finding grooves, gashes, and rot. She fumbled for a latch, clumsy and blind.

Then the door burst open with a thunderclap, as if blown from its hinges by some unseen gale. A flood of blistering sunlight seared her eyes raw, flaying her pale skin with its warmth. She cried out and raised her arms, desperate to retreat back into the cool dark—but the door was gone. There was no dungeon, no cell, no trace of the stinking black stone. Instead, beneath her bare feet lay smooth cobbles she knew well. Around her rose familiar facades and peaked roofs. Cardale. The central square.

The little girl spun in delight, clapping her hands. "We're here! We're home!"

Although it was home, it was not *her* dwelling. Lucetta craned her neck toward the Westwind Citadel's tallest spire, but her small companion tugged her forward with relentless strength. The square swelled with people in great droves, just as she had seen in her visions. Her chest throbbed violently, her heartbeat staggering and skipping. Sweat prickled beneath her arms and across her brow, yet her skin grew as cold as winter stone.

"No… no!" Lucetta pleaded. "Not again! Not this!"

She spun to flee, but the child's grip tightened like iron. When she turned back, the world had shifted. She was no longer in the crowd, but upon a gallows. Shackles bound her wrists, their weight dragging her arms to the sides. A rough coil of hemp was looped about her throat, its scratchy fibers gnawing at her skin like a serpent. Below, the teeming masses fell silent, thousands of eyes turning to her in unison, the weight of their gaze suffocating.

Out from behind a burly watchman drifted the woman in black. Mist curled around her like smoke from an unseen pyre, her grin twisted but tinged with something mournful. She passed through a nobleman as if he were air, unseen by any but Lucetta.

"Why must you keep showing me this?!" Lucetta cried, straining against her bonds. "What do you want me to know? Why did they kill you? *Why?!*"

Soft arms wrapped about her leg. She looked down and saw the little girl clinging to her, smiling with warmth and innocent love. Lucetta's heart broke—and then she dropped.

Then came the deafening snap, and the deepest blackness. No sound. No warmth or cold. No taste, no scent. It was a perfect void, a cradle of nothingness where fear and pain, even memory itself, ceased to exist. For the first time in her life, Lucetta drifted in utter stillness, free of every wound and every thought. If this were death, then death was nothing to fear at all.

But the peace shattered like glass. She awoke sprawled on the filthy floor of her cell, face caked in grime, hair clotted with pieces of moldy straw. The stench of mildew, rot, and human waste clawed up her nose—a rancid reminder that her nightmare had not ended. Worse, it had left her yearning for that brief serenity, for the freedom of oblivion.

"Mother..." Lucetta whispered hoarsely, tears leaking into the dirt. "I want to join you in the dark. Please... let me be free..."

"No, child."

The voice rose from the far corner, low and steady. Orange-red eyes flickered like dying embers, revealing the woman in black's silhouette.

Her presence was colder than stone, yet her words trembled with something almost tender.

"You must press forward," she said. "Bring your destiny to fruition. You must learn... the truth of me..."

UDORN VII

THE LAND ITSELF RECOILED BENEATH THE UBNERI HOST, AS IF THE old gods had stirred to witness what doom approached. Thousands of boots crushed brittle grass and churned loose soil into mud as the horde marched south, smoke from the sacked city curling behind them like a funeral pyre. The sun was already cruel overhead, casting long shadows from helms and spears. Flies buzzed like carrion spirits, drawn to blood, unsated.

Udorn rode at the front, not as a commander by title, but by presence. Every glance, every word whispered among the ranks drifted to him. Not Ragruk. Not anymore. His horse moved with grim patience, each hooffall measured, as though the beast understood the weight of what followed. Dust clung to Udorn's armor and hair, but he made no effort to brush it away. Let them see him as he was: battle-worn, sunscorched, alive when so many were not.

Behind him, the great war column stretched across the hills like a living scar, banners swaying limp in the heat. Every raider bore wounds, trophies, or both. Some dragged plunder in sleds or packs, while others carried the weight of their own dead in silence, refusing to leave kin behind even in death.

Ragruk rode further in the back after commandeering a horse, lips pressed in a sour line as if the air itself had betrayed him. He barked orders now and again, but they carried no weight. Not with Udorn riding ahead, his mere presence a challenge the chieftain had yet to answer.

He felt Ragruk's glare through the dust and heat, a festering thing that clung like sweat. The chieftain had not challenged him openly, not yet, but the silence between them was growing teeth. Udorn knew the look of a wounded wolf well enough. Pride stung worse than any blade, and Ragruk's pride had been gutted in front of the entire host.

Let him seethe. Let him stew in his humiliation. I did what he would not. I led when he faltered. And now they see me for what I am... what he can never be again.

Still, he kept one hand near the axe at his side. Glory made men bold. It made chieftains foolish, especially when mixed with pride. And Ragruk was the epitome of it. He cast a glance over his shoulder, scanning the host for a familiar figure, Dulkin One-Eye, never far from his side. But the warrior was nowhere to be seen.

Odd...

Dulkin was many things, but he was not absent. Not without cause, and there was scarcely a cause great enough to come between them. Udorn shifted in the saddle, rising slightly in the stirrups to peer over the ranks. He spotted Thaul, Gaxas, and even young Brorek limping along against a broken spear haft. But Dulkin was absent from the sea of bodies and banners.

His brow furrowed beneath the weight of it. Had the insult of sitting idle during the raid cut so deeply? He had kept Dulkin from the slaughter not out of cruelty, but necessity. A one-eyed man in a night raid, especially while under strength and in unfamiliar territory, might have cost him his life. But such mercy was as foreign to an Ubneri as the land they traversed.

Udorn's fingers drummed once on the pommel of his saddle. *Do not expect the worst,* he told himself. *Do not borrow shadows from a sun that hasn't set.*

Dulkin might simply be brooding, after all, licking unjust wounds until they scabbed over. But the absence lingered like a stone in his boot—small, but impossible to ignore.

Hours came and went, each distinguished by a gradual shift in the terrain. The northern forests thinned into open woodlands, then gave way to rolling meadows speckled with poppies and low, sun-bleached brush. Trees grew sparser, their limbs gnarled and sunburnt, reaching skyward like starved hands begging the heavens for rain.

The soil beneath the Ubneri's boots turned from black loam to dry ochre, cracked in places where the heat drank too deeply. The air thickened with a scent of wild herbs and distant salt, carried on gusts from the unseen coast. Cicadas droned in the grasses, their hum rising like a dirge beneath the rhythmic trudge of the war host.

It was a beautiful land, in its way—soft hills and wildflowers, the kind of place men might build lives instead of burn them to ash. But to Udorn, it felt like a painting left out in the sun. Faded. Fragile. Made to be ruined.

The sea was drawing closer. He could feel it in the wind, taste it faintly on his lips. Soon, the towers of Dellhaven would rise before them, proud and pale against the coastal bluffs. And with them, resistance. Desperation.

A low grunt pulled Udorn from his thoughts.

"Still brooding, or just counting the clouds?" Thaul rode up alongside him, sweat matting the hair at his brow. He offered a skin of water, which Udorn took with a nod but did not drink.

"They thin as we head south," Udorn said, eyes on the sky. "Soon there will be no clouds left to count."

"And no shade to march under," Gaxas chimed in, trudging beside his horse, helmet in one hand and a freshly bandaged cut across his jaw. "If the heat does not kill us, the stink of our own asses might."

Thaul chuckled. "Aye, and yet, not one man turns back."

"Glory smells worse than death, but it is more addictive," Gaxas muttered, giving his shoulder a roll. "Still no sign of Dulkin?"

Udorn gave a slow shake of his head. "Not yet."

Thaul glanced over his shoulder. "He had better. I have seen the way some of Ragruk's men look at you. If Dulkin has gone soft or sour, you will need every back that still bends toward your name."

By late afternoon, the Ubneri host had slowed, their vigor tempered by heat and humidity. Armor clinked with fatigue rather than fury, and what few songs had echoed in the morning were now replaced by the dull rhythm of boots and the groan of laden sleds.

At sunset, the order was given to halt. The host spread out across a wide basin sheltered by a ridgeline to the west. Fires were lit, lean-to shelters erected from salvaged planks and canvas. Meat was roasted, mead uncorked, wounds cleaned in silence. They had survived another day in a land not their own.

Near one of the larger fires, Udorn sat with Thaul and Gaxas. The flames carved long shadows across their faces, making each of them seem older, more worn than they were that morning.

Thaul tore a hunk of meat off its bone with his teeth, then tossed the scrap into the flames. "It is too quiet here," he muttered. "This land feels wrong."

"It is the kind of silence that hides a blade," Gaxas said, licking grease from his fingers. "I would rather be deafened by screaming than lulled by that."

Udorn said nothing at first. His eyes flicked across the firelight, scanning the encampment. Men laughed, drank, bickered, but there was a tension under the merriment; thin, stretched like muscle on the verge of tearing.

"The gods know we are here," Udorn said at last. "And so do the Southerners. That silence you hear? It is not peace. It is preparation."

Meat crackled in the flames, but the conversation had quieted. Gaxas chewed with the grim focus of a man trying not to think, while Thaul idly stared into his ale mug, churning it slowly and rhythmically. A lean raider with weathered cheeks and a crooked nose drifted near the fire. Udorn did not know his name, but recognized the face; one of Ragruk's less distinguished men.

"Bold choice for you to wander over here, Tarnak," Thaul said sourly. "Keep to your own kind."

The man crouched beside the fire and extended his palms to the flames, as if the cold had suddenly found him despite the summer heat. "Do we not sail under the same banner, kinsman?"

"I would no sooner call you kinsman than the rats hiding in our hold," Thaul shot back.

Tarnak's eyes danced between them, his smile thin and humorless. He was not here for warmth or company, that much was clear. He had come to be seen, to listen, perhaps to carry words back to those who dared not speak them aloud.

Udorn let the silence hang a moment longer, weighing the tension like a blade in his hand. Then, without looking at Tarnak, he spoke.

"Let the fire warm your hands, not your tongue."

The words were calm, almost dismissive—but they struck with precision, like a stone tossed to still troubled waters. A warning, thinly veiled in courtesy. The kind of line that told everyone watching who still held command.

"Heard a thing or two today," Tarnak said without looking at anyone in particular. "Whispers. Rumors…"

He trailed off, letting the words drift like smoke. Gaxas gave a low grunt and reached for his weapon, but Udorn's hand stilled him with the faintest gesture.

"Only the craven speak in riddles," Udorn said curtly. "Be precise. Or be silent."

Tarnak scratched his jaw, feigning thoughtfulness. "Only what is spoken freely. That Ragruk rides in the shadow of another now. That some men follow a different voice."

Udorn leaned forward slightly, just enough to show he was listening, but not enough to show concern. "And do these whispers have names? Or do they hide like cowards behind smoke and mead?"

A few heads turned from nearby fires, eyes drawn like moths to the flame of conflict. Thaul shifted in his seat, his expression unreadable. Entertaining a known disciple of Ragruk was as wise as feeding raw meat to a starving bear—it invited blood, and rarely just one drop.

Tarnak tilted his head, eyes glinting in the firelight. "No names. None spoken aloud, anyway. Only looks. Questions. Men wondering why the true chieftain trails behind while another drinks the glory. Food for thought, Udorn. Your survival is more dangerous than you could imagine."

And with that, he slunk into the dusky evening. Not a man left beside the fire suspected anything other than treachery of the highest order. Years of hard-fought friendship and laughing in the face of death gave them a keen sense of smell, and something about Tarnak reeked.

"He seeks to sow discord in our ranks," Gaxas observed. "Let us pay him no heed."

"Men like Tarnak know which way the wind blows," Udorn said somberly. "Perhaps he seeks not to drive wedges, but to secure a place for himself."

It was unnerving to think that Ragruk's grip on power could be undone not by battle, but by whispers. That mere survival could be so threatening. He had bled, endured, and won... and that alone made him a rival. No crown had changed hands, but already knives were being sharpened in the dark.

Thaul spat into the dirt. "Little rat talks like a man, but I have seen him piss himself in a squall."

Gaxas grunted. "He does not matter. Not truly. It is the one who sends him that does."

The fire snapped, sending a plume of sparks skyward. For a while, none of them spoke. The crackle of fat on meat, the hum of insects, and a soft murmur of distant fires filled the quiet. Above them, stars blinked into view, indifferent witnesses to the quiet unraveling of men and loyalties alike.

"It could be a test," Udorn said finally, eyes fixed on the glowing embers. "Ragruk might be feeling the walls closing in. If he means to make a move, he will want to know who stands in his way."

"Then he already knows," Thaul said. "We do."

Udorn's gaze shifted to his friend, sharp and thoughtful. "Or he wonders if I will strike first."

Gaxas shifted his weight, lowering his voice. "You will not, will you? Not yet."

"No." Udorn's answer was firm, though the fire in his voice had cooled. "But I will not kneel again. I will not pay tribute to a man who seeks to destroy me."

Sleep came in fits and starts that night, broken by the clatter of shifting weapons, the dry wind in the grass, and the restless stir of uneasy men. Campfires dimmed to embers, casting only ghostly glows across huddled forms wrapped in cloaks and ambition. Some men dreamed of plunder—others of blood. But many, like Udorn, did not sleep at all.

He lay awake beneath the stars, one hand always near the axe at his side, the other clenched as if to hold back something darker: doubt, perhaps. Or destiny. Tarnak's words had not struck like a blow, but they had sunk in like rot beneath the skin.

Ragruk's silence had grown too long, too pointed. And the horde could only follow one master for so long before choosing whom to obey, and whom to forget. Morning would come soon. And with it, the next move.

Or nothing at all, he thought. *Perhaps I am overestimating that bloated fool. After all, a few trinkets will pacify him well enough. Gold will not buy me safety, but it will buy me time. And time will do… for now.*

The embers had nearly died, but Udorn remained awake, staring into the dark. Power did not need to be taken; it only needed to be held long enough for others to forget who once wielded it. And if morning brought blood, then he would make certain it was not his own.

ALEKSIUS IV

M ORNING FOUND ALEKSIUS UNREADY, THE HUMID AIR BITING AS IF to remind him that nothing would wait—not war, not sorrow. He stood in the courtyard as wagons were readied, a clatter of hooves and iron wheels carrying more weight than any war drum. Kyra lingered at his side, her cloak drawn tightly against the wind, while Magia and Sakis clutched each other in silence.

"Larssa will be safer," he said, though the words felt hollow even as they left his mouth. "Everything will be alright. I promise."

Magia pressed her face into his sleeve. He smoothed her hair with a trembling hand. Sakis stared up, jaw set, trying to look like a man. Aleksius bent until his knees complained and set a palm to the boy's cheek.

"You will watch over your sister. I am counting on you, my son."

"Yes, Father… I will," Sakis said, though his voice faltered.

Kyra's gaze held him fast, calm and resolute, though he could see the storm beneath. "We will wait for you," she whispered.

He wanted to answer, to give her some promise that he would return, that the world would hold together long enough for them to share another morning like this. But no promise he could make would be true. So he only kissed her brow and watched as she mounted the wagon, her figure straight-backed against the sorrow pressing down on them all.

The wagons rolled through the western gates, and with them went the last light of his home. Aleksius remained long after they had vanished from sight, the courtyard cold and empty, until one of his captains approached with a bow.

"Sire," the man said softly. "The council awaits."

Aleksius turned at last, his joints stiff from standing too long in the wind. The gates groaned shut behind the wagons, their low rumble echoing long in his ears.

"Let them wait no further," he said, sighing.

The officer fell in beside him. Together they crossed the keep's long corridors, torchlight licking damp walls, each step carrying him farther from family and closer to duty. The council chamber waited at the keep's heart, a round hall of pale stone worn smooth by centuries of debate and decree. Torchlight licked across a domed ceiling painted ages ago with scenes of kings long dead, their colors now faded to the hue of old ash.

A heavy table dominated the center, scarred and grooved by years of elbows, goblets, and the endless pounding of fists. Chairs ringed it close, so that men sat with knees nearly touching, their tempers made sharper by proximity. Tapestries hung between tall windows, their once-bright threads dulled by smoke and dust. Outside, a dry wind pressed faintly against the glass, but inside the air was thick with voices, already raised in argument.

They rose when Aleksius entered, though only half-heartedly. The murmurs stilled, and eyes turned sharp, as if knives had been left on the table with their owners' tongues. Aleksius took his chair, the old wood creaking beneath him. He folded his hands and let silence hang until it became heavy enough to bow heads.

"Thank you for gathering here today," he said at last. "As I am sure you are all aware, we stand at the precipice. I believe the fate of our people will be decided in the coming weeks and months. Betanthia is at war, and their great stronghold at Castle Morden was sacked and ruined one year ago."

A young noble spoke first. Aleksius searched his face and found no memory of it—one of those upstarts who had clawed a seat at the table through coin and marriage rather than service. His name was Dorellos, broad of shoulder but still soft in the jaw, his polished cuirass gleaming as though it had never seen rain. The man's voice cracked with eagerness.

"King Bethard grows bolder by the day," he said. "If we do not answer fire with fire, they will take it as weakness. I say we march before the harvest. Strike first, and drive them back across the Plainhold!"

Murmurs followed. A few heads nodded, others frowned. Aleksius said nothing, his eyes lowering to the old grooves cut in the council table. Tasos leaned forward, scarred knuckles resting on the wood. The man had fought through three wars, and he wore his service like a cloak—blunt, practical, with no taste for theater.

"Bluster will not feed the ranks," Tasos said, his voice like gravel. "Half our levies are still in the fields, pulling what little harvest they can. We call them now, and they come hungry. We march without bread, and the army starves before it bleeds. You want fire? Build a hearth first."

Dorellos shifted in his chair, muttering something about cowards. Aleksius felt the weight of a gaze and found it waiting for him across the table. Tiberion sat in silence, composed, gray eyes fixed on nothing and everything at once. His silence pressed harder than words.

The Senate's man was composed as ever, robes of black trimmed in deep crimson, his silver clasp polished to a mirror's shine. Lean, deliberate in every motion, he seemed carved from something colder than flesh. His eyes—pale gray, rimmed by dark shadows—watched the room as if he were already drafting a record of the meeting for the Senate archives.

But at last, Tiberion stirred. He did not rise; instead, he adjusted his clasp as though aligning it with some unseen mark. When he spoke, his voice was calm, measured, and without strain.

"Bluster and hunger will both kill us," he said. "But the greater danger, Sire, is paralysis. Naxonnos cannot endure another season of hesitation. The Senate entrusted me with one charge: to ensure this city does not fall. I mean to see it kept."

The chamber quieted. Even the upstart noble leaned back, chastened. Tasos scowled but said nothing. Aleksius felt the weight of the words settle on him like a mantle he had not asked for. Tiberion had not shouted, had not pleaded. He had simply spoken, and in that measured tone the Senate's will was laid bare.

Aleksius drew a slow breath. His fingers tightened on the table's edge until the old wood bit into his skin. "I have already given the order for riders. They will scour the hills and cross the plains, and bring back what truth can be found. I will not gamble the lives of my people on rumors."

His voice carried more iron than he felt, but it stilled the room. A few of the younger men shifted uneasily, as if they had not considered that truth might look different than the tale they wanted.

Aleksius sighed, hands clasped tight. "If Betanthia readies to strike our lands, we will know it plain. And if they have not… then let us not be the ones to set the fire. Our people cannot endure any more suffering."

Dorellos scoffed loud enough to turn heads. His polished cuirass creaked as he leaned forward, eyes flashing. "Scouts and scribes will not hold the line, Sire. Every day we wait is another day King Bethard sharpens his blades. You think him idle? Heh! He will not wait for our truth to return on weary horses. He will march. He already has…"

A few voices muttered agreement. The young man's words had fire, even if they lacked weight.

Tasos's scarred hand thumped the table. "You've never marched a day in your life, boy. An army that moves too soon is already dead. Your hunger for glory would see us starved before we meet the enemy."

"Better to die with a sword in hand than rot behind walls like frightened old men," Dorellos said defiantly.

The insult hung sharp in the air. Aleksius's gaze swept the chamber, steady but heavy with warning. Silence stretched until even Dorellos shifted in his chair, heat draining from his face.

How many feel the same, but hold their tongues out of fear or duty?

Aleksius let his gaze linger on the chamber—the scarred table, the faded banners, the painted kings staring down from the dome above. He wondered what mark his own reign would leave. Not a mural or a tapestry, but the memory of choices made when the realm teetered on the brink. Too many already whispered that he was the architect of decline, the man who would preside over ruin. If he faltered now, that would be his legacy: not wisdom, not caution, but failure writ large across his people's graves.

"Riders are already scouring beyond our borders," he said. "They will bring back truth—not rumor, not frightened tales, but truth. If Betanthia means to strike us, we will know it plain. Until then, I will not gamble away lives needlessly. Caution is not cowardice."

A few of the younger nobles looked down at the table. Dorellos only scowled, lips tight. Tasos leaned forward, scarred knuckles pressed to the wood.

"Scouts are well and good," the Loxarchon said, voice rough and booming. "But truth takes time to return, and men grow soft while they wait. Best we start the drill yards at once—put spear and bow back in their hands. If war comes, better they march sore than stumble unready."

Without rising, Tiberion drew the room's attention as surely as if he had struck the table. His words came cool and exact, the kind that admitted no argument.

"Caution is wise. Yet do not forget, most of the men drilling in these yards are not yours alone. They are the Senate's, sworn to their authority before all others. I am here to see that they are not wasted."

His pale eyes lingered on Aleksius. Not hostile, but unyielding. "Raise them too soon, and the Senate will know. Bleed them for pride, and the Senate will not forgive."

Aleksius rubbed at his temple, the voices beginning to blur into one another. Dorellos snapping for war, Tasos harping on grain and drill, Tiberion with his cold reminders of Senate oversight. It was all the same song, played in different keys.

He shifted in his chair, the old wood groaning with him. "We pace the same ground like hounds chasing their tails," he said, voice low but edged. "How many countless meetings have we spoken in circles and gained nothing for it? Truth will come when the riders return. You have my orders. See to them. Unless there is more to speak that is worth the breath, this council is ended."

Aleksius pushed back his chair, the scrape loud in the chamber. He rose slowly, each step heavy as iron, and did not wait for protest. By the time he reached the doors, the voices behind him had already swelled again, a tide he no longer cared to stop.

Tasos followed close, the old soldier's boots striking hard against the stone. The doors groaned shut behind them, muffling the chamber's clamor to a dull murmur. For a time, Aleksius said nothing, his steps carrying him down the long corridor. Then, low enough for none but Tasos to hear, he spoke.

"I will not suffer this pointless bickering any longer," he said, each word tinged with venom. "For too long, our people have remained content to squabble and crow like roosters with nothing to show for it. Naxonnos will choke on their empty words long before Betanthian spears pierce our flesh."

The Loxarchon gave a rough snort, half laugh, half growl. "Words do not win battles, yes? Steel does. You give the order, and I will see the men sharpened. Let the council wag their tongues. We will not be caught sleeping when Betanthia comes."

Aleksius's mouth bent into something between a grimace and a smile. "See them sharpened, yes. And when Tiberion retires to his chambers, I will walk the yards myself. Let the Senate hear it if they must. I will not sit idle while darkness closes in around us."

Tasos's scarred hand clenched into a fist and thumped his chest. "That is the leadership they need, Sire. The men will stand straighter with you among them."

By nightfall, the keep had quieted, the corridors emptied of servants and councilors alike. Only the tramp of guards' boots echoed through the stone halls. Aleksius did not retire to his chambers. With Tasos at his side, he crossed the courtyard toward the garrison barracks, lanterns throwing long shadows across the yard. The air smelled of oil, sweat, and steel, the scent of men half-prepared for a war that already pressed at their gates.

Inside, the barracks stirred to life at their arrival. Soldiers straightened on benches, dice forgotten, boots snapping to the floor. Some looked startled, others wary. Their sovereign had not walked this hall in years.

Tasos barked the first order, his voice cracking like thunderbolts. "On your feet, all of you! Spears in hand! Shields up! Let's see if you can stand longer than a harvest wind!"

Aleksius watched them scramble into formation, the shuffle of boots and clatter of arms filling the hall. The first rank stumbled into place, shields banging against one another in a crooked line. Aleksius frowned, though he tried to mask his discouragement. They looked more like farmers clutching doors than warriors meant to bar an enemy charge.

"Lock them, damn you!" Tasos roared, striding down the row like a storm made flesh. He seized a shield by its rim and slammed it tight against its neighbor, the crack echoing off stone. "You leave a gap wide enough for a dog to slip through, you may as well dig your own graves!"

The line tightened, spears jutting forward in uneven angles. Some men braced firm, shoulders square, and feet planted. Others sagged, grips loose, the hafts quivering in their hands. This was not the army of his father, nor his grandfather. To even call it an army was questionable at best.

Aleksius stepped forward, his shadow falling across the line. "Again," he said, his voice level but sharp as steel. "Raise them as if King Bethard himself were thundering down upon you."

The shields came up once more, this time with more strength, the spears bristling like a field of iron stalks. Boots stamped into place as Tasos barked the cadence, and for a moment the hall rang with a rhythm that stirred something long dormant in Aleksius's chest.

"Better," Tasos growled. "But a wall that holds once must hold a hundred times. You do not get to falter on the second charge."

The men broke into squads, drilling under the torchlight. One row practiced advancing with shields locked, their spears stabbing in unison. Another row rotated through shield-bearer and spearman, learning to hold formation even when comrades fell. The clash of wood on wood and the guttural shouts of effort filled the hall until the sound felt like battle itself.

Aleksius moved among them, his gaze sharp, noting who stood steady and who shook. He offered no speeches, only corrections. A raised chin pressed down. A shield lifted higher. A spear angled to the gap between helm and breastplate. His silence carried more weight than a dozen shouted orders.

When a man stumbled, Aleksius caught his shield before it fell, pressed it back into his chest, and fixed him with a look that burned hotter than any reprimand.

"The line does not break," he said quietly. "Not while Naxonnos still breathes."

By the time the torches burned low, the hall was thick with sweat and an acrid tang of oil lamps. Men sagged on their spears, arms trembling, but their lines were straighter, their rhythm sharper. The Droethien war machine, ancient as the hills, had begun to creak back into motion.

Tasos looked to his sovereign, his scarred face split in a wolfish grin. "They'll be ready when the horns sound. You've put the fear in them, Sire—not of death, but of failing your eye."

Aleksius stood silent for a moment, listening to the echoes of spear and shield that still lingered in the stone. He thought of Kyra's steady gaze, of Sakis's trembling vow, of Magia's small hand on his sleeve. Then he looked to the men before him, sweat-streaked and weary, but standing tall.

"We will not break," he said at last. "Not here. Not now. Not ever."

The words carried through the hall, quiet but firm, and the men thumped their shields against the floor in answer. The sound rolled like thunder in the deep, and Aleksius let it echo—a promise forged in sweat, steel, and the shadow of coming war.

EINARR V

M OR SEVEHT CREPT INTO VIEW LIKE A SCAB ON THE EDGE OF THE world. Low, sun-bleached hovels slouched in the dust, their walls bowed with age and neglect. There were no gates, no guards, no welcoming eyes. Just wind, grit, and a silence that did not care whether a man arrived crawling or crowned.

Einarr pulled his mount to a halt, or perhaps the beast stopped of its own accord. The horse's sides heaved, foam and blood matting its flanks. It would not carry him another step. Behind him, his companions rode hunched and swaying, little more than shadows wearing armor. They had lost too much blood, time, and hope.

To his surprise, Hyleth appeared largely unfazed by the Plainhold's brutality. The Zylmacian sat upright, a tattered cloth draped over his head and coiled around his face. The heat bowed to him, or so it seemed, leaving the others to suffer in its stead. It was a quiet testament to a life carved from wilderness—brutal, unforgiving, and remote: the Bymist, a place where even death looked over its shoulder.

It was strange to see civilization appearing in the distance, though Einarr first suspected it was his mind playing tricks. But there it was, Mor Seveht, slouched against the earth like a drunk too stubborn to fall. Even from afar, it looked half-dead.

By the gods! Could it be so?

Einarr smiled, but his cracked lips tore and stung. He winced, then grew frustrated and desperate for a gulp of fresh water. His waterskin had been empty since morning, and his tongue felt like dry leather. Still, he urged his horse onward, for if Mor Seveht was truly ahead, then relief, however meager, waited at its edge.

"We have arrived," Hyleth said. "Trust not anyone who is not among our company. Men disappear here, and the dust forgets them by morning."

The land gave way slowly, almost grudgingly, as if the Plainhold itself refused to release them. Scrub brush thickened, and jagged outcrops of stone rose from the earth like broken teeth. A scatter of crude markers lined the path ahead: weather-beaten planks, bone totems, and rusted blades jammed into the earth. Warnings, perhaps. Or trophies. The wind shifted as they neared the outskirts, carrying with it the scent of smoke, old sweat, and something fouler still… civilization.

They passed between leaning shanties and crumbling stone huts, their footsteps stirring clouds of red dust that clung to skin and tongue alike. Mor Seveht had no walls, no gates—only the husks of forgotten ambitions and the stench of unburied sin. The streets were little more than dry veins through the wreckage, crowded with gaunt-eyed wanderers and merchants who watched them with the same interest one might give a wounded animal.

A pair of shirtless boys chased a feral dog through the alley ahead, their laughter sharp as knives. One clutched a length of rope, the other a broken bottle. Nearby, an old woman sat cross-legged beneath a warped awning, muttering to herself and shaking a cup that held more teeth than coins. No one stopped them. No one greeted them. Mor Seveht did not welcome guests; it merely endured them.

Einarr tightened his grip on the reins. Every gaze felt like a blade testing his armor. And though no sword was drawn, he sensed the weight of unseen ones, tucked behind cloaks and beneath rotting tarps. Survival here was not measured in strength, but in suspicion.

Valerick's lip curled as he scanned the shantytown. "This place reeks of corpses and cowardice," he muttered. "We should not linger in the open."

Dolsigg nodded grimly, adjusting the torn strap of his satchel. "Aye. I've seen dead men with warmer welcomes than this."

Hyleth dismounted slowly, dust trailing from his boots as they hit the ground. "Then seek shade near the stables, all of you," he said. "Speak to no one. Look no one in the eye. I will return with food and water… if such things still exist in this forsaken place."

He turned without waiting for a reply, vanishing into the heat-warped haze and the meager crowd beyond. The others hesitated only a moment before trotting off, following the jagged street past stacked crates, bleached bones, and sagging doorframes. Einarr lingered at the rear, scanning faces that disappeared just as quickly as they emerged—narrow eyes in shadowed doorways, silent figures hunched over crates of copper and broken glass.

At the stables, troughs of water sat stagnating in the blistering sun. Their horses lurched forward, desperate for a drink. The water was warm and unpleasant-looking, but their beasts cared little. They dunked their snouts in, guzzling gallon after gallon until little remained. Einarr and his companions sought shelter in a nearby shack, long abandoned.

Tattered cloth hung across a single window, cracking and snapping in a fierce western wind. Inside, the air was thick with old hay, dung, and the musk of creatures long gone. Flies buzzed lazily in the rafters. Valerick dropped into a squat near the wall, his armor creaking as he peeled off a gauntlet and inspected a blistered palm. Dolsigg remained near the door, his axe across his lap, eyes fixed on the street as if daring it to blink.

Einarr slumped against the far post, letting his weight settle into the shadows. His limbs ached. His mind swam. Yet here they were, alive—and in Mor Seveht, that counted for more than most could say. He glanced about the others, some faring well, and others barely clinging to life.

Darmund sat slumped against the wall, his leg bandaged high above the knee, blood having soaked through in jagged lines. He gritted his teeth as the wound throbbed, but said nothing. Beside him, Mardek lay half-conscious, lips cracked and eyes sunken from thirst, whispering prayers to gods that had never once heeded him.

Only Vexar seemed untouched by the Plainhold—tall, lean, and alert, his dark eyes watching the doorway like a hound waiting for trouble. He gave Einarr a curt nod, the kind that needed no words.

"This place stinks worse than a battlefield left to rot," Valerick said, grunting.

"Worse than that," Einarr reflected. "At least battlefields don't pretend to be cities."

Valerick glanced back. "Your faith in this Bymist rat is generous. I am uncertain which is more treacherous: him or this gods-forsaken hellscape."

A fair question, and one Einarr was beginning to consider. No Nothanek had ever come this far. If a Rhivothi had, Mor Seveht had buried him beneath the dust without a whisper. The town felt ancient, but not in the way of ruins or history. It was old like rot, like a wound left to fester. Every creaking board and sun-faded shutter told him they did not belong here. And yet, here they were, bleeding into a place that had no room for strangers.

They waited in the shade, pressed close together in the sweltering shack, watching the street through a slit in the hanging cloth. Time crawled. A man with a wicker basket passed by twice, whistling tunelessly. Somewhere nearby, a scuffle broke into shouts and the crunch of fists on bone, but no one intervened. Flies buzzed thick in the heat, and even the horses stood motionless, too spent to swat them away.

Einarr began to wonder if Hyleth had vanished into the haze when the Zylmacian returned, arms burdened with wrapped bundles and two sloshing skins of water. He looked untouched by the filth of the streets, as though Mor Seveht itself dared not to lay a finger on him.

"Long have I mastered the southern tongues," Hyleth said, his voice sounding like anything but his own. "Their accents are my camouflage."

He dropped a packet of hard bread and dried figs onto the floor and looked around at them. "Eat. Drink. Regret it later, if you must."

Valerick eyed him warily as he bit into the bread. "Strange, how a man from the wild can walk these streets unscathed."

"I am not the only predator here," Hyleth replied. He tore a strip of fig and chewed without expression. "But I am the one who knows when not to bare his teeth."

Einarr drank deep from the waterskin. It was warm and tasted faintly of iron, but it might as well have been wine. "Let us not linger long," he said, wiping his mouth. "This place is watching."

They ate in silence, save for the crunch of hard bread and the wet gulps of water passed from hand to hand. No one complained. Even Darmund, whose arm was bound in a crude sling, devoured his share without pause. The air inside the shack was thick and foul, but it was shelter—and in Mor Seveht, shelter was not to be questioned. Valerick eventually lay back and closed his eyes, one hand on his axe hilt. Dolsigg and Thaen leaned against the walls like dead men propped for burial.

Outside, the world moved in strange rhythms. A child screamed. Laughter followed. Then silence again. The day grew no cooler, but the harshest edge of the heat had dulled. When the food was gone and their nerves had settled, Einarr stood and fastened his belt.

"Come," he said quietly to Hyleth and Valerick. "Let us find this town's rot and scrape what we can from it."

They slipped into the street with hoods drawn low and blades hidden beneath worn cloaks. The dust swallowed their footsteps as they moved through the crooked alleys of Mor Seveht, passing beggars with missing fingers and traders hawking rusted trinkets from sun-warped stalls. A one-eyed man spat near Valerick's boots, but said nothing.

At the edge of a cracked plaza, beneath a slanted awning draped in tattered sailcloth, the tavern appeared—no sign, no name, just a warped door and the dull throb of voices behind it. Hyleth pushed it open with the ease of a man who had walked into darker places and lived.

The door groaned on its hinges as Einarr pushed it open, a gust of heat and stink wafting out to meet them. Inside, the tavern was dim and narrow, the ceiling so low that even Hyleth had to duck slightly. The air was thick with pipe smoke and unwashed bodies, the scent of old mead soaked into the beams. A dozen tables leaned at odd angles, many of them occupied by pale-faced drifters and cloaked figures nursing drinks like secrets.

A minstrel strummed a broken-tuned lute near the hearth, playing to no one. Near the back, a few armored men sat together, their gear too clean, their bearing too crisp for this place. Betanthians, no doubt, given their much lighter complexions. Einarr noticed them in a heartbeat, and Valerick's gaze fell upon them like a hungry bear.

"There," Hyleth said softly, motioning to a table nearest to the door. "And avert your eyes."

Valerick grunted, steaming with resentment. Were they not knee-deep in hostile territory, he might have clobbered Hyleth for daring to direct him in such a manner. But there was more than life on the line; there was fresh ale, as well. The Zylmacian smoothly approached the bar, patronized by bedraggled locals, men who were just as weathered as their surroundings. Behind it stood a wiry man with sunken eyes and a permanent crease in his brow, wiping out a mug that looked cleaner than most things in the room. His apron was stained, his sleeves rolled past scarred forearms, and a crossbow sat half-hidden beneath the counter.

After a few muffled words were exchanged, Hyleth slapped a trio of coins onto the dingy bar, then returned to the table. Einarr watched as the barkeep poured out several mugs of frothy ale. His mouth watered so aggressively that it sent jolts of lightning through his jaw.

The barkeep carried the mugs over on a dented tray, setting them down with the efficiency of long habit and no particular warmth. Einarr took one of the mugs, savoring the first bitter gulp like it was spring water. He waited until the man made to leave before speaking.

"What's the good word in Mor Seveht?" he asked casually.

The barkeep paused, studying them for a beat too long. "Good word, is it?" he muttered. "There isn't much of that left these days."

Einarr reached into a belt pouch and slid a gold coin across the table. It spun once before stopping flat. "Then let's settle for the honest kind."

The man's hand snatched the coin, but he did not pocket it. He turned it between his fingers, shoulders easing ever so slightly. "Betanthians are pulling out. Fewer patrols. Fewer questions. If you ask me, someone's bracing for a storm… and they don't want their boots in the mud when it breaks."

Einarr nodded slowly, then tipped his chin toward the armored men at the far table. "And them?"

"Blackthorn," the barkeep said, lowering his voice. "Rotating out of Naxonnos, by the looks of it. You can always tell. The ones who stay wear dust. The ones who've seen the front wear ghosts."

A faint patter of feet sounded from the ceiling above—quick, light steps, followed by a muffled giggle. Einarr's eyes flicked upward, then back to the barkeep. "You've family here?"

The man hesitated, then gave a slow nod. "Aye. A wife and little ones." He wiped at the same spot on the table, though it was already clean. "There's nowhere else to go. The Plainhold will swallow you whole if the heat doesn't kill you first. This place may be cruel, but at least it has corners to hide in."

Einarr stared into his mug, watching the foam settle. His conscience twisted like a knife in the gut. If they moved on the Blackthorn, blood would follow—it always did. But the war was no longer a distant worry. It was here, clawing at the edges of a town powerless to defend itself.

He looked up at the barkeep. "Keep your family close, and may the gods watch over you."

"You must be new in town," the man said before starting back to the bar, "for there are no gods here. They have forgotten this place exists."

It was disheartening to hear any man sound so defeated. He looked away, then across the tavern. The room breathed with quiet despair. Men drank not to celebrate, but to forget, their eyes hollow, their spines bent from burdens no one cared about. The fire offered no warmth, only smoke. Conversations, where they existed at all, were murmured things—sparse, suspicious, and clipped. It was a place where hope had not died loudly, but had simply stopped showing up.

Einarr's gaze swept the room again and landed on a worn leather dispatch satchel tucked beneath one of the Blackthorn's boots. The man leaned back in his chair, laughing at something his comrade said, but his foot never strayed far from the bag. Military issue. Reinforced seams. Brass latches dulled with grime, the kind that carried orders... or secrets.

Einarr's eyes narrowed. No need for confrontation. Not yet. "Let's go," he said, quickly gulping down his ale. "We follow. Patience will draw blood better than steel."

They slipped outside discreetly, the tavern door creaking shut behind them like a breath held too long. The sun had begun its descent, casting long shadows across the broken street. Mor Seveht did not grow quieter with dusk, only meaner. Voices grew sharper. Faces more guarded. Somewhere down the block, a bottle shattered. No one looked up.

They found a sliver of shade beside a shuttered stall, its canvas canopy flapping like loose skin in the wind. From there, they could keep one eye on the tavern door and another on the street beyond. Time crawled. Dust settled on their boots and cloaks. A trio of barefoot children passed by, arguing over a piece of dried fruit. A mutt with three legs pissed on the tavern's stoop, then limped off toward the alleys.

An hour passed before the door opened. The Blackthorn stepped outside, four of them, helmets tucked beneath their arms, laughter still clinging to their voices like the stink of ale. One of them carried the dispatch case slung over a shoulder now, unbothered by its weight. They turned up the road, speaking in low tones, boots stirring grit as they moved.

Einarr gave a subtle nod. "Now," he muttered, and they followed. Quiet. Patient. Like wolves behind a wounded deer.

The knights led them through the winding arteries of Mor Seveht, deeper into its frayed edges, where the hovels thinned and the dirt turned coarse. The sun dipped low, casting blood-red streaks across the sky as the shadows lengthened. At the town's fringe, past a cluster of tilting sheds and a dried-up well, the Blackthorn entered a squat, stone lodging with warped shutters and soot-stained walls. A faded crest above the door had long since been scratched away.

Einarr and the others found a hollow behind a crumbled wall, just close enough to observe without being seen. They crouched low as the evening gave way to darkness. The scent of roasted meat drifted on the breeze—goat, perhaps, or something stranger. Inside the lodging, the knights laughed and shouted over one another, their voices swelling with drink and stories of battles already growing mythic in the telling.

"They've grown comfortable," Hyleth said in a hush. "Too comfortable."

Einarr studied the building, eyes narrowed. "If we're quick and quiet, we can slip in while they sleep. In and out. No blood. Come sunrise, they will never know what happened."

Valerick the Red said nothing, his gaze locked on the scant dwelling like a predator. Then, without a word, he rose and walked toward the door, hands twisting at the handle of his axe. At first, Einarr was too dumbstruck to realize what was happening.

"Valerick—" Einarr reached to stop him, but the warrior had already passed beyond the reach of caution. He strode across the parched earth like a man going to fetch firewood.

The door groaned open. Light spilled across the yard. A burst of laughter greeted him, and then, silence. Followed by shouting. Then screaming. Then wet, meat-thick sounds of steel splitting flesh. Einarr stood frozen. Hyleth leaned forward, lips parted in disbelief.

Moments later, the door opened again. Valerick stepped out, breath heaving, axe dripping. The dispatch bag hung from one hand. His brow was painted in blood, none of it his own. The Red Rhivothi had proven his Soul Name true yet again. He strode once more across the dirt, then tossed the dispatch bag at Einarr's feet.

Panting and with a deep frown, Valerick grunted. "Problem solved."

SYLVIA VIII

SHE LAY AWAKE BESIDE A DWINDLING FIRE, STARING WIDE-EYED AT Ruin. The greatsword sat propped beside Damien's body, its core pulsing with a deep, ominous glow. Soft screams of the vanquished radiated from its steel, as if the blade had trapped every soul it ever cut down. Not only men's voices cried there, but the wails of women and children, woven into its chorus of death.

Such an object could only be cursed by the gods. With every waking moment, Sylvia wondered if taking it from its resting place had been wise, knowing the blood price paid to put it there. Even when she rolled over and pressed her hands tight to her ears, the screams still clawed at her.

When exhaustion finally dragged her under, her dreams became a blur of chaos, death, and battles fought centuries ago. Each time her mind's eye tried to focus, the vision shattered, shifting again and again until the images flickered like lightning across a stormy sky.

One thing remained constant: a crippling fear of death. Sylvia felt the horror of every life Ruin had claimed, their final moments seared into its cursed steel. Its bloodthirst seemed as endless as the heavens, and she feared the weapon might one day consume them as well.

A deep hum rippled from the greatsword's fuller, resonant as a voice beneath the earth. In her dream, Sylvia somehow understood its intent. Ruin was no servant of men, no instrument of justice. It was hunger given form, a ravenous will to devour life wherever it found it.

The blade's ghostly light flared, burning hotter until it seared her skin. She screamed, trying to shield herself, but there was no escape from the soul-destroying heat. Her flesh peeled back in ribbons, fingers blackening to bone, hair catching fire until her scalp blistered. A sudden burst of flame erupted from Ruin's fuller, engulfing her whole.

She woke with a strangled gasp, dripping sweat, her body trembling as though the fire still licked her. Though her ghastly death had been only a nightmare, Ruin's demonic oppression pressed on her chest as if it had followed her out of sleep. The torment eased only when Damien knelt, bound the weapon in cloth and leather, and shouldered its weight again.

"Are you unnerved, Stormguard?" Damien cocked his head.

"That sword…" she replied, breathless. "That sword is evil. I've seen it in my dreams. I've witnessed the terrible things it has done—and what it will do still. We never should have taken it from the mountain."

There were mysteries in the world far beyond mortal grasp. Whatever unholy bargain Kuggvord had struck to bring such a weapon into being had damned him for centuries. Now Damien's fate was tied to that same darkness. The thought was not lost on him; his manner had grown heavier, his words slower, as though each carried a burden.

"Perhaps you are correct," Damien muttered. "Either Ruin will bring us victory over our enemies… or it will herald our doom. Only the gods know."

The screams ebbed as the blade disappeared beneath its wrappings, but their absence birthed something worse—a suffocating dread, like a canopy of night spread over her soul.

"What if the gods have no foresight of our actions?" she whispered, her voice shaking. "Lazilyth was blinded on the Plainhold fields. What if we've meddled in powers too great to control?"

Her question gave Dreadfire pause. His black eyes lifted toward the sunlit clouds. "Let us speak no more of this, Stormguard. I have come too far to turn back. My fate was sealed at Borjifa. I walk already as a ghost."

After a meager breakfast, they returned to the hunting trail, its dirt worn hard by generations of feet. Mile after grueling mile, they trudged through the snow-dusted forest. Never had Sylvia known the Hinterwood so still. No birds sang from the branches, no squirrels rustled in the underbrush. Even the wind seemed to hold its breath.

The silence unsettled her, but worse still was Damien's leg. Gone was the seeping wound, gone the limp that had slowed him. His stride was steady, strong, as if a near-mortal injury had never been. She stared in quiet dread.

I fear to see what Ruin will do to him in time…

Even standing near Dreadfire became unbearable. The closer she drew to the cursed blade, the more her stomach soured and her strength withered. Though she had rested, she felt as if she had marched a hundred miles without pause. Yet a few steps farther back, and the sickness lifted, her breath returning.

Near midday, a disturbance rolled through the forest — the thunder of hooves pounding earth, so heavy she felt it in her ribs. She froze, heart racing, until she recalled whose lands these were. Rhivothi domain. Neither she nor Damien reached for steel.

Moments later, riders broke through the pines—a band of fifteen, surly as wolves, some bearing the marks of their chieftain's guard.

"Hail, Stormguard," called Kaldor Wolfbane, his face sharp with familiarity. Yet unease marked his voice, a rare crack in his stony demeanor. "Why are you unmounted?"

On any other day, her kinsmen would have chuckled at her expense.

At Rej Rhivoth, it was tradition to mock a horseman who returned without their mount, whether by battle or carelessness. But now, no one dared laugh.

"They fled when we reached the mountain," she said quietly, forcing her eyes away from the bundle that was Ruin.

"Perhaps you should have done the same," Sigvald muttered, his gaze locked on the wrapped sword. His voice carried no jest, only suspicion. "You bring a great darkness to our kin."

"Worry not," Dreadfire answered, his tone low and even. "I have found the greatsword Ruin; forged in the underworld, gifted to Kuggvord by the gods. I saw his corpse rise, his bones crawling with life again. But by my hand, and by the will of the Dread Fires, I struck him down and claimed the weapon as my right."

Silence fell. None of the Rhivothi dared reply. Some narrowed their eyes, doubtful; others looked stricken, as if superstition had clawed into their hearts.

Damien pressed on, unbothered. "The sword seeks only the blood of our enemies — the enemies of the gods. It claims one soul alone. You need not fear its hunger."

Still, they studied him in wary silence, their mounts stamping uneasily as he walked past. Every step of his boot seemed heavier than the last, thudding against the earth like the tread of something more than mortal.

Fear and uncertainty crept through them all. None had expected Dreadfire to return from Morvhalgr, let alone carrying an artifact thought lost to legend. For generations, the elders of Rej Rhivoth had told tales of Kuggvord and Ruin. Few believed them more than campfire fables.

And now, today, their world has been shattered. Every tale they have heard since childhood has come true. Surely, even the most pious among us will be examining their faith.

A long-familiar scent drifted through the tree —smoke and pine, hearth and earth—wrapping Sylvia in the warm comfort of home. Rej Rhivoth lay just ahead, its presence marked by runes carved deep into the bark of ancient oaks. These paths were seldom traveled, but their shapes were known to her heart. Soon, smoke curled above thatched roofs, rising steadily into the sky.

For the first time in what felt like a year, a smile touched Sylvia's weary face. After the mountain's horrors, home seemed worth more than gold. For a fleeting moment, she thought of staying, abandoning the march of war, and laying her sword aside. The right was hers, yet honor whispered otherwise.

After all we have suffered, after all we have endured, how can I break faith now? By the gods' grace, I have come this far. Surely, they are not yet finished with me.

But as they drew nearer, her smile faltered. Something was amiss. A host was gathering between the hovels and along the dirt streets. At first, it seemed no more than a few hundred — not unusual for a settlement the size of Rej Rhivoth. Yet the further they pressed, the more the crowd swelled. Hundreds became thousands, bodies pressing shoulder to shoulder, eyes fixed upon them.

"What trickery is this?" Damien muttered, unease threading his voice. His hand hovered near Ruin's bindings, as though expecting an ambush.

"It is no trick," Kaldor answered, his expression unreadable. "Your name has spread across the Hinterwood and beyond. Kin and companion, friend and foe — all have gathered to witness what was once only myth. Many believe. Many doubt. But none will ignore what stands before them."

No revelry greeted their arrival. Sylvia's heart sank; even here, where she should have felt safest, unease crept cold along her spine. Dozens of banners rippled in the breeze, their strange beasts and runic crests unfamiliar to her eyes. Tribes and warbands had come from every corner of the wood, each bearing their colors like judgment cast against her and Damien both.

Though their banners were strange, their blood was not. These were Rhivothi, every one of them, marked by the same lean faces and wild eyes of those who lived hard among the trees. Even the shieldmaidens bore that familiar ferocity, shoulders squared, jaws tight, gazes unflinching. Yet beneath the stoicism, Sylvia glimpsed the truth: fear coiled in many hearts, however well it was hidden.

"The gods must still be with us, Damien," she whispered, awe mixing with unease. "Surely they have borne witness to what we accomplished."

"Not all gods approve, Stormguard," Dreadfire said, his black eyes sweeping the crowd. "And those who do are not the ones your kin pray to. The gods I serve move toward their own ends—not yours, not mine."

The words settled like a chill wind, and silence fell heavy over the gathering. Hundreds of eyes turned upon him as he loosened the bindings at his hip. Sylvia's stomach lurched as his fingers traced the shrouded steel. Ruin pulsed faintly, as if recognizing the moment. The very air seemed to recoil; no breeze stirred the trees, no bird dared to cry. It was as though the Hinterwood itself held its breath.

When the cloth fell away, a ripple of unease shuddered through the clans. Sylvia felt it in her marrow. Dark was the day when a Rhivothi faltered, darker still when a shadow like this was invited into their midst.

I have never seen such fear in our people before. Gods... what have we done?!

The screams of the souls Ruin had devoured still clung to her ears. Its cursed steel throbbed with a low hum, like the beating of a monstrous heart. For an instant, crimson light bled from the fuller, pulsing before it dimmed again. Damien's black gaze lingered on the blade, reverent and grim, before he lifted it with one hand as though it weighed no more than a hunting spear.

"Behold!" His voice crashed across the crowd. "Bear witness to

Ruin—the sword of Kuggvord the Grim, thought lost to time, cast to myth… and now unleashed upon the world once more!"

Gasps broke loose. Whispers surged. Men shifted uneasily, women clutched charms and amulets, and children hid behind shields and cloaks. Its presence alone pressed like a storm upon them, choking the air, stripping hope from their eyes. The clans recoiled, their silence louder than any roar. Then, just as suddenly, Damien veiled the steel again. The cloth muffled its malign radiance, and a shuddering exhale swept the assembly.

"What has he done?" someone shouted.

"You have defied the gods!" another voice cried.

Through the press came Taug, looming as though carved from storm cloud and iron. Fifteen spears flanked him, their tips glittering in the half-light, but not one dared lift against the weapon. Even shrouded, Ruin commanded reverence. It was steel, yes, but steel kissed by the divine, and cursed for it.

Damien stepped forward, unbowed by their fear. His tone was low, terrible in its certainty. "When Betanthia slaughtered my kin and razed my home, I swore an oath before the gods. I vowed to pay any price to see justice done, and to avenge the faithful who died in fire and blood. You cannot fathom the compact I have made. But hear me well: generations yet unborn will flourish by the cost of it."

Dreadfire stilled, gaze drifting into the distance. In his blackened eyes, Sylvia glimpsed the fire of Borjifa, the slaughter replaying like smoke upon a wind. Whatever resolve he had forged that day burned hotter than any sun, and though she pitied him, she prayed she would never know the ruin of seeing her people's world erased.

"What I have done," Damien said, his voice ringing with iron, "is not for my people alone, but for yours as well. Do not fear the horrors I summon against our enemies. Fear instead what waits if we do nothing. The hand of the gods shields the faithful."

From his pack, he drew the ossuary, cradling it with outstretched arms as though it were an altar. His eyes slid shut, lips parted in reverence. Veins crawled red across his forearms, staining from fingertips upward like rivers of blood. Even the fiercest Rhivothi warriors shifted uneasily, humbled by the sight.

With those words, his fingers cracked the lid. The ossuary's breath spilled forth. Dark clouds coiled across the sky, smothering the sun. A foul western wind tore through the village, carrying with it the stench of ash and grave rot. The earth groaned like some wounded beast, trembling beneath their boots. Warriors scattered, some screaming, others standing rigid with terror.

A surge of red light burst upward with a scream of black flies, blotting the air in a writhing swarm. The box snapped shut, the foul light dying with it, but its echo lingered, rattling the bones of all who had borne witness.

Had Sylvia not seen the horrors within the mountain, she might have bolted with the others. Even so, her flesh quivered, though her warrior's spirit kept her spine rigid. Faith in Azldyr anchored her—faith in prayers older than memory, words etched and spoken by generations who had known the gods' fire firsthand.

Damien tucked the ossuary beneath his arm and strode toward Bryndraskar, the towering great hall of Rej Rhivoth. The crowd parted as though before a funeral march, eyes wide, mouths hushed. Their awe curdled to suspicion as he vanished within the shadow of the doors, and the weight of their glares shifted to her. Dozens of eyes bore down like spears, branding her as the handmaiden of their undoing. Her pulse quickened. Alone, she might not survive their judgment. With stiff resolve, she followed Damien, slipping into the hall's dark embrace.

The heavy doors slammed shut behind her, cutting off the murmurs outside. Bryndraskar loomed vast and hollow, its rafters vanishing into gloom. Only the chieftain's council lingered, clustered in uneasy knots near the polished oak throne, voices low and urgent. Damien had already claimed his place against the far wall, a mug of ale in hand, as if he had stepped from battle into a feast. The sight of the froth curling at the rim made her throat ache with longing. She crossed the hall swiftly, joining him.

The barkeep, an elder with lines cut deep into his face, poured her a mug with reluctant hands. His eyes darted to the wrapped sword at Damien's side, then back to her with a look that was more curse than courtesy.

"We are not among welcoming company," Damien muttered into his drink. His black gaze lingered on the council's whispers. "Their faith has long been little more than ceremony. Few among them burn as we do. Now their brittle world lies shattered."

For the first time, Sylvia felt unsafe in the land she had once called home. The unease was sharper than any blade, as though the people she had bled beside now saw her as something foreign, even dangerous. These men had written her off for dead. And now, with Ruin bound at Damien's side, they were being forced to reckon with a reality they had never believed possible.

"Do not be so quick to dismiss my people," she said, her voice steady but thin with strain. "You have done the impossible, Damien. You have shifted the course of history itself. How could any man greet such upheaval without fear? Every word spoken, every step taken, will be carved into memory. This is a moment that will outlive us all. They only need time to face it."

Damien inclined his head but said nothing, a rare silence from a man who carried words like weapons. The weight of her truth lingered even with him, his dark eyes fixed on the shifting faces of the council.

At the throne, Chieftain Taug bent low with his councilors, their whispers drawn out, their glances sharp as knives. The murmured counsel dragged on until the silence in the hall became heavier than the rafters themselves. At last, Taug straightened. His voice, though calm, rang like iron on stone.

"Sylvia Stormguard," he called, summoning her forward. "Stand before us and be known."

She set her mug aside untouched, forcing her feet forward across the stone floor. Though she did not look back, she felt Damien's presence looming behind her, as steady and suffocating as Ruin itself. They halted at the foot of the oaken throne, councilors bristling around their lord like wolves with hackles raised.

"Few among us believed your expedition would bear fruit," Taug said, lifting his chin. "We thought it madness, a tale that would end as so many others have ended in Morvhalgr, with silence and bones. Yet here you stand. Your return, with this... artifact, has shaken us all."

The words were diplomatic, but the council's faces told another truth. Fear clung to their eyes, sharpened into suspicion. Some hands strayed to the hilts of their blades, their meaning plain: better to strike down the curse now than suffer it within their walls. Sylvia's stomach turned. Faith, it seemed, could be as perilous as any Betanthian sword.

"You have imperiled our people, Stormguard!" Aldrik roared, his fist trembling in fury. "You have dragged us into powers far beyond our reckoning. Truth be told, it would have been better had you perished on the mountain. Then this curse would never have darkened our doors!"

His words struck like stones, and the grunts of approval that followed cut deeper still. Sylvia's chest tightened at the sight: brave warriors, men she had once admired, reduced to trembling at shadows. These were the Rhivothi, the fiercest race in the deep north. Their songs spoke of valor, of standing unbroken before gods and men alike. Yet here they cowered like frightened children. She had thought better of them.

Her voice rose, steady and fervent. "All my life I have waited for this moment; to see faith proven true, to see the veil torn aside. And now you would shrink from it? How can a man lose heart when proof of the beyond stands before us? The gods exist! The tales of our ancestors were no mere fireside lies. This is not cause for fear, but for praise. Rejoice, and give thanks! Let us walk without fear in our hearts, for we are chosen to witness what others only dream."

Her words echoed against the rafters, bold as a warhorn, but the air in Bryndraskar remained heavy, poisoned by dread. Eyes flicked toward Ruin, then back to her, as if her fervor could not pierce the shroud clinging to the blade.

Damien moved then, stepping to her side. His hand came down on her shoulder, firm and steady. His skin was its natural hue once more, yet the presence that rolled off him was darker than iron. He met the eyes of those who glared at him with undisguised scorn, his northern spirit radiating defiance. Where they saw a curse, he stood as if nothing could shake him.

"Stormguard speaks with the wisdom of the ancients," Damien thundered, his voice filling every rafter of the hall. "We live in an age written in the heavens long before our Khorrish ancestors ever drew breath. Destiny is here. The gods themselves have summoned you to their righteous cause. And will you falter now — when they have delivered into your hands the very means of salvation?"

The hairs on Sylvia's neck rose, as though lightning had rippled through the air. The Rhivothi stirred uneasily, glancing to one another, as if some presence greater than themselves had entered the hall.

"We do not mean to challenge the gods nor their will," Taug said, raising one hand for calm. His tone was even, but the steel beneath it was clear. "Understand, Lord Dreadfire, the gravity of this moment. Do not think us cowards. If you presume so, I will carve your heart from your chest and serve it raw for supper. But what we debate now is not courage… it is course."

A fair assessment, Sylvia thought. These were men who had grown comfortable in their authority, insulated from the slaughter on the

Plainhold. Rej Rhivoth sat far from the front, far from the mud and the dead.

"Bonesplitter is gone," Sylvia said softly, her words falling like stones into the silence. "He gave his life in a battle doomed from the first charge. Yet I tell you this: he would bless the measures we have taken. Dreadfire and I act to secure a future for our people. Honor him now—honor him as he honored us—by standing as he did."

The name fell like an axe. A shadow crossed the hall of Bryndraskar. Murmurs faltered. Sigvald and Aldrik lowered their eyes; even Taug bit his lip, his bravado trembling. All of them revered Marvath Bonesplitter, and all of them shrank in his absence. He was a measure by which they all found themselves wanting.

"I am pained to learn of his passing," Taug said at last, his voice stripped of its thunder. "We shall celebrate his life this night, and mourn the loss of his grand company."

Sylvia studied him closely. The chieftain's words wavered, and for the first time, he seemed less a master of men than one wrestling with his own conscience. Bonesplitter's shadow had fallen long, and it weighed heavily on him now.

"His body was never recovered," Damien said, his tone iron and grief in equal measure. "He lies still upon the Plainhold fields where he fell. But I swear before you, before the gods, before the relics of Kuggvord himself, I will avenge his death. I will grind Betanthia into dust. Stand with me, or be remembered as the men who faltered while history was remade before their very eyes."

The words rolled through the hall like a storm. Bold. Defiant. Dangerous. And yet the silence that followed was not triumph but fear; fear of Damien, of the unholy power at his side, fear of what Ruin might demand. Taug bent close with his councilors, their voices hushed and urgent. Sylvia kept her eyes fixed on Damien, her faith steady but her stomach knotted with unease.

After long minutes, the council dispersed. Taug straightened upon his oaken throne, grasping for his warrior pride as though it were a shield.

"Tread carefully, Sylvia Stormguard," Taug began, then lifted his voice until it rang against the beams of Bryndraskar. "But let it be known, from this day until the end of days, that the men of Rej Rhivoth shall not falter. We will honor our ancestors. We will uphold the warrior's path. We will follow the road you have carved, no matter how slick with blood it runs. The wheel of fate turns ever forward, and we will march beneath it. Let the gods bear witness to our conviction!"

Tears welled in Sylvia's eyes, hot with pride and sorrow alike. This was what Marvath had died for—what he would have demanded of his people. Whether to salvation or ruin, Rej Rhivoth would not shrink from the storm.

Damien stepped forward, towering above them, and raised Ruin high. The wrappings shuddered as if alive, the steel beneath throbbing with a hellish red glow that bled through the cloth. The sound of its hungry hum rippled through the hall, setting teeth on edge and stirring both awe and terror.

"Then it is settled," Dreadfire roared, his voice shaking the rafters. "Our brethren bleed on the Plainhold even now. We march to their salvation. We ride with the might of the gods at our backs! Let us shatter Betanthia, grind their armies to dust, and quench the gods' thirst with the blood of our enemies!"

GARETH V

GARETH SAT ALONE BENEATH THE SHALLOW CANOPY OUTSIDE HIS tent, elbows on knees, boots planted firm in the dirt. A brazier hissed nearby, its embers low and orange, casting his shadow in jagged shapes against the canvas. The wind was dry, carrying the stench of sweat and horse piss and the faint reek of boiled lentils from the mess tent.

My best friend… nearly murdered. How could it have come to this? First Madelyn, then me, now Edmund…

Even though the assassin's blade was meant for him a second time, it was no less infuriating to know its benefactor had marked the elder Guardsman for death. The conspiracy had gone too far, grown too treacherous, and allowed to metastasize unchecked. Covert actions had proven ineffective, for Lord Vakaro's circle appeared to be ringed with steel.

There must be another way…

As he stared into the brazier's dancing light, an idea struck him like a lightning bolt. Patience and discretion had failed, but there was another path, loath though he was to take it. Perhaps the time for boldness and audacity had come, he thought, the same audacity that had been visited upon Sir Edmund this night.

If I allow this to go unchallenged, then I don't deserve a crown… nor friends by my side. I have to act. I must.

But how? Men like Lord Vakaro would never bow to intimidation so easily. If anything, it could embolden the Southern Commandant to the point of open rebellion. But not all men were made of iron; some were soft things, pliable and full of cracks. Commander Renald Fletch of the Blackthorn was just such a man.

He was a snake with no fangs, hiding behind emblems and protocols, eager to serve whatever master kept him fed. He had neither the spine to scheme nor the cunning to lead, which made him dangerous in a different way: he obeyed.

With the right pressure, or hands around his throat, all manner of secrets might come tumbling out of Renald's mouth. There was only one way to know for certain. Gareth rose, the firelight casting hard lines across his face. The time for whispers had ended. If blood was what they wanted, then he would draw first. Without delay, he stormed across the heavily guarded encampment, boots crunching rhythmically, and headed straight for the command tent, hoping to find his mark.

The canvas flaps tore open as Gareth stormed into the tent, dust and heat trailing him like a cloak. Inside, the air was thick with smoke and stale sweat, lanterns flickering over maps pinned with iron nails. Renald looked up from the war table, appearing almost infantile in his unease.

"My prince," Renald said evenly. "You arrive unannounced. And at such a late hour. How may I be of service?"

The only service Gareth cared for was driving his sword into the man's guts as far as it would go. His face twisted into a tight frown. "If it were service I was after, Commander, you would be the last person I would entertain."

Renald's mouth fell open. "I beg your pardon, Your Highness?"

At first, Gareth said nothing. He simply stared, eyes narrowing to slits, as if daring the man to keep talking. The silence that followed was louder than any accusation, stretched taut like a drawn bowstring.

"Sir Edmund was nearly killed this evening," Gareth finally said. "We have assassins running amok amidst our ranks. Tell me, Commander, precisely what purpose the Blackthorn serves? You have failed to locate the Northmen. And now, you have failed to secure the integrity of our camp!"

"Heavens!" Renald gasped, clutching his throat as if it were about to be slit. "Sir Edmund? I… I cannot fathom how anyone would want to—"

"Enough!" The word cracked like a whip, leaving silence in its wake. Gareth's hand moved to the hilt of his sword. "Someone tried to murder my best friend tonight, just as they tried to murder Madelyn… and just as they tried to murder me."

Renald's mouth opened, but no sound came, as if the weight of Gareth's words had stolen the breath from his lungs. He glanced toward the war table, perhaps searching for an answer— or an exit.

Gareth stepped forward, his voice low and cold. "The Order has either grown fat and lazy on ceremony, or this is more than mere incompetence. No, Commander, I suspect it's more than that. A blade does not arrive three times by accident. Thankfully, its wielders have all failed in their mission. If you intended to spill our blood, you should have sent your best."

Renald flinched as if struck. "Your Highness, please! You wound me! I've no knowledge of any such plot, I swear it! The Blackthorn serves at the pleasure of the crown, and I—I have only ever remained faithful to House Bethard! I beg you, do not confuse my loyalty with the failures of others."

There was nothing more pitiful than watching a grown man squirm. Renald Fletch was all uniform and no spine, it appeared. But even the most craven were dangerous, for their treachery lay veiled behind courtesies. His words reeked of fear, not innocence.

The tent flap stirred slightly as the wind shifted, but no one entered. Outside, the camp still bustled with the illusion of order. But in here, truth seeped through the cracks like rot. Gareth's hand remained on his sword. He had not come for justice. He had come for blood.

"Failure certainly seems to be the Blackthorn credo these days," Gareth said, scoffing. "The Order's accomplishments are painfully lacking. Although it appears we can add treason to the list."

Renald straightened his collar and cleared his throat, forcing a smile that died on his lips. "Your Highness, I assure you, no one within the Order would ever sanction such an atrocity. It's likely the work of… outside agents. Dissidents. Saboteurs. We have many enemies, you know."

"Outside agents?" Gareth said without blinking. "Hired blades who just so happen to strike three times against myself and those closest to me? That's quite the coincidence… and I am not a man who believes such things can happen purely by chance. I want names, Renald. And then, I want heads."

"These are troubled times, my prince. Loyalties shift, tempers flare. Perhaps someone misunderstood an order—acted rashly—"

Gareth stepped closer. "So, you *do* know who gave the order? Are you suggesting someone like… Lord Vakaro might be behind these plots?"

"I… I did not say that."

Renald's eyes flicked about, not in calculation, but in panic. The kind of panic born not from guilt, but from proximity to consequence. He shifted his weight, tugged at the hem of his tunic, then clasped his hands as if prayer might shield him from accusation.

"I will have names, Commander," Gareth said, twisting the handle of his sword. "One way or the other."

He turned without another word, his cloak flaring behind him as he shoved through the tent flap and out into the night. The camp greeted him with a rush of dry wind and torchlight, guards snapping to attention as he passed. No one dared speak. Word of the confrontation would spread, but for now, silence obeyed him.

The perimeter around the royal tent was tightly drawn, with double the usual guard. Spears in hand, helms glinting beneath the lanterns, the soldiers stood rigid as statues. He approached the Guardsmen without fear or hesitation, even after being challenged. But the purple cloaks recognized their prince after he drew closer, and parted like silk drapes. Gareth saw Tarren Vale, a young colossus of a man, and one of Sir Edmund's trusted Lieutenants.

"You there," he said, pointing. "I want you to place a detachment outside Commander Fletch's tent. No one is permitted to enter or exit. If anyone tries, detain them immediately. If they resist, kill them."

"Yes, Your Highness," Tarren said, his voice beating like a hammer. "It will be done."

The Lieutenant gestured for Gareth to pass the defensive perimeter, then set about barking orders and gathering spears. The Guardsmen were not to be trifled with, especially not on this night, and they appeared all too satisfied to spill Blackthorn blood.

Gareth ducked inside his tent, the heavy canvas sealing him away from the world. Sleep would not come easily, not with his blood still up and his thoughts a storm of vengeance. He paced for a time, fists clenched, jaw tight with fury. But dawn would bring fresh battles, and so, with great effort, he stripped down, lowered himself to the cot, and closed his eyes.

His dreams were little more than noise and shadow; half-shaped memories and twisted visions. Faces warped by pain. Hands slick with blood. A rush of hooves, the scream of steel. Madelyn's eyes, hollow with betrayal. Edmund's voice, calling out through the dark. When he awoke, it was with sweat at his brow and fists clenched and aching, his rage no less quiet, only buried a layer deeper.

Angry, clipped voices rose over the early light like steel drawn from a scabbard. Gareth shot awake, pushed off the coarse blanket, and rose, sword already in hand, his mind still half-sunk in blood-soaked dreams. The air outside was cooler than the night before, but thick with tension, the kind that crackled just before violence.

He threw open the tent flap and stepped into the growing light. Just beyond the perimeter, two knots of soldiers faced one another with swords half-drawn—Blackthorn on one side, cloaked in black and gold; the Royal Guardsmen on the other, purple and silver blazing in the dawn. One wrong word and the killing would begin, as quick and vicious as a dog fight.

At the center of it all stood Tarren Vale, towering like a mountain, his voice steady but stern. "You will not pass," he said. "The prince's orders were clear."

A Blackthorn knight, older and red-faced, jabbed a finger at him. "We have a right to speak with our Commander! Stand aside, or—"

"You'll what?" Gareth's voice cut through the morning like an axe. Every head turned. Though without his armor, the thunder in his voice was all the protection he needed.

The Blackthorn knight turned, face flushed and mouth half-open, but whatever words he meant to speak turned to dust the moment he saw Gareth striding toward them. The prince's eyes were hard as granite, his expression carved into a deep scowl. Barefoot, bare-chested, but burning with purpose, he might as well have worn a crown of flame.

"I gave a direct order," Gareth said, stopping beside Lieutenant Vale. "Now, disperse!"

The knight's lip curled, but he held his tongue. A younger man behind him shifted uneasily, fingers brushing the pommel of his sword.

Gareth's gaze locked onto the movement like a hawk. "If any man here believes I won't bury the next fool who disobeys me, I invite him to test his luck."

The Blackthorn stepped back without another word, outmatched by a growing congregation of loyal soldiers. They scattered in twos and threes, muttering beneath their breath. Gareth stood still until every last one had vanished from sight. He spied Lord Kenfield approaching, hands wringing and eyes wide as wagon wheels.

"Your Highness," he said, dipping his head. "I came as soon as I heard the shouting. Are you harmed?"

Gareth shook his head, still glaring in the direction the Blackthorn had fled. "No, but others nearly were. The Order's arrogance knows no end."

Anders glanced toward the perimeter where Tarren Vale now stood silent but vigilant. "They've grown too bold. Lord Vakaro's leash is long, but even long leashes can be yanked." He lowered his voice. "You were right to post guards. The Blackthorn have shown their true colors ever since Madelyn was relieved of her post."

"I have no evidence they are guilty of anything, except complacency," Gareth proclaimed. "I am merely pulling on a thread to see what unravels. Renald Fletch is the weak link. He is my path to answers... and hopefully, a confession."

Anders' brow furrowed. "Then pull carefully, Your Highness. Threads like that can snap... and sometimes, what unravels is the man holding them. He could become unpredictable."

Gareth's jaw flexed. "Then let it snap. I'm done waiting in the shadows while our enemies draw blood in the open... the blood of those closest to me. We will get answers, Lord Kenfield. If this rat won't squeal, we'll torch the nest and see who runs screaming."

"I can only imagine how Lord Vakaro will respond to such a provocation," Anders said, scratching his neck.

Gareth allowed himself a smile. "That's the point. If he takes offense, if he moves to defend the man or calls it an overstep, then we'll have our answer. Detaining Commander Fletch is an internal matter between the Order and the Crown. And any who protest too loudly will out themselves."

Anders blinked, the weight of Gareth's words settling in. For a moment, he said nothing, his mind chewing through the implications like a dog with a bone. Then he exhaled a slow, low whistle.

"Heavens," he muttered. "You're not just pulling the thread... you're wrapping it around their necks." A grin tugged at the corner of his mouth. "It's a clever trap, my prince. Cruel, but clever."

"Let's hope it catches something worth gutting."

The hours dragged like chains across stone. Gareth remained beneath the canopy, hands clasped, boot tapping a restless rhythm against the dirt. The camp bustled with the hollow droning of routine—clanging pots, whinnying horses, the distant bark of drills, but none of it reached him. His mind was fixed on one thing alone: retaliation. He had baited the trap, set it in motion, and now he waited. If Lord Vakaro meant to strike, he would do so soon... and Gareth would be ready.

But the blow never came. No messenger. No courier. No formal protest. The command tent remained still and unapproached. It was almost worse than an outright response, this lack of reaction. Gareth could feel it coiling in his gut. Either Lord Vakaro was more cautious than he imagined... or more dangerous.

At last, Gareth rose, shaking off the weight of inaction like a cloak. Waiting had become its own kind of surrender, and he'd suffered enough of that for a lifetime. He crossed the camp with grim purpose, boots crunching over sunbaked earth until he reached the command tent. Without pause, he threw open the flaps and strode inside.

"Enough with the stalling," he snapped, fixing Renald Fletch with a glare sharp enough to flay skin. "You will give me names freely, or so help me, I will force them from you."

Renald, already pale, fumbled for words, his lips moving faster than his thoughts. "Your Highness, I've told you, I know nothing of these plots! I am as horrified as you are, truly!"

The stench of fear clung to Renald like rot in a meat house. His hands fluttered at his sides, unsure whether to plead or protest, and the sweat on his brow glistened like ocean water. Gareth saw not a Commander, but a coward wrapped in fine wool and empty titles, given to him by appeasing those more cunning than himself.

"One thing we will not do is talk in circles," Gareth proclaimed. "I have neither the time nor the patience. If you will not give me the names freely, then perhaps there is someone who can convince you better."

He stepped back and peeked through the tent flap, the Guardsmen outside taking notice.

"Fetch Titan Bradshaw," he commanded.

The Guardsman gave a curt nod and vanished. Renald's face drained of what little color remained. His lips parted as if to protest, but only babble poured out. Only then did he understand the severity of the moment, not just the threat, but the inevitability of it. Whatever protection he thought his station afforded him had been torn away like a curtain before the noonday sun.

Before long, the flap parted again, and Titan Bradshaw stepped inside, broad-shouldered and scowling, his hair wind-tossed and his expression tight with irritation.

"You called?" Tylar muttered, not caring to bow.

Gareth pointed to Renald without preamble. "This man has information vital to the crown. You are to extract it. Break whatever you must, so long as he still has a tongue when you're finished."

Titan's brow raised, but only for a breath. Then he strode forward and seized Renald by the throat, lifting him off the ground as easily as one might hoist a sack of barley. The Commander squealed, boots kicking helplessly, eyes bulging with panic.

"I don't give a shit who you're protecting," Tylar Bradshaw said, his voice like gravel. "You're going to spill it real fast, or I'm going to cave your fucking head in."

Renald thrashed like a worm on a hook, babbling something

incoherent through desperate grunts. Gareth watched in silence, arms folded as if awaiting a report, not a confession. The flailing, the whimpering, the pitiful pleas, they were nothing more than background noise. He had tried civility. He had tried reason. But if blood were the only coin these traitors understood, then he would pay in buckets. One way or another, Renald Fletch would talk. Or die trying.

"Names, fucker!" Titan snarled, his grip tightening. "Is it Vakaro? Huh? Is it?"

"N-no!" Renald sputtered, choking on the word. "It wasn't Vakaro!"

Titan yanked him closer. "Then *who*?"

Renald gagged, chest heaving. "Cardale," he gasped. "The order came from Cardale…"

Gareth blinked, stunned into stillness. Of all the answers he expected, that was not one of them. Not the frontier. Not some rogue bannerman seeking favor. But *Cardale*—the heart of the realm, the throne's own shadow. A chill crawled down his spine, colder than the bitterest winter winds. The implication was staggering.

Someone close, someone with power, was masterminding treason. The thought coiled through his chest like a serpent, squeezing tight. He felt no clarity, only betrayal. Faces flashed through his mind; ministers, advisors, relatives with warm smiles and colder ambitions. Who among them had sharpened a blade behind his back? And more importantly… how many were left who remained loyal?

Titan lowered Renald to the ground, his grip loosening as if the strength had been drained from his arms. Even the brute looked shaken, his brow furrowed deep, jaw set tight with disbelief.

"Cardale?" Bradshaw muttered, more to himself than anyone else. "Fucking hell…"

Gareth stepped forward, voice like a knife's edge. "Who gave the order?" he demanded. "Name them!"

Renald coughed, crumpling to his knees, clutching his throat. "I… I do not know," he rasped. "I swear it. The message came through intermediaries, and never to me. Lord Vakaro only shares information with me when necessary. But I know the palace sanctioned it! I swear!"

"He's nothing but a useful idiot," Tylar said, spitting. "When I was in the Order, this piece of shit was the laughing stock of every officer around. I can only imagine who he had to fellate in order to become a Commander."

"Yes…" Renald admitted. "After Madelyn was ousted, the High Marshal needed someone he could trust to take command!"

"Keep fucking telling yourself that," Titan said, then turned to Gareth. "This worm was chosen because he's too stupid to ask the right questions and put the pieces together. Why do you think that cunt Vakaro didn't storm this tent and pry him out of here the second you entered? It's because he doesn't know shit, and he's of no consequence."

For a brute, Titan spoke with the wisdom of elders. Had either of them attempted to catch Lord Vakaro alone, a dozen swords would have appeared out of nowhere within seconds. That was the difference between the powerful and the protected, and those who merely existed.

Gareth said nothing for a time, only stared at Renald—crumpled, wheezing, slick with sweat and humiliation. Whatever illusion of authority the man once carried had bled out onto the canvas floor. There would be no rising from this.

He turned and strode to the tent flap. "Come, Bradshaw."

Titan gave one last scornful look before following. The canvas closed behind them, and the heat of a coming day bit against their sweat-dampened skin. Two Guardsmen stood rigid at the perimeter.

"Commander Fletch is to remain here, under strict guard," Gareth ordered. "No contact. If anyone attempts to free him—anyone, I don't care what cloak they wear—detain them. If they resist, kill them where they stand. When we break camp, keep him in a secure carriage."

The Guardsmen nodded in unison. Purple cloaks caught the dry wind. Gareth looked east, where the first fingers of sun stretched across the Plainhold.

"The Blackthorn won't take this lightly," Titan muttered. "Be ready. They may come for him."

"It's a risk I must take," he sighed. "My soldiers outnumber theirs by an order of magnitude. I have fought beside those men. I have to believe they would rise to my defense."

Titan grunted. "And if they don't?"

Gareth said nothing, but pondered the question's weight. His eyes lingered on the distant horizon, where the sun rose like a sword being drawn across the sky. Dawn spilled across the Plainhold, painted in gold, but edged in blood.

"Tylar, I need you to keep a close eye on the Order," he instructed. "You are still respected by most, and feared by many. You must do whatever is necessary to maintain the peace."

"This slippery cunt won't be missed," Tylar said, nodding. "And if any of the rabble get uppity, I'll break a few necks and set them straight."

Before long, the army stirred once more. Campfires hissed as they were doused, and the clang of steel on steel echoed through the ranks as soldiers strapped on greaves and tightened saddles. Horses snorted restlessly, and the scent of wet leather, smoke, and churned soil drifted on the wind.

Gareth moved among them like a shadow, his silver sword catching the occasional glint of light. No trumpets heralded the day's march. No banners flew. This was not a show of strength, but a movement driven by necessity and suspicion. Orders were passed quietly, and each man seemed to watch the other with a touch more caution than the day before.

The attempt on Sir Edmund's life had changed something. Word traveled fast in a war camp; faster than orders, faster than horses. Gareth had expected whispers, but not the palpable tension that now simmered beneath every glance and grunted exchange. Men tightened their grips on spear shafts, eyes scanning not just the horizon but one another, as if expecting betrayal from within.

The name "Sir Edmund" hung in the air like a prayer or a warning, and though no one dared speak of assassination aloud, the silence that followed his name was proof enough. Gareth said nothing, but the realization stung: trust was eroding, and madness was only a heartbeat away. Indeed, a civil war at such a time would spell Betanthia's demise.

Another day bled into the next, each one marked by the same monotony: dusty marches, creaking wagons, and the soft clatter of steel in rhythm with footfall. The sun hung high and cruel above the Plainhold, baking the earth and the men alike. Flies buzzed like curses, and not even the promise of battle stirred much excitement anymore. Gareth rode near the front, silent in the saddle, his thoughts still clawing back to the night before.

Behind him rode the eagle sigil of House Bethard, the fading fabric snapping and cracking like a whip in the dry wind. Although he was exposed to the greatest danger at the front, it was necessary to reassert the authority of his bloodline. Marcellus Bethard may have diminished, and his authority usurped by snakes, but on the searing Plainhold fields, the heir to the Westwind Citadel stood tall.

The hours dragged, the horizon an unbroken smear of heat and dust. Even the wind seemed tired, carrying only the rasp of dry grass and the weary creak of wagon wheels. Gareth's gaze wandered over the endless plain, each distant shimmer a trick of the sun—until the sound came. A horn, low and deliberate, drifted on the wind. Another followed, shorter, sharper.

Horsemen raced to the front as scouts rushed back toward the main column, banners flowing and horns blazing.

"My prince!" a rider called out. "We have located the horde! They are just beyond the hills!"

On their tails came black shadows, phantoms against the hazy horizon. Gareth squinted, disbelieving the truth his eyes were screaming to tell him. The Northmen were here, and their riders were upon them.

"Formation!" he cried out, drawing his silver sword. "Get into formation now!"

A chorus of horns rang out, the soldiers behind him scrambling into place, shields locking, pikes angling forward. The ground began to tremble, not from the march of Betanthian boots, but from the oncoming thunder of hooves. Dust rose like a storm cloud over the ridgeline, and within it, the first glints of steel flashed in the sun. The Plainhold, quiet for so long, was about to roar.

Gareth wheeled his horse about, seeking shelter behind a protective wall of shields. The first volley of arrows hissed through the air, thudding into shields, kicking up dirt, felling two men where they stood. Gareth raised his sword, rallying the front ranks as the Northern horse archers split, wheeling in a great crescent to loose another storm.

Their war cries echoed across the plain, sharp and alien. Then, just as suddenly as they had come, the Northmen veered away, melting back toward the hills in a cloud of dust and jeers. From the left flank, a contingent of Blackthorn rode forward, their lightly armored horse archers in front. Behind them trailed the armored fist of Bentmont; heavy cavalry with lances as long as tree trunks.

However, their weight served as a hindrance. The Northmen disappeared like morning fog, vanishing as quickly as they arrived. Another horn blast rang out, friendly in tone, drawing the heavy horsemen back. Knights wheeled about like a flock of birds, gracefully disengaging and returning to their place at the left flank. The next battle was now upon them.

As Gareth surveyed the distant hills, he spied Lord Vakaro and his retinue nearby. The Southern Commandant paid him no attention, pointing and issuing orders as if he did not exist. Even though they stood a breath away from facing down the Northmen, a secretive, more lethal battle was already being fought. Gareth stood firm and unflinching, his banners beside him.

Then, as if emerging from a dream, he spied a familiar form approaching in the hazy heat. Sir Edmund Thomas sat mounted, face and body wrapped with bloodied bandages. The elder Guardsman trotted forward, wincing with each hoof fall.

"Edmund?!" Gareth said breathlessly. "What on earth are you doing here? You should be resting!"

"How could you say such a thing to me?" Edmund Thomas replied sourly. "My heart still beats. My arm still carries strength. How could I ever explain to your mother in the next life that I left her son to stand alone against the wolves?"

Gareth felt a swell of something between pride and dread. The sight of Edmund—bloodied, stubborn, unbroken—was as much a balm as it was a burden. "You're a damn fool," he muttered, though his voice softened.

"Then I'm your fool, and that's all that matters," Edmund said, settling his reins. His gaze slid to the hills where the horse archers had vanished. "We'll be upon them soon. And you will need every ounce of strength at your side."

The horns died away, leaving only the restless clink of armor and the snort of uneasy horses. In the brief silence, Gareth looked from Edmund to Lord Vakaro, then to the empty ridgeline. The Northmen had tested their mettle and found it worth testing again. But so too had Gareth taken the measure of his own camp, and the fractures within it. When the next clash came, he knew, the enemy before them might not be the one that decided the day.

"Let them come," he said somberly. "And let this come to an end... one way or another."

LUCETTA VII

Warm rays and a salty breeze roused Lucetta from a deathlike slumber. It felt an age since she had last known rest unmarred by fear. With a groan, she pushed herself upright on a wooden bench, rubbing the crust from her weary eyes. But this was no dank, cramped cell of stone and rot.

No, this was Cardale's city square, silent as a tomb, empty of all life. Lucetta's breath caught. How had she come here? Had her captivity been only a nightmare? Or was this the work of the woman in black… or her mother's vengeful shade?

Whatever the truth, the relief was undeniable. To be free of chains and free of darkness. Dungeons were fit for criminals, not for royalty, not for her.

"Thank the heavens," she whispered, rising on shaky legs. "It was only a dream. A terrible… terrible dream."

The square looked unchanged, though its scars lingered. Scorch marks marred the stones, rubble still lay in piles; reminders of the Harbingers' rampage. That day had been all too real, the terror etched into her marrow, the memory of zealots clawing for her mother's body refusing to fade.

She turned, intent on finding her estate, but the square shifted.

Guards in purple cloaks poured in from every street, boots striking in unison. They ringed the plaza, walling her in, their shields glinting like a hundred accusing eyes. At first, Lucetta thought they had come to escort her home. Then she saw it. To her right, a gallows loomed where none had stood before. Its noose swung lazily in the eastern breeze, waiting.

The Guardsmen closed around the gallows, steel gleaming in the sun. Shields locked and spears braced, they stood like a wall of iron. Yet their presence felt less like protection than judgment.

Soon, the low rumble of voices swelled, echoing off the stones. A crowd poured into the square—peasants and lords alike, packed shoulder to shoulder. Hundreds, perhaps thousands. Why they had gathered in such numbers she could not guess, though the sight struck a chord deep within her. Something about their arrival rang with dreadful familiarity. They pressed close, but not too close, leaving a ring of space about the gallows.

I have stood here before, Lucetta realized, heart quickening. Why does this feel so familiar?

The jeers came first, sharp and ugly. Then a prisoner was thrust through the mob, wrapped in chains and rags, driven forward by the points of spears. Garbage and curses flew at her in equal measure. Lucetta strained for a better look and felt the blood drain from her face. The prisoner was a woman, slight of frame, hair cropped short.

She was shoved to the gallows, forced onto a barrel as the hangman's rope swung overhead. The coarse loop slipped over her head, settling against her throat. Lucetta gasped, her voice breaking free in a cry.

"No! Not again! I will not let you suffer this fate! Not while I still draw breath!"

She lunged for the ring of Guardsmen, but their ranks did not yield. Their boots seemed fused to the earth, their shields immovable. She beat at them in desperation, her strength meaningless against their silence.

Helpless, she could only watch as the woman in black stood beneath the rope, her fate tightening around her neck.

"Good people of Cardale!" a hulking man in a shimmering steel breastplate cried out. "You have gathered here today to bear witness to the King's justice. Before you stand the accused."

Lucetta's breath caught. She *knew* this scene. The weight of recognition pressed down on her chest, and grief surged so sharply she could scarcely breathe. Her gaze fixed on the woman in black, and she began to sob, raw and childlike.

"She is guilty of bribery, murder, and treason of the highest order," the towering man continued. "Having stood trial before the King's court, she has been found guilty on all counts and sentenced to hang by the neck until dead. Do you have any last words?"

The woman gave none. Stray locks of cropped, filthy hair clung to her face, hiding what little expression she had left. Her silence was not defiance but something colder—resignation. She stood as though she had already left the world behind, and it chilled Lucetta to see her so still, so unshaken.

"No!" Lucetta shrieked, hurling herself at the line of Guardsmen. "No, you cannot!"

She struck a shield with all her weight and bounced back as though she were nothing. Pain lanced through her shoulder, yet she staggered up and tried again, hammering at steel that would not move. The purple cloaks did not flinch, their faces blank, their stance unbreakable.

Each effort bled her strength away. Soon she could only clutch at her throbbing shoulder, eyes streaming as she stared past the wall of spears.

"I'm sorry, mother."

The hangman stepped forward, planted a boot against the barrel, and kicked. Wood clattered against stone. The rope snapped taut, jerking her body into the air. The crowd gasped as one, and within heartbeats, the woman's life was gone.

"I know not why you show me such things," Lucetta sobbed, tears burning hot trails down her cheeks. "Whatever you did in life… you did not deserve to die like a common thief."

Movement flickered at the edge of her vision. She turned and saw a cluster of purple cloaks beyond the ring of Guardsmen, far back in the haze. Their faces blurred, lost to distance and tears… all but one. A figure stood at their center, still and watching. His presence alone hollowed her chest, and terror welled in her heart until she stumbled backward.

Lucetta turned to flee. Hope carried her only a step before fire tore through her gut. She gasped, staring down at the blade driven into her abdomen. The hand clutching it was slim and pale, the hand of the woman who had just hung lifeless from the rope.

"W…why…" Lucetta stammered, voice shaking.

The corpse lifted its head, hair falling away to reveal a face ruined with rot. Milky eyes bulged, jaw snapping wide as a shriek poured out, shrill and unending. Maggots writhed from between her teeth, bile spilling down her chin in thick ropes, pattering against Lucetta's dress like foul rain.

Lucetta screamed, then awoke. Her body trembled beneath a clammy sheen of sweat. The warmth of the sunlit square was gone. The voices of thousands gone. Only stone, mildew, and shadows remained. Her cell pressed close around her: a heap of rotting hay, a rust-flecked bucket, and the suffocating stench of her own despair.

"Get up," a harsh voice commanded. "You're coming with us, Your Majesty."

Three Harbingers stood outside the bars, their chuckles cold as steel. One slid a skeleton key into the lock and swung the door wide. Lucetta thought of lashing out like some desperate animal, but her limbs betrayed her. Hunger and exhaustion had scoured her strength. Rough hands seized her arms and dragged her into the corridor's damp darkness, hauling her toward the chamber beyond.

It was a routine all too familiar. Each time Lucetta defied the Harbingers, their cruelty grew worse. For weeks, she had borne witness to atrocities no mortal ought to see. Flayings. Amputations. Bowels unspooled onto the stone. Even the most hardened butcher would have gagged at the sights that now marked her every waking hour, and today promised no different.

The chamber blazed with heat. A great fire roared in its pit, fed by dozens of braziers until the air itself seemed to sear her throat. Corpses of Guardsmen lay scattered like refuse. Some still hung in chains, their bodies blackened and cracked where the flames had kissed them. Others had been reduced to a heap in the corner, a mound of limbs and armor that grew higher with each passing day.

Dragged inside, Lucetta was shoved to her knees and forced to behold the spectacle awaiting her. Pavlos sat bound in a heavy stockade beside a pair of blood-slick tables—tables that had broken men before him and would break men after. Only the stocks could restrain him; otherwise, the Droethien would have torn the Harbingers limb from limb. Instruments lay in neat rows across the wood. Hooks. Knives. Hammers still wet with another man's life. Their gleam made her stomach lurch.

Pavlos himself was near unrecognizable. His face was pulp, beaten again and again, yet the faint flash of golden teeth marked the ghost of a grin. Somehow, through agony, he still managed to meet her gaze as if her presence alone gave him cause to mock their tormentors. She tried to return the strength in kind, though both knew there was no comfort here.

"You think she'll give in today?" sneered a lank Harbinger, his voice nasal, reeking of rot.

"I hope not," his companion replied, lips peeling into a brown-toothed smile. He spat a dark stream onto the stone, where it hissed against the heat and left a slick stain.

A cruel choice loomed before her. Without Pavlos, her fragile queendom would wither; he had been her hammer, her shield, her living banner of defiance. Replacing such a man in Betanthia would be near impossible, and even if it could be done, time was a currency she did not possess. Yet if she yielded and begged for his life, the Harbingers would seize it as leverage forever. Both paths reeked of ruin.

Hesgrin lounged by the torture rack, hideous face warped yet smug, a mask of corruption Lucetta had come to know too well. With a languid flick of his fingers, he beckoned the Harbingers to haul her forward.

"Another dawn, another round of needless agony," he complained, voice cracked and wet. "How many men have bled out thanks to your silence? Loyal men, who swore their lives to you. I wonder, princess… would they have pledged themselves so eagerly had they known the true price?"

He rose with a groan, joints popping like firewood in the flames, and drifted to the table where an arsenal of instruments lay in grim array. Hooks, brands, and clamps, each rusted from old stains yet ready to drink again. Hesgrin let his hand hover before plucking up a slender iron spike. He turned it lazily between blistered fingers, savoring the weight of suffering it promised.

His steps toward Pavlos were slow, deliberate, the gait of a man savoring a meal. The Droethien's mangled face still wore its crooked grin, golden teeth glinting beneath the blood trickling from his brow.

"You've watched your men flayed and butchered," Hesgrin rasped, coming close enough for the spike's tip to graze Pavlos's skin. "Yet your tongue remains still. Admirable, perhaps… but foolish. Do you imagine they thank you for this stoic silence? Do you think their souls linger here, singing hymns to your unbroken will?"

The spike pressed beneath Pavlos's jaw, its chill biting into torn flesh until a bead of blood welled bright against his battered skin. Lucetta's breath hitched; her body went rigid in the Harbingers' grip, every nerve straining against hands that pinned her fast.

"This one—" Hesgrin angled his head toward Pavlos, the iron digging deeper— "is no nameless Guardsman. No purple cloak whose life can be squandered like coin. This one is yours, princess. Your confidant. Your knife-hand. Your… friend."

The last word dripped with such cloying venom that her stomach knotted.

"Tell me, then," Hesgrin murmured, "what is his worth to you? Enough to beg? Enough to kneel?"

Lucetta's thoughts raced, each possibility a blade against her pride. To bend would be to surrender everything she had built: her crown, her schemes, her very name. To resist would be to watch Pavlos carved to pieces before her eyes. The weight of her queendom pressed down like a millstone, grinding her spirit between damnation and ruin.

"Truth be told, I could drag this out for days," Hesgrin went on, lips peeling into a grin. "But I've felt your indifference growing. You are resilient, Princess Lucetta. I've seen hardened men crumble when their brothers' flesh was flayed from bone. But not you. Not yet. So let us end this pageantry. The last of your Guardsmen will scream, and then… then it will be your turn."

Though half-starved and weakened by delirium, Lucetta clung to one certainty: they would not truly harm her. She was too valuable, their only leverage in prying free Queen Charlotte's corpse. And in the shadows lurked her other shield—the woman in black. Even now, Lucetta felt her presence, coiled like smoke, ready to strike should any blade dare cut too close. But Pavlos was another matter entirely. And for him, no such protection would come.

"Stop now, I demand it," Lucetta squeaked, her voice brittle as autumn leaves. "You will leave this man be—or you will lose forever any chance of my cooperation."

"Ahh…" Hesgrin's chuckle rasped like rusted hinges. "So the mask slips at last. I thought he must be worth something to you, given how close you clung when we found you. If… if I spare him, will you finally relent? Will you grant the faithful their rightful prize?"

Relenting was as foul as drinking from a swamp, yet there was no other path. Better to yield now and live long enough to scheme. Surely there was some way to outwit a clutch of superstitious zealots, even if their fanaticism lent them strength.

"I will give you what you ask," she said at last, each word a stone dragged from her throat. "I will guide your men into the palace grounds. I will lead you to the family crypt. All the arrangements will be made."

A chorus of laughter and jeers erupted from the Harbingers. They howled in triumph, stamping feet and clattering weapons in crude celebration. Yet Hesgrin did not join them. He stood apart, chin in hand, eyes glittering with distrust. Weeks of defiance had hardened her—why should he believe this sudden surrender?

"So you say, Princess," Hesgrin murmured, voice smooth as oil. "But what proof do we have? What assurance that once we step within those walls, you won't turn our faith against us and see us slaughtered like cattle? No, no… your words alone are not enough. You must offer us collateral."

Collateral. The word struck like a hammer. Bound, starving, stripped of every resource, what could she possibly offer? Gold meant nothing to zealots; jewels, even less. These were not men who could be bought.

"My life is already in your hands," she croaked. "If I falter—if I betray you—then do what you will. Cut my throat, burn me alive, feed me to the dogs. I care not. But let him live."

Her voice hardened as she spoke, brittle steel beneath fatigue. "You will have the Queen's body. If you doubt me still, bind me with your strongest chains. Guard me day and night. Take whatever assurance you crave, just keep him breathing."

The Harbingers muttered among themselves, wolfish grins flashing in the firelight. Even Pavlos, half-crushed by the stockade, managed the faintest glimmer of his golden smile.

Hesgrin leaned over the table, the lamplight catching in the wet hollows of his ruined face. "Collateral, you say? You would give us… yourself? As though you are not already ours to squander."

He let the silence swell, thick and suffocating. "No, princess. Words and chains are cheap. We require something lasting… something that will remind you, every time you draw breath, who holds the reins."

His fingers drifted across a scatter of blades, lingering over cruel points and serrated edges. Lucetta's pulse thundered, her chest tight as a snare drum. Then Hesgrin's hand closed on a small hammer, its iron head better suited for nails than flesh. He hefted it, smiling, and met her gaze.

Before she could speak, he lunged. The hammer cracked against Pavlos's cheek with a bone-splitting crunch. Teeth clattered across the floor like dice in a cup, his golden smile shattered, spilled in fragments at her feet.

Hesgrin's hunger was not sated. He brought the hammer down again and again, each blow splitting flesh, cracking bone. Pavlos thrashed in the stockade, hands clawing uselessly at the air, but the wood held him fast. The wet thumps, the snapping crunches, each one carved cold shivers down Lucetta's spine. She was watching the key to her grand designs ground slowly to ruin.

"Stop!" she cried, voice shrill, breaking. "I've given you my word… my assurances! What more do you want?!"

At last, Hesgrin staggered back, chest heaving, the hammer slick with blood. Two cultists caught him as his legs buckled, lowering him into a chair. He looked half-collapsed, but the grin smeared across his wreck of a face was the grin of a man who had feasted on suffering.

Pavlos's head slumped forward. Blood poured from the ruin of his face, spattering the boards, pooling at his feet. For one dreadful moment, Lucetta thought him dead—her last ally, her knife-hand, her lynchpin—gone. Then came a low groan, ragged, gurgling, just enough to prove he still clung to life.

"You bastard!" Lucetta shrieked, so wild she nearly toppled with the sound. "Why?! WHY?!"

Her words were swallowed by the cavernous chamber. The woman in black did not appear. Hope itself felt like it had deserted her. Betrayal upon betrayal piled high, until her will cracked beneath the weight. She collapsed to the filthy floor, sobbing, frail hands clutching her face as though she might hold it together by force.

The roar of the Harbingers receded to a muffled drone, as if she had been dragged under black water. Every nerve in her body screamed to rise, to hurl herself at Hesgrin, to seize the hammer and drive it into his skull. But her limbs hung useless, heavy as stone, her breath shallow, her strength gone.

Pavlos wheezed, a wet rasp that hovered between life and death. The sound was pitiful, frail, yet it pierced her more deeply than any blade. She had not wept for the flayed, the gutted, the burned. But for him, the tears came unbidden.

Somewhere beyond the smoke and reek, she felt it again: that gaze. Orange-red, unblinking. Watching. Waiting. Not to save her. Not yet.

Lucetta lifted her head, forcing her blurred eyes to meet Hesgrin's ruined face. Her voice cracked, but carried venom still. "You will regret this."

The fanatic only grinned, teeth yellow in the firelight. "Chain her. Feed her. We march on the palace soon."

Cold iron snapped shut around her wrists. She was dragged back into the tunnels, the light fading until Pavlos was only a shadow, head slumped, blood dripping steadily at his knees. She did not look back.

She could not. One glance would have broken what little remained inside her.

They believed her finished. They believed her broken. But as the darkness swallowed her whole, one truth burned steady through the wreckage of her soul:

I will have my revenge… and it will burn hotter than the fires of hell!

SYLVIA IX

The Hinterwood stirred with life. Sylvia Stormguard guided her mount along a carpet of damp leaves, the chill of autumn clinging to the air. Golden crowns of oak and pine stretched high above, their branches creaking like old timbers in the wind. Smoke curled from countless campfires ahead, each one marking another warband drawn to their cause.

First came scattered riders, but with every mile the trickle swelled into a flood. By noon, thousands marched beneath banners stitched with beasts, runes, and crude depictions of gods. By dusk, their number had become tens of thousands.

They filled the glades and ridgelines in every direction, tribes from across the Hinterwood gathering in one place for the first time in living memory. Shields were stacked in great mounds, spears leaned in rows that stretched farther than her eyes could follow. Some sang war chants, others feasted, but most stood silent, watching. Their eyes followed Damien and the shape wrapped across his back.

"Stormguard!" a rider called, raising a spear skyward.

"Dreadfire lives!" another cried out.

The cry rippled outward, taken up by a hundred throats, then a thousand. Horns blared, drums thundered, and the forest shook with the stamp of feet and the clash of weapons. For a heartbeat, Sylvia let the sound wash over her, pride burning hot in her chest.

The gods have answered. Our people rise again!

Yet not all voices cheered. Some fell into a hush when their eyes found the cloth-wrapped hulk of Ruin across Damien's back. The cursed greatsword pulsed faintly in the half-light, like a coal hidden in ash. Sylvia felt the weight of their stares, the fear and unease twisting beneath the chants of victory.

She forced herself to sit tall in the saddle, her voice clear and sharp as an axe strike. "Stand proud, kin of the Hinterwood! The gods have not abandoned us... they have chosen us! We are the flame that will consume Betanthia!"

The warbands answered with a deafening roar, stamping spear butts and slamming shields. Still, as Sylvia's cry faded, she caught sight of an elderly camp follower shaking his head, lips moving in prayer. Another woman spat when Ruin's glow caught her eye. Faith and fear walked hand in hand.

Sylvia tightened her grip on the reins. For all the thunder of drums and cries of glory, she could not silence the dread whisper within her: *We are gathering for war... but what are we following? A man of the gods, or a curse that will undo us all?*

Damien rode forward, black eyes sweeping the mass of tribes. He raised Ruin high, its bindings unfurling to reveal the steel within. A hush fell. Even the forest seemed to still, as though the trees themselves bent to witness. The greatsword throbbed with an unholy crimson light, bathing the host in its glow. Then his voice rang out, deep and commanding, carrying clear through the Hinterwood.

"Kin of the north! Warriors of the Hinterwood! You have heard the lies of Betanthia— that we are broken, that our spirit has withered, that our gods have abandoned us. Look around you now, and tell me if that is true!"

A thunderous roar answered him, spears rattling like hail against shields.

"I have walked through fire and shadow. I have bled on the Plainhold. I have climbed the forbidden mountain and beheld its horrors. And there, in that accursed place, I took from the hands of Kuggvord himself the weapon of our ancestors." He thrust Ruin higher, and the sword pulsed in answer, drawing gasps and fearful cries from the mass.

"This blade was forged for one purpose: to end the dominion of Betanthia. The gods themselves placed it in my hand, and by their will, it shall drink the blood of our enemies. But know this—" Damien's eyes scanned the crowd, black and burning. "The gods do not favor the faint of heart. Only those who stand defiant will share in this victory. Only those who fight will be remembered in the halls of Sjenohor!"

The tribes bellowed again, some kneeling, others raising their weapons skyward. The sound rolled through the forest like a storm tide, deafening in its fervor. Sylvia felt pride swell within her—the Hinterwood united, the fire rekindled. Yet even as the chant of thousands shook the trees, her eyes lingered on Ruin. Its glow pulsed stronger, feeding on their voices like a hungry beast. And she whispered a prayer, not of triumph, but of warning.

Zifnir, shield us. For if this sword leads us astray, then all the North shall follow it into the abyss.

The forest was alive that night. Campfires burned in the hundreds, their smoke curling into the canopy until the very air seemed thick with firelight and song. Drums thundered from every glade, horns blared from every hilltop, and the warband's chant rolled ceaselessly through the Hinterwood.

Warriors clashed cups together until mead sloshed to the earth, singing the old songs of Azldyr. Others fought mock duels with axe and shield, sparks flying from steel as cheers erupted around them. Sylvia drank it all in. After the terror of Morvhalgr, after the silence of the

Plainhold, this felt like life itself had been reborn. The fear and doubt that had gnawed at her heart seemed to have burned away in the blaze of their revelry.

She could almost feel the gods moving among them, feeding their spirits, binding their rage into one. Every shout, every drumbeat, every clash of steel sang in her veins until she was nearly trembling with it. This… this was what it meant to be Rhivothi. This was what it meant to be free.

She was still basking in the glow when a shadow stepped into the circle of firelight. The man was tall and wiry, his long coat of wolfskins trailing to his knees. Tattoos ran across his cheeks and down his throat in jagged lines, marking him as one of the nomadic tribes of the far west. His hair was bound into tight braids, and a bone talisman dangled from his ear.

"Stormguard," he said, his voice a slow rumble, heavy with accent. "I am Hrokan, Chieftain of the Veylothi. Your people howl as though the war were already won."

Sylvia straightened, embers crackling at her back. "We have cause to howl. The gods have returned their favor. Look at them. The Hinterwood has risen as one!"

The chieftain's eyes glinted in the firelight. "I see it. And yet I see fear as well. That sword Damien carries… it stirs not only the spirit, but the marrow. I have heard its whispers already. You would be wise not to mistake dread for devotion."

Her blood was still hot from the celebration, and she found herself bristling. "They answer the gods' call. What you hear is awe, not dread."

"Perhaps." Hrokan crouched, dragging a stick through the dirt by the fire. He drew a crooked line, then slashed through it. "But awe fades. Fear festers. And if Dreadfire cannot master the weapon, it will master him. When that day comes, I wonder… will the clans follow still?"

The murmuring of the warband swelled again in the background, rising into a thunderous chant of Damien's name. Sylvia's heart soared at the sound, even as the nomad's words sank cold into her gut.

She lifted her chin, refusing to yield. "If such a day ever comes, then may the Hinterwood turn to ash and our people fade from memory. Dreadfire is no ordinary man. He is the best of us."

"Perhaps…"

Hrokan's eyes lingered on her for a long moment, as if weighing not her words, but her very soul. Slowly, he reached inside a pouch tied to his belt and withdrew a small bundle wrapped in hide. He set it down on the earth between them with the same reverence one might give a blade or relic.

"Your faith burns hot, Stormguard. But flame alone does not win wars." He loosened the bundle, revealing a cluster of gnarled, pale mushrooms streaked with veins of deep blue. Their pungent odor wafted through the firelight, sharp enough to sting the nose.

"These grow only in the oldest groves of the Hinterwood, where the gods themselves are said to have walked. We call them *Skeldr's Gift*. Eat them before the battle to come, and you will see through the veil. Fear will leave you, and in its place will be fury, clarity, and the voices of those who came before."

The chanting of the warband swelled louder, the forest itself seeming to tremble beneath the roar of Damien's name. Sylvia stared down at the bundle, her pulse quickening with equal parts dread and exhilaration. She felt as though the mushrooms pulsed faintly in the firelight, their pale skin almost alive.

Hrokan leaned closer, his voice a low growl meant only for her. "Take them when the hour is blackest. The gods demand sacrifice, and through these, they will taste yours."

Then, without another word, he stood and melted back into the darkness, his wolf pelts swaying like shadows in the fire's glow. Sylvia remained where she was, the chanting rising all around her, her hand hovering over the hide-wrapped bundle. Her heart soared with the thunder of her people, but in her gut, unease gnawed like a hungry beast.

She closed her fingers around the offering. The hide was rough against her skin, the shape of the mushrooms faintly yielding beneath her grip. It felt heavier than its size suggested, as if the gods themselves had pressed their will into the flesh of those pale caps. She slipped it into the fold of her cloak, careful not to draw attention. Tonight belonged to triumph, and she would not stain it with doubts.

The Hinterwood camp was alive with fire and fury. Warriors of every tribe joined in the revelry, their shadows leaping against the towering pines. Mead flowed as freely as blood on the Plainhold, spilling down beards and staining the earth. Shieldmaidens circled the flames with hair unbound, stamping their boots and clashing swords in rhythm to the drums. The scent of roasting meat hung thick in the air, mingling with pine smoke and the sweat of thousands.

Sylvia moved among them, greeted with cheers and horn-blasts. Hands clapped her shoulders, voices roared her name. "Stormguard!" they called, some with reverence, some with drunken adoration. She smiled despite herself, letting their fervor wash away the ache of past defeats. She had begged the gods for deliverance; now, here it was, pounding like a war-drum in her chest.

Her head swam with the energy. She felt lighter than air, as if she could ride alone into Betanthia and cast their legions into the sea. The chants of Damien's name rose higher, echoing through the trunks like thunder in a mountain pass. She threw her head back and joined the roar, her voice cracking but her spirit unbroken. For the first time since Hok, she felt wholly alive.

Yet even in the heart of glory, unease whispered. Between the fires, she spied the solemn ones: warriors sitting in silence, hands clasped in prayer, eyes drawn to the glow of Ruin at Damien's back. The greatsword pulsed faintly in the dark, its wicked light flickering in time with the chants, as though it fed upon their worship. Every cheer seemed to make it brighter, every cry of devotion another breath into its cursed lungs. She turned away before the sight could sour her spirit further.

The forest drew her like a tide. Away from the fires, the night deepened into black silence. Owls hooted in the canopy, and the crunch of her boots seemed sacrilege against the stillness. She found a fallen log and sat, clutching her cloak tight against the chill. Her hand strayed to the bundle again.

Skeldr's Gift. Hrokan's words lingered: *Take them when the hour is blackest. The gods demand sacrifice, and through these, they will taste yours.*

She loosened the hide and again studied the mushrooms in the moonlight. Their pale flesh gleamed faintly, streaked with blue veins like rivers across bone. She raised one to her nose. The smell was sharp, earthy, tinged with something metallic. She imagined biting into it, the taste bitter on her tongue, the world bending sideways in a rush of god-sight. She imagined the Plainhold again, the dead piled in heaps, but this time, lit by divine fire, every blow guided by the will of Azldyr himself.

Her stomach tightened. Were these a blessing? Or poison?

A howl split the night. Then another, and another, until the forest quaked with the voices of wolves. Sylvia looked up sharply. Golden eyes glimmered from the undergrowth, a dozen pairs staring from the shadows. The wolves did not advance, nor flee. They only watched, their voices rising in harmony with the distant chant of the warband. For a moment, the howls and the drums were one, forest and tribe united in a single, wild chorus.

She closed her eyes and let it wash over her. It was no dream, no trick. This was the Hinterwood speaking, the gods reminding her she was not alone.

Sylvia pressed the hide bundle to her breast and whispered, "If this is the path, then let me walk it without fear. If the price is my flesh, then let it be taken. Only grant me strength enough to see our people free."

The howls faded, leaving only silence. The firelight beckoned her back. When she returned to the glades, the revelry had begun to die. Many lay sprawled in drunken heaps, weapons clutched to their chests, while others still sang hoarsely by the embers.

Damien had withdrawn to his own tent, Ruin propped beside him like a sentry of steel. The cursed glow had dimmed, but Sylvia still felt it pulsing faintly through the earth, as if the sword's heart was beating in time with her own.

She slept little that night, dreams broken by flickers of fire and storm. Shadows of wolves prowled the edges of her mind, their eyes burning like coals, their howls mingling with the clash of steel. Each time she reached for her axe, the vision shattered, leaving her in darkness with the taste of smoke on her tongue.

Dawn came, cold and gray. A mist hung low among the trees, muffling sound and swallowing the edges of banners as they were raised. Horns called the tribes to muster, and the camp stirred like a great beast rousing from slumber. Fires were extinguished, packs were lashed, armor donned. Voices were low, sober now, the mead-fueled frenzy burned away by the hard light of day.

Sylvia strapped her axes and mounted her horse. She looked upon the host gathered in the clearing and felt her breath catch. There were more than she had ever seen in one place—thousands upon thousands, tribes and clans that had not stood together in living memory. Their banners cracked in the wind: wolves, bears, spears, storm-runes, all lifted high. It was as if the whole Hinterwood had risen at once.

Damien emerged at their head, black armor gleaming dully, Ruin strapped across his back. His eyes swept the host, and the murmurs stilled. For a long heartbeat, the forest itself seemed to hold its breath. Then he drew the sword, its crimson glow cutting through the mist like dawn's first fire. A roar erupted from the host, spears lifted, shields hammered, voices crashing together in a single earth-shaking cry. The trees themselves seemed to shudder with it.

But not every voice was raised in triumph. At the head of his own warband stood Taug of Rej Rhivoth, the cavern-chieftain himself, flanked by his grim honor guard. His face was carved from stone, his eyes like cold embers in the morning mist. Where others stamped and roared, Taug remained still, watching Damien with the quiet weight of a man who had seen too many oaths broken and too much blood wasted.

When the clamor began to fade, his gravelly voice carried across the clearing. "You have raised the Hinterwood, Dreadfire. Now see that it does not burn. We will follow… for now."

A hush rippled through those nearest, the words biting even as banners still whipped above them. Sylvia bristled at the doubt laced in the chieftain's tone, but Damien gave no answer, only shouldered Ruin as if the matter were already settled.

And the host roared again, drowning hesitation in a tide of steel and thunder. The Plainhold had broken them, but here, in the heart of the Hinterwood, they had risen anew. They would march. They would bleed. And the world would tremble.

If this is to be our doom, then let it be a doom to shake the world!

MADELYN VI

An unseen force compelled Madelyn onward, defeated though she felt. Perhaps the gods had doomed her to wander the Plainhold fields for all eternity as punishment for a crime never committed. She began succumbing to such a possibility, for no other explanation seemed plausible.

But something different lingered in the dry air. She could sense it, nearly taste it, even. It was an amalgamation of fear and hatred, of determination and dread. It was an anticipation like a storm's coming, though not of wind and rain. Madelyn's heart began fluttering so quickly as to take her breath away.

She paused, pulling back on the reins and staring intently at the rolling hills ahead. Every instinct was screaming for her to turn away, to leave this accursed place and never return. It was the same looming apprehension often felt while growing up at Castle Thorn.

The fear of disappointing the High Marshal and of reprimand for her childish curiosities was ever-present. Many times, she received the end of a switch for snooping or playing in forbidden rooms. "No" was a word all too familiar, and its utterance only fueled the flames within her.

Even now, with death seemingly on the horizon, Madelyn remained defiant. It was all she ever knew. After all, how could an eagle know anything other than the open sky, or a fish the ocean tides? It was an inescapable nature that could not be diminished even now, in the face of nightmares made real.

I can feel you, Dreadfire, as if you were standing beside me. Our fates are entwined, you know. The suffering you inflicted upon me is imprinted on my soul. And now, I have awakened the power within me… the power to destroy you and your ilk once and for all.

Whether it was truth or only a weary mind's delusion, she had to know. Madelyn turned her horse west, into lands she seldom traveled. A haze blackened the horizon, rising like smoke from a battlefield. Dust storms were common on the Plainhold, but this was no trick of wind. These clouds heaved like waves breaking on a shore—vast, deliberate, born of marching feet.

She crested a ridge and almost recoiled. The horde stretched below, thousands strong, their banners and dust swallowing the earth. Even after Blackthorn blades had culled them, their numbers remained dreadful. Her eyes swept the mass, hunting for the glint of black armor. None. But he was there. He had to be. Damien Dreadfire, specter of her nightmares, could not be far from his rabble.

"I know you're there," she whispered through her teeth. "And I will find you.

To ride among them in disguise would be folly. Even cropped hair and blackened leather would not conceal her long enough. Recognition meant death. She reined back, slipping from the ridge, her gaze never leaving the dust plume. Like a wolf shadowing a herd, she trailed them for hours, reading their every turn, every scatter of hoof and boot.

By sunset, the sky burned crimson, streaked with gold and dying fire. The Plainhold glowed like a smoldering forge, and in that light Madelyn felt the press of fate upon her. She reached into her saddlebag and withdrew one of the fragile scrolls, the parchment flaking beneath her touch.

Perhaps within its silence lay strength. But no voice stirred, no whisper from her ancestors came to guide her. The runes remained dead.

A single tear welled, and she brushed it away with the back of her hand, scowling at her own weakness. The scroll slipped back into its case. Night was coming, and with it, the hunt would continue.

I will make you proud, for I will right the wrongs of the past and avenge the horrors I have suffered. You will see the power in my blood… the great legacy you have left to me. Watch me, now.

With a steadying breath, she urged her horse toward the barbarian encampment. From the gloom emerged three riders, shapes hardening into men with recurve bows and a lance. Their armor was a patchwork of leather and scavenged mail, steel plates hanging like trophies. Bald scalps gleamed with inked runes, their faces mapped in the crude paint of Zylmacian tribes. The sight of them made her teeth clench. Of all the creatures in this wasteland, these were the last she wished to meet.

"Who rides there?" one bellowed, already nocking an arrow. "Speak, or we'll feast on your bones!"

Madelyn refused to slow. She spat into the dust, scowling as she rode closer. A curtain of black hair veiled one eye, brushing her cheek with each step of the horse. Woad paint would have helped seal the disguise, but none was to be found in these barren lands.

"She's one of them Rhivothi whores," another jeered, lowering his bow with a sneer. "They'd rather share a bed with their shield-sisters anyway."

The third kept his lance leveled, suspicion burning in his eyes. Madelyn fixed on him, riding straight at the point, her face drawn hard with a frown that dared him to test her. Twilight cloaked her features, muting what remained of her old self. Recognition was not impossible, but the odds favored her gamble.

"Lower your spear, Bymist rat," she said, attempting a Rhivothi accent. It was a slur she remembered Marvath using.

The spearman sneered. "Fiesty little bitch. Lucky for you Jollkud's back in camp, or I'd fuck your headless corpse right here."

His companions barked crude laughter, but Madelyn kept her face stone. She thought of Sylvia Stormguard, who'd shown her that Rhivothi women could be as hard and merciless as their men. Beauty made them dangerous, but their fire made them feared. Madelyn let that fire steady her.

"But rats have such tiny cocks," she snapped back, her lips curling. The other two wildmen roared with delight, even as the spearman's knuckles whitened on his lance. "Now, fuck off back to your patrol and leave me to mine."

The barb worked. Northmen were fierce, but they rarely salted their tongue with filth. Titan Bradshaw's ghost must have left its imprint on her. Still, it bought her space. Or so she thought.

"Not so fast," the first bowman said, eyes narrowing. "Scouts and spies crawl these hills like lice. You don't pass unless you name your warchief."

An answer came quickly enough, though speaking the name of her tormentor brought bile into her throat.

The answer clawed at her throat, but it came quickly enough. "Stormguard," Madelyn grunted. The bile in her mouth made the name taste bitter. "Shall I tell her you're the reason for my delay?"

The three riders traded wary glances. Doubt rippled between them—maybe Sylvia had fallen, maybe her banner was ash. If so, they'd know, and Madelyn's mask would split. Her hand drifted to the throwing knives at her belt, fingers brushing the worn hilts.

"And how might you do such a thing, hm?" one of them asked, his smile thin as a blade.

Such a cryptic question could mean only three things: the warchief was dead, broken, or cast aside. Madelyn knew her next words would either grant her passage or trigger her execution.

"I'll be certain to inform her when she returns," she hissed. "And I'll stand beside her when she mounts your head on a pike for daring to delay me."

That landed. The Zylmacians stayed their hands, though their eyes burned with hunger for blood. They were brutes, every one of them, but there was a savage sharpness in their kind. Madelyn remembered the night they nearly tore into Marvath Bonesplitter, perhaps the only man who could trade blow for blow with Titan Bradshaw.

"Nasty little cunt," one spat, his lips curling. "Go on, then. Stop wasting our time."

They wheeled their mounts, laughter and curses trailing like carrion birds as they vanished into the dark. Madelyn pressed on, her pace unbroken, though her fingers still hovered near her knives. Smoke thickened in the air, acrid with sweat and horseflesh, until her tongue tasted of iron. She clenched her jaw and endured. She had withstood worse than the taunts of vermin.

At last, the camp unfolded before her. A thousand fires glimmered across the hills like fallen stars, each one throwing hard light on faces that did not sing or celebrate. No drums, no horns, none of the revelry the Northmen were known for. Only the low murmur of voices, heavy with defeat, and the stink of too many bodies packed too close. Madelyn's stomach turned. She had seen this before at Castle Morden, in the days after its walls came down. The barbarians stood low in spirit, yet they were not broken. Not yet.

There was little merriment to be found, though not wholly absent. Rhivothi were easy enough to distinguish: towering frames, wolf pelts on their shoulders, and mugs of mead in hand. A gang of them gathered around a fire, trading boasts of past glories.

Madelyn scowled and strode past without pause. To linger was to risk recognition, and though her cropped hair and black leathers masked her well, a single word might undo her. A few lifted their eyes as she passed, but none called out. Even among brutes, there was respect for the shieldmaidens, and that respect had always been earned with axe and blood.

Much as she loathed them, Madelyn could not deny the brutal symmetry of their ways. Every woman who bore steel was treated as an equal, no matter her birth. Perhaps Betanthia, for all its polish and pageantry, might have learned something from such harsh simplicity.

Now, where are you?

Dreadfire had to be here. Somewhere in this sea of fire and smoke stood his command tent, the largest of all, hemmed in by his fiercest warriors. But every step closer was agony. The press of bodies, the guttural laughter, the stink of sweat and hide—it clawed at her nerves until she felt flayed raw. Each glance seemed to linger too long, each grunt of laughter twisted into mockery.

They know. They all know. They are only playing with me.

As the wagons came into view, her breath shortened. A suffocating weight coiled in her chest, squeezing tighter with every step. Her skin prickled, her heart hammered. She could feel it, something foul and familiar moving just ahead, prowling in the dark like a beast that had scented its prey. Not friend. Not ally. A force that knew her as surely as it despised her.

No, it cannot be, Madelyn thought, sweat forming across her brow. Short locks of black hair turned wet with perspiration.

Sweat broke across Madelyn's brow, dampening the short locks that clung to her cheeks. Her eyes fixed on the carriage nearby—less a transport than a hovel on wheels, its wooden panels blackened with age and bound by cruel bands of iron. A lantern swung from its doorframe, its thin flame fighting the dusk. But it was not the sight that froze her—it was the dread pulsing from within, steady as a heartbeat, a rhythm that gnawed at her soul. Lazilyth.

The name itself coiled like a snake in her mind. In the Fate Realm, the crone had been all-powerful, a shadow that bent time and form. But here, in the realm of flesh? Here, steel ruled. Even the most cunning sorcery bled when kissed by iron. Madelyn whispered that truth to herself like a prayer, yet the question burned all the same.

Or could she?

The thought festered, quickening her breath. Yet, an opportunity like this would never come again. The chance to strike her tormentor, to carve away the nightmare at its root. Madelyn swallowed her fear, hand slipping to the hilt of her short sword. Each step nearer was a battle; nausea rolled through her gut, her legs heavy as lead. The air thickened with cedar, sage, and smoke that curled from the chimney above, carrying with it the stench of sorcery.

You will torment me no longer, monster!

She drew her blade, clutching it with both hands until her knuckles ached white. A bitter wind rose through the camp, rattling the tents, tugging at her cloak. The incense smoke stirred, torn from the chimney and whipped into the open air. It twisted upon itself, swirling, gathering, until the wind itself seemed to bow. The cloud coalesced before her, and against all reason it took form—an unnatural shape, its features blooming in defiance of the gale.

At that terrible moment, Madelyn recognized the image before her. A face, gaunt and hollow, its cheeks sunken, its eyes two pits of despair. When it smiled, the mouth was a black void that seemed to stretch forever.

"No," she gasped. "It... it cannot be..."

A mournful wail rose on the wind, carrying with it an eerie laugh that clawed at her spine. Lazilyth's shade had seen her. Somehow, the crone knew she was here, as though the Fate Realm itself had whispered her arrival. Panic seized Madelyn. She had to flee before the trap closed.

Her vision clouded as black mist filled her eyes. The shadows answered, cloaking her form, swallowing her into darkness. Yet even hidden, she felt those hollow sockets fixed on her, following her every movement.

She ran. The ground felt brittle beneath her boots as the cloud above writhed and split apart. With a deafening roar, Lazilyth's shade unfurled—long, spindly arms tearing free of the smoke, skeletal wings sprouting in jagged arcs. The crone shrieked, the sound like steel dragged across stone, surging forward as if to rip Madelyn's soul from her flesh.

"Get away!" she cried helplessly. "Begone you… you beast!"

Then, light. Faint, but certain, gleaming from the shadow of her horse. The scrolls. They were calling her, guiding her through the nightmare. She flung herself toward the glow, scrambling into the saddle as her horse reared in terror.

"Ride!" she hissed, driving her heels hard. The beast bolted, cloak whipping behind her like a tattered banner. Wind screamed in her ears.

She dared a glance back and nearly lost her breath. Lazilyth's shade soared above the wagons, wings of smoke stretched wide, shrieking so loud it rattled her teeth and set her bones humming.

The scrolls pulsed faintly at her side, each hoofbeat echoing their rhythm. She clutched the saddlehorn until her knuckles ached, praying the horse would not stumble, convinced at any moment the crone's claws would tear her from the saddle. Her soul felt strung on a thread, swaying between worlds.

Then, suddenly, the pursuit broke. At the edge of the camp, the shade halted, its ghastly frame writhing against some unseen tether. It clawed and wailed, smoke unraveling in furious tatters, but could go no further. The wind scattered its remnants into the night, and silence rushed back like a tide.

Madelyn emerged from shadow, her form solid once more. Her horse bucked and tossed its head before recognizing her touch, and she drove it harder until the horde's fires shrank to sparks on the horizon.

Only then did she pull the beast to a halt, her chest heaving, her eyes still blackened from the shadow's touch. With trembling hands, she tore a scroll from her bag, desperate for guidance. The parchment lay still, yet she swore warmth flickered against her skin, faint but undeniable.

"Not yet," she whispered, her throat raw. "But soon… soon you will answer me."

She cast one final glance northward, where the horde spread like a plague across the Plainhold. Somewhere in that sprawl, Damien Dreadfire sharpened his ruin. Somewhere in those wagons, Lazilyth waited, proof that her enemy's reach stretched far beyond mortal steel. Madelyn tightened her grip on the scroll. A fire sparked in her eyes.

"You will not take me," she swore into the wind. "Not here. Not ever."

She turned her horse westward. The glow of the horde dwindled behind her, swallowed by the hunger of the night.

UDORN VIII

T HE UBNERI MOVED SOUTH IN A COLUMN THAT STRETCHED LIKE A black scar across the land. Drums marked their pace, steady and relentless, the cadence of a people hardened by exile and blood. Spears rose and fell with each step, the hafts catching the pale light, their steel heads dull with the grime of old slaughter.

Yet for all their discipline, the horde was not whole. Grief gnawed at them from within, the death of Rennek heavy on their backs, and the silence between their ranks grew louder with every mile. Udorn felt it as keenly as the weight of his axe—the sense that their next battle might not be fought against Dellhaven's walls, but in the shadows of their own camp.

Eyes lingered too long on him. Whispers passed like smoke through the ranks. Some still clung to Ragruk, their faith as unyielding as stone. Others studied Udorn with something else in their gaze: doubt, hunger, perhaps the ache for new fire to lead them. He had no need of omens to know it was true. The air itself trembled with unrest, a host marching south, yet ready to fracture at the first true spark.

I did not survive the maw of the beast to be slain by those who call themselves kin. Nor will I see my brothers die in vain.

510

Never had survival felt so treacherous. Better to have been dashed against Dellhaven's rocks, Udorn thought, than to march beneath such a shadow, for now it was not only he in peril, but all who bore his trust.

Udorn let his gaze wander across the horde. Shields swayed at their sides, spears rising like a forest stripped bare, helmets dulled with dust and ash. Faces were hard, unflinching, yet in their silence, he read more than weariness. There was division here, cracks running unseen through the host… some carved by grief, others by ambition. Every step southward pressed against those fractures like a weight that might split the stone.

From Ragruk's ranks, a figure broke free. He moved with the stride of a predator, tall and broad as if the earth itself had shaped him for war. Hair and beard burned the color of flame, cropped short, his shoulders thick as quarried rock. Eyes, sharp and restless, fixed on Udorn. Whispers stirred as he drew near, low voices carrying a name that moved like a shadow through the column. Joven Krenn, he was.

The Ravenking…

The name passed from mouth to mouth, never shouted, never bold, only breathed as if it carried weight enough to summon omens. Udorn had heard it before, though never so near, never spoken with such quiet awe. He was one of Ragruk's most infamous brutes, and his mere presence was enough to invite dread and suspicion among Udorn's men.

For a moment, Joven said nothing, only matching Udorn's stride, his shadow falling long across the field. The silence weighed heavy, broken at last by Thaul's voice from among the host.

"What business have you here, Ravenking? Have you come to do your master's bidding?"

A ripple of unease stirred the ranks. Few ever questioned Joven

Krenn, fewer still to his face. The giant's gaze shifted, slow and deliberate, until it settled on Thaul. His reply came like stone rolling down a mountain.

"Master?" Joven said. His half-scowl, half-smile was as unsettling as rotten flesh. "The only master I serve is death."

Were such words spoken by any other man, they might have been met with amusement. But none dared to mock the Ravenking, for he was born of fire.

Murmurs rippled through the ranks, the kind that could curdle into violence if left to grow. Thaul's hand tightened on his axe, and the Ravenking's eyes gleamed with something perilous, neither threat nor welcome. Udorn felt the air strain between them, taut as a bowstring.

"Come now, kinsmen," he said, breaking the tension. "The road south is long enough without brothers quarreling. What brings you over to us, Joven?"

The Ravenking's gaze lingered on Thaul, unblinking, a furnace of quiet hatred that made even the seasoned warrior shift beneath its weight. For a heartbeat, it seemed the giant might lunge, and the column itself seemed to hold its breath. Then, as suddenly as a flame guttering low, he turned away.

"They say a wise man feels the wind before the sail does," Joven said, "and hears the tide turn long before it reaches shore."

Udorn had braced for bluster, some rough boast or threat to match the man's bulk. Instead, the words landed with the weight of an old truth, spoken like a sailor who had spent his life reading storm and sea.

"You speak as though you know the course already," Udorn said, his tone measured. "Tell me then… what do you see in these winds?"

Joven lifted his gaze skyward, watching a lone cloud crawl across the pale expanse. The silence stretched long enough for the tramp of boots

512

and clatter of arms to fill the gap. When he spoke at last, his voice was low, almost reverent.

"The winds do not answer to men… yet they carry us all the same. Best to be ready when they change."

He gave no further glance toward Udorn or Thaul. With the same steady stride, the giant drifted back into the ranks of Ragruk's warriors, his broad shoulders swallowed by the column. Udorn and his companions exchanged uncertain looks, the proverb clinging to them like a shadow. For a time, none found words to break the silence. Then Gaxas let out a snort, shaking his head.

"Bah. Winds and tides. I trust a man's axe more than any breeze."

A few chuckles followed, thin as the wind itself. Udorn did not join them. He kept his eyes on the road ahead, the Ravenking's words turning over in his mind like stones beneath the surf.

He knew the tale well enough. After one of Ragruk's bloodier raids, it was said Joven Krenn had stood unscathed amid a ring of corpses, his axe slick with ruin. As the cries of the dying faded, a great black raven descended and perched upon his shoulder, calm as a tame hawk. The men who saw it swore the bird was no creature of flesh, but a spirit come to mark him.

From that day on, none spoke his name without a shiver, and few called him Joven at all. He was the Ravenking, a man touched by death itself. Udorn wondered now if the tale was truth, or merely the shape of truth forged into legend. Yet as he recalled the fire in Joven's eyes, he could not wholly dismiss it.

But what unsettled him most was not the legend, but the man's choice to break the silence at all. Why seek him out now, on the long road south? Was it a warning, a test, or the first crack of dissent within Ragruk's own camp? Udorn could not yet tell. The thought gnawed at him as surely as hunger—that somewhere behind the stoic faces and iron discipline, the horde was shifting, and Joven Krenn might be the sign of it.

The horde pressed on through the fading day, the rhythm of boots and drums their only song. Night fell heavy, and still they marched until darkness swallowed even their whispers. When dawn broke at last, pale and cold, the Ubneri crested a low rise, and the land opened before them.

Dellhaven rose against the sea, its stone walls plain and pale, built for strength rather than beauty. No farms or hovels sprawled beyond them; every roof and street lay tucked behind the curtain of defense. From a distance, it looked less like a city than a fortress, a place meant to shield Cardale's wealthy from the world beyond.

Udorn's jaw tightened at the sight. He remembered the stifling press of those walls, the hunt through narrow streets where every shadow promised death. He had shed blood in Dellhaven once, fighting like a cornered beast to see another dawn, and the memory clung to him now as sharp as any scar.

Suddenly, Ragruk's voice carried over the ranks, rough and commanding, leaving no space for question.

"By the gods, it is magnificent!" he bellowed. "Imagine the riches these Southerners sit upon. Fall back and make camp out of sight. We attack before sunrise tomorrow."

The Ubneri withdrew in silence, their column folding into the low ground like a dark tide retreating from shore. No horns sounded, no voices lifted in song. Camp took shape in whispers. Shields were stacked, weapons laid close at hand, and the earth sat scarred with the weight of so many feet. Not a single fire was lit, for fear the city's watchmen might spy the glow against the coming night.

When the work was done, the host lay in shadow, stretched across the plain like a sleeping beast. Udorn found himself apart from the others, seated on a rise of stone beneath the pale moon. The air was cold and still, and the quiet bore down on him heavier than the march had.

Tomorrow would bring blood, he knew, yet it was not Dellhaven's walls that haunted him most, but the question of what storm might break within the horde itself.

At last Udorn lay back upon the hard earth, finding what little sleep the night would yield. Dreams came shallow and broken, filled with the press of walls and the caw of unseen birds. When his eyes opened again, the moon was fading, and his kinsmen moved like wraiths through the dark. Blades were strapped to belts, helms pulled low, shields lifted without a word. The host stirred as one, silent as the tide before a storm.

Udorn rose and slung his axe across his back, moving through the shifting mass of warriors until he came to where Ragruk stood. The chieftain was ringed by his chosen men, their voices low, their faces hard in the waning dark. A crude map had been scratched into the dirt at their feet, the walls of Dellhaven etched in rough lines, arrows drawn where the horde would strike.

Ragruk's hand swept across the markings as he spoke, his voice a growl meant to carry no farther than the circle. "We scale here, just beside the towers nearest the gate. Those dogs within will not expect us before dawn. Once the gates are seized, the city will break like a rotten hull."

All around, the Ubneri listened with grim intent, nodding as each order was given. Udorn kept his silence, watching the plan unfold, his thoughts dark with memory and doubt.

"Udorn!" Ragruk said, grinning. "You have seen inside the city. You know its inner workings better than anyone. You will lead the incursion along with your closest shield brothers."

The words struck like a fist to the ribs. Udorn felt the eyes of the circle turn to him, weighing, measuring, some with pity, others with cold expectation. Ragruk's grin was too wide, too eager, the look of a man already savoring another's death.

Udorn gave no sign. He only inclined his head, the gesture slow and steady, though inside he felt the trap close tight around him. To refuse would mark him a coward, yet to obey was to step into the jaws Ragruk had opened. He lingered within the circle for but a moment before turning away silently.

Men parted for him without a word. As he passed, his eyes caught Dulkin—the warrior lowered his gaze at once, shame burning in his face. Udorn felt the weight of it, though whether it was shame for him or himself, no one could say. He found Thaul waiting with the others, their gear already in hand. The barrel-chested warrior stepped close, his voice pitched low.

"What is it, Udorn? What game does Ragruk play?"

Udorn lowered his voice so only his brothers could hear. "We are to be the first over the wall. Ragruk has named us to lead the incursion."

Gaxas gave a sharp scoff, spitting into the dirt. "A fine honor, that. Let the chieftain wrap it in ribbons and call it glory, but we all know what it is."

Thaul's face hardened at once. His eyes flicked past Udorn, toward where Ragruk still conferred with his chosen men. "He means to have you killed," he said flatly. "To bleed you out on Dellhaven's stones while the rest watch."

"It is not only I whom Ragruk seeks to cast aside." Udorn's gaze swept over their faces, steady and grim. "Any man who has bent his back toward my name will be fed to Dellhaven's walls. He would see us all broken in one stroke."

Thaul's jaw tightened, and Gaxas muttered a curse under his breath. Around them, the camp stirred in silence, warriors sharpening blades and strapping shields, unaware of the snare being drawn tight.

Gaxas leaned closer, voice low and urgent. "Then what is our plan, Udorn?"

Udorn drew a long breath, his eyes fixed on the pale walls glimmering in the distance. "I do not know," he admitted. "But the answer will come soon enough."

The first light of dawn crept across the plain, painting Dellhaven's walls in pale gray. Udorn and his shield brothers stood at the fore, the vanguard tense as ladders were brought forth by the dozen. Around him, he felt the weight of a hundred eyes, some eager for his death, others watchful, curious to see whether he would rise or fall.

From the rear, Ragruk's roar split the morning air. "Forward! Take the city!"

Yet Udorn did not move. His axe fell limp in his hand, his boots rooted to the earth. Slowly, he turned, fixing his gaze upon the chieftain. There was no anger in his face, no fear, only the flat indifference of a man who had seen and survived too much.

The stillness spread like wildfire through the ranks, and Ragruk's face darkened with fury. The chieftain lumbered forward, his voice breaking like a whip over the host.

"Coward!" he bellowed. "Move, you wretch! Or I will have your carcass nailed to the city gate!"

The horde stirred uneasily, but Udorn did not flinch. He stood as stone, his eyes fixed upon the chieftain. No words, no gesture, only the quiet, steady weight of defiance. Ragruk's face twisted crimson, beard bristling like flame in the wind. At last, he wheeled on one of his retainers, a thickset warrior clad in battered mail.

"Then you, Varald! Take the ladders forward! Show this traitor what it means to serve your chief!"

The retainer barked to his men, and the vanguard surged toward the wall with a thunder of boots and iron. Udorn did not join them. He remained still, his gaze locked with Ragruk's across the field, contempt burning hotter than any fire.

The first crash of ladders against stone rang out, followed by a hiss of arrows and the screams of men. Dellhaven's walls came alive with defenders, their shouts and steel cutting through the morning air. Blood spilled on pale stone as Ubneri claws scraped for purchase, their war cries drowned in the clash of battle. Yet Udorn remained at the fore, unmoved as the slaughter began without him.

Behind it all loomed the silent war between chieftain and warrior. Udorn's stare never wavered, and neither did Ragruk's. The walls of Dellhaven might decide the fate of the Ubneri, but it was the fire burning between both men that promised a greater reckoning still to come.

EINARR VI

THE MOUNTAINS CLOSED AROUND THEM, RIDGES OF PALE LIMESTONE stacked one over another. The trail climbed narrow and crooked, sliding between cliffs where thornbush and wiry pines clawed at the stone. Every step jarred their horses on loose stones, and the air tasted of resin and sun-baked rock.

Everyone was worn thin. Dust caught in their eyes, and sweat traced white lines through the grime on their faces. Packs sagged. Tempers frayed. A curse here, a violent threat there. Einarr rode in silence, eyes moving from ridge to ridge. The mountains offered no kindness, only blind corners and narrow cuts where a handful of men could bar the way. He felt the unease rippling through his company, as steady as the rhythm of hooves.

Hyleth pressed on at the fore, shield strapped across his back, reins loose in his weathered hands. Their Zylmacian guide carried himself with the patience of one who knew these passes better than his own kin.

"Not far now," he called, voice carrying against the rock. "The road narrows to a gate in the cliffs. We'll make the crossing before night."

A few men grumbled their disbelief, but none dared raise it louder. They had followed Hyleth this far, and in the mountains, there were no better choices.

"Fucking heat," Valerick grunted. "For the life of me, I cannot imagine why you creatures would choose to live in such sordid places."

The insult rolled off Hyleth's back like pebbles down the mountainside. "These lands belong to old Droethia, Northman. The Bymist is far less forgiving."

Valerick spat into the trail, his horse tossing its head at the rein. "At least there, you know the land wants you dead. Here, these rocks only bleed you slow."

Einarr listened to the exchange without a word. Complaints, curses, insults—all the same notes of weariness. Men too long in the saddle, too hot, too hungry, looking for something to hate. The mountains gave them plenty, but Einarr knew hate was wasted unless it was aimed true.

They pressed on, the trail tightening between walls of stone. Horseshoes struck sparks on the rock, reins creaked, and the only water was the sweat running down necks and seeping into collars. Even the horses seemed to breathe heavier, sides darkened with lather.

Then Hyleth lifted a hand. Einarr saw it too, a pale plume rising against the hard blue sky, dust drifting above the far bend. Riders, most likely. He motioned sharply, and the company peeled off the trail, crouching low among thornbush and broken stone while the sound of hooves grew clearer.

Dolsigg leaned close, sweat falling in beads down his cheeks. "Best not be Droethien. If they are, they'll smell us like wolves in a pen."

Einarr's eyes stayed on the ridge. The plume thickened, shapes beginning to break through the glare. Banners of black and gold emerged, tall and rustling. Blackthorn Knights.

Valerick hunched beside him, one hand pressed to the stones. "I hope you have a plan, Rolffson," he whispered.

Einarr scanned the trail; sheer wall to one side, drop to the other. Nowhere to slip away, nowhere to vanish. The Knights would ride straight over them if they stayed hidden too long.

"We take them," he murmured. "Fast and clean. Spears to the lead, blades for the rest. Not a cry, not a horn. I want arrows on the riders furthest to the rear. We'll trap them."

The men shifted in the brush, eyes flicking to him, to the narrowing pass, and to the banners swaying closer with each beat of hooves. Einarr raised his hand, palm flat, holding them in check. The Knights came into view in full now—ten riders, cloaks heavy with dust, helms gleaming in the sun. Their horses clattered on the stone, easy in their pace, unaware of eyes watching from the rocks.

His hand fell softly. A bow groaned gently as it was drawn back, followed by another. The sound was soft as breath, but it carried. Arrows hissed from the brush. The rear rider toppled sideways, a shaft jutting clean through his neck. Another arrow thudded into a horse's flank, the beast screaming as it crashed against the wall of stone.

Einarr surged from cover, arming sword in hand. "Now!"

Spears thrust into the lead, wood shattering on steel and bone. The first Knight reeled back in the saddle, helm ringing as iron split his brow. Horses reared, eyes rolling, hooves clattering frantically against loose rock.

The company poured in low and fast, blades flashing, axes hewing flesh like firewood. Black cloaks whipped in the wind, banners pitching as riders fought to wheel, but the trail was too tight, too sudden. A horn lifted—Einarr cut the man down before the note carried, steel biting deep into his throat. Blood sprayed the stone, dark against pale rock.

The last Knight swung wildly from the saddle, blade carving only air, before an arrow struck his flank. He hit the stone hard, helm ringing once before a spear pinned him down for good. Silence fell as suddenly as the strike. Only the horses remained, snorting and stamping, reins tangled in the fallen. Blood streaked the rock in crooked lines, already drying in the heat.

Einarr wiped his blade on a cloak and scanned the narrow pass. Ten bodies, gear scattered, banners half-crushed under hooves. A scene loud enough to draw eyes if left.

"There," he said, pointing to a dark cut in the cliff face, a shallow cave opening just above the trail. "Drag them in. All of them. Strip their arms, their cloaks, their shields. Leave nothing here that speaks their name."

The men worked, silent but quick. Cloaks torn free. Shields stacked. Helms wiped clean and passed down the line. One by one, the dead were hauled into the cave, swallowed by shadow and stone. When it was done, only the echo of hooves remained, scattered up the pass like memory. Einarr stood at the mouth of the cave, watching his men shoulder stolen gear.

"Wear it well," he said. "From this point on, we are Blackthorn."

Valerick smirked, his kinsmen chuckling softly. The sound was low, rough, not quite laughter but close enough. To them, dead men's cloaks were no worse than any other trophy. Dolsigg tugged at the silver-banded helm in his hands, face pale beneath the grime.

"And when the Droethiens see us in these colors? What then?"

"Nothing," Hyleth said sharply. "Their Governor at Naxonnos is a cautious man, slow to provoke, and slower to give chase. My people have crossed into his lands a hundred times over. He has yet to lift a hand against it."

The cave swallowed the last of the bodies. Only the clink of buckles and a rasp of leather straps broke the stillness as the men set about their grisly work. Cloaks were fastened over shoulders, helms pulled low, shields slung in practiced hands.

Einarr gave no speech, only pointed with the flat of his blade. Six men in Blackthorn garb took the fore, lances tilted just so. Another four rode at the rear, heads bowed beneath borrowed helms. The rest, stripped of the disguises, fell into the center with bound wrists and lowered eyes, prisoners in a play too convincing to question.

The formation settled into motion, hooves ringing against the stone. To the eye of any watcher, it was a patrol returning from victory, captors and captives alike. Einarr rode at the fore, helm shadowing his face. He kept his gaze fixed on the winding pass ahead, the stolen banner snapping in the wind above him.

The trail bent downward, curling out of the high passes into broken hills. Pines thickened in the gullies, their scent sharp in the cooling air. Behind them, the mountains loomed gray and jagged, watching like old sentries. By nightfall, they found a hollow by a stream where the horses could drink. Fires were coaxed from thornwood, thin smoke vanishing into the dusk. Men stripped off their helms, rubbing sweat and grime from their faces, but kept the Blackthorn cloaks around their shoulders.

Hyleth crouched by the stream, filling a skin with steady hands. "The border lies just ahead," he said. "By dawn, we will cross it. And not far beyond, there is a Droethien village, small, unwalled, unnamed."

The fire burned low, throwing long shadows against the rocks. Einarr sat apart, helm at his feet, the stolen cloak heavy across his shoulders. The men muttered among themselves, trading jibes and curses, but his thoughts ran elsewhere.

The Droethiens had no love for Betanthia, yet neither did they hunger for another war. They guarded their highland passes with a zeal born of centuries, but beyond their borders, they were slow to rouse. To draw them into bloodshed, to set their spears marching, would take more than whispers of enemy strength. It would take outrage.

Firelight glowed along the edges of the parchment spread across Einarr's knees. Maps, scribbled orders, patrol schedules, all stripped from the Blackthorn dead at Mor Seveht. He traced the lines with a finger, following passes and rivers, weighing strengths and weaknesses. Numbers were thin in some places, thicker in others, but none of it gave him what he needed. The papers spoke of walls and garrisons, not the hearts of men.

There must be a way…

Einarr stared into the flames until the light blurred, and there it was again—the great cat, the ethereal beast that had stalked him across Caldakas. A great shape of smoke and sinew, its mane rippling though no wind stirred. Its eyes fixed on him, pale and unblinking, as though it weighed his soul.

It prowled just beyond the fire's edge, each step soundless, its form wavering between ash and flesh. The men did not stir, but Einarr seemed to see it. When its jaws parted, no roar came, only a crackle of flames, rising and falling in time with the beast's breath.

His jaw tightened. "A beast fights when its den is threatened," he whispered, half to himself. "Not before."

The thought slid into place like a blade finding its sheath. If Droethia could be made to believe their homes burned under Blackthorn banners, their wrath would come swift and certain. Einarr looked down at the cloak across his lap, the polished helm glinting faintly in the firelight. The great cat's gaze lingered in his mind, silent, unyielding, driving him forward.

Then we will give them a den to avenge…

Valerick's voice carried from the far side of the fire, rough and edged with impatience. "What now, Rolffson? We've cloaks on our backs and stolen steel at our belts, but what do you mean to do with them?"

Einarr lifted his eyes from the parchments, gaze drawn past the flames. The great cat still lingered in his mind, mane rippling in unseen wind, eyes pale and merciless. But when he turned, the fire showed him only rock and shadow. The vision was gone.

He set the papers aside and rose, the Blackthorn cloak falling heavy around his shoulders. "We cannot creep and nibble at the edges," he said. "If we mean to wake Droethia, we must be bold… bold enough to do what even the gods may not forgive."

The words settled over the camp like a burial shroud, leaving only the hiss of the fire and the restless shifting of men who did not know what shape their leader's boldness would take.

Dolsigg's brow furrowed. "And what does that mean, Einarr? Bold enough for what?"

Einarr tapped the parchment at his feet, the inked columns of patrol routes and sigils. "We have the Blackthorn's schedule. Where they ride. When they change watch. Every gap in their guard. They've given us the place and the hour."

Hyleth leaned forward, firelight carving deep lines across his face. "I think I see your meaning, fisherman. The Droethiens will not march for whispers, nor for pleas for assistance. They need to bleed. They need to burn. Only fire at their door will drive them to the spear."

A hush spread around the circle. Even the fire seemed to crackle softer. Einarr straightened, the stolen cloak falling into place around him.

"We know there is a village just across the border, small and unwalled. We ride as Blackthorn, take it, sack it, and leave one man alive to run for Naxonnos. He will tell the tale, and the city will rouse as if they had been struck themselves."

Valerick gave a low laugh, harsh in the stillness. His kinsmen grinned, eager for blood. Dolsigg only stared at the fire, the reflection dancing in his eyes.

"You are a curious one, indeed," the Red Rhivothi said. "I would never have expected such savagery from the mind of a Nothanek."

Einarr's gaze swept the men, cold and unblinking. "I have seen a great many things, Valerick. Things that, perhaps, I was not meant to see. But I understand the greater picture now. What we do may stain our souls, but it is necessary. It will not be clean. It will not be forgiven. But it will be remembered. And it will start the war we came to make."

TITAN V

THE HORNS STILL ECHOED WHEN TYLAR SPURRED HIS HORSE FROM the line, Conrak and a gang of Blackthorn racing beside him. The barbarians had vanished over the ridge in a storm of dust, their jeers clinging to the wind like gnats. Tylar would not suffer it. Not today.

"After them!" he roared, his voice ragged, half-swallowed by the thunder of hooves. "After those fuckers!"

The knights fanned out as they crested the rise, sunlight flashing across polished plate and drawn steel. For an instant, it seemed the Northmen were already in flight, a ragged column of riders scattering across the plain. Easy prey. Cowards fleeing the field. But then the bows came up.

Dark-feathered shafts hissed from every angle, a storm of wood and iron. Horses screamed and staggered, knights toppled from the saddle, armor ringing like struck bells. Tylar raised his shield as two arrows thudded into it, one splintering through the rim to score his cheek.

"Archers!" Conrak's warning was nearly drowned beneath the chaos.

The Zylmacians did not stand and meet the charge. They wheeled and circled, loosing as they moved, their mounts swift and tireless. Every moment Tylar pressed forward, another storm of arrows drove him back. Rage seared his blood, but even he could not close the distance.

"Stand and fight, you sons of whores!" he bellowed, skewering one rider who strayed too close. The man tumbled lifeless from the saddle, but three more arrows sang past Tylar's helm in the same breath, one biting deep into the mail of the knight beside him.

A dozen Blackthorn horse archers wheeled into the fray, loosing shafts skyward in ragged volleys. The first shots forced the barbarians to break their rhythm, a few saddles emptied, dust rising where bodies struck the ground. For a heartbeat, it seemed the tide might turn. Then the savages answered in kind.

Their bows bent with terrifying speed, arrows whistling in from every angle. The Order's archers were singled out as if painted with a mark. One knight pitched backward, a shaft buried through his throat; another sagged forward over his pommel, gurgling as blood spattered the mane of his horse.

"Gods damn it!" Conrak cursed, taking shelter behind his shield.

The plain echoed with screams and the hollow thump of bodies hitting earth. The Blackthorn line, already frayed, began to crumble in earnest. Where once the Zylmacians had scattered like frightened prey, now they closed like wolves, circling the stragglers and plucking them off one by one.

Tylar's shield quivered as another arrow punched into it, splinters stinging his knuckles. He ripped it free with a snarl, ready to drive his spurs and plunge deeper into the maelstrom.

"Bradshaw!" Conrak's voice cut through the chaos. "Fall back! We'll be slaughtered if we linger!"

"Then let them fucking try!" Tylar roared back, cleaving a rider from his saddle with a savage swing of his sword. Blood sprayed hot across his face, spattering his visor. The moment's triumph was hollow; already the Zylmacians wheeled away, drawing fresh arrows to string.

The Order's line buckled. Knights who had ridden in so boldly now veered back down the slope in broken groups, horses frothing, men screaming for their brothers to follow. Arrows rained in cruel volleys, finding backs and unguarded flanks.

Conrak surged in beside him, seizing Tylar's reins with a gauntleted fist. "Enough! We fall back, or we die for nothing! Remember Madelyn!"

Tylar wrenched against him, teeth bared, every vein in his neck fit to burst. But another knight toppled nearby, an arrow through the eye, cutting his death scream short, and Tylar knew the truth of it. No fury, no vow, no oath of vengeance would stop this rout.

With a guttural curse, he wheeled his horse about, shielding Conrak as they tore back down the slope. Around them, the shattered remnants of the Blackthorn cavalry streamed for safety, the jeers of the wildmen chasing them all the way to the plain below. Tylar spat a gobbet of blood, the sting of retreat burning deeper than any wound.

The wildmen wheeled back into the hills as suddenly as they had come, their laughter carrying on the wind like a curse. Arrows ceased. Dust thinned. Only the broken and the bloodied lay strewn across the slope, their horses wandering riderless back toward the lines. Both sides had broken contact, neither holding the field, neither claiming victory.

Tylar rode at Conrak's side, jaw clenched so tight his teeth ached. Blood smeared his cheek where a splinter had cut him, and his knuckles were raw from clutching the reins. Every step of his warhorse's hooves beat out the same refrain in his skull: cowardice, cowardice, cowardice.

Conrak's voice was low, almost measured, as if unwilling to feed the storm. "They were never trying to win. They meant to bleed us, Bradshaw. To test our bite and break the line where we were weakest. Call it what you will, but that was discipline, not defeat."

"Discipline?" Tylar howled. "I call it pissing from the shadows. If they had the stones, they'd have stood and fought me. I'd have ripped their fucking heads off one by one."

Conrak chose not to argue further, though the look in his eyes said all. Survival had demanded retreat. Even the mighty Titan could not stand alone against a storm of arrows.

The two crested the last rise and found the Betanthian host spread before them in full battle formation, banners rippling in the Plainhold wind. Shields locked, pikes angled forward, archers nocking fresh shafts. The whole army stood braced, waiting for the next charge. A haze of dust still drifted where the horsemen had vanished, but already the order of battle had re-formed.

Tylar pressed through the ranks, the stares of men following him. Whispers of "Titan" stirred at his passing, some in awe, some in doubt after what they had seen on the ridge. He ignored them all and rode hard for the royal banner.

Prince Gareth sat mounted at its center, his face grim and set. At his side loomed Edmund Thomas, bandaged and bloodied, yet unbroken, and behind him, the silken colors of Lord Vakaro's retinue snapped in the wind. Tylar dropped from the saddle, boots thudding against sun-baked ground. With his helm under one arm, he pushed through the ranks, his voice rasping from strain and exhaustion.

"They run scared," he said, huffing. "Fucking cowards refuse to stand and fight. Their horde can't be far away now. I say we press on and smash them once and for all!"

"Agreed," Gareth said. "We need to force a conclusion here and now. This ends today."

"Press on, is it?"

The words slid into the space like oil on water. Lord Vakaro guided his stallion forward, his retinue parting the ranks with hardly a stir. Where Gareth's men dripped sweat and Tylar's armor was scored with grime, the Southern Commandant sat immaculate, as if no battle had ever touched him.

"You saw what happened," Ridley continued, his tone low but carrying. "They draw us out, bleed us with arrows, and vanish before we can land a killing stroke. If we hurl the host into the hills, we invite disaster. Patience will break them, not reckless charges."

Tylar fumed, clutching his helm as if to heave it. "Patience? While they pick us apart like carrion birds? You sit on your fat ass at the rear and talk of patience? I'll show you patience when I ram your words down your—"

"Enough." Gareth's voice cracked like a whip. He wheeled his horse, meeting Tylar's burning eyes first, then Ridley's cold ones. "This is not the time for quarrels. Lord Vakaro, ride with me. We'll weigh our options away from the men."

The Southern Commandant inclined his head ever so slightly, a courteous gesture that reeked of condescension. "As you wish, Highness." He tugged his reins, withdrawing with his retinue in neat order.

Gareth spurred after him, his cloak snapping in the dry wind. Tylar growled low, throwing his helm back onto his head. "Snake's got the prince's ear," he muttered, and without waiting for leave, he mounted and set off in pursuit.

Lord Vakaro drew his reins, guiding his horse toward a low rise overlooking the plain. His retinue fanned out behind him, disciplined as a sword wall. Gareth trotted behind, his jaw like iron. Tylar came last, ignoring the glares from Ridley's men as he rode to his prince's side.

"You saw it as well as I did," Lord Vakaro said, his tone cool, unhurried. "Their horse archers are the key. So long as they harass us at range and melt away into the hills, we will spend our strength and gain nothing. To press into that is folly."

"Folly?" Gareth snapped. "They toy with us, Lord Vakaro. Every hour we hesitate or get distracted by skirmishers, the horde slips further away. We end this now or not at all."

Ridley's eyes narrowed, but his voice remained soft. "A commander's duty is not to appease his pride, but to preserve his host. The Northmen want us to chase them. They want us scattered and broken. You would do well to remember that."

Tylar barked a harsh laugh. "Preserve the host? Tell that to the men bleeding on that ridge. Tell it to the poor bastards rotting at Castle Morden. They don't need a lesson in patience, Vakaro; they need vengeance."

The Southern Commandant's gaze slid to him at last, cold as stone. "And what do you know of command, Bradshaw? You're a sword. A useful one, but still only a sword. Leave the thinking to men who carry more than steel."

That was enough. Tylar swung down from the saddle, boots striking hard earth, his hand already closing over the hilt at his side. "Say that again, and I'll ram that silver tongue down your throat, you fuck!"

"Enough!" Gareth's shout cracked like thunder. His stallion side-stepped at the force of it, ears laid back. "I'll hear no more threats among my own. Lord Vakaro, return to your command. Tylar, you will hold your tongue, or I'll have you bound like a common brawler. Do I make myself clear?"

The two men glared at one another across the space, one calm, the other seething like a furnace. Then Lord Vakaro inclined his head again, that same slight bow that dripped with mockery. "As you wish, Highness." With a flick of the reins, he turned his mount and rode back toward the banners.

Gareth exhaled slowly, eyes fixed on the plain where the horsemen had vanished. "I need you to temper yourself, Tylar. Events are unfolding behind the scenes, each a matter of life or death. Sir Edmund was nearly assassinated the other night. I believe Ridley was responsible."

For a moment, Tylar thought he'd misheard. He blinked, jaw tightening. "That snake? I knew he was poison, but to strike at Edmund?" His hand flexed on the hilt at his side. "Say the word and I'll open his throat before the sun sets."

"No." Gareth's reply came quick and sharply. He turned his horse, cloak snapping in the dry wind. "I need proof, not blood. If Ridley is guilty, I'll not have him slip free because we moved too soon."

Tylar spat into the dirt. "Proof or no, he reeks of treachery. Men like him don't stop at one try. You'd be wise to keep him where I can see him."

"I intend to," Gareth said, voice dropping low. "But I need you steady, Bradshaw. Not reckless. If we're to survive what's coming, I must know you'll hold your fury until I give the order."

Tylar ground his teeth, staring after the banners where Lord Vakaro had vanished. Patience was the one thing that Titan had never mastered. But for Gareth's sake—for Edmund's—he forced a slow nod.

"If you insist," he said. "But don't expect me to remain idle forever."

The army pressed forward, the plain swallowing them mile by mile. Hooves drummed a steady thunder across the parched earth, banners snapping high overhead. Northward the host went, chasing the shadow of the barbarian horde, each man knowing the next clash was only days away.

Tylar rode close to Gareth, never more than a horse's length from the prince. He loathed to be anywhere near Lord Vakaro's retinue, their crimson silks and polished helms gleaming like they were marching to a feast instead of war. But Gareth's words weighed heavily in his skull.

Edmund was nearly cut down in the night: Ridley Vakaro, the serpent with the knife.

His hand strayed to the hilt at his side more than once. One quick thrust, one gush of blood, and the threat would be ended. But Gareth had been clear: not yet.

"You truly believe it was him?" Tylar asked at last, keeping his voice low.

"I believe he had cause," Gareth murmured. His gaze never left the road ahead. "Ridley came to this war for more than the crown's glory.

He seeks power, and to get that power, he needs to dismantle the protection around me. I'm the only thing standing in the way of his coup."

"Then why let him ride free at your shoulder?"

"Because snakes bare their fangs when cornered," Gareth said softly. "Better I see his strike than feel it in my back."

Tylar's brow lowered. The idea of keeping Lord Vakaro close felt like bedding down beside a wolf, but he forced himself to swallow his protest. He was no schemer, no court-bred hawk. His trade was blood and steel. Still, if Gareth needed a blade ready when the trap was sprung, then by hell, he would be that blade.

The column slowed as a line of wagons creaked across a shallow ravine. The air thickened, churned into a cloud by thousands of boots and hooves. Through the haze, Tylar glimpsed Lord Vakaro riding with his chosen men, every one of them armored and ordered, their crimson banners cutting clean against the dreary world. The Southern lord sat straight-backed in his saddle, his face as still as carved stone, issuing commands with the smallest flick of a hand.

"He knows," Tylar muttered.

Gareth's head turned slightly. "What do you mean?"

"No man rides that calm in the middle of this storm unless he thinks he holds every card. He's daring you to call him on it."

"Perhaps." Gareth's eyes followed the red banner cutting through the haze. "Or perhaps he thinks me blind. Either way, the day will come when the masks are torn off. Until then, we march."

The host surged again, faster now, scouts riding ahead in clouds of grit to harass the enemy's trail. Rumors flew as quickly as the wind: the Northmen's baggage train was days ahead, their horde slowing under its weight. Some swore they'd seen Damien Dreadfire himself on the ridges at dawn, watching like a hawk.

Tylar only half-heard them. His gaze stayed fixed on Lord Vakaro and his sycophants like an attack dog. Every false smile, every courtesy, every bow of the head stank of treachery. His fingers drummed on his sword hilt, hungry for the command Gareth would not yet give.

"Careful, Bradshaw," Conrak muttered as he rode up alongside, his horse lathered from the pursuit. "Keep boring holes in him like that, and the snake might just shed his skin. Then where would you be?"

Tylar gave him a sideways glare. "Better off. I'd crush the fucking thing before it slithered back to its hole. Haven't you heard? That Southern cunt nearly had Sir Edmund assassinated. And instead of claiming his treasonous head, I'm forced to stand idle."

The Sacrithon nodded, his voice dropped low. "Aye, I have. It's difficult to keep secrets from a man such as myself. The prince plays a long game, and he'll need you steady when the time comes. Patience is not a virtue I ever expected from you, but you'd best learn it fast."

"I've no patience for traitors," Tylar growled.

"And yet here you are," Conrak said, gesturing at the endless line of marching men, the banners, the dust hanging like a pall. "Riding in lockstep, waiting for the next horn. If you can stomach this, you can stomach watching Ridley Vakaro a little longer."

Ahead, Gareth raised his hand, urging the host to quicken. The column stretched north, a serpent of steel and flesh, its head driving hard toward the horizon. Rumors of baggage trains and shadowed ridges pulled them onward, the promise of battle tightening every rein and jaw. Tylar's eyes narrowed on the red banner cutting through the haze. He said nothing more, but his grip on the hilt remained, knuckles pale beneath the grime.

The day would come when masks slipped and blades were bared. When it did, he would be ready. Not to argue, not to wait—but to kill.

LUCETTA VIII

CHAINS BIT INTO HER WRISTS AND ANKLES, THEIR COLD WEIGHT dragging her down the tunnel like a condemned prisoner on the way to the gallows. The Harbingers spoke little, their boots crunching in gravel and filth, their torchlight casting warped shadows along the dripping stone walls.

Pavlos was nowhere to be seen. The last image she had of him, slumped in the stockade, his golden teeth scattered like coins, clung to her mind like the stench of the sewers.

"Move faster," a fanatic barked, jabbing her in the back with the haft of his truncheon. She stumbled but kept her footing. They would not kill her, she reminded herself. Not yet. She was too valuable.

They hauled her into a side chamber she had not seen before. It stank of stagnant water and rot, the walls lined with rusted racks and the skeletal remains of unfortunates long forgotten. A table sat at the far end, cluttered with maps, candles burned low, and a scattering of crude talismans. Hesgrin toddled in behind her, then hunched over a table, tracing a bony finger along a route toward the Citadel.

"You will guide us," he said without looking up. "The hidden ways into the palace. The Queen's crypt. You know them better than anyone."

Truth be told, the Westwind Citadel was impregnable. It was the largest, most formidable construction in Caldakas, engineered by geniuses and madmen alike. Despite many attempts in her youth, Lucetta was never able to find a way to escape the palace grounds. If there were no way out, certainly there would be no way in.

Disclosing such information, however, would be suicide. Lucetta decided to cross such a bridge when the time came, opting to weave a tapestry of clever lies instead. "Along the coast is the safest way. The rocks are jagged and treacherous, but enough to conceal your path to the walls."

Hesgrin's cloudy eyes flicked toward her, sharp despite their decay.

"The coast…" he murmured, as if rolling the words over his tongue like a rare spice. "And the guards?"

"They will not expect an approach from the cliffs," she said, willing her voice to remain steady. "The tide is cruel there. Even at its lowest, it drowns the unwary."

One of the fanatics muttered a curse in his throat. Hesgrin ignored him, studying her as if she were some curious insect pinned to a board.

"Perhaps you do speak truth," he said at last. "But I have known liars sweeter than honey and twice as poisonous."

He gestured to the guards. "Take her back to the pen. We will test her words soon enough."

A calloused hand clamped around her arm, dragging her toward the doorway. Lucetta let her knees buckle, forcing the guard to half-carry her. The moment they passed into the tunnel, she stole a glance back at the chamber. Hesgrin was already bent over the maps again, muttering to himself.

The Harbingers dragged her through the winding, stinking arteries of the sewer, their grip bruising her arms. Her feet scraped against the damp stone as she was hauled back toward her cell. The reek of rot and rust thickened with every step until they reached the familiar row of iron doors.

A shove sent her stumbling inside. The door clanged shut, the rattle of a skeleton key echoing as it turned in the lock. Their footsteps receded into the dark. Lucetta pressed her back against the wall, willing her heart to slow, but the terrors of the dark quickly reemerged.

"Please," she whimpered to the woman in black. "Do not leave me in the dark! Anything but the dark…"

Hours came and went with no difference between them. For all she knew, it might have been a warm, sunny day in the streets above. The people of Cardale might be going about their daily routines, oblivious to the horrors unfolding beneath their feet.

Her mind clung to that word—*routine.* Against her will, Aldred came to mind. Not the man himself, not truly, but the life he had embodied. The quiet rhythm of her estate's halls, the measured order of a house that ran like clockwork. Even his dull speeches at supper and his obsession with ledgers and legacy had carried a strange sort of comfort.

She had grown to loathe him, to scorn his complacency and his insufferable caution. Yet here in the bowels of Cardale, with the smell of rot stinging her nose and the shrieks of madmen still ringing in her ears, she found herself longing for the stillness of those nights. For the sound of quills scratching on parchment, for the weight of tapestries shutting out the wind, for the predictability of a man she no longer loved. It disgusted her, that longing. But the thought remained, stubborn as a stain.

As Lucetta stared aimlessly into the darkness, a soft glow appeared down the blackened corridor. It was soft and subtle, perhaps passing torchlight. But the glow pulsed as if breathing, growing in size and intensity. A bitter chill wafted into her cell, bringing with it an old, comfortable sense of dread.

A pair of orange-red eyes emerged in the gloom just ahead, but disappeared like a candle snuffed by the wind. Iron creaked as the latch of her cell doors clicked open, the hinges groaning ever so slightly. Lucetta thought she was dreaming, but a sharp bite of bitter air on her skin convinced her otherwise.

Nervously, she stepped outside her cell like a child up after bedtime. Her bare feet made no sound on the damp stone as she eased into the corridor. The glow was gone, swallowed by the dark, but the cold it left behind clung to her like a second skin. No voices. No footsteps. Only the distant drip of water somewhere far down the tunnel.

She moved slowly, every shadow threatening to reach out and drag her back into the black. Torchlight from the main chamber bled faintly into the passage ahead. Lucetta hugged the wall, peering around the corner.

A pungent smell struck her first; iron and decay, undercut by an acrid tang of old smoke. The main hall lay before her, its braziers casting long, flickering light over a slaughterhouse of bodies. Guardsmen, stripped of armor, lay in broken heaps. Some hung lifeless from their shackles; others were stacked like cordwood in the corner.

Pavlos was slumped in the stockade, his head drooping forward, his face a ruin of bruises and dried blood. But his chest still moved, shallow and slow. Lucetta slipped inside, heart hammering. She kept her eyes from the dead, her focus only on him. The stockade's iron fittings were stiff with rust, but she forced them open with shaking hands. The latch gave with a low creak, and Pavlos sagged into her arms, heavy and limp.

"Come on," she whispered, bracing him under one arm. "You're not dying here."

He gave no reply, just a groan that rattled low in his chest. She glanced toward the tunnels, straining her ears for the sound of returning boots. They had only moments.

With his arm slung over her like a sack, she dragged him toward the nearest tunnel, every step a test of strength. Pavlos's boots scraped along the stone, leaving faint streaks in the grime. His weight threatened to pull her down more than once, but she bit back her grunts of effort.

The hall seemed to stretch forever, each flicker of torchlight revealing another bend, another shadow to fear. Somewhere in the distance, a muffled laugh echoed, too close for comfort. Lucetta froze, pressing herself and Pavlos against the damp wall. Her heart pounded loud enough to betray them.

When no footsteps followed, she moved again, faster this time, steering them into a narrow side passage. The air grew fresher here, the ceiling lower. It seemed as if an exit lay just ahead, though its whereabouts remained concealed. But every sound was against her: the faint rattle of Pavlos's breath, the drag of his feet, the low shuffle when she brushed the wall.

Lucetta gritted her teeth, hauling Pavlos forward. "Just a little farther," she hissed, though her arms screamed and her legs burned.

They burst into the drainage hall, the stench of stagnant water hitting her like a slap. Ahead, the moon's pale glow seeped through the iron bars of a grate. Freedom was there, so close she could taste the salty air beyond. Even the idea of being so close to escape made her eyes water.

The grate was rusted, its hinges swollen with age, but Lucetta threw her weight against it. Metal groaned in protest, flakes of red-brown falling away with each push. With a final heave, it swung open just enough to squeeze through. Cold night air rushed in, sharp with brine. She pulled Pavlos through, his boots clanging against the lip of the grate before they tumbled onto the stones outside.

They landed in a narrow gully where water lapped quietly against rock. In the distance, the Citadel's towering walls loomed black against a starlit sky. The tide was low, revealing a jagged path of slick stones winding away from the outflow. She dragged him along the shadows, keeping low. The wind carried the muffled drone of the city beyond, but nearer still came the sound she dreaded most—the shuffle of boots on wet stone.

"Wait," she whispered, though Pavlos seemed not to hear.

Desperately, Lucetta scrambled to close the gate, but the approaching footsteps were closing in quickly. Surely, the Harbingers in the tunnels would have heard the screeching metal already. Instead, she hoisted Pavlos to his feet, grunting and straining under his weight. She guided Pavlos along the rock wall until the gully narrowed and opened into a weedy embankment that climbed toward the lower streets of Cardale.

Her legs screamed with each step, but she forced them to carry both their weight. At the top, the cobbled streets glistened with the night's dampness. A drunk staggered past an alley not twenty paces away, muttering to himself, a clay jug swinging from one hand.

Lucetta waited until he turned the corner before slipping into the shadows. Cardale's streets were never truly empty—dockworkers, gamblers, and the city's rats in human form prowled at all hours. Every intersection was another risk, each figure in the dark a possible threat.

They ducked behind a fishmonger's stall, its tables bare but still stinking of the day's catch. A pair of cloaked figures passed, speaking low in a language she did not recognize. When they were gone, she pressed on, keeping to the narrowest lanes, hugging the walls to hide their shapes from any watchful eyes.

Somewhere ahead, a dog barked, sharp and sudden. Pavlos stirred at the sound, his weight shifting heavily against her.

"Stay with me," she whispered, not sure if she meant it for him or herself.

They slipped deeper into the labyrinth of backstreets, where the smell of brine gave way to woodsmoke and rotting refuse. Above, the Citadel's black silhouette shrank behind them. They were still in danger, but for the first time in weeks, Lucetta felt the cold night air on her face without iron bars between her and the sky.

The city closed in around them, its alleys narrowing, the buildings leaning like eavesdroppers over the street. Somewhere to the east, a ship's bell tolled, its mournful note carrying over the rooftops. Lucetta's eyes swept every shadow, searching for a haven, but Cardale offered none.

She found a recessed doorway half-hidden by hanging laundry and eased Pavlos into it. His breathing was ragged and shallow, and his head drooped against the wall. He would not last long without food, water, and a place to rest. Somewhere in the endless maze of streets, she would have to find help, or at least a place where the Harbingers would not think to look. But help came at a price in Cardale, and she had nothing left to bargain with except her life.

A faint sound carried down the alley; the slow, deliberate tread of boots on cobblestone. Too even to be a drunkard, too quiet to be a merchant making an honest round. She froze, eyes searching the darkness until the footsteps faded. She looked once more toward the Citadel, a black tooth against the night, and turned away.

"Just... a little... further..." Lucetta grunted, straining to keep Pavlos afoot.

The wind shifted, bringing with it a whisper of movement—too soft to name, too brief to trust. Lucetta's breath caught. Was it boots on stone, or only the sigh of the night through narrow alleyways? Every shadow seemed to lean closer, every corner seemed to hide an unseen watcher. She tightened her grip on Pavlos and pressed on, refusing to look back, for fear she might find the answer.

MADELYN VII

MADELYN WAS UNCERTAIN HOW LONG SHE HAD BEEN ASLEEP OR IF she was even sleeping at all. There was blackness, to be certain, but not the sort of dreamless limbo she had often experienced. It was more like waking from a dream, but not to a reality of light and warmth. Perhaps it was waking from one dream into another, as she had sometimes done.

The air was hazy with sage smoke, a slight tinge of must from two rows of tall bookshelves dampening the aroma. Their contents appeared ancient, spines and faces cracked, slowly disintegrating from the relentless rot of time. It was difficult to tell one apart from the next in the flickers of faint candlelight, but something about the texts felt familiar.

A library? she thought, glancing around in disbelief.

A shadow danced across a nearby bookshelf, its form distorted yet decidedly human. From an adjacent room, the soft sound of pages turning in an old book was evidence that she was not alone. Madelyn stepped forward with nervous anticipation, knowing she was a foreigner in this unknown place, yet feeling strangely at home.

"Come in," a deep voice said, its tone like distant thunder, its cadence slow and measured. "Come, and sit."

At first, Madelyn made to turn and flee, but something about the man's voice calmed her deepest fears. She peeked around the corner and spied a man sitting on a simple wooden chair, a lit lantern resting on a worn wooden table. He appeared middle-aged, perhaps late forties, though his eyes carried the knowledge of centuries. Lengths of long, brown hair were swept back, tinged ever so slightly with silver strands. His dark, straight beard was thick yet neatly groomed, streaked with the dust of memory.

"Who… who are you?" Madelyn asked, drawing her hands up to her chest. "And where am I?"

"You are in the place between," the strange man said, "where breath no longer stirs the body… yet the soul still resists its reckoning."

He gently closed the cover of an old book, its leather binding cracking ever so slightly. The man rested his hands on top of it reverently. Dark blemishes blotted his fingers, though it was unclear if they were ink stains or tattoos.

"I have known many names," he continued. "But to you, I am only what I must be—a keeper of what was, and a witness to what may yet come. Some have called me the Lanternbearer—the Keeper of the Still Voice. But names are of little consequence. Sit, Madelyn. You've run long enough."

Despite her uncertainty, Madelyn entered the ancient study and sat at the weathered table, the chair beneath her squeaking and shifting under her weight. Although a foreigner to this place, something about her host felt familiar. It was an energy she had experienced before, although she could not quite place a finger on where.

"Have we met before?

"You have felt my presence in recent times, yes," the Lanternbearer said. "Only when your mind's eye opened have I been able to make myself known."

A flutter took hold in Madelyn's chest, stealing her breath for a second. "It was you I saw on the Plainhold! And… and.. it was you I felt

at the Ivornorium! I knew it… I knew you were real. But… where am
I? What is this place?"

"This is the hall of memory," the man said, his voice like worn stone,
yet flowing like gentle water. "Where the echoes of those before you
linger, not in flesh… but in consequence."

He peered at one of the many shelves, eyes slowly scanning its contents. A faint ember appeared to flicker within the spine of a cracked
tome, yet it vanished as quickly as it arrived.

"Every path walked. Every choice carved. They are written here—not
to judge, but to remain. You, Madelyn… you are not the first to pass
through this place. But you may yet be the last to leave it unchanged."

Tightness gripped Madelyn's chest. It was as if a parent were speaking to her, the familiarity of his voice oddly comforting. Yet, there was
a separation she could feel but not describe.

"Unchanged?" she asked, emotion welling within her. "What are you
trying to say? Speak plainly."

She stared long into the man's eyes, who appeared to look not at her,
but through her. His gaze did not shift, though his brow creased ever so
slightly—whether in sadness or recognition, she could not tell.

"I *am* speaking plainly," he said. "But when a soul is already bound
to a path, even truth sounds like riddles."

He rose slowly, stepping to the side, gesturing subtly toward a nearby
shelf. The wood was warped and ancient, bowing beneath the weight
of its contents.

"These tomes," he said, arm outstretched, "are not written in ink
alone. They are memory… consequence… blood. Every time a choice
is made, the page turns. And yours…"

He let the sentence hang unfinished, like a noose half coiled, each
word tinged with an emotion she could not quite describe. It was not
sadness, nor frustration. Perhaps disappointment, she supposed, for it
appeared the stranger knew more than he was alluding to.

Madelyn swallowed hard. "Then tell me what it says."

He turned back to her, voice gentler now. "It does not *say*. It *shows*."

The Lanternbearer moved to a tall, narrow book—its cover a deep, weathered gray, scarred with cracks like old bone. He laid a hand upon it, and a breath of cold air stirred the dust.

"This is yours, Madelyn."

She stared at it, unwilling to step forward. "And if I open it?"

"You will see the thread you've spun to its fraying end. Not prophecy. Not promise. Just the natural weight of every step you've taken. You asked for plain words. Here they are: you are not wrong to want justice. But you are mistaking your pain for purpose. And if you continue forward believing they are the same…"

He stepped back, his hand falling away from the book. "…you will not recognize yourself at the end."

"I recognize myself less each day," Madelyn admitted. "And I have Damien Dreadfire to thank for that. He corrupted not only my flesh, but my spirit. There is no light left in me, only vengeance. Only the need to see him suffer as I have, and to stop him before another suffers my fate."

The man's expression remained unchanged. If her words wounded him, he did not show it. But the silence between them was not indifference —it was mourning, not with weeping and gnashing of teeth, but the quiet, reflective sort one buries deep within oneself.

"Then you have already begun to fade," The Lanternbearer said softly. "Vengeance burns hot… but leaves nothing to warm you when it's done. It feeds on what remains of you. And when it is satisfied—if it is ever satisfied—you will look for yourself, and find only ash."

He turned away, hands clasped loosely behind him, head bowing slowly. "You are not the first to say what you've just said. Not in this hall. Not in this bloodline. Every soul who believed vengeance would complete them left behind a story written in ruin. The only question now, Madelyn, is whether yours will end the same."

A strange sensation washed over her, as if something was deeply amiss. Perhaps he was more than an ancestor or a living memory—for all Madelyn knew, he might have been a god. Regardless of the truth, the crossroads before her still stood. Tears began stinging her eyes, then dripped down her cheeks like spring rain.

"I have no good left in me," she said, sniffling. "I was violated in the most heinous ways. I was forced to bring a child into this world, made from suffering, not love. And I was betrayed by the man I called father. How can I allow the world to inflict such wrongs upon me and not seek to right them?"

The Lanternbearer did not turn. He let her words echo, filling the chamber like smoke thick with remembrance. When he finally spoke, his voice was quiet, less than thunder now, more like the rustling of old pages.

"You were wronged," he said. "And no justice in this world will ever make it right."

He turned then, slowly, deliberately, his eyes not pitying, but present, as if he were standing within her pain rather than above it.

"What you carry… no soul should be asked to bear. And yet you do. You endure. Even if only in fury. There is something I must tell you," he said, his voice threaded with something heavier than sorrow. "The form you see before you—the face, the voice—is not my own."

A flicker of light passed across his features, and for a moment, he seemed older, or younger, or many—as if the flesh itself were made of memory.

"I have taken the image of the man who fathered you. Not the one who raised you, but the one whose blood first stirred in your veins. I do not wear him to deceive… only to be recognized. For though he was lost, you were not forgotten. And in the eternal house where your forefathers dwell, he sees you… and prays you turn back from this path."

Madelyn's composure shattered like falling glass, her sobs and wails echoing throughout the library. All of her strength, all of her will and resolve, crumbled as she collapsed to her knees. Every painful event from her past came cascading back with the same unrelenting weight as when she first felt it.

"He left me…" Madelyn sobbed. "He forced me to grow up in a household not of love or warmth, but of duty. Stern… rigid… and unloving. And for what? Only for Jensen to try and slit my throat when I was no longer of use to him?"

The Lanternbearer did not move as her cries filled the hall. He let them rise and fall like waves against stone. Only when her sobs slowed, when the weight of her grief pressed her breath into silence, did he speak again.

"Your true father's actions I cannot commend nor condemn," he said, devoid of emotion. "It is easy to judge the actions of another without knowing their reasoning."

"Were they discovered? My parents—" Madelyn blurted between sobs. "Did the same people who tried to kill me find them? What were they running from? If I am the last of the Eveldanyr, then one of them was as well. My mother… or father… what secrets were they trying to hide?"

Silence filled the grand library, and the Lanterbearer remained still. "There are truths so bound in shadow," he said slowly, "that dragging them into light would do more harm than good. Some names carry weight not because of who bore them… but because of who hunted them."

He looked at her now, not with sorrow or sympathy, but with the quiet burden of one who had carried too much. The tragedy and triumph of millennia played out behind his unblinking eyes.

"Your bloodline was not merely royal," he continued, "it was dangerous. Feared. Misunderstood. Perhaps even by those who carried it."

Madelyn's breath caught. "So they *were* running."

The man's jaw tensed slightly. Not an answer. *Not quite.*

"Running, hiding, fighting… There are many words for the same motion. It is not for me to say what they fled. Only that they tried, in their flawed and desperate way, to shield you. Sometimes… surviving is the only answer you're allowed. Should you choose to turn away from this dark path, perhaps you might learn the truth of your parents' fate."

He stepped toward a high, narrow window. The candlelight stretched toward him like a shadow trying to catch a ghost. A kiss of raindrops pattered gently against the pane, as if the heavens themselves were weeping over what had transpired.

Madelyn sat, chin pressed against her knees, arms wrapped tightly around her legs. She studied the bookshelves and their ancient, dusty tomes, each containing memories and deeds of countless ancestors. What mysteries and revelations could be awaiting her, she wondered. But such sentiments were short-lived.

I am the only one who can slay Lazilyth… and I am the only one who can stop Damien Dreadfire and his horde. If I fail, and forces of darkness march across Caldakas, it will be as if my ancestors never existed at all. Every trace of their legacy will be snuffed out. And how many countless others will endure the same fate? I cannot let that monster claim any more than he already has.

The Lanternbearer watched the rain trace rivers down the glass, his expression unreadable, as if he too were trying to make sense of a world that no longer fit the shape of its promises.

"I can sense your mind is made up," he said, finally. "I will not stop you, that is not my purpose. I can no more change your destiny than I can rewrite the pages in these books."

He turned to her one last time, and in the flickering light, his face appeared impossibly old, like stone remembering what it once was before the chisel.

"But know this, Madelyn Everly… there are victories that cost too much. And some monsters do not die when you slay them. Some… take root in the one holding the sword."

He took a step back into the gloom, and his voice softened, barely more than a breath.

"If ever you forget who you are, return here. Even if only in memory."

And then, like a shadow retreating from dawn, he was gone. Only soft rainfall against the windowpane remained, a final, sorrowful lament from those whose voices would never be heard again. Madelyn wept and curled into a ball, the strength in her body waning. The lantern light began dimming, its precious fuel finally exhausted. Darkness draped over the hall, until neither sight nor sound remained.

She awoke to insects gnawing and stinging her face and arms. How long she was unconscious was a mystery, though it appeared not to have been more than a few hours. The library and its magical aura had faded like a dream, quickly vanishing from memory. But her sorrow was real.

Both eyes burned as fresh tears still moistened her cheeks. Perhaps it had been real all along, much the same as the dark void of the Fate Realm. But there was little time to be certain. In the dreary distance, the ground trembled with thunder, though the sky bore no heavy clouds. The horde was drawing near once again.

"I'm sorry, forefathers," Madelyn said, sniffling. "I've come too far now to turn back. I was so close last time to ending that monster and his soothsayer. What would you think of me if I failed now… if I gave up and allowed this evil to continue unchecked?"

A wounded resolve began to harden within her spirit. Madelyn rose on unsteady legs, brushing off dirt and insects from her leathers. Who was to say what the future would hold with Damien dead, she wondered. Perhaps a new life could be waiting on the other side, either at Gareth's side or in peaceful solitude somewhere far away.

"Guide my hand in battle, and lead me true," Madelyn said as she hastily mounted her horse. "Soon, this will all be over… and I will avenge us. All of us."

EINARR VII

THE MORNING BROKE PALE, THE MOUNTAINS BEHIND THEM CAST IN cold shadow. Einarr stood by his horse, fastening the Blackthorn cloak at his throat. Around him, nine others did the same, helms drawn low, armor fixed and ready. The rest of the company waited in the hollow where they had camped, horses tethered, faces drawn. They would not ride this part. Too many cloaks missing, too many accents roughened by northern ice. Better they remain unseen.

Einarr swung into the saddle and let his gaze measure the disguised riders. "Helmets on. Cloaks straight. Speak not a word unless I give it."

The men nodded, shifting in the strange weight of stolen steel.

Hyleth came forward, weathered eyes steady. "The village lies just beyond the border," he said. "Small, unguarded. The smoke from their hearths will guide us."

Valerick raised a lance bearing the Blackthorn standard. Black cloth rippled in the chill wind, the golden horse within its crown of thorns clear against the morning sky. It snapped once, sharp as a whip, before settling.

"Who among us speaks in the best Southern accent?" Valerick asked. It was a good and fair question, one Einarr had yet to consider.

A few of the riders exchanged uneasy glances. One muttered

Mardek's name under his breath, while another shrugged and looked to the ground. None volunteered outright. Einarr's mouth thinned. He had not thought of it, and he despised the weakness it showed. Still, the answer mattered little. The Blackthorn were feared, not loved; they were men of few words, and fewer courtesies.

"Then it falls to me," Einarr said, sighing. "Perhaps a Nothanek's tongue will be so foreign, they will assume it's Betanthian."

A few of the men chuckled nervously, though none too loudly. Valerick smirked, reins taut in one hand, the banner lance steady in the other.

"Foreign enough to pass, I suppose," Hyleth said.

Einarr pulled the reins tight and looked over the line of riders. "Remember, we do not chatter like farmers on market day. If we are hailed, let me answer. If we are doubted, then let steel do the talking."

They rode out of the hollow two by two, hooves striking stone in steady rhythm, the false patrol vanishing westward into the broken hills. Behind them, the remaining company watched until their banners dipped below the ridge, leaving only smoke from the campfires and an uneasy silence of men who knew they were waiting on a lie.

The trail bent lower with every mile, the air warming as they left the heights behind. Brush gave way to fields tilled in narrow strips, the soil thin but stubborn. A few goats scattered at their passing, bells clattering on their necks.

By midmorning, the village lay before them: a cluster of stone huts, thatch roofs gray with age, smoke from cookfires rising in slow, straight columns. Children chased one another in the square, their laughter sharp against the stillness. A mill wheel turned on a stream, creaking steady as a heartbeat.

A dog barked and ran a few paces toward them, then stopped, tail stiff, hackles raised. One of the villagers, a graybeard with a limp, called it back, shading his eyes against the sun. He squinted at the riders but did not flinch; cloaks and banners told him all he thought he needed to know.

"See how they don't scatter?" Valerick muttered under his breath. "They think we are here for a routine shakedown." His smirk held no humor.

Another rider spat his disdain. "Too easy."

Einarr said nothing. He let the silence build, let the weight of it press on his men. The villagers had begun to notice now, a woman drawing her children close, a pair of men setting down their tools, their hands uncertain at their sides. No one ran. No one screamed. It was trust, unearned and fragile. And it would damn them.

Einarr slowed his horse, the stolen cloak heavy on his shoulders, and lifted a hand. The riders closed in tight, the banner swaying above them like a dark omen. He sighed, looking to the heavens and feeling the weight of the atrocity he was about to commit.

Kholdyr, forgive me for the wicked deeds I am about to do. Let the souls of the vanquished find peace, and let them know their deaths were not in vain. Together, they will have saved a continent.

Suddenly, his hand fell like an axe. The riders surged forward, hooves pounding like war drums. Goats scattered, children froze mid-laugh, and the square erupted in screams as Blackthorn cloaks swept down upon them. Einarr's blade flashed like lightning, cleaving through a man clutching a shepherd's crook. Another rider trampled a woman beneath his horse, the crack of bone lost in the chaos.

Doors slammed as villagers scrambled for shelter, but the Northmen broke them down with iron-fit hooves and axes driven through weak wood. Thatched roofs caught fire as torches were hurled. Smoke rose fast and thick, mingling with the shrieks of the dying.

Einarr rose in the stirrups, his blade a silver arc. It sheared through the miller's shoulder, sending him sprawling across the stone. The mill wheel turned on, creaking steadily while the stream below ran dark with silt and blood. A woman clutched her child to her breast, but Dolsigg's axe split them both before she could scream.

The village was broken in minutes. Its square lay in ruin, strewn with bodies. Only the fire had a voice now, crackling as it devoured thatch and beam of the modest hovels. Horses stamped and snorted, restless among the dead.

Reining in, breath steady, Einarr's eyes scanned the wreckage. A door sagged open on its hinges, flames licking at the frame. From within stumbled a boy, no more than fifteen, soot streaking his face. He coughed once, then bolted, bare feet slapping against the dirt roads.

Einarr spurred after him. His horse closed the ground in heartbeats, steel whispering as he wheeled his reddened blade overhead. He rose in the stirrups, sword raised, and the lad skidded to a stop, terror writ across his smoke-reddened eyes.

The boy was halted with the edge of polished steel, close enough that he could see his reflection in its sheen. His chest heaved, ribs near splitting, eyes darting to the ruin behind and back to the blade before him.

"Run," Einarr said in a clean Southern accent, his voice an octave lower. "Run and tell them what you saw. Tell them what happens when you defy Marcellus Bethard!"

The boy's lips trembled. He nodded once, too frightened to speak, then stumbled backward before turning in a full sprint, legs pumping, vanishing into the smoke and hills beyond. Einarr lowered his sword and let out a slow breath. Around him, the square smoldered, roofs collapsed, bodies sprawled in pools of blood, the air thick with ash and the stink of burning flesh.

He raised his voice over the crackle of flame. "It is done. Mount up. We ride before the smoke carries word faster than that boy's feet."

The riders wheeled about, hooves splashing through blood and ash as they pulled away from the ruin. Behind them, the village sagged in fire and smoke, the mill wheel still turning, indifferent to what it had witnessed.

Valerick rode up alongside Einarr, banner swaying in the heat. He grinned through the soot on his face. "A ruthless gamble, Rolffson. Perhaps we underestimated the wrath of a fisherman."

Einarr gave him no smile. It was a terrible act to have committed, one that would surely stain his soul.

Dolsigg pressed close on the other side, his helm pushed back, eyes hard. "What now, Einarr?"

"We fall back to the hills," he said, "and retrieve the bodies from the cave when the time comes. They'll wear Blackthorn colors again when Droethia comes to see what's been done. But for now, keep them cool in the stone. I don't want rot spoiling our story."

The men exchanged uneasy looks but said nothing. Cloaks snapped in the wind as they urged their horses up the trail, the burning village fading behind them, the weight of a lie heavy on their backs.

They climbed from the valley, the hills closing in again, until they came at last to the hollow where their kin waited. The men without cloaks rose at once, relief and unease written plain on their faces as they counted those who had returned.

Einarr spoke only a few words, enough to quiet the murmurs. "Mount up, and be quick about it. We go to the cave and wait."

There was no argument. The men gathered their things quickly, their faces grim, and together they wound along the ridge trail. By dusk, they reached the stony hill where the corpses lay hidden. Einarr dismounted without a word and strode to the cave mouth. The stench of old blood and horse hung there, cool stone swallowing sound. Inside lay the bodies, stiffening but still whole in the shadow.

"Bring them out," he said.

The men obeyed, dragging the corpses one by one into the pale light. Helms and breastplates were returned to their former owners, cloaks pulled across cold flesh. Armor buckled, straps tightened, swords laid at hands that would never grip again.

It was slow work, grim and silent. Even the Northmen muttered less than usual, their rough voices dulled by the weight of what they had done. From a distance, the dead might have passed for sleeping Blackthorn, slumped against the stone.

Einarr stepped back, arms folded, eyes unreadable. "Good, they look as they did before. Keep them here in the cave. The cold air will keep the bodies from spoiling. When Droethia comes, we will place them again in the open as if they had only just been slain."

The men shifted and groaned, glancing to the horizon where smoke still stained the sky. No one spoke. The lie was made, and now there was nothing left but to wait for the truth it would summon.

"The blood will long be dry by the time they arrive," Valerick pointed out. "How do you propose to keep your charade going then, Rollfson?"

A fair question, but one Einarr had already considered. It was unsettling to know just how easily he could mastermind such evil, and it spoke to the dark cunning the gods had instilled in him.

"We'll need to cut the throat of a horse when the time comes," he said. "And we'll have to do butcher's work on these bodies."

"Just recognizable enough to tell they are Southerners," Dolsigg grunted.

Einarr nodded. "Aye. Not so mangled they can be mistaken, but enough to make the story true. The stench will do the rest."

A few of the riders grunted in agreement, the rest silent but steady. They had seen worse, and if this was the price of war, then so be it. Dolsigg stooped to drag a body further into the cave, muttering about keeping the cloaks clean. Valerick adjusted the banner-lance against the wall, its black cloth catching what little light filtered inside.

The cave held the dead like a vault, cool air rolling out from its depths. Armor clinked, boots scraped, and the work was done without complaint, each man knowing his part. Einarr watched them for a time, arms folded, his face hard as the stone around him. Beyond the hills, smoke still bled into the sky from the village below, but his eyes were fixed further on the war yet to come, and the fire he had set to summon it.

At length, Valerick sank to a flat stone and ran a hand through his sweat-matted hair. "We've struck the match, now we wait for the blaze. But if Droethia sends no answer… if they swallow the insult and do nothing?"

"That is not their way," Hyleth said. He crouched by the fire they had rekindled at the cave's mouth, his weathered face caught in the glow. "Droethia may be slow to act, but they are not cowards. Their Governor will march, if only to keep his honor intact."

Dolsigg spat into the dirt. "Or he'll shut his gates and leave the villages to burn."

A silence followed, the fire popping in the stillness. Einarr finally spoke, his words cutting through the doubt. "Whether they march or whether they cower, it serves us the same. Either we rouse their wrath, or we show them their masters cannot protect them. Fear will drive them to the spear if pride does not."

Vexar tugged at a strap on his vambrace, uneasy. "And what of us? We wait here in the dark with rotting Southerners for company? How long before the stench draws wolves down from the hills?"

"Then we will feed the wolves," Valerick said with a grin. "They can gnaw on a Blackthorn or two while we count the days."

Laughter came, rough and short, but it died quickly. The men shifted, settling themselves against stone and saddle, each lost to his own thoughts. The night gathered in around them, heavy with smoke and secrets.

Einarr stayed on his feet, gazing out over the black horizon. In the distance, a glow still lingered where the village had burned. He felt the weight of it pressing on his shoulders, the memory of wide eyes staring back at him in the steel. The boy would run, yes. And with his words, the first stone of war would be set rolling.

UDORN IX

STEEL SHRIEKED AGAINST STEEL, DROWNING THE DAWN IN A STORM of blood. Ladders splintered beneath stones hurled from the battlements, warriors tumbling backward into the masses below. Arrows fell like rain, punching through mail and hide, each shaft carrying a scream to the earth. The plain before Dellhaven's walls had become a killing ground, dirt slick with blood, bodies writhing underfoot, the air thick with death.

Udorn stood and watched indifferently, his shield brothers at his side, the roar of battle battering his ears. He had seen cities fall before, but never one so fierce, so swift to bare its teeth. Dellhaven fought not as pampered lords, but as men desperate to survive. And with every heartbeat, the cost of Ragruk's pride mounted higher, the dead piling at the base of the wall like driftwood against stone.

He held the line, axe idle in his grip, while the slaughter raged on. His kinsmen clawed and screamed upon the ladders, only to be dashed down by stone and steel. Blood poured onto the earth as quickly as water into sand, and still Ragruk's voice roared for them to climb, climb, climb.

Every instinct in Udorn screamed to join them, to bury his axe in the enemy and stand shoulder to shoulder with his brothers. But he saw the truth too plainly—this was no charge of glory, only a grave dug deeper with each heartbeat. To throw himself upon the walls now would be to serve Ragruk's design, to die not for honor but for spite. The weight of it pressed on him heavier than any shield.

How many brothers must be fed to pride before the gods are sated?

Beside him, Thaul's voice cut through the chaos, tight with urgency. "What are we doing here, Udorn?"

It was a question to which he had no answer. Seeing his kinsmen dashed senselessly against the walls ignited something within him, but charging into the fray would serve little purpose.

"This is madness!" Gaxas said, his eyes wide. "We will be killed to the last by midday! Udorn! We must do something!"

Udorn's eyes swept the field. Ladders splintered, bodies tumbled, shields cracked like eggshells against the stones of Dellhaven. The air was a chorus of dying men, his men, and each scream twisted deeper into him than any blade could. Pride demanded he join them. Duty demanded he preserve what was left. Between the two lay a chasm vast enough to swallow his soul.

He drew a long breath, steadying himself against the tide of rage that threatened to pull him forward. No—to climb those walls now would be to play the fool in Ragruk's game, and the chieftain's laughter would carry longer than any song of glory. There was only one way to stem the slaughter.

"Very well," he sighed. "Steel yourselves, brothers. Better to climb the city walls than face what lies ahead of us. Our lands, our homes, and our families will be put in peril."

He looked to his men and found them standing firm, their faces set as stone, their eyes unflinching. They asked no further questions and offered no protest. Whatever end awaited, they had chosen it together. In that moment, Udorn felt the bond between them stronger than any oath sworn in a mead hall. They were his brothers and would not waver.

As they pushed through the press of men and toward Ragruk, Udorn caught sight of a familiar figure lingering near the ranks. Dulkin stood apart, his one eye fixed on the chaos at the wall, his face hard as weathered stone. When he noticed Udorn's approach, his lip curled.

"What brings you before me?" Dulkin asked, crossing his arms. "We have no business to speak of."

Udorn halted before him, meeting his gaze without flinching. "I wronged you, Dulkin, aye. But hear me now. This is not about glory, it is about brothers. Every man who falls today is a thread cut from the cloth of our people. I would see us stand together, not broken and scattered. Whatever comes, I need you at my side. Not for me alone, but for all who call themselves Ubneri."

Dulkin's jaw tightened, the bitterness still sharp in his eye. Yet beneath it, something flickered; the memory of battles shared, of blood spilled shoulder to shoulder.

"Very well," he muttered. "But do not mistake me… I follow for the sake of brotherhood… not for you. If I fall today, let it be known I did so with my kinsmen, not as some castoff skulking in the rear."

Udorn laid a hand on his shoulder, the gesture firm. "That is all I ask."

With that, Dulkin fell into step beside them. The rift was not healed, but the bond was not broken, and in the shadow of Dellhaven's walls, that was enough. Warriors paused to glance their way as they pressed on, eyes narrowing as the shield-brothers moved as one: Udorn at their head, Thaul and Gaxas at his flanks, Dulkin now grimly beside them. It was not a warband, nor a retinue, but something harder to name… a knot of men bound by a fire that no chieftain's word could quench.

Step by step, they carved a path toward the rear, where Ragruk's booming voice still lashed across the host. Udorn's hand never left the haft of his axe. Whatever end awaited, it would be faced in the full sight of gods and men.

"Look at them!" Ragruk roared to the men gathered near. "The Southerners cower already! Each body at their gates is a stone broken from their wall! By nightfall, Dellhaven will be ours, and all Mot will sing of triumph!"

A handful of warriors cheered weakly, more out of fear than conviction. Udorn saw it plainly—the hollowness in their eyes, the doubt gnawing behind their clenched jaws. That was when he stepped forward, shield-brothers at his side, their presence cutting a sudden silence into the circle.

"Triumph?" Udorn thundered. "Open your eyes! Our brothers are not breaking the city's walls; they are breaking themselves upon them! Every scream you call victory is the death-rattle of men you swore to lead. Do you not hear it? Do you not see it? This is not glory… it is slaughter!"

The circle wavered, warriors shifting uneasily beneath the weight of his words. Some averted their gaze, others stared openly, their loyalty pulled taut between chief and kinsman. Ragruk's face darkened, his lips curling back to bare his teeth.

"Coward!" Ragruk spat, his voice cracking like a whip. "You speak of slaughter because you shrink from it! You would cower at the sight of blood, whimper like some milk-fed whelp while true warriors carve their names into eternity! Look at you, trembling before the wall, too craven to climb!"

Udorn stood unmoving, the weight of his axe steady in his hand. He knew the trap well enough. Ragruk's words were barbs meant to draw blood, to drive him into some rash fury before the eyes of the host. But Udorn was no whelp to be baited. His stillness was its own defiance. When he spoke at last, his voice cut low and steady, carrying farther than any roar.

"Trembling? No, Ragruk. I do not tremble. I watch. I see. And every man here knows what I see is truth. The walls will not break for your pride. They will break us instead."

Ragruk's beard bristled, his face a mask of rage as he shoved through the circle of men. Spittle flew with every word, his chest heaving like a bellows stoked to bursting.

"Lies!" he roared. "Poison from a serpent's tongue! You would break the spirit of our people because your own spirit is weak! You would have us slink back to our hovels, humbled by Southerners, remembered as beggars and cravens!"

He jabbed a thick finger toward Udorn, voice cracking with the strain of his fury. "You would damn us all to shame, just to spare your own skin! Better to die upon these walls in glory than crawl home in disgrace!"

Udorn's gaze scanned the circle, measuring the faces turned toward him. Some glared with Ragruk's fire, others watched in silence, their eyes clouded with doubt. He saw the strain in them; men weary from the march, bloodied from the walls, caught between pride and the pull of survival. It was not cowardice he read there, but the hunger of warriors who longed to return with spoils, not empty hands and broken bodies.

"Our raids were never meant for this," Udorn said. "We strike for wealth, for ships laden with plunder, not for the pleasure of corpses stacked at another man's gate. We are not equipped to batter down such walls, nor to bleed ourselves dry against them. This is folly, not glory."

A low murmur rippled through the host, faint at first, then spreading like fire on dry grass. Men lowered their spears, others casting glances back from the ladders where blood still rained down. One by one, they began to fall away from the wall—limping, dragging the wounded, or simply turning their backs on the slaughter. No order had been given, no horn had sounded, yet the retreat had begun all the same.

Ragruk's face twisted as he watched it unfold, his fury boiling into disbelief. His voice thundered like storm clouds, but for the first time, it did not carry as it once had.

Through the clamor, Thaul's voice rose, steady and unflinching. "The men see it, Ragruk. This is no path to glory. You drive them to death, and still you call it victory."

A hush fell over those nearest, the truth in his words impossible to deny. Before Ragruk could answer, a shadow moved at the edge of the circle. Joven Krenn strode past, his red beard catching the morning light, his great frame cutting silence into the air around him. He gave no word of greeting, no sign of fealty, only a long, measured look—first at Ragruk, whose fury burned unchecked, then at Udorn, who stood like stone among the storm.

For a heartbeat, it seemed as if he might speak, but instead, he turned aside, drifting from the press of men. Without haste, without concern, the Ravenking walked away from the slaughter, his broad shoulders vanishing into the haze of dust and blood.

Ragruk's eyes tracked Joven's retreat, and for the first time, his rage faltered. The murmurs pressed close, no longer whispers, but a tide he could not shout down. The ladders still clung to the city walls, but fewer men climbed them now, for too many had already turned back, and too many lay broken on the stones below.

His jaw worked furiously as if chewing the taste of ash. Then, with a violent sweep of his arm, he gave the signal. Horns moaned across the field, long and hollow, calling the warriors from the walls. The assault faltered, men peeling away in weary silence, leaving behind only the dead and the dying at the victorious fortification.

So it begins, Udorn thought, watching the raiders stream back from the walls. *Our men are splitting before my eyes. Every step we take from this field will carry the weight of that fracture, and sooner or later, it will break us. Ragruk's fury is not spent… it is only waiting. I have never stood in greater danger than I do now. Gods preserve me…*

The silence that followed the horns was thick, broken only by groans of the wounded. At last Ragruk's voice cut through, raw but unyielding.

"Enough for today," he growled. "We make camp. The city will fall—if not now, then soon."

The men obeyed, moving with the weary resignation of soldiers who knew the morrow would bleed them again.

Udorn's gaze drifted back to the walls. The defenders moved with grim efficiency, loosing arrows into the backs of the wounded who crawled for safety, casting stones down on those too slow to flee. From above, their cheers rolled like thunder, mocking the blood-soaked plain below. Banners rippled proudly in the salt wind, their colors bright against the pale stone, while the Ubneri dragged themselves from the killing ground in silence.

By midday, the horde had settled into the low ground beyond bowshot. No songs were raised, no voices lifted in boast. Tents sprouted like thorns, and the wounded were laid out in rows, their groans carried on the hot wind. Smoke curled from cookfires, though none could mistake it for comfort. It was not a camp of conquerors, but of men who waited for the next order to bleed.

Udorn sat among his brothers, his back against a splintered shield, the sounds of the camp droning like distant surf. Thaul busied himself with sharpening his axe, his brow furrowed, though he made no complaint. Gaxas gnawed at a strip of dried meat with the stubbornness of a man who would not let hunger see him beaten. Even Dulkin lingered close, his single eye dark and unreadable, though he made no move to turn away.

None spoke at first. The silence between them was heavy with the memory of that morning—the ladders toppling, the screams from the wall, the faces of men they would never see again. Udorn let it linger before he finally broke it.

"This day will be remembered," he said quietly. "Not for what we took, but for what we lost. Our people have been bloodied, and it is not the Southerners alone who cut us."

Thaul looked up from his work, his voice low. "Then tomorrow will bring worse, unless something changes."

Gaxas spat the last of the meat into the dust, his jaw working as though the taste soured him. "Changes? Aye, Thaul. The only change Ragruk knows is how to grind more bones beneath his heel. That lunatic will bleed us until nothing is left, then call it glory."

He thumped his fist against his knee, eyes burning. "I've seen chiefs mad with pride before, but never one so eager to spend his own kin like coin. All for the sin of surviving his foolish orders. If this is the path he leads, then it ends in ruin."

Dulkin shifted, his mouth half-open as if to loose some bitter retort. But instead, he closed it, his jaw tightening, and gave only a slow, reluctant nod. The fire in his one eye was not for Udorn alone now; it was for all that had been wasted at the foot of the city walls.

The four of them sat in grim accord, no further words needed. Each knew the truth: they had been marked for death, cast as fodder to sate Ragruk's pride. But worse than that, their people were paying the price. Every raid, every march, every drop of blood spilled was meant to bring back wealth and strength to their kin. Instead, they had won only graves and ash.

A shadow loomed at the edge of their circle. Joven Krenn stood there, his red beard catching what little light remained of the day. His axe was clean, untouched by the morning's blood, yet there was no mistaking the fire in his eyes. He had not joined the slaughter, but he had watched, and the weight of his judgment was plain. When he spoke, it was not with the bark of a warrior but with the calm weight of an old truth.

"Men are not stones to be hurled until the wall breaks. They are the flesh and spirit of a people, and once spent, they cannot be gathered again. Ragruk mistakes butchery for strength and pride for wisdom. That path ends only in ruin."

He stepped nearer, his gaze drifting from one to the other before settling on Udorn. "The wind shifts, and a fool does not raise his sail. I will not walk in folly any longer."

Udorn rose slowly to meet him, his eyes never leaving the Ravenking's. For a long moment, he said nothing, weighing the man who stood before him—brute in form, yet speaking with the weight of a sage. Then he inclined his head, the gesture solemn.

"Your words carry truth, Joven Krenn," he said. "We are bound not by the walls we break, but by the brothers who march beside us. If you would stand with us, know that we do not walk an easy road. But it is the only one worth treading."

The Ravenking's half-smile was unreadable, but he gave a slow nod, and in that small movement the circle felt stronger than it had a moment before. For a time, the only sound was the wind tugging at the canvas of the tents. Then, Dulkin stepped forward unexpectedly. He had listened in silence long enough, bitterness his shield, but the air had shifted; he felt it as keenly as the rest.

"What would you have us do, Udorn?" One-Eye said, his face awash with humility.

Udorn regarded him for a long moment, a feeling of pride welling within him. At last, he nodded, slow and deliberate.

"What comes next is patience," he said. "Ragruk still holds the fate of our people in his fist, and we would be fools to strike before the time is ripe. But make no mistake… the day will come when his grip falters, and when it does, we must be ready."

His gaze softened as it settled on Dulkin. "I am glad you stand with us now, brother. Whatever lies ahead, we will face it together."

Dulkin gave a sharp nod, the bitterness not gone, but bent into something sturdier. For the first time in many nights, the circle felt whole. Thaul rose to his feet, his voice steady but edged with iron.

"Then our patience has met its limit, I say. If we wait too long, there will be none left to lead. We must confront Ragruk before more of our people are fed to the slaughter."

Udorn turned his eyes to Joven. The Ravenking met his gaze without a word, then dipped his chin in a slow, deliberate nod. That single motion carried more weight than a hundred oaths.

The circle rose as one. Together, bound by a new and fragile accord, they moved through the camp toward the glow of Ragruk's bonfire. Night settled over the host, the shadows deepening, as though the gods themselves held their breath for what was to come.

They found Ragruk at the heart of his circle, a great fire snapping high into the night. Around him, his chosen men drank deep from brimming horns, greasy meat clutched in their fists. Laughter rose above the crackle of the flames, loud and jarring against the silence of the wounded that filled the camp beyond. Ragruk himself sat like a lord in triumph, his beard shining with fat and his eyes bright with drink, as if no blood had been spilled.

He noticed their approach at once. His grin widened, showing teeth, and he raised his horn in mocking salute.

"So," he rumbled, voice thick with mead, "the stoic, the scarred, the grumbler, and the Ravenking himself. Come at last to join me by the fire? Or do you bring me more sour words to spoil the meat?"

Udorn stepped into the firelight, his shadow stretching long across the trampled earth. He did not sit, nor take meat or drink, but met Ragruk's drunken grin with cold steel in his voice.

"You call this victory, yet the city stands unbroken. These walls are too vast to be starved, too strong to be battered down by ladders and stones. You cannot surround such a place, nor keep its lifeblood from flowing in. Every day we linger, supplies and reinforcements pour through unseen gates while our own strength wanes. This is not conquest, Ragruk—it is folly."

The laughter around the fire dulled, the crackle of the flames filling the silence that followed. For a moment, Ragruk only stared, then he threw back his head and roared with amusement, spraying mead onto his beard. The sound was harsh, jagged, full of mockery.

"Folly?" he barked. "You speak like some old fishwife, fretting at shadows. Do you think I sailed across leagues of sea and marched for miles with no thought for what lay ahead? You think me blind, Udorn? Ha!"

He slammed his horn down, splashing drink across the dirt. His eyes gleamed in the firelight, no longer dulled by mead but burning with cruel delight.

"Even now, fresh warriors from Mot close upon the southern gates, their axes eager for Southern blood. And from the sea, ships heavy with steel and fire bear down upon this harbor. While you prattle on about walls and supply lines, I have already set the jaws of the trap. This measly city is surrounded."

A murmur surged through those gathered, some eyes brightening with hope, others narrowing with suspicion. Udorn's lip curled, his voice cutting through the growing hum.

"Lies," he shot back. "You speak only to cover your shame. No ships prowl these waters, no host marches in the south. You waste lives and call it cunning."

Ragruk leaned forward, his grin wolfish. "Lies? No, you fool. I sent word before we struck; after the harbor bloodied us, I called for more. Did you think I would leave Mot's claws sheathed while we tore at these walls alone? Even now they march, even now their sails fill. You will see them with your own eyes, and then you will know who commands this war."

The circle held its breath, every man caught between the fire's glow and the weight of Ragruk's words. If reinforcements truly marched from Mot and sailed from the sea, then the jaws were already closing, and Ragruk's grip would tighten like iron on the horde. But if he lied, then they bled for nothing, and each day's delay dragged them closer to ruin.

Udorn felt the ground shift beneath him, as though the fate of their people teetered on a blade's edge. The mighty walls loomed, unbroken and cold, but the greater battle had already begun—not for stone or plunder, but for the very soul of the Ubneri.

So be it. The gods have decided my fate, but I will not go quietly into their ledger. Only I shall write my destiny, and I will carve it with fire!

SYLVIA X

WITH EACH PASSING DAY, SYLVIA'S ANTICIPATION GREW LIKE looming storm clouds. Although every mile brought them closer to their kinsmen on the Plainhold fields, it also compounded a growing dread in the back of her mind. Would they find the warband intact, or had the pursuing Betanthians wiped out their remnants?

A flutter took hold in her chest as the Hinterwood gave way to green, rolling fields thick with a palette of wildflowers. Gradually, the safety of mighty trees and craggy passes was left behind. Such a moment was not wasted on the accompanying Rhivothi, some having never seen the lands beyond their own.

Damien Dreadfire rode in a distant lead, separating himself from those who flocked to their cause. His pace was swift and deliberate, as if guided by the gods' hands. The significance of his estrangement was not wasted on Sylvia, for his days as a free man were numbered. It was as if he were studying the land and soaking in its peculiarities one final time.

As troubling as such thoughts were, Sylvia did well enough to drive them away. The warband's fate was at stake, and only a clear head focused on steel and blood would be of use. Others, however, were keen to sense Dreadfire's conspicuous state.

"What do you believe he is thinking?" Taug asked, riding beside her.

His long, chestnut hair was drawn into a single braid beneath his helmet. "Tell me true, Stormguard. You know him better than any man here."

"I would never profess to know what runs through Damien's mind," she replied. "If I were to hazard a guess, I would say he is communing with the gods and visualizing the battle to come."

It was a plausible answer, but speculation all the same. Kaldor Wolfbane drew up alongside them, clad in ringmail, steel gauntlets, and greaves. Atop his head was a steel nasal helmet crested with horsehair, his mighty shoulders draped with a massive wolf pelt.

"I pray it is not too late," Kaldor said," I shudder to think of our kinsmen and all they have lost… if they even remain at all."

"Speak not of such things," Taug commanded. "We are subject to a power far greater than ourselves. Evidence of the gods rides with us, and yet you doubt? I would expect such talk from a Nothanek!"

Kaldor clicked his tongue and let the matter die, but the men around them had not. A few riders jostled shoulders, old feuds flaring at nothing more than a look. It would not take much to turn pride into a brawl. Damien never glanced back. He rode like a man walking ahead of his own burial pyre, and somehow that steadied them more than any shouted order. Sylvia felt the line between panic and purpose thin to a blade's width.

A looming dust cloud drifted on a western breeze, its veil thick and unnatural. Sylvia's heart paused at the sight of it, for beyond a distant hill marched either friend or foe. Damien raised his hand and halted the riders, though Sylvia and Taug raced to join him.

"We are not alone," Dreadfire said, pointing forward. "Send forth your swiftest scouts. We must know the truth of what we face."

Taug stood in his saddle and waved an arm in a wide, arcing motion. A team of horsemen galloped forth, their arms and armor light and suited for skirmishing. Sylvia and her brethren sat breathless as the riders surged toward the unknown.

Gods... I pray to you. Let our people be safe...

It was close, far too close to the Hinterwood to be encountering a force on the move. Were they friends and allies, then perhaps their situation had grown more dire, and retreat was the only option. Were they foes, then truly, there would be no stopping Betanthia from marching all the way to the Forlorn Sea.

Time came to a slow, grinding halt as she watched the hilltop. Her hand gripped and twisted the leather-bound handle of her axe until it hurt. Perhaps soon enough, northern steel would drink once more on heathen blood.

After what seemed like an eternity, a sharp horn blast rippled across the plain. The riders waved their arms about before disappearing over the hill. To everyone's relief, the warband had been found. Sylvia roared in excitement, drawing her weapon and hoisting it proudly.

"Glory to the gods!" she exclaimed.

Shields hammered in answer. A hundred voices broke into a ragged hymn, then a thousand. Dust crested the ridge in a brown wave and poured down its face as if the hill itself were spilling men. Banners appeared first, torn and smoke-stained, then the riders and footmen beneath them—gaunt, dusty, but upright. Survivors. Their survivors.

Cheers erupted from the warband as their kinsmen crested over the hill in astonishing numbers. Sylvia beamed with pride, having succeeded in a mission most considered lunacy. At that moment, she remembered Einarr, his visions, and the road he had to travel to receive them. Shame and guilt quickly filled her heart, for she considered him a coward for abandoning their cause.

I apologize for ever doubting you. Truly, the gods share a special affinity for the Nothanek, and you were the vessel for their direction. I pray you are safe wherever you are.

Many throughout the warband appeared bedraggled, but all celebrated the arrival of reinforcements. Arik Akselson leaped onto his mount and charged toward them, hardly believing what his eyes were seeing.

"By the gods!" Arik said, too stunned to breathe. "How… how did you ever find us?"

"For a pious bunch, you seem naive to the truth, fisherman," Sylvia replied, smirking. "We have much to discuss and little time for it. Tell us, how fare our kinsmen?"

"Hungry," Arik said, still staring as if afraid the vision would vanish. "We've been at half rations for a fortnight. We burned the slow carts. The wounded are lashed in sleds. Scouts say Bethard outriders circle wide. If not for Jollkud hitting them crossways, we'd be bones on the plain by now."

Sylvia's gaze swept the weary host and caught a familiar banner snapping in the breeze—black silk, the scorpion stinger painted in crude crimson. Jollkud sat his horse beneath it, helm tucked beneath one arm, eyes burning with the defiance of a man not yet forgiven. His riders lingered close about him, lean and ash-stained, their armor mismatched but their spirit unbroken.

She felt her jaw tighten. This was the same man whose flight had nearly doomed them on the Plainhold, the coward who carried a stain no mead-hall tale could wash clean. Yet here he stood, alive, bloodied, and proud, as if daring the gods themselves to call him craven.

"You have done well, Akselson," Damien said, nodding. "I am relieved to hear Khorrtal is no more, and Jollkud has not abandoned our cause. Take your leave and tend to your kinsmen, for I have returned with a mighty host… and the sword of Ruin."

Sylvia glanced at the blade on Dreadfire's back. It glowed a deep crimson, grown ever brighter, for it seemed to sense the bloodshed soon to come. Many who gazed upon the mythical weapon diminished in fear, whispering and pointing in wonderment. Even the fiercest brutes were made humble, though some appeared unconvinced.

Word of Damien's arrival swept through the warband with the swiftness of falcons. Despite their weariness, the Northmen reveled in the return of their leader. Though it remained to be seen what effect it would have on the war effort, many felt hope return to their hearts.

The first laughter gave way to murmurs. Heads tipped toward Ruin like iron filings to a lodestone. Some men recoiled at the sight. Others spat into the grass. A gathering of Nothanek fell to their knees and began a low, urgent prayer. The joy that had burst from the ridge settled into a taut hum. Sylvia heard the word "cursed" hissed once, twice, and saw hands slip to weapon hilts without meaning to.

"Taug!" a Rhivothi warrior cried out. "What is the meaning of this? Why have you come now when all hope is lost? We are defeated, and now you would sacrifice the last of our strength for a hopeless cause?"

Taug's voice rumbled low, carrying easily across the gathered men. "Mind your tongue. You spit in the faces of every warrior still breathing. The gods have not abandoned us—we abandoned them with our weakness. Yet here we stand, with steel in our hands and kinsmen at our side. Do not shame yourself further."

The Rhivothi's lip curled, defiance burning in his eyes. He shoved past two of his fellows and pointed an accusing finger at Damien.

"It was the gods who left us on the Plainhold! Where was Azldyr when our sons coughed blood into the dust? Where was he when the Blackthorn trampled our dead? We bled, and Sjenohor watched!"

He jabbed his finger harder, his voice rising into a shout. "And now you bring a witch-blade into our camp and ask us to kneel? I'll curse any god that asks a man to love his own doom!"

Venom coursed through Sylvia's veins. She had conquered Morvhalgr and survived combat against Kuggvord himself. She felt her hands itch for the haft of her axe, to silence his blasphemy with steel. She stepped forward to challenge the belligerent Rhivothi but was stayed by Dreadfire's hand.

"Steel yourself and be silent," Damien cautioned the warrior. "I have seen beyond the living veil. I have witnessed horrors unfit for the sight of mortal men, things spoken in riddles by old men. You know not what has been sacrificed… or what has been endured. I will not be challenged by the likes of you."

"The likes of me?" the belligerent warrior scoffed. "I saw how you retreated from the battle. You should have stood and died as so many of my kinsmen did. Instead, you took flight on the back of a mare!"

With a fiery roar, Dreadfire drew Ruin, the greatsword groaning and crackling like burning firewood. The Rhivothi took up his shield and axe, scowling and spitting, then charged. Sylvia stood emotionless, knowing what terrible fate her sword brother had invited. Both men closed distance like beasts, sizing up each other.

Damien hoisted Ruin aloft, the blade steaming with otherworldly rage. The Rhivothi charged in, shield at the ready, axe cocked back and ready to strike. With a massive swing, Dreadfire brought the sword down cleanly through the Rhivothi's shield as if it were made of parchment.

Before the Rhivothi could realize what had happened, Ruin wheeled about once again, lurching and shifting into a hellish poleaxe. Its iron head glowed like magma; its jagged speartip shaking and smoking mere inches from the warrior's face. Never before could such hatred be seen and felt from an inanimate object. Knowing he had been bested, the Northman surrendered his arms and stared wide-eyed at Ruin.

"By right, your blood should be spilled for your impudence," Damien grunted before drawing Ruin back. The weapon shifted back into its familiar form. "What is your name, Rhivothi?"

"Hrodan, son of Fjorric."

"The gods have chosen you for this moment, Hrodan," Dreadfire said. "Will you take heed of this lesson? Or shall I send you to meet them?"

Wide-eyed and too stunned to speak, Hrodan stepped back a pace and nodded. Those who witnessed the exchange fell to their knees in disbelief, some mouthing silent prayers to the gods. Ruin's return was met not with revelry but instead with fear. Every doubt and every blasphemy against the divines was suddenly made real.

A band of dark clouds began manifesting overhead, churning and swirling against the northern skyline. With a guttural roar, they began creeping and slinking across the heavens, drawing ever closer. Slowly, they began coalescing above the warband, an ominous sign if there ever was.

"We must keep moving, Damien," Sylvia cautioned. "Every second we delay imperils us further."

"Which is why we will make pause and rest," Dreadfire said, scanning the area. "We must recover as much strength as possible, Stormguard, for battle will soon be upon us. Spare the tents, they will not be needed. This place is as good as any. Spread the men out and station cavalry on both flanks. Spears and pikes at the center. We will be ready."

Such orders seemed reckless, given the warband's weary state. It would have been better to continue putting distance between themselves and the pursuing Betanthians, she thought. Then again, running would only serve them for so long, for eventually, there would be nowhere left to run to.

"Agreed, Damien," Taug said.

The order spread quickly. Riders wheeled out to the flanks, posting in pairs along the ridges. Pikes were set into the hard earth, files straightened, shields stacked in neat rows. Fires burned low, enough for warmth but not higher. No tents. No songs. Only the shuffle of men settling to the ground, sharpening blades, and muttering prayers. Sylvia walked among them, offering what words she could, though she felt the same weight pressing on them all. There was no more running left.

Damien sat on a blanket of dry grass, then lay on his side. With Ruin sitting close by, he ate a heel of fresh bread, eyes fixed intently to the south. The fortress of clouds overhead brought cool winds, soothing the weary warband from the Plainhold's ferocity. They looked to be storm clouds, dark and foreboding, though they refused to part with a single drop of water.

The massive baggage train carrying the spoils of conquest and wounded men was brought to the rear. There seemed little point in defending it now, given the decisive battle soon to come. Trinkets they were, for the real treasure was the men and women gathered here, the last of the free north's strength.

Sylvia made for an ale cart, so thirsty it was anxiety-inducing. Although its contents were low, she was given a proper mug, for her Soul Name commanded reverence in any situation. As she gulped down the frothy beverage, she stole a moment to bask in the glory of companionship. Here they stood, Rhivothi, Nothanek, and Zylmacian alike—some unwitting allies, other sworn enemies, but all fighting for the same cause.

An elderly camp follower toddled through the assembled masses, leaning hard on a worn cane carved with runes. His brittle, white hair and gnarled beard danced in the breeze like cobwebs, a single, glassy eye staring accusingly. He pointed a gnarled finger, cursing and spitting.

"Repent!" he hissed. "Repent, you wicked dogs! Shame on those who have forsaken the gods. The arrogance of youth will avail you not!"

Countless dozens bore their shame openly and lowered their heads. It was easy to remain faithful during better times, Sylvia thought; the true test lay in adversity, when faith is affirmed or abandoned. So many, sadly, had chosen the latter. But not her. Not on the Plainhold fields, nor on Morvhalgr.

She pushed through the rows of warriors and nearly dropped her mug when two familiar figures came rushing toward her. Hilde and Ingryd Bjornsdottir—shieldmaidens she had not laid eyes on for what felt like a lifetime. For a heartbeat, she thought them phantoms, some trick of exhaustion, but then they were on her, laughter spilling as they seized her in a crushing embrace.

"Sylvia!" Hilde cried, squeezing the breath from her. "By the gods, we thought you dead a hundred times over!"

"And you still live!" Ingryd said, shaking her head in disbelief. "Stormguard herself, standing here before us. We prayed for this!"

Sylvia laughed through the sudden sting of tears. They clung to one another like sisters long parted, the noise of the camp drowned beneath the flood of joy. For that moment, there was no war, no blood, no Ruin… only the miracle of reunion.

"Come," Hilde said, her cyan eyes turning red with emotion. "The three of us stood together on this accursed plain once before. We shall stand together again when the horns sound."

Ingryd grinned, teeth flashing in the firelight. "Aye, and when the field is ours, we'll drink until the skalds forget their songs."

Sylvia barked a laugh, wiping her eyes with the back of her hand. "Then the gods had best grant us victory quickly. I'll not be denied a cup with you two when this is over."

They laughed again, loud and free, their voices mingling with the deeper roar of the warband around them. For that heartbeat, the weight of the Plainhold, the long marches, and even the cursed glow of Ruin seemed to fall away. These were her sisters, her kin, proof that the Hinterwood still had life worth fighting for.

Knowing time was short, Hilde and Ingryd broke away, eager for a meal and some well-earned rest. Sylvia stood grinning after them, heart hammering with renewed vigor. The gods had spared them all for this day, and she would not waste it.

Not far off, Damien prepared in silence. Piece by piece, the black plates swallowed him whole. The armor caught firelight and seemed to consume it, leaving only the smoldering gleam of his eyes. Ruin rested across his knees, restless as a chained beast. Sylvia's smile faltered as she watched, joy giving way to awe and unease.

Sylvia turned from Damien just as the ground began to tremble with hooves. A team of Nothanek riders came thundering in from the south, their faces turned pale like a northern winter.

"My lord! They are here! Betanthia has come!"

Dreadfire turned and gazed into Sylvia's eyes, an unspoken understanding between them. As he collected Ruin, she opened a leather belt pouch and retrieved Skeldr's Gift, the forest mushrooms inside. There was no time to perform the proper ritual associated with their use. Undoubtedly, the gods would understand her indiscretion. She stuffed a handful into her mouth, the taste sour yet sickeningly sweet.

"Sound the horns and form battle lines," Damien commanded, retrieving Ruin and signaling for a horse. "By the gods, we will make our stand and fight!

A chorus of shrill blasts rippled across the plain, stirring a frenzy within the warband. As Sylvia choked down the mushrooms, she saw Ruin's fuller erupt with crimson light, the blade seemingly aware of the slaughter yet to play out.

She took up axe and shield, then raced into position at the warband's center. Reinforcements from Rej Rhivoth flocked to Taug's banner on the left flank, their voices rising in chants of his name. The sound steadied Sylvia's pulse; the clans still stood united, even with doom bearing down on them.

Slowly, a forest of pikes and banners appeared in the distance, subtle at first, as if emerging from a morning fog. From over the horizon, Betanthia came, their numbers frightening and seemingly without end. Their battle line stretched for miles in either direction, flanked on both sides by thousands of heavy horsemen.

Such a sight could humble even the fiercest Rhivothi. Indeed, the warband stood silently and watched as their southern foes took to the field, the ground trembling beneath their march, dust rising like smoke from a burning plain.

A fiery rage began building within Sylvia, an anxious bloodlust as familiar as the weapons she held. Fear quickly evaporated like desert rain, replaced by the most profound hatred she had ever experienced.

I will avenge you, Marvath… or tonight we will dine together in Sjenohor!

Peals of thunder shook the Plainhold, the black clouds swirling overhead like a whirlwind. Perhaps Azldyr had made his presence known on the battlefield, for his appetite could never be sated.

Rabid cheers erupted throughout the left flank as Damien raced by on horseback, Ruin held aloft in one hand. The sight of him stoked a fire within the Northmen, laid dormant by the shame of defeat. But no longer. Sylvia grinned, then laughed, then smashed axe against shield and loosed a mighty howl.

"Dreadfire! Dreadfire! Dreadfire!"

Hundreds joined the warcry's chorus, then thousands. Even the humblest Nothanek saw their spirits lifted by such a sight. Damien continued his ride along the battle line, barking and shouting like a rabid beast. Once again, his black eyes burned with the Dread Fires of Borjifa, the eternal flame of hatred that could not be extinguished.

"Men of the free north!" he bellowed, silencing the warband. "You have bled on the Plainhold. You have buried fathers and sons in the cold earth. You have seen the gods turn their faces from you. But hear me now—they have not abandoned us! They have given us this day, this hour, this field, to prove we are not yet broken!"

He raised Ruin high, its crimson glow spilling like fire across their faces.

"Look upon the horde that comes against us. Betanthia thinks us scattered, beaten, ready to crawl into our graves. Today, we show them what it means to rouse the wrath of Kholdyr's chosen people! Today we repay blood with blood, and the ground itself will drink its fill!"

A roar shook the line, shields hammering, voices rising like thunder.

Damien's voice rolled above them still, cutting through the noise. "Stand fast, men of the North! Men of the West! Stand with me! For our dead, for our gods, watch us now from Sjenohor! We do not yield, and we do not fall!"

A ripple of weapons against shields rattled down the line like an avalanche. Faces painted with fear now hardened, jaws set, eyes burning with a promise of blood. They stood ready, free men to the last, braced for whatever hell marched against them.

The Betanthians continued their approach in eerie silence, a deep, synchronized crunching of steel armor pounding like drums. A forest of banners snapped and cracked in a churning wind, the eagle standard of House Bethard flying highest of all. It was every nightmare come true, though the sight of Ruin tempered the warband's fear.

Each meter they traversed seemed to become slower until Sylvia felt as if she were trapped in a lucid dream. Perhaps it was the mushrooms taking hold, she thought, or it was genuine terror in the face of certain death.

In a sudden flash, archers appeared from behind the fortress of Betanthian kite shields, their numbers well into the hundreds. They drew back their bows and loosed without hesitation, sending forth a dense swarm of arrows. In Sylvia's intoxicated state, she saw every projectile with incredible detail, down to the fine tips of their fletchings.

"Shield wall!" she screeched, bringing her thick Hinterwood spruce to bear.

Her cries were echoed throughout the battle line. In seconds, an impenetrable wall of painted shields was formed with little time to spare. Arrows rained down, thumping and thwapping against wood, earth, and flesh. Some were felled, though most remained unharmed. Peeking through the gaps between shields, Sylvia saw the Betanthians closing in ever quicker. Before she could speak, horn blasts rang out, followed by the beating of war drums.

Cavalry on both flanks drew back and away from the incoming salvo but remained close enough to counter-charge if necessary. The sight sent flashbacks of the crushing Blackthorn charge jolting through Sylvia's mind. She prayed their riders would not be caught unawares a second time.

From atop his horse, Damien barked commands for their archers to respond in kind. With arrows still raining down, Northern archers drew their bows and unleashed a volley of their own. It was difficult to see the results of their attack, but it did little to stop the encroaching Betanthians.

Both armies continued trading volleys at increasingly closer distances, neither content to charge. That was, until a nasally sounding horn shrieked like a wounded elk. Sylvia craned her head and saw the black scorpion banner of Jollkud surge forward from the right flank. The Zylmacian warchief had either succumbed to bloodlust or perhaps sought redemption for his cowardly retreat from the previous battle.

"Damned fool!" Sylvia said, breathless. "He's going to get himself killed and take all of us down as well!"

Thankfully, Jollkud's charge disrupted the Betanthian archers, who instinctively fled behind a protective wall of spears. If anything could be said about a Zylmacian, they were reckless and rabid, unafraid to throw themselves into any fire. The unexpected attack allowed just the opportunity to emerge from the shield wall and press the advantage.

With heavy drums beating, thousands of warriors on the right flank broke into a sprint, roaring and cursing, the earth thundering underfoot. Spears and pikes at their center were slow to advance, careful not to disrupt their formation too greatly. The left, comprised of Nothanek and some Rhivothi, remained disciplined, looking to their warchiefs before committing. At first, the wild attack appeared to be a blunder, but Damien was quick to sense an opportunity. He galloped over to Sylvia, Ruin pulsing with ravenous red light.

"These wildmen may have given us an opportunity," Damien said, pointing to the west. "We may be able to roll their line. I will send our best warriors to reinforce the right and drive forward. If we can shatter their flank, they will have to withdraw or commit reserves."

Sylvia nodded in sudden understanding. "By the gods, you're right! I will keep our men back to preserve our left, but we must commit our cavalry to the right! If they are flanked, then the battle is lost!"

Dreadfire stood in his saddle, surveying the battle line, then whistled for a messenger. As orders were exchanged, Sylvia turned to the Nothanek beside her. Some appeared confused, perhaps even afraid, for they were students of theology and not the sword.

"Steady, men, steady," she said reassuringly. "We will strike when the moment is right!"

Hopefully sooner than later, she thought. An overdose of forest mushrooms polluting her body had driven her to an insatiable bloodlust that could barely be controlled. Sylvia began grinding her teeth and growling like a beast, then bit the edge of her shield. It was all she could do to remain disciplined.

Give the order, Damien. Give the order, or I will cut their line to pieces myself!

Spears and pikes at the center met their Betanthian counterparts, a forest of twenty-foot timbers having at one another in the most vicious ways. Thus far, the haphazard battle formation appeared to be holding, though it was too early to know for certain.

Sylvia was soon overcome by an anxiety so great it could no longer be contained. The faces of those beside her appeared something out of a nightmare. Melted flesh and exposed bone provoked a murderous desperation within her. She muscled past the horrors surrounding her and stood outside the protective shield wall.

Screams and clattering steel rattled in her ears, the all-too-familiar symphony of death she so adored. She stole a moment and closed her eyes, basking in the blood-tinged air, arrows splashing down around her.

It was the most serene moment she had experienced in ages, being one with the shadow of death.

An arrow thumped into her shield, breaking her near-unbreakable trance. Sylvia glanced to the center and saw their pikes heavily engaged. Thankfully, the exchange appeared to be a stalemate. The deep right was holding, and thanks to Zylmacian ferocity, cracks in the Betanthian line began slowly emerging.

The opportunity seemed ripe for the taking. As soldiers shifted about to stop the Northern onslaught, she hoisted her one-handed axe high, screeching like a pit demon.

"CHARGE!"

Without knowing if the Nothanek gave pursuit, Sylvia Stormguard sprinted toward the enemy soldiers, thoughts of Sjenohor filling her mind. Undoubtedly, Marvath had prepared a place for her at Kholdyr's table and was beaming with pride at the sight of her fearlessness.

Do you see me, my dearest friend? May my death be as glorious as yours must have been.

With her shield raised and screaming, Sylvia collided with the Betanthian line. To her surprise, she was not alone. The Nothanek had found their courage, digging it from the depths of their pious souls.

A Southern armsman pushed back, then quickly thrust with his arming sword. The blade passed mere inches from Sylvia's face and served only to ignite the smoldering battle rage within her. She raised her axe and delivered a powerful downward swing, but a soldier's shield beside him absorbed the blow. Still, she continued hacking and chopping at anything in front of her in a fit of bloodthirst.

Tears of anxiety and anger coursed down her cheeks, a symptom of the mushroom's indomitable grip. But their magical properties afforded her unexpected clarity of sight. An opening appeared in the enemy shield wall, the face of a smooth-cheeked soldier presenting itself. Sylvia raised her axe and brought it down with crushing force, her biceps burning as if prodded by hot pokers.

The axe planted itself in the hapless lad's face, shattering his jaw into a mess of broken bone and mangled flesh. In an instant, he fell from sight and was trampled underfoot by the ranks behind him. One man lay dead, but it was but a drop in the ocean of what Betanthia had mustered.

Each strike felt more and more like a dream; her axe blows appeared as little more than colorful blurs against a backdrop of chaos. Even the screams of battle were little more than background noise, for all Sylvia could hear was the pounding of her heart and fluttering of her breath. In that terrible, bloody moment, only the vastness of the universe remained. It was as if she were watching the battle from the heavens, disconnected from the butcher's work playing out around her.

A deep crack of thunder shook Sylvia from her mystical trance state. The clouds overhead had turned nearly black as pitch and swelled like chaotic ocean tides. Perhaps Alzdyr was indeed watching and had grown ravenous in the face of such wanton slaughter. Another crash soon followed, though this one was of flesh and steel. Northern cavalry clashed with their Southern counterparts on the right flank. Indeed, the Betanthians had attempted to overturn the powerful Zylmacian assault, but thankfully, their riders had countered the charge.

Horse and rider fought and died in frightening numbers, but the warband's flank held steady. Damien was nowhere to be found, a troubling development if there ever was one. With fatigue setting in, Sylvia withdrew from the front line and was quickly replaced by a Rhivothi brute twice her size.

Gasping and fighting for fresh air, she trudged away from the fighting to locate Dreadfire. The clash of steel dulled behind her, swallowed by the ringing in her ears. She stumbled past the wounded crawling through churned earth, past corpses already stiffening in pools of blood, her shield dragging at her side. Every breath cut her lungs like glass.

She pressed on, forcing her eyes through the haze of dust and smoke. Horns rang out from the ridges, shouts carried across the field; orders, pleas, death-cries, all one. And there, beyond the heaving line, she saw him: Dreadfire, standing apart as if the battle had carved a circle around him.

"Damien!" she huffed, the mushroom's effects waning. "What are your orders? I fear the tide will soon be turning!"

He said nothing at first, instead scanning the breadth of their formation. Despite reinforcements, the warband was still perilously outnumbered. Spears bristled thin where whole cohorts should have stood, and every gap in the line gaped like a wound waiting to be struck. Yet the men held their ground, eyes fixed on him as if sheer will could turn despair into strength.

"Your concerns are well-founded, Stormguard. Jollkud's advance is stalling, and our cavalry cannot stand against their knights for long. There is only one thing left to do."

With a grunt, Dreadfire dismounted and opened one of his saddle bags. From within, he retrieved the ossuary of Kuggvord, its ominous energy causing his horse to rear and whinny. Yet again, the heavens roared with thunder, a sharp, dry wind whipping up dust clouds. Sylvia grew wide-eyed as the veins in Damien's forearms turned black, his skin a shade of reddish-purple.

"Sound the horns and withdraw," Dreadfire said, striding toward the enemy. "And harden your spirit, Stormguard. The gods will soon do battle."

ALEKSIUS V

Tiberion was waiting at first light. The Senate's man stood with hands folded at his clasp, black robes drawn neat, the silver catching the dim sun. Behind him, the drill ground lay scarred with boot marks and scuffs where shields had slammed through half the night.

The yard still carried echoes of the night before. Trampled dust hung in the air, stirred by the faintest breeze. Splintered shafts lay in a heap by the wall, their broken tips sharp as teeth. The scent of sweat and oil clung to the stones, heavy as incense in a temple. A shield forgotten in haste leaned against the rail, its rim dented where a spearhead had struck true.

Aleksius knew what Tiberion saw: disorder, waste, the remnants of toil that did not pass through the Senate's ledgers. To him, though, it was proof that Droethien steel still had edge enough to bite.

"Sire," Tiberion said. "You held the yards after dark."

Aleksius came down from the keep's steps without slowing. "I did."

"That was not sanctioned." The words were even, almost gentle. "The drill lists route through my office, so rations and pay are aligned. You moved cadres outside of the schedule. You spent grain and oil without writ."

The words cut sharper than they were meant, and Aleksius felt his brow furrow. To be spoken to as though he were some steward tallying bushels rather than the Governor of Naxonnos set his blood alight. He commanded a city older than the Senate's current dynasty, a people who had bled in wars before Larssa ever raised its marble walls, and yet here stood a clerk in fine robes daring to measure his authority in barrels and writs.

"I spent sweat," Aleksius said, closing the gap between them. "Not grain. Not oil. Sweat. And I'll spend it again if it keeps these walls from falling."

Tiberion's pale eyes stared back, unblinking. "You made a point. The Senate prefers order to points. If you have concerns, submit them and we shall—"

"If *you* have concerns," Aleksius said, voice flattening, "take them to Larssa."

For a heartbeat, the mask slipped. Tiberion's lips pressed thin, his eyes narrowing in a flicker of surprise that he smothered almost as quickly. He was not accustomed to defiance, least of all from Aleksius— the cautious Governor he had long dismissed as pliable, a man to be managed rather than challenged. To be rebuked so bluntly unsettled him, and the smallest crack showed through the lacquer of composure.

When he spoke again, his tone was still even, but rigid now, clipped at the edges. "Naxonnos survives because the Senate measures what others forget: grain, steel, temper. You risk that balance with every whim."

Aleksius let the words wash over him, heat rising in his chest. Whim. That was the word the Senate's hound had chosen, as though drilling men for war was some indulgence of pride. Perhaps there were nefarious dealings at work, he thought, for Tiberion seemed all too comfortable with the situation.

"These are my people, he said, frowning. "My walls. My dead to count if we fall. You want Larssa's order? Go back and fetch it. Until then, I will take the counsel of men who have seen blood on more than just parchment. Leave me."

Tiberion did not flinch, though his jaw worked once before the words came. When they did, they were cool and clipped, every syllable weighed like a coin. "Then pray, Sire, that your defiance wins you more than ashes. The Senate's memory is long, and it does not forgive those who squander what belongs to all of Droethia."

He adjusted his clasp with deliberate precision, as though restoring balance to a thing disturbed, and turned without bowing. Aleksius remained in the yard until the pattering of footsteps faded. His hands curled into fists at his sides, the taste of iron hot on his tongue. When at last he turned, it was not toward the drill ground but toward the keep.

The corridors swallowed him in cool stone, torchlight glimmering faintly along its walls. In his chambers, a flagon already stood waiting, half-full from the night before. He poured into a bronze cup, the wine thick and red as blood, and drank deep until the burn reached his chest.

He sat in a high-backed chair near the window, watching as morning crept across the city rooftops. The exchange replayed in his mind, every word a thorn. Tiberion had spoken as though Aleksius were a child, yet it was Aleksius who would answer to his people when the horns of war sounded. He wondered if Kyra would hear of the quarrel in Larssa, and whether she would see it as courage or folly.

Another swallow, another burn. For the first time in years, he felt less like a Governor in gilded halls and more like a soldier, preparing for a battle he could not yet see.

I am fighting for us, my love. For all of us...

He set the cup down with a dull thud and rose, restless. The chamber felt too small, the walls pressing in with the weight of old stone and older ghosts. He paced to the southern window, gazing out over the tiled roofs and market streets, already stirring with carts and cries of vendors. From the western arch, he looked down upon the drill yards, scarred earth still bearing the marks of last night's toil.

At last, he came to the northern window, overlooking a road threading out from the hills. Beyond the outer wall, meager farm fields stretched pale under morning haze, the furrows drawn like scars in the earth. There was a lone rider, a dark speck against the road, driving hard toward the gates. Aleksius's breath stilled. No rider came at such speed bearing good news.

He gripped the sill, eyes narrowing as the figure drew nearer, the hoofbeats faint yet audible. Whatever tidings rode in, he knew they would weigh heavier than any quarrel with the Senate's man.

Moments later, the courtyard below rang with commotion. Aleksius left the window and strode down through the keep, the echo of his boots chasing him into the yard. The rider was already there, lurching from the saddle, face gray with dust and streaked with sweat. He dropped to one knee, chest heaving as if it might split.

"Sire," he gasped, bowing so low his brow touched the stones. "From the border… smoke! A village near the Furrowed Stones… burned!"

Aleksius's stomach tightened. He stepped forward, looming over the man. "Who is responsible for this?"

The scout shook his head, eyes wide. "I know not, Sire. I saw only fire… and bodies. I did not linger to count them all."

The words struck like hammer blows, each one driving deeper into the dread that had stalked Aleksius for weeks. This was the shape of his nightmare made flesh—villages burning on the border, his people cut down while councilors argued and the Senate measured grain.

He had told himself caution would hold the storm at bay, that reason would guard Naxonnos longer than steel, but now the fire had come all the same. Smoke on the horizon meant more than death; it meant the war had already crossed his threshold. He thought of Kyra's last look as the wagons rolled west, of Magia's tears, of Sakis vowing to watch over his sister. What promise could he keep them now, if Droethien soil smoldered beneath foreign hooves?

Aleksius's hands clenched until they ached. He drew a long breath through his nose, steadying the anger that threatened to break loose in front of the men. The scout's words were too little, too vague, and yet they painted a picture he had dreaded all of his life.

"Guard!" His voice thundered across the courtyard. A sentry snapped to attention, spear butt striking stone. "Summon the Loxarchon. At once!"

The soldier saluted with his fist to his chest and hurried off through the archway. Aleksius kept his eyes on the rider before him, the man still kneeling, sweat dripping from his chin to the dirt.

"Drink," Aleksius said curtly. "You will tell it again when Tasos arrives. Every detail, no matter how small."

The scout bobbed his head, still gasping, and took a waterskin thrust into his hands.

My worst fears come true. I knew this day would come. I knew it in my bones.

Aleksius turned away, pacing the edge of the yard while the scout drank. His mind leapt unbidden to the borderlands, tracing the rivers and gullies, the barren fields clinging to stony soil. He could see the villages in memory, scattered and stubborn, each one a lantern at the edge of Droethia's reach. If one had been snuffed out, how many more would follow before the Senate agreed to lift a finger?

The Furrowed Stones. He had ridden there once in youth, when his father still held the governor's seat. He remembered the stream, the creak of the mill wheel, the way the rock formations leaned together like broken teeth. But now, the nameless village was gone, erased from the world in the blink of an eye.

Boots struck hard against stone. Tasos entered the yard, cloak thrown over one shoulder, helm in the crook of his arm. His eyes scanned the scene, falling at once on the scout.

"What is the meaning of this?" Tasos said in a near whisper.

Aleksius turned toward him, face carved from stone. "Smoke rises on our border. A village near the Furrowed Stones has been burned to the ground. This man saw it."

Tasos's gaze slid to the scout, who shifted uneasily under the weight of it. The Loxarchon stepped closer, the scarred lines in his face deepening as he crouched before the kneeling soldier.

"Tell it," he demanded. "Everything you remember. Do not spare detail, not a single one. I must know the truth of what you have seen!"

The scout licked cracked lips, water dripping from his chin as he tried to find his voice. "The village... huts, thatch and stone. A mill wheel on the stream. When I crested the ridge, the roofs were already burning. The square was full of bodies. Some... some were children..."

Tasos rose slowly, every motion deliberate, and met Aleksius's gaze. The silence between them carried more weight than words. This was not rumor. This was war.

Aleksius felt fire rise in him, hotter than any wine he had swallowed that morning. Rage pressed against his ribs, demanding release against the faceless butchers who had lit this spark, against the councilors who prattled while his people bled, against the Senate that measured lives in ledgers. His tongue was already shaping orders when a disturbance echoed through the gate tunnel once more.

The thunder of hooves returned before Aleksius could speak, louder this time, urgent as a drumbeat. Another rider tore through the gate, horse lathered with sweat, eyes rolling white. Slumped against the man's back was a boy, more dragged than carried, his small hands clutching at the soldier's belt. His skin was gray with ash, his hair matted, his face hollow with shock.

The rider hauled the reins hard, his horse skidding to a halt in a spray of dust. He slid from the saddle, steadying the boy with one arm before bowing low.

"Sire," he called, voice hoarse from the ride, "I found him stumbling on the border road!"

Aleksius crossed the yard in three strides. The boy's legs buckled as soon as his feet touched stone, and Aleksius caught him by the shoulders, feeling the tremor that ran through every fragile bone. He was light as a bundle of reeds, his clothes scorched and stiff with soot.

"Water," Aleksius barked. A servant rushed with a skin, pressing it into the boy's shaking hands. He drank greedily, spilling half of it down his chin, gasping between gulps.

Aleksius knelt so his gaze was level with the child's. "You are safe now," he said. "Tell me your name."

The boy swallowed hard. "Ren."

"Ren," Aleksius repeated softly, steadying him with a hand. "You did well to reach us. Now tell me what you saw."

Ren's lips trembled as he tried to speak. For a moment, only a rasp came out, his throat raw from smoke. Aleksius waited, hand firm on the boy's shoulder, giving him the steadiness he lacked.

"They… they came all at once," Ren whispered. "Riders. Black cloaks. I saw a banner…" His eyes darted wildly, as if searching the yard for it. "Black… a banner of black…"

Tasos drew in a sharp breath beside Aleksius, but the Governor kept his focus on the boy. "How many?" he asked, his voice quiet but iron-edged.

Ren shook his head. "I know not. They split in the square. Some broke down the doors, some set fire. My mother…" His voice cracked, and the rest was lost in a shuddering breath.

Aleksius tightened his hand on the boy's shoulder. "You need not finish that part. I know enough."

The child's wide eyes brimmed with tears, and there was no doubt in them, no hesitation. Whatever else he saw had blurred in smoke and panic, but the banner he had seen remained burned into his mind.

The boy's words fueled the fire in Aleksius's soul so fiercely that no Senate decree could quench it. Blackthorn, here, on Droethien soil, cutting down innocents while Larssa counted ledgers and nobles squabbled over harvests. The thought seared through him, burning away doubt, burning away caution. He would not be remembered as the man who let his people die while he measured grain.

"Bring my armor and horse," Aleksius commanded. "Summon fifty riders with bow, spear, and sword. We ride under arms, and we ride now."

Tasos stepped forward without hesitation, helm tucked beneath his arm, the old scars on his face deepened by the morning light. "Then I ride with you, Sire. The men will stand straighter with you at their head."

"See it done." Aleksius met his eyes and gave a single sharp nod.

The Loxarchon was already moving, his barked orders cracking through the courtyard, scattering servants and guards into motion. Armor was hauled from the racks, saddles thrown across restless horses, quivers counted and filled.

"Bring out the old standard," he commanded, turning sharply to a nearby herald. "The hour is upon us."

The man blinked. "Sire… it has not flown in years!"

"Then it will fly today," Aleksius snapped. "Raise the lion. Let all who see us know Droethia does not cower behind walls."

A hush rippled through the yard as the banner was unfurled. The white fabric was heavy, its threads darkened by age, but the sigil still blazed—a lion rampant, mane streaming, claws outstretched as though to rend the very sky. When the wind caught it, the beast seemed to leap alive, its golden form defiant against the morning haze.

The men whooped, shields thumping in rhythm, their voices rising until the yard thundered with renewed spirit. For a moment, the clamor felt like a heartbeat, one body answering the lion's roar.

Alexius donned his full complement of armor for the first time in ages. He swung into the saddle, the weight of steel settling across his shoulders like a second skin. He guided his horse toward the boy, who sat awkwardly before a rider, reins clutched too tightly in small hands.

"You will show us the way, Ren," he said. The boy nodded quickly, eyes wide but steady. "You must show us where they went."

Tasos raised his helm high, voice booming like thunder. "Form up! Lances to the fore, bows to the rear!"

The lines tightened with a clatter of steel and leather. At Aleksius's signal, the gates groaned open, spilling them onto the road. Fifty riders thundered forth, the standard snapping above them, dust billowing in their wake.

Aleksius did not look back. The city's towers fell behind them, and only the horizon lay ahead—hills, smoke, and the promise of blood. The company drove their mounts hard, hooves drumming a steady thunder as they pressed north. Dust clouds rose in their wake, clinging to armor and cloak until each dulled to the same ashen hue. They paused only to water the horses, to gnaw at hard bread and dried meat, to let the boy rest his head against the soldier who bore him.

Aleksius felt each mile in his bones, though he gave no sign of weariness. He rode at the fore beside Tasos, his eyes never leaving the horizon. Time was the enemy now, as much as the cloaked horsemen who had left fire in their wake.

By the second night, their mounts steamed with exhaustion, flanks streaked white. They made camp by a stream, men slumping to the ground with shields for pillows. Aleksius sat apart, the boy curled near a fire, already drifting into shallow, broken sleep. He drank sparingly from his waterskin, eyes fixed on the smudge of smoke that still lingered faintly on the distant sky. Two days, and still it marked the border like a wound that would not close.

At dawn, they rode again, the sun a red coin burning in the haze.

The air thickened with the stink of ash the nearer they came, until even the horses tossed their heads, uneasy with what they scented on the wind. By midmorning, the road dipped into a shallow vale, and there the smoke lay heavy. It clung low over the fields, acrid and sour, stinging eyes and throat alike.

What met them was no village, but a husk. Roof beams jutted like ribs from heaps of ash. Stone walls stood blackened, their mortar split by heat. The mill wheel groaned as it turned, half its paddles charred, creaking endlessly over a stream gone dark with soot.

Aleksius reined in, the lion banner rippling above him in a dead wind. He swung down from the saddle, boots crunching in cinders that still smoked faintly. The silence was worse than the sight—no voices, no cries, only the crackle of ruin and a distant whimper of a single starving dog.

Gods be good. My worst nightmare has indeed come true…

The men dismounted one by one, their armor clinking hollowly in the empty square. Tasos came to his side and removed his helm slowly, his scarred face grim but set. Aleksius did not speak at once. He let the horror fill him, sear itself into memory, so that no councilor, no senator, could ever again tell him the danger was not real.

"Where did they go, boy?" Tasos barked, wrapping his fingers around Ren's soiled tunic. "Tell me!"

Ren flinched under Tasos's grip, his soot-streaked face twisting. He lifted a trembling hand and pointed toward the jagged hills rising beyond the fields.

"There," he whispered, voice raw. "They rode that way. Into the stones."

Aleksius moved past them, his boots carrying him to the bodies that lay scattered throughout the square. Some were sprawled where they had fallen, others huddled together in a final embrace. A woman's arm still reached across the charred remains of a child, bone and ash fused as one. Aleksius knelt, lowering his head, the weight of their silence pressing into him like earth into a grave. He touched two fingers to his brow, a soldier's salute, and rose again with fire in his chest.

"Mount up," he said, voice low but fury-bound. His gaze flicked to the lion banner snapping above the ruin, bright even through the haze. "Furl the standard. Let no Blackthorn see who rides against them until the moment demands it."

The herald lowered his staff at once, rolling the great cloth tight against the pole. The beast vanished into folds of white and gold, its roar silenced for now. Fifty riders swung back into their saddles, dust and ash rising as they turned toward the hills Ren had shown.

Aleksius set his heels to his horse, and the column moved as one, steel and leather groaning in rhythm. The village smoldered behind them, a wound in the earth, while ahead the hills waited, jagged and silent, like teeth ready to close. In his heart, he carried the weight of the dead, the eyes of the boy, and the lion's roar still echoing in his blood. War had found Droethia, and now he meant to meet it head-on.

TITAN XI

T YLAR CROUCHED BESIDE THE KING'S BANNER, SHOULDERS TIGHT, jaw grinding. He looked every bit the beast they named him, a wolf straining at the chain. Beyond, the field seethed with bodies as Betanthian lines clashed once more with the northern horde. Superior numbers meant little; the savages threw themselves at steel with a ferocity that made mockery of discipline. They had not learned their lesson.

"They've charged again, my prince," Lord Kenfield said, disbelief thick in his voice.

Tylar's gaze locked on the Zylmacians tearing into the Betanthian flank. The sight of their tattooed scalps, gleaming with sweat and blood, sent a familiar fire through his veins. No matter how many they cut down, more always rose screaming from the earth.

"They are spent," Lord Vakaro said flatly. "Their strength will die before ours does."

A prudent man might have found comfort in the Commandant's calm. Tylar only bristled. Better to put a blade in Ridley now and cut out the rot before it spread. But no order had been given, and until it was, he held his hand.

"Do not underestimate them," he growled. "Rabid dogs fight hardest when cornered. The only way to stop them is to kill every last one."

Ridley's eyes rolled skyward, his disdain as sour as old wine. The gesture nearly drew Tylar's hand to the knife at his belt. One thrust under that sagging chin, and Gareth's greatest danger would be ended.

Why Gareth insisted on dancing around the matter gnawed at Tylar like rust in steel. He was heir to Westwind Citadel—the men would follow him whether or not Ridley Vakaro still drew breath. A knife between the ribs here, on the field, and the problem would vanish. Vakaro's lickspittles would fall in line quickly enough.

But it was not Tylar's hand to act. The gallows had nearly claimed him once; Gareth had stayed the rope. Loyalty demanded obedience, and obedience demanded restraint. He flexed his fingers on the hilt, then forced them away. If Gareth were to be king, Tylar would serve as his fist, not his shadowed dagger.

"I will not spend good men needlessly," Gareth said, his voice calm but edged with command. "This is not about the glory of a field. It is about the war. If our losses climb too high, I will break engagement."

Tylar inclined his head. The Prince spoke like a ruler already, hardened by necessity. Nearly fifty years of blood had taught Tylar that no man's spirit endured without suffering. Better Gareth be tested now than broken later.

"True words, Your Highness," Conrak cut in, pointing with his gauntleted hand. "Look there—their maneuver is plain. If we swing against their left, we'll collapse under their weight. We must bolster our own left and grind them down where they stand."

Insufferable though he was, the Sacrithon was right. Tylar would rather cut his own throat than admit it aloud; Conrak's pride was swollen enough without fuel.

Together, the prince's guard watched as the clash thickened. The Zylmacians surged forward in their hundreds, bald heads gleaming like skulls in the firelight, pressing deep into Betanthian ranks. Reserves slammed into place to hold the line, plugging gaps with shield and spear. But attrition was a cruel master, for it bled both victor and vanquished alike.

Northern cavalry thundered into the fray on the left, only to be met head-on by the Blackthorn Knights. Horse crashed against horse in a storm of steel, the shock of impact rolling across the field like thunder. Lances splintered, breastplates crumpled, and men were crushed beneath churning hooves. Screams of rider and beast alike split the air as blood sprayed and soaked into the churned mud. For every savage thrown down, another clawed his way up the corpses to strike anew. The ground itself seemed to quake beneath the fury of their clash.

Yet on the enemy's right flank, silence reigned. Standards trembled in the wind, but the warriors beneath them stood locked in disciplined ranks, shields braced, spears leveled. They did not advance, did not so much as shout. They waited. Watching. Their stillness was almost worse than the slaughter unfolding beside them, as if the butchery on the left were nothing more than an offering to soften Betanthia's heart.

"Why do they sit idle on the right?" Lord Kenfield demanded, pointing with his gauntleted hand. "Have they lost their nerve?"

"No, my lord," Conrak said flatly, eyes narrowing. "They hold while the left collapses. Look."

Sure enough, the Betanthian line groaned under the savage press. Shields bowed and shattered, pikes snapped like kindling, and men were driven back step by bloody step. Standards tottered and fell, their bearers cut down in the crush. What had been a line was fast becoming a wound, the Northmen driving into it like knives.

"Titan," Prince Gareth said sharply, wheeling his horse. "The left buckles. You will go. Hold the line. Drive them back. Your presence will give the men heart again."

Any reason to kill Northmen was reason enough. Tylar kicked his horse forward, iron flashing in the sun. The beast surged into a gallop, and he welcomed the rush of the charge, the promise of slaughter. But another set of hooves drummed close behind. He glanced back, and his lip curled. Conrak rode in pursuit, lance leveled, eager to share in the glory.

"The fuck are you doing?" Tylar bellowed. "This is my task, mine alone! You're meant to keep the Prince safe!"

"He's safe enough with Sir Edmund at his side," Conrak replied, his grin as insufferable as ever. "Besides, I can't have you taking all the glory. I'm overdue for some of it myself."

Arguing with that arrogant wretch was like wrestling a pig in mud—pointless and filthy. Tylar spat to the side, rolled his eyes, and drove onward. He flung himself from the saddle just short of the contact line, drawing steel as his boots struck earth. Sword and shield in hand, he shoved through the press of battered infantry, their faces alight with disbelief. The purple cloak. The scars. The giant himself. Titan had come.

"Out of my way!" he roared. "Stand firm or get trampled! I'll teach you sorry bastards what a real fight looks like!"

Even the Zylmacians faltered. Their charge slowed, eyes widening as the colossus loomed before them, his blade gleaming like judgment itself. Whispers passed in their harsh tongue, but fear was fear in any language. For one heartbeat, the horde wavered.

"Tylar tilted his head, sneering. "Remember me? I was the one who split your kin on Morden's walls. The shadow that stalked your march. Do you remember me now, you bald-headed fucks?"

He swung, a vicious slash that blurred in the dying light. One Zylmacian tried to duck aside, but was too slow. Tylar's blade carved him from shoulder to hip, spraying gore across his fellows. The corpse collapsed twitching at their feet, and the Titan bared his teeth in a savage grin.

With a mighty bellow, Tylar wrenched his blade free from a Northman's collarbone, crimson running from point to crossguard.

Another savage lunged, axe raised high. Tylar stepped in close and drove his sword straight through the man's eye, steel crunching through bone into brain. The corpse sagged on his blade before he ripped it free with a snarl.

The sight stirred the Betanthian line. Finding courage in the Titan's fury, infantrymen surged forward, voices raw with curses and war cries. Step by bloody step they pressed, their boots sinking in earth sodden with gore. Not even the fiercest Zylmacian berserkers could break through where Tylar stood. The left began to steady, the tide grinding slowly back.

"Push, you fucking cowards!" he roared. "Push!"

"That's the spirit, Bradshaw!" Conrak cackled nearby, cleaving down another half-naked brute.

The press broke at last. The horde faltered, then gave ground, stumbling back over their own dead. Retreat was no stranger to war, Tylar knew—men withdrew, rallied, then came again, each clash bleeding both sides thinner.

The respite was brief. A whistling filled the air, then the storm struck. Arrows hissed down in sheets, rattling like hail on iron. Tylar lifted his shield, oak planks thrumming and shuddering as shafts hammered deep. Protected by steel and plate, he stood fast, but not all shared his fortune.

Men screamed as arrows found soft flesh. Dozens fell, some thrashing on the ground, clawing at the shafts jutting from their ribs. Bodkin heads punched clean through mail, snapping bones and spilling blood. The cries rose in chorus, sharp and ragged. Tylar ground his teeth, unmoved. Such was life on the field.

"Hold steady!" Conrak barked, raising his voice above the carnage. "They'll be on us again soon. Steady!"

Cavalry broke from the fighting on the far left, their clash ending without a decision. The Blackthorn, ironclad and brutal, had met their match in Northern horsemen who fought with the same ferocity as their kin on foot. Riders fell on both sides, some shot from the saddle by Zylmacian horse archers, the same carrion fiends who had harassed them for days. For a heartbeat, the field exhaled—a brief reprieve.

"Bring me ale!" Titan bellowed, voice carrying far and wide. "I'll skin a man for a pint!"

Camp followers darted forward, some dragging the wounded back, others carrying skins of water and ale to the parched line. A boy no older than sixteen rushed up with one held high. Tylar shoved past a pair of infantrymen, snatched it from the boy's hands, and drank until half of it was gone. Foam dribbled down his chin. He gasped, then flung the rest aside.

"Steel yourself, Bradshaw," Conrak warned, his grin a blade's edge. "The day isn't done. No sense rushing to your grave."

Tylar spat, already searching for his next kill. He expected another push; the rhythm of battle never left him guessing long. But the barbarians did not advance. They pulled back instead, their mass shifting like a tide in retreat. Then the sky changed. Clouds boiled and thickened, black walls swirling overhead until the day dimmed to near twilight. Lightning danced soundlessly in the churn, a storm born without wind.

From the enemy's center, a figure emerged. Taller than any man had right to be, clad in black plate that drank the light. In his hands, he held a square container, and at his hip, a greatsword pulsed with an eerie red glow, as though it drew breath. Tylar felt the hairs on his neck rise. His fingers tightened on the hilt of his sword.

"What the... fuck..." Tylar whispered.

He shoved past the soldiers at his side, Conrak dogging his heels. Were it not for the horde massed across the plain, Tylar might have hurled himself at Damien then and there. Yet something in the warlord's form gave him pause. His black eyes had sunk to cavernous pits, and his hands had darkened to a sickly red-purple, marked like bruised fruit.

"Azldyr!" Dreadfire bellowed, raising the box toward the storm. "Cthenir! Unleash your torment upon the unbelievers! Accept their flesh as a sacrifice. Feast—FEAST!"

The lid came free, and the sky answered. Clouds flared with blood-red light, as if the heavens had been cut open. A thunderclap hammered Tylar's chest, followed by a bolt of black lightning that split the bleeding sky. Damien drew his cursed sword, kissed the hilt, whispered words none could hear, and with a howl drove the steel down into the vessel.

The earth convulsed as a pillar of fire speared upward, the clouds whirling into a cyclone around it. Warm droplets spattered his faceplate—blood, raining from the heavens. Tylar froze as a long, skeletal arm clawed up from the vessel, its fingers jagged hooks scraping at the air.

Then it came. A horror of bone and rotted flesh wrenched itself free, shrieking with the voices of a thousand tortured souls. It rose higher and higher until it towered nearly twenty feet, its form writhing, its maw gaping wide enough to swallow men whole.

Tylar's mind reeled. For a heartbeat, he prayed it was an illusion, some trick of smoke and terror. But the stench of decay filled his lungs, and the ground shook beneath its steps. Every nerve screamed for flight, yet his boots held fast.

Both Betanthian and barbarian alike fell back from the line, the clash forgotten in the shadow of the colossus. Tylar alone did not yield. For if he turned now, the army would break. This was the Plainhold's reckoning, and only a man willing to stare into hell itself could hope to meet it.

To his surprise, Conrak stayed close, though the shock on his face mirrored his own. Even the Sacrithon's faith wavered before such a sight — for this was not meant for mortal eyes. He stumbled to Tylar's side, mouth working, trying to make sense of the madness.

"Tell me something witty, you righteous fuck," Tylar growled, his armor trembling around him.

"I wish I had an answer, Bradshaw," Conrak muttered, glancing over his shoulder. "Look at the men. They're ready to bolt. They stay because they see us standing."

The truth was less noble. Tylar's legs were locked by terror, rooted as though iron spikes had been driven through his boots. Never in all his decades had fear bound him so completely. And yet, in that paralysis, something struck him like a spark.

This was no chance meeting. Every step of blood and misery had carried him here, to stand before a god's judgment made flesh. He had cursed the heavens, doubted them, spat in their name. Now, here they were, undeniable. And somehow, in all their cruel wisdom, they had chosen him to face this horror.

Loath as he was to admit it, Tylar had become more than a man. He was a banner, a wall of flesh and steel to which others could cling. Nearly fifty years of reputation bore down on his shoulders, and to waver now would be to betray every brother he had buried.

"I've wished for death longer than half these lads have been alive," Tylar said, his voice low but steady. Then his scarred mouth curled into something between a grin and a snarl. "And you know what, Conrak? Fuck it… what better way to go? Because you know damn well we're going to fucking die here."

"We may, very well." Conrak nodded, his voice steadier than his eyes. "But before we do, let me say this, Bradshaw: I was wrong about you. I thought you a coward for deserting, for crawling into the underbelly of the world. I'm a proud man, as you've no doubt seen. But I'm not too proud to admit when I'm wrong. I'm honored to stand with you—at the end, if this is it."

Platitudes meant little on the edge of annihilation. The bone colossus had fully torn itself free of the ossuary's curse. Its cavernous sockets burned with hellish light as it scanned the field, and when it fixed on them, the ground shook with a roar. Arms as long as siege beams swung ponderously, dragging gouges in the earth.

"Don't get all sentimental on me, you cunt," Tylar snapped. "I've lusted for death longer than I can recall. I've seen better men butchered while I kept breathing. But now I know why I survived—it was for this moment. For this fucking thing. None of my brothers would have the balls to face it. But I do."

"Cheers to that," Conrak said, kissing his sword hilt like a priest at an altar. "Then let's make this an end worthy of remembrance. Not for nobles and their songs, but for fallen friends. For us."

A laugh tore out of Tylar, rough and real. His first in years. Maybe his last. He met Conrak's wild grin with one of his own, then surged forward, shield high and throat raw with a war cry. To his surprise, the Sacrithon charged beside him, competing to see who would land the first blow.

The colossus reared, its arm sweeping wide, a blow fit to shatter towers. Tylar and Conrak split, one left, one right, its strike smashing onto empty soil. Tylar roared his defiance, blade flashing as it slammed into the monstrosity's leg. Steel rang against rotten bone, a sound like a hammer on a coffin lid.

Conrak hacked at the beast's hollow abdomen—first a slash, then a jab—but both blows skittered off uselessly. The colossus swung a spindly arm with startling speed, forcing Conrak to dive aside or be crushed. Tylar tore his sword free from bone, but a sudden kick caught him square. He flew back like a rag doll, armor clattering as he hit the dirt.

"Fuck!" he spat, the impact rattling his teeth.

A howl split the Plainhold, shrill and piercing, as if winter itself had screamed. The monster's fiery gaze lingered on them for a heartbeat, then turned toward the clustered ranks of Betanthia's army. Chunks of rotten flesh sloughed from its frame as it lumbered forward, hunger written in every staggering step.

"Got any brilliant fucking ideas?" Tylar barked, scrambling to his feet. "Any of that Sacrithon wisdom hiding up your arse?"

Conrak shook his head, pale with exhaustion. "I wish I did, Bradshaw. They don't prepare you for this at the Ivornorium. The best we can do is slow it down. There… pikes!"

Scattered along the ground lay the long spears of fallen men. Tylar seized one, Conrak another, and together they raced to intervene, two gnats against a storm.

"Fuck… fuck me!" Tylar laughed, the sound high and mad as he hefted the twenty-foot shaft. Terror needed a mask, and laughter was the only one he had left.

He spared a glance over his shoulder. The barbarian horde was in full retreat, their zeal curdled into fear. Not even Zylmacian piety had the stomach for this. Only Damien Dreadfire remained—a black figure rooted in the mire, his greatsword driven into the soil, his eyes fixed coldly on the horror he had conjured.

Tylar's grip tightened. For a fleeting instant, the colossus faded from his mind. There was the warlord, Madelyn's tormentor, the butcher who had unleashed this nightmare, standing motionless, wide open. If fate had ever offered him a chance, this was it.

I see you, fucker…

His knuckles whitened on the hilt. Every muscle screamed to ride the bastard down, to split his skull and drag him through the muck for what he'd done to Madelyn. Dreadfire stood motionless, almost daring him, black eyes lit with an unholy fire as the colossus he birthed clawed free of the abyss. One strike. One thrust of steel, and Tylar might end it all.

But the choice weighed heavier than the sword in his hands. Slay the warlord, and the beast would still stalk the field. Turn his back on it, and the line would collapse, Betanthian men ripped apart while he chased vengeance. His breath came ragged, heart hammering against his ribs as the truth struck him like a lash: he could not have both. Not today.

"Bradshaw!" Conrak's voice cut through the haze. "Snap out of it! I need you with me!"

The cry dragged him from the brink. He remembered the voices of old comrades, men who had begged for help on other fields, their pleas silenced by steel and failure. Not this time. Not another man abandoned to die.

Tylar roared, the sound tearing from his chest like a war drum, and charged the colossus with pike leveled. His heart pounded so violently it threatened to burst; his hands poured sweat; every instinct screaming at him to run. Black-fletched arrows peppered the beast's corpse-flesh to no avail, but they told him something vital: his countrymen still stood with him, still fighting, still believing.

Sweat stung his eyes, his breath rasped like fire in his lungs, and the pike quivered under the weight of terror. The colossus loomed higher than any siege tower, each step rattling marrow and shaking courage loose from the men around him. Soldiers faltered, some clutching weapons only to stave off shame, others breaking already.

"Hold the line, you bastards!" Tylar thundered, his voice cracking with rage. "If you run now, you'll never stop running!"

Conrak planted his boots beside him, shield braced, though even the Sacrithon's grin had faltered. His eyes flicked skyward, as if the bleeding heavens might yet yield some mercy. "Gods help us, Bradshaw," he muttered. "I think we've truly found the end of the world."

Tylar bared his teeth in a snarl, refusing to yield, though terror clawed its way up his chest. "Then let it end with us standing."

The monster roared, the sky bleeding with light, and the field shook with the promise of slaughter. If this were to be his last breath, then by all the gods, he would spend it defying hell itself.

MADELYN VIII

A DARK SKY SEETHED ON THE HORIZON, BURNING RED AS CLOUDS churned into a crimson maelstrom. Madelyn reined in, her breath catching as the heavens twisted and writhed, a stale wind carrying with it the faint screams of battle. After months of wandering, of hunger and dust and visions, the moment of reckoning had come.

"At last," she whispered. "Ancestors, guide me. I will have my vengeance this day."

With a sharp cry, she spurred her horse into a gallop. The wind tore at her cropped hair as she thundered down the slope, each pounding hoofbeat dragging her closer to the storm. The ground itself quaked with the clash of steel, with cries of the dying, with banners snapping like whips in the blood-lit air. She searched the chaos with fevered eyes, seeking only one figure—Damien Dreadfire. He was there. He had to be. Nothing else mattered.

The field stretched vast below her: two armies locked in slaughter, neither yet yielding. Though diminished, the barbarian horde still surged with a ferocity that made her stomach lurch. Madelyn's heart faltered, then hammered hard enough to choke her. Somewhere down there, amid the smoke and carnage, walked the man who had broken her.

Corpses already carpeted the plain, Betanthian and barbarian alike. The battle raged undecided, its end still unwritten. Madelyn's fingers tightened on her reins. It was not too late. Her presence might still bend fate, might still decide the war before the sun fell.

Then the sea of warriors split. From the northern line stepped a giant in black plate, a shape she had seen in every nightmare. Damien Dreadfire. Her breath left her in a hiss as her eyes fixed on the vessel he bore in both hands. She could not make out its shape from afar, but when the lid was drawn back, the sky itself seemed to rupture— and from it burst a monstrosity pulled straight from the deepest pit of her soul.

The behemoth was unlike anything Madelyn's darkest visions had conjured. A giant wrought of bone and dripping flesh, its frame shambled upright, towering nearly twenty feet tall. Ribbons of rot sloughed off its limbs, steaming where they struck the ground. Its screech tore through the crimson sky, a chorus of the damned that rattled her teeth and set her horse rearing in terror. Not even Lazilyth, in all her horror, had struck so deep a chord of dread.

Yet dread or not, Madelyn knew: this horror was hers to face. Through smoke and drifting ash, two figures held their ground before the abomination. At first, they seemed little more than shadows, dwarfed by the wall of carrion bone. Then the beast shifted in the firelight, and she saw them more clearly—one broad and scarred, purple cloak ragged, his great spear clenched in fists white with strain. Madelyn's heart lurched.

"Tylar," she whispered, the word breaking into a gasp. "Gods, no… you fool…"

Always chasing death. Always defying fate. But to stand against this? He would be the end of himself.

Only then did she see the second figure—Conrak, the Sacrithon— planted firm beside him, terror plain on his face yet refusing to yield. Both men leveled scavenged pikes, bracing them like reeds against a storm. They jabbed, thrust, and scrambled aside as the monster's limbs swung down, each strike powerful enough to crush horse and rider together. The weapons looked pitiful in their hands, no more than kindling before the abyss, but still they fought. Still, they defied.

The beast lashed out with one grotesque arm, faster than anything so massive had a right to be. Tylar met the blow head-on, his pike snapping like a twig before the Titan himself was hurled backward thirty paces. He struck the ground with a crash of dented steel, the breath torn from his lungs. Conrak staggered aside, narrowly avoiding being crushed beneath its heel, his own weapon spinning uselessly into the dirt.

Madelyn's heart clenched—and then she was moving. She flung herself from the saddle, sword bared, sprinting straight into the storm. Each step dragged her deeper into the veil, shadows bleeding into her eyes until the world dimmed to shades of night. She felt the half-realm wrap around her, that cursed place where she alone walked.

The colossus loomed, a wall of bone and rotting sinew. Madelyn struck without hesitation, her blade a blur. Steel split flesh, gouged deep into ribs, shadow dripping from its edge. But the monster only howled louder—not in pain, but in fury. Its cavernous eyes rolled in their sockets and locked onto her through the veil.

Gods… it can see me!

She faltered, stumbling back, the darkness unraveling as a massive arm swung down. The strike missed by inches, the shockwave sending her sprawling.

"What in all the hells—?" Conrak's voice rang out, wild with disbelief. To him, the beast lashed at nothing. "Bradshaw! It's striking at ghosts!"

Behind her, Tylar groaned, struggling to rise. He managed to prop himself on an elbow before collapsing again, blood streaking his battered face.

Conrak turned at once. "Stay down, Bradshaw! I'll—"

The beast lunged with sudden speed. An arm swept low like a

battering ram, catching Conrak full in the chest. The Sacrithon soared through the air before crashing down with a brutal thud, his shield spinning away from limp fingers. Both men lay sprawled in the dirt, stunned and broken.

Madelyn's pulse thundered in her ears. There was no one left. She bared her teeth, shadows writhing up her blade as she hurled herself at the abomination, slashing with every shred of fury her soul could summon. Black scars split across its bones, each strike a wound in the dark. Yet the colossus howled and pressed on, its cavernous eyes fixed on her as though nothing else in the world existed.

She carved another gouge deep into its side. The beast did not falter. With a guttural roar, its arm swept across the field, a wall of rotted flesh and bone. The blow smashed into her mid-swing. She flew like a rag-doll, slammed to the earth with bone-cracking force. Her sword spun away into the dust. The breath tore from her lungs, leaving her writhing, clawing at the dirt for air that would not come.

The colossus lurched closer, claws curling, its shadow falling across her broken form. Stones shattered under its steps. Her body trembled, her vision darkened at the edges. She clung desperately to the shadow realm, but even that bled thin, her strength draining away.

Memories began flooding back: the High Marshal's cold, judging eyes at Castle Thorn. Lonely years spent aching for warmth. The faces of brothers who lay long in their graves. Gareth, proud, unyielding, standing in torchlight like a beacon. Tylar, the man too stubborn to die.

Is this what it comes to? After all the pain, all the wandering, I end broken in the dirt?

The beast loomed over her, maw splitting in a howl that shook the marrow in her bones. Then, through the haze, motion caught her eye. A lone rider tore across the field, cloak snapping like a banner in the storm. Time seemed to slow—hooves hammering, dust scattering in crimson light, a lance leveled like a bolt of heaven itself. Prince Gareth.

Madelyn's heart seized, torn between terror and disbelief. No... not him. Not here. Not like this!

She could only watch, paralyzed, as Gareth thundered into the monster's frame. The lance struck with bone-splintering force, the shaft driving deep into the colossus's chest. Rotten marrow and clotted flesh burst outward in a grisly spray as the beast reeled back—shaken, but not undone.

To Madelyn's eyes, it all came in fragments: Gareth's cloak whipping like a banner of defiance, his teeth clenched in grim resolve, the ribcage of the abomination splintering like an ancient tree under an axe. Slow. Terrible. Unstoppable. The colossus staggered but did not fall. With a shriek that split the sky, it lurched to tear him from the saddle. Gareth wrenched the broken lance free and hurled it aside, his hand flashing to the hilt at his hip.

Madelyn's breath froze. Silver steel leapt into the crimson haze, the crossguard's twin gemstones bursting with a brilliance so fierce it seared through the veil of shadow clinging to her. The radiance scorched her skin, burning away the darkness like frost under the sun. She shielded her eyes, stunned and terrified.

She shielded her eyes, stunned and terrified. *The sword... the light... gods, what is he wielding?*

The abomination reeled, its cavernous eyes narrowing against the blaze. Smoke curled from its rotting hide as Damien's creation bellowed in agony, forced to acknowledge the weapon's fury.

Gareth spurred forward, cloak streaming, the sword blazing in his hand like a fragment of the heavens. With a cry that rang like thunder, he slashed across its torso. The silver edge tore deep, searing rot and marrow alike. Black smoke belched from the wound as flesh sloughed away in great sheets. For the first time, the abomination bled.

But triumph was fleeting. The monster swung with shocking speed, its arm colliding with Gareth's horse in a bone-snapping blow. The stallion shrieked and collapsed, crushing earth and rider in a tangle of steel and flesh. Gareth rolled clear, coughing, clutching the silver sword as the colossus bore down with cavernous eyes aflame.

Madelyn's heart stopped. Panic tore through her veins. Before she realized, she was on her feet, stumbling, screaming his name. "GARETH!"

The Prince looked up, his face pale but his eyes blazing. As the monster reached for him, he hurled the silver sword with all his strength. The weapon spun end over end, its brilliance painting arcs of light across the sky.

Madelyn charged forward, her hands closed around the hilt as if fate itself had guided it. The impact rattled her bones, but she did not falter. With a ragged cry, she drove the sword into the creature's back.

The gemstones in the crossguard flared blinding white, then shattered, exploding in a burst of radiant fire that tore through the abomination's frame. The shockwave knocked her back, searing the air with a scream that seemed to come from a thousand broken throats.

The colossus convulsed, howling as its rotten frame split apart. Flesh sloughed in torrents, bones cracked like timber, black smoke pouring from every wound. Its towering form collapsed into a writhing heap, dissolving into sludge and shards that hissed as they sank into the earth.

Madelyn staggered, her grip trembling. The sword's light faltered, its gemstones gone, its brilliance spent. The once-mighty blade slipped from her hands and struck the dirt with a hollow clang. Its work was done.

For a long moment, silence gripped the battlefield. Both armies stood frozen, divided by the mire where the colossus had fallen. Fear lingered heavy in the air, too thick for either side to break. Slowly, almost as if bound by an unspoken pact, the barbarians began to fall back. Betanthian horns answered in kind, calling the weary host to hold, not press.

Madelyn's eyes roved across the plain. Conrak was on his knees, swaying like a drunkard, blood plastering his hair. Even so, he braced Titan's massive frame, the giant groaning but refusing to remain down. Relief cut through her exhaustion like a knife: they still lived. And then she saw him.

Gareth staggered upright beside the broken ruin of his horse. Madelyn lurched forward, stumbling across churned mud and gore until she reached him. His head lifted. Their eyes met.

Whatever iron composure he had carried into the battle dissolved in that instant. His eyes welled as he seized her, pulling her into his arms with a desperation that left her breathless. His fingers tangled in the hair at the back of her head, clutching her as if he feared she might vanish again. His chest heaved against hers, his voice breaking.

"Why?" His voice cracked, raw as an open wound. "Why did you go away?"

Her lips parted, but no answer came. No words could ease the grief etched across his face.

He drew back just enough to cradle her cheeks in both hands, his thumbs trembling as they brushed across her skin. The touch was tender. Fragile. Aching.

"Madelyn," Gareth whispered. "You stop this. Do you hear me? Stop this… and come home."

Madelyn's lips trembled as she searched his eyes. Every part of her longed to say yes, to yield, to come home, to lay down the burden she had carried for so long. His arms felt like safety, his voice like truth. But justice still burned in her veins, a hunger that would never be sated within palace walls.

"I want to," she whispered, her voice breaking. "Gods, I want to. But I can't. Not yet. Not while he still lives. You'll never understand."

"You're wrong," Gareth said fiercely, his hands tightening against her cheeks. "I understand more than you think. Enough blood has been spilled. Please... stop this. I have thought about you every day, Madelyn. I've marched across Caldakas to bring you home!"

Tears welled in her eyes. She shook her head slowly. "I'm sorry."

Before he could answer, she pulled him into a kiss, fierce and desperate, pouring every ounce of longing, regret, and love into it. For a moment, the battlefield and the war vanished, and they were only themselves again, bound by something neither could sever.

Gareth had always loved her that way—wholly, without condition. From the days of her loneliness at Castle Thorn to the nights she doubted her worth, he had been there, steadfast and unyielding. He never asked her to change, never sought to bind her, only to share her burdens as his own. Even now, with the world crumbling around them, that love burned as fiercely as the first time he had spoken her name.

Then suddenly, she pushed hard against his chest. Gareth stumbled back, tripping over the corpse of his fallen horse, sprawling into the dirt with a cry. Madelyn turned, sprinting across the churned field toward the barbarians. Her form darkened, bled into smoke, and in the next instant, she was gone, swallowed by dust and shadow.

"Madelyn!" Gareth's voice broke into a raw, tormented scream that carried across the silent field. "Madelyn!"

His cries lingered even as the storm winds tore them apart, echoing in the ears of all who heard. They carried the weight of a love unbroken, even as the woman who held it turned from him once more.

EINARR VIII

Patience, Einarr reminded himself as days came and went. *The gods have led you here for a reason. You must not lose heart now.*

Yet patience was no armor against the gnawing silence of the hills. Smoke still marked the valley they had burned, a black smear drifting across the horizon, but no riders came, no horns sounded. The men grew restless. Valerick spat curses at the flies. Dolsigg brooded like a storm cloud, and even Hyleth's steady eyes betrayed unease.

They had gambled everything on this lie. If Droethia did not answer, then all they had left was blood on their hands and corpses rotting in a cave. Valerick kicked a stone down the slope, watching it clatter into the brush.

"Day after day of hiding like frightened hares. Perhaps the boy tripped in the smoke and fed the crows instead of reaching their gates?"

A few of the men chuckled darkly, though there was no amusement in it.

Dolsigg leaned on his axe, sweat streaking through the grime on his brow. "Or perhaps the Droethiens saw the smoke and chose to let it die."

The mutters carried through the camp like sparks in dry grass. Some grumbled about riding deeper, others about turning back altogether.

Only Hyleth remained still, crouched at the cave mouth with his eyes on the horizon.

Einarr finally rose, brushing dirt from his knees. "Hold your tongues. The gods will answer. And when they do, we must look like wolves, not carrion."

The mutters died down, but the silence that followed was no kinder. Einarr sat again at the cave mouth, eyes fixed on the haze drifting over the valley. Patience. Always patience. He told himself the gods had not shown him the lion in vain, that the vision meant more than shadows and smoke. Yet doubt gnawed at him all the same.

If no riders came, then he had slaughtered innocents for nothing. No battle won, no alliance forged, only ash on his hands and blood soaking into Droethien soil. It would not be the gods who were mocked, but him: Einarr Rolffson, butcher without purpose, cursed by his own gambit.

He closed his eyes, forcing his breath to steady. *No. The lion waits. The lion watches.*

Einarr's mind drifted unbidden to the long road behind him. To Skaginlef, where Alina's face had come to him in dreams, her voice soft and sorrowful, a reminder of the life torn from him. To Khorrtal, where the streets ran red, and he first felt the gods pushing him toward something greater than vengeance.

Then to the Plainhold, vast and merciless, where silence itself seemed to weigh on his soul, and where the lion stalked him unendingly. Each step had carried him further from the man Alina had known, further from her embrace, and deeper into a fate that now pressed heavily on his shoulders.

His sight wandered back to the haze over the valley. For a moment, he thought it was only a trick of smoke and sun, a shimmer on the horizon. But then he saw it—movement. A faint line rising from the plain, dust curling in pale ribbons.

Einarr narrowed his eyes, heart thudding. It was riders, perhaps. Or perhaps nothing at all, his mind gnawed by wish and memory until it painted shapes where none existed. He rubbed at his eyes, blinked hard, but the smudge remained, thickening, solidifying into a faint gleam of helms beneath the haze.

"Do you see it?" he muttered.

Hyleth lifted his head slowly, his weathered face unreadable. "Aye," he said at last. "They come."

The camp stirred at once, men crowding to the slope, shading their eyes against the glare. A ripple of unease passed through them. Some whispered prayers, others spat into the dirt. Valerick only smirked, though his jaw clenched tight enough to crack stone. Still, Einarr doubted, even as the hoofbeats reached him across the wind. Riders, yes. But whose?

"Bring them out," Einarr commanded. "We must set the scene."

The men obeyed at once, rushing into the cave's cool shadow. One by one, the bodies were dragged into the light, stiff limbs creaking as they were laid out upon the stone. Cloaks were pulled straight, helms fitted over bloodied heads, shields propped against still chests. From a distance, they might have been soldiers only sleeping, waiting for a horn to wake them.

Valerick knelt, tugging a breastplate closed over a corpse's caved chest. "He looks the part," he muttered, though his tone was brittle.

"Better than the truth," Einarr answered.

He strode among the dead, adjusting a sword here, a clasp there, each small gesture driving the lie deeper into shape. His men moved fast, sweat streaking their faces, mutters giving way to silence. By the time he straightened, the bodies lay in grim order along the slope, black cloaks stirring faintly in the wind. From the valley floor, no approaching rider would doubt what they saw.

He turned to his men, voice low but hard. "Back to the rocks, all of you. And keep your tongues sheathed. Let them choke on the sight before they hear a word from us. When the moment comes, I will speak."

The company scattered into cover, crouching behind thorn and stone, leaving only the corpses to hold the slope. Einarr lingered a moment longer, studying their grim handiwork.

The lion waits, he reminded himself. Then he melted back into the shadows with the rest.

The hoofbeats grew louder, rolling like thunder against the hills. Soon dust rose in fresh plumes, curling along the trail that cut upward from the valley floor. Fifty riders came into view, spears glinting, armor dull with travel, the air around them alive with heat and iron. At their head rode a man in full plate, helm crested, his bearing unmistakable even at a distance—a dignitary, a ruler of Droethia, a man of weight and authority.

The riders slowed as they neared the slope strewn with Blackthorn dead. Horses balked at the scent, ears flattening, nostrils flaring. Men muttered in shock, guarding themselves against the grotesque omen. And there, as the hoofbeats faltered, Einarr stepped forward from the rocks, cloak stirring, sword hilt visible at his side.

"Halt!" the unknown leader said, drawing a saber. "Do not move!"

Einarr paused, his heart slamming violently, although his composure remained cool. He studied their ornate armor curiously, for it was unlike anything he had seen. Droethiens were an old people, yet their sophistication was no less for it.

"Do you speak the common tongue, savage?" the Governor asked, his horse rearing at the stench.

"Indeed, I do," Einarr replied, to the surprise of the Droethiens.

A ripple passed through the foreigner's riders, mutters of surprise mingling with suspicion. Spears lowered a fraction, shields lifted against Einarr's calm reply. The Governor kept his saber leveled, though his voice carried more command than fear.

"Then answer me plainly. Who are you, and what are you doing in these lands? What happened here? Speak!"

He let the silence draw for a breath, measuring the man who challenged him. "I am Einarr Rolffson of the Nothanek, born of Skaginlef in the deep north. My people are good and gods-fearing. As to why we are here… you are looking at the reason. I would have your name as well, friend."

The man's eyes narrowed, his saber still raised. "I am Aleksius of Naxonnos, Governor of the east of old Droethia. This boy here speaks of Blackthorn raiders who destroyed the village before you. Are you telling me you had a hand in their undoing?"

Einarr inclined his head slightly, careful to let neither pride nor deceit show too strongly. "I am saying only what lies before you, Governor. The Blackthorn are sworn enemies of our people. We make war against Betanthia, even now. We have buried Cedric Valens and his army. These hands built the engine that brought down Castle Morden's walls."

A ripple went through the Droethien riders—suspicion, but also relief, even admiration. A few lowered their spears a fraction, eyes darting to the sprawled corpses clad in black.

Aleksius's voice cut sharply through the murmurs. "And why would a northerner care for Droethien soil? What stake have you in our villages, Rolffson?"

"My companions and I have traveled here on urgent business," Einarr said, stepping forward. "For all of our success, we have suffered terribly on the battlefield. The war stands at a precipice, for we are but a breath away from driving the Betanthians back… or from final defeat. We have come to seek the aid of your people."

A stir broke out among the rocks as cloaks shifted and steel glinted. One by one, more figures emerged from hiding—Einarr's men, tall, hard-faced, and bearing the scars of long war. Their armor was a patchwork of spoils, their eyes sharp, their silence heavier than words.

Aleksius's horse snorted, hooves pawing at the earth as the Governor's gaze studied them. Then his eyes fixed on one man in particular. Hyleth stood at the edge of the group, his bald head glistening with sweat, the cut of his features unmistakable.

The Governor's face hardened. He raised his saber once more. "A Zylmacian?" he thundered. "You keep these dogs in your company?"

Grunts of outrage rippled through his riders, some shifting forward in their saddles as if to strike. Einarr did not flinch. His voice carried cold and steady across the slope.

"Yes, we do. Zylmacian, Nothanek, and Rhivothi as well. And others besides. Our coalition is vast, and men who once hunted each other now march as brothers. Old hatreds burn away when a greater enemy looms. Betanthia has made itself that enemy."

"I see," Aleksius said skeptically. "Which brings us full circle. What happened here with these men?"

"We came seeking an audience with your people," Einarr replied. "One day, we saw smoke rising in the distance. Our guide was confident we had neared Droethien lands. When we drew closer, we saw these men, Blackthorn, sacking and pillaging. We waited in the hills for them to retire, and now... now they will stay here forever."

Aleksius studied him for a long moment, eyes narrowing. "You ask me to believe a wandering band of exiles did what my own captains have failed to do for years? That you broke Blackthorn steel and lived to tell it?"

Valerick the Red stepped forward then, thumping the butt of his axe into the earth. "We lived it," he growled. "Ask your boy... he saw their banners as clear as the sun. He ran because his people were dying. We stood because someone had to."

The Droethien riders stirred uneasily. A few looked to their Governor, others to the sprawled corpses littering the slope. The stink of blood carried stronger now, cutting through the heat, proof enough that men had died here, though whose hands had struck the blows remained cloaked in shadow.

Aleksius lowered his saber a fraction but did not sheathe it. His tone was iron. "If what you say is true, Rolffson, then your quarrel may align with mine. But I have seen too many lies dressed as gifts. Until I know the truth, I will treat you as both guest and prisoner. You will come to Naxonnos and stand before my council. There, you will speak again."

Einarr nodded, calm as stone despite the line of spears pointed his way. "We are unbothered by your terms. The gods see past walls and councils. They know our purpose is pure, whether you believe it or not."

The words landed like a boulder in the dirt. No defiance, no fear, only certainty, carried on the steady voice of a man who had already measured his soul against fate. Aleksius blinked, taken aback. He had expected protest, or swagger, or some plea for mercy. Instead, he found himself staring at a Northerner who spoke as if the weight of destiny itself stood at his back. The Governor lowered his saber another inch, though suspicion still burned in his eyes.

Aleksius held his gaze on Einarr, unwilling to yield an inch. His eyes flicked to the men arrayed behind him, noting the details as a soldier does. Their armor was mismatched, scarred, and hammered into shape more times than he could count. Their weapons bore the weight of use—edges nicked, hafts darkened by sweat and blood. Yet there was nothing of rabble in their bearing. They stood as men accustomed to killing and surviving, their silence heavier than any boast.

"You speak of purity," Aleksius said at last, voice carrying across the rocks. "But purity is no shield against lies. Tell me, Rolffson, if the gods willed you here, what is it you seek from Droethia? Grain? Gold? Or would you bleed my sons and brothers for your Northern quarrel?"

Einarr did not flinch. His eyes, cold and steady, stayed fixed on the Governor. "We seek only allies who have not forgotten their own strength. Betanthia's shadow lengthens, and it will not stop at your borders. This, you know. It is better we stand together, here and now, than die alone tomorrow."

A murmur passed through the Droethien ranks, some frowning, some nodding, all uncertain. Aleksius leaned forward in the saddle, steel glinting at his side.

"And if I refuse? If I send you in chains to Larssa, to let the Senate weigh your honeyed words?"

Einarr's mouth bent into something that was not quite a smile. "Then the Senate will hear what you hear now. We do not beg, Governor. We stand where the gods have led us. Whether as guests, as prisoners, or as brothers-in-arms, we will not turn aside."

The boldness of his words sent a ripple through the Droethien riders. Some spat into the dirt, contempt sharp on their faces. Others shifted in their saddles, eyes narrowing, weighing him as though uncertain whether he was a madman or a prophet. Einarr held their gaze without blinking, letting the silence work for him, daring them to decide.

"By all rights, I should cut you down where you stand," Aleksius said, the edge of his saber gleaming. "Yet something in your manner…" He broke off, shaking his head. "It reeks of either madness or destiny. I know not which."

Einarr did not waver. "It is neither, Governor," he said evenly. "It is faith. The gods have already chosen the path before us. All that remains is whether we have the courage to walk it."

The words hung in the air like a drawn bowstring. Some of the Droethien riders scoffed aloud, but others went silent, staring at him as though weighing an omen they had not asked for. Aleksius's saber lowered an inch more, his jaw tight, his eyes unreadable.

"Very well," the Governor sighed. "You will ride with us to Naxonnos, and I will offer you the hospitality of my house. These are strange days, Einarr Rolffson. Dark and strange. I pray your arrival portends brighter days. Come."

Aleksius sheathed his saber, then gestured for his riders to fall in line behind him. Einarr's men stood tense at his back, watching as the Droethiens formed their column. He moved to mount, gathering his breath, steadying himself for what lay ahead. Out of the corner of his eye, a sudden motion caught his attention. A foreign standard-bearer tugged at a knot, freeing the banner that had been bound against its pole.

With a sharp snap, the cloth unfurled. White silk billowed wide in the morning wind, and upon it roared the sigil of Droethia: a lion rampant, mane wild as flame, jaws bared in silent challenge.

Einarr froze where he stood. His heart hammered, the sound of it drowning out the tramp of hooves and clatter of armor. That beast, the great cat that had stalked him across Caldakas, who had haunted his dreams and pressed upon his soul, now glared down at him from mortal cloth. Not vision, not smoke, not madness, but flesh and thread carried by men who had no inkling of what it meant.

The Droethiens raised their voices in pride, spears lifting as the banner snapped high. Einarr heard none of it. He stared at the lion, awestruck, certain that the gods had not misled him. His path and theirs were entwined now, bound beneath the gaze of the same relentless beast. An incredulous smile crept across Einarr's face, eyes beading with tears—and then he sighed.

LUCETTA IX

S HE STUMBLED TOWARD THE GATE OF TRACE'S BANK, HALF-DRAGGING Pavlos with her. His weight hung heavy as stone, his ruined mouth leaking a steady stream of groans. Blood soaked the rags clinging to him, each step draining more life until it felt as though she carried a corpse rather than a man.

"Just… a little… further…" she gasped, her thin legs quivering with every pace.

Lantern light spilled over the wet cobbles, their glow blurred by the salt mist rolling in from the sea. The air carried a tang of ocean water, sharp and clean, and for a fleeting moment she longed to stand beneath a true rain—to feel the filth wash away, to be human again. But the reek of her tattered gown clung stronger, a stench of waste and rot so vile it was the only thing keeping Pavlos awake.

They wove through narrow streets and shadowed alleys, the city sprawling strange and unknown around her. Cardale had been the jewel of House Bethard for a thousand years, yet Lucetta knew almost nothing of it. In another life, her ignorance might have been a minor shame. Tonight, it was a death sentence waiting to fall.

"P…prin…cess…" Pavlos gurgled, his knees buckling. Together they toppled, Lucetta slamming hard on her hip, pain flaring hot enough to bring tears.

She tried to rise, but her body betrayed her. Weeks of captivity had stripped her to little more than skin and stubbornness. Pavlos sagged at her side, too broken to rise, too stubborn to let go.

"Get up!" she pleaded, clutching his wrist with trembling fingers. "We did not escape that nightmare only to die here! Please... move!"

Such words could not conjure the strength to keep Pavlos moving. His skin had turned pale, his eyes glassy and vacant. There was no fear of death in them anymore—only a dull shadow of regret. Blood streamed from his mutilated face without end, and even to glance at the wound made Lucetta's stomach twist.

I cannot lose him. Not now. Not after everything...

Though despair threatened to swallow her whole, she thought of the woman in black, of the visions and lessons granted in her captivity. Surely, they had not been given only for her to perish nameless in the gutter. No, this could not be her end.

"Please," she whispered, voice thin as parchment. "Please... give me strength..."

She tried to rise again, but her body refused, collapsing back into the muck. Then, a sound stirred in the distance. At first, it was faint, a hollow *clack* that echoed between the narrow streets. But as it drew closer, the tone shifted—harder, heavier—the unmistakable crunch of iron boots on cobblestone.

Her heart lurched. Soldiers? Watchmen? Forcing herself to turn, she realized where they had fallen. Towering over the square loomed the gaudy facade of Trace's bank, its columns rising like a temple to greed. Providence, or some cruel trick of fate, had brought her here.

"Help us!" she screamed, dredging the final strength from her lungs. The cry shattered the stillness, rattling shutters and bouncing off the close brick walls.

The crunching quickened. Shadows moved at the edge of the lanternlight; four men-at-arms in polished mail, weapons drawn as they rushed forward.

"Princess… Lucetta?!" one of the guards gasped. "How… what…"

Their eyes fell on Pavlos, sprawled motionless in the gutter. Shock hardened quickly into fury, for their ignorant eyes could only grasp what they saw.

"Him!" the officer barked, pointing his spear. "Look at what this swine has done to our princess! Run him through!"

Lucetta threw herself across Pavlos's chest, summoning every shred of strength she had left. Her arms barely held her up, but she clung to him like a shield. A faint grunt rumbled in his chest, proof enough he still lived, though death hovered close.

"No!" she cried, her voice raw, her body trembling. "He is my bodyguard. We were prisoners, held for weeks by those filthy fanatics, they… they…"

The words withered on her tongue. Exhaustion crashed over her like a wave of stone. Her vision swam, her eyelids heavy. She sagged, darkness flooding in.

"Stop your prattle," a second man muttered. "She's spent. Get her out of sight. You two, grab him. He's half-dead already."

Strong arms swept her from the cobbles as her senses frayed. Lanternlight flickered past in blurs; the clatter of boots and echo of orders rose and fell like voices underwater. She smelled fishmongers' refuse, then salt air, then the clean bite of rain-washed stone.

For a moment, she heard Pavlos groan; a low, wet sound, more gurgle than breath. Then even that slipped away. The warmth of an interior hall closed around her, heavy with oil and oak, her head pressed to a breastplate as her bearer carried her onward. The world narrowed to that steady stride, the rhythm like a lullaby dragging her under. The black tide of sleep rose, and Lucetta let it take her.

Warm rays of sunlight kissed her cheek, rousing her from a sleep that felt endless. Lucetta shifted weakly against the bed, silk sheets sliding cool against her battered skin. Her arms and elbows were swaddled in clean linen, a pungent bite of salve seeping into her sores. For a fleeting moment, with the dull ache muted by comfort, she could almost believe the past weeks had been nothing but some fevered dream.

A salt breeze drifted through thin curtains, jasmine mingling with the sea air in a way that felt almost cruel in its gentleness. She was alive. She was free of the Harbingers' filth. And yet the memory of Pavlos struck like a knife. His ruined face, his blood loss—had he survived the night? If not, then every ounce of her endurance had been for nothing.

I... must... find him...

Her joints cracked as she forced herself upright. Even her feet felt brittle, each step like glass splintering under her weight. She limped toward the door but faltered at a mirror standing from floor to ceiling. The reflection was scarcely recognizable.

Her auburn hair had been brushed smooth and braided, though its color was darker now, thinned and frayed from neglect. A plain white gown clung to her frail frame, more servant's garb than a princess's. The sight gnawed at her pride, but there were heavier concerns than dignity.

The door creaked before she could push it open. Trace waddled into the chamber, his jowled face split by a smile. A servant girl shadowed him, and behind her came an elderly physician burdened with a satchel of instruments.

"Sister!" Trace spread his arms as though welcoming her to some great feast. "This is a surprise. We had just come to check on you. But I see your fire has not guttered out. Heavens be praised, we feared you would not last the night."

"The night?" Lucetta asked, frowning. If she had truly been so near to death, standing should have been impossible. "How long have I been here?"

Trace's smile faltered. "You have been here three days."

A pit opened in her stomach. Three days were gone as though stolen in an instant. And yet she could still feel the cold grime of her cell's stone floor, still smell its rank stench clinging to her skin.

"Three... days?" Her voice shook. "And my bodyguard — what of him?"

Trace and the physician exchanged a look. The old man lowered his eyes and gave a solemn shake of his head.

"He lives, my princess," the physician said gently. "But grievously disfigured. I did all that could be done to preserve what remains of his face."

"I must see him at once!" Panic rose sharply in her chest. She stumbled toward the door, but her legs betrayed her, buckling under the strain. Trace's bulk caught her before she collapsed. His silk robes reeked of vetiver, a regal scent, but poured on so heavily it made her gag.

"No, sister," he murmured, easing her back. "You must rest. Trust us. Your man will survive, and he shall be honored for his service. A hero of the Kingdom, if ever there was one."

Her fragile body could endure no more. Blackness folded over her vision until no light remained. She sank into a dreamless sleep, her mind mercifully blank.

When she woke again, it was near midnight. Candleflame burned low, and a pale shaft of moonlight carved long shadows across the chamber. Lucetta eased herself upright, her body frail but restless. Hunger gnawed at her. On the table lay a flagon of water and several slices of stale bread. She stumbled to it, seized the vessel, and drank greedily, water spilling down her chin to soak her gown.

The bread could wait. Pavlos mattered more than hunger, more than anything. Lucetta staggered into the corridor, the plush carpet doing little to steady her trembling legs. A dozen shut doors loomed on either side, each a dark sentinel in the gloom. Ahead, one stood ajar, lamplight spilling in a pale strip across the floor.

She pressed a hand against the wall, inching closer. The air changed as she neared—sharp vinegar, boiled linen, and beneath it all, the iron tang of blood. A basin sat on a table just inside, the water stained pink, rags crusted black with use. From within came the creak of a bed. Her breath caught.

"Pavlos!?" she gasped.

The Droethien sat hunched at the edge of the mattress, his massive frame bandaged to the brow. Thick linen wrapped his head, leaving only slits for his eyes and nose. Fresh blood seeped through the wrappings at his chin, drying in dark, stiff patches. He turned to face her, the movement slow, deliberate.

Their eyes locked. No relief. No sorrow. Only a seething, murderous rage burned back at her, so fierce it made her knees weaken.

"Pavlos..." she whispered, stepping hesitantly inside. "I am so thankful you live. I never meant this—gods, I never meant for this to happen. Those foul beasts will pay for what they've done to you. I swear it. Once I am whole again, I will unleash every soldier at my command into those sewers, and they will burn the filth from this city. And you..." She forced a trembling smile. "...you will have your revenge."

Her words fell flat against the silence. Pavlos did not soften, did not yield. His glare only deepened, eyes bloodshot and unblinking, filled with a promise of violence. Lucetta felt the weight of it sink into her bones. Even broken, even ruined, he was every bit as dangerous, perhaps most of all to her.

"Very well," Lucetta murmured, forcing steadiness into her voice as she backed into the hall. "I will leave you to rest... and see to it you are brought every comfort."

The door clicked shut, and her mask collapsed. Tears welled, hot and stinging, spilling as fast as she could wipe them away. Another life ruined. Another soul she had dragged into her storm. Every good intention had soured into rot, every promise of fortune from the woman in black revealed as nothing more than a cruel jest. Sobbing and delirious, Lucetta limped through the darkened corridor.

Each step was heavier than the last. Shadows warped on the walls, twisting into the shapes of those she had failed: her mother, her guardsmen, even Aldred with his cold scorn. By the time she reached her chamber, her legs gave out beneath her, and she fell against the door for support. She slipped inside, shut out the darkness, and crumpled into the bed's embrace, sleep swallowing her like a grave.

When she woke, it was like clawing back from death itself. Her body hummed with a strange contradiction —refreshed, yet hollowed, her strength still slow to return. She stretched, wincing at the ache in her limbs, then caught sight of the mannequin by the desk.

A gown of teal silk draped across its frame, delicate white flowers stitched into the fabric. It shimmered faintly in the morning light, unfamiliar and out of place. It was not from her estate. Not from the palace. Such finery came at a steep cost, and only one man in Cardale had the purse or the motive to provide it.

Trace…

It was not in his nature to be generous without reason. No, this was coin spent to soften a blow, a gift to buy her gratitude before the knife slid between her ribs.

Even so, Lucetta dressed. The silk sighed against her skin, a fleeting illusion of royalty restored. For a moment, she allowed herself to remember who she had once been. Her hair had been washed, brushed, and braided while she slept; neat, simple, peasant-like. She stared at her reflection, regal dress above a gaunt face, and thought: better this than rags, though still far less than what she deserved.

Her stomach erupted in a sour churn, the ache of hunger twisting into nausea. Food felt like a relic from another life; roasted meats, spiced cakes, sweet wines, all reduced to half-remembered dreams. A pitcher of water, a plate of bread, nuts, and fruit sat waiting on the corner table, yet Lucetta resisted the urge to gorge like some starved wretch. No, she would not eat in desperation. She would eat with dignity. She mustered the strength to sit, straighten her spine, and take her meal as though she still presided over the palace table.

Surely, Trace would not stoop to interrogation over a banquet. Such matters were unbecoming of royalty. Not that it mattered, she had stared into the eyes of death and survived. Enduring her brother's prattle would be no worse than a stroll through the Citadel's gardens.

When she emerged, two of Trace's men awaited her. Their steel breastplates gleamed with meticulous polish, chased with carvings of eagles and swords. Heavy black cloaks trimmed in dark blue hung across their shoulders, while crested nasal helms of polished steel obscured their faces. Gauntleted fists rested on ornate sword hilts, the posture of men eager to impress their lord's power.

"My princess," one said, bowing his head ever so slightly. "It is good to see you standing. Come. Your brother is most eager to see you."

Lucetta forced a smile, though bile burned her throat. Trace's company had always been insufferable; after her ordeal, it promised to be unbearable. Yet she strode forward with chin high, heart steady.

Let him try to wound me with words. Let him wield that silver tongue as a weapon. I will gladly rip it from his mouth with my bare hands.

They led her through the corridor and down a sweeping flight of stairs, each step shooting fire through her wasted muscles. Her legs trembled like a child's, yet the scent of roasted meats and fresh wine wafting up from below was enough to dull the pain.

The banquet hall sprawled wide, its center dominated by a long oaken table. At its head sat a chair built for Trace's girth; more throne than seat, upholstered with purple velvet cushions. Mounted above it loomed a grotesque painting of her brother, made absurdly handsome and lean by a sycophant's brush.

Lucetta's stomach turned. Vanity was no stranger to her, but this was mockery. She had often heard whispers of her own pride, and perhaps they were not without merit. A Bethard princess was meant to be as radiant as dawn itself, a reflection of her mother's elegance. Yet she had learned there was power in beauty, power sharper than steel. And unlike her brother, she wielded it knowingly.

She studied the grotesque painting for only minutes before Trace waddled into the hall. Dressed in green and silver silks, his swollen belly strained the delicate fabric to near-tearing. Gold and jewels clung to his neck, wrists, and fingers in gaudy excess—enough treasure to pay the wages of an army, yet wasted on his gluttonous bulk. The cloying stink of vetiver clung to him, so thick it turned her stomach.

"Ah, sister!" he said, hands clasped with mock delight. "How pleased I am to see you upright again, and looking more your old self!"

The words were tired, hollow things, the same thin pleasantries Lucetta had endured since childhood. They were all he possessed. Trace wheezed into his oversized chair with a grunt, joints cracking as he lowered himself onto purple velvet. Once seated, he offered her a smug smile and gestured to a servant for wine.

The sight of the garnet liquid pouring into crystal nearly undid her. Weeks of deprivation left her body screaming to snatch the chalice and drain it dry. She mastered herself with effort, sitting regal and rigid as stone. Only her iron will kept the beast of hunger caged.

"I feel more like myself with each passing moment," she said smoothly, raising the chalice in delicate fingers. She sipped with calculated poise, though the wine was ecstasy on her tongue. "Tell me, my bodyguard… is he well?"

Trace waved a jeweled hand. "He lives. I set the finest surgeons upon him, though even they cannot work miracles. But he breathes."

Cryptic words, barbed with meanings he would not say aloud. Still, relief curled through her chest. Pavlos lived. His face mattered little; it was his mind, his ruthless cunning, and his unflinching loyalty that gave him value.

"He must be honored as the hero he is," Lucetta pressed, her voice sharpening like steel hidden in velvet. "And when his strength returns, I would see him lead a purge of those fanatical vermin. The filth who dared defile me must be burned out to the last. You cannot imagine the horrors I endured."

Trace's face was a blank canvas, elbows on the table, hands interlocked. The stillness was unnerving, for it reminded her of childhood, of the silent judgment that followed mischief at the palace. Her father's eyes had always lingered like a noose over her neck, inescapable. And now, Trace looked on with that same quiet weight, trapping her in place.

"Sister," he snapped his fingers. "Let us save such talk for after dinner. I have ordered a fine banquet. You must eat."

It was a fair point—her body already felt light, adrift, comfort blooming in her belly from the wine. No sooner had the words left him than a small army of servants swept into the hall in perfect unison, each bearing platters and steaming bowls piled high with roasted pheasant, fresh vegetables, and jeweled fruits.

The air filled at once with spice and smoke, clawing at her hunger. Silver platters clinked onto polished oak in deliberate sequence, every movement rehearsed and mechanical beneath Trace's smug gaze. Lucetta forced her spine straight, feigning aloof indifference, though her every nerve ached to seize the feast and devour it like a gutter-born beggar.

They ate in silence, broken only by the scrape of cutlery and the hearth's low crackle. Lucetta kept her gaze fixed on her plate, refusing

Trace the satisfaction of her attention. Each bite dulled her hunger but sharpened the unease twisting in her gut.

At last, Trace dabbed his lips with a spotless cloth. "Now. If you are satisfied, I would like to continue our conversation."

Anxiety surged so violently that it nearly tore through her ribs. Her heart was a pounding beast, sweat pearling cold on her brow. If she did not escape, the stress alone might kill her.

"You must excuse me, brother," she said, her voice smooth despite the tremor beneath. "I feel unwell. I must rest."

Before she could rise, Trace slammed his palm on the table. The crack resounded through the hall like thunder, rattling goblets and sending a shiver down her spine. It was an uncharacteristic eruption from a man usually too timid to raise his voice. Something in him had shifted, and she knew it. If only the woman in black would appear, cloaking her in courage and clarity, as she had in darker hours.

"Enough of your games, Lucetta," Trace snarled, his jowls quivering. "You have not been yourself these past years. Each day, you become less the sister I once knew. First, you galavanted into a riot and nearly had your skull cracked. Then, as if unsatisfied with survival, you threw yourself into the clutches of fanatics! What has become of you!?"

"Have you no decency?" Lucetta spat back, her voice like a whip. "I am exhausted and beside myself with grief over what I have endured. Good men died before my eyes, butchered like livestock. And you would sit there, wagging your tongue at me as if I were some common criminal? I will not have it!"

Her fury boiled over. She hurled her wine chalice against the wall, the crystal exploding into glittering fragments that caught the candlelight like shards of fire. Though her outrage was real, such outbursts had long been her sharpest weapon, honed over years of dealing with brothers too soft to withstand her wrath. Neither had ever known how to withstand Lucetta's temper—and Trace, bloated and cowardly, was no different.

She stormed from the hall, her steps as sharp as her words, grateful to be free of his prattling judgment. Still, the evening had yielded one useful truth: Pavlos lived. That assurance, at least, was worth the performance. By morning, she would plan their departure, resume the hunt for Draxios, or seek out mercenaries in his stead. The north was aflame, and time was slipping through her fingers.

In her chamber, she paced, mind racing ahead by a dozen steps, weaving and unraveling plots in rapid succession. But before her thoughts could take shape, the door creaked open. Trace lumbered inside without invitation, shutting it behind him with an unsubtle slam. His very presence was an insult.

"I was not finished," he said, breath heavy, eyes gleaming with irritation. "You will not weasel out of this. Our family went to great lengths to find you. I spent a fortune on trackers and spies, combing the city for weeks. And you will answer to me."

"I never asked for you to save me!" Lucetta shrieked, the walls seeming to shake with her fury. This was no performance, no calculated outburst. The anger boiling within her was pure and raw. "I have borne the consequences of every choice I made. I have suffered for them, endured them, and will continue to endure them. But the cause I fight for is greater than myself. It will carve a legacy to outshine your selfish little pursuits!"

Trace narrowed his eyes, the folds of fat around his face sagging into a mask that made him appear far older than his years. He twisted the heavy signet ring on his pudgy finger, rolling it back and forth as if weighing the thought of striking her. The moment stretched taut, but in the end, his courage faltered. With a huff, he turned his back and waddled toward the balcony, pulling in a deep breath of the cool night air as though it might restore his dignity.

For a fleeting moment, Lucetta felt the ache of pity. They were bound, after all, by the same curse: Gareth's shadow. Both of them had clawed desperately for scraps of destiny, for some chance to matter beyond their brother's brilliance. Neither had children. Neither would be remembered save for the works they left behind. History was cruel that way — it etched the names of kings, not their lesser kin.

She thought, just for a heartbeat, to step forward, to soften her tongue, to offer an apology that might soothe the fracture. Trace's loyalty, however petty, was still worth something. But the words never left her lips. In the far corner, two orange-red eyes kindled in the dark, their glow unmistakable. The woman in black had returned at last, silent and waiting. Lucetta's breath caught, not in relief but in rage.

You, she seethed inwardly, her thoughts sharpened to a knife's edge. *Where were you when I needed you most? You left me to rot in that pit, to bleed and break in the dark. Pavlos is ruined because of your absence, and my strength is nearly spent. You promised me power, yet all I have gained are scars and grief. These lessons you weave are nothing but torment!*

The woman in black drifted forward on an icy current, her lower form dissolving into a haze of swirling ash. Lucetta held her ground, unflinching. What more could the spirit do to her that the world had not already inflicted? Death itself might have been a kindness.

"The lessons I teach have carried you far," the woman in black said, her voice cold and smooth. She paused in the center of the chamber, her hollow smile a razor's edge. "Now you are ready to take the next step. The door to your destiny lies within reach. All you need to do… is claim it."

Your riddles weary me, demon, Lucetta thought, her defiance sharpening. *Enough with veiled promises and vague threats. Speak plainly, or leave me forever.*

Trace cocked his head, baffled, watching her glare into the empty air. Had he seen the specter that drifted inches from his sister, his heart might have failed then and there.

"You are about to discover my meaning," the entity whispered, grin widening. "This very moment."

And then she was gone, vanishing as if she had never been.

"Sister," Trace said, his voice low, heavy. "A great many things trouble me. Your behavior, your absences, your secrecy. Tell me plainly—what have you been doing in the north?"

It felt as though the floor had vanished beneath her feet. A dizzying plunge gripped her, but she forced herself upright.

"I have been away from Cardale for my health," she answered smoothly, the lie rolling easily from her tongue. "You and everyone else know this. It is hardly a mystery."

Trace's expression remained flat, unreadable. "I am a calculating man, far more than most believe. And I cannot ignore the timing of our misfortunes. Mother dies — while you are at her side in Dellhaven. And then… the rumors. Strange movements, strange company. Always circling around you."

Her heart hammered. Words, her only weapon, suddenly felt blunt, useless. Still, she pressed on.

"There are always comings and goings from Dellhaven. You cannot place every shadow at my feet."

Trace pinched the bridge of his nose, sighing as though the weight of the world hung on him. "Since you insist on deception, I will be blunt. I suspect you are involved in… unsavory acts. Your movements in Cardale are irregular, unbecoming of a princess. And I hear whispers that you consort with low men in low places. I would have the truth of it."

Lucetta's temper flared, and before she could stop herself, the words were out: "Is that why you conspired with Sir Tristan to have me followed? To pry into my life, as Mother once tried?"

The chamber went still. Trace's eyes snapped to hers, sharp with sudden recognition. The air between them grew thick with unspoken truth. Lucetta cursed herself inwardly—she had given him a weapon, and she could already see the wheels turning in that bloated skull.

"And how do you know Mother was attempting to spy on you?" Trace's voice was low, sharp as a knife. He crossed his arms and leaned forward, looming like a judge ready to deliver a sentence. "How did you come by this information?"

Her first instinct was to lie, to spin an elaborate tale so intricate even the gods themselves would struggle to unravel it. But Trace had known her all her life. He could read the twitch of her fingers, the tremor of her breath, the cadence of her voice. He knew when she lied.

"Devin told me," she blurted, too fast, too brittle. "He said Mother had grown paranoid. That she believed I was informing on her to Father."

Trace lifted his chin, eyes narrowing with satisfaction. "And how curious it is that Devin has not been seen since your last stay in Dellhaven." His words dripped like poison. "All of these strange coincidences… and all with one common denominator."

Lucetta's skin prickled cold, her stomach twisting to stone. The woman in black reappeared in the corner, smirking, shrugging as though to say *I warned you.* Every escape closed around her like iron bars. Her silver tongue, her sharpest weapon, suddenly felt dulled to uselessness. If Trace left this room, suspicion would harden into certainty.

Her mind clawed desperately for a diversion, a lie keen enough to cut him off at the root. But the harder she searched, the more hollow she felt. Trace's suspicion had already sunk its teeth in. Words would not shake it loose.

The woman in black tilted her head, her grin widening, eyes glowing like coals. "Why do you even endure this?" she purred, though only Lucetta heard. "For all you have suffered, would you let your bloated brother chain you with doubt and accusation? He is nothing. And yet you tremble before him."

I know what truths you've shown me, Lucetta thought fiercely, hands wringing in her skirts. *And the more I doubted, the harsher the lessons became. Enough of lessons. I am ready now. Ready to embrace my purpose.*

To destroy those who would do me harm. No more games. No more delays. Only… destiny.

Her body moved before her mind could temper it. In two quick strides, Lucetta closed the space between them, her hands snapping out to seize his coat. Trace's eyes barely had time to widen before she drove him backward over the balustrade. His bulk vanished into the night air, and he struck the ground below with a sound so final it seemed to drain the room of air—no cry, no plea, only the dull, distant thud of an ending.

Lucetta stepped to the edge, the cool stone biting against her palms as she peered over. Trace lay twisted on the manicured lawn, his limbs sprawled at unnatural angles, the pale oval of his face turned toward nothing. She waited for the rush of guilt, the horror she thought would come, but all she felt was the faint hum of her own heartbeat and the night wind against her cheek. Somewhere deep inside, a small voice whispered that she should care. Yet another voice, colder and steadier, assured her there was no reason to.

The woman in black appeared at her side, a scent of ash and old smoke rolling off her. "Do you feel it now?" the entity asked softly, almost tenderly. "The freedom of cutting away what would bind you?"

Lucetta's gaze lingered on the broken form below for one final moment. "Yes," she said at last. "One by one, I will see them fall… until nothing stands between me and what is mine. And when I am finished, even their ghosts will kneel before me."

GARETH VI

HE SAT SLUMPED BESIDE AN ABANDONED SUPPLY CART, HANDS trembling as he nursed a mug of bourbon. The taste barely registered. His mind circled the same impossible image: a colossus of bone and rotting flesh, towering thrice the height of a man. Such things belonged to fever-dreams, not to the waking world. Yet he had seen it. Fought it. Survived it.

Across his knees rested the sword. Once brilliant, its silver edge now lay dulled and lifeless, the crossguard's twin gemstones nothing more than shattered sockets rimmed in blackened scars. Gareth brushed his thumb across the ruined setting, haunted by memory—the radiant flare when Madelyn drove it home, the blinding brilliance that had ended the abomination. A weapon of legend, spent. Hollow, as hollow as he felt within.

The beast had been real, birthed from Damien Dreadfire's unholy will. How could a war be won against foes such as these? The thought gnawed him raw. Hours earlier, he had struggled to hold together what remained of his army, dragging them back from the edge of collapse. Thousands had broken and fled before the monstrosity; only his reckless defiance had shamed the rest into holding.

Yet one thought outweighed all others. Madelyn. At first, he had not recognized her—hair cropped short, turned black, a shadow of the woman he once knew. She had become something else, something changed. And yet, he prayed, somewhere deep inside, she was still the woman he loved.

"Why…" His voice cracked, hoarse and low. "Why did she run again? I was so close. So… close…"

Though his men needed their prince, Gareth knew he was in no state to face them. His heart had shriveled further still, leaving him hollow, a shell somehow still breathing. Not even bourbon's familiar burn could scour out the emptiness gnawing at him.

"Ah, there you are," came Sir Edmund's voice. He appeared with his helmet under one arm, silver hair damp and disheveled, sweat streaking his lined face. "I've been hunting for you all over."

"Tell me," Gareth muttered, eyes hard and sunken, "in all your years, have you ever seen such a thing? What manner of abomination was that?"

The elder Guardsman lifted the half-spent bottle Gareth had been working through, sniffed its contents, and took a long pull before lowering it with a sigh. "By the gods, lad… I've no answer. That's the damnedest thing I've ever seen. Even now, I wonder if my eyes tricked me."

Gareth rose with a grunt and shoved his mug forward for more. "Is this what our war has become, Edmund? A struggle not against men, but against terrors clawed up from the pit itself?"

"Every minute since," Edmund admitted, pouring, "I've prayed what we saw was naught but delusion… or exhaustion of a long campaign."

The words had barely left him before Edmund's hand cracked across Gareth's cheek. The blow staggered him sideways, more from shock than pain. For a moment, he stood frozen, trembling, then rage boiled up red and sharp.

"Have you lost your mind!?" Gareth roared. "How dare you strike me so! I ought to—" His hand shook around the hilt of his silver sword. "I ought to—"

"What?" Edmund interrupted coolly, arms folding across his chest. "Execute me over a slap? Perhaps over a closed fist. But that?" His eyes narrowed, unflinching. "Is that how you wish to be remembered, lad? A prince who cuts down an old man for a slap?"

It was an insult no royal should suffer, yet Gareth knew drawing blood over it would make him look more insecure than sovereign. He was no pampered monarch, no spoiled prince who had never tasted dirt or steel. He had bled on battlefields, nearly been murdered a dozen times, and earned every scar.

"I'm going to assume you're either drunk or delusional," he growled, working his jaw back and forth. "Now tell me, Edmund—why did you think it necessary to strike me?"

"For charging like a madman into the maw of death!" Sir Edmund barked, jabbing a finger toward his chest. "Have you lost your wits? If you had fallen to that beast, what would become of us? The men stayed only because they had their prince to rally behind. You are the reason they did not scatter halfway to Bentmont. Explain yourself!"

But Gareth's thoughts had already drifted from the battlefield to a single figure. Madelyn. Even now, he could smell her hair, feel the press of her lips, the fire in her eyes. The slap, the monster, the chaos—it all fell away, leaving only her.

"Because I saw her, Edmund," Gareth whispered, staring through the old knight as if into memory. "She was there. Changed… but it was her. Titan and Conrak were moments from death, and she hurled herself at that thing without fear. How could I stand idle? How could I watch my wife—my love—be torn apart before my eyes?"

The old Guardsman's fury faded like smoke in the wind. His shoulders sagged, and the finger that had jabbed so fiercely now curled into a fist before resting on Gareth's shoulder. He sighed, his weathered face softening.

"I had no idea she was there, lad," Edmund admitted quietly. "I glimpsed someone, yes, but when you spurred forward, I lost all sense of who was who. I made to follow, but my horse refused to budge. So I ran, as far as these old legs would carry me. By the time I reached the line…" He trailed off, shaking his head. "It was over."

"I held her in my arms." Gareth's jaw tightened until it creaked. "And for a moment, the world made sense again. All of my sadness, fear, and doubt… gone. She held me back, Edmund. She kissed me the way I always dreamed she would. But then… I lost her again."

The weight of it drove him to his knees. The mug slipped from his hand, bourbon soaking into the dirt. He clawed at the earth as if he could dig a hole deep enough to bury the pain, gasping for breath that would not come. His heart hammered like a smith's mallet, each beat striking harder than the last.

His father's cold lectures. His mother's gentle hand. His oaths to Betanthia. All of it seemed hollow beside the absence of her. He was no longer prince, commander, heir to a kingdom—only a man, gutted by love and left to bleed inside himself.

Edmund knelt beside him, the weight of a mailed arm wrapping around Gareth's shoulders. "It'll be alright, lad. She's still alive. Still out there. And closer than you've ever been. We'll bring her home, safe."

"Is this what love is, Edmund?" Gareth's voice was hoarse, but steady enough to carry. A single tear slid down his cheek, but his face remained hard as stone. "Is it only suffering? Is it chasing something that runs forever ahead? The harder I reach, the further she drifts. It seems her heart belongs to vengeance now, not to me. And here I sit, on the edge of oblivion, staring at horrors no man should see… and all I can think of is her."

Such despair could have broken even Lord Vakaro's stony heart.

Never had Gareth felt so hollow, so utterly alone. His life seemed nothing but a chain of tragedies, one after another, stretching on without end.

"Then you've something left to fight for," Edmund said firmly, thrusting out a hand. "Stand up, lad. There's a woman out there counting on you. I know love feels like it tears more than it mends, but it's what's kept you here. Kept you from breaking. Don't lose that."

Gareth let Edmund pull him to his feet. He glanced down at the purple cloak draped over his shoulder, its edge caked with mud and blood. His voice was ice when he finally spoke. "I don't believe in love anymore. Love is supposed to heal, not carve wounds that never close."

"Then what do you believe in?" Edmund asked, his head tilting, searching.

"I believe in nothing." Gareth's words were a blade, cold and final.

A commotion cut through their exchange—low at first, then swelling into shouts and curses. It was not the usual squabble of men fraying at the edges of campaign life. This was heavier, angrier. Gareth's stomach sank as Lord Kenfield appeared at full gallop, his face the color of ash.

"My prince!" Anders gasped, reins jerking as his horse skidded to a halt. "The men—they're leaving! Entire platoons! They've packed up their kit and are marching for home!"

Dread hollowed Gareth's chest. Desertions had already bled them after the stalemate on the Plainhold. To lose men now—scores, hundreds—was a disaster. The campaign would crumble, and Betanthia with it.

Edmund cursed and limped toward his horse, every step betraying the stiffness in his battered leg. "Come on, lad. If you don't stop this, no one will."

Gareth's anguish gave way to raw fear, not only for Betanthia's kingdom, but for Madelyn. If the army splintered here, he would lose her forever. No, he thought, such a destiny cannot be allowed.

With grim resolve, he seized the first horse at hand. The beast balked, nearly throwing him, but Gareth yanked the reins hard and forced it under his control. He spurred into the chaos, weaving between knots of fleeing men, his purple cloak snapping like a banner of defiance. Thousands of eyes followed him, wavering, searching for a reason to stand.

"Hold fast, men!" Gareth roared. "Do not flee! We must remain together!"

But even a prince's command seemed powerless. Men streamed away by the dozens, some even among Vakaro's own sworn disciples. The host was unraveling, and with it the fate of Betanthia. His legacy, his family's crown—Madelyn—all slipping into ruin

"Stand your ground!" His cry split the night like a thunderclap. "By my blood, by the crown of Betanthia, I command you… STAND!"

His throat rasped, raw from grief and bourbon, yet the desperation in his tone was unmistakable. He drove the horse into the ranks, battering shields with the flat of his broken sword until the deserters turned to face him.

"Why do you run?" Gareth bellowed, voice cracking. "Would you wait for the wildmen to crash through your city gates? Would you fight them at your own hearthstones, with your wives and children behind you? That is what your cowardice will bring!"

He wheeled his horse, glaring into every pair of eyes that met his. "You would see Bentmont burn? Cardale burn? Then flee! But know this: if you leave now, you will not flee barbarians. You will flee me."

Many paused and looked on, though some continued their dejected march south. From the mass of weary men, a giant form pushed forward—Titan Bradshaw. His armor was gouged and dented, the mail on his arm torn to ribbons, his scarred face streaked with dirt and blood. Sweat and fury clung to him like a cloak, his gray hair matted against his brow.

"Out of my fucking way!" he bellowed, shoving men aside with the force of a bull. Deserters stumbled from his path, some spitting curses, others dropping their gaze like whipped dogs. He strode through them like a wounded beast, every step ringing with the jingle of broken mail, his eyes burning hotter than the battlefield behind them.

"You think you can just slink off?" Titan roared, his voice crashing over the crowd. "Run home to your mothers and let the Northmen gut them while you hide beneath their skirts? Go on then! Run! But I'll remember your fucking faces, every one of you. And when this war's done, I'll come for you myself!"

The words struck like a hammer blow. Men froze in place, looking at one another with unease. Some cursed him, others shifted their weight, but a handful stopped outright, planting their shields in the dirt as if ashamed to move another step.

Gareth spurred his horse forward, seizing the moment before the silence curdled. He rode up beside the Titan, holding aloft his broken sword.

"Hear him!" Gareth shouted, his voice carrying like a trumpet blast. "This blade is spent, dim and shattered… but it stood against a nightmare no man was meant to face. If one ruined sword can do that, what do you think an army can do? Stand with me, stand with him, and we will finish what was started!"

The two men—the prince with his dulled relic, the Titan with his wrath—stood side by side, voices cutting through despair. Slowly, the tide began to shift. Men who had been streaming south turned back, shame burning in their eyes. Horns rang from the rear, captains shouting as ranks reformed, shields locking once more into a wall of steel.

Still, hundreds were lost to desertion, their figures dwindling into the haze of dust and smoke. Yet thousands more stayed; shields locking, banners stiff in the ashen wind. For now, Betanthia still stood, though its footing was perilously thin.

Titan's curses still rang when another figure pushed through the throng. Conrak emerged, helm tucked under his arm, his armor shredded and dark with blood. His face was wan with exhaustion, but his eyes remained sharp as a drawn blade.

"A fine display, my prince," Conrak said grimly, nodding toward the long column of deserters streaming south. "But even with your fire, look how many still slip away."

Gareth's jaw clenched. "Damn them. Every man who leaves now shortens Betanthia's life by a year." His gaze swept the battered host, despair biting at his words. "How am I meant to hold this army together when their fear outweighs their duty?"

"You cannot do it alone," Conrak answered, voice steady, almost clinical. "As much as it sickens me to say it, we need Lord Vakaro. His disciples have not broken. At least, not fully. To the men, he is still a pillar. Without his weight, this army collapses before dawn."

Titan spat in the dirt, growling. "That snake? I'd sooner break my sword across his skull."

"And if you do," Conrak snapped back, "you'll be left to face the barbarians with a company of ghosts. We all know what Vakaro is. But until the last banner falls, he must stand with us, or at the very least, look as if he does."

Gareth fell silent, his eyes lingering on the dust where deserters still vanished. The ruined sword weighed heavy at his hip, cold as his thoughts. At last, he slid it into its scabbard, his voice low but firm.

"Very well. If the kingdom's survival demands that I stand beside Ridley Vakaro, then so be it. Come. We'll find him together."

Prince, Titan, and Sacrithon shouldered through the milling ranks until they came upon the red banners of the Southern Commandant. Compared to the chaos of the main host, Vakaro's camp was eerily precise. Retainers stood in rigid lines, their armor polished as though the battle's grime dared not touch them. Eyes flicked uneasily as Gareth and his companions drew near.

Ridley Vakaro sat beneath a canopy, helm set neatly on the table, goblet of wine untouched. For once, he did not look chiseled from stone. His features were taut, jaw locked as if even he felt the weight of what had risen from the Plainhold.

Titan snarled. "On your feet, you piece of shit."

"Enough," Gareth cut him off, his voice sharp. He stepped forward, every line of his body trembling with exhaustion and fury. "This is no time for posturing, Tylar. Lord Vakaro… you know as well as I do what we saw today. No army of men can withstand it. If we cannot hold the line, Betanthia itself will crumble. Do you understand me? This is bigger than your pride, or mine. Bigger than crowns and titles."

Ridley's eyes lifted at last, cold and calculating, but the silence lingered. When he spoke, it was without bravado, as if the wind had died in his sails.

"This is not a war of men," he said softly. "And not one that can be won here, on this plain. You saw it yourself. That… thing. What sword, what shield, what courage can stand against such nightmares? We continue to march north, and more of those horrors will come. That much is certain."

Conrak's brow furrowed. "So what do you propose?"

Ridley's eyes flicked to him, cold but not cutting. "I propose survival. The army is fraying. Half a campaign more, and you will have no host left to command. Better to withdraw, to fortify our cities, to prepare for a war against creatures that men were never meant to face. To continue here is to bleed ourselves dry against shadows."

Titan growled low in his throat, his hand tightening on the hilt of his sword. "So you'd abandon the field after all we've spilled? After what *she* bled for? What's the matter, Lord Vakaro? Aren't you supposed to be some tough son of a bitch?"

Ridley's head snapped toward Titan, his eyes flashing. "Do not mistake pragmatism for cowardice, Bradshaw. I have shed more blood in this war than you have curses, and I will not waste the lives of what remains simply to appease your thirst for vengeance. You think me soft? Then you are a fool. I fear nothing—not Northmen, not you, not even that abomination. But I know when a field is lost."

He rose slowly from his chair, the weight of his presence settling over the canopy like a storm. "If you wish to die here, so be it. But do not drag Betanthia with you into the grave."

Titan's hand tightened on his hilt, his teeth bared. "Say that again, you fucking—"

"Enough!" Gareth's voice cut through the air like steel. He stepped between them, every fiber of him screaming against what he was about to say. His heart told him to draw steel and finish what the shadows had started; to cut Ridley Vakaro down where he stood. But his mind, cold and weary, knew better.

"You're right," Gareth said, the words tasting like ash. "We cannot bleed ourselves dry fighting demons across the Plainhold. Not if we hope to see another season." He turned his head toward Ridley, forcing himself to meet that cold gaze. "I do not trust you. I may never trust you. But Betanthia cannot stand if its commanders fall to squabbling while the enemy waits at our throats. So I will stand beside you… for now."

The words sickened him, each one a betrayal of his instincts. But there was no choice. He needed Lord Vakaro's banner, his men, his influence… even if it meant clasping hands with the very snake who had nearly struck him down in the dark.

Vakaro nodded, the gesture precise, almost regal. "Wise words, my prince. You may yet prove yourself a king after all."

There was no smugness in his tone, no smirk tugging at his lips, only the cool acknowledgment of a man who recognized necessity when he saw it. Still, Gareth felt sullied by the exchange, as though he had shaken hands with a corpse.

Titan muttered a curse under his breath, glaring daggers, but said nothing further. Conrak's eyes flicked between the two men, seeing the fragile thread that bound them together and knowing it could snap at any moment.

As the canopy fell silent, Gareth let his gaze drift beyond Vakaro's banner to the dark horizon. Out there lay the Plainhold, scarred and soaked with the blood of his men. Somewhere beyond it, the barbarians gathered, emboldened by terrors not born of flesh. And somewhere in those shadows, Madelyn walked—his love, his ruin, and perhaps the key to everything. The world had shifted in a single day, and he was left to bear its weight.

Gareth drew a slow breath, the taste of dust and smoke bitter on his tongue. "We thought we were fighting a war… but this is no war. This is the ending of all things. Come now, gentlemen… the fate of our nation awaits us."

EPILOGUE

Commander Albin Marrick had walked the walls a dozen times that morning, and every time, the sight of the barbarian camp across the fields brought a new weight to his chest. Ragged banners fluttered above a sprawl of tents, their fires coughing black smoke into a gray sky. Even beaten back from the gates, the bastards showed no signs of leaving.

He muttered under his breath as he paced the parapet, tallying pikes, checking the tautness of bowstrings, the readiness of the ballista crews. The men straightened at his passing, not out of fear, but because Albin had a way of making men want to look sharper than they were. He did not shout often, and when he did, it was not with venom—just enough iron to remind them the walls were worth dying for.

Albin himself was built like the walls he patrolled: broad-shouldered, thick around the middle, but still hard as quarried stone. A beard of iron and black framed a face lined deep by wind and years of salt air. His eyes, a pale gray, missed little; sharp as a hawk's when angered, but softened often by a dry humor his men had come to expect. He carried his age without shame, armor worn but well-kept, the purple of Betanthia faded but never sullied.

When he barked, it was to keep his men sharp; when he smirked, it was to remind them they were still human. The garrison trusted him because he trusted them, and in Albin's mind, that was the only way a city stood.

"Eyes front, lad," he said to a spearman who lingered on the horizon too long. "Staring at them won't make them go away."

When the circuit was done, he descended into the city. Dellhaven lived in defiance of the horde outside its walls. The fishmongers still haggled at the harbor, silk-clad merchants still strutted through the square, and laughter still drifted from the taverns. The elite prided themselves on showing the barbarians that no siege could break their spirit, though Albin knew full well how thin that pride could wear when the bread ran out.

At the harbor, he found three of his watchmen slumped against a piling outside the tavern, a skin of wine being passed between them. One scrambled to his feet when he saw the Commander, the other two trying and failing to hide their drink.

Albin fixed them with a flat stare, then sighed through his nose. "If you're going to drink on my watch, at least do it standing. The enemy may not be storming the docks today, but heavens know they're watching. You want to look like lambs waiting for slaughter?"

The youngest of the three stammered, "S-sorry, Commander."

Albin plucked the wineskin from their hands, took a long swallow himself, and handed it back. "Keep your heads, lads. When the next horn sounds, I expect you sober and ready. Till then… best drink it while you can."

Relief and sheepish grins spread across their faces. Albin left them to it, pushing open the tavern doors. Inside, warmth and noise hit him like a wave. Soldiers crowded benches alongside merchants and fishmongers, mugs slamming against tables, dice clattering across boards. The tavern keeper shouted for more barrels to be rolled up, while a fiddler in the corner scraped out a tune loud enough to drown the storm outside.

When Albin stepped through the threshold, a cheer went up. Men raised their cups, calling his name, voices rough but filled with a kind of affection. He gave a curt nod and a wry smile as he made his way to the bar, every back straightening a little, every voice rising louder at his presence. He hated to admit it, but taverns like this kept a garrison together better than any inspection. Steel held walls, but ale and laughter held men.

Albin eased onto a stool at the bar, the wood groaning beneath him. The barkeep slid him a mug of frothing ale before he could ask, and he raised it in a half-hearted salute. The men nearby pounded their cups in rhythm, shouting his name again, the cheer swelling until it seemed the walls themselves might rattle loose.

"Commander Marrick!" a man called out, his voice as sloppy as the front of his tunic.

He took a long pull, the foam catching in his beard, and let the warmth spread through his chest. The fiddler struck up a quicker tune, cards shuffled and slid across tables, and a pair of off-duty pikemen started some bawdy song that drew laughter from even the silk-robed merchants. For a moment, it almost felt like peace. Almost.

Because underneath the revelry, Albin heard the cracks. Laughter pitched a shade too high. Cups emptied too quickly. Dice thrown too hard, as if rolling them could shake away the memory of black banners and war drums beyond the walls. The storm still roared outside, and no amount of ale could drown it forever.

A group of sailors beckoned him over, clapping for him to join their hand of cards. He waved them off with a smile.

"If I start winning, you'll accuse me of cheating," Albin said. "If I start losing, I'll accuse you. Best we spare the barkeep a brawl."

The room erupted again, good-natured jeers hurled his way. He smirked, drained the last of his ale, and set the mug down with a thump. "Drink while you can, lads, tomorrow may not give us the chance."

The cheer faltered for a heartbeat—just a heartbeat—before the fiddler's tune pulled it back. But Albin saw the shadows in their eyes, and felt the same in his own bones. The city still stood. The men still laughed. But the threat was not gone. It was only waiting.

Albin leaned back on his stool, letting the sound of the tavern wash over him. The warmth, the laughter, the stink of sweat and spilled ale. This was Dellhaven as much as the stone walls or the harbor itself. A city holding fast, pretending the horde outside was just a passing storm. For the sake of his men, he let them pretend. Heavens knew, he wished he could.

The doors burst open, spilling dying sunlight into the tavern. A rider stood framed in the threshold, cloak dusty and dirty, boots heavy from the road. The cheer wavered, faltered, until the fiddler played louder to drown the silence. The messenger's eyes found Albin at once.

"Commander Marrick," the rider said softly, glancing over his shoulder. "Might we have a word in private?"

Albin pushed back from the bar, the legs of his stool scraping against the floorboards. The room had gone half-quiet, all ears straining for news, though no one dared ask. He gave them a hard look and a small wave of his hand.

"Drink. That's an order."

The fiddler picked up the tempo, dice clattered again, and laughter tried to recover its footing as Albin followed the rider outside.

They walked in silence toward the docks. The air was sharp with tar and salt, gulls crying overhead as a high tide lapped against the pilings. Out beyond the harbor mouth, faint smudges of smoke from barbarian fires clung to the horizon, a reminder that Dellhaven was a city under siege.

The rider drew a folded letter from his cloak, its wax unbroken. He glanced around to be sure they were alone before passing it over. Albin's stomach tightened. After the assault on the harbor, he had sent the rider north to Brimnora, begging the Northern Commandant for aid. Dellhaven could hold for a time, but not forever. Not alone. This was the answer he had waited on for a fortnight.

"From Brimnora, Commander."

Albin broke the seal and read quickly, his pale eyes scanning each line, his face tightening as though each word pressed weight upon him. When he finished, he folded the letter once, twice, and tucked it into his belt with a grunt.

"They refuse," he said flatly. "Brimnora won't spare a man. They claim their own walls may fall if they strip them for Dellhaven."

The messenger shifted uneasily, voice low. "What shall I tell the men?"

He stared out at the dark water, where the tide met the haze of smoke lingering overhead. Albin drew a slow breath, his face hardening to stone.

"Tell them nothing," he muttered. "They'll know soon enough. Until then, we do what we've always done. We stand."

He dismissed the messenger and walked the streets back toward the square, his thoughts weighing heavier than his armor. Dellhaven bustled in its strange defiance—silk-robed nobles strolled arm in arm, servants laden with baskets of fruit and wine, merchants haggling as if no horde crouched beyond the walls. A jeweled couple paused as he passed, offering him warm smiles and words of thanks for his vigilance.

Albin returned the courtesy with a nod, even a faint smile. It felt good to be seen, to be appreciated. But when their perfumed laughter trailed behind him, his shoulders sagged. Praise would not feed the city when the granaries thinned, nor stop the savages when they came again.

He looked once more toward the walls, their purple banners rippling in the sea wind. The people still believed they were untouchable. Albin Marrick knew better. He walked on, the cobbles ringing beneath his boots, his mind still on Brimnora's refusal. The laughter of nobles and the clamor of merchants faded into a dull murmur, a city pretending at peace while the noose tightened around its neck. Then came the shouting.

Boots pounded from the direction of the walls, soldiers sprinting toward the harbor with panic in their eyes. Albin stopped dead, brow furrowed, before breaking into a run to intercept them.

"What in the hells is this?" he barked, snagging one by the arm as he rushed past.

"They're here, Commander!" the young soldier gasped, eyes wild. "Ships—hundreds of them!"

Albin released him and thundered toward the docks, his heart hammering in his chest. As he broke through a crowd gathering along the piers, the sight froze him in place.

Out beyond the harbor mouth, the sea was thick with sails. A vast flotilla of ships, black against the dying light, rolling closer with the tide. Barbarians? Pirates? He could not yet tell. All he knew was that Dellhaven's nightmare had only just begun.

Albin stared, disbelieving, as the flotilla grew clearer with every heartbeat. Dozens upon dozens of hulls, sails billowing like the wings of carrion birds, bearing down on Dellhaven with grim purpose. For the first time in years, he felt his throat go dry. Then instinct took hold.

"Raise the chain!" he roared, voice cutting through the panic. "I want every length of iron hauled until the harbor mouth is shut tight!"

Runners scattered at once, shouting the command down the piers.

"Ballistas loaded and at the ready! I want every damned bolt we've got brought up—I don't care if the crews drop where they stand!"

Men scrambled, sweating as they cranked great winches, the groan of timber echoing across the docks.

"Archers on the walls! Spears to the waterline! If it floats and it isn't ours, you sink the bastard!"

The garrison snapped to life, the drunken ease of the taverns gone in an instant. Boots hammered cobblestones, chains rattled, the dockside transformed into a hive of desperate activity. Albin planted his boots at the edge of the quay, eyes fixed on the approaching fleet. His gut churned, but his voice carried iron.

"By every god above and below," he muttered, "let them break on Dellhaven's stones."

Even as the harbor bristled with steel, Albin's thoughts turned north. Beyond the walls, the savages still watched, their campfires smoldering in the fields, their drums silent but waiting. If the horde struck the gates while the fleet pressed the harbor, Dellhaven would be torn apart from two sides. The city had endured the first assault by grit and luck, but against this, there could be little hope.

"Commander Marrick!" A voice cracked through the chaos, shrill and panicked.

A rider galloped down from the southern road, reins flapping, his horse foaming at the mouth. The man nearly toppled from the saddle as he skidded to a halt, eyes wide, face ashen.

"Commander," he gasped, barely able to form the words. "They've landed… heavens help us, a party of them has come ashore just south of the city. Dozens, maybe hundreds. Raiders moving inland already!"

For a long moment, Albin stood frozen, staring at the messenger as if the man had spoken madness. North. Harbor. Now south? His mind reeled, the weight of it pressing on his chest until he thought it might crush him.

"Three fronts…" he whispered. His pale eyes shifted from the sea to the walls, and then to the southern road swallowed by dusk. "Three devils' hands around our throat."

For a heartbeat, he thought of Brimnora, its Commandant clutching soldiers tight behind his own walls, deaf to Dellhaven's pleas. Cardale, too crippled and bled dry by riots and war in the west, with nothing left to send but sympathy. No help was coming. Not from the south. Not from the heartland.

Albin Marrick drew a long breath, the salt and smoke bitter in his lungs. Around him, men shouted, chains rattled, and the sea itself seemed to quake with the approach of sails. He squared his shoulders, knowing the truth in his bones—they were staring into the impossible. And yet, by the heavens, they would face it. Dellhaven would stand alone.

A WORD FROM THE AUTHOR

THANK YOU SO MUCH FOR TAKING THE TIME TO READ "THE QUEEN OF Scorn"! I hope you had as much fun reading it as I did writing it. If you enjoyed the book, please leave a great review (or rating, at least) on Amazon or Barnes & Noble, as well as Goodreads. It only takes a few minutes, and it's the best way for you to support my work and get the word out. Doing so will help ensure that I can continue publishing for a long time into the future.

From the bottom of my heart, thank you for all of your fantastic support!

—Chris

www.ingramcontent.com/pod-product-compliance
Lightning Source LLC
Chambersburg PA
CBHW030325010826
48973CB00004B/865